Bloodwars

"Concluding the darkly hypnotic Vampire World trilogy, this red-blooded offering from British Fantasy Award winner Lumley also brings to a close the epic narrative begun in Vampire World's prequel, the five-book Necroscope series.... Though this is the last of the trilogy, readers must hope that Lumley isn't putting a stake through the heart of his vampire universe—which is so vivid, with characters so real, that even the undead seem alive."

—*Publishers Weekly*

The Last Aerie

"This complex, fast-paced, and challenging novel is a highly successful blend of genres and should appeal to fans of horror, fantasy, and espionage. Lumley's creatures are so horrifyingly real they make the Transylvanian version seem little more than a shadow of the real thing.

"Lumley deserves a wide audience among those who love both Anne Rice and John Grisham ... and [of course] Stephen King."

—*VOYA*

"Outstanding. A vigorous novel that draws strength from both its depth of world-building and the psychology of its characters. The genre of fantastic literature is greatly improved by the publication of this work, which is very highly recommended."

—*Wilson Library Bulletin*

Blood Brothers

"Lumley's new series should attract major attention [from] those looking for a series comparable to the Anne Rice "Vampire" books. Lumley is that good."

—John Farris

"Among the best of [the] genre ... rivals Anne Rice's vampire saga.

"Lumley never oversteps the delicate line between blood-chilling horror and cold gruel. An accomplished wordsmith, Lumley wields a pen with the deft skill of a surgeon, drawing just enough blood to titillate without offending his readers."

—*The Phoenix Gazette*

"Lumley's cleverly crafted wamphyric saga crackles with the author's sense of high adventure and panache."

—Rex Miller

"The voice of the vampire—powerful, unscrupulous, passionate—is sometimes the most enjoyable aspect of any vampire novel. [Brian Lumley's new novel is] at its strongest when the monster speaks.

"Lumley's love of his pulp-horror subjects is gleefully apparent. He revels in every telling detail, in stories within stories and convoluted histories of the self-mutating vampires."

—*San Francisco Chronicle*

TOR BOOKS BY BRIAN LUMLEY

Bloodwars

Brian Lumley

TOR
HORROR®

A TOM DOHERTY ASSOCIATES BOOK
NEW YORK

This is a work of fiction. All the characters and events portrayed in this book are either fictitious or are used fictitiously.

BLOODWARS

Copyright © 1994 by Brian Lumley

All rights reserved, including the right to reproduce this book, or portions thereof, in any form.

Cover art by Bob Eggleton

A Tor Book
Published by Tom Doherty Associates, LLC
175 Fifth Avenue
New York, NY 10010

www.tor.com

Tor® is a registered trademark of Tom Doherty Associates, LLC.

ISBN: 0-812-53628-2
Library of Congress Catalog Card Number: 94-21746

First edition: October 1994
First mass market edition: November 1995

Printed in the United States of America

0 9 8 7 6 5

For Steve Jones.
Thanks for giving me the
magic words. You'll note
that I gave them back
... to Zek!

PART ONE:

EARTH

I

Outside, Inside

Returning from an early lunch at an Indian restaurant just a five-minute walk away from E-Branch HQ in the heart of London, Ben Trask sweated inside and out. Inside from the curry which was still searing his mouth and throat, outside from the unusually warm May weather. The noonday sun blazed down on him from a sky as vast and blue as the Ionian which he hoped his visitor from another world was enjoying, because Trask sure as hell was not! In fact, ever since Zek Föener and Nathan Kiklu (or Nathan "Keogh," as the Necroscope preferred to be called now) had gone off to the Greek islands a few days ago, Trask had been right out of sorts with himself, and with everyone else in his top-secret ESPionage organization.

He thought about the two, worried about them equally . . . but for different reasons. About Nathan, because he was probably the most valuable and certainly the most— what, unique?—man in the world; even in *two* worlds. And about Zek because he loved her. At his age (Trask snorted), finally to have fallen in love! Not that he was ancient, and he certainly wasn't "past it," but . . . it *complicated* matters. And with Zek in the Greek Islands, things seemed even more complicated. That silly old saw that has it "out of sight, out of mind" had it backwards as far as Trask was concerned. She was out of sight, all right, but she'd never been more in his mind than right now . . .

And even as he thought it, the thought itself was like an invocation:

Deep water . . . the salt sea . . . weeds and sediment obscuring Trask's vision—no, Zek's vision!—and the pain in his/her chest . . . heart hammering, vision blurring, lungs screaming for air! Sweet Jesus, she was drowning! And she was letting him know about it in the only way she could . . . for Zek was one of the world's finest telepaths.

BEN! *The word exploded into his mind like a bomb.* TRY NOT TO FEEL . . . TOO . . . BAD . . . ABOUT . . . IT.

"Zek!" *he yelled out loud, and could actually* taste *the water flooding into his/her mouth.*

GOOD . . . . . . BYE . . . . . . BEN . . . . . . !

Trask staggered, whirled, fell, and felt his knees slam down hard on the dusty pavement. But it didn't hurt. Nothing hurt except the fact that Zek's telepathic voice was dead in his mind. And that Zek herself—?

Across the road, people were staring. A car's horn blared, and its astonished driver gazed down at Trask where he kneeled half on, half off the road. Then the car swept on by and people came running, questioning. Someone asked if Trask had been hit. He shook his head, got to his feet and staggered again. A young couple grabbed him, held him upright, and the girl asked:

"Are you all right?"

Numb, he nodded. He was all right, yes. But Zek—?

It was mid-May 2006, and under the hot sun Trask was cold. Sweat rivered his face and stuck his shirt to his back, yet he was cold. Cold in his mind, from the *feel* and the *taste* of the deep salt water, but far colder from the memory of Zek's telepathic voice, crying there and dying there, in his mind. Cold from the sudden emptiness of . . . everything. "Zek!"

He shook the young couple off, shouldered people aside, started to walk along the pavement and ended up running, and ran sweating and shivering down the side street to the back of the hotel whose top floor housed E-Branch HQ. He found the private door; after the sunlight it was like night in there; there was only the darkness until he used his pass-card to enter the elevator with its electric ceiling light. And even then it was dark; but that was in his mind, and he knew that the darkness was only the absence of Zek. In which case it might last forever.

Then the elevator shuddered to a halt, the doors hissed open and Trask stumbled out into the main corridor ...

... Which was—*flooded*?

An inch of water went sluicing into the elevator! *Now what the holy ... ?*

There were espers in the corridor. Trask recognized faces without considering the amazement—the relief, the ... what? triumph, jubilation?—written on every one of them. There was a smell of ocean, seaweed, salt. The smell matched the taste of Zek in Trask's mind. So that once again he asked himself: *Now what the holy ... ?*

The tall, cadaverous, usually melancholy figure of the precog, Ian Goodly, loomed into view; but now his eyes were alight with elation. He grabbed Trask's arm, husked: "Ben—he's done it! Nathan's *done* it!"

"Done it?" Trask found it hard to gather his thoughts, concentrate his mind. Goodly was wet, splotched; he smelled of sea water just like the entire corridor smelled of it. His trousers were drenched from the knees down, and clung to his thin calves. And now David Chung, Branch locator, had arrived on the scene; he, too, was soaked from head to toe, and grinning like an Oriental lunatic. "Done what?" Trask demanded, looking from one to the other of them. "What has Nathan done? And anyway, he's somewhere in the Ionian with ... with Zek." And finally losing it: "Why doesn't someone tell me what the fuck—is—going—*on*—here!?"

"They *were* in the Greek Islands, Ben." Goodly suddenly saw how close Trask was to shock. But he also knew how difficult it would be to shock a man who always knew the truth, a human lie detector like the current Head of E-Branch. And looking at him, Goodly thought to himself: *He's improved, hardened with age and time. Oh, Ben has soft, human edges, too, but the man inside—the mind, soul, and personality, the* id—*is diamond-hard.*

Trask was about five-ten, just a pound or two overweight, mousey-haired and green-eyed. His broad shoulders sloped just a little, his arms dangled somewhat, and his expression was—what, lugubrious? Or maybe that was as a direct result of his talent; for in a world where the simple truth was increasingly hard to come by, it was no easy thing to possess a mind that could not accept a lie. This was an election year, and Trask's current gripe was with politicians. Watching party political broadcasts, he would frequently burst out: "The trouble with these people is that they *never* lie! But they never tell the truth, either!"

And now he was staring hard at Goodly, asking: "What was that you said? They *were* in the Ionian? What the hell do you mean?"

Goodly knew there was only one way to tell it, and so answered: "They were there, yes, Ben. But just a few minutes ago, Nathan brought them back!"

Trask's jaw fell open. Not without an effort, he closed it and said: "He brought them—?"

"—Brought them back here, yes." Goodly nodded. "Through the Möbius Continuum."

And now Trask's jaw dropped open all the way, so that once again he had to close it before gasping: "The ... Continuum?" At which the truth finally dawned on him; if not in regard to Nathan, certainly in respect of Zek. The fact that she was alive! He'd known it was the truth, of course, even as Goodly said the words, but it seemed so far beyond his wildest hopes and dreams that even Trask had held back from letting it register. Just a moment ago he'd known that Zek Föener was dead—he had literally *heard* and *felt* her die—and yet now ...

As Trask's feet touched earth again, he snapped out of it and demanded to know. 'Where are they? Are they okay? And Zek—is she okay?"

David Chung answered him. "They're sedated. We've fixed up a couple of beds in the Ops Room. But it was a close thing. They were in the sea. And when they came through ... I thought half of the Mediterranean was coming through with them!"

Trask grabbed him, said: "But how did it happen? Don't

we know anything about it? Christ, I take an hour off for lunch, everything goes mad!"

"Nathan said a few words before we put him under," Chung answered. "But we had to put them out of it for a while. They were exhausted and in shock—especially Zek—and it might easily have developed into something worse."

"So what exactly did Nathan say?" Trask headed for the Ops Room with the others in tow.

"It seems it was a party of Tzonov's thugs," Goodly took up the story. "Nathan's Special Branch minders were taken by surprise—and murdered! Nathan and Zek ran for it, into the sea. More of Tzonov's people were waiting for them; they had wet suits and spearguns and were already in the water; for all we know at this stage, the entire operation was launched from the sea. But when the chips were down and there was no other way out, Nathan did his thing. Except . . . there was probably a lot more to it than that."

"Oh?" Trask glanced at him, and pressed on into the Ops Room, where a small knot of espers was gathered around a pair of six-foot tables.

Goodly followed on behind, nodding. "There had been some pretty weird stuff going on here. Stuff that told us these two were in trouble." He gave a shrug. "So we did what we could for them." Goodly was wont to understate things: his British phlegmatism. But the precog's "pretty weird stuff" statement told Trask a lot: namely, that there was still a lot he hadn't been told.

"All of this in an hour?" he said, as the espers around the tables moved aside to make room for their Head of Branch, and Trask came to a halt between a pair of prone figures apparently asleep in hastily made-up beds.

"In a lot less than an hour," David Chung put in. "Let me tell you about it . . .

"Myself, Ian, Geoff Smart, we all got the message at the same time: that something was wrong. With me it was Nathan's earring: the thing came *alive* in my hand! I can't say what it was for Smart, but he's an empath and he's done a lot of work with Nathan; maybe he sensed the trouble they were in even at that range. And of course Ian reads the future, and apparently he'd 'seen' me plugging in the computer in Harry's room. So we went there, and I plugged it in. Then—

"—It was the same as before: the numbers, equations, whatever; I'm no mathematician, so you tell me! But it was all on the screen. Except it wasn't *quite* the same. For this time the numbers came together, fused, formed into something else. Something that was . . . I don't know, solid? Well, almost solid."

Trask had taken Zek's wrist; feeling the steady pulse, he issued a sigh of relief. *Zek, you spoke to me. When you thought it was all over, I was the one you spoke to!* It meant an awful lot to him. Then, as if it were his first breath in a week, he filled his lungs to bursting; and finally, frowning, he looked at Chung. "Something solid, you say? On the computer screen?"

Goodly took up the story again. "Do you remember those golden darts, Ben? I mean, when Harry died?"

"Of course I remember them."

"And the one we saw entering into the computer? In fact, the computer showed it to us, right?"

Trask nodded, stepped away from the tables and beckoned the others back. "Let them breathe, for Christ's sake!" And to Goodly: "What about it?"

"The way I see it," Goodly answered, "that dart or whatever it was, it's been waiting in there. Before, the computer seemed to be running off its own power; you'll remember, it wasn't plugged in? Well, whatever it was that powered the display that time—call it a 'ghost,' if you like, or an 'echo' of Harry Keogh—it must have just about burned itself out. But this time it was tapping a legitimate power source, which boosted what was left of it. So . . . this is what we saw:

"The numbers stopped dead on the screen and, like David said, formed into something solid: a golden dart! Oh, it was faint as a wisp of yellow smoke—pretty insubstantial stuff—but it was real. And then . . . it left the screen!"

"It what?" Trask's frown knotted his forehead.

"It left the screen," Goodly repeated. "And it passed out through the wall of the room and was gone."

"Gone? Gone where?"

Geoff Smart the empath had arrived from somewhere. Having heard what had been said, he now put in: "I think that's something you'll have to ask Nathan, when he comes out of it."

Trask glanced at the speaker. Smart was something less than six feet tall; sturdily built, red-haired, crew-cut, he looked like a boxer, aggressive, but was in fact mild-mannered. What he lacked in looks found compensation in what Trask called his "withness": his intense ability to relate. His talent was empathy, in which capacity he had worked very closely with Nathan. It was odds on that Smart would be correct in his as yet unspoken estimate of what had occurred. But unspoken or not, Trask read the truth in it anyway.

"You're telling me that this dart—went *looking* for him?"

Smart nodded. "And found him! That's my bet. I think it's been in there—in the computer—just waiting for him. Which is why none of you ever messed with Harry's room all this time, because you could sense it in there. Why not? You're all espers after all. But when Nathan got here, the thing revealed itself. And given a power source at last, when Chung plugged it in . . ."

". . . The dart went home." Trask finished it for him. "Went home to Nathan."

Again Smart nodded. "That's how I see it, yes."

"It finished the job that we had started on him," Trask continued almost to himself, staring in something approaching awe at the young man on the second bed. "It gave him the Möbius Continuum and made him complete. But . . . this was his first time ever? And still he was able to find his way back here—*and* bring Zek with him?"

David Chung spoke up. "He wasn't entirely on his own. I mean, I think maybe I had something to do with it. Or rather, that *this* had something to do with it." He held up

Nathan's golden earring in the warped shape of a Möbius loop. "A vampire Lord called Maglore gave this to Nathan before he escaped from Turgosheim. I think Maglore was using it to spy on him. But as a locating device the earring works both ways. Nathan must have homed in on it, and that's how he found his way back here . . ."

Trask looked at them all standing around him. Looked from face to face, and then at Zek Föener and the Necroscope Nathan Keogh, lying tranquilized in their makeshift beds. Finally he grinned and shook his head in wonder. And to Smart, Goodly, and Chung he said, "So, all three of you had a hand in it, right? God, what would we do without you? What would any of us *anywhere* do without you?" His steady gaze spread to encompass the rest of his espers. "And I do mean all of you."

It was the finest compliment he had ever paid them . . .

The plan was simple:

Nathan had revisited Sir Keenan Gormley's resting place to "fix" its coordinates in his mind, and also to tell the ex-Head of Branch that he was experimenting with the Möbius Continuum. Now, having returned to E-Branch HQ, he would attempt a Möbius jump to Gormley's Garden of Repose. In the event that something went wrong, David Chung would be ready with Nathan's sigil earring to guide him home. And so that it would be more in keeping as a genuine scientific experiment, other Branch members would be *in situ* at Gormley's memorial, to time any lapse between Nathan's jump from HQ and his arrival in the Kensington cemetery.

All was now in place; it was 9:00 A.M., and the mid-city temperature was already climbing; Nathan, Trask, and a majority of E-Branch agents were in the Ops Room, every single man of them with a film of sweat on his brow despite the fact that the air-conditioning was up full. Finally Trask said, "Well, son, and now it's all yours."

Nathan smiled nervously, looked at them each in his turn, and last but not least at Zek. She smiled reassuringly, reminding him: "You've done it once."

He nodded. "When I had to, yes."

Trask was anxious and said, "Look, if you want to postpone this . . ."

"No," Nathan cut him off. "Let it be now. There's no time left. If I can do it, it will give me the edge I'll need back on Sunside."

David Chung stepped forward, grinned self-consciously, and said: "Nathan, I . . ." and stuck out his hand. They clasped forearms in the Szgany fashion, and Chung stepped back again. Then, as if at a signal, the espers backed away from Nathan where he stood in the center of the room.

And it was time.

Utter silence fell, and the expressions on all faces grew tense, expectant. Nathan felt the force of their minds concentrated upon him from where they stood in a circle but at a safe distance. And feeling their eyes—their minds—on him like that, and concerned that they might in some way interfere with the process, he closed his own eyes to shut them out. But he couldn't close his mind. Indeed, he must *open* his mind—

—Open it, and conjure the numbers vortex!

And at once—instantaneously, so rapidly that the effect almost unnerved him—Möbius equations commenced to mutate on the screen of his metaphysical mind. It was the vortex, and yet it was not the vortex. The numbers, characters, and symbols were the same but the pattern was not. There was no actual whirlpool of numbers as such but an *ordered* march of evolving calculi and ever-changing equations, like the emerging answer to a question of immense complexity unravelling onto the screen of some gigantic computer.

But the big difference was this: that Nathan was no longer ignorant, no longer innumerate. He now *knew* what he was looking for, and how to control and use it. And suddenly it was there, and he froze it: the Big Equation, framed on the screen of his mind like a page of printout.

Frozen there, yes, for a single moment, before it dissolved and warped . . . and formed a door.

A Möbius door!

And Nathan sensed that it was here, that it was real. His eyes snapped open and he saw it; there in the room with him, a single pace away. And he knew he was the only one—the only man in the world—who *could* see it.

The next scene would be remembered forever, by everyone who witnessed it. They were intent upon Nathan; they drank in every aspect of him, his looks, dress, stance, even something of his feelings, perhaps, until the picture of the man entire was etched into their extra-mundane minds:

Standing erect, head high, staring a little to one side and with his bottom jaw falling open a fraction as he became aware of something far beyond the sensory range of the rest, Nathan Keogh was an imposing young man of twenty, twenty-one years. His simple clothes, of this world, were nothing special, but the man inside them was. He was the Necroscope, who talked to dead men in their graves and so had access to all the secrets of the past—perhaps even of the future—and yet had no real time to explore or use such knowledge to his own best advantage. Not yet, anyway.

Nathan was something more than six feet tall. He had an athlete's body: broad shoulders, narrow waist, powerful arms and legs. His eyes might be very slightly slanted, or perhaps it was only his frown, the look of rapt *attention* on his face as he gazed at the mainly Unknown, which to the rest with the exception of Zek was completely unknown. His nose was straight and seemed small under a broad forehead flanked by high cheekbones. And over a square chin which jutted a little, his mouth was full and tended to slant downwards a fraction to the left. In others this might suggest cynicism, but not in him. Rather the opposite.

For looking at Nathan, Ben Trask knew the "truth" of him, which had to be revenant of his father, Harry Keogh: a natural innocence and compassion, the soulfulness of the mind behind the face. So that without being Keogh's spitting image, still the visitor "felt" like him. These had been Trask's thoughts the first time he'd laid eyes on Nathan, and nothing had occurred to change them. As for what was happening here: that could only confirm them beyond any further doubt.

Nathan viewed the Möbius door and stepped forward. The act was almost robotic, automatic, instinctive; as if he were drawn to the door; as if the place beyond it lured him irresistibly, which of course it did. Then, glancing just once at Trask and the others—

—He took a final, unsteady, but resolute pace . . . right out of this world.

He was there—and he was gone! They saw his right foot, calf, thigh, half of his body and face disappear, and the rest of him follow into nothingness. The Necroscope Nathan Keogh was no longer in the room. Just motes of dust drifting in the sunlight through the window blinds, flowing into the vacuum where he had been.

Easily stated, but astonishing to the witnesses. An agent on the briefing podium almost forgot to say his magic word into his handset, and only just remembered in time: "Now!"

And the answer came back at once from the Kensington crematorium: "Now!"

The man on the podium frowned at his handset. "Yes, *now*, for Christ's sake! Why are you repeating me? He's just done it. He's just gone in."

And again the answer, in a brief burst of static: "Who's repeating you? I'm *telling* you! He's just come out! He's here, now!"

No time lapse at all, not to them. But to Nathan:

He stepped in through the metaphysical Möbius door, and entered a place beyond all places, beyond all times, yet encompassed by and encompassing space-time itself. It was not the same as—could not be likened to—any experience he'd ever known before. Even the first time he'd been . . . *here*, with Zek, less than twenty-four hours ago, it had been different. At the very least there had been water then, a great spout of Ionian Sea water that had entered the Continuum under its own pressure, dispersing to . . . wherever. Now there wasn't even that.

There was nothing!

It was a place of utter darkness: perhaps even the Primal Darkness itself, which existed before this universe or any parallel universe such as Nathan's began. Except there wasn't only an absence of light but an absence of everything. Nathan might well be at the entirely conjectural core of a black hole (his E-Branch tutors had dealt with certain of the basic theories of cosmology, at least); except a black hole has enormous gravity, and this place had none. No gravity, no time (and therefore no space), no light. *Not* a place obeying one single Law of Nature or Science, and therefore a place outside the Universe we know. And yet existing *within* the Universe we know, for it had twice been conjured by a common—or an uncommon—human being; by the Necroscope Nathan Keogh. As for Nathan's father: Harry had been a habitual user, almost an inhabitant, of "the place."

Both central and external, the Möbius Continuum was nowhere and it was everywhere; from such a starting point one might *go* anywhere, or go nowhere forever. And it *would be* for ever, for in this timeless—environment?— nothing would ever age or change except by force of will . . . which was a fact that Nathan knew without knowing how he knew it. But then, how does a moorhen chick know how to swim? It was in his mind, his blood, his genes.

A "place," then, this Möbius Continuum: which might well be its best, indeed its only description. But Nathan's tutors had also touched upon theology, especially that of the Christian religion. And Nathan sensed that in some way this might even be a "holy" place. If so, then little wonder he'd been put to such pains to discover it. For it must be a very private holy place, in which no God as yet had uttered those wonderful words of evocation, "Let there be light!" Or if such words had been spoken . . . then this was the source of everything, the initial singularity from which THE ALL had shone out in a great and glorious beginning!

And as that thought dawned, at a stroke, so Nathan hit upon the greatest secret of all, which had taken his father a veritable lifetime to discover. But it was *only* a thought, which he hadn't recognized as the truth . . .

What he did recognize was this: that empty as this "place" was—and as far removed from man's laws as could be—still it had laws and forces of its own. For even now he could feel one such force working on him, trying to move, *re*move, or dislodge him from this unreal place back into the real. But Nathan had a will of his own and wasn't about to be moved except in the direction he desired.

"Behind" Nathan, if mundane directions had any meaning in such a place, the Möbius door closed. And remembering his purpose here he pictured the Garden of Repose in Kensington which was his target destination. It had been his plan to "picture" Sir Keenan Gormley's memorial marker, to focus upon the plaque and use it as a different kind of marker, but he now saw that this wasn't necessary.

For no sooner had the crematorium in Kensington entered his thoughts than he found himself in motion and knew that he was headed in that "direction." It was as if he were drawn along a route, though whether in a straight line, a curve, up or down . . . it was impossible to say or even guess. But definitely he felt the first tentative tugging of some force other than the Möbius Continuum's rejection forces. Not even a tugging, as such, but more a gentle pressure that seemed to want to guide him. He'd known something like it before when tracking the Möbius loop symbol from Zakynthos in the Ionian back to E-Branch HQ. Then it had been his lifeline—Zek's, too—and remembering that, he felt in no way threatened.

He simply went with the motion, the feeling, following it to its source: the coordinates of Keenan Gormley's Garden of Repose in Kensington. And like seeing a light at the end of a tunnel, so Nathan sensed the way ahead and accelerated his metaphysical motion by willing himself . . . *that* way, towards it. And as if he'd been walking and had suddenly broken into a run, he sensed that he was moving that much faster. So incredibly fast indeed that he was there!

And going from the incalculable "velocity" of thought

to stationary in less than a second—yet feeling no discomfort whatsoever—Nathan conjured another Möbius door and stepped across the threshold.

Light! Such brilliant light that he gasped and screwed his eyes tight shut. And gravity! Nathan staggered a moment as his feet touched solid earth and his legs trembled where they took his weight. Then someone said, "Now!" And eager hands reached out to steady him.

And despite the fact that time had seemed to pass during Nathan's trip from E-Branch HQ to Kensington, this was that same moment when the voice of the esper on the podium made his all-important mistake, and asked his all-important question: "Yes, *now*, for Christ's sake! Why are you repeating me?" Which sounded now from a handset in the Kensington crematorium where Nathan stood. Important for this reason: it was the first proof positive that "time" in the Möbius Continuum is nonexistent.

"Well done, Nathan!" Someone gasped his amazement, his congratulations. While in the Necroscope's deadspeak mind:

Well done, son! Sir Keenan Gormley applauded his efforts. *And now . . . more than ever you feel like your father.*

In answer to which Nathan was quick to inquire: *As he was in the beginning, or at the end?*

For a moment the other was silent, but Nathan sensed his shudder. Then: *It's true, Harry made mistakes.* Sir Keenan gave a deadspeak nod. *But don't forget, mistakes are what make us human.*

And almost as if his experience in the Möbius Continuum had soured his mind, making it caustic and cynical (though in fact it was simply nerves), again Nathan's rapid riposte: *Oh? But surely, Harry's mistake made him* inhuman! *It's what* cost *him his humanity!* But he knew that the other wasn't going to let him get away with that.

A clever man learns by his mistakes, Sir Keenan answered in a little while. *By his own mistakes, and by those of others. In your case, by your father's. You have a long way to go yet, son, but Godspeed. And take care along the way, Nathan. Take care along the way . . .*

* * *

After that, and during the next twenty-four hours, which was all the time he had left:

Nathan used the Möbius Continuum and the markers or coordinates which were his ever-growing coterie of dead friends constantly, until the geography of this strange world was no longer just a series of contour lines, trigonometrical points, watercolour oceans or bland white ice caps in the pages of an atlas, but a living, breathing source of constant wonder, astonishment, even awe. For the difference between this world and his own was like that between garlic and honey; and not simply in the sense that one was sour and the other sweet (not necessarily, for Sunside had its sweetness, too), but that in almost every other instance they were poles apart. Indeed, they were parallel *dimensions* apart!

Only in the mountainous regions was there any real similarity, of flora and fauna if nothing else; but even the mountains were different in a world where the sun shone on *both* sides of the range! For this Earth was one world—a complete, continuous system; *one* system, like a living creature in its own right—while Sunside/Starside, as its name might suggest, had often seemed like two. Sunside was a place of light, warmth, love, and life; while Starside was cold and gloomy, full of obscene black hatreds, bitter feuds, and loathsome undeath. How could it possibly be otherwise? The one housed the Szgany, Nathan's people, while the other was home to the Wamphyri.

But Earth—this parallel Earth—*was* wholly beautiful, notwithstanding the fact that certain of its people were not. So Nathan thought at first, anyway, before he'd seen the industrial wastelands of Eastern Europe, and those regions closed off to men forever because of their seething nuclear pollution . . .

Harry Keogh had had a great many friends among the dead, and now they all wanted to speak to Nathan. In one way it was new to him: the Szgany dead of his homeworld had wanted nothing to do with him, despite that he had often heard them whispering to each other in their graves.

But on the other hand it seemed very familiar, for the ostensibly "primitive" Thyre of Sunside's furnace deserts had been eager to know him from the first, when he had gone out into the sweltering desert to die only to find the will to live and a goal or worthwhile direction in which to aim his life.

The realization of his deadspeak had supplied the will to live, while his goal had been the Möbius Continuum (though at that time he'd had no knowledge of it, except that it was some great secret that hid itself in the mathematical maze of the numbers vortex). Well, and now that he had tamed the vortex, the Möbius Continuum was his to explore at will.

So the two talents went hand in hand, while Nathan's telepathy was a bonus that his father had not known; or at least, not until the last of his days. But as for other esoteric talents: Harry Keogh had not gone wanting. Indeed he had explored and practised one such "art" (namely, the resurrection of men out of their immemorial dust) which, in the light of what Nathan had learned of Earth's religions, might only be considered blasphemous. For it was one thing that rotting cadavers should feel empowered to will *themselves* up from their graves for the love of others, but another entirely that the long dead should be *called* back into life against their will, and raised up out of their very salts, dust, and ashes by a sorcerer for his own dark purposes.

Yes, a monstrous talent, this necromancy. And yet without it . . .

. . . . In a town called Bonnyrig not far from Edinburgh, there had lived a small boy who lost his puppy under the wheels of a speeding car. But for Harry Keogh's "skill" the pup would have stayed lost. Who could gauge the enduring pleasure that a mongrel dog's life had brought into the world of a boy, a youth, a man, even a family? For Paddy was alive still—the dog and his master both, grown up now—and Nathan had been to visit them.

But while on the one hand Paddy was only a mongrel dog, Harry Keogh's first experiment with necromancy, on the other there had been men, too, called back into life by his "art"; even a pretty young girl called Penny. All of whom had known the hell of dying twice, needlessly, because of Harry. And yet, not all of the people he'd touched in this way had been victims.

In the Zarandului mountains of Romania, Nathan talked to a Thracian warlord called Bodrogk, and to his wife, Sofia; or rather, to what remained of them. For they were no more of the flesh but a few handfuls of dust blown away on the winds of the world. But because they'd died here, they remained here still, to tell Nathan of his father's works. And none of the dead that he had spoken to or would speak to had more praise for Harry than Bodrogk the Thracian and his wife Sofia.

In the dark of night, in the ruins of an old castle under a waxing moon, their deadspeak voices thin as air apprised him of Harry Keogh's works: how the Necroscope had gone up against the last of the fabled Ferenczys here—Janos, the bloodson of Faethor—and won! And Nathan knew the story must be true, not only because the dead were telling it but because the very name Ferenc was a curse in his own world, too. As were all the names of the Wamphyri!

But when Nathan learned of the things this Janos had done—of the men he'd called up from their sacred dust to torture them for their secrets, and of their long-dead women which he'd used for other purposes—then finally his mind was decided on the subject.

Necromancy was a talent he would not pursue. In any case, it was abhorred by the Thyre and the dead of the Szgany alike, which was why the latter had avoided Nathan: because he was the son of the hell-lander, Harry Keogh. It was the last legacy of his father, which in his own world at least Nathan still must live down; either live it down, or prove that Harry's reputation in this respect was unwarranted.

But in *this* world, now that the Great Majority had finally befriended him:

Nathan visited a graveyard outside of Ploiesti in Roma-

nia, whose dead had risen up on his father's behalf against
Securitatea thugs in the days of Ceauşescu. They were still
there and they still remembered, and made him welcome.
His father was a legend to them, and they swore that despite the timidity of the Great Majority in general, they
had *never* turned their backs on Harry Keogh.

What? But Harry had been responsible for the removal
of a great cancer out of their earth: the termination of
Faethor Ferenczy himself, and his expulsion into the infinite abyss of future time—indeed, into Möbius time. For
within the Möbius Continuum, Harry had sent the incorporeal spirit of the master vampire Faethor winging down future time-streams with only his mind intact and no
possible hope of rescue. Such had been the Necroscope's
loathing of vampires . . . and such was his son's loathing
of them.

He visited a cemetery not far from Newcastle in England's northeast, to talk to a prostitute Harry had known.
Pamela's one regret was that she had never known his father "that" way . . . but she had known and liked him
enough to dig her way out of her grave for him when he
was in trouble. It had happened at a time shortly before
Harry had been driven out of (or had chosen to leave) this
world for Starside, when the Necroscope had been up
against a monster in human guise by the name of Johnny
Found. With Pamela's help—and the help of others of the
teeming dead, Found's victims all—Harry had destroyed
him right there in that graveyard.

So Nathan learned of his father's works, from the living
and the dead alike: from his friends in E-Branch and from
the teeming dead in their graves across the world. And so
he spanned the world in his efforts to track down any who
had known Harry Keogh, in order to vindicate his father
and reestablish his reputation.

In point of fact, it wasn't an absolute requirement that
Nathan visit their last resting places in order to talk to the
dead; it would be far easier to reach out a deadspeak
probe, seek them out across all the miles, and do it that
way. But that had not been his father's way; the first

Necroscope had never been the one to "shout" at the Great Majority; when he had desired to speak to a dead man, then he had gone to "see" him. Except in matters of extreme urgency, it had seemed the polite thing to do; and so it seemed to Nathan.

In this respect, too, he must use extreme caution. A good many of Harry Keogh's dead friends lay in graves or other resting places within perimeters that had enclosed the once USSR. Even with the Möbius Continuum to command, Nathan knew enough to restrict his visits to places such as these. Just as there were espers in the West, so there were "talented" men in the East—and most of them belonged to Turkur Tzonov!

But so many dead people to visit, because this might be his last chance; so many of them whom he *must* talk to. And all to be seen to in little more than twenty-four hours: a day, a night and a morning. Because that was all the time Nathan had left . . .

. . . In this world, at least.

To most men his itinerary—the amount of work he packed into those few short hours—would have been exhausting; without the Möbius Continuum it would have been impossible. Nathan was Szgany, however, and accustomed to the seemingly interminable hours of day- and nighttime on Sunside/Starside, where each day/night cycle was equivalent to a week in the parallel world of Earth. In this respect he could and did drive himself to an almost insomniac extent.

But when all or as much as possible was done, and Nathan returned to E-Branch HQ after one last trip—to a graveyard in the northeast of England where he'd talked awhile and said a fond farewell to a personal friend, the revenant spirit of a small girl called Cynthia, dead before her time—then, even he was weary. It showed in his face as he stepped out of the Möbius Continuum into Harry's room, where David Chung was no longer required to act as a homing beacon, for Nathan had the coordinates now.

And it also showed when he reported to Ben Trask, as he had been instructed to do after each Möbius trip . . .

II

Trouble at E-Branch—
The Möbius Route

The Head of Branch wasn't looking too good himself. Trask's voice was more than a little testy when he reminded: "It's Friday, Nathan, and we've a plane to catch—you, me, and a couple of minders. There'll be more of our people waiting in Belgrade, in case Turkur Tzonov is watching and has agents there. In fact, you can bet your life he has! And while we're on the subject of Tzonov: you may not know it but I worry when you're away from here on your own—that you might stray too far into his territory, that he might somehow trap and kill you. So maybe you'd like to tell me why you've kept me waiting? I was beginning to think you'd left it too late. Our plane leaves in just three hours' time. It's a standard flight of around two and a half hours; maybe you can catch up on some lost sleep in the air. Frankly, you look like you could use it."

But Nathan shook his head and said, "No, I don't think so. Flying isn't for me. I don't really care for airplanes."

It took the wind right out of Trask's sails. He frowned and said, "What the—?"

"I wasn't much for riding on Wamphyri flyers, either." Nathan's smile was wan, despite the tan he'd picked up in the Ionian. "And in a way planes are just as bad—perhaps worse. It was exciting enough at first, I suppose, but . . . let's face it: nothing that heavy should jump that high! So why don't you take David Chung to Belgrade, and I'll do my sleeping here and catch up later?"

"You'll catch up—?"

"Later," Nathan repeated it. "My way. As soon as you're in the Refuge at Radujevac . . ."

After a moment's silence: "Your way . . ." Trask said. The way he breathed the words, they were like a sigh. And in that same instant of time both men realized how much the older envied the younger. But then, perhaps in an attempt to disguise the fact, Trask asked: "Does it come that easy to you now?"

"It's getting easier, yes."

"With Harry, it was like walking, talking, breathing. But he'd had practice."

"And I'm getting it."

"You . . . you brought Zek here that way. I mean yesterday." Trask had had plenty of time to think about it; the idea should be old hat to him, but it wasn't and never could be. "You just, well, *brought* her here, from Zakynthos."

"That's right, I did." Nathan wasn't boasting; in the main it was still a mystery to him, too; he was just stating an anything-but-simple fact. And even without his telepathy, somehow he knew what was on Trask's mind, what was coming next.

"Son, do you think . . ." Trask began, and squirmed a little in his chair. He hated to obfuscate and liked all things clear-cut. Perhaps it was his talent working in reverse. "—I mean, in his time your father took quite a few people with him along the Möbius route. But it's something strange to me, an experience I can never know . . . Isn't it?"

"It's still strange to me, too," Nathan answered. "And yet attractive, maybe even addictive. Do you want to try it?"

"I . . . I don't know." Trask began to shake his head, then stopped and nodded. "Yes, I want to try it. This could well be my one and only chance."

"And do you trust me?"

This time there was no hesitation. "Yes, of course I do. You know I do."

Nathan shrugged and smiled again. "So be it," he said. And so it would be . . .

Nathan slept, but Trask was too excited to do anything but sit at his desk, shuffle paper and try to keep his mind off what was coming next, in just a few hours' time. For to dwell upon it . . . he knew he'd get no work done at all! Trask had been in a good many strange places and had done a good many strange things—the strangest!—but this was to venture into a place where only a handful of men had ever been, one that shouldn't even exist, except in the fevered dreams of theoretical physicists or abstruse mathematicians. The Möbius Continuum! Only let him think of it . . . off he would go again, into crazy dreams and fancies of his own. But *only* fancies, because there was no imagining how it would really be.

In the end he pushed the paperwork aside and went to the Ops Room. This was to be the stepping-off point for Romania. It was empty now, but in about three more hours . . .

They would all be here, E-Branch in its entirety, or with the sole (the soul?) exception of Anna Marie English, ecopath, who for some months now had been working with the kids in the Romanian Refuge, and at the same time making the way ready for Nathan. Even the Minister Responsible would be here, because this was something he'd never seen, either.

But Ben Trask *had* seen it, even before Nathan:

That time at Harry Keogh's place not far from Bonnyrig, his "last refuge" on Earth, when the Necroscope had reached the end of his time in this world. Trask had seen Harry in his Wamphyri mode—had witnessed something of a vampire's weird metamorphosis—and sometimes he nightmared about it still. But as for the Möbius Continuum: that was something you *didn't* see, unless you were the one who conjured it. But you could see it in use, certainly.

Remembering the way Harry had looked that night when the Branch burned his house, Trask shivered again. Jesus! The Wamphyri overlords of Nathan's world—or of Starside at least—were like *that*? He knew that they were, of course; indeed that they were worse than that. For Harry had fought the evil within himself all the way down the line, and according to Nathan even into Starside itself. But the Wamphyri: they gave free rein to their passions, their lusts, their evils. They *were* evil incarnate.

As so often before, one last picture of Harry Keogh came floating to the surface of Trask's memory. It was a scene from that same, sad, terrifying time when the Necroscope had almost but not quite succumbed to his vampirism:

An esper called Geoffrey Paxton—a treacherous telepathic dog who should never have been inducted into E-Branch in the first place—had tried to kill Harry, tried to shoot him with a crossbow. Failing, he had fallen prey to Harry, and almost to the creature within him.

There in the garden of his burning house, the vampire—the Wamphyri Lord, Harry Keogh—had picked Paxton up like a stuffed toy, examining him eye to eye, face to face. One fragile human being, albeit a piece of trash, up against someone who had been the *most* human being and was now a monster. Paxton, gape-jawed and bulge-eyed; his trembling, cold-sweating flesh only inches from the white-gleaming, salivating gates of hell.

Harry's face, his *mouth* . . . that crimson cavern of stalactite, stalagmite teeth, glistening and jagged as shards of broken glass. What? The gates of hell? All of that and worse.

And Trask had thought:

Paxton is a piece of candy, a sweetmeat, a coconut flake. He's something to munch on. Why, Harry could bite his face off if he wanted to! Following which the thought had occurred: *Maybe he does want to! Maybe he will!*

The memory persisted, with Trask shouting: "Harry, don't!"

And the Necroscope slowly closing those monstrous,

mantrap jaws, looking up in the ruddy illumination of the burning house and glaring at Trask across the misted garden. Then:

Your world is safe, Ben, Harry had told him in his mind. *I'm not staying here.*

And: *Starside?* Trask had wondered.

Harry's mental shrug. *There's nowhere else.*

At which he had released Paxton and let him fall to the earth like the piece of rubbish he was, and at the same time let Trask know that the war was over. But it hadn't been over for Paxton.

Snatching up his crossbow, again the telepath had tried to shoot Harry, at which the Necroscope had disappeared into the Möbius Continuum. And that had been the first time Trask had ever seen it, close up, in actual use:

With the deceptively sinuous grace of the Wamphyri, Harry had stepped or flowed backwards away from Paxton and into ... nothing! And to Trask and the E-Branch agents in the garden, it had seemed that he had simply ceased to be. Paxton's bolt had shot forward into the misty swirl of Harry's vacuum and been eaten up by it, leaving the telepath panting: "I got him! I'm sure I *got* the bastard! I couldn't miss!"

But the mist where it had closed on the Necroscope opened up again, and a clotted, gurgling, apparently incorporeal voice had come out of it, saying: "How sorry I am to have to disappoint you."

At that, Trask had snatched a breath of hot, smoky air as a clawlike hand with nails like rusted fish hooks reached out of empty space, closed over Paxton's head and dragged him shrieking out of the garden and out of this world. Then ...

Harry might oh so easily have killed the telepath, but he hadn't. Instead, moments later, he'd delivered him back to the garden: a man bereft of his telepathy. Which was the last favour that the Necroscope had ever done for E-Branch and the world in general.

Following which:

A brief exchange of words—an acknowledgement of the

friendship they had known—and Harry had said: "Look after yourself, Ben."

Trask remembered it so well. The way he'd felt: confusion, pity, shame. And his last futile attempt to find another way: "Harry, wait!"

But again the Necroscope had used a Möbius door to make his exit, and for the last time Trask had seen him step sideways into another place, space, time. If there'd been a rope, it might well have been the Indian rope trick ... if there'd been a trick! But there was no trick, and the magic was all mathematical.

Look after yourself, Ben ...

Again, in the eye of memory, Trask saw Harry standing there—a monster, yes, but a man for all that—followed by a replay of his eerie disappearance. Then dreams and memories gradually fading ... until suddenly, even startlingly, the Head of Branch was back in the empty Ops Room—

—Where now a hand fell on his shoulder!

Trask gave a massive start, half-turned, saw the Necroscope standing there! But it was a newer, younger Necroscope, himself startled by the older man's reaction to his presence, and drawing back from him. Until Trask regained control and took his arm.

"Nathan, I'm sorry! I was just thinking about your father, and ..." But here he paused, as the look on the other's face gave him away. Nathan already knew what Trask had been thinking about.

"Your thoughts, memories, were so strong ..." He shrugged by way of excusing himself, but in no way negligently. Nathan knew better than to enter another man's mind unbidden. "I knew they'd be about me, or about my father. You should learn to guard your thoughts, Ben. Especially in your line of business. Better if you'd kept that hypnotic guard on your mind, which you had in Perchorsk."

Trask gave his head a rueful shake. "No, I made mistakes in Perchorsk. A few, anyway. It seems that the act of blocking access to my mind took the edge off my talent.

Tzonov and company couldn't see in too well, but my vision was obscured, too! I'm only interested in the truth, Nathan. Half-truths aren't good enough. Anyway, this is E-Branch. There isn't a man here I wouldn't trust with my life, let alone my thoughts."

"Your mind was very clear," Nathan told him. "So clear, it was like I was there with you. You were frightened when you saw my father. And seeing him in your mind, I knew why."

Trask nodded. "He was Wamphyri, yes—but he was strong, too. He never gave in to it, not once."

"That's what everyone keeps telling me," Nathan answered. "It's as if you were saying: 'If it should come to the worst, remember that your father never gave in to it.' "

"Maybe we are saying that." Trask didn't deny it. "Nathan, even now you don't fully understand what a weapon you are. And if you were Wamphryi, too? If you should *become* Wamphryi . . . ?"

There was no way Trask could know it, but quite apart from Tzonov and the Opposition, there were other men, right there in London, who had thought that selfsame thought. The big difference between those men and Trask was this: that he was able to live with it.

With the exception of Zek Föener, out in the city arranging a flight home to Zante in the Ionian, the majority of E-Branch's available agents were gathering in the Ops Room when Ian Goodly on the Duty Officer's desk took the call from the Minister Responsible. As soon as the caller's identity was confirmed, the precog asked him: "But aren't you supposed to be here, sir?"

"Listen," said the other, urgently. "Don't ask me if I'm supposed to be there. Tell me if *they* are still there?"

"They? Trask and Nathan?"

"Of course! I mean, have they gone into . . . has Nathan . . . are they on their way to the Refuge?"

"In another fifteen minutes, yes. They're waiting for a call from Chung to say he's arrived. He's Nathan's beacon, as you should know."

"I *do* know! Now listen . . . Mr. Goodly, isn't it? We may be in for some trouble."

Suddenly the precog knew what had been bothering him all day. It was this, and the Minister Responsible was on the point of telling him about it. "Shit!" he said, which wasn't like him at all.

"What?"

"Get on with it," Goodly snapped. "Make it as fast as you can. And don't worry: I'll follow what you tell me." Of course he would, for he knew the gist of it already: that Trask and Nathan—certainly the latter—were in great danger. And so he would be attentive as never before.

The Minister took the precog at his word. Speaking rapidly, breathlessly, he said: "Goodly, other people know about Nathan. They know about him, and they have come to . . . a *decision*! But I don't agree with them. It could cost me my job, but I don't agree. Do you understand?"

"Yes. Go on."

"You don't know how relieved I was when Trask spoke to me just a couple of hours ago and said that Nathan was taking him along the Möbius route. Because these people had fixed it that Nathan wasn't going to make it out of the airport in Belgrade! That way they could blame it on the Opposition."

Goodly sucked in air so that it hissed between his teeth. "They were going to stop him going home. But . . . with prejudice?"

"Extreme! So when I heard that Nathan would be— what? making his own travel arrangements?—it was a weight off my shoulders."

"I imagine it would be!" Goodly growled, which wasn't like him either. "How come you haven't mentioned this . . . this Belgrade reception before now?"

"What would it profit anyone? I *would* have told Trask—of course I would—if he hadn't brought these other arrangements to my attention. But don't you know the risk I'm taking right now?"

"You're only risking your job. *Not* to have mentioned it would be to risk—"

"—I know," the Minister cut him off. "But I'm *doing* it, right? Give me credit for that at least!"

"So go on."

"The flight had a tailwind and got into Belgrade fifteen minutes early. And of course, Trask and Nathan weren't on it. So CMI smelled a rat."

"CMI?" Goodly frowned at the phone. "Are we talking about Combined Military Intelligence?" CMI was supposed to have shut down all of twelve years ago, but among the other intelligence agencies it was common knowledge that they were as strong and devious as ever.

"Nathan is a big gun on the loose," the Minister answered. "Nobody is in control of him. He's not even of this world, and his only interest is to get back to Sunside—*at present*! But what we've always been worried about is this: Will that be the end of it? Will he stay there? We had the same sort of problem with his father, do you remember? How many times has Ben Trask said what a weapon Nathan would make? And now he's *just* such a weapon! Of course CMI is interested. They were going to make him an offer: seduce or 'recruit' him, if you like, away from E-Branch. But that was before he got the Möbius Continuum . . ."

"Wait," Goodly cut in. "He only *just* got it. So how come they got to know about it so quickly?" On the other end of the line, he could almost hear the Minister's groan . . . which was as good an answer as any. The Minister "Responsible," indeed! Then:

"For Christ's sake, Goodly! I have a job, too, you know! I mean, do you think I'm a law unto myself? Man, there's always someone watching the watchers! If anyone should know that, you people should."

Get to the point," Goodly snapped. "So Trask and Nathan weren't on the plane. What's next?"

"Your place is next. By now they'll know we're trying to give them the slip. Just suppose *you* were looking for Nathan, where would you go next?"

"My place? You mean this place? E-Branch HQ?"

"Of course! The Belgrade party will have spoken to

their London controller, who will have seen to it that others are on their way to you even now. What's more, by now their orders will be quite specific!"

"*Christ!*"

"What is it?"

"Nothing," said Goodly, slamming down the handset. But in fact it was quite a lot. For the precog's talent had been galvanized into action, and in his mind's eye:

The elevator doors bursting open . . . a handful of muscular, hard-eyed, grey-uniformed paramilitaries spilling out into the corridor. Some of them carrying stubby automatics, others with machine pistols or folded down submachine guns. Goodly running towards them, being stopped and pinned up against a wall by two of them. Their voices clipped, gritty, as they asked him: "Your boss, and the one called Nathan—where are they?"

And him telling them: "In the Ops Room!"

Jesus! The Ops Room!

Before the precognitive vision had cleared from his mind, Goodly was out of his chair, out from behind the Duty Officer's desk, and into the corridor. The spinal corridor was a little less than fifty yards long, thirty from the Duty Officer's room to the Ops Room at one end. As he raced that way, Goodly's eyes were drawn to the elevator's indicator lights. Originally, the elevator had been part of the hotel downstairs. Now there was only one stop: the top floor, E-Branch HQ. But the floor indicator lights still worked as before, and the cage had just started on its way up!

It could be, of course, that this was an E-Branch agent, a late arrival, coming to see Trask and Nathan off. Except Goodly didn't think so. Bursting through the swing doors into the Ops Room, he saw a circle of espers standing there, shaking hands with Nathan and the Head of Branch. No one seemed in a hurry; Goodly was moving and thinking so fast that everyone else appeared to be stationary; their heads turned in a weird sort of slow-motion to see what all the fuss was about.

The fuss was about him, shouting: "Ben, Nathan—get

the *hell* out of here! I mean now! The Minister was on the blower. CMI has men on their way here, and they're after Nathan!"

"What?" Trask's mouth yawned open in a gasp, but he knew Goodly like his own brother and his mind was quick to pick up the precog's warning; he recognized the truth of what Goodly had said. And to Nathan, urgently: "Son, can we go now?"

Nathan closed his eyes, frowned his concentration, shook his head. "No. It's early and Chung is still mobile. Also, he was supposed to call us and we haven't heard from him yet. He could be in a car or something; there could be people around; we have to emerge somewhere safe."

In his mind's eye, Goodly saw the elevator doors hissing open! "Then go somewhere else!" he yelled, as he rushed back out into the corridor. "I'll stall them."

And they were already there: a handful of paramilitaries, with weapons enough to start a small war! But Goodly knew how to handle it, because he'd already seen it. Careering down the corridor, he flew straight into a pair of them. Grabbing him, they pinned him to the wall and asked:

"Your boss, and the one called Nathan—where are they?"

"In the . . . in the Ops Room!" Goodly gasped through a compressed windpipe where an arm was pressed to his throat.

"Where?"

"Down there." He flapped an arm towards the wrong end of the corridor. But at that end, CMI agents were already checking out the rooms. While at the other end, the Ops Room doors had been thrown open and a group of espers was emerging into the corridor.

Goodly found himself thrust aside, and followed on behind the paramilitaries as they ran crouching towards the Ops Room. Esper protests were ignored; Ben Trask's mind-spies were pushed out of the way as the CMI men went through the swing doors with Goodly right behind them—

—But in the room ... there was only a swirl of dust motes spiralling in a stray beam of sunlight through the slatted windows.

"You." A CMI agent prodded Goodly with his machine pistol. "You lied to us." He was about five-ten, blocky, broad-shouldered, red-haired and crew-cut. A typical bullyboy, he had to weigh about one hundred and eighty pounds. His green eyes were set a little too close together, and his lips were fleshy, the bottom one slightly pendulous.

Goodly scowled and brushed the gun aside. Other espers had come back into the room to stand watching, silent, with their arms folded on their chests. Now that Trask and Nathan were out of it, things were different. It was as the Minister Responsible had said: these men had specific orders.

"Did you hear what I said?" Sputtering and suddenly red in the face, the man with the machine pistol—their platoon commander?—again turned his weapon towards Goodly.

"I heard," Goodly answered in his piping but in no way intimidated voice. "I *always* lie to people who break into private property, and to thugs who threaten me! So do all of the people here. You and one of your men assaulted me in the corridor. And you'll pay for it. You're CMI, right? Well, you'll be dragged over some pretty hot coals for this."

The other cocked his weapon; and his men followed suit and pressed forward. But Paul Garvey, a full-blown telepath, had stepped up alongside Goodly. Now Garvey grinned and said, "He's wrong-footed, doesn't like being accused, can't do anything about it. They came to do a job and came too late. They have no more business here. Anything else would be right outside their jurisdiction. And this one is already worried about your threats. He cocked his gun to show you how big and brave he is, but now he's worried that maybe we'll report him for that, too. Because in fact he's chickenshit!"

Goodly knew that Garvey was reading the CMI leader's mind. But that one was staring—no, grimacing—at the expression on Garvey's face. For the telepath was still grinning, and deliberately. Which was a sight to see; or a sight not to see, if you weren't in the know.

"You," said the platoon commander, prodding Garvey with his weapon, but carefully. "Shut—your—*face!*" He continued to stare at Garvey's ... what, *expression?*

"Or what?" said the other. "You'll murder me? And all the rest of us? This is E-Branch HQ. Don't you know everything you say and do here is being recorded, including the fact that you wrecked the elevator's security system to get in? Not only you but the people who sent you—you're *all* in the shit!"

Paul Garvey was tall, well built, and still athletically trim despite his fifty-one years. Sixteen years ago he had been good-looking, too ... before going up against one of Harry Keogh's most dangerous adversaries, a necromancer called Johnny Found, and losing most of the left side of his face. At the time and on a number of occasions since, some of the best plastic surgeons in England had worked on him until he looked half-decent again, but a real face is made of more than just flesh scavenged from other parts. Garvey's face had been rebuilt from living tissue, true, but the muscles on the left didn't pull the same as on the right, and even after all this time the nerves still didn't connect up too well. He could smile with the right side but not the left. For which reason, and even though the other espers were used to it, Garvey would normally avoid smiling altogether—and avoid all other facial expressions, too.

But when Garvey stopped smiling and actually scowled, like now:

The platoon commander gulped and made a visible attempt to pull himself together. Then he applied the safety catch on his weapon and backed off a step. He blinked, looked away from the telepath, took out a plastic-laminated card from his shirt pocket and handed it to

Goodly. And quoting parrot-fashion, he began: "This was a CMI operation. You are required by law not to reveal—"

"—Out!" Goodly cut him short. "You and your gorillas, get your backsides out of here—now!"

The other grew yet more red in the face, puffed himself up . . . and let it all out in a grunt of frustration. He turned to his men, scowled, and indicated with a jerk of his head that it was time to leave. But Goodly wasn't finished with them. "Think about this," he said. "*You* are required by a law that makes the Official Secrets Act look like a joke from a Christmas cracker to forget you were even here! Why, you might even be persuaded to forget you were born! Because for all you know, your boss—or maybe *his* boss—is fitting you all up for prefrontal lobotomies right now!"

The CMI agents filed out of the room, along the corridor, into the lift. It was Goodly's first chance to count them: a half-section, eight men. The espers had had them outnumbered. But Paul Garvey said, "We had them out-everythinged! Not much brainpower there. And yet, if Nathan had been here, they had orders to take him. Or if they couldn't do that, to kill him."

"You got that out of their minds?"

"Yes." Garvey nodded. "But just Nathan, which meant I could afford to mouth off a bit. No big deal, for like I said: their leader was chickenshit."

"I have to report this." Goodly's face was grim; heading for the Duty Officer's room, he looked even more cadaverous than usual. But as he got there the phone started cheeping.

It was David Chung at the Refuge in Romania. And when he heard Goodly's voice: "Okay, Ian, I'm home and dry. There was a spot of trouble at the airport, but finally I'm here. Nathan and Trask can . . . they can come on in."

Goodly breathed a sigh of relief, said: "Yes they can."

Except—

—Where the hell *were* Nathan and Trask?

From deep in his mind, unbidden, it was as if some inner voice answered with a query of its own: *And where will they be this time tomorrow? For that matter, where will* you *be, Goodly my boy?* It was his talent working, he knew, except even a precog can't see too far into the future. And sometimes, like now, he was loath to even try . . .

Nathan was used to it by now, but not Trask. And after a single glance, Trask's first taste or feel of the Möbius Continuum, he doubted if he ever would be used to it. Or if he would want to be.

What do you think? Nathan asked him. For even thoughts had weight in the Möbius Continuum, and Trask "heard" them as sharp and clear as speech in the more mundane world. Quick to catch on, he answered:

When I'm a-a-able to think, then I'll let you know!

Nathan's chuckle was his only answer. But Trask was too busy sensing the Möbius Continuum all around him—absorbing or experiencing what he could of it—to feel any real resentment. And it was for him much as it had been for only a handful of human beings who had travelled here before him, so that when he was capable of thinking, he thought much the same thoughts as they had; even the same as Nathan himself had.

I was in the Ops Room, with Nathan, until we took a step—out—of there. Now we're here, on the other side of a Möbius door. Except . . . where the hell is "here"!?

For "here" lay darkness, the Primal Darkness itself, as it had existed before the universe began. It was a place of absolute negativity, not even a parallel plane of existence, because nothing existed here. At least, not under normal conditions. If there was ever a place where darkness lay upon the face of the deep, this was it. And Trask was struck by the thought: *Perhaps this was where God was born, before He took his first step into the universe of light. Perhaps that's how the physical universe started, when He split it off from this dark and metaphysical void.* For indeed the Möbius Continuum was without form, and void.

To say that Trask was "astonished" would be to belittle

the range of emotions that swept over him; indeed, and apart from that same handful of fellow voyagers, his was a new emotion, designed to fit an entirely new experience. Even the Necroscope Harry Keogh (despite the fact that he had been first), and his Necroscope son Nathan, had never felt like this. For they had understood at least *something* of the Möbius Continuum—they had imagined and conjured it—while Trask's mind was of the world, albeit a world in which Truth was the guide and Truth the gate.

And if anything that made it worse, for he understood the Truth of the Möbius Continuum: that it was *apart* from the world of men, and apart from all human existence and even conjecture, except in the secret minds of long-dead mathematicians and the "magic" of mystics and metaphysicians.

And yet he was here, and he *felt* it!

There was no air, but neither was there any time, so that Trask didn't need to breathe. And in the absence of time, space itself was absent. These essential ingredients—these prime constituents of any ordinary universe of matter—had no existence here! Yet Trask remained intact. He didn't rupture, disintegrate, and fly apart, because there was nowhere to fly to.

Trask knew the truth of it: that he was NOWHERE. But that it was also the place where Every-Where and -When had had their beginning. The birthplace of universes! The womb of worlds! The singularity before time began!

He might have shouted his alarm, his shock, his own version of "Eureka!" Except Trask was only one discoverer, not *the* discoverer. But he believed he knew now what men meant when they said they'd "seen the light." For he had seen the darkness.

And in that darkness, suddenly he was afraid. His grip was tight and growing tighter on Nathan's unseen arm. Unseen, yes, yet remembered on the photographic negative of his retinae like a slowly fading flash of light. Nathan, his sole remaining link with Sanity, Reality, Humanity. Trask couldn't actually see him but he could feel and sense him there. He knew the truth of the other. And for the moment that was all he knew in this awesome no-space-time.

Exhausted of mundane thought (or thoughts that made sense in a nonsense or extramundane environment), Trask's fear rapidly expanded into a kind of hysteria, but one that lacked the frantic motion of commonplace panic. He simply *dared not move*, because he couldn't be sure where motion—even the smallest motion—would take him. Moving . . . from *here*, one might go anywhere if one knew the route, or go nowhere forever. Which might well be Trask's fate if Nathan deserted him. And to be lost here would *mean* lost forever; for in this timeless, spaceless nonenvironment nothing ever changed except it was willed, and there was no will here unless it was brought here by someone who strayed into this place, or someone who came here and knew how to manipulate it. Someone like Nathan.

And at that a new thought occurred to Trask, or new to him at least:

Nathan, we shouldn't be here. It isn't our place. Rather, it isn't mine. His mental whisper was frightened, which Nathan sensed at once.

Easy. His own thoughts were calm, controlled. *Take it easy. Weren't you the one who wanted to do it? Well, and now you're doing it.*

But I'm not meant to be. I shouldn't be here.

Are you sure of that?

Trask wondered about that. Was he sure of it? But why wonder, when he knew the truth of it at once. *Yes, I'm sure. There are forces here. It isn't such a—what, vacuum?—as you've painted it. I feel . . . currents? And they're beginning to move me, trying to repulse or expel me.* Trask's "voice" was tremulous with his ever-increasing panic.

Calm down, Nathan told him again. *I have you. You're safe. I've wondered about those forces you feel. You know when you're waiting at a red light? How you feel the energy in the throb of the car's engine, just waiting to thrust you forward? Well, I think this is the same thing. It's your* own *power you feel. It must be, because nothing happens here except by force of will.*

It wasn't exactly the truth—only a guess at best—but Trask was in no fit state to repudiate it. Being here, his only desire was to be out of here. Like a small boy riding a roller coaster. *Where are we going?*

In a little while, Perchorsk.

That pulled the older man together in a moment. *WHAT?* But he sensed Nathan's shrug.

The last place anyone would expect us to turn up. At the core. But only for a moment. In and out again. Let them see us, then not see us. Nathan's mental voice was cold, grim now, reminding Trask very much of his father. *I want Turkur Tzonov to know who he's been dealing with. After what he's done to Siggi Dam, and what he would have done to me and Zek, I want him to worry.*

But why? You won't be here.

He doesn't know that. Anyway, I'm Szgany and I owe him.

But Perchorsk!

In and out, that's all, Nathan replied, determined. *Sufficient that they see us. It can't do you any harm, either. Turkur will think twice before he tries any more fast ones on you or E-Branch.*

Do you know the ... the way there?

Oh, yes. I was there, remember? But on the way, there's something else I would like you to see.

Trask was calmer now, but found difficulty in not being able—in not requiring—to breathe. *Really? And what would that be?*

The past, Nathan answered. *And the future! For I've discovered Harry's time-doors, but I haven't crossed a threshold yet. And don't worry—I'm not going to. Not yet. I just want to see it again. And Ben, just think what Ian would give to be in your shoes right now.*

Not a lot, Trask answered, sensing movement. *Ian Goodly doesn't much like the future. It's just something that happens to him. Come to think of it, it's something that happens to all of us. It's inevitable as dying.*

Maybe that's what he doesn't like about it. He'd much prefer to take his chances not knowing . . .

They moved rapidly towards a point of light that expanded in a moment into a shimmering door. And Nathan brought them to a halt close to the threshold. Light sprang forth from beyond the time-door, a pulsing blue light that was yet warm and in no way artificial. The light of life! Trask would have known the truth of it, of course, without being told. But standing or *being* at the threshold with Nathan, both of them silhouetted in the warm blue glow, he asked anyway:

The future? Our future? Man's future? And the blue threads?

After a short pause Nathan answered, and his whisper was no less awed than Trask's. *The threads . . . are men!* he said. *They are the lives of men . . .* And drawing Trask closer to the threshold—indeed, onto the very threshold—he added: *See! That's you, Ben, the blue thread of your future life!*

Beyond the future time-door, all was a chaos of millions of filaments of blue light, and Trask saw that one of them had its origin in his own being, streaming out from him like some weird ectoplasmic extension and dwindling to a bright blue thread as it hurtled into the future—*his* future. Another sped out from Nathan, out and away into the ever-widening haze of tomorrow . . .

For some time they gazed upon the panoply of the future; a minute or an aeon? . . . Trask couldn't say. But eventually:

Even here, time grows short, Nathan said. *At least, I feel it's so. Anyway, I know well enough where my future is leading me. Back to Sunside/Starside.*

Trask made no answer. Suddenly dumbstruck by the beauty (and not least by the knowledge) of what he was seeing, he'd become aware of a sound: an almost angelic chorus, an orchestrated, interminable *Ahhhhhhhh!* It could only be in his mind, for he guessed that time must be as silent as the Möbius Continuum itself. Of course, for if the sound of all the future were present, that would be an unbearable tumult.

And all of those blue life-threads weaving away into tomorrow and tomorrow, sighing in Trask's mind; and some of the threads growing dim and blinking out as men died, while others burst from nothing into brilliant neon-blue life as their owners were born. Trask felt he could stand here watching for all time. He *was* standing here for all time—all future time, at least.

But there's the past, too, Nathan told him, guiding him to a past-time door. Except that beyond this new threshold, instead of multiplying, spreading out and away forever as the human race expanded, the neon life-threads narrowed down, condensed, fell back into a well of nebulous light at the dawn of Man's ascendancy. And now the mystical *Ahhhhhhhh* sound seemed reversed, fading into the history of humanity . . .

In a little while—or maybe after a long time—Nathan said: *And now Perchorsk.*

Before Trask could protest he found himself mobile again, and experienced what felt like a split second of intense acceleration as his guide and companion simply *went* to Perchorsk in the Urals. They were there in a moment, coming to an instantaneous, effortless halt.

Nathan conjured a Möbius door . . .

. . . *Which warped and fluttered like the flame of a candle in a draft!*

And suddenly Trask remembered. *"Too close!"* he shouted at the top of his voice, a crushing, deafening, devastating avalanche of sound in the Möbius Continuum! "We're too close to the Gate!"

Numb from the vibratory effect, Nathan hugged Trask close. *I know,* he said. *Everything is wrong here, even the flux of the numbers vortex. But please, Ben, don't shout. Don't even think. I have to get the coordinates right, that's all.* Then, letting the door collapse in upon itself, he backed off a little and conjured another. This one was less unstable, but not entirely so; volatile and slowly consuming itself, it seemed to smoke, drifting a little as Nathan fought to hold it in place. Finally it firmed up; Nathan immediately stepped through and took Trask with him—

—Into Perchorsk. Into the complex under the Urals. Into the mighty cavern sphere known as the core!

III

The Gates: Perchorsk and Radujevac

Trask and Nathan had been here before and knew this nightmare place only too well: this alien cavern, eaten out of the solid rock of a mountain where the Gate was formed in the awesome vacuum of a nuclear implosion, this subterranean terminal or subway station to a parallel world called Sunside/Starside.

It was *like* being in a cavern, but that was where any similarity ended. The rock had been hollowed into the shape of a perfect sphere, a giant bubble well over a hundred and twenty feet in diameter. The curving shiny-black wall all around was glass-smooth except for the gaping mouths of energy "wormholes" that riddled it everywhere, even in the domed ceiling. And at the centre of the core ... the Perchorsk Gate itself, encased in a huge carbon steel shell some thirty feet in diameter whose three welded sections were supported on massive hydraulic rams. Those rams could apply terrific pressure to hold the fused sections together in one mass, if that were ever necessary. While within this protective (defensive?) shell of steel, the Gate supported itself, floating there dead centre, right where it had been born in a melting pot of alien energies.

At least, that was the scene which the two Möbius intruders had expected to see; that was what they *had* seen the last time they were here. But now:

Around the spherical steel "egg" that contained the Gate, a suspended catwalk ten feet wide had been drawn back in sections to allow for the egg's hatching. The catwalk was equipped with consoles, computers, viewscreens, but was empty of people with the exception of a handful of white-smocked, red-splashed bodies where they lay grotesquely crumpled and lifeless close to the master console. They had been scientists and were only recently dead, a minute or two at most. Nathan knew this with the sure instinct of a Necroscope; he *felt* the confusion, disbelief, panic, of people who had known that death was a thing that happens only to others ... which is what we all believe until it happens to us.

Nathan and Trask had emerged from the Möbius door on the outermost rim of a Saturn's-ring system of platforms, where a perimeter catwalk encircled the core around its equator. And as good fortune would have it, they'd emerged behind a shielding plate of aluminum fixed to the walkway's rail, making it a vantage point where they were hidden from the view of the rest of the core. The shield had smoked-glass windows through which, if ever the Gate should be opened up, it could be viewed without the customary dazzle. But of course the Gate wasn't likely to be opened up ... was it?

Some ten feet higher and sixty feet away around the gradual curve of the glossy-black wall, a landing fronted the perfectly circular mouth of a shaft running at forty-five degrees upwards into the rock. A railed stairway clung to the wall, with wide steps descending from the landing to the catwalk. Reaching out from the perimeter, a spidery gantry with an overhanging walkway formed a bridge to the inner catwalk with its consoles, computers, and corpses—and its glaring white light.

Light, yes: three giant cat's-eye slits or wedges of light shining out like solid bars from the four-foot *gaps* in the carbon steel shell, where the mighty rams had drawn back and torn the welded sections apart, leaving strips of weld hanging down like the rind of some strange metal fruit. And the alien light came flooding from the Gate, of course, exposed like the blind, free-floating eye of a gigantic Cyclops. Or the all-seeing orb of some colossal shewstone. Or maybe the seething evil of Pandora's box—standing open!

But this was the static picture, a first impression following the darkness of the Möbius Continuum, as when a light is switched on and the contents of a room print themselves on the viewer's eyeballs. Static, motionless, soundless ... until, as Nathan and Trask realized they were actually here, suddenly it erupted into life! Then—

—A veritable chaos of sound, motion, and deadly action!

The men on the inner walkway were not the only dead bodies here, and more were being made even now, so that it was immediately apparent what was happening: that Premier Gustav Turchin had done with his softly-softly approach and was going straight for the throat; he was attempting to beard Turkur Tzonov in his den. Beard him? He was trying to kill him!

"Christ!" Trask yelped, as automatic gunshots echoed and bullets ricochetted from the metal trim of the catwalk. "We've walked into a war! And Turchin ... not a word of warning from him!" As more bullets spattered, he grabbed Nathan's arm. "God almighty! Let's get out of here."

But Nathan, crouching down, said: "Wait! I have to see."

"See what?" Trask gasped, but in fact he already knew what. Nathan wanted to see Turkur Tzonov, what he was up to, what was going on here. The Perchorsk Gate connected with Nathan's world in a parallel universe, and the Gate stood open. The Russian's intention had been to invade Sunside/Starside with a crack infantry platoon loyal to himself; to colonize the vampire world, open it up as a vast new satellite of Mother Russia and sack it for its precious metals, thus financing a resurgence of expansionism and old-style communism here on Earth in what had become a politically, ecologically, and financially bankrupt USSR. During the course of which, Premier Turchin would be assassinated and replaced by a new, "democratically elected" leader of that vast region's polyglot peoples—Tzonov himself, of course!

That had been the state of play some four months ago. But then, when Nathan had come through the Perchorsk Gate from Sunside/Starside, Tzonov's plan had been discovered and passed on through diplomatic channels to the Russian premier; since when nothing much had appeared to be happening. Now it was becoming apparent that indeed things *had* been happening. Gustav Turchin had been busy and this was to have been the culmination of the premier's efforts, the realization of Turchin's goal: to catch Turkur Tzonov and his people red-handed and round them up. But it was equally obvious that Tzonov, the head of the Opposition—Russia's E-Branch—had seen it coming; this firefight in Perchorsk had to be the result of his contingency planning.

There were five uniformed, heavily armed men on the gantry. Under fire from the railed landing above the perimeter walkway, three of them strained to haul a trolly laden with an assortment of weapons and ammunition towards a gap in the steel shell—in fact towards the Gate—while their two colleagues gave them covering fire.

Now that Trask and Nathan's eyes had grown accustomed to the sudden brightness, the brilliant glare of the Gate itself, which was dazzling even through the smoked-glass window, they could see that these would not be the first of Tzonov's men to cross the threshold. Others of his soldiers had already passed through the "skin" of the dazzling sphere, its event horizon, and were visible on the other side as glowing slow-motion silhouettes against a uniformly milky backdrop. They were strung out, a straggling line of burdened, luminous figures dwindling into the alien white distance, leaving only a handful of their colleagues in the foreground to beckon eerily, with an agonizingly slow urgency, to those still outside where they crossed the gantry.

A white-smocked technician or scientist emerged from hiding behind the curve of the Gate. With his hands over his head to signify surrender, spread-eagling his body against a section of the steel shell, the frightened man inched his way into view. One of the men on the gantry saw him, turned the ugly, blued-steel snout of a machine pistol in his direction, and let go with a burst of a dozen rounds. It was murder pure and simple, totally unnecessary; obviously the soldier and his colleagues had been handpicked by Tzonov. The scientist jerked and shuddered as smoking-hot lead stitched him across and back, passed through him and fragmented against the carbon steel, and ricochetted from the metal back into his body. His white smock turned scarlet in a moment. And staggering forward, crumpling as he went, he fell to his knees at the rim of the platform, then tilted forward and nose-dived into sixty feet of thin air between the stanchions and rams. And his querulous deadspeak voice was added to that of the others near the console.

Nathan had no time to comfort them, could only watch.

More men came at the run down the circular shaft onto the landing. They joined those already there in firing at the soldiers on the gantry, pouring lead at them. One of the latter was hit in the chest, went down kicking and screaming, twitched and lay still. But they had almost got the trolley to the Gate and a few more paces would do it. Sparks flew from the gantry where bullets splintered against the metalwork, and the two covering soldiers returned fire.

As yet more men came through the entry shaft onto the landing, so a group of eight broke off from the original party to go clattering down the stairs onto the perimeter walkway. But when they were only halfway down, that was when things really started to heat up.

Nathan had been hoping that he would see Turkur Tzonov, and that Tzonov would see him. He had wanted to remind the man just who it was he'd treated so badly, and might still have to deal with in the future—also of the price to be paid for what he had done to Siggi Dam. So far the Necroscope had been disappointed, but no longer. The Russian was here after all; except now, if Nathan were to show himself, it might easily work out that he'd be the one who paid. Trask, too, of course, because they were together.

Beyond the stairway to the entry shaft, on the far side of the gantry spanning the gaps in the Saturn's rings, a twin-mounted Katushev cannon suddenly swung into action. The weapon was situated against the wall on a supporting platform; it sat there like an armoured blister of steel on a tripod of shock-resistant legs. Quiescent until now, its electric motor droned into life, the grey-domed hood cracked open, and as the assembly telescoped back on itself the operator in the heavily plated bucket seat came into view. Seeing who the gunner was, none other than Tzonov himself, Nathan and Trask gave simultaneous gasps of shock. This man would be menacing enough without deadly armaments, but at the firing controls of a Katushev ... ?

Turkur Tzonov was part Turk, part Mongol, all man. Definitely an "Alpha" male, his was an outstanding mind housed in an athlete's body. His grey eyes were the sort that could look at and into a man—literally. They were the instruments of his telepathy.

The Russian's eyebrows were slim as pencilled lines, silver-blond against the tanned ridges of his brows. He was bald, but this was so in keeping with his other features as to make it appear that hair was never intended. Certainly it wasn't a sign of ill health or aging; he glowed with vitality, and the only anomaly lay in the orbits of eyes whose hollows seemed bruised from long hours of study or implacable concentration. The purple was a symptom of his talent.

Tzonov's nose was sharply hooked, probably broken in some accident or fight. Most likely the latter, for the head of Russia's E-Branch was devoted to the martial arts. His mouth was well fleshed if a little too wide, above a strong square chin. His small pointed ears lay flat to his head. It

was undeniable that Tzonov was good-looking, but the
overall picture was of a too-perfect symmetry.

Even as the shock of seeing him receded, so the
Katushev's motor whined as Tzonov traversed the twin
barrels of his weapon from its target at the core's centre
until it lined up with the scaffolding supporting the railed
landing under the entry shaft. The men on the landing and
those descending the stairs had seen the movement and
were frantic to take whatever cover they could. Those still
on the landing made to dive headlong into the shaft;
those on the stairs hurled themselves over the rail to land
on the perimeter walkway.

And Tzonov ignored the squad on the walkway, aiming
right *through* them at the spidery scaffolding.

Nathan and Trask saw the expression on the Russian's
face as he applied pressure to the Katushev's triggers, and
"good-looking" or not, it was a look of sheer malice. His
lips drew back from his perfect teeth in a death's-head
grin, and the cords of his neck stood out in ridges where
they met his collarbone. Then . . . the grin turned into an
animal snarl!

And the Katushev went *whoof, whoof, whoof*!

Men were blown apart as exploding steel gutted them
and used them to colour everything yellow, scarlet, grey,
brown. Their liquids splashed everywhere as the scaffolding was reduced to so much twisted, smoking metal.
Those on the landing who hadn't made it into the shaft
went sliding from the slumping structure into the bowl of
the core, or hung on like grim death to the warped metal
rails or the teetering skeleton of the platform.

Tzonov laughed his scorn at them, glanced at the Gate
and saw that his men were through its skin with their
trolley-load of arms. Two of them waited on the far side,
beckoning to him in the Gate's weird slow-motion. He
would be the last of them to go through. Whatever else the
Russian was, he wasn't a coward. The savage grin slipped
from his face as he elevated the snouts of the Katushev's
barrels and put two more rounds into the screaming, mangled mess on the landing platform.

Behind their fragile shield, Nathan and Trask ducked down and covered their ears as shrapnel flew everywhere. A six-foot length of scaffolding pipe whipped end over end through the air and tore the top half of their aluminum cover away in a shriek of tortured metal. The smoked-glass window went with it.

"Now can we get out of here?" Trask yelled, surprised that he could hear himself over the ringing in his ears.

Pale-faced, Nathan nodded. He stood up, however shakily, closed his eyes, conjured a door. Trask also stood up, and as their top halves came into view, so Tzonov saw them.

They saw his mouth fall open, and a moment later the mad delight that lit in his eyes as his lips formed a single word: *"You!"*

"Shit!" Trask said, as the Russian traversed his weapon and lowered its smoking barrels.

Nathan tried to hold the door but couldn't concentrate. He could *feel* the Russian's eyes on him where they centered him in the Katushev's crosshair gunsights. Also, the proximity of the Gate was interfering; the door wouldn't form properly; his grip on the thing was too shaky.

"Nathan," Trask breathed. And again—but much more urgently—as Tzonov squeezed the trigger-grips, "Nath-*aaan*!"

. . . And the firing pins slammed forward onto empty chambers! They knew it immediately from the look of instant fury on Tzonov's face: the Katushev's magazine was empty.

It gave Nathan the breather he needed. As Tzonov swung out of the bucket chair down onto the perimeter ring and made a run for the gantry, so the Necroscope collapsed the first door and conjured another, also unstable, against the solid rock wall of the core.

But in the smoke and turmoil—with the agonized screams of the dying in his ears, and the moans of the dead in his metaphysical mind—Nathan's concentration was still lacking; he hadn't yet mastered the Möbius Continuum, couldn't afford to be distracted. And as Tzonov ran out midway onto the gantry, paused to unsling an automatic rifle from his shoulder and balance its butt on his hip, so Nathan's door slid sideways along the wall until it overlapped the mouth of a thirty-inch-diameter energy wormhole, a smooth-bored shaft in the otherwise solid rock. The door's outline at once shrank to a circle and seemed sucked into the narrow shaft . . . where it immediately firmed up.

Nathan had taken a step after the door. Looking into the wormhole, he could see that it was now stable. Having receded these few extra inches from the influence of the Gate, it was safe to use. And: "Ben," he called out to the older man. "Let's go!"

Trask came from behind his aluminum cover, saw Turkur Tzonov crouched on the gantry, aiming his rifle. And: "Shit!" he said again.

"You first," Nathan told him, as Tzonov opened up on them.

"First what?" Trask howled as bullets buzzed all about and *spanged* from the wall. Nathan made no reply but thrust him headfirst into the wormhole, and as Trask disappeared yelping into Möbius space-time, the Necroscope took one step back and dived headlong after him . . .

On the gantry, Tzonov's eyes bugged and his jaw fell open. For long moments, almost absentmindedly, he continued to hose a vicious stream of lead down the wormhole into which he'd seen Trask and Nathan disappear. Then his jaws snapped shut and his face darkened, twisting in fury. He knew it simply wasn't possible for men to wriggle out of sight that fast. They weren't in the wormhole, not any longer. They were . . . somewhere else.

And Tzonov knew where; or if not where, he at least knew what. Obviously Nathan had inherited his father's talents, or Trask and British E-Branch had helped him to rediscover them. Like Harry Keogh before him, he too had learned the secret of teleportation; he could *move* himself instantly, at will, from one place to another without physically covering the distance between. Or rather, he knew shorter, faster routes.

Tzonov's finger came off the trigger and the gun's obscene chattering died away, leaving only its echoes and the moaning of wounded men. But from the shaft behind the shattered, smoking landing stage came a clatter of booted feet. Time was running out for Tzonov, and he had a journey of his own to make.

He lifted the muzzle of his gun, fired a short burst into the shaft, then fell into a crouch, spun on his heel and hosed lead at the main console. Hot white sparks flew from metal, and Tzonov used them to trace a path across the shattering instrument panels. He knew where to hit, and when he found his target was rewarded with a display of arcing blue electrical fire. Corroborating his accuracy, there came a squeal of straining metal and triple jets of steam from the bases of the hydraulic rams. And the three massive sections of carbon steel eggshell began to crank shut.

Bullets fragmented into hot splashes of lead where they struck against the superstructure of the gantry close to the Russian's feet. Cursing, he turned and fired a long burst into the entry shaft, then raced for the narrowing glare of the Gate where two of the sections were slowly coming together. Desultory, sporadic fire followed him as he passed through the event horizon and seemed sucked into the unknown. But as the huge metal sections ground closer together and the light was reduced to three flickering arcs or fans, which were finally shut off, so the firing died away.

Then, apart from a feeble glimmer of white light from gaps in the shell where torn welding had fallen away, all was darkness. And as the rams shut down and hissed into quiescence, all was silence, too . . . except for the moans of the dying, and the unanswered, unanswerable queries of the recently dead . . .

Moments earlier:

Even within the Möbius Continuum, still Nathan could feel the disturbance of hot lead from Tzonov's weapon. Until he collapsed the door behind him. And then all he could feel was Ben Trask.

Na-Na-Nathan? Trask's query was a telepathic pant, a half-snatched breath, a prayer issued into the alien darkness. But in another moment it became a cry of panic: *Nathaaaan!*

The Necroscope went after him, grabbed him, said: *It's okay! Take it easy, Ben. I'm with you.* And reaching out with his metaphysical mind: *And David Chung is at the Radujevac Refuge. We can go there now.*

Jesus! Trask gasped. *Nathan, thank God you're there! I mean, I was wondering: "What if Tzonov hits him?" I'm sorry, son, but it wasn't you I was thinking of. I was thinking of me, stuck in this place forever. I'd go crazy in an hour. No, less than that. I'd probably already be crazy!*

Even as he "spoke" they were in motion, as Nathan tracked his earring sigil to Romania. And in another moment (or in no time at all, whichever way one wishes to think of it) they were there. Nathan conjured a door and stepped through it, dragging a stumbling, staggering Trask after him.

The light was subdued; Nathan's eyes accepted it without blinking; David Chung stepped forward and helped support Trask, whose face was drawn. "Trouble?" Chung was at once solicitous. "A bad trip?"

"You could say that," said Nathan, grimly.

He and Trask had emerged from the Möbius Continuum into a small square box of a room no more than three and a half metres across, with dim fluorescent lighting in the low ceiling and no outside windows or furniture. Just four white-painted walls and David Chung, and Nathan's golden Möbius loop earring. Seeing it in Chung's outstretched hand, Nathan took it back, slipped it into place in the lobe of his ear.

Trask was his own man again, despite the fact that his voice was still a little shaky. "Put it this way," he said. "I won't be volunteering for the Möbius route again!" Then, seeing the look on Nathan's face: "But that was only one bad thing, and there's much worse."

Nathan took it up. "We had to get out of E-Branch HQ in a hurry. I would have come here directly but you weren't *in situ*. There are a good many places I could have gone to, but I wanted to see Perchorsk again. So we went there, and ... we saw." He looked at Trask.

The older man cleared his throat. "Turkur Tzonov and, oh, I don't know—maybe a full platoon of his men? Maybe more—have gone through the Perchorsk Gate. When we got there, there was a small war going on! Premier Turchin must have decided to pull the plug on Tzonov, but Tzonov had wind of it. Being who he is, the talents he employs, that wouldn't be too hard. So no more softly softly catchee monkey. Tzonov is on his way to Sunside/Starside right now, with enough men and firepower to blow hell out of just about anything that gets in his way!"

Nathan gave him a strange, knowing look—perhaps a look of derision, certainly of denial—but said nothing.

"Which means," Chung said, "that Nathan will be wanting to get on his way, too. And as soon as possible."

And another voice, female, said: "Maybe even sooner than that."

Anna Marie English, an ecopath (and probably the *only* ecopath, sui generis, because for all Trask's years with E-Branch, he had never come across another talent like hers), had entered the room silently. Looking at the two arrivals, she said, "Ben, Nathan." Then, speaking directly to the former, and with a deal of urgency in her voice: "Have you talked to David? Do you know about the problem at the airport? CMI?"

Trask looked at her and thought what he'd thought so often before. Anna Marie was a Branch esper: English by name and nationality, but scarcely an English rose. She was invariably ... what, lacklustre? Well, that would be putting it mildly. Enervated, pallid, dowdy; even this current bout of urgency seemed a strain, almost too much for her to handle. It was her talent, Trask knew, and felt sorry for her. But on the other hand, maybe he shouldn't. At twenty-four the woman had looked fifty, and now at forty she *still* looked fifty! Which had to be good news for Mother Earth.

Ecologically aware, Anna Marie's premature aging had been held in abeyance by the planet's partial recovery from the industrial and nuclear ravages of the last century. As the Earth shrugged off its illnesses, so she caught up with her true age—but in reverse! She had been "worn out" as a teenager, and was now an "old" forty. But at the current rate of remission the day might yet dawn when she was a "young" sixty!

As for her talent (could it really be considered a "talent," Trask wondered, or was it more properly a curse?): as an empath feels for others, so Anna Marie felt for the world; she was as one with Mother Earth. As Antarctica was drained of its mineral wealth, so she was drained of energy. As the rain forests were raped for workable timber or even fuel, she too felt violated, burned up. She knew a little of the agony of every dolphin still being killed illegally by the Japanese, and could count the number of kills in the liver spots or wrinkles on the dry, desiccated skin of her spindly arms. When a huge, nuclear-powered cargo vessel sank in the Pacific, her bones ached to the slow seepage of radiation outwards across the ocean floor. And as fresh holes gaped in the ozone layer, so her ulcers ate their way through Anna Marie's guts.

But working out here at the Refuge in Romania, at least she was doing something good, worthwhile. And as well as helping these poor kids and young people, she was also helping herself. They were Earth's children, after all, and she was caring for them. Trask liked to think that maybe, in its own way, the Earth was returning the favour . . .

"CMI?" Finally he answered her. "I know about them in London. But . . . have I missed something?" He looked questioningly at Chung.

"CMI were at the airport in Belgrade, too," Chung told him. "And they were obviously disappointed that I'd showed up without Nathan—*very* disappointed. They questioned me for quite some time. It's why I was late getting here."

"It could mean a lot of trouble still to come," Anna Marie took it up. "And then of course there's Turkur Tzonov.

He has men in Romania, too. So the way I see it, we can't keep Nathan here too long. He won't be safe here. Not if CMI or the Opposition—or both—are desperate enough."

Trask grunted and said: "Tzonov was pretty desperate the last time I saw him, about . . . what, two minutes ago? He's out of it by now, though: on his way to Starside. But I know what you mean: his agents will be active as ever, carrying out whatever policies he left behind. As for CMI, I expect Ian Goodly will be stirring it for them right now! But in any case, don't worry, Nathan won't be held up here. Not if all goes according to plan." He looked at her questioningly, and she nodded.

And leading the way out of the room into the Refuge's complex, she answered: "It's all in hand. Except . . . wasn't Nathan going to take arms with him?"

"I still am," Nathan told her. "Everything I need is back at E-Branch HQ. Until I go back for it."

But Trask was quick to point out, "Ah . . . maybe it won't be as easy as that, Nathan. Not after what's happened." And to Anna Marie: "The plan was that once Nathan had the Refuge's coordinates, he'd be able to come and go—" he shrugged, "—at will. Then he would ferry his arms in piece by piece along the Möbius route. That's all there was to it. Maybe he'll still be able to do it; it all depends on E-Branch, the situation back home."

As he finished speaking, they arrived at the administrative office in time to catch the first chirrup of the telephone. It was E-Branch from London, Ian Goodly asking for Trask. Anna Marie handed the telephone over.

"Ben here," Trask said. "And: "Are we scrambled?"

They were, and Goodly told him about the rest of the visit by CMI. "They were after Nathan," he finished off. "With orders to take him if they could, or to kill him!"

Trask nodded absentmindedly, and said, "Someone's afraid of him, even as we were afraid of his father." And glancing at Nathan: "And just as mistakenly. But how did they know we were getting ready to ship him home to Sunside/Starside?"

"Would you believe . . . our Minister," and Goodly

coughed an imitation cough, "Responsible? I have to admit, though, that he seemed genuinely upset. And you have to remember, it *was* the minister who warned me that CMI would be calling on E-Branch in the first place. Thinking back on it, I recall that he mumbled something about setting watchers to watch the watchers?"

Again Trask nodded at the telephone. "Right. At E-Branch we're all big fish. But when it's something as important—or as potentially dangerous—as this, then there are even bigger fish, even sharks! They're called Advisers to the Inner Cabinet: top-level, stone-cold 'thinkers' specializing in finance, world affairs, and security internal and external. Lots of brain but not an ounce of heart in the whole bunch. You can bet your life that somebody up there, someone a lot bigger than our minister, set this ball rolling. Well, that's as may be, but whoever he is, he's obviously as prone to making mistakes as anyone else. Killing Nathan would have been one hell of a big mistake, and for a hell of a lot of reasons!" Turkur Tzonov was just such a reason, of course, but Trask wasn't going to talk about him right now, not even on a scrambled telephone.

"So what's next?" Goodly asked. "And is there anything we can do at this end?"

"Nathan's arms and ammo," Trask answered. "Still safe and sound?"

"Hidden away," Goodly said. "CMI didn't find them. And if they had, so what? We're E-Branch; we're entitled."

"And where are CMI now? Are they watching, listening, interfering?"

"Not that we can discover."

"Right," Trask grunted. "This is what I want you to do. Temporarily immobilize the elevator, and make E-Branch secure. Put a man on the roof to watch for choppers. And others on the street, just watching. Also, I want you personally on the telephone to me from start to finish, continually, so we can talk each other through all Nathan's comings and goings, until he's got all of his stuff out of there. I know it's highly unlikely CMI could get a team back in there before Nathan could get out, but I'm not going to take any chances. The merest hint of danger at your end, and we wait it out until he can start again."

Nathan touched his elbow. "You'll be wasting your time on the telephone," he said, quietly.

Trask looked at him. "Eh?"

"Zek is still there, in London," Nathan reminded him. "Have her called in. She can be my early warning system. No need for the telephone. Phones can be put out of action."

Trask thought, *Yes, and so can Zek!*

Nathan read it not only in his mind but in his eyes, too. And he was quick to agree: "You're right, of course. Use the telephone."

On the other end of the line, Goodly had managed to catch a little of what was being discussed. Now he said, "Zek walked in just a moment ago. She's been in town, making arrangements to fly home. She's with me right now and says she wants in on this."

Trask uttered a disgusted, barely audible, *"Oh, fuck!"*

And Goodly said, "Zek asks me to say, and the same to you!"

"Very well." Trask knew he wouldn't get the best of it with Zek Föener. Having fallen in love with her, he didn't even want to. "So break down the weapons into easily handled batches. The Ops Room will be perfect; plenty of room for Nathan to work in. Zek can give him the okay as each batch is made ready; he'll home in on her and, well, do his thing." Glancing at Nathan, he offered an apologetic shrug.

"Okay," Goodly answered. "Give me time to secure this place, and then Zek will get back to you—or rather to Nathan. Say, fifteen to twenty minutes?"

"Right," Trask told him, and put the phone down. And turning to the others: "We have maybe twenty minutes." He looked at Anna Marie. "Is that time enough for us to see your end of the operation?"

She nodded. "Come on."

The Refuge was a school, a hospice, a sprawling home

in the woods for fifty Romanian kids aged sixteen to twenty. Following the collapse of the disastrous Ceauşescu regime back in the late eighties, as Romania gradually opened herself up to Western influences, so E-Branch had worried certain Powers-That-Be into building a place here on the wooded banks of the Danube not far from Radujevac. The siting of the Refuge had not been arbitrary: it stood guard over the mouth of a resurgence, where a subterranean river, a tributary of the Danube, surfaced after its dark journey from a source somewhere in the foothills of the *Carpatii Meridionali*, the Transylvanian Alps. And the resurgence itself was the source of all Earth's vampire myths and legends indeed of all vampiric *infestation* of this planet.

For it was here, some miles up the lightless borehole of the sump, that a second Gate opened into this world. And this Gate, too, connected with Nathan's parallel world of Sunside/Starside. Thus the Romanian Refuge served two purposes: it *was* a refuge for a handful of victims of Ceauşescu's nightmarishly draconian policies, whose traumas had been such that after all these years they still required help; but more than that, it was a barrier against further incursions of the yet more nightmarish Wamphyri, and all the horrors of Starside.

In the bowels of the place, beneath its foundations, the river's rush had been diverted, channelled, controlled. There were monitors down there, to register the presence of anything that might prove inimical to mankind. And there was ... *machinery*, which permitted the entry but not the exit of anything bigger than a minnow or small eel. Any man or creature not of this world, coming from the underground Gate and flushed down the river, would find other than safe refuge here. And alive, dead, or undead, the thing would undergo something other than a metamorphic change. Electrocuted, gutted, boiled, and ground down, eventually he, she, or it would emerge as so much mush or paste to be dried out and incinerated. In this matter as never before, E-Branch had been very specific ...

Above ground the Refuge sprawled in three tiers, like a

modern, half-buried ziggurat against the face of a cliff once carved by the Danube but now standing well back from the river's swirl. The lower level was built on pylons sunk into the scree; between the pylons, reinforced concrete walls had been frescoed into autumnal patterns and shapes. An outsider would probably think it unlikely that there was a cellar back there, though certainly anyone approaching the wall too closely would hear a low whine of turbines when it rained or the cloud ceiling lay low on the foothills; especially in the winter months, when the resurgence powered the Refuge's heating and lighting systems. Outsiders, however, were kept well back behind gardens and a high perimeter fence right on the rim of the river. The entire location was a "Sovereign Base Area," a small British enclave on foreign soil.

Having first run the gauntlet of the Refuge's security or "purification" systems, water from the subterranean sump now resurfaced below the east-facing wall into a large lily pond. From there it made its way to the Danube via a deep concrete sluice, forming a slow, shallow stream in the dry season but running to something of a torrent when the rains came.

So the Romanian Refuge fulfilled its prime objective, and its staff only half-jokingly referred to themselves as "Guardians of the Gate." But the kids in their care weren't simply a cover. They had always been well cared for, and as long as Anna Marie English was in charge the same level of care was guaranteed. Orphans, cripples, socially deprived kids (one might call them all of these things, and even "inmates" in certain cases): they occupied the Refuge's two upper tiers. Their classrooms, workshops, and recreational facilities were in the lower tier, along with the staff accommodations, directly above the site of the original resurgence. But the infrequent whine of turbines was lost in a massively reinforced and soundproofed concrete floor.

The room where Trask and Nathan had emerged from the Möbius Continuum was little more than a storage room off the inner corridor of the central tier. Anna Marie had ordered it cleared out so that Nathan would have ample room in which to work. Her admin office was on the same level, with a huge window facing south. Looking out of that window, Chung, Trask, and Nathan had gazed across the sunlit river into Bulgaria on the one hand, and Yugoslavia to the east. But borders no longer mattered a great deal, and so the scenery was simply "country."

From the admin office they had gone down into the Refuge's lower level, and in a gymnasium where an instructor worked out with some of the kids they'd looked east through patio windows across a wide balcony set with tables and chairs, to where the gravel drive wound across gardens and into the trees, right up to iron security gates set in the high fence. The place would be generally secure, at least. But not from determined men.

And that was when Trask had decided: "It all looks far too peaceful out there—but it isn't!" It was his talent working, telling him that this was all a lie. "We're observed. The Refuge as a whole is under scrutiny. Probably Tzonov's people. Or CMI—" And quoting Anna Marie: "—Or both. You're right: we have to get Nathan out of here ASAP."

They didn't bother to visit the basement (Anna Marie told Trask that in any case it was all very quiet and ominous down there, like the stomach of some hungry, patiently hibernating beast), but left David Chung back at the admin office to take calls and went up to the Refuge's top level. There Trask met some of the staff, people who actually *were* what they appeared to be: teachers, nurses, physio- and psychotherapists, people who cared what they were doing, and for the kids they were doing it for. But among these specialists were others ostensibly "under instruction." And these were Trask's men, seconded to E-Branch from Special Forces, security-vetted and sworn to secrecy.

They were ex-navy men, cavers, speleologists, experts in subterranean exploration and underwater equipment, and Trask had been rotating their duties here for as long as the Refuge had existed. These were the men who would handle the machinery down in the guts of the place, if ever that should become necessary, and they were also the men who would escort Nathan to the Gate in the lightless bowels of the foothills. (Lightless with the exception of the Gate's own enigmatic glare, of course.)

There were five of them, three of whom had already visited the Gate. That had been two weeks ago, when the water level had gone down after a long dry spell. But the good weather had continued and they now considered it safe to take both Nathan and his weapons up the resurgence and into . . . into another world. Into his own world, of course. Or at least take him as far as the threshold of that world, from where he would go on alone.

As Nathan was introduced to them, a Romanian youth came running with a message from Chung: E-Branch was secure. Nathan could commence ferrying his weapons into the Refuge . . .

The Möbius jumps were no problem at all, and each time Nathan used the Continuum, it got easier. There was no longer any sensation of "speeding" to a place; he simply "went" there.

And E-Branch HQ was where he went, where Ian Goodly had seen to the readiness of what was to become his Sunside arsenal. Nathan had picked up a case of fragmentation grenades; compact flamethrowers normally used in rat-infested sewers; nite-sited, infrared, laser-guided machine pistols; three 11mm SLRs, inches-accurate to three-quarters of a mile; a pair of lightweight, 30mm rocket launchers; ammunition galore. He had also developed a certain fondness for a new model all-metal crossbow used in quarrying, forestry, and the Canadian logging camps. The half-inch bolts were full of plastic high explosive and could bring down a pine tree faster than any chainsaw. Fired into a trunk from a safe distance, the core of the bolt would detonate 1.5 seconds after impact. On Sunside, crossbows were weapons Nathan had always known and respected, but this model was something else. He'd picked up six of them.

All in all the weight of these armaments came to around five hundred and eleven pounds, but Goodly had bagged them in lots of one hundred pounds. Five trips to and fro, with espers loading Nathan's arms *into* his arms at the London end and Trask and Chung offloading them in the Refuge. If CMI or anyone else knew about it they weren't making any noise, and the job was done in less than five minutes . . .

IV

The Way Home

"That's it," said Nathan breathlessly after the last trip but one. "That's the weapons part of it, anyway."

"What's that you say?" Trask cocked his head on one side quizzically. "What else is there?"

"Just someone who wants to say good-bye to you before she goes home for a while. And she's asked me to take her there—my way. But she wants to stop off here first."

"She's asked you to—?" Trask drew air in a gasp. "Nathan, wait . . . !" But too late, for the Necroscope had disappeared into thin air. A moment later he was back, setting down Zek on the floor as dainty as a dancer. And she passed from his arms into Trask's just as easily. Nathan was also carrying her suitcase.

"Zek doesn't seem to have your problem with it," he told Trask. "With the Möbius Continuum, I mean."

"Ben." She smiled, never giving Trask a moment to regain his equilibrium. "I'm going home for a while. Back to Zante. I want a little time to think over what we talked about."

David Chung coughed self-consciously and slipped silently from the room, but Nathan stayed. He knew what it was all about and felt no embarrassment.

"What we—?" Trask looked at her in his arms and drank her in. Zekintha Föener was beautiful; she always had been and Trask supposed she always would be. At five-nine she was about an inch shorter than he himself, but where looks were concerned he had been at the back of the queue while she'd been right up front. Named by her Greek mother after Zákinthos, the island where she had been born, Zek was slim, leggy, blond, and blue-eyed. It was obvious that in her colouring she'd taken a lot more after her German father. Or maybe she'd taken after her Greek island birthplace itself, for Zákinthos was the Isle of Flowers. She must be, oh, some forty-nine or fifty years old now; not that anyone would ever guess; she could just as easily be thirty-six or -seven.

Zek had her faults . . . but they had always been there, and for Trask's money they only served to enhance her. It was these smallest of small flaws that made her perfect— perfect in his eyes, anyway. Her mouth, for example, with its soft, naturally moist lips just a fraction too full, which tended to tremble a little when she was angry. And the uneven jut of her jaw, also when she was upset, which seemed slightly more prominent on the right . . .

Abruptly, she brought him right back down to earth:

"Don't tell me you've forgotten?" Again her smile.

And Trask at once reddened up. "No, I haven't forgotten. But . . . will you be safe back home?"

"Nathan is the one everyone is out to get," she answered, her smile fading. "Once he's gone, they'll soon enough forget about me. And probably about all of us."

Two of the cavers came into the room to collect a bundle of arms and ammo. One of them paused a moment, looked at Trask and Nathan—and at Zek, wonderingly— and said, "Anna Marie says it has to be soon. Well, we just want you to know: we'll be ready anytime you are."

"Give me a minute," Nathan told him.

"You're that eager?"

"Wouldn't you be? I'm going home!"

The other smiled, however uncertainly. But Trask thought: *Would you still smile if you knew what he's going home to?* And as the cavers left the room he released Zek and told her, "Be careful, and stay in touch. Let me know when you're ready. Or not ready? I mean, I know I'm not that much of a catch, but—"

"You're an awful lot of a catch." She kissed him. "You're . . . true? That's not just a talent you've got there, Ben Trask. It's a lifestyle. Sometimes when you look at me . . . I have to admit, I've looked into your head once or twice. And there was only one other person who ever thought of me like that. Well, I've spoken to Jazz, and he doesn't want me to be alone."

Trask's heart gave a leap. "You've made up your mind?"

She nodded. "I think so. Now I need a break to just . . . well, to think about it. The logistics of the thing. You see, I love my island, too, and I have to say a long, slow good-bye to it."

Nathan was getting impatient and Trask knew it. He returned Zek's kiss and said: "But right now a fast good-bye, right? Very fast!" And to Nathan: "Okay, she's all yours—so to speak. And look after her!"

Nathan smiled his slow, introspective smile and said, "You needn't worry, Ben. I love her, too—but differently. Apart from her colours, Zek could be my mother." An outsider hearing that would probably find it strange: her colours *were* Nathan's and in that respect she could easily be his mother. Except he thought of himself as Szgany, and so her colours were alien to him. Moreover, Nana Kiklu (his real mother) was dark-eyed and raven-haired, a Traveller, a Gypsy. But speaking his mind was part of Nathan; so that the way he'd said it, Zek knew his comment had nothing to do with her age, everything to do with his feelings. And she felt complimented.

"I'm ready," she said. And again Trask watched it happen:

The way the Necroscope's eyes changed from a deep

sapphire blue to the cloudy blue—the near-mystical blue—
of English summer skies, as he conjured a Möbius door.
And he nodded just once at Trask as he drew Zek to him
and guided her in a certain direction, stepping to one side
with her almost as if they were dancing—but stepping into
nothingness. Then:

There was a sudden rush of air into the spaces they'd
occupied, and apart from Trask the room was empty.

David Chung, with a cordless telephone in his hand,
beat Nathan back into the small room by maybe a second
and a half. "It's Ian Goodly," he told Trask. "For you—
urgent!"

And a moment later Goodly was piping in Trask's ear:
"Ben! Something bad is on its way!"

"At E-Branch?" Trask's voice rasped his anxiety.

"No. Out there. At the Refuge!"

Trask trusted the other's talent to the limit. He didn't
question him further, except to say: "When?"

"Any time now!"

"Who is it?"

"I can't see it too clearly. Just explosions—shouting—
violence! And, Ben . . . I don't see you. You and David
Chung, you're not there!"

"But we *are* here!"

"Not in the immediate future."

Trask felt the short hairs at the back of his neck stand
on end. "Death?"

"God, I don't know! But where before I've always
known you'd be there—in my future, I mean—now you're
not . . ."

Nathan saw the expression on Trask's face, said: "What
is it?"

"Get down to the basement, the cellars, whatever the
hell they call that place down there . . . the sump, yes. Go
now, Nathan, And you, too, David."

"And you?" Chung's face was suddenly shiny with
sweat. He knew it must be bad.

"I'm coming, too," Trask nodded. "But not without one

of these!" He snatched up a machine pistol from the floor, one of the few remaining items of weaponry in the room, and slammed a full magazine into its housing. "Now come on, let's go!"

The phone was dead in Trask's hand; he hooked it into his breast pocket and let it dangle.

Nathan tucked a box of ammo under his arm and slung an SLR over his shoulder, and Chung grabbed up a pair of black-metal crossbows still in their oiled wrapping. And that was it: only a small ammo box to go, and a package of spare parts for the SLRs. An ex-navy type, checking to see that they'd got it all, picked up these last few items.

But in the corridor, as they headed for the sump . . .

. . . They bumped into Anna Marie. "I equipped some of the instructors with walkie-talkies, sent them out into the woods and approach roads," she said breathlessly. "Mercifully, there are damned few roads up here! But I'm getting reports of furtive strangers in the neighbourhood, and a couple of call signs haven't got back to me at all. Ben, I don't like it."

On their way down to the basement he told her about his call from Ian Goodly. "None of us likes it," he said. "Not you, me, or Ian. If this is Turkur Tzonov—I mean, if his people are involved—then they're taking one hell of a risk. Something that could blow up into an international incident. And if it's CMI . . . I understand how Nathan could frighten people: a man with his powers, coming from an alien world of vampires. But how come they're *suddenly* vindictive? How come we've had no wind of it? It's why we're in the intelligence game after all: so we can know what's going down before anyone else. But not this time. It's as if someone had been hiding, watching, waiting, looking for the main chance. But the main chance to do what?"

Anna Marie hobbled on spindly, hurting legs, having difficulty with the concrete stairs down to the lowest level. "Have we grown lax, Ben?"

"The Branch? Possibly. But once Nathan's out of here

we have to tighten up again. *I* have to tighten up—if they give me the chance."

"They? The manipulators? The puppeteers?" There was more than a little scorn in her voice. "We should have taken it all away from them long ago. Our world still needs saving, Ben, and no one is making the effort. Not much of an effort, anyway. It makes nonsense of everything. If we can't do anything for our own world, isn't it a bit presumptuous of us to try and save someone else's?"

"But if we were the bosses" (Trask had thought it over a good many times), "who would there be to watch us?"

"Who watches them?" There was logic in her bitterness, but Trask knew the "truth" of his argument. Absolute power, and all that . . .

"As for Sunside/Starside," he ignored her retort to examine the rest of her question, "you know as well as I do that if the vampire world is taken by the Wamphyri, ours could well be next. It's Nathan's world that's under threat now, yes . . . but tomorrow and tomorrow?"

Before she could make an answer, if she would:

The phone hooked in Trask's pocket chirruped insistently, causing him to start.

By then they were down into the sump of the place, where through the course of centuries the resurgence had eaten away the bedrock of the cliff into an overhanging, echoing grotto. Now the mouth of the cave and the course of the gurgling, shallow stream it emitted were roofed over and enclosed in an electrified wire-mesh "tunnel" hung with powerful lamps. And away from the roots of the cliff the watercourse had been diverted, lined with reinforced concrete, and channelled into a system of man- or vampire-traps.

A door in the wire mesh stood open where warning lights showed a reassuring green; the power was off. Men were waiting in the tunnel, and some of them had pulled on the trouser bottoms of rubber wetsuits in preparation. Nathan, Trask, and the others joined them, and in the mouth of the cave Trask paused to answer the phone. He recognized the Minister Responsible's voice immediately, and at once said:

"Thanks a lot!" His voice was bitter, choked.

"Trask, there's no time for recriminations," the Minister told him. Which served to corroborate what Goodly had said: it was coming soon. "Now listen and listen good. This is from the very top. D'you understand? The *very* top. You're not to go any further with your plan. Nathan isn't to use the Gate. You have to hand him over now, without any fuss . . ." The Minister paused a second as if to think something over, and in the next moment the pitch of his voice went up several notches, almost to a hysterical level:

"Trask, CMI are out there, at the Refuge! They're listening in on this, at your end and in London both. I'm not party to it, Trask, you have to believe me. But if you don't cooperate, they have orders to . . ." And the phone went dead.

Trask understood. It was supposed to have been an order, but the Minister had turned it into a warning. Following his pause, his last words had been rushed, almost shouted, near-hysterical, and at the end Trask had heard a second voice—perhaps military? Certainly authoritative, angry—as its owner snatched the phone from the Minister's hand.

"Shit!" Trask said, under his breath. But not so quietly that it went unheard.

"It's all coming to a head, right?" David Chung's face was shiny now with sweat.

"Let's see Nathan off," Trask nodded. "Then it's our necks we'll have to worry about." He was thinking about Ian Goodly's warning, that he and Chung had no immediate future. But Nathan had read his mind, and:

"I can take you out of here," the Necroscope said. "I have the coordinates of a dozen different places. Anywhere you want to go. E-Branch?"

"Christ!" Trask groaned. "The Möbius Continuum . . . again?"

But Chung was all for it. "Why not?" he asked eagerly. "I mean, if you think we're in danger here . . . ?"

"Both of you," said Nathan, as his eyes went through their weird metamorphosis. And catching hold of their arms, he drew them through a Möbius door—

—And out again into E-Branch HQ.

—The Ops Room.

—Now an encampment of the enemy!

Ian Goodly was there, his face a mask of shocked realization. So was the Minister Responsible, red and raging. (Trask hadn't known his call was from E-Branch HQ; it was a place the Minister visited only rarely). And half-a-dozen espers wearing as many expressions; *and* a handful of CMI thugs, their weapons to hand but mercifully not at the ready. The Minister had his back to the trio where they appeared out of thin air. He was flailing his arms and shouting something unintelligible at a uniformed man with a cordless telephone in his hand.

But the precog Ian Goodly had "known" where they would come through and was looking directly at them, yelling: "For God's sake go! Get *out* of here!"

Even as Goodly shouted his warning, the Minister Responsible turned and saw them. Still a few years from retirement, he was small and grey, sparse but still sprightly. Red-faced one minute, in the next he turned pale as he recognized Trask, Chung, and Nathan, and his single atypical comment was:

"Jesus!"

"Out of here!" Trask grated in Nathan's ear, repeating Goodly's expert advice. But at the same time, as the muzzles of CMI weapons swung in their direction, he cocked his machine pistol, which made a typical ch-*ching* sound as the first round was picked up and rammed into the breach. He couldn't fire the thing—wouldn't, not while there were espers in the room; and whether for good or bad reasons the CMI men were only carrying out their duty, after all—but it was a warning. If this was to be a firefight, it *would be* a firefight. The bullets would be flying in both directions.

And the warning was taken. CMI agents scattered in all directions through the Ops Room; espers hit the floor, taking what cover they could; the Minister Responsible and senior CMI officer present, who were closest to Trask and his party, took staggering steps backwards and put up their fluttering hands.

It was all of the distraction Nathan had needed. He conjured a Möbius door, grabbed Trask's and Chung's elbows and swung them off-balance, aiming them at the invisible metaphysical portal. But CMI weren't just playing a game; they did have their orders, and Nathan was at the heart of it. From beneath the podium, an ominous, answering ch-*ching* sounded over all other sounds, and just as Nathan propelled his companions over the threshold of his door, so a stream of deadly lead scythed across the room, accompanied by the deafening, snarled obsenities of rapid fire.

Even as he entered the Möbius Continuum, Nathan was hit in the shoulder. It spun him over and over in darkness, lighting up his mind with flashes of red pain. And Trask and Chung, holding grimly to him, likewise spinning and actually feeling it: his lack of coordination, the sickening whirl of Nathan's psyche, until he was able to steady himself and ask:

Where now?

That he had asked told its own story: his shock, disorientation. The fact that he'd been hit. The pain was in his mind as surely as it would be in his words if they'd been spoken.

How badly? Trask was anxious for him—for Nathan this time, not himself. And this despite the fact that if the Necroscope's wound was fatal, the head of E-Branch might easily be stuck in the Möbius Continuum forever. It was a measure of Trask's friendship for, his dedication to, even his love of the son of Harry Keogh. Likewise of David Chung's when the locator said:

"Nathan—hang on! Don't go under . . ." And yet again the insane gonging, the painful reverberation of spoken words in the elemental, echoing nothingness of the Möbius Continuum.

I don't think it's bad, Nathan told them. *But I need to know where to take you. Time's running out; I mean, at the Refuge. What about Zek's place on Zante?*

No! Trask cautioned him against it. *Whatever this thing is with CMI, she's not involved in it, not yet. And you're right, we're running out of time. Goodly foresaw trouble at both ends, and no future for me and David at* any *end! Not in this world, anyway . . .*

With which his talent took over and showed him the whole picture, the whole "truth": that while there was no future for them in *this* world, Earth wasn't their only choice. What about Sunside/Starside?

Nathan read Trasks's thoughts; but one didn't need to be a telepath to do that, not in the Möbius Continuum. *You want to . . . to come through with me?*

That has to be it, Trask answered. *It's the only answer. I don't feel about ready to die, but if there's no future for me in this world . . . ?*

Chung had understood all of this, by which time the fact had also dawned that it wasn't a good idea to speak—and certainly not to shout—in this place. So that now he thought: *Couldn't Ian be mistaken?*

But Trask said: *Oh, and can you remember the last time he was mistaken?*

The Möbius Continuum was getting to Chung, plus the knowledge that Nathan had been hurt and might well need attention. And it was a fact that Chung couldn't remember the last time Goodly had been wrong. For which reasons: *Back to the Refuge*, he groaned.

Nathan had the coordinates—

—And they were there, as quickly as that.

—He guided them through his fresh-formed door.

—Into chaos!

They emerged in the cave mouth at exactly the same spot where they'd been all of a minute earlier. And they emerged in time to experience at firsthand Ian Goodly's "explosions . . . shouting . . . violence!" But not for thirty seconds yet.

Anna Marie English and an ex-navy type were waiting, their expressions (even Anna Marie's) showing pure astonishment as Nathan, Trask, and Chung appeared out of thin air, the first stepping light while the others stumbled, gasping their relief at being back. Two of the cavers had moved deeper into the sump; the remaining pair were outside the wire-mesh cage where they worked at the dials on an instrument panel, setting them to automatic for the duration of the coming expedition.

That was how it was for a moment. Then . . .

. . . Trask's phone chirruped insistently and it was one of Anna Marie's men out in the grounds of the Refuge; he had had his walkie-talkie patched through by someone in the administrative office. "Anna Marie!" His voice came over high-pitched, excited. "There are men out in the grounds. I don't recognize them. They're doing something at the frescoed wall. Oh Christ, they've planted . . . charges? And now they're taking cover!"

Ian Goodly's "explosions" sounded clear in Trask's imagination. But not only in his mind, for a moment later:

The awesome blast sounded, then filled the hollow, acoustical echo chamber of the Refuge's basement and cavern-housed sump with hammer-blows of concussed air, and was accompanied by a fireball that blazed into blinding existence in the far, front-facing wall. In the next split second the wall burst inwards, allowing the fireball to expand into a star of incandescent destruction, while the force of the initial explosion hurled flaming debris— chunks of concrete, masonry, and twisted metal—deep into the basement. Pieces of hot-smoking concrete cartwheeled between floor and ceiling and came crashing through the wire mesh to splash down in the shallow stream or land at the feet of Trask and the others where they shrank from the shock of the blast.

The two ex-navy types who had been working at the console that controlled the sluice and various unseen engines and devices had been picked up and tossed aside, disappearing behind a mushrooming wall of fire and smoke. Perhaps they had screamed as debris rained down to bury them, but if so their screams had gone unheard, lost in the reverberations of the explosion and a burst of automatic gunfire from the gap in the shattered wall, where now the daylight was filtering in through a black smog of smoke and dust.

"Jesus Christ almighty!" Trask shouted over the din. And: "What the hell? God, someone is going to *pay* for all of—"

"Sir!" An urgent voice echoed from the back of the cave. "This way. If you're coming, come now."

"Come on, let's go," said Anna Marie, her face pale as death.

"Those two men back there." Nathan held back. "They were going to help me. And now they're gone." His voice was shaky from more than the mindless violence; he could hear the whispers of the recently dead, all the fear and the doubt and the dread of the endless dark.

Trask saw how he held his left shoulder, and the scarlet seeping through his fingers. "Are you okay?"

"Yes . . . no," the other answered, shaking his head undecidedly. "I mean, this was for me."

"So don't waste it!" Anna Marie hissed. "Now let's go."

She's stronger than she looks, Trask thought, following after her. And behind them in the reek and the turmoil, more gunshots and shouting as men came clambering over the rubble, their faces smudged but their eyes eager as they scanned the basement all about.

At the back of the cave, unseen until now, a solid plug of concrete stood wall to wall and floor to ceiling. It was fitted with a steel manhole or air lock three feet in diameter to the left of the stream. The stream itself came gushing out of a steel spout of roughly the same diameter but set lower in the wall, some twelve inches above the sluice. Two more outlets where they flanked this central jet were dry: the outflow was insufficient to warrant their operation.

The air-lock door stood open and Trask helped Anna

Marie to slide through, then directed Nathan, Chung, and the caver to follow after. Trask went last, and as he grasped handles on the door and swung his feet into the tube Anna Marie called back to him from the other side:

"Close the door after you, Ben. Just yank on the handles." He reached out again and did so, feeling the circular door settle onto oiled hinges. But before swinging it shut he saw shadows mobile on the wall of the cave as two armed, gas-masked men entered at the run. Silhouetted against the smoky lighting of the wire-mesh tunnel, they wore civilian clothing, the anonymous grey of CMI. As yet, however, they hadn't seen Trask. Then . . .

. . . A third man, unmasked, joined them; and Trask froze as he heard this one say: "Okay, where are they?" For it was a voice he recognized. A lot older than he remembered, true (of course it would be), but the same clipped, efficient, cynical and self-serving voice he had known all those years ago. Yet even though his talent told Trask it was so, still he had to be sure; even at the risk of life and limb. Which was why he waited with the door only half-closed, knowing that if they spotted him and started shooting—and if a few lucky rounds should get into the tube—then he'd be finished.

"A bunch of them came running in here," a gruff, muffled voice answered the first. "They can only be back there. If the three of us open up together, hose the place down, we'll probably get them all. And remember, our orders concerning the one called Nathan are clear: we're to kill him. If the others get taken out in the process, so what?"

"I don't much care about the others," that eager, oh-so-well-remembered voice snarled in return. "But as for the alien—*my* orders are to take him alive! Now cover me . . ." The owner of the voice crouched down and came loping through the writhing smoke into the cave, following the course of the sluice. Trask had his machine pistol, and it was still cocked. Apply a gentle pressure to the trigger . . . this one would bother him no more. But he couldn't do it, even though he now knew who or what he was dealing with. For if Harry Keogh had spared this man—despite all he'd done or tried to do to him—who was Trask to take his life?

And still he waited.

Tendrils of smoke cleared, and now the man was only a few paces away. Trask's eyes were accustomed to the gloom; he looked, saw, knew that he was right. And at the same time the man spotted him on all fours in the air lock. Their eyes met, narrowed, bridged a gap of years. And Trask remembered again that scene in the garden of the old house outside Edinburgh.

The Necroscope, Harry Keogh, monstrous in his drooling, Halloween, halogen lantern-eyed Wamphyri mode, holding in one hand a small, thin, dried-up, withered-looking prune of a man . . . called Geoffrey Paxton!

Paxton the mind-flea, an E-Branch telepath, but treacherous to a fault; indeed, to every fault in the book! He had been maybe twenty-seven then, was in his early forties now. But while the weaselish face and eyes—and certainly the voice—were the same, Paxton's body appeared to have undergone something of a metamorphosis of its own. Deprived by the Necroscope of his telepathy, Paxton had had to develop other talents; not mental or paraphychological but physical. Forced to work for a living, he'd been obliged to become more nearly the man. And Trask thought: *Why, he's looking in good shape! His body, at least . . .*

But the mind was the same as ever. Still devious, still full of hatred, still lusting after revenge. Revenge against Harry Keogh . . . or his heirs! And once again Trask recognized the truth of it, and as easily as that the mystery was solved. Paxton of CMI! Sixteen years it had taken him to get in shape, climb to the top, become a high-ranking officer in the Department of Dirty Tricks. And all that time he'd been watching E-Branch and waiting, always waiting.

Vindictive: *God, yes, he was!* Trask thought. But as vindictive as this? To have worked all these years for this? Or was there more to it than simple revenge on Harry Keogh and whoever followed after him? Harry had considered Paxton a mind-flea, an irritation, an itch he couldn't scratch without surrendering to the monstrous parasitic Thing inside him, whose prime objective had been to make him Wamphyri. But in the end he'd found a way, had entered Paxton's mind and made a few adjustments there. So that when at last he'd scratched the telepathic itch, Paxton's talent was no more. The Necroscope had erased it.

Trask knew how he would feel if he were suddenly robbed of his talent: he would want it back. And Paxton? Did he want his telepathy back? Or did he want more—a whole *lot* more—than that? As an esper with E-Branch he had read the Keogh files, of course. And he'd been right there at the finish, during Harry's last days in this world.

So . . . Paxton had known the Necroscope's capabilities; indeed, he'd experienced Harry's talents firsthand. He knew about the Möbius Continuum (Harry had taken him there, to the most private place in or out of the world, where he had fixed his mind), and about Sunside/Starside, the vampire world. At the end, he'd known too that Harry was a vampire. One of the undead—but the only one who could talk to the truly dead. The only one in the world, yes . . .

. . . At that time.

But now there was another, Nathan. And Paxton knew about him, too. Thrown out of E-Branch, the ex-esper had wormed his way into CMI, which with the exception of the Branch was the last of the covert government intelligence agencies. And he'd done it specifically to keep a watch on the mindspies. For if there was a way—any way at all—for Paxton to get his telepathy back, it would have to be through Trask's E-Branch. And if there was a chance to add to that talent or enhance it . . . ? Then be sure he would take it.

Well, and now his time had come; opportunity had knocked at last; perhaps this son of Harry Keogh could put right what his vampire father had put wrong. But that wasn't the end of it by a long shot, for it was also Paxton's chance to take his revenge! Right here and now, looking at the man face to face, Trask knew the truth of it: that that was *exactly* how it was. Paxton would use Nathan if he could, and if he couldn't he'd kill him. Trask knew it, yes . . .

. . . And Paxton knew he knew.

To recognize and evaluate Paxton had taken only a second, and a lot less than that to forcast his reaction. Next to the Necroscope himself, Trask had been Paxton's worst enemy. Obviously he still was. So that as the ex-telepath swung his weapon towards the air lock and squeezed the trigger, Trask was already closing the door on himself and yanking the handles to lock. He heard only the start of it as the cavern filled with the lunatic chatter of sudden death, but certainly he knew when the door itself was hit: the clamour was deafening as bullets flattened themselves on steel only a few inches from his face.

Trask pushed at the shut door and slid backwards down the smooth bore of the tube a few inches until eager hands grabbed his legs and pulled him through. The tube was about seven feet long, the thickness of the concrete wall, and fitted with handles at the sides to give purchase. Trask supposed that the air lock would be the weakest part of the system. The doors could be blown off. It wouldn't take Paxton long to cut or blast his way through.

Nathan, Chung, and Anna Marie were waiting with the three remaining cavers. In the white, artificial light of the inner cave, the faces of all six looked drawn, with features etched in fear. And looking at them, Trask thought: *Only one way out now*, but again Nathan had been listening.

"I can still take you somewhere else," he said. "It would only take a moment to set you down in Edinburgh or Hartlepool. Or the Greek Islands, if you like!"

Trask shook his head. "Son, we all have our talents. Anna Maria, Chung, myself, and you. Especially you. Well, Ian Goodly is talented, too, and I trust him as well as I trust myself. If he says I have no immediate future here, then obviously I can't stay here. And anyway, can't you see what a strange thing that was for him to say? No 'immediate' future? Does that mean there is a future for Chung and me, but a distant one? And does *that* mean we're to make our way to Sunside/Starside, and then return at some later date?"

Nathan nodded. "I was faced with the same problem once. My future was foreseen, and I was told it would come about even if I tried to avoid it. The future is like the past: immutable. It can't be avoided, wherefore it's better not to know it."

Anna Marie had locked the inner door and was crouched with her ear to it. "They're doing something on the far side," she said. "Preparing more charges, maybe? But it will take longer. They have to be careful not to bring the whole place down."

And one of the cavers asked nervously: "So, who's going?"

"The three of us," Trask answered at once, but he glanced at Anna Marie, waiting for her to say:

"Four," as she straightened up. "I witnessed that mayhem back there, that cold-blooded murder! Whoever was responsible, he won't want witnesses."

Trask gave it only a moment's thought, then:

"Okay," he said. "I was going to ask you to come anyway."

"Oh?"

"Yes. You see, the leader of that rat-pack back there is Geoffrey Paxton. Apparently he's with CMI now."

"Hold on a second," another caver growled. "I mean, we've been pretty patient here, but don't you think it's time someone told us what the hell's going on? Nobody told us we were going to war! As for this bloke—" he stared at Nathan, "—the way he comes and goes . . . shit, we're completely in the dark! All we know is that we're working for you, Mr. Trask. But are you doing something wrong here, or what? Isn't CMI a government outfit?"

"Let's get under way," Trask answered, "and I'll tell you as we go."

As the cavers made ready their equipment, Anna Marie applied a field dressing to Nathan's shoulder. His wound was a deep groove along the firm, rounded muscle of his upper arm. Almost a burn as opposed to a cut, the bullet had self-cauterized its own damage. Criss-crossing an earlier burn he'd come by only two days earlier in the Greek Islands, the result was a stiffening of the shoulder. Mercifully, that was all.

And in a little while the party set out up the course of the underground river.

Twenty-five minutes later, following the main watercourse deep into a subterranean cavern system, the seven were up to their thighs in ice-cold water and Trask had told a much-abbreviated story of an alien world and the vampire creatures who dwelled there. Where he might have erred, Nathan was there to correct him. Also, Trask had detailed the reasons why Nathan must get back there—not only to save his world, but possibly ours, too—and had even put forward his theory about Paxton: the ex-telepath's reason for wanting to take Nathan alive ... or dead, if only for revenge against Harry Keogh.

At first the thoroughly down-to-earth trio of cavers had seemed sceptical, but Trask's talent occasionally worked both ways: he not only read the truth but the truth was read *in* him. This was one such occasion; gradually his demeanour and tone of voice got through to them, so that as the party sloshed its way upstream they heard him out without comment. In any case they'd seen the cavern of the Gate—and what it contained—following which ... Trask's explanation seemed as good as any. And when finally he was finished.

"But didn't Miss English say that those CMI people wouldn't want any witnesses?" The caver spokesman's voice echoed in the cathedral acoustics of the place, and his face in the light of powerful torches told of his fears. "Well, we're not just witnesses, Mr. Trask: those were our colleagues, friends, who died back there. And what about us? Do we get to enter this other world, too? Or will you leave us down here to face whatever's coming?"

Trask looked at him, then at Nathan, and said: "Things

have moved too fast. I haven't had time to think it out. I can't say what will or won't work."

"They can come through with us," Nathan answered. "They're sending me home, and carrying my weapons, after all. I wouldn't want them to come to any harm. And anyway, Lardis will be able to put them to good use; he'll be needing good weapon-training instructors."

"And when it comes to coming back home again?" This from one of the other cavers.

But Nathan could only shake his head, shrug, and say: "I can't make any promises. If you knew the Wamphyri like I do, you wouldn't make any either."

"But there's a chance?"

"Better than a chance. There *is* a way back for all of you, but for the moment it's blocked. And anyway, we can't be sure of the reception you'd get at this end. But later, if there's to be a later, I can always take you back to the Starside Gate, yes."

The cavers looked at each other. And in a moment: "Then it looks like we're coming with you," their spokesman said.

Which coincided with a muffled roar like distant thunder from far back along the way they'd come. And: "There goes the air lock," Chung groaned.

By now they were waist-deep in blackly swirling water, heading for a dry ledge to one side of the watercourse. Behind them they towed a pair of lightweight rubber dinghies with tiny but powerful outboard motors, and a long buoyant rubber sausage fitted with zipper pockets. At a push, each of the dinghies could take three passengers; the sausage was a floating transporter: Nathan's weapons and other goods had been stowed in its pockets.

"Seven of us," the caver spokesman said. "Six in the dinghies, and one hanging on behind the sausage. I'll kit up." And as they climbed onto the ledge: "This is where we lose our pursuers, for now anyway. There are spare dinghies and air tanks in the Refuge, but if they want to follow us beyond this point they'll have to go back for them."

There were six prop-assisted Aqua-Lungs on the ledge, and Trask found himself feeling a little claustrophobic just looking at them. But as the caver spokesman struggled into a wet suit vest, again he reassured Trask: "For the final leg of the trip. A sump some fifty feet end to end, but totally submerged. We'll assist you through, of course. And believe me, we're lucky. The water table has never been this low. Any other time, we'd have been swimming long before this."

From back along the course they'd followed, as they got carefully into the dinghies and started the motors, they could hear echoing sounds of splashing and hoarse voices; these were left far behind as they lowered their heads and entered a long lake of black water, where the ceiling came down to only a few feet.

And feeling the weight of the Carpathian foothills miraculously suspended overhead, as they followed a string of luminous bobbing corks into an apparently endless darkness, each and every one of the seven fell silent. And it was as much as they could do not to hold their breaths . . .

But the darkness wasn't endless.

For a full half-hour they forged at low speed against the flow of the river, sometimes with the walls in sight and at others when even the ceiling receded out of view. But eventually the cavern narrowed down into something of a bottleneck, where a dark shingle beach rose inches out of the water. And to one side of the beach where the wall was split with a massive crack, there the water had a glowing, milky sheen to it, as if lit by some strange submarine fire.

Nathan recognized that soft but somehow unwelcoming glow well enough. "Beyond that crack in the wall there," he said to Trask, "stands the Gate." And to prove it, if only to himself, he conjured a Möbius door—which at once warped and collapsed in upon itself. As it had been in Perchorsk, so it was here in the bowels of the earth: the close proximity of the Gate interfered with the space-time matrix, and with the Möbius Continuum, of course.

After beaching the dinghies, two of the cavers pulled on

vests and fins and set off at once into the water. Swimming to the crack in the wall, they upended and disappeared into glowing depths. Behind them they trailed a luminous nylon line made fast to a knob of rock projecting from the wall of the cave. In only a minute or two they were back and signalling that Nathan, Trask, and Chung should enter the water. In wet suits and wearing Aqua-Lungs, the three took up positions between their guides and hauled themselves hand over hand along the line. So they came to the cavern of the Gate. There on a dry ledge they stripped down, and one of the cavers took the smallest of the wet suits and a lung back through the sump for Anna Marie. Assisted by the caver spokesman and his 2/IC, she was the last to come through.

Before entering the water with her, Anna Marie's escorts partially deflated the sausage transporter and made it fast to the end of the line. As for the dinghies, they were simply cast off and left to drift downstream. And finally all seven of the party stood in the cavern of the Gate.

The cavers had been here before; however strange, this was nothing new to them. While they hauled on the line and recovered the sausage containing Nathan's small arsenal and various items of dry clothing, the other four stood gazing all about, plainly in awe of the place. Mainly they looked at the Gate—or rather, they shielded their eyes from its glare.

"The Gate." It looked nothing like a gate in the common meaning of the word. Instead it was the very duplicate of that gigantic sphere of alien white light down in the core at Perchorsk. Except here the bulk of its mass seemed lodged in the low ceiling, or grown there like a massive blister of cold fire.

"The way home," Nathan said simply, but his words were a sigh, perhaps even a prayer.

Looking at him Trask thought: *And this time there really is only one way out.*

If Nathan heard him, he made no answer.

PART TWO:

SUNSIDE/STARSIDE

I

Starside

Staring with squinting eyes all about the cavern of the Gate, Trask thought: *We might already be in another world! And those* (he shrank from the shapes of several dripstone anomalies) *must be its inhabitants.*

"Once inhabitants," Nathan told him in a whisper that somehow managed to echo. "But not of this world, Ben. Starside. And no, we're not there yet."

The cavern was roughly the shape of the interior of a rugby ball half full of water and big as a church. The black, inward-curving walls were ribbed like a gigantic throat, with cracks and crevices here and there where the water had eaten into the rock strata, shallow ledges at various levels, and black tunnels two to three feet in diameter where the mouths of a great many magmass wormholes— alien energy channels—disappeared into the otherwise solid bedrock. And seated, crouched, or crammed into several of the higher niches, where they had doubtless escaped from rising water in times of flooding, Trask's "inhabitants" leered out in stony silence.

Or at least, they were silent to Trask and the others. But not to the Necroscope. For when Nathan had spoken to Trask out loud, of course his words no less than his thoughts were deadspeak. His words and thoughts alike, they always were deadspeak—except when he shielded them. And the long-dead creatures of the cavern had heard him. Moreover they knew him, or his sort at least, for he was not the first living man who had spoken to them in that way. Another had been here before him. And because of that other, the dead of the cavern responded in a way that Nathan had grown to expect.

Hah! Returned, are you? Well, and the first ever, be sure. Ah, but it took you long enough! What? Nigh on a thousand sunups, I'd suspect. Still, what is time to such as us? This from a nightmarish mummy-thing jammed tight in a niche, where dripstone had fused it in position like a weird embryo in a womb of gleaming calcium. A hideously misshapen skull, whose empty eye sockets reflected the glare of the Gate, protruded from the grotesque stalactite. Frozen in true death, the yawning jaws were wolfish and toothed liked a carnivore. And indeed this had been a carnivore—Wamphyri! Or a lieutenant on the brink of ascendancy, at the very least. But now it was just a dead thing. Yet still it seemed to leer at Trask and his party with a permanent, imperishable malignancy.

Startled at first, Trask now stepped closer to the wall of the cavern and gazed up at the monster. Obviously it had crouched there like this for a very long time. "What, a statue? Or is it the real thing?" Even asking it, he knew that the creature was or had been real, alive, of course. His talent told him that much. But he did *not* have Nathan's talent, could scarcely imagine that even now the Necroscope and the ossified thing were conversing:

"Oh, it's the real thing," Nathan quietly answered. "Withered away, shrunken down and encased in stone, but definitely real." And then, to the long-dead lieutenant: *I'm not who you think I am. That one was my father. He passed this way before me, on his way to Starside. He was Harry Keogh, and I am his son, Nathan.*

Indeed? And like father like son, you would follow in his footsteps, eh? Well, if he went to Starside, then your father's long dead and gone from both worlds! Now begone. For this is a private place.

It wasn't usual for the dead to be so surly, abrupt, rude. But this wasn't one of the usual dead. Unperturbed, Nathan inquired: *Whose man were you, anyway?*

The other seemed astonished. His very presence—his

previous nature—was enough in itself to cow the thoughts of most of the other dead people here. What was this Nathan anyway but a pup, and a human pup at that? *Whose man was I? Why, I was my own man, of course—called Cezar Bitesthrall.*

But Nathan knew well enough how the Wamphyri named their thralls, and so could work it out for himself which Lord this one had served. *Bitesthrall? But you've given yourself away, Cezar,* he said. *You were in thrall to Menor Maimbite, who died in the battle for the Dweller's garden on Starside. Yes, and it was my father who killed him!*

Now the other really was astonished. *You are little more than a boy,* he gasped, *and yet . . . you know so much! How is it you know so much? When a man passes through the Starside Gate, he is gone forever. Yet your knowledge of Starside is plainly considerable. But . . . did you say that Menor is dead? Truly?*

The caver spokesman, suddenly aware of a strange silence, said: "Well, what now?" His colleagues were equally mystified, not least by Nathan's expression where he stared at the freakish thing in its high niche.

But Trask, Anna Marie, and David Chung all knew what now: that Nathan was speaking to a dead man, or something that had once been a man. Espers, they sensed something of it at least. "In a minute," Trask whispered, stepping back a pace from Nathan but not taking his eyes off him for a moment. "But right now . . . would you mind keeping quiet awhile?" Among the several things he hadn't told them was this, that Nathan was a Necroscope. The concepts of teleportation and parallel universes were difficult enough, without that he should ask them to also believe in a man who conversed with the dead!

Dead, yes, Nathan had meanwhile answered Cezar's question. *A thousand sunups ago, aye. And all of the olden Wamphyri with him.*

A deadspeak gasp: *What, all of them? Shaithis, Fess, Lesk? Not Lesk the Glut, surely?*

All of them, Nathan told him. He knew the names Cezar

mentioned, for they were like old curse-words among the Travellers of Sunside.

And that one who was here that time, your father, he did all this?

He helped to do it, certainly.

And suddenly Cezar guffawed. *But that old bastard Menor Maimbite, dead, eh? Oh, hah hah hah!*

You didn't much care for your master, then.

Cezar stopped laughing on the instant and grunted: *Care for him? I hated his black heart! He caught me licking a woman of his, cut out my tongue and made her eat it. And: "There," he told me. "Now she's tasted your tongue with both her mouths—as I'm sure she's tasted your sex!" Then . . . he throttled her, and took me to the Starside Gate.*

Nathan had real experience of the Starside Gate and knew what that last meant. At least, he had experience of the Gate whose dome showed *above* the ground. Something over three years ago he'd seen it when accompanying Lardis Lidesci on his annual pilgrimage into the gaunt, aching emptiness that was then Starside. And just a few months ago he'd passed through it into Pershorsk. Moreover he'd had E-Branch's Keogh files read to him and knew there were two Gates. The upper Gate had been created when a Russian experiment, the Perchorsk Projekt, backfired and blasted a grey hole between parallel dimensions; the second was a thing of nature, lodged beneath the first in what was once a pit and so invisible from the surface by virtue of its manmade twin. Since time immemorial the lower, natural, original Gate—which had its exit here in this subterranean cavern in Romania—had been used infrequently and according to circumstance as an instrument of Wamphyri punishment, revenge or simple cruelty, into which the Lords of Starside had tossed enemies, vanquished foes, and disobedient thralls.

So you were hurled into the white gaping maw of hell, Nathan nodded grimly, *through which you sank down into this place.*

Aye, the other grunted. *But when I got here the water was high and dark and swift. And so I crept up here onto this ledge and waited, waited, waited. Soon I was too weak to swim, even if I could swim, and the cold and the damp had stiffened all my joints. Starvation.... I was not yet Wamphyri but a lieutenant ... even a vampire's longevity could not sustain me through the rigours of this place. And like all of these others, I feared the water mightily. Finally I was as you see me now, stiffened to a stone, or very nearly so. And that was the end of Cezar Bitesthrall ...* He uttered a deadspeak sigh, and after a moment continued:

And you? Do you really intend to go in the other direction? What, and are you then a madman? Ah, but it will take real magic to keep you alive in Starside! Except—(and yet again his gasp)—No, not so! For They are no more, the Old Wamphyri, dead and gone forever, But ... is it really so?

They were gone for a while, Nathan answered.

Eh? Explain!

The Old Wamphyri are dead, aye. But in the east, beyond the Great Red Waste, others were waiting out their time. Now they are back in Starside, in the last great aerie of the Wamphyri. I go as my father went before me: to destroy them who destroy mine.

But your name: Nathan Keogh? The first, however rare, is a Traveller name, be sure ... but Keogh? Ah! I remember: your father's name. And he—

—Was a hell-lander, yes. Nathan nodded. *But my mother was a Kiklu, Szgany.*

The other sighed his partial understanding, and said: *Myself, I was of the Szgany Stengi, based fifty miles east of the great pass. There were Kiklus in my tribe, too ...* He fell silent, as if memories of the olden times were proving too much for him. But in another moment his deadspeak voice had turned hard as his calcium sheath:

Huh! All such things are done with now. Even life itself, done with. I was Szgany ... I was made undead ... possibly, I might even have been Wamphyri! But all of these years in this place, frozen in the true death ... it's as if all my life were a dream. And you have disturbed it. Because of you I know the truth of it: that it was wasted. You've brought me no comfort, Nathan Keogh.

At which another voice—but a much harder, darker, even angry voice—broke in:

Comfort? Is that what you're all about, Cezar Bitesthrall? Comfort? What, and you a lieutenant of the Wamphyri? Hah! But Menor erred when he apprenticed you! Even here in this dreary place, we have comforts enough. And we've had enough of talk, too. Now still the chatter and let this fool go to his sure death in Starside.

Nathan located the source of the voice: a dripstone bulge in the wall, where a gleaming calcium "candle" seven feet tall seemed lodged in an ancient crevice under fanglike festoons of stalactite formations. The sheath was semi-opaque, glasslike; beneath it, frozen ferocious features were barely visible. But now that Nathan knew the source of the voice, he also knew the nature of its owner:

Wamphyri!

"Nathan," it was Anna Marie, breaking into his thoughts, drawing him back from his deadspeak communications.

He glanced at her. "Yes?"

"We can't stay here. The cold. And the time. We'd planned for you to go through in three days' time; by our calculations—based on what little we know—that would make it sunup on Sunside. But right now ... the sun is sinking towards the barrier mountains even as we speak. And we don't know how long the journey through the Gate is going to take."

Nathan turned to Trask. "While I talk to them, you could begin by passing my weapons up into the Gate. According to the files, they will be drawn up, go right through, slide down the dome of the underground Gate in Starside. And we won't be far behind. We'll go through together, or as close together as possible."

Then, as Trask and the others set to it, he turned again to the dripstone thing in its stalactite tomb. *Who were you?*

Bah! (The vampire Lord's voice was sour.) *Rather what am I now, that a mere child has power over me while I stand impotent, a stone which was once a man and more than a man, even a Lord of the Wamphyri!*

"But that was then and this is now." Nathan lapsed into common speech, which in his case was deadspeak of course, but easier. "You were a man. You *were* Wamphyri. But now you are a fossil. This is probably your last chance to talk to a man of the living world, even of two worlds. Will you waste it?"

The other considered his words; while from behind Nathan:

"Now *what* the hell—?" The caver spokesman snatched back his hand from where he had passed a box of ammunition up into the glare of the Gate. He'd been distracted by the sight and sound of Nathan talking to something locked in the dripstone; talking to it as if it lived and might even answer him back. "The light . . . seemed to *suck* at me!"

"Of course," Trask told him. "In the same way that it takes these weapons from us, so it will take us. It's like an invisible conveyor belt, or an elevator to another world." He passed up a self-loading rifle butt-first, watched the stock disappear into the glare and felt first the attraction, then the fierce, irresistible suction as the weapon was drawn from his hand and into the Gate. "Just don't let your fingers touch the surface, that's all—unless you want to be the first of us into Starside . . ."

Who is there now in Starside to remember me? The ex-Lord of the Wamphyri wondered in Nathan's mind.

"No one, in Starside," Nathan answered. "But weren't you a Traveller first? Didn't you ascend in the usual way? You must have had your tribe like everyone else. Maybe sons of your sons are alive even now, on Sunside?"

I was a Ferenc, said the other, gloomily. *We were outcasts, supplicants. Metalworkers, we made war gauntlets for the Wamphyri. We had a "pact" with them—hah! I was taken when I was seventeen. No human offspring from my loins, Nathan Keogh.*

But as the thing in the stalactite had mentioned the name Ferenc, so a massed groan of horror had gone up from others of the cavern's inhabitants who until now had been silent. Ferenc! A curse in itself, the very word. And the object of their terror had heard their deadspeak moaning.

Aye, a Ferenc! he told them. *And even now ... well, quite obviously it means something, to be what I have been. That is why I find comfort, however cold, even in a place such as this. The very knowledge of your fear comforts me ... that·as a dead thing, even now I strike terror into your hearts. You quaking leathery trogs and Traveller cowards! For such as you, even to be in the same company with myself ... it's an honour! And for as much as a stone thing may have thralls, all of you are my thralls from this time forward. So be it!*

Nathan bridled. This dead thing—Ferenc, Wamphyri, whatever—he should *not* have named Travellers cowards. The Szgany were never that. And so: "Pay him no heed," he told the ghosts of everyone who was ever trapped here. "For if he is the greatest of you all, then he is also the greatest coward! What, Wamphyri? Strong and fearless as ten men? Oh? But if so, how is it he's still here? Or is it that he feared the water as much as the rest of you?—Aye, and maybe feared it even more! Now let me tell you something:

"Since time immemorial this watercourse has been the route by which certain 'brave' Wamphyri Lords invaded the hell-lands, so becoming a pestilence in both worlds. But in *this* world they were small" (which wasn't entirely true; small in number, perhaps) "and *kept* small by the efforts of mere men! But this one—this *Ferenc*—was too small even to venture into the water! His supplicant blood ran true to the very end, aye. And how is that for a coward? Such as you could *never* be thralls to such as this. What? Why, he was even usurped and thrown from his seat in Starside, else why is he here at all?"

Occasionally deadspeak conveys more than is said. But now the Ferenc's fury couldn't be more in evidence if he were alive and free of his stalactite sheath. *Why ... you ... insolent ... little ... pup!!!*

"Oh, be quiet." Nathan climbed up to the encysted figure and rapped with hard knuckles against the dripstone. "And think on this, Ferenc. If ever I should pass this way again, I might easily bring a hammer and chisel with me and chip away at you until you're no more. And when all of your pieces are rounded to pebbles in this dark river, and your evil essence dispersed far and wide, what will you have of 'comforts' then, eh? And how many trembling thralls?"

But from the other there was no answer at all, except perhaps a far faint whimper . . .

"Nathan," Anna Marie was looking up at him. "The time."

And Trask said, "Son, it's not getting any warmer in here. We'd best be on our way."

Nathan got down, said, "Very well. But that"—he glanced up one last time at the horror in the crack, and glared at the thing—"was something I had to do. And anyway, my time wasn't wasted. Like my father before me, I've learned something."

"Oh?"

"Yes. That in death—even the true death—the Wamphyri are just as loathsome as in life or in *un*death!"

"How . . . how do we go about it?" The caver spokesman's voice shook a little.

Trask shrugged. "You came close to answering that one yourself just a few minutes ago. Reach up, jump, and let the Gate do the rest. It will take you in, pass you through."

"Which will take . . . how long?"

"We're not sure," said Anna Marie.

And Nathan told her, "If you go first we can help you."

She moved between him and Trask; they lifted her up; she held up her arms and was taken effortlessly from them. And as she slid into the white glare, they heard her gasp, drawn out almost interminably as she disappeared. Trask followed immediately, so that as Anna Marie's feet passed into the glare, he was already jumping and reaching out after her.

"Quickly!" Nathan told Chung and the cavers. "Let's all go through together." The cavers jumped almost as a man, and as a man were taken up. And Nathan and Chung were last.

But as the others had disappeared into the sphere of white light, so Nathan had remembered one who wasn't here. And also, he remembered his own Misha: the misery she must be experiencing, not knowing what had become of him. No need for Zek to go through that. Quickly he reached out for her, and made contact in the moment before he felt the Gate sucking at him. Then . . . it was the work of that single moment to pass on the information: that Ben Trask was on his way to Starside. But Zek's answering mental cry—of denial, astonishment, pain—was shut off even as she issued it . . .

After the initial suction, that first weird tug-of-war between gravity and the Gate's attraction, the feeling of being drawn up, of the defeat of gravity itself, disappeared completely. It was simply a drifting sensation, but of drifting upwards, like a swimmer surfacing after a dive.

Looking up—or ahead?—Nathan and Chung could see the others as in a shaft of white light, seemingly floating there, unsupported. Anna Marie was in front, followed by Trask, then the cavers in a triangular formation. And they were all looking down or back at Nathan and Chung.

In its way, Trask thought, *it's as strange as the Möbius Continuum: the weightlessness . . . the sensation of emptiness . . . the effortless mobility. But now, instead of moving from place to place, we're moving between worlds!*

Unlike the Möbius Continuum, however, such thoughts had no weight at all. This place was real enough; no metaphysical continuum this but a physical reality, the crossover between parallel universes. And where the Möbius Continuum might have been that Element in which God said, Let There Be Light, this might well be the Light itself. A misty light, white as snow but of an even temperature, so that the cold of the cavern was soon left far behind.

And so the seven fell upwards into an apparently endless white somewhere. And such was the silence, each of them could hear the uneven, nervous breathing of the others, and perhaps even the beating of their hearts.

Even knowing it must come, their resurgence was something of a shock. Anna Marie first: she passed through the skin of the Gate, then half-slid, half-rolled down the curve of the resilient dome onto the heaped jumble of Nathan's armoury, where his weapons had come to rest on a bed of stony debris that formed a shelf around the sphere's perimeter. And in those same few moments she saw that the sphere of white light was lodged like a plug in a massive hole, or a child's marble pushed down into sand by the weight of a finger.

Directly overhead, the lower hemisphere of a second globe seemed suspended in the same shaft, looking almost identical to the Gate as it had appeared in the ceiling of the cavern of petrified monsters. A distance of only five or six feet separated the two singularities, so that Anna Marie couldn't help wondering: *Or should I think of it as a duality?* But in any case, she knew that the top half of that uppermost Gate stood open to the air, glaring out on the vampire world of Starside.

And all around her in the scree and rubble, and cut in the wall of the shaft itself, those alien energy wormholes that she had seen in the cavern of the Romanian Gate—so that as Trask came through she found wind to shout: "Ben, look out! The wormholes!" For they were glass smooth; only fall into one . . . it might take a long time to get out again. If ever.

But in a moment Trask was on his feet, assisting the disorientated cavers as they came through, and finally Chung and Nathan. Then, as they dusted themselves down:

"From now on we have to mind how we go," Trask told them, his voice steady but echoing. "When Harry Keogh came this way he tried several of these wormholes before he found one that connected with the surface. But he was only one man and there are seven of us. Avoid holes that slant downwards; they twist and turn, could easily make a sudden descent. Look for upward-leading holes. But in any case go slowly, and take no chances. And the first man to see daylight overhead—"

"Or starlight," Nathan put in, grimly.

Trask looked at him and nodded. "Or starlight, yes . . ." And he left it at that.

They separated along the scree ledge, chose wormholes, went headfirst into them first in the glare of the Gate, then in the light of pencil pocket torches. And Trask was the one who found the way up. There were probably several, but he was first, and the route that his wormhole took fitted Harry Keogh's description (which Trask had read time and again) precisely:

It climbed gently at first, not so steeply as to cause him to slide back. In a little while it swung left, then rose marginally more steeply. A short, claustrophobic climb, before the bore levelled out and swung right. Following which . . . it shot up almost vertically! And looking up as from the bottom of a shallow well—

—Starlight.

Trask backed off, returned to the main shaft and the glare of the Gate, called for the others. Anna Marie, Nathan, and one of the cavers were already there. Chung and the other two cavers soon came crawling backwards out of wormholes.

"This is it," Trask told them, indicating the mouth of the exit into Starside. "As to how we go about it:

"Nathan goes first, and I'll be right behind him. I'll help him up out of the well onto the surface. The rest of us string ourselves out along the route, and pass the weapons along and up to him. Finally he helps us to get out, me first, then Anna Marie, and the rest of you in whatever order you prefer.

"On the surface, we each take what weapons we can carry and get clear of the upper Gate. That might take more than one trip, but it has to be done. It's not simply that the weapons are important—of course they are—but it's also that Nathan can't . . . er, he can't work to best ef-

fect too close to the Gate. But I warn you now: we won't
have any time to look about and gawp. When I looked up
the last nine or ten feet of wormhole, looked into the sky
of Starside, I saw stars up there. If it isn't sundown it's
pretty damned close! Now, are there any questions?"

The caver spokesman said: "That second Gate, on the
surface? That's our return route, right?"

"Right, but not yet. Oh, we could use it all right, but we
can't guarantee our reception at the other end. In Perchorsk, they've learned to be extremely cautious of things
that come through the Gate. *So* cautious they might easily
kill you in half-a-dozen different ways before you even got
to say hello! Especially now. You've seen that stuff back
in the Refuge, down in the sump? Well by comparison,
that's pretty tame . . ."

"And once were away from the Gate—what then?"

Trask looked at Nathan, who said, "Then it's my problem. But this is my world and I know . . . oh, several
routes out of here into Sunside."

And before they could ask any more questions, Anna
Marie said, "We're wasting time. And there's also something you may have forgotten."

"Oh?" Trask looked at her.

"Turkur Tzonov and his men could well be in the vicinity. How long is it since you saw him enter the Gate in
Perchorsk? And how long would it take him to walk
through? Or haven't you worked it out?"

Trask did so, and quickly. "Maybe three and a half
hours since we saw him go through—it's hard to gauge.
But we know he was walking, while we were transported.
Also, my watch stopped during transit, and—"

"—All of our watches stopped," the caver spokesman
told him.

And Anna Marie said: "Whichever way we look at it,
Tzonov can't be too far away from us." She inclined her
head upwards. "Either he and his men are closing with the
Gate's exit right now and will soon come through onto the
boulder plains . . . or they're already here, somewhere

overhead, perhaps heading for the barrier mountains and the great pass into Sunside."

Trask nodded. "First priority, then: as soon as we're out, we choose personal weapons and hang on to them. But the last thing we need is a firefight on Starside! Okay, let's move . . ."

Twenty minutes later they were out, and Nathan's single glance all about had confirmed the fact that he was home, or close to it. For of course Starside of the barrier mountains could never be considered "home" in the real sense of the word. Not to men, anyway.

As for the six newcomers to this place:

All very well for Trask to warn against gawping. But this was a different world, and weird. Staring all about, what Trask and the others saw was this:

First, the Gate.

The dazzling white hemisphere was perhaps thirty feet in diameter and set in a crater like the raised rim of a volcanic blowhole. All around its perimeter, penetrating the earth and the crater walls alike to a radius of over sixty feet, magmass wormholes gaped everywhere. The seven had emerged from one such hole and now must be careful where they stepped; the walls of the holes were glass smooth, and some were very nearly perpendicular. Their depth was entirely conjectural.

Away from the Gate itself:

The perceptions of the visitors were at first baffled, disoriented by the contrasts of what might easily be considered a surreal or even hallucinogenic landscape; except it was all too real. Perhaps because of the alien nature of the place, their eyes were first drawn to those one or two features that were most readily acceptable. Like the mountains.

Behind the Gate, maybe two miles south, the barrier mountains rose gaunt and grey from foothills and scree escarpments, up sparsely clad slopes, over crags and buttresses, through ravines and saddles to sloping plateaus and sharp-fanged peaks that were rapidly fading from amethyst to ash-grey silhouettes in the twilight before true night. The immense range sprawled east on the one hand, west on the other as far as the eye could see; its peaks marched away to far horizons, merged with them, passed into purple velvet distances and disappeared at the rim of the world. But for all that the range displayed many of the mundane features of earthly mountains, still *these* peaks were most obviously alien; they *felt* cold and alien. And Trask found himself thinking, as at least one, other had thought before him: *Only take away the trees under the timberline ... these could well be the mountains of the moon!*

Closer, maybe two to three miles south and a little east, the mouth of a canyon—the great pass—opened onto the barrel boulder plains. Apart from this pass, where in ages past the barrier range had cracked open, the march of the mountains seemed entirely unbroken. And so the mountains and the great pass through them, and the hush of twilight, were in the main acceptable to human perceptions. But as for the rest of Starside:

To the west there was only the sparsely wooded flank of the mountains, and at the foot of the range the boulder plains rolling north, turning blue then dark blue into a mainly featureless distance. But directly to the north, to the far north, the blue turned. smoky black and the earth was a darkness shot through with dull silver streaks. There under the weird weave of ghostly aurora, and the glitter of unknown constellations like blue ice-shards frozen in the vaulted dark of the skies, the surface of what might be a sullen sea, or possibly a sheet of glacial ice, made a misty mirror-image of the alien heavens. And if the mountains belonged on the moon, then this was a picture of some cold and dying planet way out beyond Arcturus. . . .

A chill wind had come up; blowing from the north, it was gradually eating its way through the clothing of the seven to their very bones. They felt it and shivered, but not alone on the outside; for it was a chill of the soul. Sensing (or perhaps reading) their thoughts, Nathan told them:

"That wind blows off the Icelands. In the olden times, when a vampire Lord was found wanting, sometimes the others would banish him north. Such errant Lords suffered various forms of punishment: to be driven north, possibly to a freezing death; or to be buried alive out on the boulder plains; or maybe to be hurled into the Hell-lands Gate, from which no one ever returned. Well, not until now."

The seven had taken up Nathan's weapons. As he led them away from the hemisphere of white light, he paused for a moment to point east and a little north. Now that the painful glare of the Gate was behind them and their eyes had grown accustomed to Starside's preternatural gloom, their view of the boulder plains was that much clearer. And there to the northeast of the Gate, of all they had seen so far, the barren boulder plains—and what stood or lay in a vast jumble upon them—were the most surreal of all.

The boulder plains were just what the term implied: seemingly endless plains reaching out from the barrier mountains to the northern horizon under its writhing dome of shimmering auroras. They might be the bed of some aeon-dead ocean, like the misnamed *mares* of the moon. But scattered far and wide across them, like clods of earth thrown haphazardly down on the bed of a dried-up lake, boulder piles and individual rocks stood starkly silhouetted in the glare of the Gate, casting concentric rings of shadows outwards from the central point of illumination. Well away from the Gate they were like eery white sentinels, and farther still they were grey ghosts gradually merging into the powder blue background.

Weathered into weird shapes, many of the boulders were grotesque as gargoyles; so that the overall effect *was* surreal, like a painting by Salvador Dali. All it would seem to lack was a focal point, an "object" of form or structure so striking as to distract the eye from what might otherwise be considered its monotony. And out there, some eight or nine miles east and two to three north, indeed that singularity existed.

For even at that distance the seven could make out a nest of squat, mist-wreathed columns like some immense

Stonehenge—like the stumps of a ring of gigantic, petri-fied mushrooms, or the mighty pedestals of toppled, cyclo-pean statues—rising up from vast heaps of scree and stony debris. And tumbled down on the alien earth itself, half-buried in the riven soil, the shattered bodies of the fallen gods, all formed into tumuli or strewn into dog-legged mounds of rubble about the bases of the naked stumps.

But central in this primal fossil forest a mighty stack re-mained, unscathed by earthquake or any device of man or monsters: the last great aerie of the Wamphyri! "Karen-stack," Nathan whispered, in awe of that incredible fang. "Or whatever they've named it . . . now."

And Trask and the others gazed their fascination, how-ever morbid, across all the misted miles to that lone kilometre-high sentinel rock, still standing there in the east among the rubble of the fallen aeries, where Harry Keogh had brought them crashing down onto the boulder plains. Then Trask, Chung, and Anna Marie were given to won-der: *But if this is only the last of the aeries—and not the greatest by any means—then how must it have looked when* all *of the stacks were standing? And all of their in-habitants alive . . . or undead?*

Trask couldn't take his eyes off that alien skyscraper tower, so that he stumbled over small rocks as Nathan led the way even farther from the Gate's glare. Possibly the stack (or stacks as they once were) had weathered out from the barrier range and been left standing there like a series of mighty buttes as the mountains themselves re-treated. Certainly they had been a natural feature of this place, at least until the first of the vampire Lords had com-menced work on them. But now, especially in its upper sections or levels, this last great aerie of the Wamphyri looked anything but natural. What? With all of those chim-neys and causeways? Those towers, turrets, and flying but-tresses? Those landing bays, balconies, and . . . windows? Behind which, even as Trask gazed, faint glimmering lights were flickering into being one by one!

Or was that simply a whim of his imagination, a trick of

the spectral light, a mirage of the twining mists that draped
the distant menhir?

"No mirage, Ben," Nathan told him. "Look the other
way, across the barrier mountains." Trask and the others,
they all looked, and saw that the sky over the mountains
was now indigo shot with fading shafts of gold, and that
the shafts formed a slowly turning fan like the spokes of
a phantom wheel. Then the fan seemed to fold in upon itself, and faded in a moment to a memory in the mind's
eye. And:

"Sundown," Nathan told them. "The true night. And
time we were gone from here. Those lights in Karenstack:
the Wamphyri are up and about. Perhaps they're already
abroad in Sunside. But if not they soon will be, and we
stand directly in their path. Now wait a moment . . ."

He conjured a Möbius door, which shrank a little from
the proximity of the Gate, then firmed up and stood steady.
"Good, we can go." He turned to the cavers. "You first. If
not for me you wouldn't be here. So I want to make sure
you're safe. Form a ring and hold on to each other; and,
well, just hold on. But no questions, and no talking. Just
. . . bear with me."

Then, expanding his door, he guided them through it,
and stepped in after them—

—And Trask, Chung, and Anna Marie were left alone
on the boulder plains.

But not for long; maybe a minute and a half, at most.
And then . . .

"Jesus!" Trask gasped, as a ragged shadow flitted close
overhead. His eyes scanned skyward and his machine pistol made its typical metallic ch-*ching* sound as he instinctively cocked it. And: "Bats!" he whispered, as he spied
what spied upon them.

"*Desmodus.*" Anna Marie's breath was ragged. "Pretty
much the same as the vampires of Earth, but big." She,
too, cocked her weapon.

"Big?" David Chung was quick to follow suit. "Why,
those things must be three feet across, wingtip to wingtip!"

"But not especially dangerous." Anna Marie had regained her composure. "Oh, if there was only one of us, injured, then they might attack. But right now they're merely curious. We're strange to them. They didn't expect to find us here. *Shh! Listen!*"

There were half-a-dozen of the giant bats, and now they were circling, calling to each other with shrill, barely audible whistles; barely audible to human ears, that is. But miles across the boulder plains their cries would certainly be heard by others of their ilk ... and perhaps by others not quite of their ilk. And maybe not too many miles away at that.

"The advance guard," said Trask, his throat suddenly dry. "Aerial observers, trackers, bloodhounds."

"Right," Chung choked the word out. "And look, here come the masters of the hounds!" He pointed a shaking hand.

In the sky barely half a mile away, a pair of weirdly pulsing manta shapes blotted out the stars as they descended from on high ... and they were headed directly for the three espers where they stood frozen like rabbits in the glare of headlight beams, on the cold uncaring plain of boulders ...

II

On the Plain of Boulders

Twenty-five to thirty minutes earlier, in Turgosheim:

It had been that Maglore the Mage was down in Madmanse, or what had been Madmanse when the Killglance brothers, Wran and Spiro, had resided there;

down in that haunted, cobwebbed, bat-shrouded mausoleum of a place, inspecting it as a prospective extension of
his own Runemanse. He'd been there with his lieutenant,
Karpath Seersthrall, making diagrams of the manse and
measuring certain of its rooms which he might use as
metamorphic vats. For Maglore had many monsters to
fashion, and the space in Runemanse was all but used up.

But down in Madmanse—where even now the dread
spirit of its murdered one-time master, Eygor Killglance,
seemed to waft on a gloomy aether—suddenly the grey fur
at the back of Maglore's neck had tingled and stood erect,
and for a moment however brief a symbol had blazed up
bright in the eye of his seer's mind. *This* symbol:

It was Maglore's sigil, by which every other Lord and
Lady of the Wamphyri knew him. But it was also the sigil
of another, gone from Maglore's ken for some seventeen
sunups now. And now ... returned? Was it possible? The
Seer-Lord's window on Olden Sunside/Starside returned to
life, or undeath?

But now that Vormulac Unsleep and his aerial vampire
army were flown west on their crusade against Wratha the
Risen, and Maglore left to his own devices in the mighty
gorge of Turgosheim, this was just the stroke of good fortune he'd been seeking! Indeed, for if that oh-so-crafty
Nathan was back in Olden Sunside, why, then Vormulac's
progress might yet be spied upon, and Maglore heir to all
the lore of a hitherto unknown land!

"Nathan!" Maglore had stood up straight and sniffed at

the air, gazing all about in the gloom of deserted Madmanse. "Why, it is as if I can even smell you!"

"Nathan Paleblood?" The hulking Karpath's eyes had narrowed as Maglore rubbed clawlike hands together, chuckled and headed for an upwards-leading stairwell. "What of him, master?"

At which Maglore had paused and looked back, his crimson eyes flaring up in the dark. "Paleblood? Nathan Paleblood? But you mean Nathan Seersthrall, surely?"

And Karpath had backed off a pace. "I . . . I used to *think* of him as Paleblood, master—because he *was* so pale, and his blood so weak."

"Oh?" Maglore's voice was deep, dark, clotted. "But this . . . this *urge* to apportion names worries me somewhat, Karpath. For it's outside your jurisdiction. In Runemanse, only Maglore names the creatures which are his. In all such matters the Wamphyri are jealous to a fault, which I'm sure you know. So . . . is it perhaps that you anticipate your ascension? Do you lust after my egg, Karpath?"

"Master." The other trembled. "Master, I—"

"—This much I promise: when I decide that the time is ripe to invest another with my powers, you shall be the first to know."

Following which, without pause, the Seer-Lord Maglore had proceeded alone to his room of meditation . . .

. . . And in that room:

Maglore's "shewstone" stood upon a slender onyx base to one side of a workbench. Seated at the bench, he might simply turn and place his hands upon the instrument of his scrying or far-seeing talent. Except the device was of no stone or crystal as such, but a metal precious in the world beyond the Starside Gate yet common in the vampire world. Shaped in gold, it was in fact a weighty model of Maglore's sigil: a twisted loop ten inches long and five wide, compact yet massy—and potent! This was the medium through which Maglore concentrated enhanced Wamphyri powers to contact and "speak" to his various spies in Sunside, and with which he had hoped to follow the adventures of Nathan in Olden Sunside/Starside.

To that end, when Nathan had lived here awhile in Runemanse—not as the Seer-Lord's thrall or familiar, but more nearly as his "friend"—Maglore had made him a gift of a golden earring in the same design but only an inch long; not only a practical but also an appropriate gift, for the Möbius loop was Nathan's symbol, too. Indeed, when first he had come here, the youth had worn a twisted leather strap upon his wrist.

And some four months ago, when the Seer-Lord had arranged Nathan's "escape" from Turgosheim on an aberrant, ill-tempered flyer, then the earring had gone with him: Maglore's "window" on a far-off land of legend. And the youth all unsuspecting of the Seer-Lord's motive. At least, that was how it was supposed to have been. But scarcely had Nathan arrived in Olden Sunside in the west than contact had been broken. And now Maglore remembered how it had been:

How then as now he had sensed . . . something, *rushed to his room of meditation and placed trembling fingers upon the golden sigil. How he had let his mind drift out from Turgosheim, then hurtle west at the unthinkable speed of thought! A flight which he had terminated when he'd seen how lifeless was the sigil, a strangely twisted mass of heavy metal and nothing more . . . for the moment, and as far as Nathan was concerned, anyway.*

So the Seer-Lord's "window on an unknown world" had been closed. But it was a weird thing, because despite the fact that Nathan's aura was gone, the feeling had persisted that he was not dead. And Maglore had wondered: *What, then? Undead? Is he locked in that metamorphic sleep which ever precedes the vampire condition? Has he at last succumbed to the seduction of vampirism? Does Wratha or one of hers have him?*

He had not known the answer then, but now:

"Ahhh!" For as his hands touched the sigil and his mind sped west, there surely burned Nathan's flame! The youth was alive, he was—back?—from wherever he had been.

And Maglore's lodestone earring still secure in his ear, mere inches from the centre of his brain.

Maglore closed his burning eyes and concentrated, concentrated—and in a moment looked out through Nathan's eyes . . . and looked upon the boulder plains of far Starside, and in the distance that looming menhir which was the last great aerie of the Wamphyri. He looked and knew it as the home of Wratha and her renegades, even as Nathan knew it. More than this, he knew what was uppermost in Nathan's mind: the utter destruction of Wratha and all like her, and everything they stood for. And:

"Strong," Maglore sighed. "Ah, *strong*! What, Nathan 'Paleblood'? No, not this one." Then—

—The picture of the mighty stack faded, and in its place . . . an ephemeral portal formed of golden shimmering smoke! That was how Maglore saw Nathan's Möbius door. And as Nathan stepped forward and entered that door, so the Seer-Lord felt something of its power:

A whirlpool of symbols, which Maglore had known before. The esoteric guardian of Nathan's secret mind: the incredible numbers vortex. But not quite the same, no, for now those symbols were ordered; they had intelligence and flowed with a will of their own. Or perhaps with Nathan's will? Yes, for Nathan was their master!

But as Nathan had stepped through that metaphysical door, so he'd been snatched from Maglore's mind, had disappeared out of this universe. Yet however tenuously, their minds were still linked, so that Maglore felt himself moving with Nathan . . . *but at such an astonishing speed!* Indeed, even as fast as Maglore's thoughts themselves. And as before, Nathan was in control . . .

Maglore gasped, snatched his stiffened fingers from the loop and staggered back a pace or two. Shocked, his eyes stood out from their orbits in vast amaze. For he knew that Nathan had moved himself—or had physically *removed* himself—from the plain of boulders to some other place. And he had been in complete command; he'd known what he was about.

Then, much like a child whispering in the dark, Maglore

reassured himself: "But didn't I once say he had powers, this one?" And recognizing if not understanding his fear— gazing all about his room of meditation, to make sure no one had seen—he quickly regained control of himself.

But as his mind cleared and his breathing grew less ragged, suddenly he felt weak . . . made weak, perhaps, by Nathan's strength? Or by abstinence? Well, at least there was a remedy for that.

He reached out for Karpath where he went about his duties elsewhere in Runemanse, and asked him: *Karpath, are there fresh ones?*

Indeed, master, the other answered at once. *Men and women both.*

Then send me a strong man. Later, seek out Orlea and tell her . . . I am young again, and I have my needs.

And Karpath answered: *So be it, master.* But when Maglore withdrew his probe the lieutenant grinned in his morbid fashion, for he knew what were the Seer-Lord's needs. As for the first, the blood is the life. And as for the second—

—To live is to lust . . .

While down in Madmanse, in an airless, diseased, disused refuse pit, sealed up for more than fifty years:

That which upon a time had been Eygor Killglance sat or slumped against a nitre-streaked wall. But while up above in Runemanse the Seer-Lord Maglore's appearance was more or less human, that of Eygor in his pit was nothing less than a nightmare.

For the long-exanimate ex-Lord of Madmanse was a vast and monstrous *anomaly*, an *amalgam*, a welding together of everything unwholesome into one being, one creature. Anthropomorphic, yes; man*like*, in outline at least; but with that any past or present connection with humanity must surely be at an end. For Eygor's metamorphism had long since "absolved" or removed him from the frailties of form and aspect of mundane mankind.

Much like the beings in the Romanian cavern of the Gate, Eygor Killglance might at first be mistaken for a strange stalagmite formation, a fantastic dripstone creation of Nature. But on closer examination (if any person were morbid enough that he might actually desire to examine such a thing), one would soon discover feverish differences. For example: the petrified creatures in the cavern of the Gate were not eighteen feet tall and composed of fused bone, black mummied flesh, knobs of gristly cartilage, and plates of gleaming-blue chitin. Nor had they additional mouths in their dripstone bodies and limbs, to complement the ones in their faces. But there in that gloomy Madmanse pit—a cobwebbed cathedral of a place, vast and high-vaulted, whose walls dripped slime and nitre—such were Eygor's form and aspect.

The floor around him was a clutter of anomalous debris, humped, fibrous, boggy. Spongy bones and white-shining cartilage remains gleamed everywhere, like a boneyard of extinct monsters; of which the ex-Lord of Madmanse had been one, of course. And because he had been intelligent, Wamphyri, he had also been the worst of them.

The *shape* and delirious *design* of this thing slumped in a kneeling position and half-welded to the wall were terrible in themselves: its horny fossil feet, shrivelled, leathery thighs, arched back and shoulders, and misshapen, screaming skull. The huge head was thrown back, jaws frozen in some unending rictus; a withered arm lay upon a ledge, ending in a talon that drooped from a wrist thick as a man's thigh; blackened bones protruded from dusty, fretted flesh.

This was Eygor the once-Lord, and once feared more than any other creature in all Turgosheim. Eygor, whose contemporaries had named him Killglance because of that mordant talent which enabled him to murder men with the sheer poison of his looks alone; whose own bloodsons Wran and Spiro had so feared him that in the end they'd murdered him in this pit. Except there is murder and murder, and Eygor's had lasted long and long.

That he'd deserved it was undeniable, for Eygor was the cruelest of creatures. He had desired that his sons should be powerful, feared in Turgosheim even as he himself was feared. But in order to *make* them strong he had been ruth-less and his brutalities unbearable. Wran and Spiro had feared their Lord and father, aye, but more than the man they'd feared his evil eye.

For they had seen him use it against the Szgany, and had watched his human victims shrivel and die in the with-ering furnace of his gaze. And for all that they were Wamphyri in their own right, they too had tasted the bile of Eygor's glance, and knew that his power was exponen-tial; the more he used it, the stronger it grew. Today he killed only men, but tomorrow . . . ?

And so for him there *was* no tomorrow. His bloodsons had deadened his senses with strong drink, poisoned his food with silver; and while he lay in his stupor they blinded him! When he leapt shrieking awake, then they'd taunted him and led him blundering through Madmanse right to the rim of this very pit . . . and over it! And at the last, when he lay broken at the bottom, they had choked the pit with boulders and sealed it.

But Eygor was Wamphyri and did not die. Well, not im-mediately. For a sixmonth he lived on muck and bones, and while his metamorphic flesh remained pliable gathered to himself the remnants of dead constructs: the armour of warriors, debris of cartilage creatures, marrow of monsters. Planning to break out, he made a giant of himself. But the refuse pit was as deep as his sustenance was bad, and Eygor's strength waned even as his size increased. And of course he was blind.

He fashioned eyes for himself, but they were poor things and lacking in power; all of their special evil had been burned out of them. Finally, starved and stiff-ening, Eygor had slumped against the wall and moved no more. But while the evil and hatred were gone from his eyes, still they burned bright in his undying mind. For just like the minds of common men, those of vampires, too, go on beyond death. And just as the evil power of his mind had been vast during life and undeath, so it continued in the true death. Which perhaps explained the morbid atmosphere of Madmanse; for if only in mind and spirit, Eygor Killglance dwelled there still . . .

When for a while the Necroscope Nathan Kiklu lived in Maglore's Runemanse, Eygor had spoken to him in his dreams, lured him down into deserted Madmanse, even attempted to bargain with him. For the thing in the pit had eavesdropped on the deadspeak conversations of dreaming Thyre ancients in their cavern mausolea under the drifted sands of Sunside's deserts, and he understood Nathan's power over the dead: that they would even leave their graves at his command. And his proposition was this:

If Nathan should see fit to bring him back to life—if only long enough to take revenge upon his sons—then the Necroscope could ask what he would of him, and be heir to Eygor's greatest mystery: the secret of his killing eye! That had been Eygor's Wamphyri vow, his promise for the future, which Nathan had spurned.

But . . . Eygor knew that the future was a long and devious thing, and that what stands today often falls tomorrow, or most certainly the day after that. At the moment Nathan did not need an extra talent; he had sufficient of his own. But tomorrow and tomorrow . . . ?

Then what had been Eygor's killing eye in life became his seeing eye in death, so that he followed the youth's adventures from that time forward; even up to the time when Nathan fled to his old home in the west. But after that—

—Nathan's passing, or what Eygor had taken for his passing, had been like a cold wind blowing in the pit-thing's mind. And like the guttering of a distant candle in the dark night of death, Eygor had seen Nathan's light go out. Which could mean only one thing: that the Necroscope was no more.

Except (and as Eygor himself had once pointed out): the future is a long and devious thing, and history often repeats. And in that selfsame moment during Maglore's inspection of Madmanse, when he had paused and lifted his head, sniffed and sensed Nathan's return . . . so too had Eygor sensed it! But where Maglore had breathed Nathan's name, Eygor in the bowels of the place could only deadspeak it: *Nathaaan!* Like the soughing of the wind in an aerie's battlements, or the sighing of a ghost in its refuse pits.

For Nathan was there in Eygor's mind; far away, true, but shining with his unique light as before, so that Eygor knew him at once. And the pit-thing's all-but-forgotten desire to be up and about in the world of the living returned immediately, for the Necroscope Nathan was his one hope of revenge against his bloodsons, Wran and Spiro.

And as if the thought of his sons had galvanized Eygor's dead flesh, albeit momentarily, there had sounded in the pit a creaking as of rusted hinges; and before all fell still and eerily silent again, a single streamer of dust had come drifting down from the high, cobwebbed ceiling.

The Wamphyri Lord Maglore of Runemanse and the ex-Lord Eygor Killglance were not the only ones who knew that the Necroscope Nathan was back. All the dead of Starside knew it, too. And as his aura washed out from him, as it was felt and his light was seen in the otherwise uttermost darkness, so would the dead of Sunside know it.

But there were others yet more special who had known of Nathan's return from the moment he moved away from the influence of the Gate onto the plain of boulders. His nephew wolves knew it: Blaze, Dock, and Grinner. He had named the first and wisest of these for the white, diagonal stripe across his grey forehead, as if the fur there were marked with frost. Dock was the one with a stump of a tail, where an angry vixen had found cause to chastise him when he was a cub. While Grinner was the one with an uneven temper, whose black-gleaming upper lip was wont to draw back from his teeth, so that it might *seem* he was grinning. All three of them, they knew he was back for sure.

And waking in their barrier mountains den—blinking triangular yellow eyes and yawning, knowing in their way that it was twilight, and their mistress moon would soon be sailing on high—they simply acknowledged his return and were glad, or as glad as wolves may be. Nor were they the last of Nathan's "relatives" to know . . .

But perhaps most special of all, dreaming in their cavern mausoleums, the revered and mummied Ancients of the Thyre knew that he was back; for among the dead of the desert folk he was as great a legend as his father had been to the Great Majority of mundane mankind in an alien world an entire dimension away. Nathan, who had brought light into their darkness, translated their works, and apprised their living descendants of a continuity of sorts in a place beyond death.

If there was a single place in Sunside more safe than any other, it must be with the Thyre. For dwelling so close to the sun, they had never known the terror of the Wamphyri except in the lore and lives of the Szgany, with whom they occasionally traded. Being telepathic—albeit secretly, so that men had never suspected their talent—the Thyre and their dead had more readily accepted Nathan's deadspeak, thus enabling him to become their spokesman among the living.

Which was how he knew exactly where to take the cavers for their safety, and who would welcome him in that place.

So that even as Maglore the Mage recoiled from the power of the now-purposeful numbers vortex, drew back clawlike hands from his golden sigil, and wondered at Nathan's *velocity* as he sped—where? And through what weird medium?—the Necroscope had already used the Möbius Continuum to reach his destination. And guiding his charges out through a Möbius door, and holding on to them as they staggered this way and that, gasping their amazement, he sighed his relief that the coordinates had not misled him. Except, of course, he knew that it was more than mathematics that had guided him safely here. Then, as if to confirm it:

Nathan! And this was one deadspeak voice he would never forget, the first such voice that had ever deigned to acknowledge him. *Nathan . . . you were absent, gone away from us, even out of the world. Then, a moment ago, you came back, but far away on Starside. I cannot be mistaken, for I sensed you there. Yet now . . . you are here! Or is it that your telepathy has outstripped you? If so then your instructors among the Thyre should be congratulated, that you have learned to project your mind with such clarity. For I would swear that you are more than a mere thought.*

It was the philosopher Rogei, a Thyre Ancient; and this was his resting place and that of many another like him. The Cavern of the Ancients, one of the many mausoleums where the Thyre entombed their most revered: a great, glowing cave buried deep in a desert gorge, but a cave unlike any other.

Overhead, splitting the sandstone ceiling wall to wall like the slit pupil of a cat's eye, a slash of white quartz seemed carved from light. The cave was cracked right across its width, but the slow seep of centuries had filled the gap with crystals which had hardened to stone. Light still found a way in from somewhere overhead, but to get here had to pass through the quartz; hence the hazy, softly luminous glow. Stalactites of crystal festooned the ceiling, and glowing dripstone mounds like candles of light reached up from the floor. And all around the cave's perimeter, in alcoves and niches, on shelves and ledges carved from the stone itself, lay the Ancients of the Thyre in their last resting places, slowly becoming one with the dust of ages.

While the three cavers got a grip on themselves as best they might, the Necroscope quickly crossed the floor to Rogei in his niche. Finding him among all the others was no problem; the Ancient's deadspeak led Nathan directly to him. And close up, as Nathan drew near, Rogei knew that indeed this was more than a mere thought.

You . . . you really are here! His deadspeak gasp of astonishment was as real as if Nathan had heard it with his ears.

"Yes, I really am. But I can't stay, not just now. I will be back, though, if only to collect these friends of mine."

You have brought others here? Of your own kind? But now Rogei was frowning.

"There was nothing else for it," Nathan told him. "I came at a time not of my choosing, and even as we speak—or if not now, then very soon—the Wamphyri will be raiding on Sunside. I've got to help my people, but I can't look after these others at the same time. They're simply not prepared for Sunside ... I can't take them there ... not when the Wamphyri are there. And so I propose to leave them here, for now."

You would help your people? But how?

Nathan showed him a variety of weapons—showed him how they worked, and their effect—but all in his mind. And they were a wonder to Rogei, who could scarcely believe their devastation. And at last he understood something of the places Nathan had been, and the things he must have seen.

These weapons are not of Sunside, he said. *No, and neither are they of Starside. And so, if they are not of this world ... ? The hell-lands?* And he saw in Nathan's deadspeak mind that he was right.

"That first time I was here," Nathan let his thoughts fly back in time, "you told me I was a Necroscope. Well, and so was my father before me. I discovered his world, his people, their weapons—the means by which to save *my* people! Now I'm back, and I've brought those weapons with me. For the first time the Szgany can meet the Wamphyri on their own terms—with blood and fire!"

Rogei drew back from the pictures in Nathan's head, which were a tumult. For deadspeak often conveys more than is spoken or visualized, which in Nathan's case meant all of the pent-up hatreds of his young manhood. "I saw my tribe decimated and my home destroyed," he growled. "It was a miracle that anyone survived, a miracle called Lardis, our chief. Well, now I have to see if he *still* survives, and do what I can to even the score."

For a moment Rogei was silent, his empty eye sockets gazing blindly on Nathan where he stood. But then he said: *And is this the youth who came wandering into the desert to die, only to find purpose in the Cavern of the Ancients?*

"The same youth," Nathan answered, "and the same purpose. It has always been the same, I suppose, but I lacked the drive and the means. Life seemed hopeless, even pointless; I thought I'd lost everything; I was wrong, much had been saved. And now at last I've *found* the means—all thanks to you, Rogei."

To me?

"You gave me a reason to live, showed me the way. Through you I met Shaeken, and through him sought out Ethloi the Elder, who knew numbers. It was Ethloi who told me that if one day I could find a way to control the numbers vortex and show it ordered in my mind as pictures upon a tapestry, then I might discover a key. Well, he was right and I did discover it, not in this world but in the hell-lands. But how would I ever have got there in the first place if not for Thikkoul the Astrologer, who read my future in the stars? And so you see, it was you who set my feet upon the path."

Should I be proud of it? Rogei sounded gloomy now.

"You were proud of me, upon a time."

I still am. Indeed, I love you! But with all of this blood and thunder in your heart, what will be the end of it? You seek to destroy the Wamphyri, you say. But is that possible? Or have I found my lost son only to lose him again in a great and terrible bloodwar?

"Am I a son to you, then?" It was an incredible honour.

I wish you could have been. You felt *like one, when you were here and working among the Thyre.*

"Then . . . you won't lose me," Nathan promised, and hoped he could keep his word.

But before anything more could be said:

"Nathan!" The caver spokesman had stopped worrying about Nathan's penchant for talking to dead things. "Someone is coming . . ."

Nathan knew where from. The Cavern of the Ancients had an exit out onto a sheer cliff face, with worn and crumbling sandstone steps descending into a gorge. But there was also a tunnel that connected to a Thyre community called Place-Under-the-Yellow-Cliffs. Out of great respect for their dead, the Thyre kept a discreet watch over their resting places. This would be a guardian, whose duty it was to attend the Ancients in their mausoleum.

The cavers were hushed now; Nathan, too, as soft, cautious footsteps sounded from an ascending shaft. A moment later and a figure rose up into view. Female, she blinked curious olive eyes with large, lemon-green pupils. But just inside the cavern she paused, froze, poised herself as if for flight. She leaned forward on her toes, lifted her chin and sniffed at the cavern's musty air. In her slender hands she carried a bow at the ready, nocked with a long arrow. She saw the three cavers—saw Nathan, too—only a moment after they had seen her.

She wore a red skirt and sandals, nothing else. Her small breasts were loose, pear-shaped, slightly pendulous. Her ears were large; mouth and chin small; nose wide and flattened, with dark-flaring nostrils. Alert, she held herself trembling erect. Graceful, her demeanour was somehow regal. And she was young.

Her youth showed in her large eyes, shining there with a brilliant clarity under the horny ridges of her eyebrows; also in the gleam of her limbs, whose sheen was the natural product of Thyre body oils. Brown as a nut but at the same time smooth, like all her race she was slender to the point of emaciation.

"Atwei!" Nathan recognized her at once, and stepped forward. Her mouth fell open and she shook her head in disbelief. At the same time he felt her probing his identity, and knowing she was not mistaken. She *had* known for some little time, but had scarcely dared to believe. Now . . . she took a trembling step towards him, then paused and looked at the cavers.

"Friends," he said.

At which she dropped her weapon and flew across the floor of the Cavern of the Ancients into his arms . . . but in the next moment drew back and stood upright, head down, hands clasped in front of her. And: *That was unseemly,* she said.

He took her into his arms again anyway, and said, "Little sister."

"Brother," she answered. Which was as much a compliment as Rogei calling him son.

But Nathan had no time, and she saw the turmoil of interests in his mind. His people, however, were uppermost. And she knew why. Outside in the open desert, and in Sunside, and especially in Starside, it was sundown.

"Care for my friends here," he told Atwei, releasing her. "And don't worry, I'll be back for them." It seemed very little by way of explanation—little enough to say after almost two years' absence—but explanations must wait. Meanwhile, there were other matters that could not.

He chose weapons for himself, conjured a Möbius door . . . then paused and looked at Atwei again. And: "Sister," he told her. "I've been to strange places and learned strange things. Don't be afraid . . ."

Because he willed it, his words were deadspeak—which Rogei heard and to which he answered: *Take care, Necroscope!*

Atwei knew nothing of that, but in Nathan's mind she felt the rush and roar of the numbers vortex and *was* afraid despite his warning . . . especially when he turned to one side, stepped forward a pace—

—And disappeared . . .

. . . And reemerged on the boulder plains, in the vicinity of the Hell-lands Gate. And indeed it *was* as if all hell had been let loose!

The scene was fantastic. A few minutes earlier there had been only the glaring hemisphere of white light, the boulders ranging outwards across the gaunt wastelands, and in a misted distance the toppled aeries of the Wamphyri, where Karenstack or what had been Karenstack stood tall and central among the stumps of the fallen stacks. But now:

Ben Trask and David Chung were each down on one

knee, aiming into the sky and hosing fire and steel at a circling Wamphyri flyer. And skimming towards the pair, weaving from side to side as it avoided the jagged crests of rock jumbles and the jutting fangs of lone boulders, a second manta flyer reached out its prehistoric neck and spatulate head, and the pouch in its underside yawned open where the neck joined the body.

Seated in ornate saddles at the bases of the flyers' necks, Wamphyri lieutenants leaned forward and urged their mounts on. Having no knowledge of guns, they heard the hellish chattering of the weapons but had no idea of their firepower. So far they had been lucky; despite the awesome size of their mounts, neither the flyers nor their riders had yet taken a hit. Or it could be that the shooting had only just begun—or that the aim of the gunmen was off—or perhaps that the flyers *had* been hit but it hadn't registered.

Nathan looked for Anna Marie; she stepped out from behind a boulder and started firing; the recoil of her weapon was such that it threw her backwards, so that she stumbled and fell. And the flyer swooping low over the boulder plains veered a little and headed straight for her!

In the moment after stepping out of his Möbius door, Nathan had loaded his weapon. Now he called out: "Anna Marie—to me!" She saw him and came stumbling in his direction. And again the flyer veered from its course, arching its wings and settling towards them where she tripped and fell against him. Forward of the corrugated belly, its underslung pouch opened wider yet.

Chung was still firing at the other creature, where now it had stopped circling and was side-slipping this way and that like a flat stone sinking in water, bearing its rider gently to earth. But Trask had seen Anna Marie's and Nathan's danger and had turned his machine pistol on the beast and rider threatening them. The flyer was hit in the leading edge of a wing, and its tapering neck reared up and back as a neat line of holes stitched themselves into its rubbery grey flesh. But still it came swerving between the last pair of boulders, its air-trap wings actually brushing their domes as the beast closed with its would-be targets.

By now the rider knew there was something wrong; he had heard the spattering impact of bullets, felt the shuddering of his mount as it skewed this way and that. And in his mind he'd felt something of the brute's dull pain, the damage to its vampire flesh. But he wasn't Wamphyri, just a lieutenant, with no real rapport with his mount. If necessary, he would drive the flyer to the limits of its endurance. Indeed he must, for his Lord and master Gorvi the Guile would require an accounting.

Dripping fluids from its wounds, the beast fell towards Nathan and Anna Marie. The saucer eyes in its hideously *human* head glared at them; its pink-lipped pouch was a yawning mantrap lined with cartilage hooks, whose fetor they could smell and almost taste, it was that close! Trask shouted something incoherent and blazed away until his magazine was empty, and still the thing bore down on them.

Nathan could see its rider's eyes: feral yellow and red in their cores—with bloodlust! The man knew he was going to drink red tonight, take thralls for his master or meat for the manse's provisioning. And he laughed as he commanded his mount: *Take them! Or knock them down, at least!*

Nathan heard him, his unsubtle telepathic command, and so knew to counter the flyer's reaction to it. "Get down!" he shouted, pushing Anna Marie aside and hurling himself in the other direction, rolling in the dust. The gaping pouch passed between them, literally scooping at the dirt as the arches of manta wings passed over them with inches to spare. Then . . . the great beast turned its head to look back as its diamond shape cleared them.

In so doing it presented Nathan with a shot he couldn't resist. He brought his crossbow to bear, squeezed the trigger. The rider lieutenant was also looking back. He threw back his head and laughed as Nathan's bolt zipped under the arched wing and entered the flyer's neck fifteen inches back from its head. What, a mere crossbow bolt? And buried in all that muscle? The sting of a stink-gnat to a creature huge and insensitive as a flyer! And he at once yanked on the reins and turned his attention to Trask and Chung where they frantically reloaded.

None of this taking more than a second.

Then—

—There sounded a muffled explosion, not a gunshot, as Nathan's bolt exploded with force enough to fell a large pine. The flyer's neck blew apart in gristle, cartilage, grey flesh and red ruin, and sent a spray of blood flying on the boulder plains. Completely severed from the neck, the head commenced a crimson-spraying cartwheel to earth, and as the neck collapsed downward and struck the stony ground, so the blanketlike body jackknifed and rose up, hurling the rider free. Behind him, even as he flew, almost three and a half tons of rubbery meat, membrane, and alveolate bone crashed down shuddering and raised a cloud of dust. The beast had been a small one of its kind. Meanwhile:

The other flyer had settled to earth and its rider had dismounted. He came at a run, but ducking, weaving, aware now that the group of people on the boulder plains weren't typical Sunsiders. Behind a rocky outcrop, he helped his fellow lieutenant to his feet. The man was shaken but not seriously hurt; metamorphic vampire flesh shrugged off minor cuts and bruises without regard.

But on high—almost as high as an aerie itself and disguised amidst the clouds—a third manta shape rode the night thermals, and its rider was different again. Nor was he alone. Behind him, mantle fluttering and propulsive orifices sputtering, an aerial nightmare pulsed like a monster octopus against the stars: a warrior, accompanying Gorvi the Guile and his men on their way to Sunside. But Gorvi was Gorvi, and having detected strangers on the boulder plains, he'd sent his lieutenants to investigate while he stood off. Now . . . he heard the chatter of gunfire, saw the flickering fire of the guns, and sensed the shock and astonishment in the minds of his lieutenants.

Gorvi knew something was very much amiss, but the

height was too great even for his vampire eyes to make out anything in detail. So now he sent: *Destroy all opposition. Take prisoners. See to it!* Then, having made contact, he at once received news from one of his men on the ground: a series of frantic, chaotic mind-pictures that brought the entire thing into something of perspective:

A flyer had been downed, crippled or dead . . . His lieutenants faced human beings, but *not* Szgany! . . . There were men and one woman on the ground, pale creatures who appeared weak, but they were armed with incredible weapons . . . Even now Gorvi's men were under fire!

All sorts of ideas ranged through the Guile's mind:

Despite what his man had said, Gorvi suspected that this could only be a party of Travellers (Szgany Lidesci, probably, if their weapons were anything to judge by) on their way over the boulder plains to make a surprise attack on the last aerie. They would know that at sundown Wrathstack was empty of all but thralls and mindless guardian creatures. With their new weapons they would attempt to destroy Gorvi's earthbound guardian warriors in the scree and rubble at the foot of the stack, enter Guilesump and poison his wells, and so forth. Maybe they could break into Madmanse and destroy the Killglance twins' gaslings in their chambers, and so bring down the entire stack with a mighty explosion! It had been done before, as witness all the toppled aeries of the Old Wamphyri. Indeed, in an age immemorial, it had even been tried in Turgosheim.

And yet . . . only a handful of them? No, even with their superior weapons their task was impossible; unless they were a suicide squad—and Gorvi wouldn't put *that* past the Lidescis, either!

Or perhaps they had simply come to discover the lie of the land for some future invasion. With the rest of the Lords (and the bitch Wratha, of course) already raiding on Sunside, the way had been clear for a covert expeditionary force to make its way unseen over the boulder plains, and so discover a safe route for later use. It had long been a matter of some concern to Gorvi that Guilesump was open to attack from the bottoms ...

... He was brought rudely back from his musing by his man's urgent mind-call: *Master, what now?*

And: *Attack!* Gorvi ordered at once. *Send in my familiar bats to flush them out and your flyer to crush them. What, do you call yourself a lieutenant? Use your head, man—or lose it! For all their weapons these people are only human, fodder! So be about your work and never fear. For I, Gorvi, am coming.*

And to his warrior: *Down!* he sent. *Down onto the plains. Deflate your bladders and descend. Prepare to create your most powerful exhaust stenches, with which to sicken them who oppose me and mine. And think on this: when all is done, there will be a reward. Aye, for I shall feed you the very best of tidbits—the ones that scream when you crunch them!*

III

Violent Homecoming

Riderless, using rocky outcrops and hillocks of stony debris to shield its bulk, the flyer came skimming across the boulder plain. It had only one purpose; its vampire master, dismounted now, had sent only one telepathic command from where he went afoot among the scattered rocks: *Fall on them!*

A command that Nathan had heard. But Trask and Chung had taken refuge in a cluster of boulders close by; it would be no easy thing to prise them out of there, or to fall on them, and their ability to fire out was unaffected. Their location was a natural vantage point.

Nathan and Anna Marie, however, remained out in the open and so were an easy target. And the flyer was headed for them. Anna Marie saw the brute coming, forming its wings into vast scoops, deliberately stalling itself. Its intention could not be clearer. Panicked, she made to hobble away; Nathan caught her arm and said, "No, not that way."

He conjured a door, pulled her in after him, took her to a place he knew. It was a flat-topped bluff to one side of the mouth of the great pass, with an easy scramble down to safety. Lardis Lidesci had brought him here once to watch the sun rising on the last aerie. And steadying her, he said: "You should be safe here. If all goes well, I'll come back for you. If not . . . well, Sunside lies beyond the pass." It was as much as he had time for.

And then he went back for Trask and Chung.

Frustrated, the flyer was making a low, hovering pass over the cluster of boulders where Nathan's colleagues were sheltering. They cradled their weapons but were saving ammunition and waiting for further developments. Emerging from the Möbius Continuum close to the nest of boulders, Nathan yelled: "Hold your fire!" But as he sprinted towards them, he saw the two vampire lieutenants creeping up on their flank.

Skidding to a halt and pointing, Nathan shouted, "On your right. Down in that hollow." Which was a moment before the lieutenants sprang into view and came loping, zigzagging towards the clump of boulders. Then:

A shadow passed over Nathan where he stood undecided . . . and a *second* shadow; and at the same time he heard a sound to fill his veins with ice water: the sputtering throb of a Wamphyri warrior's biopropulsive vents! And oh how he knew what that meant; so that his mind and blood froze as he felt himself carried back, back in time—back to that night in Settlement, when Wratha's raiders had left the town in ruins.

The night his brother Nestor had been taken by the

Wamphyri, when Nathan had seen Misha with Canker Canison and thought that she, too, had been stolen away into Starside. The night a warrior reduced Nana Kiklu's house to rubble, leaving her son to believe that his mother was ...

"Nathan—for Christ's sake!" Trask's shouted warning snatched him out of it—or back into it; Trask's shout, and the obscene snarling of automatic weapons. Nathan's eyes focussed. He saw the vampire lieutenants closing with the boulder clump, saw them hurl themselves headlong, in superhuman dives, up over the protective rock barrier ... and saw them slam to a halt in midair, even thrown backwards by the twin streams of smoking steel that slammed into them!

The two vampire lieutenants were out of it, incapacitated if only for the moment, but Gorvi's lesser familiars were not. They came shrilling from the west, no longer as mere trackers but more nearly as hounds: harriers! Not in the least clumsy for their size, the giant *Desmodus* bats seemed like a horde as they wove this way and that, while in fact there were only six of them at most. Yet such was their speed and erratic patterns of flight, as individuals they presented near-impossible targets.

Nathan had reached the jumble of rocks where Trask and Chung had taken cover. If he squeezed his way in with them, it might well prove difficult to conjure a Möbius door within the confines of their sanctuary. No, he must first get them out of there.

"Ben, David!" he called to them. "Out here, to me. Out in the open." And he worked frantically to reload his crossbow.

Then, as a pair of the bats swooped chittering on him, he ducked down and glanced skywards ... and glimpsed what he had known must be up there. Just a glimpse, for the thing was still high overhead, and there was already more than enough happening on the ground to keep Nathan occupied. But the throb of propulsors was louder now, and the first faint reminder of that nightmare stench from the past was falling like some vile rotting rain all about.

Momentarily distracted, at last Nathan finished reloading. Then, scanning the boulder-strewn landscape all around, he saw:

A flyer, coming in low; the biggest so far and armoured. And its rider, vulturelike, hunched forward in the saddle; a weird scarecrow figure with eyes so deeply sunken under jutting black brows they were little more than a crimson glimmer. Angular and deathly corpselike in his figure and riding posture—yet radiating power, a devious strength—it was perfectly obvious that this one was no mere lieutenant. No indeed, for he was a Lord of vampires. Wamphyri!

It was the first time Nathan had laid eyes on Gorvi the Guile, one of the renegade Lords who had fled Turgosheim with Wratha the Risen; nevertheless, he knew him from a description he'd had from Maglore in Runemanse:

The dome of his head, kept shaven save for a single central lock, with a knot hanging to the rear. His sallow, parchment features (again Nathan was reminded of a leprous vulture) *and shifty sunken eyes; and hands like skinny claws, but full of a true Lord's strength. And dressed in black head to toe, always, with his black cloak flapping like tattered wings . . .*

Oh yes, Gorvi the Guile. Definitely.

Braver now that their vampire master was here, the great bats formed a cloud, came shrilling in a flurry of thrumming wings. Nathan's crossbow would be worse than useless, wasted against them. Doubly frustrating, their buffeting made it impossible to set his sights on the larger, higher targets.

But the riderless flyer was also back, appearing as from nowhere, hovering into view over the tops of nearby boulders. Nathan kneeled, took aim . . . and the great bats at once struck against him, knocking him off balance. As he sprawled, so the rest of the flock fell towards him—

—And Ben Trask, seeing his chance as the bats crowded together, opened up with his machine pistol. Three of the six literally exploded in midair, torn into bloody fragments by the ferocity of Trask's firepower. And the rest of them scattered in disarray, shrilling their alarm as they swerved left and right, and made off into the maze of leaning rocks.

Why do you wait? Nathan heard Gorvi's furious mind-shout, which the vampire Lord directed at the riderless flyer. *Finish it! Settle on them! Smother them with your bulk and drive your thrusters down between the rocks to crush them!*

The thing came, arching its wings, gentling to earth. And between the segments of its underbelly, rubbery landing appendages uncoiling like quivering nests of sentient worms! Nathan knew he couldn't miss; he simply raised his gun-hand, aimed at the juncture of neck and body above the slit of the pouch, and squeezed the trigger. And as the flyer came drifting towards the clump of boulders, so the bolt flew home.

Nathan turned his face away; it seemed a long time; perhaps the detonator was faulty, the bolt a dud? But then a dull *crump*! As if a boulder had toppled and fallen to earth. Nathan looked:

Not six feet away the flyer's huge but patently human face at the end of its ten-foot neck gazed at him in vast amaze—a sort of vacant astonishment—in the moment before it twisted into an agonized mask, threshed left and right, opened its jaws and emitted an ear-piercing shriek! Then . . .

. . . The creature's membranous air-scoop wings pounded at the air as if to bear it up, up away from its pain, which was inescapable. The thing skewed wildly to the left, tilted, allowed Nathan to see close up the damage his explosive bolt had done: the gaping hole that rained pink fluids, where the flyer's head and neck had been half-severed from the body. There was scarcely enough muscle left to hold the head erect, and nothing at all of strength or will.

The beating of the wings slowed to a quiver as the beast commenced a staggering, stalling glide. A tilting wingtip got snagged between tall boulders, turning the flyer like a pivot. Its grotesque head sank down, touched crumbling earth, dug in and ploughed a furrow. The long neck concertinaed, buckled at the point of injury, and snapped with a soft cartilage *crack!* Dust rose in a cloud as the manta wings flopped uselessly and the carcass slewed to a shuddering halt.

Nathan looked at the weapon in his hand and felt awesomely powerful; he tightened his grip on it, shook it in the air, and shouted his triumph through bared teeth. His elation was short-lived, however; warrior stench thickened in a moment, and again a monstrously pulsing shadow blotted out the stars in its passing.

Trask and Chung emerged from their nest of boulders. Nathan saw the looks on their faces as they crouched down, shrank back, stared slack-jawed above and behind him. He spun on his heel and saw . . . his worst nightmare. Throbbing obscenely in midair, a Wamphyri warrior!

With its air-trap mantle fluttering and its gas-bladders fully inflated, the warrior's sputtering biopropulsors emitted clouds of stench-vapour as it turned and came pulsing and rumbling over the barren boulder plains. Like the two downed flyers this monster was "small" of its kind; but despite the fact that it flew, it was not a "flyer" as such. In its delirious design it was not dissimilar to Sunside's small, lake-dwelling, harmless freshwater octopuses: its body sac was rather more elongated, and its tentacles more properly launching thrusters than appendages for walking or groping for shrimp prey in the pebbles of a pool. But its principal *dis*similarity lay in the eyes . . . their shrieking *madness* . . . their malign *intent* . . . their *number*!

And in its size. For even a small warrior is not small.

Nathan recognized his error: one of comparison. Distance had fooled him, causing him to compare this Thing with a creature of Nature; distance and perspective. For the warrior was all of a hundred and fifty yards away, at which distance (and quite apart from its multitude of saucer eyes) the *idea* of it was still acceptable—barely. And given that the safety margin was narrowing even now, for a little while at least a man might retain sufficient of composure to think of such a thing in terms of other animals. But as it pulsed closer . . . there *was* no real comparison.

That a thing like this could lift its massive bulk even an inch from the earth, let alone fly, seemed patently impossible; yet here it spurted against the star-spattered horizon like an alien, aerial slug. Just looking at it, details were branded on Nathan's feverish mind:

Of grey-mottled flesh, with fish-scale armour gleaming metallic-blue in starshine . . . of gas-bladder clusters bulging like strange wattles or nests of morbid tumors from both sides of the segmented, flexible spine, constantly shrinking and expanding, regulating the monster's balance . . . of cartilage hooks and sawing appendages, and chitin grapples in the shape of crab claws. But over and above everything else, the evil pseudointelligence of its swivelling, searching saucer eyes, and their placement: in the sloping prow of the skull, the softer membrane of the undermantle, and flanking the propulsors in the anal region, where a spiked tail flailed like a mace and acted as a rudder . . .

. . . It was only fifty yards away now, and it had spotted the three men. Propulsors blasting, the warrior lowered its head and zeroed in on them!

Crush them! Let their pulp stain those boulders crimson! Gorvi's mind-cry galvanized Nathan to activity. Jerking erect, he glanced at his crossbow, knew there was no time to reload. Then Ben Trask grabbed his elbow and Nathan jumped six inches.

"For Christ's sake!" Trask yelled over the rumble of the warrior's propulsors. "Nathan—get us *out* of here!"

And to one side, David Chung gasped: "God! I just *don't* believe it!" Gorvi's lieutenants—their leather-clad bodies holed, and both of them leaking red from a dozen wounds—had appeared from behind the clump of boulders, staggering but yet advancing on the three. Trask on the other hand had seen vampires close-up before, and he believed it well enough.

While overhead, leaning forward in the ornate saddle of his flyer, Gorvi himself stabbed a trembling, outraged claw of a hand at the three and commanded his warrior: *Now! Crush them now! Aye, and those idiot, weakling thralls of mine with them!*

Chung was quick to get a grip on himself. Even as Nathan conjured a Möbius door, Chung turned his machine pistol on Gorvi's lieutenants; at point-blank range he literally tore them apart. His spray of bullets punched crimson lace holes in their leather armour, across and back, up and down. They were swatted like flies, knocked flat on their backs on the stony ground.

And Trask opened up on the warrior. Less than twenty-five yards away, the thing had opened its jaws. Inside . . . it wasn't so much a mouth as a cave of daggers! Trask was shaken but held his aim directly into that gaping maw. And slime-dripping teeth flew in shards as steel met bone in shattering collision, none of which deflected the warrior from its course by an inch.

Nathan had his door. Holding it steady, he grabbed Trask's arm, Chung's too.

But the warrior was almost upon them. Grunting its challenge and intent on ramming them against the clump of boulders, it came head-on. Trask snarled his fear, aimed at the foremost cluster of gas-bladders, let fly with a final spray of bullets. And as bladders exploded like grenades and the thing screamed, swerved, and turned the armoured mass of its flank to the fore, so Nathan yanked on his colleagues' arms and dragged them off-balance into the Möbius Continuum.

In the void of the Continuum, Trask panted his relief as he fingered his torn jacket and knew that the sleeve had been ripped off on one of the warrior's scales. . . .

Gorvi's warrior sprawled, for the moment winded, in the lee of the boulders. Scales had been wrenched loose, several eyes and launching limbs crushed, and more bladders burst in the collision with the rocks. The nightmare beast's air-trap mantle was holed in several places along its left flank, but not so badly it wouldn't mend. First, however, it must rest, feed, fashion fresh bladders from its metamorphic flesh; that is, if its master desired it should ever fly again.

Gorvi had landed. Furious, the vampire Lord approached and examined the space between his construct and the boulders where he hoped to find the crushed remains of his dead foes—whatever *they* had been! And yet, that space was empty.

Well, not quite empty, for the bodies of his thralls were there at least, all crumpled, broken, and dead . . . or undead. For even now they were not completely beyond repair, if Gorvi so desired it. Except he did *not* desire it, not for this pair of unworthy dogs! As well that he'd sent the best and longest lasting of his lieutenants ahead of him into Sunside, to fight alongside Wratha and the others, else it might just as easily be Turgis Gorvisman lying here all full of holes and his blood leaked out!

On the other hand . . . well, he was a one to look out for, that Turgis. Gorvi *could* have left him in charge of Guilesump, except by now he'd probably have been at it with one or another of Gorvi's females—or several of them! *Huh!* A man couldn't trust anyone these days.

But the strange and sudden absence of these alien interlopers—or their corpses at least—was a puzzle. Gorvi had seen them here; he was *sure* he had seen his warrior crash into them. As for their awesome weapons, why, for all he knew they could be trained on him even now . . .

. . . He at once crouched down, sent a cautious vampire probe into the maze of boulders. Their aura—their scent—would soon give these humans away if they'd somehow managed to wriggle back in there: the warm salty scent of untainted blood. But no, they weren't there; only an oily smell now, and a trace of their human breath hanging sweet on the still air . . . and lingering smells of cloth and hot steel, too, from their clothing and their weapons. Alien smells all, but nothing of the flesh-and-blood people who had made them.

Gorvi snarled his frustration, cursed his misfortune: to have lost two flyers, a pair of lieutenants, a warrior damaged and depleted. Well, at least the last might still be salvaged. And so: *Feed!* he commanded the beast.

The monster's permanent prow eyes (permanent as opposed to the rudimentary metamorphic sensors in its underbelly and other parts of its anatomy) immediately swivelled in Gorvi's direction. Blank black disks that should scarcely be capable of reasoning intelligence as such—more properly receptors for the tiny brute mind with-in—they yet displayed all the evil of a warped mutant sentience, a deviousness whose source lay in Gorvi himself. The warrior was after all his construct, and therefore imbued with the Guile's essence.

Feed? He could sense the beast's querying hesitation, its dull apprehension. *But surely these are yours, Master?*

Gorvi snorted, nodded his skull-like head. *They were mine, aye, but now I give them to you. So feed and grow strong. Take these thralls of mine but leave the flyers where they are; let them rot here! Do not glut but fuel and repair yourself. Then, when you are fit for it, make your way back to Guilesump.*

The warrior's launching limbs surged into motion, turning it about. The saucer eyes in its great armoured head focussed as one on the gutted lieutenants. Powerful jaws gaped and saliva slopped from leathery lips as a forked tongue thick as a man's thigh tasted, than snatched, first one shattered body and then the other. As a chameleon takes flies, so the Guile's battle-construct took the dead lieutenants.

And if Gorvi's promise of a few minutes ago had ever registered at all, it was now forgotten—wiped out, obliterated from the monster's one-track mind—in the brief but passionate rapture of its feeding frenzy. For these "tidbits" neither screamed nor made any sound at all when they were crunched. But their flesh was soft and succulent for all that.

While his construct refuelled itself, the Guile returned thoughtfully to his nodding flyer, climbed into the saddle and urged the beast aloft. So far the night was a disaster. First, in Guilesump, there had been several unforeseen ad-

ministrative tasks: morbid fluids to draw off from a still-
born warrior lest the thing go rancid in its vat; quarrel-
some thralls to cow; an ill-tempered woman to chastise.
(Well, these things would form the substance of Gorvi's
excuse, at least, if ever Wratha and the other Lords should
find fault with him or query his tardiness. But that was unlikely; for knowing he would be "delayed," Gorvi had dispatched not only Turgis but others of his lieutenants and a
good many aspirant thralls ahead of him to join the Lords
and Lady in this their joint venture: an all-out attack on
the Szgany Lidesci.)

But . . . he'd felt *uneasy* about tonight's mass raid right
from the start. What, to join up with Nestor and Canker,
both of whom hated him, Wratha who despised him, and
the Killglance twins who were mad, on this less-than-
predictable soiree (more likely a bloody campaign) against
the resourceful Lidescis? It had been, indeed, more than a
feeling of uneasiness: rather an aura of foreboding, a
doom-laden atmosphere hanging over Wrathstack itself,
ever since the so-called Lady had broached the thing, this
onslaught against the Szgany Lidesci. Or perhaps it was
simply that dwelling in the stack's "basement," as it
were—in Guilesump, level with the scree jumbles and so
open to attack from the ground—Gorvi had come to feel
more and more vulnerable. Whichever, tonight he'd held
back, determined to be last into the field of battle.

Huh! Much good it had done him, for now this. And
perhaps this, too, was an omen, a warning that he was as
well out of it. And certainly he *was* out of it; for there was
no way he would join in any grand battle without a strong
force of lieutenants, thralls, and warriors about him. Not
for the sake of the battle itself, at least. Oh, let the others
seek glory all they would . . . Gorvi could do without
battle-scars! What, cowardice? No, never, for he was
Wamphyri! But he was also the Guile, and he well deserved his name.

Wherefore he would watch the others a while and see
which way it went; and however it went, at the end of the
night Gorvi would have his own tale to tell: of how he had

quashed a sneak attack on the last aerie, while Canker and Nestor and the rest were rutting, counting coup, and glutting themselves on Sunside booty. And aye, this way he'd yet be a hero in his own right!

Sunside, he ordered his flyer as it gained height. *Cross the dome of the Hell-lands Gate, climb on the wind off the Icelands, and follow the foothills west. Then up into the western peaks and through them, and down onto Sunside's flank. There we'll land in the foothills and see what we shall see. . . .*

From their vantage point on the flat-topped bluff in the mouth of the great pass, Nathan, Trask, Chung, and Anna Marie—all four of them together—had watched Gorvi's takeoff and had seen him set his course west. Down on the boulder plains, however, his damaged warrior was still very much in evidence; its roaring and grunting echoed up to them, and puffs of exhaust gasses rose like vile smoke rings from its venting.

The four couldn't know it, but the bodies of the vampire Lord's lieutenants were even now undergoing a process of digestion, their leather gear and all. But they had merely whetted the warrior's appetite and his attention was now centered upon the vastly sprawled corpses of the flyers. Both were as "dead" as undead vampire things can be, despite the fact that they had that in their blood which would keep them "alive" for a long time yet. But since a good deal of that blood had been spilled, the flyers *were* dead to all intents and purposes. Depleted, dead . . . and deserted. But the warrior was mindful of Gorvi's last command— that it must *not* glut itself—and dared not disobey it. The creature felt very little of and understood even less about physical pain; but even as an "infant" or unformed thing still waxing in the morbid fluids of its vat womb, it had felt the sting of its master's corrective mind-darts, and knew how he could bring all of its functions to a shuddering, cringing halt with just a single stab.

So the flyers were out of the question, and meanwhile the warrior had clear instructions which it must follow as a duty to Gorvi the Guile, its master, and to Guilesump, his manse: to rest awhile, replenish its gas-bladders and propulsive system, and let its metamorphism seal the holes in its membranous aerial mantle. Then to fly back to the last aerie and its pen in the stem of the stack. And since sleep is the best way of conserving energy and the greatest aid to any healing process—for vampire flesh no less than human—the monster closed its eyes, slowed its metabolism, shut down the bulk of its sensory apparatus, and slept.

Only two "scanners" remained active, and then barely: a pseudo-eye in the thing's blunt prow skull, and another at the base of a spine in its flail-like rudder. Linked to the rudimentary brain, these would keep watch. Any abrupt or inexplicable change in the warrior's immediate surroundings, it would come snarling awake!

Nathan knew that much, at least, for he'd learned a lot about Wamphyri warriors and guardian creatures in Turgosheim. And now, atop the bluff, he asked Trask and Chung: "I take it you left the weapons hidden away in those boulders?" The two men glanced at each other, could only shrug. And Trask said:

"We couldn't go on the offensive *and* look after the weapons. Survival had to come first, Nathan."

The other's nod. "I understand, of course. But until that warrior heals itself and moves off—which could easily take as long as the rest of this sundown, or three days Earth time—I daren't go back for the guns. So we have to make do with what we've got."

"But our friends the cavers took their loads with them," Chung pointed out. "Er, wherever you took them, I mean."

Again Nathan's nod. "Right. But before I can go back for them, I have to carry you to safety in Sunside. Or what should be safety, except . . . well, it's night now. And so I have one or two things to check out before I can move you. It shouldn't take too long, but until I'm done you must keep a low profile and wait for me here."

He conjured a Möbius door, stepped through it and disappeared . . .

* * *

. . . And reappeared in the Cavern of the Ancients.

Atwei and the three cavers were still there, also a young Thyre male. And so were the sacks of arms that the cavers had brought with them. Nathan had no time for explanations. "Atwei, stay here with my friends," he told her in her own tongue. And taking up one of the bundles he was gone again—

—To the bald, rounded plateau of Sanctuary Rock where that landmark refuge backed up on Sunside's foothills at the edge of the forest to the west of ruined Settlement. Nathan had chosen the Rock because its dome was a vantage point from which he should be able to spy out the lie of the land east and west along the flank of the barrier mountains, the region he'd once called home. And travelling there through the Möbius Continuum, he had remembered it as he had known it all of his young life.

The dome of the Rock towered more than two hundred feet over the slope of a stony hill. It was like a huge oval boulder, toppled over on its side, half-buried in a hillside that climbed through pines and birches, and bramble and blackthorn undergrowth. Above the rock the greenbelt was narrow, shaded, and gloomy where it wound with the contours of the foothills. Rising steeply across its width, its foliage grew sparse at the feet of frowning cliffs. Below, the patchy woods descended into a thinly swirling mist, levelled out and thickened into forest proper, finally faded with distance into a grey-green fuzz of soft-edged canopy and the gently mobile concentric contours of false, misted horizons.

As to why the place was called "Sanctuary" Rock:

In the olden times—indeed since time immemorial—the Szgany had hidden from Starside's vampires in the roots of the Rock; hidden in the guts of the boulder, which was mainly solid in its body and dome, but hollow as a rotten tooth in its base. And now the Szgany Lidesci not only hid there but lived there, too. They also "lived" in Settlement, which was no great distance away, but at night invariably withdrew to the safety of the Rock.

Over the years the Lidescis had burrowed extensively to make the place more nearly liveable. And they had opened up a maze of passages, granaries, animal pens, private habitations for family units, storage facilities, even recreational areas. They had tunneled their way from a huge overhung entrance and various connected cavern systems under the eastern rim of the Rock, right through to the rear and the far side. Also, they'd strategically mined all of the major entrances with barrels of crude but effective gunpowder. Thus the Rock was now a sanctuary, makeshift encampment, lethal trap, and escape route all in one.

As for the Rock's location:

For fifteen to twenty miles around this was Lidesci territory, which Lardis Lidesci had always guarded jealously and protected with his life—especially against the night raids of the vampire Lords of Starside. And it was the Necroscope's guess that if tonight the Wamphyri could be found anywhere on Sunside, then that . . .

. . . But in the moment that Nathan emerged from the Möbius Continuum, he knew that there was no "if" about it. For they were here even now. They were actually *here*—at Sanctuary Rock!

Far to the south, across the sprawling expanse of night-dark woods and the furnace desert that lay beyond, a curved horizon was silhouetted against a band of molten yellow light fading upwards into pink and amethyst, then light and dark blue, finally black reaching back to the sky overhead, where the stars were as shards of blue ice frozen in alien (but to Nathan familiar) configurations. Or at least, the sky *should* be black—

—But it should *not* be shot through with lances of coloured light, and dotted with nightmare shapes that sputtered explosively or glided silently through the black smoke rising from oily fires and the exhaust trails of careening rockets! Sanctuary Rock was suffering a concerted attack, and following the silence and darkness of the Möbius Continuum, it was as if Nathan had stepped forth into hell itself!

Down there on the sparsely wooded slopes at the foot of

the Rock, close—too close—to the gaping entrance to the main cavern system, there were warriors on the ground. One of them, the biggest one, seemed crippled. It was burning, roaring and hissing like a herd of rutting shads, and heaving its forequarters this way and that on an apparently broken spine. Its hindquarters were writhing, a mass of flames where Travellers had poured oil on the thing and fired it. But there were lesser warriors, too: smaller, less cumbersome, undamaged as yet and very, *very* dangerous . . . and enraged, of course.

Even as Nathan watched, one of the things rose up on its forward-thrusting limbs and fired a short burst from its propulsors. Seeming to bound in the air, it crashed down among a group of the Rock's defenders, crushed several of them to the earth, commenced snapping at the rest. Its chitin clubs, pincers, and stabbers wove menacingly in all directions.

Nathan also saw flyers down there on the ground, half-a-dozen of them at least, but they were all positioned well back from the forward edge of the battle area. Ideally situated for relaunching, facing downhill on the narrow trails leading to the Rock, they waited for further instructions. Their masters, lieutenants and senior thralls, had dismounted and went afoot like infantrymen, shadowing and directing the battle-engines that were the warriors.

Other flyers and warriors were in the air, probably less than two dozen of them in all but seeming to Nathan to swarm in their hundreds. They were not quite the height of the dome of the Rock, so that in fact he looked down on them silhouetted against firelight and the flaring, multi-coloured trails of rockets. Only a handful of the warriors were big ones, but the smaller variety was versatile and full of a terrible vitality. Nathan saw two of them go spiralling down, propulsors sputtering, thrusters uncoiling, to land near the base of the Rock on its western approaches. Well, they'd achieve very little there. Uninhabitable and therefore undefended on that flank, the Rock was solid and its face sheer; it sank straight into the stony ground. On the other hand, it wouldn't take long for the warriors to get airborne again and turn their monstrous energies to the eastern flank. . . .

While overhead, maybe two hundred and fifty feet over the dome of the Rock and six hundred above the forest—circling like vultures over some soon-to-be corpse—the Wamphyri generals themselves rode the night air, blotted out the stars in their wheeling, and gazed down through red and rapacious eyes on the efforts of their army. There were five of them mounted on armoured flyers, and five first lieutenants in attendance on lesser beasts.

Aware of their presence from the moment he vacated the Möbius Continuum, Nathan had automatically taken cover in a clump of gorse growing in the scant soil of a deeply scarred depression. Now, having apprised himself of the situation, he looked skyward again to see what the Lords were up to—

—And none too soon, for they were spiralling down towards the dome of the rock, approaching the flat, central area of its plateau as they prepared to land. This was to be their command position, from which they'd manoeuvre their men and monsters on the ground.

The entire scene had been stunning to Nathan's senses from the very first moment. The roaring of beasts and screams of men carried up from below on air warmed by fear, fire, and fighting. The shrill whistle or occasional shriek of unreliable missiles, and the deafening blasts of sound and blinding explosions when they burst against vampire flesh, or more frequently empty air. The stench of sulphur, and of warrior exhaust gasses, drifting in poisonous grey and yellow clouds through the night; and the mind-searing sight of nightmare shapes throbbing or undulating in the star-spattered sky. But over and above everything else, the knowledge that they were *his* people down there, fighting and dying for the Rock, and for human existence itself.

Stunning to Nathan's senses, yes . . .

. . . But the vampire Lords would soon be landing!

For long moments frozen, at last Nathan was galvanized to frantic activity. Shaking out some of the arms from his bundle, he saw what he'd got here. Fragmentation grenades; a 30mm twin rocket launcher, fully loaded; a lightweight flamethrower, and a machine pistol and ammo. He yanked the rocket launcher free, stuffed grenades into his pockets, crammed what he could of the rest of the stuff back into the bundle and shoved it deep into the roots of the gorse.

The first flyer was coming in for a landing. It was one of the lesser beasts, commanded by a lieutenant. Nathan stood up and came head and shoulders above the gorse. He'd gone entirely unnoticed so far (or so he thought), but for some little time had been shielding his mind while intercepting the telepathic messages of the Wamphyri Lords—and those of one Lady, their leader!

Safely down on this great boulder, we'll see so much more clearly, she was saying. *But it seems to me our forces on the ground are already costing the Lidescis dear, and pushing them back into their holes. By the time we send down another three or four warriors, we'll have them in full rout. After that, if we can only get a beast inside the Rock . . . !* She left the rest of it unthought.

The Lady Wratha's great mount was coming in immediately behind her lieutenant's lesser beast; the rest of the Wamphyri Lords followed on behind, descending in a loose V formation. But next in line after Wratha the Risen was one whose thoughts grew more anxious and confused moment to moment, who now sent her this urgent message:

Wratha! Back off! Don't land! There's someone there! An enemy—even a Great *Enemy! Aye, and he's dangerous!*

Recognizing that telepathic voice at once, Nathan thrilled with a variety of emotions, not least horror. For its owner was his twin brother—Lord Nestor, of the Wamphyri!

IV

Nestor

For something less than an hour now, Lord Nestor Lichloathe of the Wamphyri had known it: the fact that his mainly unremembered brother (his real brother, aye, his "blood" brother, but a brother in name only, and his Great Enemy to all other intents and purposes) was back in Sunside/Starside. In precisely the same moment that Maglore of Runemanse had known it, and the mummied, monstrous Eygor Killglance in his refuse pit, and the dead and dreaming Thyre, and Nathan's nephew wolves, so too had Nestor known it, and just as surely as the rest.

Except, and paradoxically, Nestor *had* found it harder to credit, for he had believed that he was his brother's murderer! Indeed he had *known* that Nathan was gone forever, banished from this vampire world into the Starside Gate, from which neither man, monster, nor any creature of nature or the vats had ever yet returned. It *must* be so, for all of seventeen, even eighteen sunups ago, Nestor's first lieutenant Zahar Lichloathe had reported the fact of it: that acting on Nestor's orders, he'd tossed Nathan into the Gate and sent him to hell! Since when, and until this very night, Nestor had been certain of it, for with his brother's departure one other curse at least had been lifted like a yoke from his shoulders . . . which now was back!

The numbers vortex!

That cryptic, madly whirling dust-devil device of symbols, figures, and cyphers which, bursting out from the core of his twin's weird mind, had often overflowed into

Nestor's dreams, too; Nathan's mind-shield, wherein as a child he had used to hide himself away, now revealed him like a light in the night, or as the smell of Traveller campfires floating on the breeze off Sunside reveals a campsite, or the frenzied buzzing of carrion flies a piece of rotting meat.

Nestor had first sensed the thing as he and the others crossed the spine of the barrier mountains midway between the great pass and Settlement. But . . . *behind* him? Its source had been behind him, in Starside, in the vicinity of the Starside Gate. Now what would a man of Sunside be doing there? And what would a dead man be doing anywhere? But then, as they had descended into Sunside's foothills, so the mountains had blocked it out a little; and supposing it to have been a rogue memory out of times best forgotten (for what else could it be, since Nestor's Great Enemy was no more?), he had tried his best to do the same: shut it out of his thoughts.

But as the massed might of Wrathstack spurted and pulsed west like a flock of shadows against the greater shadow of the mountains, so the thing had been there again, swirling in Nestor's vampire mind and stronger than ever before! For where in past times the vortex had been disordered, chaotic, insensible, now it had direction and was purposeful.

And yet if his Great Enemy was in fact alive, then what was happening here? For first Nestor had sensed him close to the Hell-lands Gate, and now . . . far to the south, in the desert beyond the forests and savanna? It made no sense. No man (and certainly not a dead one) can be in two places at once!

Then Nestor had felt an urgent need to reprimand, or at least to question, his man Zahar, and had called him up alongside the better to speak to him. And riding the night a little apart from the main force, without so much as glancing at his great grim lieutenant, Nestor had inquired of him in his softest "voice":

Zahar, are you faithful?

"To you, Master? Always." Zahar spoke the words out

loud, knowing that Nestor would "hear" them despite the wind's bluster. But for all that he had answered in the affirmative, still he'd been concerned. What was Nestor's purpose, he'd wondered, asking such a question at a time and in a place such as this?

Then the necromancer had looked at him, a frowning, even disapproving glance across the gulf of air. And shuttering his scarlet eyes somewhat: *But—have you never disobeyed me?*

The other had given his head a fervent shake. "Nor shall I ever, Lord!"

For a moment Nestor had held his gaze eye to eye in the night, across the squalling updrafts, scarlet to feral yellow. And he'd known that his lieutenant spoke the truth. For Zahar Lichloathe feared his master's art and the pain it could bring not only in this world but also in the next. Not even the dead were safe from one such as he: a necromancer who tortured them for their secrets, causing them pain in their dead flesh as if it were alive. But in the course of the last four to five months Zahar had learned to fear him even more, when such a change was apparent in him that by comparison Zahar's previous master Vasagi the Suck had seemed a friendly, even a merry creature.

Gazing at Nestor however briefly (for it is not seemly to look upon the Wamphyri too long or too openly), staring at him where he sat forward in the saddle and leaned a little into the wind, this is what Zahar saw:

A man changed immensely. Two and a half years ago he had been a six-footer, and now was almost seven. He'd been tanned by the sun, and was now pallored by the night, and by his condition; for his flesh had taken on the leaden look of undeath. His Szgany eyes had been dark, naturally . . . but not for long, a day at most; the Change That Shapes had taken him that fast! Wamphyri, aye— he'd been a natural! And eyes red as fire.

And yet . . . perhaps not as "natural" as might at first be imagined. For he covered his leaden flesh as if ashamed of it, swathing himself in black head to toe, so that his eyes burned out over a mask of black cloth. Shame or denial, whichever; but even as a Lord freshly ascended—through all the pain, frustration, and uncertainty of his vampire metamorphosis—still Nestor had retained something of his Sunside heritage. And for a while, for all that he'd become more and more Wamphyri, still he had been the man.

Sufficient that when he went hunting in Sunside one night with the dog-Lord Canker Canison, he'd come back with a sweetheart out of earlier times: the girl Glina, who had loved him. Ah, but that had been the last of his humanity. For where now were Glina and the child she brought with her out of Sunside?

Zahar knew well enough, for he had been witness and more than witness. The child was dead, all burst into tatters from the force of his descent onto the rocks at the foot of Wrathstack; and Glina burned by the sun, and likewise fallen from on high; her body walled up with stones in a crevice west of the great pass. All of which by Nestor's command, if not his hand, and the change still taking place in him.

All of this running concurrent with his affair with Wratha the Risen, during which his step had seemed lighter, his spirit uplifted. But their "love" had been as false as Wratha herself was false . . . or as Nestor was false? In any case, it had not lasted. For by then he had discovered his necromancy: that he could speak with dead men, and torture them for their secrets. And when that had become known to him his change had taken a new direction; it was a darker Nestor who stalked the night, and moved like a ghost through the mazy ways of Suckscar . . .

Oh, they saw each other from time to time even now, Nestor and Wratha, and went to each other in their beds; for they were Wamphyri and had their needs. But the first allegiance of a vampire Lord is to himself; he seeks security, provides for his longevity. This was no time for lovers, when winds of war were blowing out of the east from beyond the Great Red Waste. There was Szgany blood to be spilled, undead armies to build. Aye, and soon there would be powerful invaders to be killed. That was the way of things: crush or be crushed.

So the delights of dalliance were put aside, and now the black-draped creature who rode the night wind alongside Zahar had precious little of the man in him but a great deal of the vampire. More than that, however, there was something that Zahar couldn't fathom. An unspeakable terror? (Nestor's lieutenant scarcely dared think it, and he must *never* be overheard thinking it!) But ... some morbid fear, perhaps, gnawing at his master's necromantic mind?

... Zahar's glance was too bold! Likewise his thoughts, however much he would shield them! Dangerously bold, aye! He knew it and looked away, forced his mind to opaque, meaningless meanderings. That way was the safest ...

Reading most of Zahar's thoughts anyway, Nestor had known that his man would never dare lie to him. But to be sure:

Zahar, he said, *now listen. That night when I crashed on Sunside, and you thought that I was lost forever. You captured him, my Great Enemy, and told me how he awakened in the moment that you tossed him into the Gate. But are you sure—absolutely sure—that he disappeared into the Gate?*

"Yes, Master—" and hastily: "—but all in accordance with your orders!"

And: *Of course,* Nestor had nodded in a little while. *Of course ...*

But after Zahar had fallen back in line:

Again that disturbance of psyche, that thrill of awareness, that recognition of the vortex! It was here! He, Nathan ... *was* here!

It came and went: a surge from far across the forest, to the southeast, then—nothing. As if a candle had been lit however briefly, then snuffed. And at once a second flare-up, but fainter, from across the mountains in Starside. So that Nestor had wondered: *One* Great Enemy, or should that be two? ... Or three? Or was it all in his head?

And then he had wondered: Was that it? Was his mind going as well as his body? For Nathan and his numbers vortex weren't the only curse on Nestor Lichloathe, and the thing in his body struck far more terror than any imagined condition of his mind. Ah, yes! For unlike the questionable nature of the latter, the thing in his body was indisputably real.

Yet both curses had the same source: a night of ill omen some eighteen sundowns gone, when he and Zahar went a-hunting in Sunside . . . hunting for his Great Enemy, Nathan, and for a treacherous Lidesci bitch called Misha.

Then, as the Wamphyri Lords and their aerial army headed for Sanctuary Rock, so Nestor's mind had drifted back in time, recalling all the terrors of that night, but scarcely wishing to remember all the fearful times passed between . . .

The dog-Lord Canker Canison, who from time to time read the future in dreams, had warned Nestor not to go; but the necromancer would have none of it. His Great Enemy was in Sunside, and Nestor intended to have it out with him.

Canker had been right and the raid was a disaster. Nestor's flyer was crippled, half of its face shot away, its small brain seriously damaged. Nestor, too, was badly wounded, half-blinded by silver shot from a Lidesci shotgun. Only sheer Wamphyri tenacity and willpower had kept him in the saddle as his dying beast glided south, losing height over the forest.

Then the crash . . . unconsciousness . . . a slow awakening. Some pain, best ignored. The Wamphyri turn pain aside, mainly; they suffer in silence while their parasites see to the mending. But the *place* of awakening: a leper colony!

Leprosy! Great bane of vampires!

Nestor had fled before the fear and loathing of it, and also before the killing rays of the rising sun, deep into the forest, to a cave in the bank of a river where he'd slept and dreamed fever dreams through the long Sunside day. And while he moaned and nightmared, so his leech had commenced a healing metamorphism deep within his damaged flesh.

With the night he'd crossed into Starside, and there in the barrier mountains had been met by his man Zahar and Canker Canison. Apparently none the worse for wear (well, a couple of scratches and a scar or two, the deepest of which he might keep as a souvenir), but saying nothing at all of how he'd survived the previous day and night, Lord Nestor had returned to Suckscar, his manse in the last great aerie of the Wamphyri.

Following which . . . he scarcely desired to remember what had come after that. Not here and now, with so many keen Wamphyri minds around him. It could well be that he'd remembered too much already—but he doubted it. The minds of the others were intent upon what was to be, not what might have been.

But Zahar Lichloathe (once Sucksthrall), flying in line somewhat to the rear of his master, remembered that time just as well as Nestor. He guarded his thoughts as best he could, be sure, but he remembered all the same. . . .

In Suckscar (named by and after Vasagi the Suck, its one-time master), the necromancer Lord Lichloathe had very quickly fallen into something of a routine; but one known only to himself, at first, and strange for a Lord of the Wamphyri. Perhaps even morbidly so. Zahar remembered the background details:

Penultimate of the stack's great manses, situated beneath Wrathspire, which was the very tip and towered more than half a mile over the rubble and scree, Suckscar had been a dingy, doom-fraught place before Vasagi's—demise?— and Nestor's ascension. Even by Wamphyri standards it had been doleful, with an aura all its own . . . or the Suck's.

A cold one—entirely unfathomable except by his peers, and often by them, too—Vasagi had been a monster among monsters. The victim of a hereditary bone disease, when a surge of growth in his jaws and teeth had threat-ened to outstrip the metamorphic flesh of his face, he'd simply extruded them. Which is to say, he'd stripped his upper jaw of teeth, unhinged the lower jaw, withdrawn all flesh from the offending bones and so been rid of them. And in their place he'd shaped his face to a tapering pink tentacle tipped with a flexible needle siphon, not unlike the proboscis of a bee. This was a weapon he'd used with remarkable dexterity and in a variety of ways: sliding it into the finest vein to draw off blood, or through an eardrum or eye deep into the whorl of a brain to vampirize, instruct, cripple, or kill.

Speechless because of his self-inflicted deformity, the Suck had become a master of mime; but he was also a mentalist second to none, so that between gestures and telepathy he was always understood . . . when he wanted to be. Keeping mainly to himself and to his manse, however, Vasagi had little use for speech of any sort but preferred his privacy. Similarly, he had seemed to prefer austerity.

When Nestor had ascended to Suckscar after Wran the Rage killed (or incapacitated?) Vasagi in a Sunside duel, he'd been dismayed at the lack of lighting, heating, the inadequate water supply, and the sparsity of facilities in general. The fixtures were all in place but mainly turned off or stopped up, for Vasagi had not availed himself of these common utilities. Likewise the lives of his thralls, be they fledgling vampires or lieutenants alike: austere. And because Vasagi was "dumb," they too were quiet, sparing of speech, cowed where they crept through Suckscar.

And while it's a fact that *all* vampire thralls fear their masters, Vasagi the Suck's (especially his females) feared him more; for with his alien features—crimson eyes, weird snout, and stabbing siphon—he looked far more an insect than a man. In the days before their Sunside duel, Wran the Rage had often taunted Vasagi that he only ever mounted his odalisques from the rear, because they could not bear to look him in the face!

Well, and they'd bear it even less after the duel. For in an act as merciless as it was monstrous, Wran had severed Vasagi's proboscis, leaving him only a red-spurting sleeve for a face. Except, of course, the vampire women of Suckscar would never see that awful sight, for this was a fight to the death . . . or rather, it should have been.

In any case, Wran had left the Suck broken and bloody, pegged out on the slope of a south-facing foothill; left him there in the twilight, in the dawn mists of Sunside, to await the rising sun and an agonizing death. Since when and to date, no one in the last aerie had seen or heard of him. There again, neither was he missed, except perhaps by the Lady Wratha, who had counted him an ally . . .

But in Suckscar (which for his own reasons Nestor had not renamed) Vasagi's aura had lingered on; his people continued to be morose, alienated, and sparing both of speech and the utilities . . . for a while at least; until they were used to Nestor. Then:

The young Lord Lichloathe had changed all that. He was no cold creature but a man out of Sunside, and his likes and lusts more nearly a man's. The vampire Lord Vasagi the Suck, when he'd taken a woman, had fucked and feasted at the same time, penetrating not only with his member but also his siphon, in breast, throat, or root of tongue. While bedding with him had been a very painful affair, with Nestor it should be a pleasure. Since he was mainly innocent of women, Vasagi's odalisques had instructed him in their various ways, and Nestor had been an avid pupil. Until soon enough, with the assistance of the Szgany girl Glina Berea, he in turn instructed them.

As for Suckscar:

Nestor turned on the water which, drawn up from Gorvi's wells, was processed by Wratha's siphoneers in Wrathspire; he had the gas inlets cleaned and refurbished as required, drawing off his share of gas from the methane chambers of Madmanse to give Suckscar additional light and warmth; and despite the fact that it might be considered a luxury, not a necessity, he even saw to the few requirements of his thralls, so that their lives, too, were not entirely lacking in comforts.

But in turn he demanded obedience absolute, from thralls and lieutenants alike, with harsh and occasionally fatal penalties for any who failed him. And because Nestor's word was law, and his law was strict, they did not fail him. And everything in Suckscar was his: his people and creatures, even Vasagi's warriors still waxing in their vats, were now Nestor's to do with as he desired.

It had been a period of adjustment in Suckscar and, for Lord Lichloathe's thralls, in large part one of contentment (though it should be understood that "contentment" and "happiness" as such have no real place in the lives of thralls). But in any case the basic needs of their existence were much improved . . . in the beginning, at least—

—Until Nestor had discovered his necromancy; and especially later, following that night when he and Zahar had gone a-hunting together, across the barrier mountains in Sunside.

Since when things had deteriorated. Not so much in the maintenance or "morale" of Suckscar itself, but more properly in its Lord and master. His moods had grown changeable as the winds (but not his expression, which was ever grave), and his thralls had commenced to go quietly again, as in the days of Vasagi. It was, as Zahar had been quick to note, as if a morbid spell was upon him . . . or a morbid dread within.

Once, hurrying to Nestor's private rooms with a message from the necromancer's friend and neighbour in Mangemanse, the dog-Lord Canker Canison, Zahar had discovered his master naked, bathing, and apparently engaged in a most minute examination of his person, the skin of his forearms and thighs. So engrossed was he, that for a while Zahar's presence had gone unnoticed. But when it was, then Nestor had been furious!

What? (he'd wanted to know as he hurriedly, tremblingly dressed himself), and did his most trusted lieutenant now spy on him in the privacy of his own apartments? Well then, from now on these rooms were forbidden to him and all others; nor would Zahar enter with *any* message unless Nestor first called for him. Moreover, there would be no more telepathic communication between the two unless Nestor himself initiated it; and should Zahar *ever* feel the need to encroach upon Nestor's mind unbidden, in however small a degree . . . let him first discover the secrets of flight, for he would surely find himself hurled from one of Suckscar's windows!

Zahar had never seen him so wroth . . .

. . . But he was aware that the replenishment of fuel for the Lord's fire-hole was an ongoing task, so much so that a thrall was employed to that end only, carrying Szgany charcoal to Nestor's bathroom. And he did know that Nestor drew off a deal of water from the catchment sluices, so as to leave siphoned water free for the use of the manse generally. It could only be that Nestor bathed himself frequently—*very* frequently! But . . . to what end? A man can only be so clean, after all.

Or perhaps he cleaned more than his body? Perhaps he would also cleanse his soul. But of what? Deeds performed that even a hardened lieutenant might find unwholesome? For Nestor was a necromancer. And Zahar had used to think: *Surely the terrors and torments of life are sufficient, without that men should be tortured in death, too.* Which were of course thoughts that he kept to himself as best he might.

Or was it that Nestor cleansed himself of innocent blood? If so, then he must be the first Lord of the Wamphyri to admit his guilt! Aye, for the others revelled in it! Ah, but there's guilt and there's guilt, and Zahar remembered the woman Glina and her bairn . . . Except that was another thought best kept to himself.

Then there was the matter of Nestor's needs. He had only ever stinted himself in respect of his women when he was going to Wratha on a regular basis, for he would save his energy for her. Before their *affaire*, however, and in the period of gradually declining passion that had followed it, Nestor had not gone short. Although Vasagi had been no great beauty himself, he'd had an eye for good-looking girls and had taken his fair share out of Sunside. Along with the Suck's leech, Nestor had inherited them and tried them all; indeed, he'd tried one of them—one of the first—too far, and depleted her even unto death, or undeath. Then, lest she rise up from her fatal sleep Wamphyri, an unwanted Lady, even a mistress in Nestor's manse, Zahar had advised that she be carried into the barrier mountains, pegged out to await the sunrise, and so destroyed. And his master had agreed.

So, no lack of women to warm Nestor's bed, neither before nor after his grand romance with Wratha. Yet ever since returning from Sunside on foot following that hunting trip, he seemed to have lost all interest in Suckscar's females; or if not all, then most.

And his appetite . . .

Nestor had never much cared for it red. When necessary, then he'd have it, but lightly cooked meats generally sufficed. Except (and here a curious thing), when he *did* take it live, then he would ensure that the donor died immediately afterwards—not undeath but the true death—that the corpse was cleansed, flensed, and the flesh *roasted* before it went to the provisioning! And always, and *only*, for the consumption of warriors whose constitution was such that they could digest and dispose of almost anything.

And yet . . . he lusted after blood like all of them. Zahar knew this quite definitely, for he'd raided with Nestor on Sunside and seen him kill with the best—*and* with a bloody zest—which is a sure gauge of Wamphyri vitality, for invariably the bloodlust of the kill runs commensurate with the scarlet thirst. So why not in Nestor? Whatever the answer, it probably explained his leaden pallor. Even for a Lord of the Wamphyri, Nestor Lichloathe was undeniably pale these days. The blood is the life, and Nestor was scarcely living it to the full.

On the other hand, he'd been looking forward with some anticipation (or . . . foreboding? It was hard to tell) to this raid on the Lidescis. And Zahar recalled how, in the early dawn twilight some hundred or so hours ago, Nestor had called him to his south-facing room of repose. It was a rare thing these days to be offered audience with the necromancer in his rooms—but it was also worrying. One could never be sure what Nestor had on his mind. On this occasion, however, he'd merely craved company, the presence of someone other than himself. Also, he had desired to talk a little.

A great window in Nestor's room of repose looked out over the boulder plains to the barrier mountains, whose topmost peaks were edged with yellow now as the sun rose far to the south. Many hours yet before that furnace orb would blaze between the peaks on Wrathstack itself, and even then only on the bleached or calcined south face of lofty Wrathspire. Long before that Wratha's black bat-fur curtains would have been drawn against even the smallest hurtful ray, and the Lady herself removed to some darker, safer place.

As for the other manses: despite the fact that the sun never shone on them, generally their vampire masters took to their beds at sunup, and slept their fill in the wake of the long night. But Nestor was and always had been different. He feared the deadly power of the sun, aye, but it fascinated him nonetheless. And he would often sit in his room of repose to watch that poisonous golden stain creeping on the distant crags, and stay there till the last possible, unbearable moment, when he would seem to hear a far faint seething as of acid eating stone.

And that was where Zahar had found his master when Nestor called for him, seated at the great open window, with the baffles thrown wide, gazing into the southwest at the gold-rimmed barrier mountains.

In a little while Nestor had said to him: "You know that I've told Wratha the location of a Lidesci stronghold, called Sanctuary Rock . . ." It had not been a question but a statement of fact.

"The stack has lesser channels of communication, as well you know, Lord," Zahar had answered, carefully. "Thralls mend the water and gas pipes between the manses, and carry out work on the high faces replenishing water catchment skins, sigils, pennants. Sometimes they strike up conversation. The word is that we attack tonight!"

"All of us, aye." Nestor's nod. "You, me, Grig, Norbis, Lexis, Asabar, and the best of our aspirant thralls; the Lady·Wratha and her lads; likewise Lords Spiro Killglance and Wran the Rage, Gorvi the Guile and Canker Canison.

Plus a force of warriors—indeed *all* the warriors, barring only those fresh weaned! The very best blood of the stack, and only a handful of trustee thralls left behind, to see to our manses in our absence."

"The Lidescis are doomed, Lord!"

At which Nestor had gripped the arms of his chair, and turned his face sharply towards him. "Oh, really? Are they? You're sure of that? But they're a tenacious people, Zahar."

"So are lichens tenacious, Lord, yet you may scrape them from the rocks on the heel of your boot."

"Yet lichens don't die in the sunlight! Look there, the barrier mountains: there are lichens in the peaks. They live where we may not."

"Likewise the Szgany, but—" (and here Zahar had frowned) "—but the sunlight is a natural thing, not a Szgany weapon."

"It was upon a time," Nestor brooded, turning his gaze on the barrier mountains as before. "I . . . I seem to remember a myth or legend—a story out of another time—when I was a small thing, or even before I was born. And the legend was this: that before Wratha and the rest of us, there were other vampires here. Quite obviously it was so; signs of their habitation are all around, and of their decline, their demise. This is but one aerie, the last aerie, but sprawling on the boulder plains for all to see lie the skeletons of others that died in a great and terrible war. And in their shattered stumps, evidence of smoke, terrific heat, explosions. For in that forgotten time, the sun also shone in Starside!"

"I know this 'myth,' Lord," Zahar had answered. "Except I am older than you, begging your pardon, and know it for a fact. I was a child in Sunside, eight or nine years old, and—"

"Wait!" Nestor had looked at him again, a curious glance this time. "First tell me . . . do you miss it?"

"Miss what, Lord?" (Zahar's frown.)

"Your childhood. Your . . . humanhood? Do you miss Sunside? You were stolen by Vasagi, and changed into . . .

you. But all so recent—a little over three years? Surely you remember how it was. Now tell me, Zahar: Do you miss what you had and what you were?"

Mystified, Zahar could only shrug. "I am a vampire, Lord. I have what I have, what Vasagi—and you, Lord—have given me. If I am fortunate . . . if I am *very* fortunate, why, I might go on forever! Or if not forever, for a very long time. But in all honesty I cannot say, I do not know, if I 'miss' anything. There are things which I crave, certainly. But then . . . I *am* a vampire, Lord."

"Then why do *I* miss it, eh?" The timbre of Nestor's voice was suddenly deeper, full of a strange melancholy. "Why is it that you remember, without caring, while I who have forgotten almost everything—care so much?"

"You care about Sunside? About the Travellers?" Zahar had offered a shrug. "Not hard to fathom. The Szgany are your livelihood, future, longevity. The blood—"

Without looking at the other, Nestor had held up a hand to still his tongue. And wearily: "Do not tell me that it is the life, for I know it. But I ask you to consider this: Could it also be the death?"

Zahar had been baffled, but then he'd braved a smile. "We . . . are playing a word game! Am I correct, Lord?"

At first Nestor had given his head a shake, but in another moment he'd nodded. "Of course."

And from Zahar, ruefully: "I'm not so good at them, Lord. Even at the best of times Vasagi spoke infrequently—not to say curiously."

"Hmmm!" Nestor had mused. And then, returning to the previous theme: "No, I don't 'care' about the Szgany, and especially not the Szgany Lidesci. Not any longer."

"Despite that they were your people?" But Zahar realized at once that that was a stupid thing to ask of one of the Wamphyri. And: "Of course not, Lord," he'd continued immediately. "You care only for yourself. And for your manse of course, and . . . those in your care?"

Again Nestor had looked at him. "Did I not care for Wratha the Risen?"

Zahar's smile had vanished. Convoluted thinking and

argument aside, he must be careful how he answered that one. "This *is* merely a game, Lord? I mean . . . am I to speak openly?"

There had been no emotion of any sort in Nestor's scarlet gaze when he'd answered, "Oh, yes. I demand it."

And Zahar had discovered his throat to have gone a little dry as he said, "Perhaps . . . perhaps it was not so much 'care' as 'lust,' Lord?" Then, wincing inwardly, he had waited.

But Nestor had not appeared to take offence, and without too much pause: "Is there no love in vampires, then?"

"I have heard of it, but I never saw it." Glad to be on a different tack, Zahar had sighed his relief.

But: "Do *you* love, Zahar?"

"There are women in your manse, Lord . . . other than your own, of course! I go to one of them, yes. But love her . . . ?"

"Women other than my own?" (Still no emotion in Nestor's voice or on his face.) "But *all* of them are mine, surely?"

"As are we all," Zahar had quickly agreed. "But you don't call on all the manse's women, for not all of them are worthy. And of course I know your preferences."

Nestor nodded. "I have my harem, yes."

"Indeed, Lord."

"But sometimes they go wanting."

"As you will it, naturally."

"Recently . . . I have denied them."

"And yourself, Lord."

Again Nestor's swift glance. "Have they gone to others? To you? To other lieutenants? Other men? Common thralls?"

Zahar had backed off a hasty step. "But . . . they would not dare! What, your women? Go to other men? And what man of yours would hope, or try, or have nerve . . . I mean—"

"I know what you mean: my reach is long, my hand is heavy and hard."

Again Zahar's sigh. "Yes, Lord."

"Am I too hard?"

(How to answer that? Say yes and be considered soft? Say no and have Nestor prove him wrong right there and then, perhaps by removing another of his fingers?!) "You are precisely as hard as required, Lord. No more, no less."

At which Nestor had looked at him and grinned mirthlessly. "Clever! You are good at word games, Zahar—well, considering that Vasagi was so difficult to speak to, or the nuances of his speech so hard to grasp. But still you've not answered my question. You averred that 'The blood is the life.' And in my turn I asked: 'Can it also be the death?' How do you answer?"

Zahar was stalled. "I have no answer. Your riddle defeats me. How can blood be death? We drink to live, not to die."

"And if what we drink is tainted?"

"Poisoned, Lord?"

Nestor's shrug. "Poisoned if you will, yes."

"With silver, or kneblasch?"

Nestor's look had been doleful, and Zahar suspected that he'd missed his master's meaning. But after a moment, abruptly, "Put all that aside," the other said. "Except you must believe me when I tell you that there are worse poisons than silver and kneblasch. . . ."

Then for a while he had sat in silence, Zahar waiting on his word. Until: "The word game is over. I won . . . but yet may lose. Now tell me about this Sunsider myth, when the sun shone on Starside."

Zahar nodded, then shook his head. "It was not the sun, but a man with the power of the sun."

"Eh?"

"The sun shone out of him!"

"Out of his eyes? His mouth? His arse? Make sense!"

"I only know what I remember, Lord," Zahar had protested. "I was but a boy, and you were not yet born. Things get warped in the retelling."

"Perhaps I *was* born after all." Nestor had sat up again. "Do you mean the time when the clouds burned red over Starside, and a wind from hell blew through the great pass into Sunside, killing men and trogs alike? This man from the hell-lands had something to do with that?"

"No, before that, four years at least. Alas, I don't know the details, or who or what was involved."

Agitated or impatient, Nestor sat back again and fidgeted. "Tell it anyway."

"The man was a hell-lander, who came from beyond the Starside Gate. He joined his son who was here before him. That one was called The Dweller and the Wamphyri feared him greatly. He kept a garden in the western heights, between the mountains and the foothills. The Wamphyri banded together against him, raided on him in his garden. They were met with fierce opposition! The Dweller and his father used the power of the sun—do not ask me how, Lord, for I don't know—to destroy the vampire army in the air. Defeated, broken, a handful of survivors flew home to their aeries on the boulder plains. Except the stacks were no more! All bar this one, the last aerie, in those days called Karenstack after the Lady who dwelled here, they lay broken on the plain. As to why this one was spared," (Zahar's apologetic shrug), "alas, I don't know . . ."

"Ah!" Nestor's sigh. "The fallen aeries!"

"Indeed, Lord. For The Dweller and his father were here first. They were magicians with the power to move instantaneously from place to place, without consideration of distance. They destroyed the gas-beasts, poured naked sunlight into the methane chambers, reduced the stacks to rubble! When all was finished, the few Wamphyri survivors flew off and exiled themselves in the Icelands . . ."

Again Nestor's sigh, for it appeared he'd been holding his breath awhile. And: "The tumbled stacks!" he'd whispered once again. "The blackening. The great stone corpses crumpled to the plain . . ." And looking at his lieutenant: "Zahar, in this regard your memory matches my thoughts precisely. For I too had heard this legend; except I had forgotten it, as I've forgotten most things." At last he had showed more than the usual animation, and Zahar had congratulated himself that he'd excited his master.

"Is it important, Lord?"

Nestor's frown; his wrinkled forehead and pursed lips. "I don't know. But one thing for sure: Wratha and the others have it wrong. For they believe it was a Szgany suicide squad, raiding through the pass at sunup, who exploded the aeries in their bases and blew them to hell! Well, for the moment we'll let them continue to believe it. But—did you never mention this 'myth' to Vasagi?"

Zahar's shrug. "As we have agreed, Lord, the Suck was not talkative. And anyway, it is generally the case that Wamphyri Lords are not much given to conversation with mere lieutenants. Er . . . which is not to say that you lower yourself, Lord, but that—"

"Yes, I know," Nestor had cut him off. "But lower myself? Of course I don't lower myself. What? It is that *you* are elevated! Consider yourself fortunate."

"I do, Lord."

"Then also consider this, but consider it an order: never speak of these matters again, except to me if or when I desire it. What I know can't hurt me, and what my 'colleagues' do *not* know won't concern them. Understood?"

"Yes, Lord."

Following which Nestor had mused darkly but out loud: "It seems there were Powers in those days, some of which might even have transferred to the present. It will bear looking into."

"Is it your thought that there may be magicians among the Szgany Lidesci even now, Lord?"

At which Nestor had given him the strangest look of all before answering, "I think there may well *have been* one, yes. At least until that night we went a-hunting together, you and I, on Sunside." And then he had very grimly repeated: "Aye, I think there just *might* have been one, at least . . ."

All of which—*uneasy*—conversation had taken place some hundred or so hours ago, in Lord Nestor Lichloathe's room of repose in Suckscar.

But now Zahar must drag his mind back to the present,

the here and now, the fact that just a moment ago he'd "heard" his master issue a mind-warning to Wratha the Risen:

Wratha, back off, don't land! There's someone there! An enemy . . . even a Great Enemy! Aye, and he's dangerous!

Danger! And the first duty of a lieutenant is to protect his Lord and master! Zahar urged his flyer forward, alongside Nestor. And he looked where Nestor was looking.

Front and left, the Lady Wratha's huge, ornately saddled manta flyer was descending towards the flat, pleateaulike dome of that great boulder or massively rounded outcrop called Sanctuary Rock. Directly in front of her, her first lieutenant's creature was about to touch down. More yet to the left—paralleling Nestor but slightly higher, so forming an awkward V behind Wratha—Canker Canison stood in his saddle, hauled on his reins, and barked a string of vivid curses. Eager as ever, deliberately stalling his flyer so that it would lose height more quickly, the dog-Lord. was anxious to be down. And following on behind these three, Wran the Rage Killglance in Nestor's slipstream, his brother Spiro in Canker's, and their chief lieutenants, of course, forming the trailing legs of the V.

But suddenly visible in a patch of crevice-grown gorse, directly in the flight- or landing-path of the foremost flyer, a man had appeared as if from nowhere. He wore a strange mask with protruding, reflective eyes, and carried upon his shoulder a device like a long box . . . which he seemed to be aiming at the lead flyer! Heeding Nestor's warning, however, Wratha was already in contact with that creature's rider:

Whoever he is, gather him up in your beast's pouch, she commanded. *Spill him into space over the rim of the rock!*

Moving to obey—jockeying his mount forward on arched air-trap wings—the lead rider closed with his victim. But in the next instant . . .

. . . Madness! And mayhem!

PART THREE:

WAMPHYRI!

I

Canker and Siggi

Only minutes ago the Wamphyri had circled high over Sanctuary Rock before commencing their spiralling descent. And mirrored in the dog-Lord Canker Canison's feral yellow, crimson-cored, night-sighted eyes as he looked down, the great weathered dome had appeared as the skull of a fallen colossus: the scant patches of gorse and bramble were all that remained of the ancient giant's hair. But apart from this coarse vegetation in the suturelike cracks and crevices, the flat pate had seemed as bald and as empty of life—and of death—as it was of thoughts; a safe high vantage point from which to observe the fighting.

That was how it had *looked*, certainly: all calm and serene on the plateau of the Rock, though there'd been no lack of war and death below. Except that had been minutes ago, while this was now.

And now . . . madness and mayhem!

Even if the dog-Lord had dreamed it in advance, if he'd forecast it through his oneiromancy—which this time he had not—still Canker would scarcely have credited its reality. But standing tall in his saddle, cajoling his stalled flyer as it formed air-traps of its manta wings and let down its coiled thrusters to reduce the shock of a forced landing, he had seen it with his own eyes and so must believe it.

A man, standing there in the night-dark gorse on the plateau of the Rock, with a long box- or tube-thing balanced on his shoulder, and wearing a bulge-eyed mask over his head and face . . . standing square in the path of

Wratha's man Goban, at that; and Goban all set to make a landing. Then ... Lord Nestor Lichloathe pointing and gesticulating, while the man in the gorse aimed his long box at Goban's mount.

It had been gloamy in the starlight on the dome of the Rock; it might even have been dark, if not for the intermittent flaring of Lidesci missiles skittering wild in the sky, and the glow of firelight reflected from a handful of clouds. But what is the night to Wamphyri eyes? Nothing, and the twilight even less. Canker had been able to see well enough.

Also, he had "heard" Nestor's warning, and Wratha's instructions to her man: that he should brush this fool from the rim of the rock. Goban had at once spurred his flyer forward in a swoop. But then:

A burst of light like a miniature sun, issuing from the box on the man's shoulder; a spear of light reaching out, but swift as a snake's kiss and tipped with bright metal. It left a vapour trail and hissed like a warrior, and its bite was yet more deadly! Goban's mount's pouch was open, to grasp this madman and sweep him before it over the rim. But flyer and rider, they never reached him.

The "spear" took the flyer in its pouch, situated where the long, tapering neck widened into the body, directly under the saddle. It sped deep into the cartilage-hooked, mouthlike pouch and was deflected upwards, penetrating the flesh of the flyer between pouch and saddle—where it detonated.

Armour-piercing and packed with ultrahigh explosive, the rocket would have stopped a half-track. By comparison, the alveolate bones and membranous flesh of the flyer were like tissue paper; they would absorb bullets easily enough, and a good many bullets at that, before enough liquid was let out that the creature was seriously hurt. But a 30mm rocket is something else. Nathan had seen the results of explosive crossbow bolts in the flesh of flyers, but he'd seen nothing like this.

The blast was star-shaped and struck out in all directions. Downwards, it unhinged the beast's pouch as easily as a man might pick off a small scab, and hurled it to earth. Sideways, it ripped through the base of the flyer's neck, shearing flesh and saddle trappings alike and stripping meat, membrane, and cartilage from the leading edges of the wings. Upwards, it sliced through the saddle like a knife . . . and sliced through Goban, too! Rider, saddle, and all were hurled upwards in two parts, literally torn asunder!

A two- to three-foot section had been chopped out of the flyer's spine. All control was gone and apart from the undead nature of its blood the thing was quite literally dead in the air. The eyes in the almost-human head at the end of its long, slowly slumping neck glazed over; its pink worm thrusters convulsed spastically, then coiled themselves up, back into their body cavities; it swerved this way and that as its wing arches began to collapse . . . but still it came gliding forward.

Nathan ducked down, scrambled to avoid a drenching rain of fluids as the flyer's rubbery bulk and nests of twitching thrusters scraped by barely overhead. And with its tapering tail vibrating like a crippled snake, tearing up the gorse as it went, the thing headed for the rim and the shattering fall beyond it.

But Nathan's headgear—the rocket-launcher's nite-site targetting set—had been knocked askew on his head. Down on his knees in the gorse, elated by his success, he worked frantically to get it realigned. Finally he was striking back . . . at the Wamphyri! There was another rocket waiting in its tube. All it required was his finger on the button.

However momentarily, the Lords and Lady were in disarray. Following on in line of descent behind Goban's mount, Wratha's creature had instinctively reared back from the flash of light and its concussion. Jolted, she clung to the twin pommels. On her left and drawing level with her, Canker's flyer was skittish, afraid. Its thrusters groped nervously for a hold on the Rock; an arched wingtip touched down, and Canker felt himself tilted in his saddle. Cursing, lashing out with a booted foot at his mount's flank, the dog-Lord leaped free, swung from the bony leading edge of a wing, let himself fall sprawling in the gorse. In another moment his flyer touched down and Canker was on his feet—

—And Nathan saw him!

They saw, and knew, each other!

The dog-Lord *knew* him, but not from where or when. Nathan, on the other hand, remembered only too well where and when. It was a nightmare he would never forget.

That night in Settlement ... the first time Wratha and her renegades raided there ... Nana Kiklu's house had been levelled by a warrior, and Nathan knocked out. Later, coming to his senses, he had found his girl, Misha Zanesti, lying unconscious in the rubble. Half-carrying Misha, staggering towards a break in the stockade fence, he'd heard a panting and a patter of padded feet from behind him. And looking back—

—It had been this one, Canker Canison!

Canker: only to look at him was to know that there'd been a dog, fox, or wolf in his ancestry. Or possibly a combination. He was loup-garou—a werewolf! And the first time Nathan had seen him, his error in this respect had been wholly understandable; for he had thought that this was one of Settlement's domesticated animals:

This great wolf-shape, coming out of the destruction of Settlement's main street and making straight for him ... seeking human company in order to escape the invasion of the Wamphyri. But then he'd noticed that this "wolf" seemed enveloped in a drifting cloud of mist, and that it was more biped than quadruped!

The thing loped towards him with an aggressive, forward-leaning eagerness ... it only paused to cock its head and turn its great ears this way and that, listening ... or when it went to all fours in order to sniff the earth. The cores of its eyes were scarlet and glowed like lamps in the dark. And then Nathan saw that the mist wasn't surrounding this creature but issuing from it!

The Wamphyri ... Nathan had heard campfire stories

about them ... their powers, hybridisms, animalisms. In that moment he knew what he was facing ... and that he was a dead man!

Canker came loping, reared up snarling, tall and taller than a man. Nathan tried to shake Misha awake ... no use. He tried to ward the dog-, fox-, wolf-thing off. Canker sniffed at him, cocked his head on one side, dripped saliva from his jaws and looked at the girl in Nathan's arms. And: "Yours?" he growled.

Nathan put Misha behind him, but the dog-Lord grabbed him and tossed him aside, as easily as that. And: "No, not yours—mine!" he said.

After that, Nathan had known no more—until he woke up to find Misha gone. And if Canker had her? It was a horror he nightmared still: the sight of Misha in this beast's arms, and Canker stripping her rags of clothing from her.

A nightmare he would never forget, flashing once again in a series of vivid, kaleidoscopic pictures across the screen of his mind. Neither would he forget the vow he'd made that night: that he wouldn't rest until the dog-Lord was nothing but a puff of black smoke and a foul stench drifting on the sullied air.

And now they were here—he and Canker were here— face to face in the gorse not fifteen paces apart ...

The telemetry was right; Nathan centered Canker's chest, his heart, in the luminous crosshairs of his nite-site lenses ... and squeezed the trigger.

Canker saw it coming. It was as if he dreamed while still awake! A flash of waking oneiromancy. A glimpse into his immediate future: *nothingness! An empty blackness. Death?*

Nestor Lichloathe witnessed the whole thing: he saw the burst of brilliant white light from the devastating boxlike weapon on his Great Enemy's (his brother's) shoulder, and the gleaming warhead extending itself at magical speed on a smoking stem of white-hot fire towards Canker. He saw the dog-Lord dive for cover as the missile *hissed* between him and his skittering mount to slam into his first lieutenant (one of Canker's "pups," as he called them, upon his flyer), still airborne but about to touch down behind him.

Well, and that one touched down, all right, but in several crimson pieces! Nestor didn't know exactly where the spear had driven home, but the lieutenant's lesser flyer was driven downwards like a swatted moth by the force of the blast, its back broken, and its rider . . . he literally rained to earth!

Then:

Fully in command again, and furious, Wratha sent her beast surging forward towards the man in the gorse. Its pouch clamped shut on his shoulder, weapon and all, and he was dragged kicking and fighting like the madman he must be towards the rim.

For a brief moment Nestor felt pride: this was his brother, Nathan, and he *was* the great and powerful enemy that Nestor had named him. No shame in being wary of this one! Nor any point in hating him now, for at last he was gone. How he'd come back . . . it no longer mattered. For he certainly wouldn't be coming back from this.

Gone, yes. Gone over the cliff as Wratha's creature opened its pouch and let him fall. For a moment he hung there, suspended against the far faint glimmer of the distant horizon, and then he was no more: a stone sent hurtling into the abyss.

But . . . Canker lay where he'd fallen in the gorse. The dog-Lord hadn't stirred! Nestor gentled his beast to earth; he dismounted, ran to his friend; there was blood on Canker's leather tunic, also in the coarse wolf's hair of his head. He'd cracked his skull hard against one of the dome's jagged suturelike fissures. Even a vampire's brain can be shaken insensible.

Nestor cradled Canker's head and looked into eyes even now glazing over, closing. Canker didn't see him; only a picture in the eye of his own mind, which Nestor clearly read there. And:

"Siggi!" Canker sighed, as he fell unconscious. "My silver . . . silver mistress out of the moon. Who will care . . . care for you now?"

After that:

Only the nothingness that Canker had forseen. The empty blackness. But it was not the emptiness or the blackness of the true death. Then, as Canker's leech commenced to work its metamorphism and heal his broken skull, so the darkness formed into a dream. And his dream was to remember how *She* had come to him, and the memory was of all that had occurred in the four months passed between . . .

It happened after Nestor was lost on Sunside, when he made his way back across the barrier mountains on foot, and called for his man Zahar to meet him in the peaks with a spare flyer. Canker, too, had been waiting for and received that call, and flew out with Zahar to greet the necromancer and congratulate him on his safe return.

But flying back to the last aerie, as they'd passed low over the Hell-lands Gate:

A diversion! A female figure had stepped down from the crater rim of the Gate, to go stumbling and fumbling out onto the boulder plain. But . . . an entirely human woman, here?

Landing, the three had approached her, Nestor and Zahar curiously, but Canker in total amazement, awe, wonder! Transfixed, the dog-Lord, as his eyes soaked up the beauty of this utterly astonishing creature. And she *was* beautiful, her colours alien, her clothes (if clothes they were and not a weave of mist and sheerest cobweb) light and lighter than moonbeams. At which Canker had known what she was, what she must be.

Szgany? No, never! Some freakish albino Traveller woman, whose colours had been absent from birth? Impossible; why, her eyes were bluer than the vault of the sky on a clear day! And as for her *design*, and the rest of her colours:

She was a statuesque, unheard-of silvery blonde, and her skin was pale, unblemished, perfect; likewise her features. Long-limbed, her flesh was firm beneath undergarments of sheer silk, which were clearly visible under the swirl and waft of a gown wispy as butterfly wings and far less than opaque. Those looks, colours, garments! Oh, yes, Canker had known what she was, all right.

Long and long now he had dreamed his oneiromantic dreams of her, his silver mistress in the moon! For the dog-Lord (no less than his grey wolf cousins running wild in the mountains) worshipped the moon on high and serenaded her in her tumbling orbit. And on a balcony in Mangemanse, in Wrathstack the last aerie, he had even constructed a mighty organ of hollow bones, whose music accompanied him when he sang to her. And all this because he had dreamed of her: that one day she would answer his call, and lured by his music step down from on high to be with him in Mangemanse—

—Which now she had!

There had been no question of arguing the point with him. Canker knew what he knew: that beyond any slightest shadow of a doubt, this *was* his silver mistress from the moon. And if Nestor or Zahar had disputed Canker's authority in this matter—especially if they had disputed his proprietary right—then there would have been trouble.

But no, they had recognized his right of ownership—or if not that, they'd been too astonished (perhaps fortunately) to deny him either his dreams or his rights—and Canker had carried her off to Mangemanse. Carried her off literally, for when he had first approached her near the Starside Gate, she had taken one look at him and fainted away in his arms. Obviously (he had thought), she was overwhelmed to have found him so soon, the one who'd lured her down from her temple on high . . . and him so handsome and all.

But in Mangemanse she had soon recovered from her swoon, and in a little while Canker had known that indeed he was not mistaken. For plainly she had no knowledge of things here in the world of men and the Wamphyri. What? But she'd seemed innocent of knowledge itself! Not ignorant, no—not with her astonishing grace and beauty; for a clod of earth is ignorant, while silver shining Luna has knowledge to light the world!—but innocent of the *ways* of the world! And yet, well, not *entirely* innocent.

Certainly she had known how to charm Canker ... but that had come later.

First he must instruct her in—oh, almost everything!

In the ways of the stack, the aerie as a whole; and then in the ways of Mangemanse, wherein she was now mistress, second only to Canker himself. Mistress, aye, and only a woman, not even Wamphyri!

Hah!—"only" a woman, indeed! But never before a woman such as this one.

And so he had set about to teach her. Except ... how to instruct someone he could not even speak to, who had no knowledge of the Szgany/Wamphyri tongue? Which had been something to give him pause. Until for knowledge Canker had substituted use. His moon mistress had no *use* of the tongue—yet understood every word!

A thought-thief, aye. A mentalist. The moon beings had no spoken language as such, because they conversed mind to mind—when they so desired. And when they did not, then they obscured their thoughts in impenetrable mental mists. It was so; Canker couldn't get into her mind for the great banks of fog that she conjured there! But only natural after all. No maiden of worth would let her beau see what was on her mind, surely? For women have their lustful thoughts just as surely as men. Canker knew *that* for a fact: his vampire women were whores from one set of lips to the other, and kissed and sucked with both!

But sex? With such as Canker's moon mistress? Unthinkable ... at first. What? But she was untouchable, a goddess! He had made her so. And she sat upon her throne of fine carved cartilage in the dog-Lord's most private of private chambers, and of all the men and monsters in Mangemanse, his was the only form she ever saw and she was for his eyes only—at first.

Except, what good is a goddess without her worshippers? And if she were a goddess, then surely Canker was a god—or would be, if he was not found wanting. And so he must woo her, win her over, convince her of his godhead; he must *become* godlike in her eyes! And not only in the eyes of his silver moon mistress, but in the eyes of the manse entire.

Well, he was that already. Or if not a god, a Lord certainly. But to own a goddess for his mate! Ah, his most improbable dream come true!

Her name was Siggi. Leaning over her as she slept her fitful sleeps, and slipping into her mind during those few, brief moments when her guard was down and the mindmist rolled back a little, Canker had learned that much at least. And in another world (the moon, it could only be) she had known an enemy whose name and face formed the core of all her nightmares. Even now, in Canker's care, she feared him, and moaned his name when silver pearls of perspiration formed gleaming on her brow.

Turkur!

Turkur Tzonov!

A strange and alien name, unheard of among Szgany and Wamphyri alike. But one that Canker's silver moon mistress would never forget; nor Canker, now that he knew it. And growling low in his throat, peering into her cringing, shuddering mind, he'd even seen the face of this moon monster as Siggi remembered it:

The broad bronze dome of his head, smooth and hairless, yet glowing with vitality to match the flesh of his face. And in stark contrast the purple, deep-sunken orbits of grey, penetrating eyes which, for all that they were human, nevertheless contained an inhuman Power. Eyes that could look into, or even through a man, which would make this one a great leader among men. Impressive . . . among men. But Canker was Wamphyri! Still, he sensed the moon-man's extraordinary fascination, his weird allure.

And quite definitely he was of the moon; where else would Siggi have known and feared him, if not in that hurtling world on high? But quite apart from Canker's "logic" in this respect, there were also the looks of the man, his colours and demeanour. He glowed no less than Siggi herself, and what little hair he displayed was silverblond as Siggi's own: his slender eyebrows, haughtily tilted, highlighting the tanned, sharp-etched ridges of his brows.

Then there was his nose, sharp-hooked (broken, the dog-Lord suspected, perhaps in a fight; it had mended that way and Turkur had kept it so, possibly as a trophy; except he was not Wamphyri and so should have no say in the matter; yet there was this Power in him that caused Canker to think of him as such, a Lord in his own right), which for all its lack of convolutions gave him the look of a war-lord.

Aye, and with his well-fleshed mouth above a strong square chin, and cheeks so very slightly hollowed, he was not entirely unhandsome, this proud and haughty warrior-priest of the moon.

A warrior-priest, proud and haughty . . .

Haughty.

Twice now that word had commended itself to the Lord of Mangemanse as descriptive of this Turkur Tzonov, and twice too often. Siggi feared his memory; or was it his reality that she feared? She had come down to Starside from the moon. And might not this Turkur follow her? What magic did he have, this moon-priest? And if he should come to claim Siggi back, how might Canker answer the challenge?

"With all my heart . . . with all my blood . . . with all my sinew. With all my Wamphyri strength . . . with my oneiromancy . . . with my lycanthropy. With everything I own, and all that I am! Neither man, monster, nor moon-thing—no child of Nature, or of the vats, or any alien world—shall ever part us. I Canker Canison swear it by my teeth, my balls, by the very blood that thunders in my veins!"

And rushing to a north-facing window, and glaring at the hurtling moon: "Let him come, this Turkur. Proud and haughty? Canker will show him proud and haughty. *I'll eat his eyes and face, and send him home on a great black flyer, blind and red and smoking from his wounds, and screaming in the night!*"

It was his Wamphyri vow . . .

* * *

Siggi got used to him. She even got used to his guardian creatures, which prowled the mazy corridors of his manse when their master was abed or hunting in Sunside. She very soon "acclimatized"; which is to say she accepted her lot, for to a mind vacant as hers, this was all she had ever known. The manse and all its monsters were home, and Canker her protector. Moreover, he adored her. And for all the knowledge that she had lost, stolen from her mind in the magmass bowels of Perchorsk by the madman Turkur Tzonov, still Siggi retained her sensuality, her overpowering animal magnetism, that essence of womanhood which was hers in abundance.

And she needed. In all her life since she was fourteen, Siggi had not gone without a man. She could not remember them now, but she remembered how; she *knew* how. And as always, and as is the case with most sensual women, she felt the attraction of power. In Mangemanse there was only one Power, one raw source of furious energy, and its name was Canker Canison. As for his "pups," his bloodsons, lieutenants, thralls: oh, they were men—despite the taint of their master's animalism—but Canker himself was magnificent! And to a mind wiped clean of ideals—of the idea of Man the beatific, the noble, the honourable—Canker *was* the ideal!

Romantic? The dog-Lord was that. He would take her to the north-facing gallery which housed his incredible instrument of hollow bones, adjust the baffles to let in the winds that blew off the Icelands, and play his mighty organ with all the verve if not the skill of a veritable maestro. And while the rest of Wrathstack groaned at the resulting cacophony, Siggi the moon mistress would laugh and applaud, and even be brought to tears by the joy of Canker's music—or perhaps by its pain. But he would never suspect it, for she knew he played for her.

And all the time he kept her upon a pedestal, far above all earthly desires, and never a single carnal thought in the dog-Lord's cesspit vampire mind, not about Siggi; for she was his silver moon mistress, whose flesh was holy of holies, and he was only a great dog. He would not corrupt her, nor change her in any way. And when she went to her bed, Canker would be there, asleep upon a pallet outside her door. For instead of a dog-*Lord*, he'd become like unto a *watch*dog. And a faithful dog at that.

But with or without her memories, Siggi was still Siggi and a lustful woman. Because Canker was all she knew (because she had nothing for comparison) she wanted him; and anyway, he was almost as much man as dog. In the end she seduced him, and even suspecting it might destroy her led him to her bed. Astonished, believing he dreamed a most marvellous albeit forbidden dream, he went to her.

Then, knowing her flesh was frail, Canker was gentle with her; perhaps too gentle, so that she must become the aggressor. At which the great and terrible beast was conquered; not alone by beauty, but also by urges as alien and powerful as his own, until he became a toy for a woman out of another world.

Innocent in her way, Siggi couldn't know it, but in toying with Canker Canison she toyed with her very soul.

Canker must show his moon mistress to the stack, to the aerie as a whole, to all the Lords and chiefest of the lieutenants, and even to the Lady Wratha . . . most *certainly* to her.

Hah! Let that one see a *real* lady!

Except it was not the dog-Lord's way to welcome visitors into his manse. Mangemanse was a secret place, and its wolfish master kennel-proud. So he spoke to the necromancer Lord Nestor Lichloathe in neighbouring Suckscar, his one true friend in all Wrathstack, and with some few small misgivings Nestor made the arrangements. The Lords and Lady were invited up—or down in Wratha's case—into Suckscar, to a grand reception in honour of Siggi, Canker's silver moon mistress.

But a reception for a commoner, a thrall, a "mere woman"? Even a woman from another world? It was unheard of! And yet the Lords were curious, each and every one of them. And Wratha the Risen even more so.

So it was that in the eleventh sundown following Siggi's arrival in Starside, her reception took place in Suckscar and the vampire Lords and Lady came to discover the nature of this remarkable creature who had so captured the dog-lord's previously rabid heart and monumental imagination. Nor would their curiosity be disappointed.

Siggi had not been seen when Canker first brought her to the last aerie. And even if she had been, then slumped across his saddle in a swoon she would have been thought just another captive taken by force out of Sunside. No one but Nestor Lichloathe knew how Canker's silver mistress looked, her stunning colours, shape, or fabulous design in general. Nor would they, until the last possible moment.

Canker was a sly showman, even as sly as the fox in his mixed ancestry; he had a sense of the dramatic and appreciated the delicious tingle of anticipation, the sudden shock of revelation, the stunned astonishment of denouement. He revelled in upstaging all other actors at every given opportunity: in this instance, Siggi's reception. And since posturing was integral to his character, Canker was never on time. He preferred the grand entrance.

Nestor Lichloathe had announced the reception (or more properly a gathering, in celebration of the success of a recent alliance of the Lords in their efforts to turn Wrathstack into a fortress proper, and their thralls and creatures into an army) following a raid on the Szgany of Tireni Scarp some eighty miles west of Settlement. Under Yanni Tireni, their leader, the folk of Tireni Scarp were ferocious as the Szgany Lidesci; they didn't have Lardis Lidesci's weird weapons, but their skill with lures and pitfall traps, and their accuracy with silver-tipped, kneblasch-soaked crossbow bolts, and ballistae-hurled fireballs was phenomenal. So that just like Lardis's people, the Szgany Tireni had survived without returning to the wild and becoming Travellers.

But on this occasion the raid had been successful, and a number of thralls had been taken alive without cost to the Wamphyri; yet another reason to celebrate. And in accordance with Canker's instructions, Nestor had mentioned in passing the fact that the dog-Lord would present the new Mistress of Mangemanse at that same affair, a reception of sorts in Suckscar, which Nestor would host. Canker had of course made himself scarce at the time, so avoiding any banter or questions in this respect. With his sense of the dramatic, he'd wanted Siggi to come as a complete surprise. Which she would . . .

The time had been set: four hours before sunup, allowing plenty of time for strutting, wagering, eating, and drinking before all must depart in the early dawn, back to their various manses and the security of their dark places. Nestor had retired to Suckscar to make the necessary arrangements. Wratha and her chiefest lieutenants would come down on foot out of Wrathspire, and the dog-Lord and his whelps were well acquainted with the way up from Mangemanse (though in fact Nestor knew they would come by flyer, and late of course, in order that Canker could make his entry in accustomed style). As for the rest:

Wran and Spiro Killglance and their men could not come through Mangemanse (Canker would never allow it) and so must fly; and Gorvi and Guile could scarcely be expected to climb almost half a mile vertical out of Guilesump, which meant he too would use a flyer. A landing bay must be made ready, with lieutenants and thralls in attendance to handle the flyers.

Nestor had seen to everything; it was no great effort; he owed the dog-Lord this much, at least.

Came the time appointed.

Deceptively dandyish, Wran the Rage was first up. Accompanied by his first and second lieutenants, Wran was magnificent in a wolf-grey cloak, crimson cummerbund, black bat-fur trousers and leather boots; he sniffed the air superciliously and tweaked the small black wen on his chin. His brother, the ever-scowling Spiro Killglance, followed close behind. As was his wont, he dressed in rags; likewise his men. Nestor greeted them in the landing bay, instructed his thralls in the temporary stabling of their beasts, and had a lieutenant escort them down into the great hall beneath his private quarters.

Minutes later as the gauntly sinister Gorvi the Guile and his lieutenants made their approach, Nestor's man Grig reported Wratha's arrival by internal stairwell. The Lady was acquainted with this route into Suckscar; Nestor's guardian creatures were accustomed to her; in any case he had ordered that there be no let or hindrance, and so she had passed in safety with two of her men.

Which left only Canker and his pups, and his silver moon mistress, of course. But all of the others were in Suckscar a good half-hour before Canker put in his appearance, and during that time Nestor had done his best to entertain them, despite that in the main he despised them.

Well, he scarcely despised Wratha the Risen but appeared more than a little wary of her, and kept his mind shielded from her probes at all times. Being female she was curious, and more than mildly peeved; in the last few weeks their *affaire* had all but fizzled out; she was unable to explain the change come over her former lover. Not only was Nestor's attitude radically different but also his character, even his mien. He seemed to have assumed the guise of a mystic, a recluse, like one of the gaunt old men of Turgosheim; or rather, like a young Vormulac Unsleep or a Zolteist ascetic like the Seer-Lord Maglore. Indeed, Nestor's change was startling, especially to one who had known him as Wratha had known him. Nothing remotely ascetic about *that* Nestor, not as Wratha had known him. But:

This sudden *fad* of his for wrapping up, keeping himself covered, like a child in swaddling clothes—almost as if he were ashamed of his flesh—

—Or as if he were shy of some blemish or other . . .

But on the other hand, well . . . Nestor's ascension to a Lord of the Wamphyri *had* been lightning fast, when the Change That Shapes had moulded him like a soft candle in a flame. It had seemed that he was a natural, a vampire born, but perhaps it had been too fast and something had been burned out of him other than his humanity. Or there again, it could be that recognition, *awareness* of his vampire condition had changed him, the fact that his universe had now expanded beyond all previous boundaries. It was ever traumantic, the Change That Shapes, but sometimes more so. In which case he might yet change back again and be what he had been (not human, no, for that was gone forever, but vigorous and . . . what, alive again? Well, undead, at least), when finally his blood had settled down and his vampire leech had determined his destiny.

Or was it something else entirely? Where now was the zest and the lust and the dark thrill of being: the thrill of being Wamphyri!? It had been vibrant in him; he had revelled in it; even without his parasite's drive, his own had been as a roaring fire in him, so that he'd blazed with its heat and glowed red in his dark heart. Wratha knew, for she had felt it there. And she had loved him, in and out of her bed. Loved the touch and the smell and the very thought of him. But all gone now. And ah! . . . She missed it.

She missed it but . . . not that much. For one erection is much like another, and a man is only a man after all. The fire had burned too brightly, that must be it. Which was a concept that Wratha could accept: the idea that perhaps *she*, the Lady herself, had sucked it out of him; that *she*, Wratha the Risen, had reduced him to less than her needs, until she no longer had need of him at all.

She could accept that, yes.

And yet—

—What if she was wrong?

What if Nestor shielded his mind not to hide his weakness but to protect a strength, a passion beyond her comprehension? Beyond her *Wamphyri* comprehension, because everything that was human in her had long since fled the seething, searing corruption of her leech? Was that it? Did he yet retain a capacity—an entirely human capacity—for love? For the true, living love? For love inadmissible by virtue of his nature? For love unrequited?

For a love out of his mainly unremembered past . . . ?

Which was a concept Wratha could *not* accept, never!

That she had exhausted him—fine. But that some other had distracted or abstracted him—never!

There had been this Szgany wench, Misha, a Lidesci bitch out of his vague and shadowy past. When Nestor's mind had been more accessible, Wratha had discovered her there, still in his thoughts despite that he was Wamphyri. And for all of the past that his damaged mind had forgotten, he'd remembered her well enow, *and* his hatred for the one who had stolen her from him.

That was why he'd gone with Zahar that time into Sunside, to settle an old score. Almost three months ago, aye, and he'd never been the same since. For all her much-vaunted mentalism, Wratha never had discovered what happened that time. But now that she remembered it, she could clearly see how it coincided with his change. All of which had gone unnoticed at the time, for events of moment had been crowding thick and fast—

... Such as the reunification of the aerie under Wratha, the foundation of supplicant Szgany tribes east of the great pass, the creation of a tithe system similar to the one they'd known in old Turgosheim, from the proceeds of which to build their armies against the chance of some future invasion.

Events of moment, aye, and all coming at more or less the same time. Not to mention a few of lesser importance; such as the dog-Lord finding his so-called silver moon mistress all lost and alone, wandering on the boulder plains in the vicinity of the Starside Gate ...

... Which was a timely recollection, for surely that was Canker's great bark of a laugh even now?

As the echoes of that uproarious laughter came drifting down into the banquet hall, the Lady Wratha gave a mental nod of recognition and exasperation. For aye, indeed it was Canker's laugh, preceding the dog-Lord as lightning precedes the thunder ...

II

Wratha, Wran, Spiro

As the echoes of Canker Canison's laughter died away, Wratha returned from her mental meanderings, glanced all about Nestor's banquet table, and contained herself as best she could. The heat of her inward conjecturing, specifically with regard to Lord Lichloathe (the resurgent possibility of a rival lover in Sunside), had not been so great that it had wrought any noticeable physical change in her. To all intents and purposes—and with the acceptable exceptions of her conchlike ears, convolute snout, scarlet eyes, and divided tongue—she was just like a young and beautiful girl; the practiced and effortless metamorphism of her leech hid the monster under the skin.

Indeed it hid it well, so that no one—not even a Lord of the Wamphyri—would suspect the century of time that she had lived, not until she was angered sufficiently that the monster became ascendant and the facade of her skill was stripped away. Then . . .

. . . The Lady's change at such times was legendary, a veritable transformation, an incredible catabolism: like watching the ten-day decay of a ripe apple to a spotted mouldering fungus lump, but all accelerated or compressed to a period of ten nightmarish seconds. And then it would be seen that indeed the female of the species is the most dangerous, and the most venomous! But for now:

The monster was hidden, and Wratha *was* beautiful. Nothing of the leadenness of the Lords about her! Her skin was pale as milk, unblemished. Her jet-black shining hair fell in plaits to her shoulders, which were fitted with a torque of finely worked gold. Depending from this golden harness, ropes of plaited bat fur formed a smoky curtain to her knees, but by no means opaque. For as she moved, so the ropes would sway, revealing a soft curved breast or brown nipple, rounded hip and smooth thigh, delicate arms and hands where they broke through. And so (and quite deliberately, for Wratha was proud of her skill), she scarcely kept herself secure from viewing. It was a distraction, which kept the Lords from scanning her mind by occupying theirs.

Paradoxically but not unusually, Wratha's eyes were least in evidence. Protected by a scarp of carved bone upon her brow, their fire was subdued by the ornamentation of blue glass ovals at her temples and matching earrings in the fine-furred lobes of her ears. This, too, was deliberate; for if Wratha's deceit were at all visible, then surely it was in her eyes. Which is to say that however inarticulately, nevertheless the Truth of her being was shouted from them, so that she must make every effort to deaden their unquiet voice and disguise their undead evil. Slightly protuberant—until she was enraged, when they bulged—they gave away that which the lady would keep secret or at least hidden, and so formed her most vulnerable feature. But in any case, hers was a grotesque deceit.

Apart from which, and the usual anomalies of vampirism, Wratha might well be Szgany (which indeed she had been, upon a time): a clean-limbed Gypsy girl from Sunside, whose flesh was still untried. But beauty is only skin deep, and so much for looks . . .

The Lady sat at one end of the long table with her chief lieutenants flanking her. Gorvi and his two sat along one side, which they shared with Spiro and his ruffians. Nestor, Grig, and Zahar occupied the other side, along with Wran the Rage and his pair. But at the dog-Lord's request, the head of the table had been left free for him. Spread before them were various appetizers: halved wolf and bear hearts floating in blood; suckling shad basted in its mother's milk; various joints, rare-roasted and thick-sliced, from the same mature beast; bowls of fruit and pitchers of weak ale. Spoils of the tithe, naturally, but nothing ostentatious; not so much a banquet as a buffet.

Nestor Lichloathe was on his feet; he too had heard Canker's laughter from on high, and his gaze rested upon a balcony overlooking his great hall, with a corridor behind that led to the landing bay. Sure enough the dog-Lord was there, and with him his silver moon mistress . . . what little was to be seen of her, as yet. Why (Wratha thought), she was as much covered—all swathed and shielded from the sight of men, and of Wratha—as Nestor himself!

The Lady stared, as did the others, but Nestor paced to the sweep of his great stone staircase and called up to Canker: "Come down, my friend. Alas, but you're late and the food is cold."

"I had a little trouble," Canker barked, lying with great proficiency. "A creature of mine went mad, and I saw it as my personal duty to slaughter him for the provisioning. But—" he shrugged, "—it was bloody work, and afterwards . . . all to be made tidy. And so you must excuse us that we're late."

He led his mystery woman down the stairwell, with two great shaggy lieutenants—a pair of his "pups"—following close behind. These were not the dog-Lord's bloodsons as such (his children born in Mangemanse were all infants as yet), but when Canker took thralls out of Sunside, he usually picked wolfish-looking ones, so that in other circumstances these two might easily have been his bloodsons. As leader of the pack—patriarchal, as it were—all of the dog-Lord's thralls and lieutenants were his "pups," of course.

At the bottom of the sweeping staircase Canker paused for effect, turned to Nestor and bowed stiffly. He was dressed all in red: red vest and cloak, and baggy red breeks. The hair on his head shone red to match the cores of his eyes; it was the fox in him, of course, but startling nevertheless. Nestor had never seen him so well groomed. But in another moment the dog-Lord's wild wolf laughter rang out again, then turned to howling as he threw back his head, went to all fours and, in order to give full vent, shook from head to toe. Finally the ringing echoes died away; Canker fell silent and flowed upright, shook himself again—an entirely voluntary action this time, as if to shake off a mood—and glanced all about his host's great hall. Then:

"My Lord Nestor," he panted. And to the rest: "My Lords, and Lady. I am genuinely sorry I'm late, but as you know I've no sense of timing. Why, I was probably late at my own whelping! And if I'm lucky I may even be late to my grave. As for these little gatherings of ours, too infrequent by far, it must seem that I'm *always* late! Wasn't it so at Wran's reception in Wrathspire that time, when he'd rid us all of Vasagi the Suck? Two and a half years ago as I recall, but I remember it well!

"That was when the young Lord Lichloathe first came among us out of Sunside, and fell heir to Suckscar. Aye, and fortunate for Canker that he did. For it was Nestor who taught me the moon music, with which to lure my silver mistress down from the moon. And I learned his tune and perfected my art, and likewise perfected my organ of warrior bones hoisted up from olden battlefields. But it was at Wran's reception that I first broached the idea, tootling a small Szgany flute for your amusement. And you *were* amused, of course, for you thought me mad . . ." His lips curled back from great wolf jaws and he grinned a toothy grin, then held up a massive paw.

"Now don't deny it—" (though no one had) "—you thought me crazed, a victim of the moon as my father before me. But no, the moon is not my tormentor but my friend and *mentor*, who sent me dreams of a silver mistress: a message from the moon! For I have a talent— oneiromancy, with which I read the future and the truth in dreams—and knew that she was real. And hour on hour, night after night, I played my moon music and sang to her on high, knowing she would heed me and come down to be mine in Mangemanse . . .

". . . Which she did!

"But here I have been remiss, for I've kept her to myself. Indeed, I shall continue to do so—and let him *die* most agonizingly who dares so much as lay a hand, or even considers such an act!" The soft black leather of his lips again drew back, to display the gleam of elongated canines, and a low, threatening growl escaped his throat. But a moment later: "As for the *fact* of her being," he continued, "it's high time you all knew what I've done, what Canker has achieved with his moon music and in his 'madness.' Wherefore, lo and behold, I give you Siggi!"

Until now she had been wrapped in a robe of purest white albino bat fur, her face hidden behind a shimmering veil hanging from a crown of figured cartilage. As the dog-Lord finished speaking, however, he took the crown from her head and gave it to one of his whelps, then carefully unfastened the robe and lifted it from Siggi's marble shoulders; until she stood there almost exactly as first seen in the dim false dawn of Starside and the preternatural glow of the Hell-lands Gate.

Almost exactly as first seen. But of course that had been some three months ago ...

And: "Behold!" Canker said again. *"She is awake!"* And to a man, and a woman, they knew what he meant. For despite the fact that as yet she was still his silver moon mistress, and her colours alien and beautiful beyond reason, they could each of them see that this would not, could not last.

Silver-blonde her hair, and skin a fading gold ... aye, for now. And desirable in her various parts to drive men wild, true. But rumour had had it that her eyes were blue as the sky under the northern auroras, and plainly they were not. So that Wratha knew she was no longer the only Lady in Wrathstack.

"Awake!" Canker barked again, a single word—but all of them knew what it meant:

That Siggi had been asleep. And a long, cold, breathless sleep at that: the sleep that changes life to undeath. Moreover, he'd drained her to the dregs, or if not that, then his passion had been such that ...

"... Indeed!" he snarled, cutting all such inference

short. "For just as I lured her down from the moon, so she has lured my egg out of me. Accept her, for she has ascended, this Lady, and *is* Wamphyri!"

Crimson-eyed she clung to the dog-Lord's arm, smiled however vacantly yet in no way naively, and showed them her pure white teeth. And they saw in the ribbed deeps of her scarlet, yawning mouth, how already the dark cleft of Siggi's pointed tongue was deepening for division . . .

The dream had been Canker Canison's and yet it had involved others—especially the Lady Wratha—and had been dreamed as from their point of view, as if seen through their eyes as well as Canker's own. Though rare, this was hardly strange to him; it had happened before and was phenomenal of his oneiromancy, which allowed him to see the truth of his dreams. This time he'd seen how Wratha's concern for Nestor Lichloathe was much like his own, despite the fact that their motives were different. For while his was born out of love for the man (so far as the Wamphyri are capable of brotherly love), hers was based mainly in love of self, which nevertheless requires the confirmation or consummation of another. That was why she could be dispassionate about Nestor one moment and furious the next, when she wondered if there was some other and remembered this "Lidesci bitch" in Sunside.

As for Canker: he *knew* there was another, also that Nestor's old scars were itching again, those mental scars out of his mainly forgotten youth. However obliquely, Canker and Lord Lichloathe had even talked about it on occasion: about Nestor's Great Enemy among the Szgany Lidesci. What's more, the dog-Lord knew that Nestor had tried to put this unknown rival down, with near-disastrous results! So that Wratha the Risen's suspicions had only confirmed what Canker already knew: that indeed there was an unknown woman in Nestor's past.

But . . . it was all a very tangled skein, and anyway Canker's head hurt . . . and the night wind was cold where it whipped back his hair, driving a thin trickle of blood into his eye . . . and—

—What?

He tried to sit up and couldn't budge but an arm. Loosely lashed to his saddle, he was facedown on the one side, bent in the middle, and legs all a-dangle on the other. And viewed down below before it faded into mist and smoke and distance, a scene straight out of hell!

Explosions—bright, glaring, blasting; but louder and deadlier far than anything the Szgany Lidesci had used before—their smoke and roaring voices drifting up on the night air, along with the howl of maimed warriors and the dying sputter of failed propulsors. And mewling flyers limping aloft on blazing wings, only to go tumbling back into fire and smoke. A warrior airborne, its bladders exploding as a shrilling rocket scored a direct hit; the crippled beast floundering to earth, where antlike figures fell upon it with oil and torches, and turned it to a living bonfire. A frenzied, metallic cachinnation as of giant cicadas, accompanied by stuttering flashes of bright white light and the death screams of men and monsters . . . but mainly of thralls, lieutenants, flyers, warriors.

In short, a rout!

And: "What . . . ?" Canker wondered again, this time out loud.

Flying alongside, Nestor Lichloathe knew that he was conscious and called out, "Canker, your left hand and arm are free. I tied your left foot with a slipknot. Only reach down and tug on the rope, your leg will come free. Meanwhile, and as you've no doubt gathered, we're on our way home . . ." And then more viciously, through grinding teeth, ". . . where I suppose we'll look at each other stupidly, lick our wounds, and count our *fucking* losses!"

The necromancer was more animated, certainly in his emotions, than Canker had seen him in a threemonth. But the dog-Lord had a headache, and problems enough of his own . . .

On the left flank and a short distance to the rear, Spiro and Wran Killglance watched Canker free himself, straighten up in the saddle and loll there like a drunkard, and thought as one man: *Damn it to hell!*

Twins, it was no great feat to share their thoughts while keeping them guarded from the others. And:

The man-hound lives! Wran the Rage grunted.

What did you expect? Spiro scowled across at his brother. *That a knock on that great thick wolf head would kill him?*

Would that it had! That way, at least something would be salvaged from this night.

Aye, you're right. Spiro's mental nod of agreement. *Quite a lot salvaged, come to think of it. For I'd have been up into Mangemanse in a trice, and all that's his would be mine!*

Wran's lewd grin. *What, all of it?* He licked his lips and flashed a picture of Siggi at his brother. *Including this?*

All of it! answered the other.

Wran's grin slid away as if wiped clean off his face in the slipstream of air. Spiro's attitude irritated him greatly these days, had done so ever since he made his first kill with his evil eye. But it hadn't always been so; back in Turgosheim those many years ago, the twins had been united in mutual fear and hatred of their father and *his* killing eye, until at last they'd murdered him. But now . . .

. . . The longer Wran lived in close proximity to his brother in Madmanse, and the more he looked at him, the more he thought to see the spitting image of their father, old Eygor Killglance himself, looking back at him out of Spiro's killing eyes. Which was a thought he kept not only from the rest of the Wamphyri but also (or especially?) from his twin.

Well? said Spiro abruptly, as if ready for an argument.

And caught off-guard for a moment, Wran finally repeated him? *Well? Was there a question?*

You know there was. I said that in the event Canker had been seriously incapacitated, then I'd take Mangemanse and all that went with it. And you . . . said nothing, which seems to me to pose a question in itself. Do you disapprove?

Wran's mental shrug. *Not really. For who knows, maybe we have been cooped up together too long, both in Turgosheim and in Wrathstack. And it was always the plan that you would have a manse of your own some day. But this Siggi . . . is a lot of woman. Would you keep her all to yourself, too? A bit greedy, isn't it?*

Oh? And do you fancy her? Spiro was scowling even harder now. *But I thought Wratha was your meat?*

Again Wran's shrug. *Wratha will suit me fine, if she can be tamed. But you saw her when all went crazy back there? Oh, she can fool men looking the way she does, like a young wanton out of Sunside. But when she's wrathful . . .*

. . . And his mind flew back some ten to fifteen minutes in time, to picture Wratha as they had seen her atop the dome of the great rock in those moments before and after she forced their attacker over the rim to his death:

Her cry of rage—turning to a cackle even as *she* turned to a hag—as she urged her mount forward and issued her mental command: *Grasp him, lift him, dump him from the edge!* And Wratha's monstrous metamorphosis; not only in the tone of her voice but also in her face and figure.

Wran had witnessed it before, as had Spiro and Canker—aye, and Gorvi, too, wherever he was now— some three and a half years earlier at an extraordinary meeting of the Wamphyri in Vormulac Taintspore's melancholy Vormspire in Turgosheim, at which Lord Vormulac (called Unsleep) had presided. And Wran knew that it was Wratha's vampire leech reacting to her emotions, her shock and anger, by pumping its essence into her veins in the same way that lesser mortals pump adrenaline. It was her parasite's response: to gird the Lady for whatever trial was in the offing. But the change it wrought in her was seen as terrible even by the *utterly* terrible Wamphyri, even by Wran the Rage himself:

For the girl was gone from her saddle in a matter of moments, and in her place . . . a witch!

Wratha had gained spindly, craggy inches in height, seeming to elongate vertically, as beneath her leather armour the healthy bloom of her flesh turned leaden as a Lord's and her cheeks shrank inwards to age her to gauntness. The convolutions of her nose had taken on much clearer definition; its flat flange turning darkly moist, with nostrils that flared and gaped. The overlapping leaves of her leather breastplate collapsed like a last sigh as beneath it her breasts flopped to flaccid dugs.

But her eyes were the worst. For while Spiro had the killing eye, the Lady Wratha's were pure poison. And beneath the visor upon her brow, they had become as blobs of hellfire, as if they'd been peeled to bleeding and drawn half out of their sockets!

Even among the Wamphyri—whose mutations were many and whose metamorphism allowed *trans*mutation into endless varieties of form—few manifestations were as ghastly as Wratha the Risen's change when she was threatened and her leech took the upper hand. And:

Aye, when she's wrathful, Wran said again, musingly. *As for me, I merely rage. But Wratha*—(he could only shrug helplessly)—*is monstrous!*

Spiro agreed. *That says it all—especially coming from such as us, her peers, as it were.*

But on the other hand this Siggi, Wran returned from his reflections, *whether she hails from the moon or not, is mainly woman—albeit a* lot *of woman! Oh, she'll be Wamphyri eventually, aye, but a ways to go yet before she has the measure of such as Wratha. Then ... she'll be some Lady, Spiro. And will you be able to handle her, d'you think?*

Spiro had never been quick on the uptake, but now he was. *Bastard! You don't fool me! I don't have her yet, and already you're drooling over her!* His thoughts were vehement, almost "shouted."

And: *Be careful!* Wran's mental voice was a hiss of warning. *Guard your thoughts!*

They are guarded, damn you! Best guard your own—from 'me!

Calm down, calm down. Wran chuckled darkly (though in all truth he felt a good deal less than merry, even darkly merry). *Don't you know when your own brother is having a joke with you? As for Mangemanse and Siggi: they are yours if the opportunity should dawn. But until then . . .*

And suddenly Wran's mood as he fell silent seemed far more ominous, so that Spiro felt obliged to prompt him: *Well?*

. . . Brother, the more I consider it, Wran continued after a while, *The more certain I am we've made a big mistake: joining up with Wratha and the others again, I mean. With the Guile . . . well, that's different. We know where we stand with him: we don't give him an inch, ever! But these others . . .* He pulled a wry face.

How d'you mean?

Well, just look at the mess they've dropped us in to-night! Frankly, the reason I was having a joke with you was to take my mind off our losses. Why, there's almost half as much dead meat back there about the foot of that rock as there is undead stuff in Wrathstack!

Huh! Spiro grunted. *D'you think I don't know it? What use to build armies, just to send them into that sort of hell? The Lidescis won't break, we should have learned that by now. They won't break for Wratha or for anyone else. We should leave Lardis and his lot till last, convert the rest, then bury the Lidescis under such a mass of vampire flesh that even they can't resist!*

Wran had to agree, and admitted: *We lost some good lieutenants, some good meat, down there in the smoke and the stink. And damn it, I still haven't worked out what happened!*

Aye, it was quick. Spiro gave a mental nod. *That mayhem atop the rock, before Wratha pushed that lunatic off the edge of the cliff—him and his lightning-box! And then all hell breaking loose below. Until then it seemed our forces on the ground were doing well.*

But their weapons! Wran shook his head. *I saw warriors destroyed like clumps of rag! I mean, we know they can work metals, these people . . . but miracles?*

Spiro was silent for a moment, then said: *The necromancer knew he was there.*

Eh?

The madman on the dome of the rock. Lichloathe cried out to Wratha in the moment before she would have landed, warning her off. He knew that this—what? A "Great Enemy," he called him—was there.

Perhaps he saw him.

But no one else saw him. How so? Huh! If I had seen him first, and if I'd been quicker thinking, I might have used my killing eye on him. But things were happening so fast . . .

Wran thought about it a moment, then said, *There's more to the young Lord Lichloathe than meets the eye. Another mistake: that I ever introduced him into Wrathstack in the first place. What? In the last threemonth he's gone as weird, reclusive, and silent as Vasagi the Suck in his time! Well, we all know what happened to Vasagi. He should take care, this necromancer, lest he go the same way.*

But not yet?

Wran's shrug. *You can find fault with him, challenge him if you want. After all, it's you who needs a manse of his own, not I. Also, we're supposed to be allies, remember? And what if Wratha's and the dog-Lord's premonitions about Vormulac Unsleep are correct? It might be as well to remain unified under Wratha . . . for the time being, at least. But when things are resolved, however they're resolved—*

—That will be time enough, Spiro finished it for him.

None of which was overheard by the rest, for like Canker Canison they were all concentrating on their own problems.

It had been Nathan's plan to get off a shot at Canker, conjure a Möbius door and get out of there on the instant. But several things had conspired to stop him. His consuming hatred of the dog-Lord had demanded that he at least make an attempt on his life, but the knowledge that his brother was among these Wamphyri Lords had probably served to distract him and deflect his aim. Also, he found it difficult as yet to concentrate on physical action while exercising mental control over the metaphysical Möbius Continuum. It would come with time, but he wasn't yet the master his father had been.

And with both rockets fired, the Necroscope had been in trouble. There were grenades in his pockets, but the launcher's shoulder clasp had caught on his jacket and he was unable to rid himself of the thing. And then that monstrous woman had been there (a "Lady," he supposed, and therefore the Lady Wratha), and there had been no time left to do anything. A moment more and he'd felt himself gripped by the shoulder, driven forward, released into free fall, and then into full fall!

In one respect, however, Nathan was like his father, and *exactly* like him: when his life was threatened, then he was at his best. Knowing about death—what it was, and what it was not—Nathan had the utmost regard for life, especially his own. So that he'd found it less than astonishing how the proximity of death mobilized him for life.

Freeing himself at last of the rocket launcher's tube, kicking it away from him, Nathan had tumbled head over heels in midair while plunging towards the base of the Rock. Then, instinctively curving himself like a leaf, and after a moment of rocking from side to side, he'd found himself falling facedown, with the stony, scree-littered slope at the foot of the Rock rushing towards him at a fearful velocity!

But no hesitation this time: he'd forced mutating Möbius equations onto the screen of his mind, conjured a door directly in his hurtling path and fallen straight through it . . . into the merciful darkness of the Möbius Continuum. And none too soon, for in the next second he would have smashed down to stain the scree black with his blood in the blue starlight. And knowing how close he had come, the Necroscope was angry. With himself, yes, but mainly with the Wamphyri.

In the Möbius Continuum he controlled his still hurtling body, headed for well-known coordinates, emerged in the main entrance cavern to Sanctuary Rock, perhaps four hundred feet from where he'd been dropped from the rim . . .

. . . Into an echoing, babbling blast of noise and ruddy, torch-cast light, a smoke-wreathed turmoil of frenzied activity, and a combined sulphur, kneblasch, and sweat stench like standing at the brink of hell!

Men were at work, organized by a gangling, simian central figure who stood on a flat-topped, daislike boulder and shouted commands at teams of cursing, sweating Szgany. Lardis Lidesci, there could be no mistaking him. And as for the men he commanded:

They were his people, and they were Nathan's people. Here in the main cavern entrance, maybe sixty of them; the rest were out there in the night, doing battle with vampire thralls and warriors, risking and giving up their lives in the unequal red-raging contest between good and evil, the bloodwar between humanity and the Wamphyri. But those of them here in the cavern: they hauled small carts carrying makeshift bamboo rockets that trickled coarse black gunpowder propellant from dangerously short fuzes. Or they formed a sweating, grimy chain gang, passing buckets of kneblasch-laced oil hand-to-hand out into the fearful, lurid, hoarse-voiced night; while others on ladders rammed dangling, ropelike chains of fuze into the dark, ominous recesses of high ledges, or heaped small squat barrels in trenches along the walls. Taken as a group, these men formed a support and supply team for the frontline troops; but they were also the rear guard in the event that the action spilled back into Sanctuary Rock itself.

"Keep it moving!" Lardis's bull-voice roared out . . . and in the next moment, as his dark eyes swept across the panorama of frantic activity, so they settled on Nathan. Then his mouth fell open and his eyes bugged, and he pointed a shaking, astonished, disbelieving arm and hand.

The Necroscope had no time to spare; he broke through the garlic-reeking chain gang, ran forward, caught Lardis's arm as the other jumped down from his dais. "Lardis . . ."

"You!" the Old Lidesci gasped, his bloodshot eyes still huge and round. He scarcely believed it, but had to. "Nathan Kiklu! But . . . where from this time?" Instinctively, suspiciously, he narrowed his eyes. "And how?"

"No time to explain." Nathan shook his head. "But I have men with weapons: fantastic weapons, Lardis! Except . . . they are strangers; I mean, they *look* and *sound* strange, these men. And if I bring them here now, your own men might mistake them for enemies. There'd be no time for questions, and my friends could be killed."

"Not while I'm here." Lardis shook his head.

"Then stay here, and I'll be back," Nathan told him.

"Eh? Back?" Lardis gaped—

—And gaped even wider, actually staggering a little, as Nathan took a step to one side and half-disappeared, then stepped back and was whole again! Because in that moment, as he had been about to depart, so Nathan had heard a sputtering blast of propulsors, and there'd sounded a rumbling and roaring from immediately outside the yawning cavern entrance.

A small Wamphyri warrior had breached all of Lardis's defences and was out there even now, about to break in. Brave men came running, stumbling, retreating into the temporary safety of the cave; even the bravest of them knew that it meant unavoidable, nightmarish death to go up against something like the Thing outside. And:

"Back!" Lardis yelled, as a monstrously evil shape bulked huge against the glaring night, beyond the mouth of the cavern. "Everybody back into the escape tunnels." Recovering from what he had just seen—not the threat outside but Nathan's almost-disappearing act—he was quickly in charge again. For in any case this wasn't the first time that he'd seen it, and now that Nathan was back he suspected it wouldn't be the last. Also, he knew that what he had believed for quite some time now was proven beyond a doubt: that Nathan Kiklu *was* in fact a son of the long-dead Harry Hell-lander, called Dwellersire. For there had only ever been two who could come and go like that: Harry and his changeling son, the Dweller, both of whom were dead. But what is in the blood is in the blood, and quite obviously it had come out in Nathan, too.

The riddle was at last solved, and the solution indisputable. Which in turn meant . . . that there was hope yet!

. . . *If* Sanctuary Rock could survive the night! Lardis gave himself a shake, snatched a torch from the hand of a retreating man, looked for the dangling end of a rope fuze where it snaked down from explosive charges in the high, inward-curving walls.

But: "No," Nathan told him, taking the torch from him and jamming it in a crack in the dais boulder. "I said we had weapons."

He took grenades from his pockets, handed one to Lardis, ran towards the entrance whose walls flared red from the fires outside and reverberated to the sounds of battle. Lardis looked at the deadly egg in his hand and remembered the last time he'd held one: when the hell-lander Jazz Simmons had been here, oh, twenty-one years ago! Lardis hadn't much cared for the things then, and still didn't, but he knew what they could do. Gritting his teeth he ran after Nathan . . . to where the Necroscope had skidded to a halt in the very entrance.

Just outside, turning its great savage head this way and that, a metallic-gleaming machine of death—yet a creature of flesh and blood, a vampire construct—coughed and snarled as its small but incredibly vicious brain considered the possibilities for additional mayhem. Even as it did so, Nathan "heard" a mental order from its lieutenant commander out there in the night:

Enter the cave! In the name of your maker Wran the Rage, you are ordered to kill, ravage, destroy! Be about your work!

And as the horror bunched its thrusters beneath its bulk and prepared to propel itself forward into the cavern, Nathan held up his grenade where Lardis could see it, twisted its cap and yanked on its fuze-pin to prime it. They were small, these hand-hurled bombs: only two and a half inches long, like large eggs. Small, heavy, deadly! Effective far beyond anything that was available in Jazz Simmons's time. But Lardis couldn't know that as he imitated Nathan's actions and together they tossed their grenades right down the warrior's throat.

Then Nathan grabbed Lardis's arm and dragged him behind a stalagmite stump. And two seconds later:

Crump! Crump! Two muffled, shuddering detonations, as the grenades exploded. One of them went off on its way to the creature's stomach, ruining many of its vital organs; the other in the back of its throat, letting out a blast of hot white light, a lick of fire, and spurts of steaming plasma through a blackened hole where its thyroid cartilage had been. It also shattered the beast's spine and shocked its tiny brain to a standstill.

The warrior's gaping mouth and nostrils issued thick yellow smoke; its head was thrown up by the blast; the propulsors flanking its anus fired one last time in nervous reflex reaction, to send it in a clatter of chitin scales halfway up the external face of the Rock, where finally the thing shut down. And as its grotesque, lifeless body came cartwheeling back to earth some small distance away, so Nathan and Lardis felt the ground shudder under their feet . . .

But there was still no time to spare.

Nathan dug two more "eggs" out of his pocket and handed them to Lardis, said, "I'll be back," and left the other standing there as he conjured a Möbius door and passed through it—

—To the sentinel bluff where it stood close to the mouth of the great pass and looked out over the foothills to the boulder plains of Starside; also to Anna Marie English, Ben Trask, and David Chung, all of whom gasped and started in unison as he appeared.

"How long was I?" he asked. It had seemed like ages.

"Ten minutes at most," Trask answered him. "It's grown a little darker down there on the plains, but the stars have compensated; they seem that much brighter, bigger. Our friend down there hasn't moved much, not that we've noticed." He meant the wounded warrior. "There again, we've not been doing much moving either. Nor are we feeling any warmer." Inactivity had chilled their blood.

"I'm moving you—" Nathan told them, "—into battle! But first we need arms. Three-fifths of our arsenal is temporarily beyond reach. So first we have to pick up what's left. Hold on to each other, and if you think it'll help you might try closing your eyes." He conjured a door and guided them through it one after the other, then stepped through after them—

—And took them to the Cavern of the Ancients.

The trio of cavers were still there; also Atwei, and several Thyre males from Place-Under-the-Yellow-Cliffs. As Nathan and the others appeared as if from thin air (indeed, *from* thin air), all of the Thyre with the exception of Atwei were startled. One of them even cried out. But as Atwei stepped forward and said, "Nathan," so he was recognized by all of them, including a Thyre elder. But:

"No time." He wearily shook his head. "Not for explanations or for anything else. Later, maybe. Until then . . . Atwei, will you continue to care for my friends? These three men and this woman?"

She nodded. *Of course we will, brother.*

Nathan turned to Trask and Chung where they stared all about in open astonishment. "Ben, David—are you both familiar with the rest of these weapons?" As the cavers handed over the two remaining bundles of arms and ammunition, the espers nodded their confirmation.

"Very well," Nathan said. "But since we can't afford to lose anything else, let's do it here."

They broke open the bundles on the sandy floor and made their choice of weapons: grenades, ammunition for their machine pistols, and three crossbows, one of which was for Nathan himself. In all the coming and going, he seemed to have lost his original weapon.

But quickly scanning what was left, the Necroscope felt a sinking sensation as he realized how little there actually was. And how much time it would take to teach the Szgany how to use flamethrowers, self-loading rifles, rocket launchers. In fact, he never would be able to teach them to fire the latter; there were only half-a-dozen rockets, and none to waste in practice.

No time to worry over that now, however. A second or two more to pick up a carton of a dozen exploding bolts, and they were ready. And:

"Let's go," said Nathan, and took Trask and Chung to Sanctuary Rock—

—Where Lardis Lidesci and one other old friend of the Necroscope's were waiting for them . . .

III

The Battle at the Rock

Lardis Lidesci and Andrei Romani made an odd pair: the one a born leader, hotheaded, full of fire, vision, action; the other cool, calm, calculating, a friend and adviser. But both of them were fighters to the last drop of their blood; they'd been the closest of friends all their lives; they were united as all of Lardis's Szgany Lidesci were united in their hatred of the Wamphyri.

It was their *apparent* disparity that made their relationship so successful. Despite the fact that the Old Lidesci frequently accepted and acted upon Andrei's advice, he would never admit it, and for all that Andrei despaired of his leader's volatile temper—Lardis's tendency to leap before looking—-he knew it was the reason the Szgany Lidesci continued to survive.

Lardis came of seer stock and something of that art was in him. Andrei had seen evidence of it before: an uncanny knack of knowing when things weren't quite right, enabling him to calculate the odds in advance of calamity. Which was why Andrei kept his advice to a minimum and acted mainly as Lardis's principal support, his right-hand man, and why the other valued him above all other men, because he had the effect of cooling his too-hot blood when without him it might boil over. So their partnership worked, and so the Szgany Lidesci survived—or had survived, until this night. . . .

Their looks were different, too. Andrei Romani was a lithe, rangy man ("skinny," Lardis like to call him), with nothing of fat but a great deal of muscle on his shoulders, arms, striding legs. The years has cost him a lot of hair but little else; his dark Szgany eyes were still keen, and his aim with a crossbow deadly. That's why Andrei was back in the cavern entrance even now: to replenish his quiver with bolts. For outside, the hand-to-hand fighting was fierce and bloody!

And: *Hand-to-hand,* he thought, hurrying to a wooden barrel of ironwood bolts close to Lardis's command position. *Aye, and it's all down to crossbows these days, now that the last of the Dweller's shotgun shells are used up.* But for all that Andrei's shotgun—his "weapon out of another world"—was alien and more than twenty years old, it had long been his pride and joy and he still kept it clean, oiled, polished . . . "just in case."

As for "old": well, men grow old faster than machines, and they're that much harder to repair, too. Lardis Lidesci could tell you all about that, who for the first time in his life had commenced to feel rheumatic twinges, or "growing pains," as he was wont to call then, in his knees and elbows.

But . . . *What else can he tell me?* Andrei wondered spying his leader through the smoke and turmoil, and noticing a certain look on his face—as if he'd seen a ghost.

Andrei went to the other where he had moved to the central boulder and leaned against it, took his arm and stared into his eyes, and fired off questions without saying a word. And he wondered about the Old Lidesci: how he was, his heart, health; his mind, stability. The hell of it was, that was all he ever did: wonder. For there was never time to inquire.

Lardis was short, barrel-bodied, near-apelike in the great length of his arms. His lank black hair framed a weather-beaten face, where a flattened nose sat uncomfortably over a mouth missing several of its worn, uneven teeth. Under shaggy eyebrows, Lardis's dark brown eyes glittered his mind's agility, even as the man himself remained agile despite his stumpy shape, rheumatism, and the inescapable fact of his mounting years.

For he *was* old now, or at least starting to show his age. Two-thirds of a lifetime spent fighting the Wamphyri would age any man before his time. Another year or two of his only son, Jason, would have stepped into his shoes, except . . .

. . . Jason had been taken in that very first raid almost three and a half years ago, since when no man had heard of him. Seeing Nathan tonight had brought it all back to Lardis; alas that it had brought more than Jason back; and the thought that he too might be alive. For Nestor Kiklu, Nathan's brother, had also been taken that night—and he *had* been heard of!

Lardis had seen it for himself, some seventeen, eighteen sunups ago:

Nathan Kiklu had returned from allegedly fantastic adventures in the mythical east, beyond the Great Red Waste, where he'd dwelled a while in the gorge of Turgosheim as a companion or "familiar" to Lord Maglore the Mage in the self-styled magician's Runemanse, an aerie of the Wamphyri. There, discovering that the powerful Vormulac Unsleep and the other would-be warrior-Lords of Turgosheim were intent upon the imminent pursuit and punishment of the Lady Wratha and her renegades (in short, an invasion of Nathan's own Sunside/Starside, and the unthinkable bloodwar that must accompany or even precede it), Nathan had stolen a flyer with which to make his escape west.

That he had come out of Turgosheim unscathed, untainted, had seemed a miracle in its own right . . . but that he'd done so in the saddle of a Wamphyri flyer? A *fantastic* adventure, indeed, but one that Lardis had heard from Nathan's own lips, so that he'd accepted it . . .

And no sooner had the youth returned than he had taken a wife; or rather, she'd taken him! His girl, Misha Zanesti, had waited for him long enough and her father, Varna, had seen to it that she would wait no longer. Then, in the deep twilight before the night, as the couple had returned from their nuptial trek, back to Sanctuary Rock—

—Disaster!

Lardis had gone out from the Rock into the night to meet them and hasten them home. And so he'd seen it for himself and had witnessed the weirdness of it:

Nathan and Misha, returning along a foothills track to the rock; but descending towards them out of the twilight's mist, a pair of Wamphyri flyers! Their riders could be Lords . . . lieutenants? Lardis didn't know, but he knew what they were after. And these young lovers out in the open, unprotected and unsuspecting. Then . . .

. . . They'd felt the throbbing of the mist-damp air, glanced skywards, seen hell descending out of the stars! One beast and rider had gone after Misha, the other after Nathan. Lardis had seen the girl take a tumble into a covered pit, a trap for flyers and warriors alike. She might be shaken, even a little hurt, but at least she was safe for the moment. And so Lardis had gone after Nathan, head over heels down a scree slide!

Slithering on his rump and heels, he had actually passed under one of the flyers where it floated down upon Nathan, its great manta wings formed into air-scoops! Then Lardis had collided with Nathan, and a moment later the pair of them had come to a halt at the bottom of the slope. But relentless as some grotesque, sentient shadow and almost as close, the flyer had been right there behind them.

Lardis was first on his feet; he'd turned his shotgun on the flyer, discharged it point-blank into the creature's eyes—once, twice! The thing's high-pitched scream; the frenzied lashing of its bloodied head, left and right; the in-

sane pounding of its wings! Immeasurable satisfaction! And yelling like a madman, the Old Lidesci had reloaded and aimed his weapon again—but this time at the vampire Lord himself where he fought to control his injured mount.

Which was when the mist had lifted a little, and Lardis—and Nathan, too—had seen just exactly who it was rocking in the saddle of his agonized beast:

Nathan's brother, Nestor!

Lord Nestor, of the Wamphyri!

But in that precise moment Lardis had got off a shot that he was certain found its mark. Whether or no, the injured flyer had lifted off into the mist, and nothing more seen of beast or rider.

Following which, it should have been over—but wasn't! For breaking through the mist, the second flyer had snatched Nathan up and made off with him! And just like Jason and Nestor before him, neither had he been seen to this day, so that Lardis had suspected he was dead . . .

Until tonight.

But if Nathan still lived, then what of Jason, Lardis's son, lost so long ago? And what of Nestor—the *Lord* Nestor as he was now, or as Lardis had last seen him: with his face torn to a splash of blood against the mist-grey night?

Except . . . Lardis hadn't really recognized him then. Not then, and not for some little time. It was only later, when he went to his bed, slept, and nightmared the thing through, that he'd seen that awful face again: scarlet-eyed and bloated with black hatred; but young and proud for all that, and in outline at least the very image of the one he'd come to kill! Then, in his dreams, Lardis had known.

He'd suspected that Nathan knew, too, but Nathan had no longer been here to ask. And of course Lardis had never dared speak to Nana Kiklu about it, and certainly not to Misha . . .

. . . Poor Misha! She'd got back her lover, only to lose him again! The strength of the girl, that she hadn't fallen apart from it all. And all of it beginning to connect up in Lardis's mind, solidifying there, making sense at last:

Nestor Kiklu: a vampire Lord ... And this sudden attack on Sanctuary Rock, which had always been the Szgany Lidesci's best-kept secret. Of course Nestor had told them! But why not before? He'd probably been one of them since the time he was stolen away! Nestor and Nathan ... rivals for Misha Zanesti. Was that it? Nathan's love had brought him back, most definitely—and against all odds, at that—but Nestor?

Nathan's love and Nestor's—what, hatred? But they were twin brothers, born of one womb in the same hour! Ah, but Nestor was Wamphyri now! Blood brothers, aye ...

"What is it, my friend?" Andrei Romani's anxious inquiry drew the other out of it; out of the past and his morbid reverie both, and back into the fear-fraught present. "What have you seen? What's wrong, eh?"

Lardis looked at him. "Not what I've seen, but who."

"Who?"

"Aye." Lardis's curt nod. "And not what's wrong, but right—I hope!"

"Will you explain?"

"Let these explain," said Lardis, and showed him Nathan's grenades. But before the other could say a word: "No, let *him* explain." And Lardis pointed across the cavern.

Nathan, Trask, and Chung had emerged from the Möbius Continuum against the wall of the cavern, where Nathan had put in his first appearance. Andrei took in all three at a glance, but mainly Nathan. And like Lardis, he knew him at once. "What? But that's Nathan Kiklu!" he gasped before falling silent, lost for words.

The three came hurrying through the hustle and bustle, but this time not unnoticed. A group of sweating, grimy, sharp-eyed men stepped forward, pinioning their arms as they drew close to Lardis. The Old Lidesci quickly cautioned them: "Now hold! For I know these men. They're friends. Be about your business."

Andrei still couldn't speak, and he noticed that the two with Nathan (one of whom, the small yellow man, looked a very strange specimen indeed) seemed similarly shocked, stumbling, incapacitated. But it only lasted a few seconds. Then—

—Nathan and Andrei grasped forearms in the customary Szgany greeting—and so did the strangers, with Andrei and Lardis both! Not so strange after all. And:

"Andrei," said Nathan, "put that down." He took Andrei's crossbow and handed him a new one—*brand* new, the oil still gleaming on it. "As for bolts," Nathan held up a fistful, "use these—but careful how you handle them, and don't drop them! When you go out, stick close to Lardis and watch his back."

"When we go out . . . ?" Andrei's mouth had difficulty staying shut, even when he wasn't speaking.

"That's right," Nathan nodded. "Into the thick of it. Now listen: if you come up against warriors, Lardis has the answer right there in his hands." He indicated the grenades. "As for these bolts: they'll kill thralls, lieutenants, even flyers—and they'll kill them dead!"

Lardis pocketed the grenades, took the second of Nathan's three crossbows and a fistful of explosive bolts, and growled: "Is there a plan?"

Nathan shook his head. "Only to destroy our enemies, and save the Rock."

"Sounds like a good one to me." Lardis and Andrei headed for the cavern entrance, where again the sounds of battle were on the increase. But when Nathan and the others didn't follow, they looked back—

—And saw that the Necroscope and his hell-lander friends were gone . . .

. . . Up into the foothills directly above the Rock, from which vantage point to look down on the fighting and take their pick of opponents. And:

"Those flyers," Trask pointed, "down there on the trails where they lead to the Rock. There must be seven or eight of them, maybe more. With all this smoke and fire, it's hard to tell. But if we could take out the flyers . . ."

Nathan shook his head. "Not all of them. There are lieutenants down there too. If we cut off their escape route, they can only stand and fight . . . I mean to the very end. And that would mean more Szgany losses."

"Half of them, then," said Chung. "Then, when those monsters see what's happening to their mounts, they'll likely make a run for it! Okay, take us down there, Nathan, and let's see what we can do."

Perhaps surprised, the Necroscope looked at him, frowned. "You're ready?"

"Not really, but as ready as I ever will be." Chung's grin was nervous.

Now Nathan seemed worried about it. "There's still so much you don't know. I mean, there are traps down there, camouflaged pits in the earth: flyer traps, mainly, but warrior traps, too. Don't make a mistake and fall into one. And don't get too much blood on you! It isn't especially active in itself—unless it's from a Lord or senior lieutenant, which could be dangerous in your eyes, nose, mouth—but, well, you can't be too careful . . ."

"Son," Trask told him "you had better *believe* that we'll be careful! We fought with your father on Earth, remember? And we were careful there, too. Just get us down there. The sooner this is over the better."

"Very well, but all within hailing distance. Then if you see lieutenants or thralls coming, you can call for me." Without more ado he conjured a door, guided Trask through it . . .

. . . And out into a part of the flyer launching area that was farthest from the Rock, where monstrous grey shapes nodded in the mist not very far away. Then: "Good luck, Ben," Nathan told him, leaving him there.

It was Chung's turn, and Nathan dropped him off a little closer to the rock, but in a place where there was no sign of human—or rather inhuman—activity, just continuing sounds of fierce fighting from the near-distant Rock. And finally the Necroscope located himself at the head of the column of flyers, so that he would be the first to note any retreat of the lieutenants from their frontline positions.

Nathan chose a flyer, ran towards it through drifting

smoke and reek, lobbed a grenade that bounced and rolled to a standstill directly under the flyer's nodding head. A moment later ... the detonation was so vicious that it stripped the creature's face of flesh, hurling back its head so violently that the tapering neck was broken in the whiplash.

And again Nathan felt the *power* of these weapons from another world, and thrilled to it! Well, and why not? As the Wamphyri and their creatures, thralls, lieutenants took pleasure in destroying men, so he could rejoice in destroying them. What was their war cry? Wamphyri! *Wamphyri!* Nathan felt like shouting, "Human! *Human!*"

He chose another target: a second grey head, nodding and mist-wreathed, maybe thirty yards away. Except ... someone was coming, crouching low, panting. Someone whose eyes were feral yellow, glowing like gold in the dark. A lieutenant!

Nathan snatched his crossbow from his belt ... nocked its wire, loaded the bolt ... was aware that the vampire was almost upon him. He lifted his arm and hand, head and eyes, and saw a flame-eyed demon with jaws gaping and arms outstretched, rushing at him!

He squeezed the trigger—then hurled himself backwards and to one side. The lieutenant mewled like a mad thing as he staggered, snatched at the bolt in the right of his chest and tried to draw it out. Sprawling in the dirt of the trail, Nathan turned his face away. And with a sound like a *crack* of doom, flesh and innards went flying in all directions and half a man staggered this way and that upon the old trail, before collapsing in grotesque and bloody disarray ...

Behind Nathan, lost in the smoke and rolling mist, there were other explosions, dim flashes of light. But these weren't the soft-sounding pyrotechnics of Lardis's inferior gunpowder. They came with a series of crisp *cracks*, which even the swirling mist couldn't deaden. It had to be Trask and Chung, about their deadly work. Good!

From the other direction, however, towards Sanctuary Rock: hoarse cries of rage and terror, screams, the throb and sputter of warrior propulsors, the occasional whine and careening flare of a rocket run wild. But Nathan knew that Lardis was there; he had heard at least two explosions which could only be caused by grenades. The Old Lidesci had already expended his most effective weapons—necessarily, Nathan was sure.

The Necroscope's blood was up, and up there in the front line he knew that blood was being spilled—good clean Szgany blood, some of it; spilled or perhaps changed forever. The idea of transferring himself into that zone was terrifying, but that was why he was here. If he didn't at least try to make Sunside/Starside safe for his people, then what was the point?

He used the Möbius route back up into the foothills for orientation, then transferred down onto the approach trail to the main cavern entrance.

Maybe one hundred and twenty yards from the foot of the massive outcrop, a defensive arrangement of covered pits and trenches had been dug in the hard earth and rock. In plan, the pits formed two concentric semicircles ringing the entrance in. They were eccentrically positioned so that any advancing enemy who avoided the first row must run right into the second.

On the ground, however, and due to the declining terrain, the Rock's defences presented an even more complicated picture. Enemy forces approaching from the forest (the south) must push uphill towards the Rock, while those from the east could follow the more or less even flow of the foothill contours. Lardis had known this, too, when he'd dug his pits; it was why he'd dug in addition a trench behind the pits on the level ground. And that was where the thick of the fighting was taking place even now.

But pits and trenches were not the Rock's only defences. Thirty yards within the inner circle, a low drystone wall had been built, with upward tilting, kiln-glazed pipes of clay cemented in position every other pace, providing launchtubes for the stems of Lardis's rockets: the Old Lidesci's missle battery. The wall was mainly drystone to allow for rapid rebuilding in the event that it was breached, flattened by the sheer bulk of a warrior. And every *other* pace, stout wooden stakes with their points sharpened to needles, also facing outwards to impale onrushing monsters.

Also, at the base of the Rock itself where that colossal boulder's roots buried themselves in the earth—half-hidden in the natural camouflage of scree-grown vines and shrubbery—a second battery; this time of stone-hurling engines, and giant crossbows with bolts formed of young, arrow-straight, stripped-down pines.

While *inside* the covered pits:

Beds of slender stakes, harpoon-tipped to catch and hold any flyer, warrior, or vampire thrall that might fall on them; and recesses in the walls, where men could wait with buckets of oil, and flints and candles at the ready.

Most of the pits on the level were on fire, their withe frames of twisted straw and gorse camouflage going up in smoke and flame into the reeking night. *Meat* ... was steaming in several of them, while others were simply smoking, blackened holes in the earth. The hot air was full of death smells that caught in men's throats, making them choke, retch ...

Nathan had emerged from the Continuum behind the Rock's defenders, where the fortified wall faced first the trench, then the twin rows of pits. Since the men on the Rock's side of the wall were all facing the other way, he'd stepped (as it were) into existence all unseen. And now for the first time he saw evidence of the hand-to-hand fighting: how it had washed to and fro over this very spot. Obviously the warrior he and Lardis had dispatched in the cavern entrance had been accompanied by vampire thralls led by lieutenants; there were a number of corpses littering the stony ground ... many of them without heads. The ones *with* heads were human, his own people: Szgany killed in the fighting.

Their wounds were horrific, the work of Wamphyri gauntlets. Flensed faces; chests laid open through flesh and ribs; throats ripped out, *literally*! Even through a swirling ground mist it could be seen that the earth was stained black in the fire- and starlight, and the whole area stank of brutal butchery and blood . . .

. . . It had been scenes such as this—scenes as violent, mind-stunning as this—that had driven Nathan from his cause and course in the first place, out into Sunside's furnace desert to die; only to discover the Thyre, his ability to talk to the dead, and fresh hope for the future. And now . . . this *was* that future, and he must fight to come to terms with it, get a grip on himself, his soaring emotions. He didn't have the time to stand and consider what had happened here; it could all too easily happen again, if he simply stood still and let it!

But terrible memories had been set in motion, and terrible scenes out of a none-too-distant past. Inescapable as a recurrent nightmare, Nathan viewed them as a ghostly tableau against the equally swirly-smoking backdrop of mist, fire, and blood-splashed night:

That time when he'd searched for his brother, stolen by a flyer out of ravaged Settlement . . .

The Szgany Sintana, true Travellers in Sunside's forests, had befriended him. And in turn Nathan had made them a promise: if he couldn't find Nestor, then he would join them where they planned to establish a permanent camp at the edge of the sprawling savanna dividing the forest from the furnace deserts. The reason they would settle there was simple: that much closer to the sun, and distant from the barrier mountains, it had seemed unlikely that the Wamphyri would venture there. That had been the reasoning, anyway.

And when Nathan was done with his searching, that's where he'd found them—or what was left of them.

Nikha Sintana, and Eleni, his sister: their faces and the faces of their people haunted Nathan still.

Nikha: young in years, old in his ways, wild as the woods and gentle as its creatures . . . but hard in the ways of survival. So it had seemed. The actual number of his years had been a secret hidden in the agelessness of his penetrating, intelligent brown eyes, and in skin weath-

*ered to a supple leather. He had seemed like part of the
landscape, at one with Nature. His hooked nose, sharp as
a kite's beak, but lacking its cruelty; his brow, with the flat
slope of a wolf's, yet broad enough to accommodate a
good brain and wide, inscrutable eyes; his thin lips, and
dark grey, shoulder-length hair. Nikha had reminded Nathan of nothing so much as a lean and rangy hunting owl.*

And Eleni . . .

*Maybe twenty, twenty-one years old, and typically
Szgany. All lithe and sinuous; movements smooth as oil;
shiny black hair, and skin tanned to a glow. She'd seemed
as wild—even wilder—than her brother; given the chance,
and in a better world, Eleni would be ever vivacious and
live her life to the full. Her mouth had been generous and
sensuous at one and the same time, with a laugh that was
husky and teasing, but never quite seducing. Because when
finally she did love, the chosen one would get it all.*

*And because at that time Nathan had thought that
Misha was dead (or worse far, stolen out of Settlement into
Starside by Cánker Canison), he had even considered be-
coming that one. But it hadn't worked out that way.*

*Following their trail through the night to where the
forest met the prairie, at last he'd seen the carts and caravans of the Szgany Sintana sheltering under mighty ironwoods. Their fire had been a welcoming splash of leaping
light holding back the shadows in the space under the
trees.*

*It had welcomed Nathan, aye . . . but in the same way
that it had welcomed others before him!*

The Wamphyri!

*They weren't there now, but the evidence of their having
been was unmistakable. Nathan remembered it as if it were
but a moment ago:*

*He stood under the ironwoods, where the dusty ground
had been swept free of needles to form a small clearing in
its own right. But in the shadows, bloated black shapes
like windblown weeds went lumping and fluttering low
along the ground, hiding from him in dark places.*

Then, as he heard a chittering in the night and started

in recognition of the sound ... something wet dripped down and splashed on his forearm where his sleeves were rolled up. Looking down, he saw that his arm was red; likewise the earth under his feet. And looking up—

—He saw the tree's strange ripe fruit, all dripping their juices, strung up by their heels with their throats slashed ear to ear!

The drained corpses of the Szgany Sintana, swaying there on creaking ropes under the branches of the iron- woods ... and all festooned with black Desmodus bats, Wamphyri familiars so glutted with blood they couldn't fly ... and these loathsome, bloated monsters falling or flop- ping to the ground and scuttling off into the shrieking night!

The shrieking night ...

Instinctively, Nathan crouched down and shot a terrified glance overhead—as if expecting to see a body, dangling by its heels and dripping blood. But it was only a Szgany rocket gone off course, which showered sparks on him and whistled off into the mist. Its shrieking had startled him to life, except it wasn't the only thing that shrieked—or roared?

Looking around, perhaps in desperation, Lardis had seen the Necroscope. "Nathan, quick!"

He ran to the knot of defenders at the wall, joined Lardis and his men. Lardis pointed east, to the trench, pits, and the swirling mist beyond. "We've fought them off once, twice. The first wave came with the warrior that we destroyed at the entrance, and the second was made up of thralls on a suicide mission. Those who are left are mainly lieutenants, but they are the most dangerous. And they've called down another warrior. Look!"

A handful of tall grey figures moved in the mist around the perimeter of one of the innermost pits. From the sinu- ous, loping flow of their movements they were plainly lieutenants. Along with them, a half-dozen vampire thralls held up leather shields against incoming bolts from the de- fenders at the wall, so protecting their superiors. And shouting instructions, all of them urged action from a warrior where it had fallen into the pit.

A small one of its sort, the creature floundered. It was caught on harpoon flukes and several of its gas bladders had been ruptured. In the event of its freeing itself, however, this superficial damage wouldn't impede its fighting ferocity, its monstrous thirst for blood, war. Indeed, its frustration would make it yet more ferocious! But jammed awkwardly in the hole, it had difficulty bringing its thrusters and propulsors into play. Hence the thing's roaring, the occasional sputter of its propulsors and jets of noxious fumes issuing from the pit.

Even as Nathan and Lardis watched, so the creature got its monstrous head up over the rim, and the glare of the red eyes in its bony, prowlike, chitin-scaled slope of a forehead threatened the defenders at the wall with a nightmarish death. Its propulsors fired again, and the horror jerked halfway out of the pit.

Nathan had two grenades left. Handing one of them to Lardis, he said, "Now!"

They squeezed through a breach in the wall, ran forward, were met by eager lieutenants loping the other way, in anticipation of their warrior's imminent attack. But Andrei Romani and other defenders were right on their leader's heels; crossbow bolts flew in the night, passing far too close by Nathan's reckoning. A lieutenant was swatted from his feet, and blew to bits before he hit the ground. A flame-eyed thrall cursed and spat where he writhed upon the earth, tugging frantically at ironwood bolts in his chest and belly. Snarling men fell on him with sharp knives, hammers, stakes.

Nathan and Lardis left the hand-to-hand fighting behind, arrived at the pit, armed their grenades. Lieutenants came at the run out of the smoke and mist; the pair lobbed their grenades into the pit, then turned and fled. Andrei was still with them; he fired the last of his explosive bolts into a lieutenant's shoulder and joined them in flight.

Behind them there was an explosion, the sharp *crack* of a bolt. And: *Now!* Nathan thought.

The warrior roared its triumph as it bunched its thrusters and its propulsors sputtered into life. But just a moment too late. Twin blasts tore the night, accompanied by brilliant flashes of light and an agonized mewling, as chitin scales and chunks of raw flesh shot skywards. The detonations had cracked the thing's carapace, setting fire to its mantle and gas bladders. Lesser explosions and the flames that roared up to hurl back the shadows—and the mewling that climbed the scales to a continuous high-pitched screaming—signalled the monster's finish.

Then, arriving back at the wall, Nathan "heard" it: the Lady Wratha's raging, and her final command from her vantage point on the dome of the Rock.

Fools! Weak fools! What? And have mere men—the Szgany Lidesci—defeated you yet again? Get out of there, those of you who may. Flee! Flee for your lives, aye! For we your masters and I your mistress would have words with you—back in Wrathstack! Wratha's promise, or threat, was all too evident in the grating of her hideous mind-croak.

Nathan took Lardis's arm. "They're pulling out. They've had enough. It's all over. For now, anyway . . ."

Lardis looked, snarled his triumph, then shook his fist and laughed like a lunatic. Nathan was right: lieutenants and thralls were vacating their positions, slinking back into the mist, making for their flyers. But from back along the trail, out of the blood and sulphur reek, the night and its leaping shadows, there sounded a sudden stuttering of automatic fire: Trask and Chung, picking off vampire thralls where they tried to make their escape.

Nathan used the Möbius Continuum, picked up his friends, transferred them back to Lardis and the defenders at the wall. They were safe now, all of them . . . well, from the Wamphyri at least, if not from the nightmare of what must follow.

In that respect: it would be as well if Anna Marie English and the others were at least offered the opportunity to see it, too, and so know what they were into. With that in mind, Nathan collected them from the Cavern of the Ancients. When they were all together again and perfunctory introductions concluded:

"Very well," said Lardis Lidesci, nodding grimly where he surveyed the littered battlefield. "And now let's be at it . . ."

All of which had been something less than thirty-five minutes ago. But on high over the barrier mountains, and heading (some limping) home, the Wamphyri were still feeling bruised by their defeat; and Wratha was still raging, albeit in her secret mind. Raging and rotating the facts of the night—those known, and others as yet unknowable, but facts nevertheless because they had happened—in the depths of her secret vampire thoughts.

She should be grateful to Nestor, that he had warned her not to land as she made her descent, but she was not. How had the necromancer known there was danger? How had he, a veritable infant among the Wamphyri, seen or sensed that which she had not? What? But he'd been a Lord for less than three years! So, he spoke to dead men—so what? That one on top of Sanctuary Rock had been very much alive! But no longer.

What *was* this thing with Nestor and the Szgany Lidesci? Again a picture formed in the Lady's mind: of the one on the Rock, him and his deadly tube . . . Nestor's Great Enemy? And much like Lardis Lidesci before her, Wratha wondered at the connection:

Nestor, Misha, and a Great Enemy. Or a Great Rival? Was that it? Was he still mooning over this Traveller shad Misha? Was that why he'd finally set himself against the Szgany Lidesci, because he had a rival among them? But if so, why wait so long? Also, Wratha had thought that *that* had been all over and done with following Nestor's last abortive strike against this so-called Great Enemy. And it still didn't explain how he had known there was danger on the Rock's roof. Was Nestor using her to his own ends, she wondered? Using the rest of them, too, as a punitive force in some private feud? In which case tonight's losses were all down to him!

And raging still, she told herself: *Very well, let's see how he reacts to this.* Then, opening her mind for all to see and hear, and using her mentalism to the full, she cried:

Now hear my vow! I Wratha the Risen make it, and I shall keep it. From now on it is sacred to me, and I make it so that you all may know it and call me Wratha Vow-breaker if I do not keep it. I shall destroy the Szgany Lidesci. By skill or trickery, wit or sheer unbendable will . . . by the blood that is the life, I shall destroy them! Wratha had made such vows before, but never out in the open where she could be held to them. Ah, but no one would have to hold her to this one, be sure!

As she had spoken, so Wratha had cast a sideways glance at Nestor. At him, and *into* his mind—or at least she had tried. But his mind was clamped shut as a lichen to its rock, impenetrable. He sat there pale as new lead in his saddle, his body swathed and his face cowled, and rode the night wind. And never a sign that he had even heard her, he was that cold. Or seemed to be. Until:

All mine who are able, to me! he called abruptly. *There's a deed must be done. Any who are injured, damaged, get on back to the last aerie and wait on my return.*

He and his peeled off, swooped southwards; and letting a tail wind off the Icelands take them, they quickly dwindled to gnats in the clouds scudding high over Sunside's forests. Astonished, Wratha and the others let them go and carried on homewards. But the Lady wondered: *What now? Is he also a madman, this necromancer?*

Before she could consider it further:

"Ho, Wratha!" came a shouted (yet somehow restrained) greeting across the gulf of air. "And all you others there! But a sorry-looking lot if ever I saw one!" It was Gorvi the Guile, wheeling on the wind and coming up alongside to where Wratha and the Lords spearheaded their reduced forces. Gorvi and his flyer, alone. "Have I missed something, I wonder?" he continued, quieter now. "Well, perhaps it were better missed at that! It appears you had problems." He seemed to commiserate, but in fact they knew he gloated . . .

. . . Until he looked back at the tattered remnants of the army that had left Wrathstack, and especially at what was left of his own contingent. Then:

"What!?" Gorvi gasped. "But . . . how have you protected my men and creatures, Wratha? What has *become* of them?" His words were supposed to be accusing yet sounded as a wail: the cry of a wrongful child who knows he's about to be smacked.

Where—were—you—Gorvi? Wratha's growl sounded in his mind, and the mental voices of all the others with her.

Gorvi would babble an answer—a well-rehearsed excuse concerning a deadly force of strangers on Starside's boulder plains—but before he could do so there came a diversion:

A giant *Desmodus* bat, one of Wratha's familiars, appeared out of the east in a whirring of tired wings and settled to the neck of her mount. There the creature clung, exhausted, finally folding back its black membrane wings and chittering a faint—but not that faint—message. And Wratha at once straightened up rigid in her saddle.

The language of bats ranges from the faint to the fantastic, from barely audible to seeming silence . . . in the ears of common humanity. But to the Wamphyri each note is distinct and has meaning. And the meaning of Wratha's familiar was clear. It was one of two creatures she'd positioned as sentinels in the eastern peaks at the edge of the Great Red Waste, her early warning system against a surprise attack out of Turgosheim—

—Which was why it was here now!

So that Gorvi the Guile was the only one among them who actually felt a sense of relief as a certain dreaded name took form in the suddenly whirling chaos of Wratha the Risen's mind. But even his relief was only temporary, for the worst fears of each and every one of them were suddenly come true. Then . . .

. . . The Lady's jaw fell open and her eyes stood out like lamps in her gaunt and haggard face. And she beat her

breast and cried her frustration: "Why now? *Why now?*"
Until finally she croaked the very last name that any of her
colleagues had ever wanted to hear:

"Vormulac!"

What of him? Wran the Rage "gasped" in her mind, unwilling to believe it despite that he knew.

He's crossed the Great Red Waste, she answered, speaking to all of them at once. *He's here, in the east of Olden
Starside, even now. Our mortal if not our im*mortal enemy
. . . *Lord Vormulac Unsleep, of Turgosheim. Him and his,
aye. And they are many!*

IV

Vormulac

In Turgosheim, Maglore the Mage had been busy for a
night and a day; which was the equivalent of an entire
week in a parallel world currently beyond Lord Maglore's
ken. He'd been busy ever since the warrior-Lord Vormulac
Taintspore (called Unsleep) had ventured forth from melancholy Vormspire, and from the gorge of Turgosheim itself, into the unknown west with his vampire army. That
had been in the twilight before the night; and how Maglore
had gloated where he watched from the roof of Runemanse, as his supposed "colleagues" and all their creatures
vacated the gorge to fly west in the shadow of the mountains, bound for a legendary land of plenty beyond the
Great Red Waste.

In the eye of memory he could see it even now: the
beginning of that grand crusade, and all the pomp and
splendour of Vormulac's marvellous exit from Turgosheim.

(Marvellous, aye, especially in the greedy eyes and heart of the Seer-Lord Maglore, who had vowed in the hour of their departure that once they were out, Vormulac and the others would *never* get back in!—which were thoughts he'd kept to himself, of course.) But quite apart from his ambitions, to actually witness that exodus *had* been a wonderful experience.

To stand there on the roof of promontory Runemanse with Karpath Seersthrall, his right-hand man, watching first the flypast, then the departure; to see the massed might of Turgosheim "on parade" as it were, under its many generals, and all of them under Vormulac's overall command. The gradually burgeoning whorl of that aerial army within and level with the rim of the gorge as, emerging from the landing bays of individual spires and manses, the contingents filled their spaces within the soaring ranks. Awe-inspiring!

The gleam of polished leather body-armour, iron-studded trappings, golden ornamentation; the raucous banging and blaring of drums, gongs, and horns from the various aeries, where common thralls made noise to speed their masters (and mistresses) to victory in far foreign places; the rumbling cough and sputter of warrior exhausts . . .

Then to see the great spiral unwind as Vormulac Unsleep himself led the column westwards out of the gorge; to recognize and check off the various sigils, standards, and pennants fluttering in the vile slipstream of propulsive gasses, where they passed level with Maglore and dwindled into distance:

Vormulac's own "hanging man" emblem, Grigor (the Lech) Hakson's odious "rampant rod," the virgin grandam Devetaki's "grin-scowl mask," the Lady Ursula Torspawn's "Szgany bells," Lord Eran Painscar's "spiny gauntlet," Lord Tangiru's "warrior tooth necklace," Zun's "bloodied tusks," and Lady Zindevar Cronesap's "spitted pig" (in fact a spitted man, right down to the apple in his mouth!) and many another.

They had all been there:

Lom Halfstruck, Lord of Trollmanse; Lady Valeria of Valspire; Black Boris, who kept trog mistresses; Lord Wamus (pronounced "Vamus"), whose far-reaching, folding claw-tipped arms were in fact membranous pinions, for his metamorphic skill was such that he effortlessly maintained the guise of a great bat; Lord Freg of Fregscarp; Laughing Zack Shornskull of Zackspire, oh, and at least a dozen and a half more.

Noticeable if only by their absence (curiously, Maglore had actually found himself *looking* for them) were such as Wran "the Rage" and Spiro Killglance, Wratha the Risen, Canker Canison, Vasagi the Suck, and Gorvi the Guile. But since ostensibly they had been the spur for this allegedly punitive expedition, that was only to be expected. For in fact all six of them were fled into the unknown west where they'd hidden themselves away for more than three years now, and where Vormulac and his army hoped to seek them out to punish them for treason against all of Turgosheim's Wamphyri.

But in fact they had committed no such heinous crime, nor any crime at all, or only a middling one at best. For in truth Wratha and her gang had only ever sought to be what they were: Wamphyri! Which by reason of Turgosheim's politics was a sort of treason in itself. Against Zolteism.

And: *Hah!* Maglore thought. *Zolteism, indeed!*

Turgo Zolte had been the father of them all, the founder of Turgosheim, who had fled with his children out of the west from the wrath of Shaitan the Unborn. But all of that was history, an immemorial legend. As for Zolteism: that was Turgo's legacy, and some would say his curse. For of all the Wamphyri who had been and were to be, Turgo was the one who had denied himself to do battle with his leech. He had been and had continued to be his own man even unto death, following which the creed of Zolteism was passed down to them who survived him in Turgosheim.

The blood is the life, aye—but in moderation. To lust after power, territory, thralls, and possessions is the *way* of life—in moderation. The thrill of the kill is a joy—but all in moderation and according to rules. That was the essence of Zolteism: to deny one's parasite, keep it in its place, and be master of one's own urges, one's own destiny.

Moreover, Turgo's creed had been seen to make sense; the Szgany of Turgosheim's Sunside had become so reduced in number that the bloodwars *must* cease, or the Wamphyri themselves die out from lack of nourishment. For in the beginning, in Turgosheim's youth, the interstack wars had been many and the toll in human lives, in Szgany beasts and vitals in general, enormous. If Zolteism were not enforced the blood itself would soon become enfeebled, run cold, run out! Thus, if the vampire Lords would live, so must the creed. And of course the weakest of them had been eager to embrace it—or if not the weakest, the wisest, certainly.

It was all history now, aye, but the creed had survived, and Maglore the Mage had been a "true Zolteist," an "ascetic," all of his days. Well, within limits, of course. Maglore, and Devetaki Skullguise, even Vormulac Unsleep himself: ascetics of sorts. For these three had been Turgosheim's secret triumvirate, its regulators, who recognized the folly of depleting Sunside to the dregs. And besides, life had been good for them in their mighty manses, towering high over Turgosheim's lesser knolls and hovels—

—Until Wratha the Risen and her renegades had made warriors that flew, and with them had flown out of Turgosheim into the fabled west! That was their crime: that of their own admission, Wratha and her outlaws had stolen forbidden flesh out of Sunside from which to build millennia-banned constructs. Also, that they had cheated in the tithe in order to further improve their get. But it was *not* why Vormulac had ordered his massive war effort, culminating these three years later in a so-called crusade. No, for that had been done out of fear.

Fear that indeed a fabulous land of plenty lay far to the west, beyond the Great Red Waste, and that the Lady Wratha would utilize its riches to build an invincible vampire army of her own. And fear that she would return one night, and wrest Turgosheim from its rightful leaders. For in her time she'd made a habit of rising up and returning, this Lady; which was why they had named her Wratha the Risen.

In his room of meditation, these were some of the thoughts that passed through Maglore's mind as he gazed upon his golden sigil "shewstone" and considered putting it to use. Where was Wratha now, he wondered, and where Vormulac? And how would it go when they met—or collided? And where for that matter was Nathan, Maglore's "window on an unknown world"?

That was why the Seer-Lord merely considered using the Möbius loop sigil: because the last time he'd done so . . . well, it had been to discover that the crafty Nathan was oh-so-much more crafty than Maglore had ever guessed. Oh, he had long suspected that Nathan was a weird one, but never the *extent* of his weirdness! Still, with all of those unknown miles between—and the Great Red Waste itself as a buffer zone—where would the harm be? But being a "mage" of sorts, and certainly a seer, Maglore respected the talents of others; and despite that he was Wamphyri and knew no real fear (or so he told himself), for the time being he kerbed his curiosity with regard to Nathan and turned instead to Vormulac.

For prior to Lord Taintspore's departure, his old "friend" and colleague Maglore had given him a good-luck piece: a golden ring for his ear . . . in the shape of a twisted figure of eight, Maglore's sigil! Surely a sign of undying, even undead friendship, that a man honour another with his own talisman, the sign of his house and being? And so, in precisely the same way that Nathan Kiklu wore a ring of gold six inches from the centre of his brain, so now Vormulac Unsleep, absent vampire Lord of melancholy Vormspire, wore another.

An hour and a half had passed since Maglore last expended psychic effort on that powerful image, that abstract symbol of alien mathematics; during which interval he'd taken sustenance and satisfied . . . other appetites. Now replete and a deal more relaxed, he would try again.

Vormulac, yes.

So thinking, and closing his mind to everything else, he rested long, talonlike hands on the massy, gleaming, strangely twisted loop of gold, and sent his seer's probe winging west in search of the warrior-Lord Taintspore.

And in another moment . . .

Vormulac Unsleep's mood was black as his soul would be, if he had one. The flight out of Turgosheim and across the Great Red Waste into these unknown western parts had been arduous to say the very least; in fact and in proper perspective, it had been a hair-raising, nail-biting, apparently endless *nightmare* of a journey!

Of course, Lord Vormulac would never dream of admitting such to any of the lesser Lords (and certainly not to a Lady); throughout, he had appeared the Great Leader, entirely unshakable, utterly inscrutable: the warrior-Lord Vormulac of Turgosheim. But to himself . . . on several occasions he had wished that he'd never set out, and there'd been as many times again when he'd thought he would never see it through.

Known for his fits of melancholy as well as for his might, now that most powerful Lord of the Wamphyri looked more morose, withdrawn, and doomfraught than ever; yet at the same time—seated upright and solid as a rock in the saddle of his flyer, at the head of what *had been* an awesome army—he seemed more determined, too. For he'd made a vow of vengeance those three long years ago, after Wratha had flown the coop, and he wasn't about to deny himself the pleasure of sealing it now.

Vormulac was a huge man, almost seven feet tall. He was no strict adherent to Zolteism, but neither was he a glutton. He had not dealt his fellow Lords ill, not even in his prime. His forces had never attacked—other than in the defense of Vormspire—but when on occasion he had been *obliged* to make war, then it had been utter and ruthless; Vormulac was a hard man. Eighty years ago, he'd lain Gonarspire and Trogmanse to waste, bound their masters in chains and hung them out to dry where the sun's hot smelt would discover and dispose of them. Since when the gorge had stayed relatively free from internal feuding.

Despite the fact that Vormulac had ascended to Vormspire all of one hundred and twenty years ago, he kept his head shaved and wore the forelocks of a common thrall. A creature of lifelong habit, what had suited his old master Engor Sporeson in an earlier age continued to suit Vormulac to this day. His thralls, his lieutenants, and even his women were similarly cropped, and several younger Lords had emulated the fashion, not least Laughing Zack Shornskull of Zackspire.

Vormulac's forelocks, having lost most of their jet sheen through long years of sleeplessness, were iron-grey as if covered in dust; they were plaited and finished with lead weights which dangled onto his nipples. His eyes, not quite uniformly crimson but marked with yellow flecks, were close-set and deep-sunken in ochre orbits. His nose was long, slender, and sharply hooked at the bridge. Its convolutions and the gape of its nostrils were less marked than in most Lords, but its great length was a singular anomaly; its tip came down almost to the centre of his upper lip, lending his looks a hawkish severity.

Severe, yes, yet melancholy, too. Some said it was a lost love that had robbed him of seventy years' sleep; others had it that he feared to sleep, lest starting awake he might find himself a leper, as his old master before him. Only combine the two theories, and something of the truth would be known. Vormulac himself had mastered the art of *not* dwelling upon it . . . except when he slept. Which was why he didn't.

Nor had he slept this last sunup, but had weathered out an entirely wretched day in the shade of the barrier mountains, sitting in a cave with only the meat of trogs and a cup of vile mushroom wine for consolation; and thoughts of red revenge, of course. Against Wratha, whose fault it was that he was here at all.

Now, flying west again in the early hours of sundown, he found himself looking back on the misadventure—so far as it had proceeded—with something of relief, and thanking whichever star he was born under that things had not been worse. . . .

First the planning, which had not been of the best. But Vormulac's generals had thought: *If Wratha the Risen managed it in total secrecy, with mainly untried men and monsters, and no apparent effort all of a hundred and fifty sunups ago, then there can't be that much to it! How can we fail with all the thought and effort that* we're *putting into it, and having the choicest materials out of Sunside with which to work?*

Then, as if simply thinking these things had been enough, the very idea of failure had been put aside; thought and effort had become less than adequate; liaison and cooperation between the manses had broken down as the vampire Lords vied to create the finest contingent of men and fighting creatures for Vormulac's aerial army. The thrill or "glory" of the coming venture (and anticipation of its successful conclusion, or course) far outweighed any niggling doubts with regard to the possibility of failure. In short, the Lords and Ladies of Turgosheim were grown overconfident.

But contrary to their beliefs, and prior to Wratha's departure from the gorge, she *had* worked in close (albeit covert) liaison with her conspirators. And because their departure had been an escape from dire punishment, they'd put that much *more* effort into it. It had only looked easy by virtue of its simplicity:

A handful of aerial warriors and a dozen or so of lieutenants and flyers . . . not much in the way of logistical problems there; a fuelling stop in the western heights of the mountains, before attempting the Great Red Waste; finally the mighty leap westwards, into the unknown.

Simple, aye . . .

The differences had been these: that Wratha the Risen's party had been small, while Vormulac commanded a polyglot and potentially unruly army. That her constructs were comparatively light creatures and built for flight, because she had dispensed with weapons, ornamentation, and almost every other unnecessary encumbrance or accessory of war and death in favour of the basic requirements of life; while the warrior-Lord Unsleep's creatures were weighty, and armoured to the hilt for battle. And that while she pursued ambition, she was *herself* pursued out of frustration, revenge, and fear. Not only differences, but positive advantages—to the Lady, that is.

And one more advantage, which Vormulac was only now beginning to take into account: Wratha had fled *knowing* that she would be pursued. So that by now—

—Surely three years had been time enough for her to take adequate precautions? Wherever she was now—in whatever manse she called home—the place would be a fortress, be sure. But fortresses have fallen before, and so would this one when Vormulac found it. Then ... there *would* be war: a bloodwar, aye, if only to pay the Lady back for all of his troubles.

Now, in the eye of memory, the warrior-Lord reviewed those troubles, which had started as early as stage one: the refuelling stop on the westernmost jut of the eastern range ...

Wratha had stopped there, too, at the beginning of her flight into the west. After she'd gone, Vormulac had sent his lieutenants to check the place out. They'd found signs of her halt: spilled meal from her flyers' feedbags, beast droppings, various other signs. Yes, her creatures had refuelled themselves there ... and so had Wratha and her renegades, as witness the discarded clothing of several thralls. After she and her lads had drained the thralls of their lifeblood, then their cadavers would have gone to the warriors. There had been just four of those, one of which Vormulac remembered very well indeed.

The handiwork of Canker Canison, that had been a terrible construct. It had all but wrecked the Great Hall in Vormspire, and would have wrecked Vormulac and the others, too, if they hadn't escaped into bolt-holes! It had been as a direct result of *that* nightmare that the Lords had proved so zealous in the construction of their own warriors. But Lord Unsleep couldn't fault them there; he had built a Thing or two himself in the last three years. And not all of them successful, either.

But of the seventy fighting creatures that did finally set out that night from Turgosheim with Vormulac Taintspore, his fellow Lords and Ladies, and their one hundred and twenty lieutenants and thralls—*they* had been warriors . . . !

. . . *Aye* (he thought gloomily), *and two-thirds of them too hungry, too hot-blooded, too loaded down with armour-plate and all manner of fearsome but unwieldy appendages, too! Chitin-plated gouges, grapples, retractable claws . . . Huh!*

Just how unwieldy had been seen at that first landing.

Wratha's choice of a refuelling stop had been a flat summit, a mainly sheer-sided plateau, where the last of the peaks and rockpiles tumbled to the smoking ochre desert that formed a skirt around the Great Red Waste. For her purposes the place had been ideal, because she'd landed less than two dozen creatures in all. But as for Vormulac . . . a disaster! For he was attempting to land one hundred and seventy, and there simply wasn't room.

There might have been space enough, if the generals had proceeded in an orderly fashion. But as the Lords at the rear of the column had seen those at the front landing, so it had become apparent that the choicest of the laid-up provisions would go to the first down. In all likelihood, the *last* down would get nothing at all! And between here and Olden Starside in the unknown west—*if* that alleged Land of Plenty existed—there was nothing but the Great Red Waste; neither food of any sort, nor drink, nor any sustenance at all other than what they carried. Which meant the beasts, of course . . . and the men themselves.

Then, breaking ranks, *all* of the Lords and Ladies alike had vied to be first in line for food after Vormulac. And in the ensuing melee . . . the warrior-Lord himself had been fortunate not to get run off the edge of the plateau!

What a mess!

It *should* have been orderly, yes—but the Wamphyri are

greedy and territorial; each man or woman for him- or her-self, and to hell with the hindermost! They had practiced rattling their gauntlets, aye, and parading their creatures, the issue of their vats, but knew nothing of cooperation. Also, a good many of them were rivals; there were old feuds to be settled, and old scars still itching. Why, they would never have come together at all, if not for Vormulac's crusade. And what with all the jostling, the jibes and the taunting . . . the suddenly electric tension . . . the throb of hot blood . . . nerves balanced on a knife-edge . . . tempers fraying!

Flyers tilting this way and that, their vampire riders cursing, shouting, hauling on the reins; all desperate to discover a patch of dust in which to flop down. Warriors accidentally colliding as they made their approach runs, then doing it again, but deliberately, as finally the tempers—of men and beasts both—shattered into shards! *Wamphyri!*

And in the mist of the melee, the first bloody scuffle; then two, three . . . an uproar! While on the rim of the rock, many of the thralls, lieutenants, flyers, and warriors who were already down found themselves pushed into space as a massive tug-of-war over the provisions milled to and fro, this way and that. The plateau was a high one; some who fell from the rim (those of them skilled in meta-morphosis) had time to form airfoil shapes and save themselves. Most of the flyers survived, of course, and several of the warriors; but others injured in the fighting simply plunged to the scree and boulder bottoms, where for them the crusade came to an abrupt end . . .

Finally the dust had settled, and Vormulac stamped here and there, shouting, clouting, browbeating the rest into submission and demanding the presence of the idiot planner whose idea it had been to refuel here, en masse. That task had gone to Zestos Kalkas, a lesser Lord who now appeared to be absent. There was a man of his, however (Gaul Kalksman, a minor lieutenant), doing his utmost to look fierce as he stepped forward in answer to Vormulac's call. Then it had come out how Zestos and his senior lieu-

'tenants had been swept from the rim; Gaul had witnessed it with his own eyes, which now were nervous, wary.

"*Huh!* Then it appears you've ascended," Lord Unsleep had told him, without further ado.

"But . . . perhaps my Lord Kalkas is alive down there!"

"He *might* have been alive up here," Vormulac had at once growled. "But not for long! For *if* he were alive, I would bind him in chains myself and hurl him from the rim! The fool!" And after a moment's thought: "I have a suggestion . . ."

"Yes, my Lord?"

"Take a flyer, descend, find Zestos. Cut out his parasite and accept its egg."

At that Gaul's feral eyes had seemed to light with a red internal fire, preempting his actual ascension. "Yes, my Lord. Indeed!"

"And listen," Vormulac had told him. "You're lucky. You're one of his and I should kill you, too, but I need a man to lead his contingent—what's left of it!"

"Yes, my Lord." With which, Gaul Kalksman (Kalk*son*, now) had scurried off to find a flyer . . .

But at that, it hadn't worked out too badly. Three flyers and six warriors lost over the edge, four more of each damaged on landing, three Lords and some seven lieutenants either killed accidentally or slain in the fighting, along with perhaps fifteen thralls. As for those injured in the fray: they had been put to death, and so became part and parcel of the provisions they'd fought over. It seemed only right.

By then the sun had been well down; the hurtling moon was up; the refuelling had been attended to. And no time to spare, for no man knew how wide was the Great Red Waste, a hundred or a thousand, or *five* thousand miles. But all knew how long was sundown. Morning must not find them in flight, but flown over the wastelands and landed in the west. Then:

"We take off. *in order*!" Vormulac had shouted for everyone to hear. "Once up, spread out, make room. The sky is wide. But keep the same ceiling. I go first, and the rest follow on. Fainthearts ... may fall out now, go back to Turgosheim, keep old Maglore company. The blood we seek is only for the strong. You Lords are responsible for your men, as they are for their beasts, within your own contingents. During the journey, any who are lost through weakness ... are lost. Make good use of them before surrendering their scraps to the Great Red Waste. We go."

With which he'd lifted off on his flyer, found a thermal, and risen up until a band of orange light cracked the southern horizon. So much for altitude; any higher and they would catch up with the sun, and it with them!

So Vormulac had headed west, while behind him the whorl of his army had straightened itself out like the coils of some strange aerial snake. And before too long, the stench of acid vapours had come drifting up from the Great Red Waste.

Vormulac couldn't know it, but despite all of Wratha the Risen's advantages three years earlier, she too had experienced difficulties. Canker's warrior had been the most heavily armoured of her party's constructs, and it had used up a deal of energy and suffered some small damage in rescuing Wratha and the others from melancholy Vormspire: the landing, the fighting, the relaunching. But out over the Great Red Waste, the Thing had paid the price in full.

Its loss had scarcely been mourned (well, with the possible exception of the dog-Lord himself, and then not for very long); its vital fluids and flesh had served to fuel the rest of them on their way.

Likewise with Vormulac's army. For less than eight hours after setting out, Devetaki Skullguise had drawn up alongside and called in his mind: *Vormulac, it appears there's a small problem. A creature of mine is nearing exhaustion. Perhaps it was injured in all that huffing and puffing at the plateau. I thought it prudent to let it fall behind a little and so conserve its energy. What would you have me do?*

Devetaki had been wearing her scowling half-mask, ample evidence of her displeasure. But there had been nothing for it except the obvious answer. *Are any of your other constructs in need of sustenance, Lady? If so, bring them up front here. If not, then as you slip back to the weak one, be so good as to pass on the word . . .*

Devetaki had understood him well enough: since her warrior was doomed, best to let the others make use of it. And as she'd reined back to let the various Lords and Ladies pass her by, so she had informed them: *I'll be sending a weary creature up front; doubtless the extra effort will finally exhaust him. If any of your warriors would benefit from a good meal . . . you are welcome. Never let it be said that the mistress of Masquemanse is mean.*

And falling to the rear, she had ordered her tired beast to speed for the front, for:

We shall be landing soon, when for you there'll be tidbits galore! Propulsors throbbing, the thing had immediately spurted ahead . . . to its doom. For as the last of its propulsive gasses were burned, several larger warriors fell to and in short order incapacitated, separated, and finally devoured it. Only a well-gnawed skeleton and half-a-dozen sections of blue-glinting carapace had been left to go tumbling into the acid reek of the wastelands.

It was a scene that would be repeated many times, until towards the end even healthy creatures would be sacrificed in order that the rest might survive. A great many warriors, aye, so that now only thirty-seven were left. Flyers had been lost, too. Weary from inhaling the reek, they had choked, stiffened, gone spiralling into a bubbling red oblivion; and nothing for it but that their riders go with them, lieutenants and common vampire thralls alike.

But as for the rest, survive they had; for a night that seemed an eternity yet felt, paradoxically, too short by far. The Lords had food in their saddlebags, which they devoured. They had water in skins, which they drank. And when these had been used they unplugged cartilage stoppers in the knuckled spines of their flyers, to sip sparingly on vital fluids . . .

Like the Lady Wratha's party before them, some had slept while others maintained the course . . .

The stars had been like foggy ice chips on high, in the poisonous vapours rising from the open sore of the Great Red Waste . . .

Vormulac had despaired, if only to himself . . .

Far faint cries had come drifting up out of the fetid fog—like the wailing of souls in hell—as even more exhausted constructs descended to the red-smouldering death of the wastelands . . .

But as the first crack of hazy golden light appeared on the southern horizon, so Lord Unsleep had spied ahead a rising moon all bitten in half as if by some cosmic monster. And despite the fact that his view was obscured by fading fumes, he knew it was no monster gnawing at the moon but the spires of distant mountains. The barrier mountains of Olden Starside!

And straightening in his saddle, he'd sent back:

We've done it! The worst it over! We've crossed the Great Red Waste! Now spare your creatures and glide, for we need to lose height. No need to worry; these poisonous fumes are thinning, and there's only the sun to fear now.

"Only" the sun! But Lord Unsleep had known that his sky-snake's tail was many a mile long, and he'd wondered if they would all make it . . .

Not all of them had.

Many hours later, alighting in the shade of the barrier mountains, Vormulac had climbed a crag to a vantage point from which to gaze east and watch them come in. And peering through eyes still sore from the reek of the wastelands, he had seen a golden stain spreading on the higher peaks, and had known that a fan of deadly light was even now lowering itself as the sun commenced its tortuous climb up over Sunside's rim.

He actually watched while that fan swept lower and lower, and saw its beams dispersing the mists over the plains between the mountains and the rough red desert. But the mists were not all that those rays would disperse.

The men and beasts at the very tip of the sky-snake's tail didn't stand a chance. They were weary (unto death?); the flyers were exhausted and the warriors depleted of gasses and substance both.

Mainly they were drifting in, on membrane wings that no longer had any lift in them, that threatened collapse at any moment; or suspended from fluttering, half-empty buoyancy bladders, whose essence had been drained off to fuel their coughing, sputtering propulsors. They knew they should lose altitude, but in fact were fighting gravity. For once down there'd be no getting up again, just a series of inevitable crashes in the rusty red earth.

Forming the very tip of the tail, four men and flyers had herded a small knot of forsaken warriors from as many different contingents. The latter had been too tired even to squabble. Of these dozen men and creatures, the very last pair—being also the highest—had been first to succumb. Yellowed by sunlight, then browned, blackened, and incinerated to smoke and smoulder, the scorched debris that once was a flyer and rider had drifted to ochre earth. Then it had been the turn of a warrior; its gas bladders exploding, mantle bursting into flames, armoured body plummeting like a stone to shattering extinction. And finally a seething of smoke in the brightening sky, even an explosion or two, as an unrelenting sun caught up with the rest of them at a stroke.

Vormulac had felt no remorse, only annoyance that his army was so depleted . . .

They had harboured in trog caverns behind the foothills. Blood of the submen wasn't much to their liking, but beggars can't be choosers. The warriors weren't fussy, and the flyers were happy to subsist on lichens licked from the rocks. Rest was what they had needed most. Only Black Boris, who back in Turgosheim kept trog mistresses, had seemed truly happy with the way things were working out. Having taken a firm young female alive, Boris was soon in fine fettle; he had food and fanny all in one.

Exhausted beasts had been seen to as best possible and

given shelter in shallow caves; thralls, too. Had circumstances been different, common vampire thralls such as these might well have expected to become one with the provisioning. A good many lieutenants had died, however, and others had ascended to the seats of lost Lords. These thralls were lucky: they would replace dead or elevated lieutenants. Some had even been "promoted" that same day; their Lords had taken small measures of sustenance from them, in return transfusing copious doses of their own vampire essence. Thus a dual purpose was served.

And thus the seemingly interminable day had crept by in the dreary dank of trog caverns and the life-preserving shade of the rearing barrier mountains.

All of these things had been "seen," "felt," or "experienced" by the Seer-Lord Maglore in his talisman "shewstone" in Runemanse. These and others: such as the onset of night, and Vormulac's mounting-up and departure from the trog territories to journey still farther west; his soaring climb on bitter night thermals into the heights, from which to gaze down on a hitherto unknown Sunside—unknown to Lord Unsleep, at any rate. The way his previously repressed Wamphyri senses came awake! How he'd smelled strong Szgany flesh down there in the dark and the silence: the very matériel and even the ordnance of the bloodwar to come.

But there was something that Maglore had not seen, which Vormulac himself had never suspected. It was simply this: that one of two sentinel *Desmodus* bats, Wratha's familiars, had witnessed the arrival of the aerial army out of Turgosheim.

The Lady had positioned them some two hundred and fifteen miles apart: one at the very tip of the range, the other in the heights where the mountains burgeoned into a true barrier. The first creature had seen Vormulac's arrival, yes, but hastening west with its warning had *failed* to see the party of trogs out hunting in the grey twilight before the dawn. And it had only become aware of their nets, hurled skywards into its flitting path, when it was far too late.

Perhaps something of its shrill, piercing cry—of fear and warning both—had crossed the many miles to its sentinel twin, but not enough to act upon; not until the warrior-Lord's invading army became visible to it, too. Which was why Wratha got her warning late; for although her second creature had near-exhausted itself in the frenzy of its flight, still Vormulac was only hours behind when it alighted to the neck of the Lady's flyer . . .

By now (having seen the warrior-Lord on his way again) Maglore the Mage was eager to scan Nathan once more. Withdrawing from Vormulac's mind, he cast his probe again, but this time with a more youthful target in mind. And a more useful one? Possibly. As yet Maglore had no great knowledge of the legendary western Sunside; perhaps by now his "window" on that unknown world had settled down and was no longer doing . . . well, whatever it was that he had been doing.

And Nathan, so rapt upon what he *was* doing, that when Maglore oh-so-tentatively entered his mind he noticed nothing at all of his presence there . . .

It wasn't that Lardis Lidesci was a normally vicious or vindictive man, but that he never missed an opportunity to glean even the smallest piece of information on the doings, the comings and goings, the evil works of the Wamphyri. It was one of his mechanisms for survival. And like his father before him, Lardis was an excellent survivor.

Anna Marie English wasn't able to watch, which was hardly surprising. Lardis gave her into the care of a Szgany woman to be taken into the Rock and instructed in its ways. These were also the ways of survival, of course. Everything was survival with the Szgany Lidesci.

But Nathan, Trask, Chung, and the three cavers accompanied Lardis and Andrei Romani as first they examined and questioned the Szgany survivors of the hand-to-hand fighting, then interrogated a badly injured lieutenant and several vampire thralls. Before that, however, there was the burning of the dead—*all* of the dead, Szgany and vampires alike. And not on any funeral pyre, but in a blazing pit: a warrior-trap that was already an inferno. Without ceremony, the bodies were wrapped in sacking and bundled into the flames. First five of the Rock's brave defenders, while many old friends looked on with lowered heads and recalled other, perhaps better times; then, after a barely decent interval, fourteen dead (or temporarily incapacitated) thralls; finally the grotesque remains of seven lieutenants. As they burned, a handful of Lardis's men tossed resinous pine branches into the pit to fuel the fire.

But as the lieutenants' bodies and pieces went into the flames, Lardis had been quick to beckon his men back from the edge. This was just a precautionary measure; the dead lieutenants had all been young men, ex-Szgany, vampirized and promoted within the last three years; it seemed unlikely that there would be much of undead Wamphyri monstrousness in them. Nor was there, but better safe than sorry. The flames consumed them without incident.

Lardis was jubilant—albeit quietly so. Tonight's toll of vampires was far and away the best that the Szgany Lidesci had ever achieved. The cost, however . . . had been great. The lives of five good men and true were too much to pay even for a victory such as this. But the discovery of the Rock by Wratha and the vampire Lords . . . that was the worst blow of all. It took the edge off the Old Lidesci's triumph.

On the other hand, Nathan's return—and these fighting hell-landers he'd brought with him (for such they must surely be), *and* the incredible weapons they had brought with them—these were wonderful things! Indeed, there was nothing in the world Lardis would enjoy more than to sit down right here and now with Nathan and the newcomers and hear their story. Except . . . there was business he must see to first. The sort of business that wouldn't wait.

There had been men hurt in the hand-to-hand. Crossbows, rockets, and shotguns (when there'd been shells for the guns) were fine at a distance, but in any melee a Wamphyri gauntlet was superior. An ironwood bolt through the eye or heart may be a clean way for a vampire to go, but for a man to have his face ripped off, or to be disembowelled, or to lose a limb and bleed to death, is something else. That was how Lardis's five brave ones had died: trying to hold their minced guts in. And it was also why they'd been first into the fire: so that their women wouldn't see them like that. A man has his dignity.

As for questioning and examining the surviving defenders: that was another precautionary measure. It was always important to ensure that the men had not been injured in any way, especially by being bitten. For the poisonous bite of the Wamphyri is often quick-acting, and even the bravest man might find himself suddenly reluctant to admit of . . . well, a slight neck injury say . . .

The captured thralls were tied to crosses bedded in the earth, not for the sake of cruelty but because it was the best way of keeping watch over them. Even tied up, they could slip away like snakes into the thinnest ground mist. Their interrogation didn't take long; they hissed and spat and writhed, but answered no questions at all. Why should they, when they knew what was their lot? Perhaps if Lardis had the time he would be much more persuasive, but since the location of Sanctuary Rock was no longer a secret . . . the Old Lidesci had other plans for tonight. Well, and hadn't he always been a Traveller at heart?

Unemotionally—having been through all of this before, and knowing there was no alternative—he ordered the grimacing, squirming thralls put down as cleanly and painlessly as possible. Shot through their hearts point-blank and by marksmen, they never knew what hit them, nor ever felt the furnace heat of the firepit.

Finally it was the turn of the injured lieutenant, except "injury" was scarcely the word for the monstrous damage he had suffered. And unlike those who had gone to the fire before him, this one was no fledgling recruit. No, not by any means. A much older man—a changeling to the point that he might almost be Wamphyri—there was no question but that he had come out of Turgosheim along with Wratha and the others.

Lardis, Andrei, and Nathan looked up at him on his

cross, waiting for him to recover consciousness. But to Trask, Chung, and the others where they stood back among a crowd of silent, watchful Szgany, it seemed unlikely that he ever would. Perhaps at that Trask should have known better, for he at least had known his fair share of horrors such as this, albeit in another world.

. In the pulsating glow of the firepit, the crucified man was as gory a sight as could be imagined. He had been brought down by Andrei Romani, stopped by an explosive bolt shot into the muscle of his right shoulder. Either the bolt was faulty or the blast went awry, else he were surely a dead thing; but in any case the detonation had cost him his right arm and all the flesh of his right breast. His upper ribs were all sprung on that side and stuck out red and black, and above the empty socket and shattered shoulder, his face and neck were a blistered black fusion of scorched flesh.

But as the men on the ground waited, so finally the left eye opened, and the merest crack in the roasted meat where the right eye should be. And there *was* an eye in there: a blob of sulphur flecked with red, just like the left. Not quite Wamphyri, no, but he might have been if he'd lived. Except he knew he would *not* live, for Lardis Lidesci intended otherwise. And as he slowly became aware and lifted his head:

"Who are you?" Lardis wasted no time.

"Go fuck a shad!" the other wheezed, coughing blood and mucus. Unlike the thralls, he wasn't merely tied to the cross but was nailed there, truly crucified. Since his right arm was missing, silver wire had been looped under his chin to support his head. But it also constricted his throat and made it hard for him to speak. No ordinary man would even have tried.

Lardis shook his head. "I'm a man, not a thrall. I don't fuck shads."

"And I'm a *lieutenant*!" the other spat. "I have pride!"

"Very well, then—Lieutenant." Lardis nodded. "I'll ask you again: who are you?"

"Since I'm doomed anyway, it can't hurt to tell you,"

the other answered. "I'm Turgis Gorvisman, last lieutenant out of Turgosheim."

"What, Gorvi the Guile's man?"

"What of it?" Turgis struggled a little on his cross, then gasped and hung still. While full-fledged Wamphyri have ways of stilling their pain, their lieutenants are not so fortunate.

Lardis shook his head. "Just a pity you're not him, that's all," he said. "For I would dearly love to have Gorvi himself up there in your place!"

The other narrowed his one good eye, stared down on Lardis and said: "You'll be the Lidesci, then. Lardis the Chief."

"Aye," (again Lardis's nod), "and I fancy it was Gorvi who took my son."

"You didn't know for sure, then?" Turgis writhed a little, then coughed up more blood. "Well, now you do. The first time we raided on Settlement, aye. Gorvi took your son; I remember it well. He sent me down into the town with the others, while he attacked the house on the knoll. He likes to keep to himself, does Gorvi. Likes to keep out of trouble, too."

"And Jason—my son—is still there, in Wrathstack?" The Old Lidesci tried to keep the anxiety, the eagerness, the need to know out of his voice, but failed.

Turgis gagged, turned his head this way and that, and vibrated for a moment like a crippled snake against the upright of his cross. Urine smoked where it dribbled from under his clout. "This *con* . . . conversation is all very— ah! *Ah!*—very well. But it gains me nothing. I desire to be dead. Will you make it clean?"

Lardis, Andrei, even Nathan, all of them had heard much the same plea before. But this was important to Lardis. "Tell me the truth, and I'll make it clean."

"*Your* . . . your boy was a brave one, but he's dead."

Lardis closed his eyes and breathed a sigh—of agony, relief, who can say? "And . . . and was his death clean, too?"

"Clean, aye." The one on the cross nodded. "He tried to

escape, failed, climbed Wrathstack to a high place, jumped. He killed himself. He was *your* son, Lardis."

Perhaps he knew more, even a lot more, but Lardis was satisfied. Truth be known, he was even grateful. "And now you can die," he said. "Except . . . will *you* die cleanly?"

Turgis looked down on him. "For myself, I say yes: indeed I *welcome* it. But I have been with Gorvi for long and long. My blood is changed, even as I am changed."

Lardis, Andrei, Nathan, all three stepped back; and more yet, well away from the foot of the cross. Lardis nodded to men on the flanks. They lassoed both ends of the horizontal bar with good ropes, and waited. Others with crossbows came forward . . . but when Turgis saw them he commenced to writhe and spit again. He was tormented in two directions, tortured by pain and terror both. *He* wanted to die, but his blood didn't!

And: "Now!" said Lardis.

Three bolts flew home—straight to Turgis Gorvisman's heart. He cried out once, then flopped down on his nails and hung still . . .

. . . *For a moment!*

Then his belly and chest *burst* open, and a nest of white worms lashed and squirmed amidst the crimson of his innards! A thing of white siphon arms like some grotesque aquatic anemone, it tossed the rags of his flesh aside, drew blood from faltering veins, sprayed scarlet all about as if pissing on unseen foes! Indeed it *tried* to—but they were out of harm's way.

The men on the ropes waited no longer but hauled on the cross until it toppled lengthwise into the firepit. And very shortly, a protracted hissing and a plume of black smoke were all that remained of Turgis Gorvisman . . .

In Runemanse, Maglore the Mage slowly withdrew his hands from the Möbius sigil, his mind from Nathan's, his seer's probe back across those thousands of miles to its home in his vampire mentality. And for a long while he simply sat there with the pictures of what he had seen gradually fading in his inner eye ... but not in his memory.

Of the things he'd seen: he might easily have guessed some of them in advance, certainly with regard to Vormulac's crusade. But others would have been quite impossible to imagine; impossible to believe, if he hadn't seen them with his own eyes. Well, through the eyes of another, at least. Nathan's *mind* might well be obscured, but his eyes were crystal clear. Maglore didn't have to know what he was thinking to see what he was seeing.

In Olden Sunside/Starside, the Szgany fought back. What's more, they sometimes won! Now that Nathan was back (from wherever he had been these months), perhaps they would win that much more frequently. Maglore had feared the return of a great army one night, out of the west. Maybe he would be wiser to fear the return of just one man. Maybe he should never have let that man go in the first place.

But what had Nathan been except a strange Szgany youth, a weird, blond-haired, blue-eyed pet, a freakish familiar? So it had seemed. And now ... a mistake?

There again, Maglore comforted himself, the man who never made a mistake never made anything. On the other hand, neither had he lived to regret it ...

PART FOUR:

FURTHER INCURSIONS— FACTIONS— SKIRMISHES— COUNTING COUP— NATHAN

I

E-Branch—Turchin—Tzonov

Fifteen hours after the battle at the Rock—in a parallel world beyond the Starside Gate, a world where it was 10:00 P.M. in London and midnight in Moscow—three heads of department had a meeting of sorts at the London headquarters of E-Branch. The three were the Minister Responsible, whose name was known to a small handful but never used; Ian Goodly, temporary head of E-Branch; and Gustav Turchin, premier of the loosely named and *very* loosely connected Soviet Alliance, also known as the USS or Union of Soviet States. A fourth person was present—not in any official capacity but because she was the only person now living on Earth who had ever been to Sunside/Starside, which was in the main the subject of the meeting.

Ian Goodly had asked Zek Föener to be there, but she had already decided to fly in on the first plane out of Zante. The others had made no objection. Perhaps they might have if they had known what was on Goodly's mind. Or perhaps, on the other hand, they'd made no objection because they *did* know what was on his mind, for something of the sort was on theirs, too.

Introductions had been brief to the point of perfunctory; communications were secure; Premier Turchin's larger-than-life image was on the big screen of the Ops Room's central console. The other three were seated in padded swivel chairs within the console's operational perimeter.

Sixteen hundred miles away in Moscow, Turchin was looking at them on just such a screen.

The Russian premier was short, blocky, and looked unshakable as a sumo wrestler. It was his image, and not only on the screen but also in real life. Considering all the problems of the massive territory he presided over, he *had* to look that way. What with escalating food riots in Kazakhstan, terrorism in the Ukraine, Mafia-style gang wars in Moscow itself, territorial disputes far and wide, and the accelerating decay of law and order just about everywhere, he must at least give the *impression* of toughness. His lips were thin and compressed under an angular nose; his dark eyes were restless under bushy black eyebrows that crushed together in a frown; the corners of his mouth were turned down—because he hated being in the wrong. But then, so did they all. And not a man of them had had anything good to report. Indeed they each of them felt a certain relief if not downright satisfaction at the discomfort of the others.

Zek Föener knew this, of course, and thought: *The Germans have a word for it:* Schadenfreude.

Each of the men had stated his position—or in effect, made his confession, if not of guilt, then of incompetence in one degree or another—but also knew that the others were at least equally to blame. Laying blame wasn't the purpose of the exercise, however, but rather untangling the very complicated skein of things back into something of order. It was imperative that they unravel that skein, and quickly, for a frightful pattern was beginning to emerge.

"Briefly, then," said Turchin, after a silence that had already lasted for several long seconds. "Clearly I was right to take my softly, softly approach with Turkur Tzonov. For as I've stated previously, I was already on to him and it was only a matter of time. As it now works out, it was your pushing me that speeded up the process. In moving my own men into Perchorsk, I alerted Tzonov and made him jump the gun. In one way a bad thing, perhaps, but in another . . . ?" He shrugged and looked to the others for their opinions.

"Meaning he's out of it now, lost in another world?" This was Goodly. But the precog's face was sour as a lemon. "Sir, I hate to remind you, but that is a nightmare scenario: that Tzonov or someone like him should pass through the Perchorsk Gate into Starside. Wonderful if we could be sure he or they would stay there, but terrifying to think they might come back . . . and what they might come back as!"

"Premier," the Minister cut in. "I know you've heard much the same thing before, but do you take our meaning? Mr. Goodly and I—everyone at E-Branch—we have had to deal with this sort of thing before; we *know* what we're talking about. You've come in on this a lot later, whereas we have been with it from the beginning, for a great many years. And you must never forget that while there are two routes into this parallel world, there are also two ways out. Now you've let Tzonov go in there with a platoon of trained men, and—"

"—As you have 'let' your Mr. Paxton go in!" It was Turchin's turn to cut in. "And with just as many trained men, if not more! What's more, it appears Paxton has brought down the roof of that underground river behind him, however temporarily. Also, I didn't 'let' Turkur Tzonov do anything. Why, the way you have it, anyone would think he had my authority!"

"I'm not accusing," the Minister held up his hands placatingly, "just stating facts. But now we have Ben Trask, David Chung, Anna Marie English, and a bunch of potholers, *and* a half-company of paramilitaries, lost between two worlds. And that's too many. Too many of them who can and just *might* come back as vampires! And if it's Tzonov? What, with his powers and ambitions?"

"And if it's Trask, Chung, or English, with theirs?" Turchin countered. "Or this Nathan, this . . . this Necroscope?"

Zek Föener said, "This is getting us nowhere. Surely the point is that good men and bad ones have crossed over, and it's the bad ones we don't want to come back. Or if they do, we want to know that we can stop them when they get here. Have I got it right? And isn't it also that we'd like to get our friends, the good ones, out of there if that's at all possible? I mean, get them out unchanged? Get them out as men?"

"Zek has said it all," Goodly's high-pitched voice fluted out. "We know what's on your mind, sir, and we agree with you: those Gates must be closed, and this time permanently. But not before we've got our friends back. What happens to Tzonov, Paxton, and their men ... we could care less. But we do care about our friends."

Turchin nodded. "So despite the fact that you've just this minute told me too many of our people have gone through already, now you're contemplating sending even more. Is that it?"

"Yes." The Minister nodded. "But a joint effort, our best shot. And if it doesn't work ... time enough then to close the Gates permanently."

"Huh!" Turchin's mouth turned down more yet. "Oh, yes: a joint effort ... but only because I have the Gate, eh? Because this Mr. Paxton of yours has blocked the way to the one in Romania?" He looked pointedly, searchingly at the Minister. "Now tell me, don't you think it is time I knew a little more about this man? Oh yes, I know: CMI—for your eyes only—and definitely *not* for mine! But aren't we in a little too deep for all that cloak-and-dagger stuff now? There's no more cold war, and certainly not between we four."

The Minister was suddenly looking uncomfortable—very. "But I still can't talk about—"

"Oh yes you can," Goodly told him. "The premier is right. The stakes are too high for cover-ups. E-Branch was less than diplomatic in its eagerness to get a hold of Nathan, and Premier Turchin was less than effective at stopping Turkur Tzonov dead in his tracks. We've owned up to our errors, so now it's your turn. Because I have to admit, I'm interested in Paxton, too. I thought he'd stopped being a thorn in our side a long time ago, when Harry left us. And now this. But let's face it, in your official capacity you have to be 'responsible' for a lot more things than just

E-Branch. So let's have it all out in the open, and then maybe we can move on."

The Minister took a deep breath, said, "Very well." And after a moment's thought:

"Originally, Paxton was my idea. A bad one, as it turned out. He had a talent—telepathy, in which he was very gifted—but he was too much of a loner to fit snugly into an organization such as E-Branch. And the fact of the matter is that I needed a watcher to watch the watchers. E-Branch looked out for my country's security, among other things, and did a wonderful job if it. But being what it was, there was always the chance that someone in the Branch might go rotten. It wasn't impossible by any means; after all, it had happened before—and to a Head of Branch, at that!—the time Norman Wellesley turned traitor. Talents such as E-Branch employed for good . . . mighty conceivably be employed in the opposite direction, and devastatingly; or for personal gain, whatever.

"Paxton would be a Branch operative, responsible to Head of Branch, naturally, but mainly responsible and reporting to me. This wasn't just my idea but fitted in well with the thinking of others higher up. So Paxton entered E-Branch. To make a long story short, he didn't fit in; the others sniffed him out almost from square one; he especially fell foul of Ben Trask, and more especially of Harry Keogh.

"Paxton . . . fucked up!" The Minister shrugged apologetically. "Excuse the expression, but right now it seems the only one that fits. Rightly or wrongly, he was responsible for the death of the then Head of Branch, Darcy Clarke, and would have been responsible for the Necroscope's death, too, except Keogh was a different kettle of fish. But we mustn't forget that at the time we were *trying* to kill Keogh! So in a way it wasn't a personal thing: you could say it was Paxton's duty to kill him. But Keogh wasn't about to die, not that easily. Paxton failed; the Necroscope was multitalented and got into his enemy's telepathic mind; he did something to him that killed his talent, robbed him of his mind-reading skill.

"Afterwards, Paxton came to see me. He was a broken man, and I have to admit to feeling partly responsible . . ." The Minister paused and shuffled uncomfortably, but in a little while continued:

"Remember, I *am* responsible for E-Branch: not only for what the Branch does, but also for its security. And Geoffrey Paxton knew a hell of a lot about the organization and all its members. I thought it would probably be a good idea to retain a measure of control over him, to continue to be his paymaster. After all, it's unusual for a dog to bite the hand that feeds it. That was my reasoning, anyway . . .

"There was an opening in CMI. I got him work there in an administrative capacity, watched him for five years until eventually I was satisfied he'd settled down and wasn't going to be a problem. But CMI has its own command and control structure—and its own rules. One of which is that when a man gets promoted to command level, he also gets a change of name; it's a simple security measure. I had already lost track of Paxton, but would have anyway as he went up in the world."

Goodly asked: "How far up?"

The Minister glanced at him coldly, then back at Turchin on-screen. He took another deep breath and said, "As an organization, CMI is split three ways. From the bottom up: Administration; Operations; Command, Control, and Instruction. Paxton performed so well on the command level that they were reluctant to let him work in a field capacity. He persisted in volunteering, however, and eventually got a transfer—and yet another new name: would you believe Smith? No one outside CMI could keep track of him after that, which is the whole idea, of course. CMI Ops has three branches, three officers commanding. And Paxton, or 'John Smith' . . . is now one of them."

"It didn't take you long to find out about all of this. About Paxton, I mean." Goodly's tone of voice sounded close to accusing, and the Minister at once rounded on him.

"Mr. Goodly, you've known me for more than twenty years! Is there no trust left?"

"Just recently? Damn little!" Goodly snapped.

"Gentlemen," Turchin said, holding up his hands.

And Zek added: "Let's keep it impersonal. If you fight now you'll only be wasting time. And it's not our time to waste but Ben's, David's, and all the others."

"Listen," the Minister told all three, a hint of desperation showing in his voice, "ever since I found out that CMI were interested in the Branch over and above what one would normally expect—and *especially* interested in Nathan—I've been trying to discover what was going on. Goodly," he turned to the other. "Wasn't it I who warned you they'd be coming for Nathan here at HQ? Look, Paxton is his own boss within the organization . . . well, more or less. I mean there is an overall officer commanding—but he no more suspected Paxton than anyone else. The raid on the HQ and the trouble at Radujevac were the first he knew of it. Paxton was doing his own thing, don't you see?" The Minister paused to mop his brow, and after a moment continued:

"Paxton has a flat in the city. We've checked it out, and at last we're beginning to understand. It's full of stuff on E-Branch, the full range of the Branch's talents; on Harry Keogh, the Necroscope's origins and what he was capable of; and on the Gates at Perchorsk and Radujevac, almost everything you have on file right here at HQ. Remember, Paxton worked here! He didn't have to lift any of this stuff; he was required to *know* it! He knew Harry Keogh well enough, for sure!"

Goodly frowned. "An obsession?"

"I think so." The Minister had cooled down a little. "He wanted his talent back. Harry Keogh had robbed him of his telepathy, and he wanted it back again. A vampire took his talent away from him, so perhaps a vampire could return it. And Paxton knows there are vampires in Starside . . ." This time the Minister thought he was finished, but Goodly didn't.

"So he was interested in Nathan, the son of Harry

Keogh. But . . . how did he find out that Nathan had come over? I mean, that he'd come through the Gate into Perchorsk?"

The Minister slumped in his chair. "Yes, you're right. I had to tell CMI. I mean, I *had* to! E-Branch and CMI are all we have left in the line of national security. If anything was to go wrong we would need a backup and CMI would be it. So I had to bring them in on it. And of course Paxton got to know about it; it switched him on; it was what he'd been waiting for. Now he could stop playing and start pursuing his real goal, to get his talent back. In this world . . . or in some other."

Turchin was looking mystified. "But if he knows about the Radujevac Gate—if all he wants to do is cross into Starside—why hasn't he tried it earlier?"

The Minister threw his hands in the air. "I don't know! Maybe he wanted to be sure. Maybe he was waiting until he had a full hand. Maybe the rest of it was literally an obsession, just a crazy idea he was playing about with—until he found out about Nathan: the son of Harry Keogh, the man who'd caused all of his problems in the first place.

"It must have seemed too good to be true; it confirmed what Paxton had always suspected, for another Necroscope had come into our world out of Sunside/Starside. And now he, Paxton, was tired of waiting. If he wanted to get his talent back—and maybe other talents, too—he knew where he had to go. But there could also be a revenge motive. He'd failed to kill Keogh, so maybe he could get his boy instead. But not until he had what he wanted out of him. Just how he would go about that, I can't say—and maybe Paxton can't either! Maybe he's playing by ear. Anyway, beyond this point it's all conjectural and you're as wise as I am. The rest of it is known . . ." The Minister was through.

"All very pat," said Goodly softly, after a while.

"You don't believe me?" The Minister looked at him again.

"Yes, I do—because my talent tells me nothing is going to change around here. You're going to be the Minister

Responsible for quite some time to come. Which also means that whatever you've done wrong, or mistakenly, was done with the best of motives. Because if it wasn't . . . the Branch has a knack of dealing with its enemies."

Turchin spoke up. "Do you threaten your superior?"

Goodly looked long and hard at the screen. "No." He shook his head. "Not a threat but a promise. And if you're unwilling to help us out of this, I make you the same promise. Look, it's quite obvious that you're a good man. Ben Trask thinks so, anyway, and that's good enough for me. You are trying to help your country, and we're trying to help our friends. But neither side can succeed alone. So in helping us you'll be helping yourself, because if you don't . . . well come what may, I personally guarantee that E-Branch won't be helping *you* out of anything again. Not ever."

Finally Turchin smiled. "That kind of loyalty means something to me. It's my kind of loyalty! But you know, Mr. Goodly, my entire country expects *my* loyalty. And between the three of you, you've made it all too plain where my duty lies. The Radujevac Gate is closed, for the moment. And now I believe we must close the one in Perchorsk, too."

Zek was on her feet at once. "But not until Ben Trask and the others are out!"

Turchin shook his head. "I can't promise that. There will have to be a time limit on it."

"But you won't stop us from going in?" Her gasp—the way her face lit up—told Turchin a great deal.

Again he smiled. "No, I won't stop you. Indeed, you'll get all the help I can give you! It won't be like the last time you went through into Starside, Miss Föener." And as quickly as it had come, his smile fell away. "How things have changed, eh?"

"For some, maybe." Goodly was quick off the mark. "Unfortunately not for others. Have you forgotten so soon? Siggi Dam was forced through that Gate, too. But we'll be damn lucky to find her!"

And frowning thoughtfully, Zek said: "Or unlucky?"

The Minister Responsible was now much more at ease, however. "Yes," he quickly put in, "but that was Turkur Tzonov's doing. Things *have* changed, and for the better, due mainly to the efforts of Premier Turchin." And then, more businesslike: "Very well, sir, you'll set a time limit. And upon its expiry the Gate will be closed. But how will you do it? I mean, it's been tried before, you know."

Turchin shook his head. "No, they tried to *destroy* it— from within, with nuclear weapons! But I said we'll *close* it, and we will—under a million tons of rock! You can thank your Mr. Paxton for the idea. *He* may have made a very temporary thing of it, but my solution will be permanent. Surely nothing of flesh and blood can withstand the weight of a mountain?"

"You'll bring the roof down on the place?" Goodly pictured the Perchorsk complex: that vast, spherical cavern at its core. Riddled with magmass wormholes, the whole place could easily be made to collapse in upon itself—and upon the Gate, blocking it forever. "But how much time will you give us?"

"How much time will you need?"

Zek ventured: "Three days?"

Turchin shrugged, seemed bemused. "Certainly, my dear. But . . . will that be enough?"

"Three, er, *Starside* days?" Returning his shrug, she tried to look innocent and failed.

"Three weeks!?" Now Turchin was plainly staggered. "After what you've told me about that place, the dangers it harbours?"

But the Minister Responsible was nodding. "They might well need all of that and more, yes," he agreed.

Eventually Turchin gave in. "As you will, twenty-one days. And when will your party set out?"

"Tomorrow," Goodly answered, "or the next day at the very latest." And despite the fact that he was cringing inside, he doggedly deciphered a brief, echoing precognitive glimpse of the future. *Tomorrow or the day after, it's got to be. After that, and for as far as I can see right now,*

*there will be nothing much left for us here. Not for me and
Zek, anyway . . .*

All of which conversation had taken place some fifteen
hours after the battle at Sanctuary Rock. By no means a
protracted period, not in the whirl of political and diplomatic activity following on the debacle at Radujevac. But
in the world of the vampires that same fifteen hours had
seemed a long, long time indeed. A great deal had happened there, involving some politics but almost nothing of
diplomacy . . .

Turkur Tzonov, along with Staff Sergeant Bruno Krasin
and his somewhat reduced section of thirteen men—not including the effeminate yet sadistic locator Alexei Yefros,
who but for his talent might best be classified "excess
baggage"—had passed through the Perchorsk Gate some
two and a quarter hours *before* Nathan and his party entered the Radujevac Gate. Therefore it might logically be
concluded that they would arrive in Starside first. But in
the context of abstract space-time mathematics, considering the complexities of white, black, and grey holes, and
passageways between worlds and indeed universes in general, there was sufficient disparity that they arrived last.
Even in Earth's mundane science, it is accepted that a
straight line is not the shortest distance between two
points. In any case, Tzonov and his men had gone on foot
carrying their weapons, while the Necroscope's party had
been "conveyed" between worlds and all of their equipment with them.

The fighting between Gorvi the Guile's warrior and
lieutenants and Nathan's party had been over for something more than an hour when Tzonov's section emerged
from the uppermost of the Starside Gates; emerged into
starlit night, naturally, and stepped down from the crater
rim onto the eerie, foreboding, blue-tinged boulder plains.
It was a stroke of bad luck, but Tzonov had always known
that the chance of it being sunup was only a little better
than two to one against.

On the other hand, Tzonov's men were trained and their egomaniac leader "knew" that Starside's vampire men and creatures could be stopped. All it took was firepower, and he had plenty of that. The once-head of Russia's E-Branch wasn't looking for that sort of confrontation, however, not at this time and certainly not on Starside; his coming here at all had been a course of last resort, which he had been forced to take. And that in turn meant that the sooner he made his way through the great pass into Sunside and safety the better. To conquer and convert a world, first conquer its weakest inhabitants.

Tzonov's knowledge of the vampire world was rudimentary, but he did know that the Gate stood close to a pass through the barrier mountains. Standing at the base of the crater wall, and shielding his eyes from the glare of the Gate, he scanned carefully along the silhouette of the star-limned range of towering peaks and high plateaux until he spied a deep cleft a little to the east of his location. It must be the pass, where the mountains were split to their roots. And as Krasin lined up his suddenly silent men in three ranks, Tzonov pointed out the way for him. Setting out, Alexei Yefros kept pace with Tzonov a short distance behind the squad.

Yefros was a thin-faced weasel of a creature, a misogynist with bright, narrow, blackbird eyes, a thin nose and lips, and a very ugly sadistic streak. His hair was shiny black and stuck flat to his scalp as if painted there. His reflexes were fast, his movements quick, nervous but rarely fumbling. Tzonov had looked into his mind on a number of occasions and knew it for a cesspool; the man's sexual proclivities were . . . unusual, to say the least.

Tzonov had never made friends easily, and Yefros was not a man he would have chosen anyway. But the locator had been in Perchorsk when Gustav Turchin made his move, and knowing which side his bread was buttered, he'd fled with Tzonov and the rest to the Gate at the core of the complex. Anyway, they were espers together and Yefros much admired Tzonov, which was why the latter suffered his company. Also, there could be no question but that as a locator Yefros was one of the best; a fact that he was now able to prove.

"Your 'alien' is here," he told Tzonov. "There can be no mistaking his signal; he throws off those esoteric numbers and symbols of his like a dog shedding fleas!" He nodded his head west and a little south, almost at right angles to their direction of travel. "He's that way, across the mountains."

"Huh!" Tzonov grunted. "He's on Sunside with the Szgany—or Gypsies to you. But you waste your talent on that one. Oh, I know, you found him easily enough up there in the Urals; but it won't be so easy the next time. Nathan had to go on foot then, but no longer. He is a Necroscope and has his father's talents. We want to get somewhere, we walk. But he ... simply goes there. He can be here, there, everywhere; you'd get dizzy just looking for him! You are a locator and I'm a telepath, and our talents come in very handy. But his are amazing—and deadly! That's the reason I issued that order on the way in here, that he's to be shot on sight."

As he finished speaking there came a weird hissing and a coughing rumble from somewhere to the left and a little behind them, an animal *articulation* as opposed to any kind of mechanical sound. Signalling the squad to keep a low profile, Bruno Krasin at once scaled a jagged, leaning boulder, put nite-site binoculars to his eyes, and scanned the land eastwards and to the rear. In another moment, as the noise sounded again, Krasin's jaw fell open in a silent gasp and he signalled Tzonov to join him. The squad kept going as Tzonov climbed up beside his senior man, while at the foot of the boulder Yefros waited nervous as a cat in the shadows.

"What is it?" Tzonov whispered, taking the binoculars from his 2/IC. In his perception, Bruno Krasin was the perfect military underling; the blood of Cossack forefathers ran strong in him. Dark-skinned, wiry, long-limbed, and as fit as Tzonov himself, Krasin was tall, thirtyish, square-jawed, hard-eyed. As a boy he had been indoctrinated in the ways of an obsolete ideology by his hard-line

Communist father, an ex-officer of the KGB. It was entirely in keeping that Krasin was one of Tzonov's most trusted men.

Now he hissed a warning: *"Shh!"* but offered no other reply. He scarcely needed to; Tzonov would have to be blind not to see the thing. His own gasp was audible—indeed visible—as his breath plumed in the cold night air and the horizontal sweep of his binoculars jerked abruptly to a halt. Then:

"A warrior!" he breathed, cold sweat gleaming on his brow. Until now the thing had been hidden by the terrain; it lay in a slight depression, in the lee of a cluster of boulders where Gorvi the Guile had left it. Tzonov could make out the heaving motion of scales as the thing breathed, the jetting of hot air through nostrils six inches wide, the glimmer of starlight on chitin. *"We had better get after the men, Bruno,"* he whispered. *"And from now on the order is absolute silence!"*

"What is it?" Yefros called up to them, his nervous voice echoing out and away. As if in answer, they heard for the third time that primal, threatening rumble of sound. And magnified in the lenses of the nite-lites, Tzonov saw an armour-plated, prowlike head lift listlessly from the earth, and a flicker of eyes like scarlet lamps in the—face?—of the disturbed monster.

Tzonov handed the binoculars back to Krasin, glanced down once, furiously at Yefros, and jumped. Landing expertly, soundlessly in the dust, he straightened up and grabbed the locator by the throat, cutting off any further questions. And: *"Fool!"* he hissed. *"Locator? Oh, and do you want to be located? If you would go on living . . . keep . . . fucking . . . quiet!"* Releasing the other, he thrust him away and told him: *"Catch up with the section—but quietly!"*

As Yefros threw a narrow-eyed, accusing glance at his superior and stumbled away rubbing at his throat, Krasin came down from his observation point. In a barely audible whisper he said, *"I think the thing's asleep! We may have disturbed it a little, that's all."*

They hurried to catch up with the rest, and in the blue-tinged night of Starside made all possible speed for the mouth of the pass. From behind but gradually fading, the uneasy rumbling of the warrior followed them most of the way.

In the pass, several surprises were waiting. Because of the low trajectory of the sun and the elevation of the barrier range, it had been night on Starside for some hours now; but it soon became apparent that on Sunside darkness had fallen much more recently.

Following a barely discernible trail through the scree of shattered boulders tumbled from the heights, in something less than an hour the squad passed through a dogleg defile and saw ahead . . . the very last trace of a sunset? Strange, until Tzonov remembered that a day and night in the vampire world were the equivalent of a whole week in his. The sun *had* set on Sunside, but a slowly fading crack of amethyst light yet remained to show where it had sunk down out of sight. Pale though that glow was, it threw the walls of the pass and the distant crest of a rising saddle into silhouette. And in so doing it became, as it were, the "Light at the end of the tunnel" for Tzonov's men. This world, even this pass into Sunside, had seemed full of morbid alien auras; rightly so. But now in the glow of this faint crack of light the spirits of the men were lifted; they even began to exchange small talk—albeit in whispers.

The second surprise was nothing of nature but an artifact, perhaps of men. But Tzonov, who knew some few things at least about this vampire world, had his doubts. For some time he had been keeping himself apart from Yefros, walking at the head of the section with Krasin. Now he called for the locator to join them, and in the light of electric torch beams they picked out the rough-hewn features of a towering edifice.

Here, where the bed of the gorge had narrowed to a bottleneck at the foot of sheer canyon walls, the east face had been carved into a rearing keep or observation post ideally sited to guard the pass; or perhaps it was a Wamphyri way station, where lieutenant slave-takers had rested during the long trek back to Starside with Szgany captives. Tzonov's understanding, however, was that the last members of the Old Wamphyri had died out sixteen years ago when nuclear missiles had been fired into Starside from Perchorsk. Which meant that this castle could only be a relic of old times and no longer in use.

But on the other hand . . . Tzonov *had* seen a warrior creature back there on the plain of boulders, and he'd had it from Siggi Dam how Nathan had been punished, even banished from Sunside/Starside, by a new breed of Wamphyri. Indeed, it had been one of Tzonov's fears (ostensibly, at least) that Nathan might be a spy for vampire masters, sent to check out the lie of the land before the Lords themselves came through. Also, as Tzonov and the section had climbed the foothills gradient to the pass, he and Bruno Krasin had paused and turned for a moment to gaze out over Starside. Far in the northeast they'd spied a distant stack, and Tzonov knew that he hadn't imagined those flickering lights and the smoke going up. There might not be as many of the Wamphyri as before, but there could be no denying that they were here. And . . . it was sundown, their time.

Tzonov shrugged off a feeling of foreboding, dismissing it like an itch between his shoulder blades, and gave his attention to the great gaunt keep. In any case, he felt sure his men had the measure of anything they might find here. Nothing that lived could possibly face up to their weapons. Except . . . he'd seen film of the early Perchorsk encounters, and now remembered some of the *things* that had come through into the core. They had been stopped, yes, but it hadn't been that easy . . .

The men were waiting for him to say something. He turned to Yefros and asked, "Well, what do you make of it?"

The locator was peering at the castle built into the face of the cliff, concentrating upon it, searching *through* its massive walls. Nervously alert, birdlike, his shining black eyes moved from feature to feature, getting the feel of it.

He took in its awesome starlit gauntness, its texture of blue-gleaming stone (which looked and *felt* more like bone), the inhuman soullessness of bleak, frowning facades; its battlements carved of solid rock, notched into gaping embrasures, or merlons thrusting up into towers and turrets; its flying buttresses, and the menacing chutes of its gargoyle corbels.

"Well?" Tzonov said again.

Torch beams reached out, swept up and up the face of the great keep. Ledges in the virgin rock had been carved into massive steps, causeways climbing from one level to the next. Vertiginous arches made bridges to parts of the architecture that were otherwise inaccessible, where the overhanging face jutted or generally obstructed; cowled window holes gloomed like dark eyes in the star-silvered stone, frowning down on the midgets ogling from the shadows.

"Well?"

"Wait," Yefros muttered, peevishly. He still hadn't forgiven Tzonov, and wanted him to know it. Also, he wanted his talent appreciated. Why should Tzonov get all of his admiration, while Alexei Yefros got nothing in return?

Looking into Yefros's black eyes, Tzonov read the locator's thoughts, his disappointment: that his superior had such scant regard for him. Maybe in the future he should treat him more kindly—while he needed him, anyway. But for the time being: he knew that Yefros was doing his job, that he was diligently "searching" the keep, and so kept his peace. And the locator continued his mental exploration.

The structure started maybe fifty feet up the cliff face, halfway to the top of a lone, projecting stack. In the chimney between cliff and pillar, stone steps were visible zigzagging upwards to the mouth of a domed cave. Presumably this cavern entrance was extensive, with its own passageways into the keep proper. Higher still, the fortifications spread outwards across the face of the cliff like a weird stone fungus, covering Nature's efforts with the lesser but more purposeful works of—men? Well, men of sorts.

But plainly the builders of the keep weren't here now. No figures moved on the battlements or on the stairways; no lights shone in the windows, turrets, or high balconies. The place was deserted, which Yefros now confirmed:

"No one is in there. It's empty. But there are—I don't know—echoes?"

"Echoes?" Tzonov waited.

Yefros shrugged. "It's as if the keep itself were undead. As if the very stones waited . . ."

"But you sensed, or located, no one, nothing?"

Yefros looked puzzled, undecided, even harassed. But finally he answered, "No, I located—no one." It was the first time Tzonov had seen him uncertain of his talent.

By now Tzonov was convinced that the place was even more ancient than he'd at first thought. In the old times there had been wars between the Wamphyri Lords, bloodwars, when this keep would have been a fortress proper. It certainly seemed unlikely that a structure like this—so well fortified and apparently impregnable— had been built to fend off common Szgany tribesmen! But there was no reason why "common" men couldn't defend it.

"That's our refuge till morning," he said. "Which in turn means we have three days here, Earth time." And turning to Krasin: "See to it."

Krasin gathered the squad to him in a semicircle, allowed those who wished to smoke to do so, told them: "The place seems deserted. In you go, search and secure— but carefully! Sort out defensive positions, and prepare a roster for guard duties. Then back out here to gather fuel. Among this rubble there are trees fallen from the heights. Gather wood and let's have some fires going. Then we'll break out the rations. Any questions? No? Then get to it . . ."

At its base, where the stack stood free of the cliff and formed the keep's foundation stone, it was surrounded by a wall whose ends joined up with the cliff face. The wall was of massive masonry, stood twelve to fifteen feet high, and was crowned with merlons and embrasures. Every other merlon had been shaped into a stone dragon, with a gaping mouth that formed a circular corbel chute. But these dragons were of no mundane design; they had the lean bodies of wolves poised to leap, the folded wings of bats, and the faces . . . of men. Well, of monsters at least.

Huge, ages-blackened, iron-studded gates leaned open on rusted hinges. Embellished with the same awesome dragon motif, their welcome seemed cynical to say the least. The squad went through them at the run in teams of four: one left, one right, two covering; a breathless pause of five seconds to secure positions, then a leapfrog movement forward as the next team followed on. Tzonov, Yefros, and Krasin came on behind, moving from one secured position to the next. And so into the "courtyard," and from there to the steps and cavern entrance; finally into the keep itself.

Sprawling across the face of the cliff, the keep's extensive surface area was greatly disproportionate to its depth. The builders hadn't hollowed out the cliff to any great extent but had used natural caves wherever possible. Quite obviously, and just as Tzonov had supposed, the place must have been a way station and observation post. Dust lay thickly layered wherever time or the elements had deposited it, with never a foot- or claw-print to disturb it other than the fresh, sharp-etched imprints of combat boots.

The men relaxed a little. Defensive points were manned; wood was gathered; in less than half an hour smoke and cooking smells went up from chimneys cold for fifty years. Tzonov said nothing, but as he looked at the great girth of the fireplaces and the size of the rusted iron spits, he couldn't help thinking: *The last time that people cooked here, people were cooked here!*

It was a nightmarish thought . . . but not nearly as nightmarish as the huge, mummified grey thing one of the men discovered in a previously unexplored observation tower where access had been difficult due to fallen masonry.

Tzonov was with Krasin when the shuddering soldier reported his find, and was at once arrested by the man's answer to Krasin's abrupt "What is it?"

"It's something I found, sir. I . . . stumbled against it—touched it—and it's dead. But what it is? Well, it isn't a man . . ."

They returned with him to his discovery, and on the way Tzonov called for Yefros to accompany them. In the tower over the gorge they shone their torches where the soldier pointed, and Tzonov understood what he'd meant. Quite definitely, the thing was *not* a man. But a long time ago, it might have been several men.

The thing was as big as a horse, but . . . there could be no further comparison with anything of earthly origin. Except perhaps men. Its many legs and feet, and single pair of arms and hands, were short and stubby but manlike. Rather: if *men* wore them, they would not look out of place.

The thing had fallen over on its side and died there. It must be dead, for it was partly mummified . . . the dry air had kept it from corruption. Tzonov got down on one knee, shone a torch on the thing close up. Take three men, cut them across their bodies about nipple height and fold them forward at the waist one behind the other. Then fuse them, chest to buttocks and so on, all three into one. Now take the excised material and mold it into a long, flexible neck, with nothing much of a head but a mouthful of grinding teeth, rudimentary nostrils and ears, and (most important) a great many eyes along the neck and tapering nub of a head, so providing your—your what? your alien, six-legged centaur? or simply your observer?—your *thing*, anyway, with the means to scan in every direction simultaneously.

That was what this abomination was: a Wamphyri construct, a sentinel whose sole function had been to keep watch over the gorge. Except its eyes were fused shut now in merciful death. So it seemed.

The entire—*creature*—was covered in thick, leathery skin; where this had desiccated and cracked open, it was seen to be more in the nature of animal hide an eighth of an inch thick. Protection against the cold, during monotonously long nights of duty in the keep? Possibly.

The most puzzling feature in Tzonov's estimation was an upward-projecting, featureless nodule at the base of the neck; its short stem was knuckled like a spine, but its bald, bulbous terminal might easily be a second cranium, with a smaller brain housed in a skull only half the size of a normal human head.

"Alexei." He glanced up at the locator. "What do you make of this?"

Yefros was standing beside him, gazing down on the thing in disgust. "I don't know." He shook his head. "But there was once a theory, mainly fallen into disrepute now, that certain dinosaurs evolved secondary brains in their spines to control their armoured tails. They were too big and lumbering; it was Nature's way of balancing the deficiency of slow thought processes and reflexes. This, however—" he shook his head again, gulping audibly as he backed away, "—is nothing of Nature. I believe it is the echo I talked about. It was made by men, and it was made . . . *of* men? Yes, and a long time ago. And one more thing, Turkur. It isn't dead yet! Not *quite* dead, anyway . . ."

In the last few seconds Tzonov had become aware of a sick smell rising from the shrivelled, crumpled thing. Externally it was fairly well preserved. But internally . . . ? Now, as an eyelid cracked open in the near-mummified neck, and others in the blob of a head, he kicked himself backwards away from it, sprawling in the dust.

Some of the eyes were black sockets, dribbling a thick tarry morbid substance; others were yellow with pus. But one at least was clear . . . and stared directly, however vacantly, at Turkur Tzonov! His talent was instinct in him. Even sprawling there, he could read the thing's feeble mind as clearly as a living man's, and actually *felt* the faint pulse of thoughts that it sent hurtling towards Starside from the telepathic ganglion in its secondary brain:

Master . . . my Lord . . . there are . . . men . . . in the . . . keep!

That was all. But the rotting eyes of the undead horror continued to follow the four as they left the turret and descended gratefully into the company of other human beings. . . .

In a little while they returned with flamethrowers and burned the watcher where it lay.

Later still, Tzonov ordered his own sentries to be especially wary for the duration of their stay. After all, he knew that the creature had transmitted a final message to someone, somewhere. In that last, however, he was mistaken. The thing had tried, certainly—but uselessly. And just like the blazing observer itself, as chemical fire reduced it to roiling smoke and greasy ashes, Tzonov had no way of knowing that its message had not and could never be received.

He himself had been able to "read" the thought by virtue of his eye-to-eye telepathy. But as for anyone else: the creature could only communicate with its master, whichever Lord had "built" it.

And the maker and master of the watcher, the great Lord Shaithis of the Wamphyri, had been dead now for more than sixteen years . . .

II

Reconnaissance

There was no way that Turkur Tzonov could know it, but a few scant minutes after he and his half-platoon had left Starside to enter the mouth of the great pass—and therefore into the shelter and doubtful safety of the gorge's shadows and shielding rock walls—the Lady Wratha and her much-depleted Wrathstack army passed half a mile beyond the glaring hemisphere of the Starside Gate on their way back to the last aerie. The dimly flickering lights that Tzonov and Krasin had seen in that solitary stack's windows were Wratha's beacons guiding her home.

But if he and his section had entered the pass only a minute or so later, then despite all of their human ingenuity and much-vaunted firepower they might never have entered it at all. For then Wratha or Canker, Gorvi, Wran, or Spiro, or even some senior lieutenant, might well have detected the aroma of human flesh, picked up human thoughts, or by some other means unique to their individual Wamphyri senses or talents become "aware" of the presence of men in Starside.

Or there again, perhaps not. Certainly the Lady and Lords had more important things on their minds; indeed, it could well be that Tzonov and his men owed their survival to Wratha's concern for her own. For the Lady's eyes scanned Starside's skies this night, not its land. And her senses were alert for intruders, not refugees.

Do you have a plan? Wran the Rage's query entered Wratha's mind undisguised, urgent and anxious. With a battle in the offing, there was no time for bluff and bluster. He could rant and rage all he wanted then, but little use for such now.

Aye, she sent back. *But only if you and Spiro, Gorvi and Canker*—and *the necromancer Nestor Lichloathe, whatever that one is up to, and wherever he is now—will agree to put yourselves, your men and monsters at my command. Then I may have a plan.*

At your command?

Of course. (Her curt mental nod, and an eyebrow lifted as if in mild surprise.) *As Lord Taintspore commands his army out of Turgosheim, so I shall command the forces of the last aerie. And just as Vormulac has his generals, I shall have mine. What? And didn't we always plan it that way?*

Huh! Spiro Killglance scowled across the gulf of air. *We should put ourselves and our men under the orders of a woman? And where has that got us so far? Tonight, for instance. Was* that *an example of your leadership?*

Wratha's scowl was no less severe. *My shell is that of a woman, aye, but my leech is a vampire no less than yours. And I am all Wamphyri! As for leadership: would you even know that Lord Vormulac was here, if not for me? And as for tonight: so the Lidescis waylaid us. It has happened to the best . . .*

Spiro wasn't satisfied. *But in a fight? You're not built for it, Wratha. Built for other things, certainly; built to be under a man, to . . . accommodate him? But did you think to fuck them all to death? Tussling with a man in your bed is all very well, Lady, but going up against a gang of them wearing gauntlets is something else again! Now tell me, what do you really know of fighting?*

To command is not to fight, fool! Her retort was stinging in its intensity. *To command is to* direct *the fighting! And we aren't talking about a skirmish or even a battle, but a war—a full-scale bloodwar! Listen, Vormulac is a warlord born . . . but you? When you and your brother were wetting yourselves if your father so much as glanced at you, Lord Unsleep was settling blood feuds in Turgosheim—and settling them his way! He bound far greater Lords than you in chains, and strung them up by their heels for the sun to fry! Hah! Only be sure he'll do it again, here, tonight, if you don't listen to reason.*

Gorvi the Guile had been silent for some time. Fallen out of favour with the rest, he had to mind his words. But at last he felt obliged to ask, *So what is this plan of yours, Wratha, and how do we bring it into being? And anyway, what makes you think you're so much smarter than us when it comes to plotting wars?* Just like his real voice, his mental sendings seemed to ooze, insinuate, and cling like glutinous tar.

Hah! she snorted in return. *And now the so-called Guile says his piece—as if he has the right! But a fairer question might be: "Where was Gorvi this night, when the best of his men were being slaughtered at Sanctuary Rock?"*

What!? He commenced to bluster. *But if you'd only hear my story—*

No time for stories, Gorvi! Wratha cut him short. *Time for action, and barely enough time at that. Very well, you ask why I am smarter and I'll tell you: because I'm a woman! All right, you have your guile—but I have my woman's wiles, all doubled and redoubled by my leech! And I was* never *the dullard, believe me. As a girl on Sunside I killed a lieutenant, and fresh risen as a vampire I did away with his brother. Then, to be a Lady, I—usurped?—Karl the Crag. All by my wits alone, where muscle would not suffice. So tell me: who better to lead you now, when sheer numbers may whelm you down, and all the tenacity and willpower of a world will not suffice? The simple truth is that none of us is experienced in war. For in Turgosheim we were too soft for too long; we have almost forgotten how to wage war! In the years since I ascended there have been damn few feuds, let alone wars! And as for the Szgany we* knew: *they were the most docile of creatures. That's why these Lidescis continue to get the better of us: because we're not used to resistance . . .*

Finally she paused and swept hot red eyes over all of them. Until: *There, I'm done,* she told them. *You may fall*

*in with me or simply ... fall. And in the morning wake
with the sunrise—to find it shining in your eyes! But make
up your minds quick, for we'll soon be home and I've orders to give. And then you'll see if I have a plan or not.*

Canker Canison was still groggy from the knock he'd
taken, but it was his turn to say his piece. *Wratha, I'm
with you!* he barked in her mind. *My head's still singing
and I can't think a damn, but you're the only thing that's
held us together so far, and individually we're finished for
sure. So what will you have me and mine do? Order away,
Lady.*

Wratha turned to scan the hag-ridden sky under its canopy of blue-glittering stars. She looked upon her "colleagues" all grim in their saddles where they rode for the
Northstar, whose pharos eye gleamed down on Wrathstack, silhouetted now against the shimmer of the northern
aurora. Silent, scowling, the Wamphyri Lords rode the
wind, and to a man they were aware of the truth in Canker's words. But the Lady would have it from their own
lips, their own minds. *And the rest of you?* she said. *What
of you others? What of you, Wran, Spiro, Gorvi? Will you
stand like giants, or fall like swatted flies?*

Wran had his pride, but he was not a fool. And in a little
while: *Say on, Lady,* came his mental grunt. Followed by
Spiro's rasped:

So be it! And finally Gorvi's grudging:

Any plan has to be better than none.

There was no time for Wratha to take pleasure in their
submission, their admission that they needed her skills as
a leader. If anything she felt a sensation of relief and nothing of elation, and so steered well clear of gloating as she
began to outline her plan. *Very well. Now listen:*

*It's my belief that Vormulac is no more than an hour
and a half away at most. Which means we have a lot to do
and very little time in which to do it. If you follow my instructions to the letter, we may survive the first assault. After that, it's in the hands of fortune and the fates, if you
believe in such. Personally, I believe in me—and so must
you! This is how it shall be ...*

And as Wrathstack loomed ever closer, so she went on to lay the foundations of survival.

In a little while, handpicked lieutenants and warriors began to peel off from the main aerial formation and go winging down to those strewn, blackened, exploded stumps of Starside stacks whose names were long forgotten, and shortly after that Wratha and the rest arrived back in Wrathstack. But even before they landed in their various bays, their orders had been received and acted upon by rear parties left in charge of the manses.

In Guilesump, Madmanse, Wrathspire, and Mangemanse—and especially in Suckscar, from which for the moment and possibly for some time to come, the necromancer Lord Nestor Lichloathe was absent; which meant that his thralls and lieutenants were more than usually anxious for their own and the manse's safety—lights grew dim and blinked out as gas jets were plugged and mantles hooded, and smoke ceased coiling from the chimneys as fires were extinguished. Cooking smells, escaping from the kitchens to the open air, were wafted this way and that, dissipated by frantic wings of *Desmodus*; all other culinary activity came to an abrupt halt.

All signs and sigils, pennants and heraldic devices were taken down and replaced by a handful of mouldering, indecipherable rags out of ages past. Water-catchment skins were removed, and likewise replaced by tattered, decaying leathers. All signs of recent usage—of external stairs and causeways, platforms, turrets and such, and, after the various parties had landed in their manses, of the landing bays themselves—were disguised or camouflaged, which included the removal of main supports and ironwood stanchions, and the indiscriminate scattering of dust and debris where bays had been polished by the constant slither and thrust of flyers' bellies. So that in less than an hour the stack had taken on an appearance of disuse to the point of dereliction . . . exactly as Wratha required it.

And not only lights and fires, smoke and smells, but even the *thoughts* of the stack's diverse inhabitants—

Lords, lieutenants, thralls, and creatures alike—were stilled. From the basement of Guilesump, up through the broad levels of the Killglance brothers' Madmanse, and from Canker Canison's Mangemanse through Suckscar and Wrathspire to the latter's topmost turret, such telepathic silence reigned as never *could* be heard. Wrathstack . . . was dead! Or seemed it.

Perhaps Lord Unsleep's great bat familiars, his aerial scouts, should have known better, and perhaps not. There was after all something of the bat in the Wamphyri, too, not to mention other creatures, such as the wolf and, in Canker's case, the fox. But more devious far, there was also that of men in them. They were or had been men; they had the *minds* of men, and therefore Man's intelligence, his cunning and tenacity, but vastly enhanced by their vampire leeches. And where cunning and tenacity are concerned . . . Wratha, of course, was a woman.

And so, to Vormulac's advance intelligence agents, his familiar bats where they scouted out the way some ninety minutes ahead of the main body of his army, Wrathstack looked as Wratha intended it to look: empty and derelict. Even her own familiars seemed wild, untamed, without purpose in their flitting, slide-slipping, weaving, and plummeting courtship flights in and about Wrathspire's towers and turrets. But sensing the approach of strangers, outsiders, the initial curiosity that these indigenous bats displayed quickly turned (or appeared to turn) to anxiety for their colony, their territory; and as three of Vormulac's creatures commenced circling Wrathspire's ramparts, so the aerie's own inhabitants bolted for familiar cranny entranceways into the stack and disappeared within.

Plainly, they weren't much for defending their territory, these great cowards! Vormulac's scouts set up a derisive chittering and made to follow the stack's bats to their very roost, where in future they would lord it over the entire colony. And so the Lord Unsleep's creatures entered Wrathstack—

—Whose massive walls muffled to indecipherable

squeaks and squeals their panic cries of shock, surprise, and sudden death, and the brief flailing of membrane wings to the fading echoes of a flutter . . .

A second trio of Vormulac's creatures had stooped on the tumbled aeries of the old Wamphyri lying broken on the boulder plains, exploring them in the exposed, exploded areas of their shattered stems and bases. But delving too deeply, they fared no better than the others. Netted by lieutenants and trampled by warriors, their cries were trapped in dust and rubble, and lost in the ruins of blackened basements. No word of Wratha's whereabouts would reach Turgosheim's army through the medium of *Desmodus*, at least.

And indeed, a half-hour later, neither a creature nor a sound, nor even a *thought* betrayed the Lady, but an effect of fickle Nature that announced her presence even a dozen miles away, and so went far beyond Wratha's or anyone else's control . . .

Ten miles east of the great pass into Sunside, Lord Vormulac Taintspore had landed his army in the heights of the barrier mountains on what was once a mighty lava flow, now a series of gently sloping plateau summits, like a giant's causeway rising from east to west and gradually angling south into the fanged caldera of the dead volcano. From there, he and his most valued confidante, the so-called virgin grandam Devetaki Skullguise, along with Laughing Zack Shornskull and Lady Zindevar Cronesap (who would much prefer to eschew her mainly derisory cognomen and go simply under the name of Zindevar), mounted fresh flyers and went up again to find a place to perch, spy out the land, and confer awhile in private.

But after they found a landing site in the topmost peaks of the ages-worn caldera—and when they gazed out from their high vantage point on all of this unknown land— what they *saw* cut conversation to a minimum. Far to the south, the rim of the world was outlined against a haze of faint starlight, its curve silhouetted by a dim sickle of amethyst light growing dimmer by the minute, residual of sunset. And at the foot of the barrier mountains, ranging out and away to the savanna and the far furnace deserts, all of Sunside's forests spread like a dark green ocean under ever-brightening ice-cluster stars. From east to west, as far as the eyes (even Wamphyri eyes) could see, lay that fertile tract with its promise, and much more than a promise, of human life.

For there in the woods, campfires! Four sets of them: two to the east, one directly below, and another a mile or so west. Not the fires of trogs, no, for here in Old Sunside the aboriginals were as their Turgosheim cousins: night creatures, cave dwellers, Starsiders. Wherefore these must be the camps of men. They could only be! Hot human blood for Lord Taintspore's army, to fuel his war on Wratha the Risen!

Except . . . if Wratha and her renegades were here, then what sort of men *were* these western Sunsiders, that they lit her way with fires to guide her to them in the night? Had she brought them to heel so quickly, then, in the space of only a year or two? Were these the fires of supplicant tribes, as the Szgany of Turgosheim's Sunside? Or was it that Wratha and her lot, like so many of Vormulac's men and creatures, had failed to make the crossing from east to west, had been devoured by the rising sun, or had fallen into the reeking acid lakes of the Great Red Waste?

In which case these people would never have suspected Wratha's existence in the first place, and so would continue their simple lives as always. Which might possibly explain these apparently careless fires, but in turn posed another question: why so *few* fires? Or was there another, entirely different, infinitely more threatening solution to this puzzle?

Back in Turgosheim, the venerable Maglore had declared these western regions free of Wamphyri influence. Indeed, the Seer-Lord Maglore had been sure that the last of the Old Wamphyri had died out some eight hundred sunups ago, in a terrible holocaust wrought by a magician in their midst who had called up Things beyond his control.

But what if Maglore was wrong and the Old Wamphyri survived to this day? What a greeting Wratha would have had from them! The theory might also serve to explain these campfires; for if there *were* vampires here—and if their reign had been unbroken since time immemorial— then of course a majority of the tribes would be suppliant . . .

All of these were points that Vormulac and his generals chewed over in the peaks, before Laughing Zack Shornskull said: "There is of course a simple way to find out. Take a handful of chosen men and monsters, fly down on the most isolated of those fires and take prisoners. It's something that must be done anyway, if we'd feed our men and beasts. Then, if the people down there aren't supplicants already, they damn soon will be! And a heavy tithe to pay, too, I fear." And Zack, a squat, barrel-bodied tub of a Lord, chuckled deep in the back of his throat, as was his wont. There was never any humour in Zack's "mirth," but he chuckled anyway.

Before Vormulac could answer, Devetaki exclaimed: "Look there!" And all heads turned north, where she pointed. Which was the moment that Wratha was discovered; or if not the Lady herself, her fortress stack at least. And: "See!" said Devetaki. "See! Now tell me, is that an aerie, or what?"

Erratic in its orbit, the pale disk of a blue and silver moon seemed on a level with their eyes over the cold northern horizon. Perhaps it was lit by the Northstar, or by starshine in general, or its own surface was of reflective rocks. Whichever, and despite the fact that the sun was down, the moon sailed over Starside like a softly glowing bubble in the sky. Except . . .

. . . It seemed stabbed in its belly by a mighty spire, by the topmost fang of the last aerie! And just as that telltale moon had informed Vormulac of his safe passage over the Great Red Waste, so now it informed on Wrathstack, which was otherwise camouflaged by night and dark and distance.

"And down there!" cried Devetaki, whose eyes were

keener than the rest put together. "There, to the west. That glowing light in the Starside foothills. What of that? See, it throws a plume of foxfire out across the plain of boulders." For she had spied the Starside Gate.

Vormulac frowned, snapped his fingers. "I sent a team of great bats ahead, along the spine of these barrier mountains," he said. "Six of them—but only five returned. They reported a great wonder: a ball of cold white light, half-buried in the foothills. The familiar who was lost strayed too close to the light, was blinded by it and eaten up. Such was my translation of their report. That—" he nodded his great head in the direction of Devetaki's pointing finger, "—is perhaps the Thing which they reported. No doubt we'll find out more as we journey west. Ah, but I sent six more to spy out the land across the plain of boulders and see if they could discover aught of Wratha the Risen. So far they've not returned—not a one of them!" He turned cold, suspicious, gold-flecked scarlet eyes on the distant stack. And as Vormulac's frown deepened, so his eyebrows drew together over the bridge of his hawk nose. Then, to Zindevar Cronesap:

"My Lady, what of your own familiars, which you brought with you out of Turgosheim? I trust you instructed them as I required of you?"

Zindevar was a "Lady" in name only; no more or less than any Wamphyri Lady, except she made no effort to hide the truth of her aspect, the facts of her lifestyle—which in any event were plainly evident in her face and form. What looks and shape she had worn on the day of her ascension she'd kept. They were scarcely desirable to men, but in Zindevar's case this was just as well. With the exception of a small handful of fighting men, her male thralls and lieutenants were eunuchs; which, apart from breeding stock, all men *should* be, according to the Lady.

"Aye, six of them," she answered. "I sent three along the Sunside flank, as far as they could go and still return in the first quarter of the night. Don't expect them back yet awhile. The others went out over the Sunside forests, to see what they could discover of secretive Szgany. With a bit of luck they'll ignore campfires such as these we've seen as being the work of supplicants, and seek out the furtive ones in the forests. If such men are to be found, then my bloodhounds will find them, be sure!"

Vormulac gave a grunt, perhaps of disappointment. "This last-mentioned trio of yours: they, too, might take hours in the performance of their task?"

She shrugged mannish shoulders. "As long as it takes. Is it important?"

The warrior-Lord glanced at her, wrinkled his nostrils a very little, otherwise was not intimidated by the Lady Zindevar's decidedly male aura. For the atmosphere about her was ever pervaded with this manly odour: a cloying stench of sweat and muscle which all her many perfumes together could not hope to obscure. Despite her years, whose number fell not far short of Vormulac's hundred and fifty, she looked youngish or in her middle span at most, which said a deal for her lifestyle. Zindevar was no Zolteist, no great "ascetic." Indeed, and in her leather armour—for all that her face was rouged and painted under her visor, and the telltale girth of her bust and behind—she looked far more the warrior than a good many of Vormulac's handsome young Lords!

Eventually he answered her: "It could be important, aye. For I would like to send a few more bats to spy on that tower there, and on those lesser mounds lying scattered all about." He indicated the lone stack far out on the boulder plains: a dark fang now and hard to make out, for the hurtling moon had ridden on and the auroral curtain wove too high to make à silhouette. And humped on the plain in disarray, those dark and enigmatic remains of which he'd spoken.

He turned to Devetaki Skullguise. "My Lady, do you have bats with you? Or if not, do you know of any other who brought his familiar creatures with him out of Turgosheim?"

Devetaki answered with a nod, her gold-filigreed, frowning half-mask glinting with reflected starshine. "Yes to your second question, my Lord Unsleep . . . probably. I can't be certain, of course, for a great many of us made the crossing and we each looked to our own contingents. But to hazard a guess: did you ever know Wamus of Wamscarp to venture anywhere without his familiars? Why, Lord Wamus is *himself* a great bat, or as close as he can get!"

"Good!" Vormulac was pleased. "As always, your advice is the very best, Devetaki, and your common sense easily outweighs the so-called talents of so many of your contemporaries." He smiled a rare, appreciative if gloomy smile at her. "I'll talk to Wamus."

The virgin grandam, probably as old and wise in the ways of Turgosheim (if not in these new, foreign parts) as Vormulac himself, had been a favourite of his for decades. She had long been a member of the gorge's covert yet governing triumvirate; its other members being Maglore the Mage, and the warrior-Lord Unsleep, of course. So Vormulac was well acquainted with Devetaki's history. He knew she professed Zolteism as a creed, and much like himself was an ascetic . . . within the limits of Wamphyri nature, at least.

Devetaki Skullguise was no girl but a mature woman, regal of stature, proud but not haughty. As to the privileges of her title: she was neither a virgin nor, in the matriarchal sense, a grandam. She desired no bloodsons or daughters to fight over Masquemanse when she was gone (not that she intended to go for a while), for she'd seen more than enough of that as a thrall.

Gifted with a rare beauty, redheaded, long-limbed, full-breasted and unblemished, Devetaki had been taken in the tithe as a girl. Alas, she'd gone to a manse whose master had daughters out of diverse females but no sons. Also, he had no special odalisque, no "wife" as such on whom to bestow his egg. His vampire daughters vied with each other, naturally, to see which one would become Wamphyri and a Lady. In all likelihood they would be Wamphyri anyway, but the one who got his egg would be first among them. Now, however, when they saw Devetaki and knew how their father was taken with her, she soon became the victim of their jealousy.

For if he should fall "in love" with her, who could say but that in the heat of passion she might not receive his egg, and so usurp them all? To cut a long story short, she was challenged by the strongest of his girls; she was offered an ironwood knife while her opponent wore a gauntlet; she stabbed the other to the heart and took her head, but in the fighting lost the right half of her pretty face, flensed from the cheekbone.

The Lord of the manse had heard the commotion and came to see. Enraged at the loss of one of his five daughters, furious at the spoiling of Devetaki's face, and driven to an absolute frenzy by the sight of so much blood spilled in his own manse, all without his permission, he suffered a brainstorm and collapsed. He was old, after all. And his leech, doubtless believing it was all up with him, produced an egg that issued from his mouth.

As the pearly thing skittered this way and that upon the floor, the surviving daughters scrabbled to attract or otherwise obtain it: by scooping it up, by attempting to fall upon it with their mouths, even by opening their bodies to it. But the *blood* is the life . . . and Devetaki was drenched in blood! Sensing her strength, the egg knew that it had found a worthy host. It turned scarlet in the moment that it touched her; it flowed like living liquid to the raw pulp of her face! And as the others tore their hair, the egg soaked into her. Devetaki was Wamphyri!

And three sunups later, when the Lord of the manse died, she ascended to a Lady . . .

Then, one by one, without too much ado, she did away with the other sisters and so became sole heir to one of the mightiest manses in Turgosheim. And from then on she made it plain how she had got her egg; not through the seduction of her Lord or by usurping him, or through any act of lust or "love," but simply because the vampire seed had "known" who should be its rightful recipient. And to this day she had never admitted to being an odalisque in the first place. Hence "virgin"; and the "grandam" in her title referred to her long years as mistress of Masquemanse, not to her progeny, for there was none.

As for "Skullguise": the cognomen resulted from a small affectation. When Devetaki's mood was good she wore a smiling half-mask over the naked bone; when it was sour or serious she wore a frowning half-mask; but when she was *most* angry—then she wore no mask at all.

Vormulac's praise had obviously pleased her. Saying nothing at all, she turned her face away and took her smiling mask from her belt to replace the scowl she'd been wearing.

On the other hand, Laughing Zack Shornskull (despite his customary chuckle) was not pleased at all. "Lord Vormulac," he said, "time's wasting. Why send more bats to look at that lone tower when you can send men? If Wratha is there, and unless she has built herself a powerful army . . . why, my contingent alone has her measure! And if she did have such an army, do you honestly believe she'd still be in hiding? No, not Wratha—she would be fighting!"

Vormulac, for all that he was the warrior-Lord, knew as much about true war as the others: very little. He was expert at settling feuds and putting down insurrections, but his knowledge of logistics, strategy—the science or basic elements of war—was rudimentary to say the least. He did know, however, that he had men and beasts to feed, and must find adequate shelter for them before sunup; *and* that he must yet fight a bloody war, whenever that should come.

But he also knew Wratha was devious to a fault, and that Laughing Zack probably underestimated her. And with regard to Lord Shornskull himself: Vormulac was finding it irksome, the ways in which this fool aped him—the way he stuck so close and copied his thrall's hairstyle, and pretended a comparable status—so that all in all it might be a good thing to put him out of sight a while.

"Are you suggesting that you personally investigate that stack out there?" The warrior-Lord's iron-grey moustaches twitched a very little where they dipped to meet his goatish beard. It was a sure sign of his displeasure (Vormulac did not care to be advised by lesser men), but Zack chose to ignore it.

"Have you something against the idea?"

"Nothing at all—on the contrary, I like it! A warlord should appreciate those among his generals who take the initiative. Perhaps you would like to command the crusade-entire?"

Now Zack backed off a little. "My only desire is to save time, Lord Vormulac."

"Good! Then be on your way. And Zindevar here can go with you, to organize a party of her own to investigate those fires. I've matters to talk over with Devetaki." It was a cursory dismissal, which this time Zack had the common sense to recognize. A nod of his head to Devetaki, another to Vormulac, and he made for his flyer. Zindevar likewise, but scowling as she went.

When they had gone, Vormulac said: "He irritates me."

"Because you're forty years older, wiser, stronger," Devetaki told him. "It's that Zindevar who irritates me—the crone! Now, what matters are these you would discuss?"

"Eh? Ah, no—that was mainly to be rid of them, though there are things to talk about, certainly. Devetaki, I think I may go down with Zindevar and see what's what with those fires. Similarly, I want you to take a reconnaissance party and go on ahead, perhaps as far as that light in the foothills. Except I would caution you: mind how you go. Aye, for I value your company and friendship as much as your counsel. And now, give me the benefit of your good advice and tell me: what else should I do to ensure that all runs smooth?"

"Two things only," she told him without pause, "and let these suffice. One: always ensure that your men and creatures are fed and watered; that they have what small pleasures are due them, and sleep out of harm's way where the sun may not find them. Two: hold tight your rein on spoilers and troublemakers; these Lords were feudal before our time, and would be again without that we curb them."

He nodded. "Devetaki, as always you are my right arm. And now let's get to it . . ."

They took a little longer coming than Wratha had thought, and there were not so many of them. Also, they came in something of stealth, or "quietly" at least. Which is to say: they, too, kept their minds shielded. Which was all to the good: no telltale thoughts issued out from the last aerie, and no sly alien probes sought entry. The telepathic aether seemed sterile. *Too* sterile.

From on high, Laughing Zack Shornskull looked down on the upper ramparts of Wrathstack and thought (to himself), *I don't like it!* Nothing *stirs—well, except for those ancient pennants, all sluggishily aflutter—neither a thought nor even a bat; yet a place as massive as that must surely have its colonies?* And he chuckled, however grimly. *A trap? An ambush? Or is she simply hiding? What disaster could have befallen the Lady, that the proud and haughty Wratha—even Wratha the Risen—has gone to earth like some Sunside fox? Or . . . could it be that the place* is *truly deserted?*

But this massive, mighty stack—deserted . . . ?

And as easily and as suddenly as that, Zack's great wide grinning mouth was moist and flowing with saliva—lust! For the aerie itself! For in Turgosheim, Zackstack was the veriest pimple by comparison; like a heap of pebbles in the bed of the gorge, and only marginally taller than Lom Halfstruck's Trollmanse! But *this* place . . . why, it could easily equal, or even *contain*, one-third of all Turgosheim's great manses! If a man were Lord here—if a *single man* were Lord and master of the entire stack—why, he could build, house, and command such an army, that . . .

. . . But then, so could a woman!

Zack's lustful territorial thoughts—the inspiration of his leech—subsided as quickly as they had risen. For in his passion he'd hit upon an inescapable truth: that if Wratha was here, then she was *here*! No Lord or Lady of the Wamphyri could ever have resisted it, the opportunity to reign over an aerie such as this. To reign supreme!

But on the other hand, this was only one stack, and all the vast expanse of this new Starside still unexplored. Wratha *and her five* had fled out of Turgosheim that time; was it possible that they *all* inhabited aeries such as this, strewn far and wide across these boulder plains? In which case they would not have had time to build their armies, not yet! As a colony, working together, perhaps, but not as individuals, constantly vying with each other.

So perhaps *one* of the rebels was here. Or in the case of the Killglance brothers, maybe two of them. But which?

Zack signalled his party to move in closer—especially his eager warriors, who had stood well off so as not to alert with the throb and sputter of their propulsors—and continued to circle the upper levels. And gradually losing altitude, he sank through the sombre night until the blue-tinged, white calcined fangs and sloping roofs of Wrathspire rose up like a castle within his spiral, and the bone-embellished base plummeted far below.

And still nothing stirred, neither a breath nor a thought. So that Zack was given to think (but far less secretively now): *Deserted, aye, it could well be.* But men and monsters had been here upon a time, certainly, as witness the windows, balconies, chimneys, flying buttresses, platforms, causeways, and . . .

. . . And landing bays!

Why send in thralls or lieutenants to examine the stack, when there were warriors to do the job? And laughing his most sinister laugh, Lord Shornskull opened his mind and called them in, and ordered the first of them down into the yawning cavern mouth of the largest of the uppermost bays.

Then, even as the creature descended, hovering at the rim of the bay with mantle fluttering, gas bags inflated, and propulsors angling this way and that, Zack "heard" it: the faintest echo of telepathic terror, a telltale gibbering in the psychic aether; like the whinny of a cornered goat as the wolves close in:

No, no! He mustn't find me here! Please let him go away . . . awaaay!

Wratha! She was here after all! Alone! Undefended!

And: *In!* Zack ordered his construct without further pause. Its propulsors fired once; landing limbs uncoiled, reached out; the great armoured body settled to the polished rim of the bay.

Fascinated, Zack's aerial troops looked on, all eyes zeroed in on the landing bays, windows, balconies, precarious causeways. If the great aerie had defenders, surely they must show themselves now? Yet all was still, silent. Somewhere within, the Lady hid: Wratha the Risen, a woman at bay! And Laughing Zack would drag her in chains, naked and begging, before Vormulac Taintspore for his not-so-tender mercies.

But Wratha had *heard* that last! Again her terror was such she could not contain it, but once more issued a futile appeal to faithless fates: *Please don't let him find me! Please make him go away!*

And: *In, all of you!* Zack ordered his troops. *There are landing bays on all levels—use them! Find her! Find Wratha and bring her to me. It's possible she's alone, but any with her . . . destroy them! Feed them to the warriors to fuel them back to the barrier mountains. But do not harm Wratha, not a hair of her head. For I fancy Lord Unsleep has plans of his own for her!*

III

Starside Ambush—Nestor's Inquiry—Canker's Discovery

All eyes were on Wrathstack, and not one of them watching the fire-blackened ruins of the tumbled stacks of the Old Wamphyri where they littered the plain of boulders for miles all around. Since the closest of these shattered stumps and the mounds and tumuli of their debris lay something more than a mile away, and the more immediate visual lure of the last aerie and the drama about to be enacted there was so strong, this was scarcely surprising. But as Zack's forces approached and carried out cursory examinations of the ledges and landing bays on the various levels, while Zack himself stood off to survey and command the activities of his party, so a massed emergence and launching was taking place from several of the fallen stacks.

Most of Wrathstack's major entranceways were in the east-facing wall of the aeire; Wratha's ambush came from the west. And as the rumble of Zack's warriors' propulsors disguised the throb and stutter of Wratha's, so the gauntly looming mass of the aerie itself served to hide their approach from view.

Zack had five warriors: three of his own and two borrowed specifically for this detail. One of the latter was a giant of a beast of Vormulac's design and construction: in Zack's estimation, too unwieldy by far. The rest of them were smaller, but devastatingly fearsome creatures for all that. He also had six flyers in addition to his own; they carried three lieutenants and six senior thralls, the latter mounted two to a beast.

Accompanied by a flyer and two thrall "minders" or commanders, the giant warrior had proceeded to the base of the stack and was about to land in a vast landing bay only a few hundred feet over the boulder plains. The remaining warriors and their commanders had taken up roughly equidistant hovering positions close to platforms, entranceways, and landing bays as suitable or available in the length of the stack. Laughing Zack himself attended his own warrior where it had landed in Wratha's main bay and was using its chitin prow as a battering ram to force massive inner doors. As he heard the doors groaning and straining under the brutal attack, Zack's grin was broad as his lustful face . . . for a while—

—Until suddenly it became apparent to Lord Shornskull just how precipitant was his laughter. For from close at hand and without warning, Wratha's mental command entered his skull with all the sharpness and force of a Szgany crossbow bolt. No timid, tremulous shuddering and cowering now, as that treacherous "voice" of hers cried:

Strike them! . . . Strike them NOW!

Zack hadn't quite landed; his flyer's wings were hugely arched air-traps, and its thruster-cum-landing tentacles were extended, reaching for the rim of the bay. But instinctively, even as Wratha's voice and message registered, Zack backed his mount out over the gulf of air away from the face of the stack—which probably served to extend his lifespan a little. Over the landing bay like lashes over an eye, heavy sections of harpoon-tipped, rusty iron grille were held aloft on ropes depending from various windows. The ropes were frayed from years of disuse, but many of the grille sections had been welded to the vertical face by the action of nitre—which did *not* include those directly above the central landing area.

Suddenly those sections were released, their ropes hissing as they uncoiled from narrow windows, and the harpoon heads slammed down in line to strike sparks from the polished rock of the bay. A moment earlier, the long neck of Zack's mount would have been pierced through— and maybe Zack himself! Even the best possible scenario would have seen him bucked out of his saddle into thin air! And:

Oh? And who laughs now, eh, Zack?—Wratha's mocking mental voice, taunting him from somewhere within.

But not for long, Lady! He answered with a snarl, turning his startled mount to one side and stalling it into a clumsy glide . . . which was a single moment before he heard the first dull rumble of angry, alien propulsors.

And around from behind the great fang of Wrathstack they came, full of deadly intent, riding a breeze out of the northern Icelands and spacing themselves to provide individual challenges to Zack's lesser creatures: four of the most nightmarish constructs he had ever seen! From their aspect alone—without that Zack could sense the fearsome *focus* of their tiny minds, or saw the scarlet bloodlust in their eager, swivelling saucer eyes—he knew the defenders were experienced in battle. And where his own forces were mainly expeditionary, exploratory, these were full of purpose, had a grim determination, and knew their enemy.

A pair of flyers, too, their lieutenant riders alert and observant in their saddles, gliding out from fortifications on Wrathspire's roof to direct the warriors. And in the last great aerie itself, a hundred minds coming sharply awake, uncloaking as their owners went to work with a vengeance!

More flyers emerging from secret exits below and rising on the Icelands wind . . . and a veritable cloud of small but deadly aerial warriors suddenly appearing as if from nowhere! (In fact there were only five of the latter: three released by the Killglance brothers from a hidden bay in Madmanse, and two sent out by Canker Canison from the rear of Mangemanse); but all appearing together, they seemed like a cloud to Laughing Zack.

Back off!—Get out of it! He sent his telepathic command with all the force of his vampire mind. *They've set a trap, an ambush!*

Too late!

His warrior, trapped in Wratha's landing bay, raged like the mad thing it was and vented furious propulsive gasses, but to no avail. Barbed pike-heads came stabbing from niches in the walls and through holes in the floor, tearing at its gas bladders and slashing at its undulating mantle. Mainly unhurt though definitely incapacitated, finally the stupid thing answered its master's command and backed out of the bay. Taking the dangling grilles with it in a jumble of buckled iron, it flopped free of the stack and fired its propulsors to stabilize its flight. But with air whistling through holes in its mantle, and most of its buoyancy gasses escaped from ruptured bladders, the doomed warrior's ungainly retreat was erratic to say the least.

Howling its frustration, it quickly capsized, commenced a spiralling, accelerating dive, slammed headlong into one of Suckscar's causeways at its junction with the stack and burst like a bomb! Steaming hot plasma painted Suckscar's slanting strata red; great gouts of blood washed outwards in a scarlet flood, and ran in a torrent down the wall of the aerie; loose scales, chunks of smoking meat, and chitin shards spun lazily in the gulf of air. And as the huge body crumpled to the near-vertical wall, clung for a moment and then began to fall, its raw flesh left a crimson skid mark where it slipped and slithered; until finally it struck a projection and was deflected outwards and down, end over end into eternity.

The rest of Zack's party were faring no better. Close to the base of the stack, Vormulac's giant construct had somehow been driven from the rim of Gorvi the Guile's landing bay and attacked in midair by speedier, more manoeuvrable creatures. With its gas bladders ruptured, and listing badly, it had been forced down on the boulder plains. Damaged in the crash-landing, it had lain helpless as all three of Gorvi's ground warriors closed in. These earthbound constructs, unhampered by the clumsy bladders and skirtlike mantles of their aerial cousins, were heavily armoured and hideously agile. Built and equipped for infighting, they grunted their exertions and roared their triumph as they stripped the giant to its alveolate bones and strewed its guts far and wide.

Several of Zack's lieutenants and thralls had effected landings in the stack's bays. Some managed to escape, others didn't. Zack saw a flyer about to launch; a handful of defenders emerged from niches to scramble beneath it and cling on to or hack at its launching limbs; the flyer tilted over the very rim, flapped its manta wings to avoid toppling, was held back and down by the sheer weight of numbers clinging to its belly. As its rider was bucked cursing from his saddle, other defenders rammed pike after pike into the flyer's belly, before its thrusters were sliced through and it was allowed to fall . . .

One of the remaining three warriors had landed on a sabotaged platform; defenders of Madmanse released chains, knocked loose weakened stanchions, sent the thing plummeting. But some clever thrall had learned a lesson from Lardis Lidesci; before the warrior fell, it had been drenched in oil and torched! Now a fireball lit the dark night air, hissing and screaming, puffing jets of blue and white fire as it plunged to earth.

Wratha's flyers, coming from above, attacked Zack's. They swooped; their riders lowered clusters of weighted, razor-sharp hooks; Zack's thralls were gripped through leathers and flesh, ripped from their saddles, and dashed against the aerie's wall . . . or simply allowed to fall. If they had been Wamphyri, they might have shaped metamorphic flesh for flight. But they were only men.

A clump of gleaming hooks swung close to Zack himself. Too close; he felt the vibration of the air as the weapon whistled by his head and ripped a chunk from his flyer's manta wing. And that was enough for Laughing Zack.

Away, and run for the barrier mountains! He called to men and beasts alike, but needlessly. Even a brave man knows when to flee, with or without orders. The survivors—two warriors, one listing badly, and three flyers, including Zack's own, one of which was minus its rider—turned away from the last aerie and made off . . . or would have.

But even Wratha had not foreseen the rest of it.

From out of the northeast, some pulsing, spurting thing zeroed in on Zack's damaged warrior, ducked beneath the listing hulk of its body and sliced its bladders tip to tail with twin rows of erectile dorsal spines! A construct of Vasagi the Suck at his monstrous best, the warrior had been designed with just such a purpose in mind: the disposal of other aerial warriors. Except Vasagi was gone now, and Nestor Lichloathe ruled in Suckscar!

Wratha had come out onto a balcony to see the last of it. It was Nestor, aye, returned now from whatever lone mission had diverted him in Sunside. Nestor upon his flyer, all swathed and cloaked as usual, his face masked except for his eyes, burning with some inner passion or incendiary knowledge. And accompanying him, his best out of Suckscar. Survivors of the defeat at Sanctuary Rock, they were eager to give a good account of themselves and so balance the odds. But with what little was left of Zack's lot, there was scarcely enough work for them.

Nestor's warriors fell on Lord Shornskull's sole remaining beast and dismembered it in short order, and his riderless flyer went the same way. One lone thrall and flyer, first away from the ambush, had put sufficient distance between to effect an escape. Which left Laughing Zack himself.

As Nestor's warriors zeroed in on his flyer, and fired on all propulsors for a multiple ram, Zack reverted to characters, threw back his great head and laughed loud at Nestor across the gulf of air. But in the moment before the collision he loosened his cloak, divested himself, and launched from his doomed flyer's back. Three-quarters of the way to earth he achieved metamorphosis, formed webbing between his arms and legs, flattened his body to an airfoil—all in vain. For even as he slipped into a controlled glide, so Nestor's flyer swooped on him.

Snatched from midair, Zack was gripped in the flyer's belly pouch with only his left arm and leg protruding.

These kicked a while, regained their normal shape, then hung still. The flyer had clamped its rubbery pouch shut on Zack to expel all air, and even a vampire must breathe or suffocate. Lord Shornskull was no exception. A moment more and . . . he was not dead, but very unconscious. So he remained until, two hundred and fifty feet over the boulder plains, Nestor hauled on his reins to bring his mount out of its dive, and commanded the creature: *Drop him!*

Zack's body fell like a stone, burst like an egg, spattered the dirt and pebbles black in the starlight. His parasite leech, itself injured and knowing it was all up for him, fled his shattered body. One of Gorvi's warriors, coming to investigate, failed to see the leech and crushed it flat.

Thus Zack suffered the true death and knew only darkness.

For a while . . .

. . . Until the necromancer Lord Nestor Lichloathe of the Wamphyri "spoke" to him in his fashion, and said:

Zack Shornskull. Ah, but you're a mess now! I might even sympathize and leave you in peace, for I never knew you in life and so have nothing against you in death . . . but alas, it can't be. For there are things you know which I must know, before I may leave you to sleep the last long sleep.

And: *What . . . ?* said Zack. *Who . . . ?*

Did you not feel me before I even spoke to you? Nestor's deadspeak voice oozed like tar. *Strange, that, because the rest of them do.*

The . . . the rest of them? The rest of who?

The rest of the dead. They know *when I am near, for I can feel them trembling in my mind! It is my art, you see. And the dead fear me for it.*

Zack had known he was dead, or at least he had very much suspected it, in that pitch-black interval before his mind was awakened again. For regaining consciousness in the last moment before crashing to earth on the boulder plains, he'd known that no man, not even a vampire, could survive such a fall. Yet now—it seemed he was alive after all! Alive, aye, but blind and crippled, and . . . empty? For he sensed that even his leech had deserted him, he'd come so close. But:

Closer than you think, Zack, Nestor told him. *For you are dead, and I am the necromancer Nestor Lichloathe.*

There was no feeling—none whatever—in any of Zack's limbs. It might even be that he had no limbs. Or that there was no life in them. Which would be the case, naturally . . . if he were really dead? *Where . . . am I?*

In Suckscar, to which I've lifted you up. In Wrathstack, which you invaded.

Wrathstack! Named after Wratha the Risen! Well, Zack had got that right, at least. And a thrall had escaped to get word of her whereabouts back to Vormulac. *Huh!* Cold comfort to Lord Zack Shornskull, who *was* either dead . . . or in the company of a madman!

His thoughts were deadspeak, of course, and Nestor heard them. *No "either" about it, Zack,* the necromancer told him, in his most gentle and his most terrifying voice. *You are dead to the world—but not to me! And now I have some questions for you, some small points which we would clarify.*

We?

Myself, the Lady Wratha, the Killglance brothers, Canker, and Gorvi, of course.

And Vasagi?

Ah, no! For he is gone, and I have taken his place, his manse.

Ah! "Suckscar!"

Correct. I like the name, which isn't out of place after all. Vasagi sucked with his beak and I with my mind. He sucked from veins and I from brains . . . even dead minds. I suck knowledge, Zack, and you have what I need! So let's be at it. The first of my questions:

How many men, monsters, and flyers, has Vormulac Unsleep, and where is he camped?

Aye, a madman! Zack answered at once. *What? I should tell you where Vormulac is? Why, he would tear out my heart and eat it raw!* And despite the weirdness of Lord Shornskull's situation (or perhaps because of it? For if in fact he were truly dead, then what harm could anyone, even Vormulac, do him now?) he allowed himself a chuckle: the worst possible error! For a moment later:

I see you need convincing, Nestor sighed. *But I'll admit, I admire your tenacity: to laugh from the throat of death.*

Don't you mean, in the face of death? said Zack.

And Nestor's answer more doleful yet, *You do need convincing, don't you? Now listen—do you feel this?*

At last Zack did feel something: a breath of air—and a sweet one at that—blowing cool in his face. Like the breath of some gasping Sunside woman, trapped on the run, stripped of her skirt and thrown flat, feeling his weight come down on her and his first probing stab in the moist sleeve of her cunt.

You've a vivid imagination, Nestor told him, quietly. *But inaccurate to say the least. I merely breathed on you. I don't take it red too often, and my breath is sweet. But tell me, why don't you breathe on me, eh? Or even spit on me, if you like! Why don't you at least try, Zack?*

I . . . I . . .

Because you can't, can you? Ah! But if only you could see what I can see! Then you'd know for sure why you can't breathe, see, feel. (Nestor's voice was the merest whisper now, but one that burned it its intensity.) *Shall I show you?*

H-h-how can you show a blind man anything?

I am a necromancer, Zack. You can hear my voice and feel my breath, my . . . touch? And when I concentrate, why, then you may even see what I see! Like so:

Zack saw—and screamed! Even Laughing Zack: screamed like that same Sunside slut he'd raped. His very first, she'd been, after he ascended and achieved his full measure of metamorphism. Ah, *that* was a fuck! Shagged dry first, then sliced to the ribs as he turned his tool to a cartilage-toothed saw! Not so dry then, but wet and hot on his quivering bone . . .

Conjured deliberately, the memory of her agony served as a balm for his own.

Really? Said Nestor, as Shornskull's mental shuddering subsided. *Did you do that, Zack? My, but you were a hard one in your time! Not so hard now, though. Indeed, you're even a bit soft in places, eh?* And again he showed Zack . . . to Zack! The wobbling, soggy mess that had been a man.

But by now the other was sobbing, and Nestor very much suspected that he wouldn't need to torture him, not this one. For he had *already* tortured him by showing him the truth of his condition. Zack knew now why he couldn't breathe: because a man needs lips and a face and a throat to breathe. And he knew why he felt nothing: because when your limbs and your body and your head are so much jelly, you can't feel anything—because you are dead! It was true, and finally he believed Nestor.

Then you may believe this, too, the necromancer told him. *Just as you felt my breath on the raw red smear of your face, so you would feel my hands on your broken body and most sensitive parts. That is my art! And believe just one more thing: I can return to you tenfold all the pain you ever gave—all the pain of this vampire world— again and again and again!*

For answer, the monster Zack Shornskull continued to sob. It was as much as he could do. Except:

Do—you—believe me? Nestor must have an answer.

Yes! Yes! Yes! Zack sobbed. And he sensed Nestor's talon hands draw back from where they were poised, and he felt that they drew back—reluctantly?

Following which, he answered the necromancer's questions, every one, and Nestor knew he answered true . . .

At the end of it, Zack wanted to know: *What's to become of me?* And he sensed the negligence in Nestor's answer, his deadspeak shrug:

What else can become? It's over.

I'll be buried? Burned? Or what? I am—or was—a Lord of the Wamphyri, after all. Have I no rights?

None. Our forces are depleted. There's the provisioning to consider. You'll be eaten.

Lords are not eaten! Zack was aghast. *Their essence may transfer! Something of them—however little—may get into lesser creatures. Is that a fitting end for a Lord? Continuity without consciousness?*

In wartime, Lords are eaten, Nestor contradicted him. *And we are at war. You won't infect any of ours . . . but if you did, so what? They are already vampires, every one. As for your Wamphyri essence: that will be well distributed. Ground down fine with the meat of lesser men . . . why, the warriors won't notice the difference!*

You . . . are a monster! Zack's final protest.

Aren't we all? Nestor's answer.

Then, as Laughing Zack's shattered remains were removed, so Wratha stepped forward, spat upon them, and cried her derision. "Who laughs last, laughs loudest—eh, Zack!"

But Lord Shornskull couldn't hear her, and Nestor didn't bother to translate . . .

Nestor told Wratha everything he'd learned from Zack: the warrior Lord Vormulac's whereabouts, the strength of his army, the fact that almost every Lord and Lady in Turgosheim—with the exception of Maglore the Mage, who had remained behind as caretaker—had joined Lord Unsleep's crusade against her; following which she went off with the others, escorted from Suckscar as was only right and proper, to make her plans. Only the dog-Lord lingered, and Nestor could tell from Canker's expression and actions (his irritable whining, the way he touched his ear tenderly, and shook his great wolf's head) that something was amiss.

"What's wrong?" he wanted to know, when he was sure that the others were out of his manse. "Where are those high spirits of yours now, Canker? Why is your bark changed to a whine?"

"But I might easily ask the same of you!" Canker

snarled by way of an answer. "Indeed, in the last four to five months, why, I might have asked it a dozen times!"

Nestor nodded wearily, beckoned the dog-Lord to a chair, himself stood gazing from a window at the black-fanged silhouette of the distant barrier range. "Aye, things have changed," he finally said. "We've sniffed war awhile now, and finally it's come. Nerves have become frayed . . . even friendships, it appears."

"This has nothing to do with fighting and war," Canker growled, coming directly to the point. "You've not wanted my friendship for quite some time now. Since it's nothing that I have done, it has to be something with you. Well, friends are for listening, so now it's my turn to ask: What's wrong?"

Nestor looked at him, opened his mouth—looked away and said, "I can't tell you. But I can tell you this: if I've kept away from you, or kept you from me, it has done you no harm."

"A riddle?"

"If you like."

"I don't!" And again Canker whined, fingered the injured side of his face and head again, especially his ear, shook his head and blinked rapidly.

"That knock you took?" Nestor was solicitous, as best he could be.

"Maybe, maybe not," said the other.

And smiling with his eyes (for they were all that could be seen of his face behind the gauze of his mask, in the shade of his cloak's high cowl), Nestor gave a wry chuckle and said, "Now who makes riddles? It's as if we played word games!"

Canker yelped, *"Huh!"* But even though the necromancer's hidden smile had seemed wan, it was all it took to perk him up a little. He grinned a foxy grin in return, sprang up from his chair, shook himself like a great dog as was his wont, and made to approach Nestor at the window. But the other at once shrank back. At which Canker was more than ever crestfallen. "Perhaps . . . perhaps if I tell you, then you'll tell me?"

"No." Nestor shook his head.

"Why not?" The dog-Lord frowned, his spiked eyebrows coming together over his snout.

"Because there's no answer to what ails me. And since it can't be helped, there's no point in mentioning it. But that's not to say I can't listen to you. Didn't you say it yourself, that friends are for listening?"

The other loped to his chair and flopped into it. And: "I hate this," he said, his voice a low growl.

"This impasse?"

"An impasse may be breached. No, this . . . *condition*!"

"Your condition?"

Canker sat up straighter, looked directly into Nestor's eyes. "My friend, you've heard how the others talk about me, behind my back?"

Nestor shrugged. "They talk about me, about each other. There's no peace or satisfaction in any of them . . . or in me . . . or in you! We're Wamphyri!"

Canker clawed at his ear again, shook his head more violently yet. But in a little while he grew calmer. "You know of course that my father went baying mad? His ear went soft on the inside, began to stink and leaked his brains. He'd seen it coming—for he was oneiromantic, too—so that when his favourite bitch dropped me, he named me after his affliction: Canker, as if I were to blame for it! Or . . . as if I were the spawn of it? When I was yet a pup, he mounted a flyer and flew off into the sun. His talent came to me through his seed, and his vampire egg through a fond fatherly kiss. But am I also heir to his madness?"

Finally Nestor understood. "Is that what's bothering you? You think you're mad?"

"*Going* mad, aye," Canker growled. "Maybe . . ."

"Ridiculous!" (But in all honesty, Nestor wouldn't have wagered on it.) "What, you, crazy? Crazy as a fox, perhaps!"

Canker's feral-cored eyes were suddenly miles away, vacant except for a distant glimmer. "But I have had such *dreams*, Nestor—such dreams as even I can't believe! My silver mistress in the moon ... I had thought there was just the one ... but perhaps the moon is full of them! To *hell* with this war! Once more I'm driven to play upon my instrument of bones, and do homage to the goddess of the skies ..."

He was on his feet again, eyes blazing now. And now Nestor most definitely would not bet upon the dog-Lord's sanity. He sent out a call to his first lieutenant, Zahar: *Come*. And said to Canker, "Mangemanse needs you, my friend. It's time you went down and saw to things. Hell will have to wait, for the war is here. My man Zahar will see you out."

But the other grabbed his arm, pleading with him, "Nestor, my dear young Lord out of Sunside, you must tell me: am I mad? *Is* the moon eating at my brain?"

Nestor saw a way to reason with him. "Did Wratha and the others call you mad when first you mentioned your silver moon mistress? Yes, they did. Even I found it strange. But tell me now: is she real or not, your Siggi? And now ... are you saying you've dreamed of others?"

"One other! More woman than girl, mature, but a beauty beyond imagining!"

"Then your madness is not yet proven. Call her down, if you must. And if she comes—"

"—Then I'll know that I'm sane!"

"Exactly."

Zahar came and Canker, at least partially appeased, left with him.

But when they were well away from Nestor's private rooms, Canker said, "Zahar, your master is my friend. Do you believe that?"

"I have seen it, Lord." Zahar's tone was cautious. "How may I doubt it?"

Canker nodded. "Just so. And I fancy that you are a good and true lieutenant and love him ... well, as much as you may. Is it so?"

"You know it is, Lord."

"Then you are concerned for his welfare?"

"Of course, Lord."

"Ah, but what *is* it that concerns you?"

Zahar was the victim of a word game, but one with a point, as he now saw. Having admitted his concern for Nestor, now he must say why . . . or perhaps not. For a "true" lieutenant would never give his master away, after all. "You know I may not tell you that, Lord," he protested. "My master would send me soaring like a Szgany kite from his highest window—except I'm a good deal heavier than a kite, and not so airworthy."

"But something ails him?—Don't deny it, for I've seen how you shun him . . . *ah!*" And Canker snapped his fingers. "But it's true: you *do* shun him! Why, this place was full of life, or undeath at least! But now, it's gloomy as melancholy Vormspire in the gorge of Turgosheim. Very well, so you won't tell me what's wrong, despite the fact that my only interest lies in putting it right. Then tell me this instead: What happened tonight, on Sunside? Where did you go and what did you do?"

Zahar was confused; the dog-Lord was so quick, his questions coming thick and fast; Zahar couldn't guard his mind and tongue both. Since his thoughts were transparent to the other, he must blank them out. But before he could do so he felt Canker's telepathic probe . . . only for a moment, until Zahar conjured thoughts of warmth and softness, safety and sleep: such thoughts as a foetus might think in its mother's womb. It did the trick, but how much had the dog-Lord seen? Judging by his disappointed expression, not much.

And: *"Huh!"* Canker grunted. "Well, and so you are indeed a good man and true—which is as it should be. Protect your master's interests, say I, and who knows but that one day you might even get his egg!"

At which Zahar Lichloathe could scarcely contain the look of horror that threatened to twist his face, the stab of terror he felt in his heart.

But no harm done, for the dog-Lord had not noticed, apparently . . .

* * *

Canker *had* noticed. And he at least had kept his thoughts to himself as he'd probed Zahar's mind and spied on all the vivid memories that flashed there; memories of Nestor's raid after the ignominious defeat of the Wamphyri at Sanctuary Rock:

A place at the edge of the forest, where the mighty iron-woods grew to the rim of the savanna, beyond which the furnace deserts sprawled south. A place under the trees, of low-roofed construction, as if huddling or hiding there. And a place that Nestor had known about, obviously.

Not so strange, Canker thought; despite the lad's amnesia, there were still things he occasionally remembered from the old days, from his time as a Szgany youth in the tribe of Lardis Lidesci. And as the dog-Lord proceeded down into Mangemanse, he scanned the screen of his own memory, recalling the rest of what he'd read in Zahar's unguarded mind:

Of Nestor's flyers' silent landing a little way out on the savanna, where a hummock of crabgrass half an acre square guaranteed an easy takeoff; of his handful of men fanning out to surround the dark huddle of lodges beneath the trees, while he brought up his eager fighting beasts from where they waited like storm clouds in the starlit sky. And of his command, that the warriors crash down indiscriminately through the forest's canopy! How they brought down massive branches with them, and crushed many of the furtive-seeming dwellings into the floor of the forest. Then:

The hoarse-voiced screams that at once went up from the wrecked houses . . . the frightened bellowing of domestic beasts in their pens, and the squawk and flutter of chickens in their coops . . . the uproar *of the warriors where they proceeded with their deadly work! Except here a surprising, perhaps even astonishing thing: the necromancer's strict mental command going out to his warriors and thralls alike, that they must not eat of the flesh of these men and beasts!*

Then what was the point of it? Revenge? But for what? And anyway, wouldn't that be the sweetest revenge of all:

to eat your enemies? But no, the necromancer Lord Nestor Lichloathe had other ideas and gave his men other orders. At his command his monsters had quit their wrecking and ravaging, and headed for the open savanna, and his men where they had spread themselves out around the low fence enclosing this secret community . . . had set fire to the place!

And as the flames roared up and the surviving inhabitants attempted to escape into the night-dark woods, instead of taking prisoners or recruiting thralls, Nestor had caused his men to throw them back into the fire!

But here a weird—distortion?—of memory; of Zahar's memory, at least, for Canker was merely reviewing what he had glimpsed in the lieutenant's mind:

Those terrified figures fleeing—some stumbling, even crawling—from the flames, but only to be thrown back again. Able-bodied? No, not a one of them! There was no fight in them. They were weak, crippled, broken people, these. But crippled by the warriors? Ravaged by the heat of the conflagration? Broken in their bones by flying debris from their collapsing houses?—Or what?

Their silhouettes against the leaping flames: grotesque, misshapen, twisted—incomplete? At first it had seemed that their clothes must in tatters, but . . . this was no distortion! For suddenly it had dawned on Zahar that they themselves were the tatters!!!

And now it dawned on the dog-Lord, too, and as simply and as devastatingly and as mind-blastingly as that, he knew:

That Nestor had burned a leper colony!

The rest of it—total understanding of Nestor's predicament—came like a clap of thunder, even as Canker descended into Mangemanse. And shivering and shuddering, he went to his rooms and called for one of his pups, a trusted lieutenant, to attend him. Then:

"The internal route up into Suckscar," he told his man in something of a whimper, or a whisper at least. "Have it sealed tonight, at once, now! No one shall pass that way again; *nothing* shall pass that way, not even air or light!"

"Yes, Lord," said the other, gawping. "Is that all?"

Canker nodded absentmindedly, then gave himself a shake. "No, something else. Wratha the Risen may call for the Lords, myself included, to attend her war council. All well and good, except I may not hear her; I'll be at my devotions in the cavern of my instrument. I want you to listen for her call, and alert me when it comes."

"Yes, Lord."

"Then be about it."

The other departed. But on his way from the dog-Lord's apartments, loping through the mazy passageways and halls of Mangemanse, he gave a massive start. Coming from behind him, passing him by, and filling all the manse with its throbbing ululations, such a long-drawn out, mournful howl of a cry as never before was uttered! Doleful and doom-fraught, finally it tapered to a sob and died away.

The lieutenant shook his head worriedly, and went about his duties as instructed.

IV

Devetaki's Lure

Some thirty-five minutes earlier, Devetaki Skullguise and her small reconnaissance party had landed on the boulder plains in the vicinity of the glaring hemisphere Gate. A cursory, purely visual examination of the phenomenon had told the Lady nothing, but acute Wamphyri senses had warned her to leave well enough alone. Whatever the Gate was, at present it was quiescent and probably better that way.

Before landing, she and her men had spied Gorvi's warrior where it lay recuperating in the lee of a boulder clump; failing to recognize her but sensing that she was Wamphyri, it had issued vile gasses and a warning honk but made no violent movement. Patently the thing was injured, which meant very little; sometimes an injured warrior was all the more dangerous.

Since she had brought no fighting beasts of her own with her, only the speediest flyers on what was mainly an exploratory trip, Devetaki ignored the creature for the moment but sent a messenger back to Vormulac to report its location. There was sufficient meat here to fuel Lord Unsleep's beasts through all the long night ahead and for some time to come. His men would have other needs, however.

Taking off again, she had ventured south for the mouth of the great pass, and rising above it to a position approximately central in the width of the range, had sensed human thoughts in the darkness of the canyon yawning below. Landing on a plateau east of the pass, Devetaki had cautioned her thralls to silence while she, a highly skilled mentalist, attempted to "listen in" on the minds of those below.

That they were not Szgany was immediately apparent, for the Szgany of Sunside had long since learned to shield their minds from Wamphyri probes. Come sundown, they were expert at suppressing, disguising, diffusing, or thinning their thoughts; they became moths, owls, or foxes in the night. Also, in olden times in Turgosheim, they'd had a trick of smearing themselves with foul oil of kneblasch, so discouraging investigation; but as often as not the stink itself had located them, and the oil could always be removed. Oh, the Szgany were wise in the ways of the Wamphyri, and vice versa; wherefore, these men in the pass were not Szgany. But if not Travellers, Starside trogs, or desert Thyre—and definitely not vampires—then what?

Ah, but these were strange new lands, perhaps inhabited by stranger people! As well to listen to their minds awhile, Devetaki thought, and see what she could glean.

But what she gleaned . . . was fantastic!

Two of the minds were powerful, talented, skilled in the psychic arts. One was a seer, a locator: he could scan afar to discover other minds, enemies. And even though he was sleeping when Devetaki "visited" him, still she must be careful not to announce her presence. Ah, and his mind was dark, too; treacherous, cunning. In the olden parlance, a "magician," this one, and sinister.

And the other . . . was little different! Except not only was his mind very powerful, he himself was a Power—or saw himself as such, at any rate. A commander of men, he should make a fine lieutenant. And all of the men with him were his; he *was* their commander! His talent . . . was Devetaki's! A mentalist, he could read minds "at a glance," and accurately. But the glance was all-important; he needed eye-to-eye contact to see in through the windows of the mind.

A pair of them, then: magicians!

And the men with them? A dozen at least, some wary, even worried, but mainly full of an alien self-confidence. Strong men: soldiers! And all of them with a good understanding of discipline, strategy, tactics—the very stuff of their profession! They had all of those skills which the Lords of Turgosheim had long forgotten; yet these were common men!

Or uncommon men?

Self-confident, aye, but an *alien* self-confidence, as she had already noted. And now Devetaki looked closer:

They had weapons and slept with them; or if not with them, they kept them so close to hand it made no difference. Several of them dreamed of war, and of using those weapons. Except . . . Devetaki could scarcely credit what they dreamed; surely these were fantasies! But then, was it also a fantasy that these men had come into her world through the portal of the glaring Starside hemisphere, that cold white globe bedded in its crater on the boulder plains? And again she thought of Maglore the Mage in Turgosheim, and what he had said of the Old Wamphyri, that there had been magicians among them who . . .

. . . called up Powers they couldn't contain, which was the beginning of the end. For in a cataclysmic war, such weapons were brought to bear against them that they were destroyed in all of their houses . . .

Then, but more carefully yet, Devetaki went back to the mind of their commander. And probing however gently, she read his purpose here: conquest! No less than Wratha when she had fled from Turgosheim, and no less than Vormulac now, this one would subdue this entire world and bring it under the sway of his homeworld beyond the Starside Gate. But no, Devetaki saw that she was wrong. It had *been* his purpose to usurp Sunside/Starside, *perhaps* for alien masters, but that was before they banished him or caused him to flee from them.

Now he had another purpose. He would still conquer this vampire world, yes—but for himself!

Why, this one's daring, his ego and aspirations, were as great as those of Wratha herself. Even as great as Vormulac's. Possibly as great as Devetaki's! Nor was it blind ambition; he *knew* what he was up to, what he went up against . . . something of it, anyway. And just like his men, he put his faith in the power of those alien weapons.

Devetaki must probe deeper, but he wasn't long asleep and she must be careful not to disturb him. That sensitive mind of his might possibly discover her there. Or if not his mind, perhaps that of his locator companion.

Thus it was that concentrating, concentrating, a Lady of the Wamphyri gazed upon Turkur Tzonov's innermost dreams and ambitions . . .

Turkur dreamed, but at first his dreams were obscured by some strange intervention, by a presence that watched albeit from afar. For a while he tried to distance himself from it, which had no more effect than floundering through a swamp to escape one's own shadow; for like a mote in the eye the presence was always there, until in the end he ignored it.

He dreamed a little of the past, something of the present, and snatches from a vague and uncertain future. The past was fact, however disappointing; the present took form as directed by past events, if not exactly as Turkur would have it; but the future . . . could yet be as he willed it, if he willed it hard enough.

And since dreams are the clearinghouses of the conscious mind—where not only the desires but all the suppressed guilt of the waking world gains expression and the balance is adjusted accordingly—much of what he dreamed was nightmarish, so that he tossed and turned a little in his bed in the keep in the pass. And all that he dreamed was "observed" by Devetaki Skullguise.

From the past, Turkur dreamed of the telepath Siggi Dam: of how she had acted and looked after he and Alexei Yefros had downloaded her brain, the night they sent her through the Perschorsk Gate. But because he remembered other times before that—remembered her body, breasts, buttocks, and the oh-so-sweet suction of her sex—his dream was a nightmare, an expression of his guilt, which he would never have admitted during waking hours. Of course not, for Siggi had been a traitor after all. Siggi the clever, the awesomely talented, the incredibly beautiful— reduced to a vegetable, bereft of all knowledge except the most basic instincts: her recognition of being, her telepathy (which in any case lay in the structure of her brain, not in anything she'd learned), her sexual awakenings. She'd been like a child again when they were through with her, a shivering, trembling innocent. Mentally innocent, at least.

It had been achieved with the aid of a machine, a "technological marvel" . . . or a monstrosity, however one chose to view it. In his dream, Turkur remembered how lovely Siggi Dam had looked, lying there drugged and mainly unfeeling, but conscious where she waited for them to switch on the machine. And he remembered Yefros telling him:

"It's much like a computer—we don't have to delete it all. We can start at the beginning, with . . . her birth?"

And his answer: *"No, let her keep it. We all need to know that, for it's part of the will to survive. Without it she'd be nothing but a bag of plasma. She has to have something of will, so that she'll know to run, hide, be afraid. As for her childhood, most of that can go. But her sex, her first arousal, and the way it has developed—or overdeveloped—she can keep those things. Siggi was good at it, and it might even keep her alive awhile, in Starside . . ."*

The dream moved on but stayed focussed on Siggi. Siggi: bundled stumbling through the Gate, caught by the grey hole's seemingly gentle but nevertheless irresistible attraction and drawn in; walking in a weird slow-motion, wonderingly into a hazy white distance, and diminishing in size as the distance increased. Then: Siggi pausing, looking back, trying to *come* back, and failing! Her discovery that the Gate was a one-way ride, and of the extra-mundane forces that allowed her to move in one direction only, forward into the unknown. But then again, almost *everything* had been unknown to this newborn Siggi. And finally the last they'd seen of her: her tiny running figure, a shimmering blue and silver and platinum-blonde mote on the solid yet hazy-white horizon, gradually disappearing into it.

Siggi gone. Through the Gate. Into Starside . . .

Then, as if Turkur's memory, his psyche, his subconscious self could bear it no longer, the dream moved on, drew closer to the present:

Snatches from the fighting in Perchorsk . . . Turkur's men against Gustav Turchin's forces . . . The sheer, unholy devastation *unleashed by the weapons of both sides . . . Turkur's escape into the Gate . . . His first astonished impressions of Starside when he and his team emerged from the glaring portal onto the plain of boulders.* Devetaki viewed all of these things, and learned something of Turkur Tzonov's aspirations, too.

He had failed to become a true Power in his own world—for the moment. But if he could somehow tame *this* world, starting first with the Szgany of Sunside, and eventually bringing the Wamphyri themselves to heel . . . !

What? Why, the unbelievable, towering ego, the stupendous audacity of the man! (But nevertheless, Devetaki made a mental note: he would make a fine thrall, this fellow, even a lieutenant, but he must *never* be offered or allowed to acquire an egg! For if this Turkur Tzonov should ever become Wamphyri . . . what chance then for the rest of them? Nor was the virgin grandam's introspective query entirely sarcastic.)

It was a new feeling for Devetaki, even a new emotion: to stand in awe of another's grandiose ambitions and be aware that he could probably achieve them. Or rather, to know that he *had been* capable of achieving them . . .

Plainly she must have him. Maybe even both of them, Tzonov and Yefros together. And she had reasons galore:

One: they must not be allowed to reach Sunside with these alien weapons and their superior knowledge of warfare. Why, the Szgany worked metals and could probably duplicate these death-dealing devices, these "guns"! With Tzonov leading an army of resurgent Szgany (*if* the men of this western Sunside had ever been under the heel of the Wamphyri in the first place, which wasn't as yet proven), then the renegade Wratha would be the very least of Vormulac's problems.

Two: quite apart from their military skills and the definite threat of their technology, these men were from another world and had full, fantastic knowledge of it. *And* there was a white-glaring gateway into that world down there where the foothills met the boulder plains! Moreover, and based on what Devetaki had read in Tzonov's subconscious mind, the many and diverse inhabitants of that world were generally weak and had little or no belief . . . in vampires! Even better, as yet only a select handful of them knew about *this* world, Sunside/Starside. Obviously there was a lot more to be learned, for instance: how could a place like that have bred men like Tzonov? But that was for the future. For Devetaki's future!

Three: these alien soldiers were newcomers here. If they should fall into Wratha's hands, their military knowledge and technology would go with them. Even Vormulac and his army out of Tugosheim would have no great advantage then—*if* he had one now!

Four: only deprive these men of their leader—and possibly Yefros, too—and they'd be like chickens without heads: running around and squawking a great deal, but without getting anywhere. That would make them easy prey; *literally* prey, for there was an army to be fed. Or, if Tzonov's men should prove too valuable for use in the provisioning, then they (and their weapons, of course) could always be recruited. And what chance for Wratha then?

Oh, the reasons why Devetaki should at least attempt to kidnap these two talents were many and obvious; not so obvious how to go about it. But the virgin grandam was a woman no less than Wratha, and her mind moved in equally devious circles. She was well aware of the weakness of men, and how to use them to her advantage. This Siggi Dam, for instance: Tzonov thought she must be dead by now, and he was probably right. But he couldn't know for sure. Perhaps Devetaki could convince him otherwise.

She issued orders to her men, mounted her flyer, and keeping well clear of the keep flew down into the pass. And winging silently through the night, she thought:

The weaknesses of men, aye—especially strong men, when they think they are safe and secure in their strength. But she was thinking of one such weakness in particular: their curiosity . . .

Turkuuur!

At first it was only a whisper in his dreaming mind, but one that grew louder and gained definition apace with its insistence. *Turkuuur . . . Turkuuur!*

Again he saw pictures of Siggi, planted in his dreams (or released from the wellspring of his memory) by Devetaki Skullguise. Siggi in the swirling tatters of what had once been her night attire, in which she'd been dressed when she went through the Perchorsk Gate; but just as beautiful as ever, and as innocent of knowledge. Or perhaps not. Presumably she had learned something of this world, or she could never have survived.

Turkuuur! . . . And suddenly her telepathic voice firmed up. . *Turkur—you're in danger!*

"What? Danger?" He mumbled in his sleep and fidgeted awkwardly in his sleeping bag by the hearth of a great fireplace, in which embers were still glowing red. Deep in his subconscious mind, however, he knew that he was safe; there were sentries in the keep's courtyard and watchers in its turrets. But human watchers now, not *Things* left over from some nightmare past.

Turkur, I'm in the pass. I saw you arrive and remembered you. And I remember Alexei . . . But I can't come to you; those men, soldiers, they frighten me. I don't want them to see me. I can't come to you because the men frighten me, and so does Alexei. But I know you. We trusted each other once. You need me now, Turkur. I know about this place . . . its daaangers.

"Siggi?" She had got through to him at last. He continued to sleep but his mind was locked on to his dream and the false images planted there by Devetaki. In fact the Lady was somewhat surprised to discover just how susceptible his mind was. Telepathic, demanding, threatening in his waking hours, he was used to contacting and probing the conscious minds of inferiors but lacked a defence against her subconscious superiority.

And Devetaki was proud of her mentalism.

In Turgosheim one time, when she'd caught the Seer-Lord Maglore creeping silently through her thoughts, Devetaki had warned him: *hands off my mind, Maglore! Drift in the shallow thoughts of others all you will and catch what sprats you can. But beware the swirly deeps, for there dwell great and vicious fishes!* And Maglore had moved on at once. For he had known her telepathic power and accepted her as his peer; while this one, this Turkur, accepted no one as his peer apparently. Therefore, he would not believe he was being manipulated; he would reason that his thoughts, even his subconscious thoughts, were wholly original to himself. And he would be curious. Ego + curiosity = weakness.

"Siggi?" Turkur mumbled again, twitching more violently yet. "Where? How?"

Devetaki had developed the theme of his dream; now she was sparing in its direction, merely guiding Turkur's stream of thought and letting him follow the trail—and hoping, of course, that he would follow it all the way. *I'm in the pass. But there's danger, Turkur. You didn't need me before, but now you do. Don't leave me here in the dangerous dark. For if you do, who will care for you in this new world, and who will care for me? Would you have some coarse Gypsy for your companion in Sunside, or would you have me?*

It was a seductive argument. Tzonov almost started awake, and Devetaki knew it was time to move on.

The beacon of Alexei Yefros's locator mind was impossible to miss. His talent worked against him as Devetaki located him in roughly the same vicinity, probably the same room as Turkur Tzonov, and carefully probed his subconscious thoughts. She pictured the machine that she had seen in Tzonov's mind, and let Yefros shape his own dream from the image.

He saw the machine, and, hooked up to it, lying on a surgical trolley, Siggi as she'd been that night: clad only in her gauzy night things, more beautiful than any woman he had ever known (or any man), and entirely accessible. Except ... Tzonov was there and anything like that was out of the question. But her mouth, so tempting ... the valley between her breasts ... the various openings of her body.

And Devetaki thought (if only to herself), *Hah! He has the mind of a vampire Lord if not the physique! Little wonder these two were outcasts in their own world. But in* my *world ... what you would have done to her, Alexei, my lads would do to you—except you would probably enjoy it!*

And in the guise of Siggi Dam, Devetaki sent into the psychic aether a message that both of these talents would hear: *I'm in the pass, Turkur. But I'm afraid of your soldiers—and of Alexei Yefros!*

Both of them came starting awake together, and both with the same name on their lips: "Siggi!"

Her picture was receding in their minds, but a fleeting echo was still there: *Turkur, I'm in the pass towards Sunside. I was on my way back to the Gate on the boulder plains when I saw you. But I'm afraid, Turkur, afraaaid!*

Devetaki had got her as nearly as possible right; she had been the very essence of Siggi Dam. Now that Tzonov and Yefros were awake, however, she knew her subterfuge couldn't continue. She could no longer *be* Siggi but only a presence, and then only to the locator. So she became a presence, but nothing more than that, in the location that she'd already chosen.

"In the pass," Yefros whispered, as they unzipped their bags, pulled on combat boots and stood up. "Definitely. I can feel her there."

"She survived!" Tzonov could scarcely believe it. "Maybe the British got it wrong and this place isn't so deadly after all. But no, I can't see that. Perhaps she's simply lucky."

"I heard her speaking to you." Yefros's voice was sibilant in the silence of the keep. "Even sleeping I located her. Her telepathy . . . the machine certainly didn't take *that* from her! She seems to be afraid of the men, and she's afraid of me, too." He licked his lips, relishing the idea. It pleased Yefros that someone feared him.

Tzonov finished dressing, glanced at the other. "She fears the filth that's in your mind," he said. "No disrespect to your talent, Alexei, but your . . . personality? That leaves a lot to be desired. To Siggi's way of thinking, anyway."

They were in a room approximately one hundred feet above the bed of the pass. The room was one of a series cut back from a natural ledge under a massive overhang and walled with masonry from the rim up to the outward-curving rock face. Beyond the wall and arched window-spaces lay empty air. An archway led out onto a walled balcony looking down on the pass.

Sharing the room with Tzonov and Yefros, and hearing

their movements and something of their conversation, Bruno Krasin had also come awake. While Krasin knew of their talents, he himself was of mundane perceptions and could scarcely comprehend them. He understood the physical well enough—especially in a military context—but ESP was metaphysical and so beyond him; he tended to forget about it until he saw it in actual use.

"Who survived?" he said, coming easily to his feet. And: "Am I needed?" He looked at the two espers, their faces glowing dull red in reflected firelight.

"Siggi Dam survived," Tzonov told him, going out onto the balcony. "She's hiding somewhere down there in the pass, in the direction of Sunside. We're going to find her and bring her in. Her telepathy is still powerful and she could be extremely useful—to us." He had almost said "to me," but didn't want to show his specific interest. Right now he wasn't ready to admit that interest even to himself, despite the fact that something of what she had conveyed to him lingered over. Something about a companion? Would he prefer the company of a coarse Gypsy woman to hers? That was a question he could answer later, and so he put it to the back of his mind.

Yefros and Krasin joined him on the balcony, stared down into darkness. South, the very faintest of afterglows silhouetted a narrow horizon; it was less than a smudge above the inky well of night. But Siggi's thoughts had been powerful and she was probably close. "Somewhere down there," Yefros mused. And to Tzonov: "If she sees you, she'll come to you."

"How do you know she's—?" Krasin started to say, frowning. He checked himself at once. A stupid question; Yefros had simply *known*, that was all.

"Do you have her?" Tzonov glanced at the locator.

Yefros's eyes were glinting bright in starlight. "A presence, that's all."

"But you know it's her, right?" This from Krasin. Without knowing it, he had asked the one question that they hadn't. And he followed it up with another: "Is she on her own?"

Tzonov blinked his penetrating eyes, glanced at his section commander and shrugged. "Siggi spoke to me, mind to mind. Alexei got something of it, too."

"A presence," Yefros said again. "Just the one, yes."

Tzonov gripped Krasin's elbow. "Come with us anyway." And to Yefros, "Check your weapon."

The locator took out a small-caliber, high-powered automatic, checked the clip, replaced it in its shoulder holster. More suited to a woman's hand, still the pistol had stopping power. Krasin tried not to sneer as he asked: "Is that it?"

Yefros answered, "If a single bullet will stop a man, I can't see much sense in using ten, twenty, an entire stream of them. It strikes me we'll be a long time in this vampire world. A little economy now may later be seen to make a lot of sense." He spoke without too much animation, but couldn't resist raising an almost effeminate eyebrow as Krasin checked out his own short-barrelled, laser-targeting, 10.2mm self-loading rifle.

Krasin didn't notice, but Tzonov chuckled and said, "Ah, yes, Alexei: nasty macho weapons for a nasty macho world! But you are right about the economy bit. We must be careful how we spend our firepower." His own weapon was a machine pistol, and as he spoke he moved a lever from "rapid" to "semiautomatic" fire. Now he must pull on the trigger for each individual shot required.

They descended to the ground floor of the keep, quietly through rooms where the men were billeted and down dark, echoing stairwells, occasionally using external stairways under a clear-cut swath of coldly glittering stars where the towering canyon walls met the sky.

In the courtyard they were challenged by a member of the prowler guard who loomed out of the shadows, his weapon at the ready. Krasin congratulated him, and quietly told him: "We're going out for a while. Until we're back make sure your weapon is on safe. You wouldn't want an itchy, nervous trigger finger to slip and blow your superiors to hell, now would you?" There was no humour in his remark, and a sharp metallic *click* in the darkness signalled the prowler guard's immediate compliance.

Another prowler was at the massive gates; Krasin spoke to him briefly, and the three moved out into the pass.

It was eerily quiet, so that even the whirring of a tiny bat's wings sounded unnaturally loud before the creature sped away into the night. Then, with their torch beams sweeping the way ahead, and following the scarcely recognizable trail along the scree-littered canyon floor, the three searchers gradually increased the distance between themselves and the keep—*and* the keep's far greater store of firepower, of course . . .

. . . Which was precisely what Devetaki Skullguise wanted. And one hundred yards farther down the pass, behind a leaning boulder where she oh-so-patiently waited, that Lady uncloaked her telepathic mind (but just a little, the merest crack, and so revealed nothing of her true identity but simply the promise of her presence). And:

"There!" Alexei Yefros hissed. The locator went into a half-crouch and pointed with his torch, whose beam dispersed with distance and fell short of lighting up Devetaki's hiding place by some fifteen to twenty yards. As Tzonov and Krasin's torch beams joined in, however, the half-buried boulder stood out as a leaning, irregular blot against the greater dark.

"A rock?" Krasin grunted.

"A place to hide," Tzonov corrected him. And to Yefros: "I heard it, too, Alexei. And you are right, she's there!"

They moved forward, left the trail, clambered towards the boulder. As they went Tzonov called out in a low voice, "Siggi, it is I, Turkur. I heard your call and I've come for you. Don't be afraid." But in the next moment . . . the female who emerged from behind the boulder certainly wasn't afraid, and she most definitely wasn't Siggi Dam!

The sight—the jolting shock—of her abrupt appearance in the glare of their converging torch beams stopped all three men dead in their tracks. Her face froze them; its "smile" was awesome. For the Mistress of Masquemanse was wearing her frowning half-mask. And while the leaden side grimaced, its counterpart grinned! And both of her eyes, in the face and the socket of the half-mask alike, were red as clots of blood and glowed with an internal, an infernal fire!

Krasin, in no way a believer, breathed, "Jesus!"

Yefros, as his jaw fell open, gasped, "Not Siggi!"

But Turkur Tzonov, cocking his machine pistol, said simply, chokingly: "Wamphyri!"

Devetaki was dressed in exoskeletal-styled battle gear, all gleaming leather and sculpted, flexible cartilage. Her gauntlet looked alive on her hand, like a vicious spiny beast in its own right; and with her long legs, proud breasts, and red hair flowing, she looked every inch a warrior queen of ancient Earth. It was a disguise, of course, the product of that metamorphic art which allowed all of the Wamphyri effortlessly to maintain a more or less human guise. But when threatened or gearing for action . . .

. . . That same metamorphism was changing her even now—into the monstrous destroyer she really was! The great gape of her jaws, and the flickering bifurcate tongue they housed; the quivering, batlike convolutions of her flattened nose; the hellfire heat of her burning gaze! And the sickly mist pouring from *her* pores, and called up writhing from the riven earth, as if the pass itself were a tortured, living creature!

Then, to add to the confusion of these three aliens in her world—aware of the mentalism of one of them, and the psychic prowess of another—Devetaki opened her own vampire mind all the way to hurl a gurgling, phlegmy thought at them:

Fools! Why, I know what you would do even as you proceed to do it!

Tzonov tested her anyway, pulled the trigger of his machine pistol and sprayed the space where she had been—or tried to spray it. But his weapon was still on single-shot and fired off just one round, and in the moment that he fired it Devetaki had acted: a flowing, swirling *dislocation* of space that moved her like a wraith—as if she floated to one side without physical effort—back behind the boulder.

So that Tzonov's lone bullet scarred the rock, struck sparks from its flinty surface and did no harm at all, while Devetaki's vampire mist swirled mockingly around his ankles, then his knees.

Then: a vicious, mechanical ch-*ching*! as Krasin cocked his rifle and ran forward in a crouch to skirt the boulder; and his harsh, practiced, authoritative cry of "Flush the bitch out!"

And Yefros's terrified, stuttering squeal, "M-m-mother of God—*more* of them!" as his talent came into play and located other minds where suddenly they sprang into sharp focus. Thus, in a matter of minutes, both Tzonov's locator and his military commander had called on deities in whom they had no faith, and who certainly would have none in them.

Before Krasin could get close to the boulder and attempt to "flush the bitch out," the psychic aether came leaping alive.

Take them! And Tzonov scarcely needed eye-to-eye contact now; Devetaki had deliberately fired her order for all to hear ... and especially Turkur Tzonov, to further increase his confusion. *And you, creature—come, take me up!*

At which the darkness came alive, too!

Something huge and grey, previously unnoticed, disguised by the night and a backdrop of rubble and jagged canyon walls, pushed itself upright on a nest of wormlike thrusters, arched its wings, stretched its neck and launched out and down from a sliding scree mound; a great manta shape drifting on the night air, angling for Devetaki's boulder.

Tzonov would line up his sights on the thing but was distracted by Yefros's shrieking; likewise by Krasin's curses and the deadly diatribe of his weapon; and in any case, Devetaki's flyer was only *one* thing! Where to fire first for best effect? At the Lady, of course, if only she were visible. But in this clinging, sickly mist, in all this confusion, in the flitting shadows of more nightmare flyers, which even now soared overhead, blotting out the stars and drawing Krasin's fire . . . ?

Tzonov found his voice at last, and in the temporary lull while Krasin slapped a fresh magazine into his rifle's housing, shouted: "Back to the keep!" His voice was hoarse, even terrified—

—But the virgin grandam's was fearless, full of a monstrous anticipation as she told him: *Ah, no, my pretty!*

Briefly—so swift and sure in her movements that Tzonov barely had time to swing the muzzle of his weapon in her direction—Devetaki emerged again from hiding, sprang skywards and grasped the trailing trappings of her beast's harness. It bore her away laughing into the mist and the darkness.

Now Tzonov's frantic gasping and cursing joined Krasin's, and both were almost drowned out by Yefros's woman's shrieks as the night and more than the night pressed down on them. And the air of the pass seemed full of swooping motion. No, it *was* full of motion!

No longer mere shadows, a pair of manta flyers came speeding along the bed of the pass, one out of the south, the other from the north. Eager figures leaned forward in their saddles; feral eyes gleamed yellow, and ivory teeth dripped saliva into red-ribbed caverns of horror.

Yefros had made his way back to the trail. Arms and legs frantically pumping, the terrified locator was heading for the sanctuary of the keep, whose eye-socket windows and cliff-hewn balconies were lit up now in the yellow-flaring light of hastily fired torches. Viewed through Devetaki's mist, however, the flickering golden fireflies seemed far away indeed—and much too far for Alexei Yefros.

One of Devetaki's lieutenants' flyers had veered from Tzonov's view into the deep shadows of the rearing east wall. The other, coming through the "tunnel" of the pass from the north, was rapidly losing altitude, stalling, arching its membranous wings as it settled towards the running figure of Yefros. Like the grasping limbs of some unthinkably huge carnivorous insect, or the feelers of a hideous, sentient anemone, a nest of wormlike thrusters was uncoiling from a belly cavity, palps quivering where they reached out after the unsuspecting locator. But as mount and rider went drifting by, fully intent upon their prey, so they presented Tzonov with a target he couldn't miss.

Falling to one knee, he took careful aim at the leatherclad back and side of the figure in the saddle . . .

. . . And just a moment too late sensed rather than saw his own doom almost upon him!

It came swooping from the shadows in the overhang of the canyon wall—the flyer he'd lost sight of! And where its tapering neck joined a corrugated underbelly, a vast scoop lined with cartilage hooks was yawning open to receive him!

Tzonov straightened up, swung his machine pistol to face the threat, squeezed the trigger. With a *rrrip* of gunfire, hot lead was hurled into the gaping belly pouch—but Tzonov might as well be firing at a jellyfish. He dropped his weapon, turned to run, and felt the shadow of the flyer falling on him like a tangible weight as its head and long neck passed overhead.

In the next moment the jutting, drooling lip of its pouch smacked into the back of his thighs between knees and buttocks, and he was folded and scooped up as neatly as that.

Before clammy, alien flesh closed on him, Tzonov had time for a single, hoarse, meaningless cry of protest. And the last thing he saw as the cartilage-barbed clamp of the pouch meshed shut was the spastically kicking figure of Yefros snatched up and jerked aloft, his head and right arm lost in a writhing of greedy, triumphant claspers . . .

Soldiers came running, the searchlight beams of their torches cutting swaths of white light through the thinning mist. Bruno Krasin heard their shouts and squeezed himself out from a clump of boulders where he'd taken shelter. Dusting himself down, he made stumblingly for the ancient trail, came face to face with one of his corporals.

"Sergeant?" The corporal glanced nervously all about,

and his party took up defensive perimeter positions. But Krasin had seen everything that had happened and knew it was much too late for that sort of thing. Too late for Tzonov and Yefros, anyway.

"Sergeant?" the corporal said again. "What about Comrade Tzonov, and that thin fellow, Yefros?"

Krasin realized how shaken he must look. He got a grip on himself, stood up straighter, and asked, "Did you see anything of it? Anything of . . . them?"

"Them?"

Krasin nodded. "Then you didn't see anything." Perhaps it was for the best. He desired to command men, not leaning towers of jelly!

"What happened?" the corporal asked, as they set off back along the trail.

Krasin paused, bent to pick up Yefros's pistol from where' the locator had dropped it, called back to the men in the rear, "Somewhere in those rocks there's a machine pistol. If you can see it, bring it in. If not, forget it. It will keep till morning." And to the corporal: "As for Comrades Tzonov and Yefros, I . . . don't think you'll be seeing them again." And he strode out for the keep.

But in the next moment he paused again, half-turned and gripped the corporal's arm, drawing him close. "If you *should* see them, however, you have my permission—no, my orders—to shoot on sight! For you see it won't be them. It might look like them, but believe me it won't be."

And there was a deep, deep shudder in Krasin's voice that the corporal had never heard before.

Back in the keep Krasin fortified himself with several mugs of good American coffee, then held an O-group with his four NCOs.

"Tzonov and Yefros are gone," he told them, "taken by the creatures of this world. From now on, that's how you will think of this place: as an alien world whose people can snatch you up just like they snatched them. Except that's not how it's going to be and we won't be caught out again. But those two . . . were talented. Their minds were different from ours. I believe it's what let them down, and lured them into an ambush.

"Well, we're talented, too—at living in the field and off the land, but especially at *staying* alive! Now, you've all been briefed; you know that this is a vampire world; you would have been sent here anyway, eventually, with or without Turkur Tzonov. And I would have been with you: your beloved Sergeant Krasin, mother and father both, to look after you! Yes, and I know what my children need.

"Now listen, the vampires of this world live on Starside. That's north to you: that barren place where we left the Gate. They live there and can't abide the sun, which kills them. So south is where we are headed. But if you ever want to *get* to Sunside, if you ever want to see its rivers, forests, and game—and chase its wild Gypsy women— first you've got to live through one hell of a long night. Of which there are at least two 'days' still to go!

"Very well, at first light we move out, for as I've said, the sun will keep them at bay. But between times we have to be extra careful. For every man who sleeps I want one awake, on the lookout. And I don't want anyone on his own. Drink all the coffee you like, but when you're on duty stay awake and alert. *They* know we're here now, and after talking to Tzonov and that snivelling Yefros—well, they'll probably know all about us, too. But they'll also know about our weapons.

"Now I saw Tzonov fire point-blank at a flying beast, and I myself fired this weapon of mine into the bellies of several, but we didn't nearly stop them. Not with a machine pistol, no, nor even with a rifle. But I'm betting a grenade-launcher would stop just about *anything* they've got! And here's something else to keep in mind: I fancy that while their flyers are just huge, dumb animals, their riders are—or were—men. If you knock *them* out of their saddles, its possible their mounts will run as wild as riderless horses.

"Okay, that's about it. Maybe they'll come back and maybe they won't, but if they do I want to meet them with force, let them know what they're up against. They have their own special brand of hell, these bastards, but they haven't seen ours yet, not by a long shot ..." Finally he paused. "Any questions?"

A lance-corporal took something from a pocket, handed it over. "Feel the weight," he said. "It was buried in the dust and dirt of my billet. I found it under my sleeping bag."

The thing was a bracelet an inch wide, an eighth of an inch thick. And it was solid gold. "Yes, that too." Krasin nodded. "Gold is a common metal on Sunside. It's one of the reasons we were coming here, before we were *forced* to come here. And it's another reason to go on living. We won't be marooned here. It won't be long before others follow us through, or until we can return through the underground Gate. After all, it was Tzonov who was on the run, while we were only following orders. If we go home carrying our own weight in this stuff ... you can stop worrying about being traitors. We'll all be heroes!" He looked from face to face. "Anything else?"

But there was nothing.

"Okay, let's get the heavy stuff set up. Two machine guns, a rocket launcher, flamers, too. I want weapons on all the balconies, and nite-sites on that ribbon of sky overhead throughout. Let's turn this place into a *real* fucking fortress!" And to himself: *We'll have to, if we want to see it through until the morning!*

For Krasin knew he'd never be able to forget the "smile" on the female's face—how her flesh had flowed and changed—as she'd stepped into view from behind that boulder ...

... And she was only one of their women!

Only? Devetaki smiled however grimly where she "listened" to Krasin's thoughts from her vantage point high on the rim of the canyon wall. *Only a woman, do you say? Well a woman I'll grant you—but* only? *Hah! Wamphyri, my alien friend, Wamphyri!*

But she liked Krasin for all that and considered him a man. Aye, and he would have made a fine lieutenant, too

. . . and perhaps still would. But two out of three wasn't bad—

—Not for starters, anyway . . .

V

A Lady Schemes

Devetaki, Vormulac, and Zindevar arrived back in the lava flow heights within half an hour of one another, and eventually came together in a vast, horizontal shaft of a cavern that was once the extinct volcano's blowhole or safety valve, now the warrior-Lord's temporary headquarters.

Lord Unsleep and the Lady Zindevar seemed well pleased with themselves (or, in Vormulac's case, and in the light of his perpetual melancholy, as "pleased" as he'd ever seemed); the fires observed on Sunside had indeed proved to be the permanent camps of supplicant or fief Szgany . . . the "tithe" they had paid this time had been in blood!

"We took half," Vormulac dolefully detailed the outcome of his and Zindevar's joint venture. "Half of everything, that is, including the people. They were docile enough, if a little surprised. Wratha and her lot weren't due for three sundowns yet, but their Szgany supplicants thought we'd come out of the last aerie—or Wrathstack, as that fang out there on the plain of boulders is known—on some special collecting round. By the time they'd got it worked out that we weren't a bunch of lieutenants out on a spree, and that in fact they couldn't say *who* we were, it was too late. Even so there was little or no resistance; Wratha, Canker, Gorvi, and the Killglance brothers seem to have them well trained. There was no word of Vasagi, though, so it seems the Suck's gone the way of all flesh. But there is a new Lord among them: a fellow called Lichloathe. Lord Nestor Lichloathe of the Wamphyri—a necromancer, apparently!"

Zindevar took up the story:

"Doubtless you've observed the constant stream of flyers, lieutenants, and thralls we're sending down? Well, they'll all get their fill. We stunned as many of the Szgany as were required—about half of them as Vormulac stated, but mainly the old, the unskilled, the barren, and the burdensome—and sent the rest into the woods while we took our fill. Drained carcasses are being brought back for the warriors, though not enough to fuel them through another complete cycle, I fear . . ."

Vormulac nodded. "But we got your message concerning the injured creature on the boulder plains. Excellent! When you've rested awhile and taken a little sustenance, I'd be obliged if you'd guide our beast-minders and their starveling warriors to the very spot. This way the entire army will be fully fuelled for the fighting that lies ahead."

At which Devetaki cocked her head knowingly on one side, and inquired: "There *is* to be fighting, then? Oh really? So is it that I'm only hearing the good news? And what about the bad? I saw no sign of Laughing Zack Shornskull as I flew in. What of him and his? I seem to recall him boasting that his contingent alone would have Wratha the Risen's measure. Can something have happened to change his mind, do you think? Did Wratha's 'measure' exceed his calculations?" She was all innocence.

Vormulac scowled down the hook of his nose. "It strikes me you've heard all about it! Am I right, Lady? Well, the man was a braggart and a fool—but at least he was our fool! His loss is sufficient a blow without all this sniping and sniding."

"He *was* our fool?" Devetaki repeated Vormulac inquiringly, though she already knew. "His *loss*, did you say? So everything I've heard is true: Laughing Zack will laugh no more. And his troops?"

Vormulac sighed. "A thrall made it back."

And Zindevar put in: "Upon a flyer."

Devetaki's scowling mask was entirely in keeping with her mood as she glanced disdainfully at Zindevar. She not only considered the other Lady her social inferior, but also a social climber who liked to have her nose—and indeed her say—in just about everything; to the point where in order to be heard she would deliberately introduce trivia into otherwise serious conversations. And in an untypically scathing tone, the virgin grandam repeated her: "Upon a *flyer*, Zindevar? Really? Well, I scarcely supposed he'd walked!" And ignoring the other's spluttering, she turned back to Vormulac. "What's the word?"

The warrior-Lord made no bones of it. "If we're to believe our sole survivor, Wrathstack's a veritable fortress. The aerie houses all of them, and they fight as one. Their creatures are lean, mean, experienced, and fighting fit; they swarm like hornets to repel their enemies. Shornskull's losses were—what, total? And Wratha's were nil. In short, it was a shambles."

Devetaki nodded. "Aye, yet I find myself in disagreement with you, if only on one point. It wasn't a *total* loss. We did get something out of it: knowledge. We know they're definitely there. Also . . ." But here she paused to glance sideways at Zindevar. Reading that glance, Lord Unsleep saw that Devetaki had something to say, but not in front of the glowering Cronesap.

"Also" (he cut in, diplomatically), "I think you're looking tired. What's more, your weariness makes you just a little disagreeable, Devetaki. But the Lady Zindevar here is well fed and her men provisioned. Wherefore I suggest that she goes to seek out the injured Wrathstack creature, and leads our hungry warriors to their supper. Also—I suggest she does it now."

Zindevar had missed none of the interplay. Still stinging from Devetaki's sarcasm, she drew apart and hissed: "*Hah!* And do you have favourites, my Lord?"

"No!" he hissed back. "But it appears I have generals who spit and snarl at each other when they'd do well to save their venom for our enemies!"

"I would hear the rest of what Devetaki has to say!" she snapped.

"And I would have you feed my hungry warriors!" He puffed himself up. "And I'd have you do it now. Unless you would prefer that I personally feed them—perhaps on your lads out of Cronespire? What, 'lads' did I hear myself say? No, *eunuchs,* most of the poor bastards! And how are we to suppose *they* will fare in the fighting, eh? Why, I couldn't put them up against women, let alone men!" His words rang true in whichever sense.

Zindevar was furious; she couldn't speak; she stormed out from the mouth of the blowhole and began screaming harshly for her lieutenants and beast-minders to attend her. Gesticulating and shouting, she disappeared from view.

Devetaki couldn't help but snigger, and even Vormulac must turn away or break into a smile. But finally he controlled himself and said, "Now out with it, Lady. What's on your mind?"

"Wratha's fortress could well end up her mausoleum!" Devetaki was down to business at once. "Consider: the place stands several miles—what, nine, ten?—out on the barren boulder plains, clearly visible for miles around. Set watchers and . . . why, she couldn't even send out a bat without we'd see it!"

"True." Vormulac frowned. "But by the same token we can't get near without she sees us. She has the elevation."

Devetaki held up a finger. "But I fancy we've taken her by surprise—our coming at this time, I mean. Her Szgany supplicants didn't even know who you were. So they weren't prepared, and I think that she's the same. It would be my guess that the Lady's had no easy time of it keeping her renegades from each other's throats, and that they've only recently joined forces in the fullest sense."

Vormulac was mystified. "But is that a good or bad thing? And if they were not unified before, but are now, what difference does it make? As individual Lords, they would have built up their individual forces. And Wrathstack is a vast place; I have our lone survivor's assurance that it could house all of us and ours. For all we know, it could be filled with men and beasts from tip to toe—just waiting to pick us off!"

Devetaki put on her smiling mask. "Just waiting, aye," she said, mysteriously.

"Eh?"

"Now tell me this: who can afford to wait the longest?"

"To wait the . . . ?"

And quietly, Devetaki inquired: "Is she not in siege?"

"What?" His great jaw fell open.

"Where is her sustenance? Where are her provisions?"

"Why, in Wrathstack!"

"No." The virgin grandam shook her head, then changed her mind and nodded. "Her *immediate* provisions, aye . . . but later? In Sunside, that's where. And how will she supply and resupply her creatures? *If* her army is huge, she'll need to feed it—and we'll be in the way, waiting for her. Except we'll be well fuelled. And I say it again: *if* her army is vast—" Devetaki shrugged, "—then I fancy we won't have long to wait."

"How so?"

"Wratha's no fool. She knows the lie of the land; we don't. By now, she'll probably know our strength; we don't as yet know hers. She has all Sunside mapped, knows its forests and favourite hunting grounds; we haven't and don't, not yet. She has all the long, long night ahead; forty hours and more to go, before she—indeed *we*—must take to the shade."

At which Vormulac got in: "But so do we have that!"

"She is settled and we are not. And where will you put *your* army when the sun comes up?" Devetaki's logic was devastating; she'd always been good at word games . . . at *tactics*, as Vormulac now saw.

He grunted and scratched his beard. "Upon a time, I had a wife," he said. "I lost her to a vile disease. Well, enough of love. Now, for all that I'm a follower of Turgo Zolte, I have my lust . . . from time to time, you understand. But

I tell you, Devetaki Skullguise, that if ever I wanted a woman for wife—which I don't—it would be you."

"Because I'm clever?"

"For one thing . . . but also because you're already Wamphyri," he growled, "and would not be obliged to ascend over my dead body! But aye, you're a clever one. Instead of explaining the meaning of the things you've been saying, and telling me what I should do, you're waiting for me to beg it out of you."

She smiled, and her mask and face alike matched up. "It's just that I like to feel appreciated," she said. And more seriously: "We're not much good at this, are we?"

"Eh? At what?" He walked her out into the night, and they stood at the rim of the lava flow, like a series of waterfalls frozen to a standstill on their way to the boulder plains.

"This warring."

Vormulac looked at her in the light of the stars. "Because we've forgotten how," he said, as gloomy as ever. "These thousands of years we've followed the ways of Turgo, because we had to. Unlike these vast western territories which we're now opening up, our place in Turgosheim and our own Sunside were small concerns. If we'd destroyed all of the Szgany to fuel our wars, in the end we'd have eaten each other. The end of the Wamphyri, aye! So we suppressed our vampire leeches as best we could and . . . grew weak! Weak in the ways of blood, the ways of war, the natural ways of the Great Vampire."

She nodded. "Between you and me, then: you're saying that Wratha was right to flee Turgosheim?"

Again his solemn glance. "Between you and me, Devetaki, the Szgany of our Sunside are grown vile! Their blood is bad. We took all the fight out of them, and all the goodness, too, a long time ago. In Turgo's *time* we lived on the blood of men—men like Turgo himself—who fought back! But now in Turgo*sheim* we've become as fleas on a dog's back. Except the dog is mangy. The blood is the life. But if it's bad blood . . . ?"

"And now?" Devetaki grasped his arm, and her slender

fingers were urgent where they bit into his grey flesh. "Is it too late, or can we reverse it? If we win this war—conquer Wratha and this new Sunside/Starside—can we stop the rot?"

His glance was more penetrating now. "The rot? Do you feel it, too, then? I thought that I was the only one. I thought it was just me, gloomy old Vormulac Unsleep."

She shuddered. "Ah, no, my Lord. For I too have felt it—and for years! And I've seen it: the way it manifests. The autisms, animalisms, mutations, and madness. In short, the decline of the Wamphyri. Did you know, I liked Wratha upon a time? Why, I believe I still do! Because she's 'clean' in a way that most of us can never be. Clean, spirited, and original. What's more, I envy her what she's had here, and what we must put an end to. For the rot's in her, too, or if not in Wratha the Risen, certainly in her renegades. The dog-Lord Canker Canison, for instance, more animal than man. And as for the Killglance brothers: why, even their father's terrible eye was a weapon! And—"

"—*And,*" Vormulac cut in, "Wratha's supplicant Szgany have it that Spiro is now *heir* to old Eygor's killing eye!"

Devetaki shrugged. "Can we be surprised? And what of Vasagi the Suck with his rampant acromegaly, his amazing miming, telepathy, metamorphism? I'm *glad* that he has gone, and not simply because he's my enemy! What? Why we're *all* our own worst enemies, and dangerous ones at that! But not as dangerous as these I've mentioned."

Vormulac nodded and said, "Our own worst enemies, aye. We always have been. It's nothing new. Isn't it what Zolteism was all about? To deny our leeches and be men? But we can't be men because we are Wamphyri! Old Maglore had it right. I remember he once told me:

" 'We're not true masters but slaves to our parasites. In Turgosheim only a blind man or a fool would ask why beings who could live as long as the Wamphyri usually live so short! Such is our nature, however, and jealousy, hatred, and lust—and blood, of course—our way of life.' "

Just for a moment Lord Unsleep had looked worn out. Now, straightening up, he said, "But Maglore must be something of a fatalist, too, for I remember he also told me—and I think I agree with him—'So be it; perhaps it is as well to leave it at that . . .' Well, and perhaps it is."

Devetaki shook her head. "I think .not. Better if we weed it out once and for all, then start afresh here in these clean western territories . . ." *Or perhaps in another place, far away, where the vampire's taint is scarcely known, and the blood of men and beasts alike is sweet and clean.* Which was a thought that she kept to herself, of course.

"Weed it out?" He looked at her, as if to gauge her meaning. "How? When? Where?"

"Here. In all the battles to come. Whenever the opportunity arises," the virgin grandam answered, drawing him aside, away from his army where its various contingents were camped. And in an undertone: "My Lord Vormulac, the rot is in us, too. Now believe me that this is nothing personal, but the Lady Zindevar is a corruption in herself, as is any creature who goes against nature to that extent."

"Eh? I can't see that. There have always been women who are drawn to women."

"Aye, but it scarcely leads to strong men! And remember, she's no underling but a leader."

"Are you sure this isn't your leech speaking, Devetaki? Is it that you envy Zindevar something or other? Her manse in Turgosheim, perhaps?"

"Do I envy Zindevar? You think I might *envy* Cronespire, when I have Masquemanse?" Devetaki shook her head. "But let me go on, let me try to convince you of this . . . this creeping *disease* that has come among us, crippling us more all the time." And after a moment:

"Look at Wamus. He's brought his bloodsons with him, and both of them the same as their father: more bat than man! Why, they're outside of nature, Vormulac—even the nature of the Wamphyri! And what of Lom the Stunted, whose knuckles drag on the floor? Or Grigor Hakson and Black Boris, whose lechery—"

But again Vormulac stopped her, saying: "—Now hold! For surely there's lechery in every man!"

"Like theirs? If something so much as *looks* like a cunt,

Grigor is into it. And Boris shags with trogs: a rival for the dog-Lord that one! Nor are they alone in their vices. And we talk of 'ascending' to a Lord or a Lady. What, ascension? But surely it's a foul descent, to disease, deformity, and madness! But we—you and I, my Lord—were never that way. And there are others among us who are likewise . . . 'clean'? They should be spared."

"Spared?"

Obviously she must speak it out loud, or in a whisper at least. "Send out the *freaks* into battle! Send them out first, so that they may take the brunt of it. When it's over, those who survive will have been weakened. That will be the time to strike, to do your weeding."

"To cut out the rot?"

"Exactly! And we'll start again, repopulate Turgosheim with our own, and develop these new territories as best they should be. But always with a tight rein on population, and a sharp eye out for freaks and degenerates."

"But Turgosheim will remain our seat?"

"Why not? The Centre of Empire, certainly, to which we'll return from time to time, for the worship of our people!"

Vormulac felt himself carried away with the idea. "I see it clearly: the Grand Triumvirate, controlling all from their seat in the Gorge of Turgosheim!"

"Eh!?" Devetaki's turn to exclaim, to question. "Triumvirate? But . . . can you possibly mean Maglore?"

"But hasn't the Seer-Lord always been one of us? Doesn't he even now keep the gorge for us and see to its servicing in our absence? Isn't he our oldest friend?"

Devetaki put on her frowning mask. And darkly and quietly she said, "I have often wondered about Maglore. For where some go too far, he goes too short. Long on lore and runes and magic, short on guts, drive, and vision. Where is he now but in Turgosheim, tending the hearth like some Szgany slut while we wage war? So I would counsel you thus: keep Maglore the Mage for a 'friend' if you like, or better by far keep him as your spy—for certainly as a seer and mentalist he has no peer—but as a leader with powers? ... That is hardly fitting. No, this is how I see it:

"Lord Vormulac Unsleep shall be the Emperor, the virgin grandam Devetaki his adviser, and the Seer-Lord Maglore his shewstone—for scrying on his lands and possessions afar to keep them safe. We can surely *value* Maglore, without that we elevate him to a position of power. For after all we're Wamphyri!" And Devetaki gave what she hoped sounded like a lighthearted laugh. "The two of us watching each other should be quite sufficient, without that we must watch him also!"

Vormulac wasn't sure. He frowned and tugged on Maglore's twisted loop sigil where it dangled from the lobe of his ear; that golden symbol of the Seer-Lord's mysticism, given to him by Maglore for good luck. But ... Devetaki was usually right, and so:

"Let me think on it," Lord Unsleep growled. "Meanwhile we have other things to talk about. And while we talk, let's walk together among my generals, and so inspire them with our presence ..."

"Devetaki!" Maglore spat out her name as if it were essence of kneblasch. "So-called virgin grandam! So-called Lady! Treacherous, scheming, back-stabbing whore! Spawn of a leprous spore! May your blood turn to acid and scorch your leech to a cinder!"

His own blood was up; he stamped, shook a fist, cupped a talonlike hand under the rim of his Möbius sigil "shewstone" to sweep it from its onyx-stemmed table. The table itself went toppling, so that Maglore had to reach out to save it before it struck the floor and shattered. And the gleaming, strangely twisted mass of his sigil thudded heavily down onto a pile of parchments and skins, and lay there all unrepentant.

Maglore was alone in his room of meditation, which was just as well. If Karpath or another lieutenant or thrall had been there, certainly the unlucky one would have suffered some small harm, and perhaps even a large one. For even as the Seer-Lord reached out to save his table, still the scarlet lamps of his eyes were glaring all about for some lesser thing on which to vent his fury . . . *and* they spied just such a thing, within easy reach at that:

His marvellously detailed clay model of Turgosheim, complete with all its spires and manses, including Vormulac Taintspore's melancholy Vormpsire—*and* Devetaki's Masquemanse, of course. And striding to the workbench where the model reposed, Maglore issued a curse through teeth like a tight-meshed man-trap, to snarl:

"A plague on your house, Devetaki! And more than a plague—a fist!" With which the Seer-Lord brought his clenched hand smashing down, so that Masquemanse was stripped from the rim of the gorge and crushed down into the meticulously molded clay of its bottoms. The clay had desiccated somewhat; the turrets and towers fell apart; the bulk of the flattened manse did not compress but flew in chunks. If this were the real Turgosheim, it could only be that a meteorite had struck home with shattering force to strew bits of Masquemanse across half the gorge.

Maglore felt something of the sympathetic "magic" of his act (though in fact his trembling sprang more from his rage), and rushed from his room of meditation and through the corridors of the vast promontory turret which was Runemanse, until he could gaze from a window on all the star-silvered bight of the gorge. He gazed at Masquemanse, of course, intact despite the destruction of its simulacrum . . . which served to promote a further bout of cursing and fist-shaking.

Eventually, exhausted by his emotions and determined upon a far more substantial revenge, Maglore called for his man Karpath, only just returned to Runemanse from certain "duties" in the shadowy bed of the gorge. By the time his lieutenant reported, the Seer-Lord had regained control of himself, though he still raged inside.

"Yes, Lord?" The hulking Karpath stood before him.

"How goes the work?" Maglore wasted no time.

"As you ordered, Lord, we work from the bottoms up. Lom Halfstruck's Trollmanse fell at once. The dwarf had left only one lieutenant in charge, whom we discovered spent from a surfeit of Lom's women. His plasma was not Wamphyri; it churns now in a vat, along with most of what we found of Lord Halfstruck's thralls. Pregnant women were dealt with, to ensure that nothing of Lom survives, and also to fuel your own creatures. Wherefore it only remains for you to imprint the stuff in the Trollmanse vats, and eventually you'll have warriors to send out far and wide across Turgosheim's bottoms."

"Good! And the lesser hovels? Mordslump, Zackstack, Wensknoll, and the rest? I hope that in all of your rendering down, you've not forgotten to do a little recruiting?"

Karpath shook his great head. "We have forgotten nothing, Lord. You'll discover all the recruits you need herded together in the base of Madmanse, the best of the stuff out of the lesser houses. With their Lords flown, they were as easily gathered up as fatherless children. Only descend, take what you will, and give back of yourself . . . your thralls shall teem!"

Maglore allowed himself a mirthless chuckle. "It seems I could easily exhaust myself, imprinting all of this good stuff into the faith—into *my* faith, that is! Why, I must be sure not to give more than I take, lest I swoon from my depletion! Very well, then let the work continue. Except—"

"Yes, Lord?"

Maglore took him to the window. "Look there!"

Karpath followed the line of the other's pointing finger. "Masquemanse?"

"The same. See to that next, and then return to your work down below."

"You want to invade Devetaki's place, and . . ."

". . . I want to *destroy* Devetaki's place!" Maglore grabbed him by the shoulder, his long nails digging in. "I want to sack it utterly, break off its balconies, knock out its windows into the gorge, topple its chimneys and leave promontory Masquemanse a veritable ruin, uninhabited and uninhabitable! And all of her thralls and creatures reduced to monsters shambling in the bottoms and guarding the passes! And her entire house a burned-out shell where the dust gathers in drifts and the winds mourn, but *only* the winds! For I most certainly shall not. Indeed and from now on I'll not hear her name mentioned, neither hers nor Vormulac Unsleep's!"

Such was his vehemence that Karpath was taken aback. "It shall be done, of course, Lord Maglore ... but as you're surely aware, Devetaki—I mean, *she*—left a strong body of men and monsters guarding the place. And Masquemanse is heavily fortified. Moreover—"

"—Her wells are in the bottoms." Maglore waved his protests aside. "Poison them! Kill off her siphoneers. Then, when her people are sick, attack from the rim of the gorge. Take up my young hungry warriors onto the rim even as I wean them from their vats, and break through the roof of Masquemanse into its heart. By then our flyers, recruited from the other spires and manses, will be too many to count. We shall strike Masquemanse full in the face, driving in through every landing bay and window! So the night shall be spent, and all resistance crumbling away as our aerial assault on the face of the manse continues. Then, as our men penetrate deeper and press on up through the manse's levels, finally we'll withdraw our forces on the rim. The last of the bitch's thralls shall think to escape by that route, up onto the roof—only to discover that the sun has risen, barring their way with golden fire!"

"They'll melt," said Karpath, shuddering.

"Too true," said Maglore with a curt nod. "They'll melt, aye—and all of the Lady's dreams of empire with them! So be it."

And so it would be, but a long night to go before then. . . .

Vormulac's army was sprawled all down the ancient lava river; where the rock formed folds like frozen falls. Behind the petrified spume and ages-stilled columnar gush, shallow caves and weathered-out pockets gave shelter and cold comfort to men and beasts alike. The various contingents kept to themselves; men hurried here and there, pursuing the orders of their Lords or Ladies; an orderly stream of flyers continued to launch—or land, whichever was the case—on their way to, or returning from, the banquet of blood on Sunside.

The belly pouches of returning flyers invariably disgorged corpses, which were dragged away to makeshift warrior pens. The flyers had been fed on Sunside greenstuff and honey laid up for Wratha and commandeered by Vormulac and Zindevar's forces, more sparingly on unappetizing lights and giblets: human flesh, naturally. Thus all creatures—manlike or otherwise, man-*shaped* or monstrous—had been or were in the process of being fuelled as best possible in the circumstances. And apart from the loss of Lord Shornskull's reconnaissance party, all seemed to be going reasonably well.

Silent for a while, the warrior-Lord and the virgin grandam walked together and approached the latter's contingent where Devetaki had made camp in the lee of a small, crumbling secondary cone. There she called for one of her lieutenants to attend her, and as he approached and bowed said to him: "The Lady Zindevar prepares to launch . . ." (And in an aside to Vormulac, "One has to admire her *scrupulously* fair attitude: only observe the way she leads her own warriors to supper first!") Then back to her man: "Go with the Lady and guide her with all speed to the injured creature which we spied on the plain of boulders. And when she's safely there, return at once."

"Yes, Lady." Her man nodded, and went to mount a flyer.

"What's this, cooperation and concern?" Vormulac raised an inquiring eyebrow. "What, for Zindevar Cronesap?"

"In her current rage she might overshoot and fly across the rim of the world!" Devetaki answered, sourly. "Not that I would care a bit, but your warriors—and mine—would go hungry."

Vormulac grinned in his fashion, but said, "Oh, well, Zindevar has her uses. Did I tell you, her familiar bats returned—most of them?"

"Not all of them?" Devetaki looked away for a moment,

and called loudly after her lieutenant: "Be sure and take a beast-minder with you, and *our* warriors also. Ensure that a chain is established, so that all of Lord Unsleep's creatures follow on in turn ..."

Now Vormulac saw the point of Devetaki's shouting. "Which were the tasks I gave to Zindevar, right?"

"But you are so sweet on her," Devetaki looked up at him, "you ignore that *she* ignores your orders!" It was true, Zindevar's fury had overriden common sense. Some two hundred yards down the lava slope she was just this moment airborne; her own warriors were spurting aloft in her wake, but not a one of the other contingents' fighting beasts. Thus she ignored Lord Vormulac's orders, apparently, or had forgotten them in the grip of her fury.

Vormulac sighed. "Very well—but you must let me handle affairs such as this in my own way. *Yes*, your suggestion with regard to the freakish and aberrant, including a certain Lady, is a good one, but I am in command here. Only let it be noticed that you have more than your share of influence ... they'll *all* be jealous—even the men—no less than Zindevar!"

Devetaki put on her smiling mask, but a moment later was businesslike again. "What of her bats?"

Vormulac shrugged. "It appears that some went missing."

The virgin grandam nodded. "A voracious place, apparently, where Lords and men and beasts alike—and even small familiar creatures—go out only to be eaten up, by Wratha or whatever! Yet some of us *do* venture forth, fulfil our duties and return; not alone with news, or bounty in the shape of crippled enemy warriors, but also with *living* tribute!"

Vormulac looked at her more closely where she led the way through a weathered, crumbling section of the secondary cone's wall into a shallow caldera. "Are you saying you took recruits? Well excellent! But why didn't you mention it before?"

"Because Zindevar was there. I trust her as far as I could throw her, and confide in her to that same extent. Yes, I found men in the great pass to Sunside, and took recruits which I now claim for my own. It is my right; for as my Lord will doubtless recall, I fuelled his starveling army on a creature of mine out over the Great Red Waste, by reason of which my forces are reduced—or were. Let this serve to even up the score. Behold!"

Watched over by a senior thrall, Turkur Tzonov and Alexei Yefros lay huddled in the shadow of the wall. The latter's eyes were closed, head lolling. Tzonov, on the other hand, was wide awake, alert, staring all about. Giving a great start as the Lord and Lady came into view, he stood up, bowed his head and kept it low, stared at the ground under their feet.

"Subservient!" Vormulac approved.

"Not a bit of it," Devetaki touched Tzonov under the chin, drawing up his head. "Clever, more like!"

The warrior-Lord stared, and Tzonov looked up and back—eye to eye! Directing her thoughts closely (which was scarcely necessary, for Vormulac's telepathy was minimal), Devetaki was into the Russian's mind in a moment: *It would not serve my purpose if this great Lord were to learn that you're a mentalist. Nor would it serve yours to have those knowing eyes put out!*

Tzonov lowered his gaze at once.

"Clever?" Vormulac repeated her. "How so?"

"Just a suspicion," Devetaki told him. Then, changing the subject: "But . . . don't you see anything strange?"

"I see a great deal that's strange! These men are neither trogs nor Szgany. Also, in my youth on Sunside—ah, but *that* was a long time ago!—I once saw a dead desert nomad, and so I know that they're not Thyre either. So what are they?"

"I've no idea," Devetaki lied, pretending ignorance. "But this is a strange region, which appears to be inhabited by even stranger races!" She shrugged. "I'll find out all about them—eventually."

Vormulac looked Tzonov up and down: his penetrating grey eyes (which once again the Russian quickly and wisely averted); his silver-blond eyebrows and tanned, healthy flesh; the broad bronze dome of his head, hinting of a formidable intelligence. His sharply hooked nose, as stern if not as long as Vormulac's own, lending him a hawkish appearance; his small, pointed ears lying flat to his head, and the too-perfect symmetry of his face as a whole, whose left and right halves were alike as mirror images. And his build: athletic, powerfully muscled, oiled to a perfect flexibility, yet tight as a coiled spring.

A handsome specimen, this one. If there were tribes such as this on Sunside, then they'd really be worth fighting over! And Vormulac could readily understand Devetaki's determination to keep him. He'd make a lieutenant and a half; possibly a decent plaything, too, after he'd put on some weight, height, and the cold grey cloak of undeath. As for his companion:

Casually, the warrior-Lord put Tzonov aside, causing him to stumble a little. And stooping, he took the unconscious Yefros by the lapels of his jacket, jerking him up off the ground and holding him aloft, legs dangling, where he could glare directly into his crumpled-seeming face. But . . . there was no comparison here. Why, the two were dissimilar as wolf and weasel! Or master and servant? And where Tzonov seemed intact, as yet entirely human, Vormulac could scarcely help but notice a pair of familiar punctures, purple gashes in the lesser man's neck. Devetaki had converted this one at least: plainly he slept the sleep of change.

As Yefros began to choke in Vormulac's grip, the warrior-Lord lowered his arm, let him crumple to the earth. Tzonov was quick to catch the locator and let him down more gently. After all, they were in this together— and up to their necks in it at that!

Vormulac turned to Devetaki. "The suits they wear: tough stuff! Not as coarse as Szgany weave, yet stronger far."

Again her shrug. "All kinds of benefits seem likely, aye."

"I notice you've not yet converted this one?" He glanced at Tzonov, who continued to avert his eyes judiciously, not alone in deference to Vormulac's stature, but also because Devetaki watched like a hawk.

"Easy to do, but impossible· to reverse," was her response. "I want him free thinking, for a little while at least. For as you're aware, as a thrall he'll say what I want him to say, do as I direct."

"Not always the case," Vormulac grunted. "He looks like a strong one to me. But I concede your point. You desire that he retain his individuality in order that you may better understand his mind."

"Before I make it mine, aye. To see as he, or as his kind sees may be of benefit." And then, because eventually she might be obliged to reveal the truth: "Also . . . I think it's entirely possible that they're talented, these two; there's something of an aura about them. And while conversion to vampirism has been known to amplify certain talents, it has the effect of suppressing others. For far too long the Wamphyri have destroyed what may not be re-created. Er, but this, surely, was one of several conclusions arrived at during the course of our recent conversation, my Lord?"

Vormulac scratched his head. "Was it? Why, yes, I believe it was . . ." He seemed satisfied. "Very well, I leave it in your capable hands, Devetaki. Do as you will, and discover what you can."

"But one thing I can tell you now," she said quickly, as he turned away.

"Oh?"

"Their weapons are devastating!"

"Really? And yet you returned unharmed."

"My superior mentalism! Entering their minds, I saw what was in store for me and mine. Avoiding it, I survived and took prisoners to boot." All of which was the truth. And leading him out of the crater, Devetaki glanced back once over her shoulder at Turkur Tzonov, her scarlet eyes telling him: *Never fear, for I shall be back, my pretty. And then we'll talk some more.*

"And they were in a pass leading to Sunside? But how many of them?"

"Oh, a dozen more at least. And armed to the teeth."

"What, with stakes of wood, knives, spears, cross-bows?"

Devetaki shook her head. "Ah, no. Their weapons *are* astonishing! I can't describe them. Best if you yourself were to see them in action."

"I should go up against them?"

Oh, if only it could be arranged! And it could *have been, if I'd had more time to think it out. But no, for if by chance you had survived* . . . . The virgin grandam's mind was shielded as never before—like an ironwood kernel in its shell—as she answered, "Ah no, not you, my Lord! As commander in chief, you would only attend as an observer. But . . . Lord Wamus, perhaps?"

They stood alone on the lava slopes. He looked at her and smiled, but grimly. "I see. You're thinking we should send out the 'freaks' into battle, to test the way ahead."

Devetaki's smiling mask was well in keeping as she slowly nodded her head and gazed unflinchingly back at him. And Vormulac thought she even looked beautiful in the starlight. Or he might have, except he knew what lay beneath the gold-filigreed lead: the leering hideousness of flensed bone, the naked truth under the lie of the Lady's mask.

But even he did not know all of the truth, and therefore none of the lie.

And despite the fact that he felt a sudden warning chill, as if a cold wind had blown on his spine, Vormulac thought to himself: *Well, and what does it matter that she's disfigured? For after all, beauty is only skin deep in all of us.* And picturing Zindevar and Wamus, and others who were even less lovely, he concluded: *Aye, and a good deal shallower in some!*

Which only served to show the warrior-Lord's own shallow nature: that his Wamphyri *awareness* was so easily confused by the virgin grandam's treacherous "logic."

And for once in her life and undeath, the virgin grandam was glad of her disfigurement and mask both; lest the scarcely concealed, self-satisfied writhing of her mouth became obvious in the ice-blue glittering starlight . . .

VI

Devetaki: Her Schemes Coalesce—Nathan: After the Battle at the Rock

All of the Wamphyri were territorial; all of them were greedy, scheming, and intent upon their own survival. With their metamorphism, their metaphysical powers, magnified emotions, vastly inflated egos, and vampire tenacity—with all of these driving forces which were theirs by virtue of their parasite leeches—they understood that success meant power meant survival! Wherefore infinite success might well mean immortality. But even in common men power corrupts, and absolute power corrupts absolutely. And in the Wamphyri?

Like all megalomaniacs, they only perceived the corruption, the evil, the perversions of others; or, should an individual glimpse an aberration in himself, his preference would be to blame it upon, or assign it to, his leech, depending on the circumstances. Thus, while acknowledging the dubious benefits of their parasites, still they decried their insatiable appetites or "vices." Contrarily, and while a victorious Lord would revel in "his" triumph, in the event of defeat he would just as readily heap curses upon his "thin-blooded" vampire.

Devetaki Skullguise, the virgin grandam of Masquemanse, was no different. In Turgosheim it had made sense to live an ordered life: to "exist" as governed by the tithe system. By no means an austere existence, it had scarcely been an opulent one. Nevertheless Zolteism had suited Devetaki: the creed made clear how each should live commensurate with his or her needs. Thus the requirements of her house, the "provisioning" of Masquemanse, had been guaranteed. The Lady's gauntly jutting promontory of an aerie was by no means a hovel; her "fair share" of the Sunside tithe had been considerable; while very occasionally her men and creatures might find it necessary to scratch and scrape, their mistress had never gone without. On the other hand, the lesser knolls and crevices of recently ascended vampires, and the middling manses of young up-and-coming Wamphyri Lords and Ladies, commanded a much-reduced get out of Sunside and frequently were shabby, even impoverished.

Thus (and especially with Vormulac in the role of tithesmaster) Turgosheim's secret triumvirate had established and kept a rein on the gorge and its inhabitants— *and* upon themselves! When one has only sufficient for himself and his immediate household, all instinctive or leech-inspired notions of feuding, territorial expansion, and empire-building become academic; finally they assume the status of fantasies. Plots are still plotted, but they are rarely acted out.

Of course, in a society whose continuity is based on principles of conservation, the rules must be seen to be obeyed by everyone. Lord Vormulac, and Maglore the Mage, too, were known to be fairly strict adherents to Zolteism: "ascetics." So Devetaki and everyone else had believed, even as her partners in the triumvirate had believed it of each other—and of Devetaki herself. . . .

Turgosheim was yesterday, however, and this was here and now. And *this* . . . was freedom! Or it could be, if she and her leech played it right. What Devetaki had disclosed to Vormulac was true: she envied Wratha and her renegades what they'd had here, and what they could have had eventually, without Turgosheim's intervention. But what she had necessarily failed to disclose was far more to the point: that if she herself could have it—*for* herself—then she wouldn't for a moment hesitate. Even now the thought made her shudder deliciously: to be Empress of these vast and sprawling territories and all that went with them . . . and perhaps other places much further afield.

Moreover, it wasn't impossible that she'd come across the key to unlock just such airy ambitions, in the shape of Turkur Tzonov. Precisely how she would turn that key—in what ingenious lock—was hard to say just yet, but it was in her hand, be sure. And Vormulac Taintspore himself approved of it there.

Vormulac: currently, and however unknowingly, he was Devetaki's tool; but a heavy one and unwieldy. If she should slip and miss her stroke, he'd prove a sharp one, too! Although he had gone along with her so far, still she must be wary. Her time would come when she'd used him to whittle the others down, removing all who might possibly have her measure. Laughing Zack Shornskull *might* have been one such, but circumstances had seen to him without her help. With any luck Wamus would be next; and as for Zindevar . . . she simply *must* go, and straight to hell if at all possible! After that:

Any and all of the other Lords would consider themselves superior over a "mere" woman (Devetaki wondered how Wratha had fared, and felt a certain kinship); but by then, hopefully the bloodwar would have worn their forces down a little. The aspirations of Black Boris went little further than a harem of trog mistresses, and Grigor the Lech had similar weaknesses; Devetaki was sure that if she struck while they were whoring it up, she could take them out with a minimum of trouble.

Eventually, of course, even Vormulac would see the lie of the land: how the virgin grandam gathered survivors of defunct contingents to her own, to reinforce it, and how she had begun to draw apart from him. This would probably split the army out of Turgosheim into two uneasy camps, both of them obliged (for the time being) to remain united and concentrate their efforts against Wratha, their main priority; at least until Wrathstack had fallen. By which time the warrior-Lord would have decided how best to deal with Devetaki, and she would know how best to use the bonus talents of Turkur Tzonov.

These were some of the Lady's thoughts (kept hidden from the warrior-Lord, of course), as the pair approached the camp of Wamus behind a time-tattered curtain of white volcanic pumice, the fragile spume of the lava river's ancient falls. And just as Devetaki became aware that she'd been lost in thought for too long:

"You are quiet, Lady," rumbled Vormulac, as if reading her mind—which mercifully he wasn't. "Quiet and thoughtful. I've seldom found it easy to fathom you. So tell me: what is it that you're pondering?"

"I was thinking," she answered at once, "how best . . . how *best* to advise you with regard to Wratha's containment."

"Is she contained?"

"Not yet, and that's the problem."

"Then have you thought it out?"

"Possibly . . ." (And now Devetaki must *really* think on it, and quickly indeed; but in a moment): "If Wamus should survive the coming battle at the keep in the pass, then we'll let him hold it. For remember: as things stand now Wratha may yet venture out unseen from Wrathstack in its lower levels, below our horizon, and keeping her head low speed for the pass. With Wamus or his survivors in the keep, we'll be able to deny her passage into Sunside via that route at least. That will leave only eastern and western routes open—which we'll also block, naturally. Even now we stand in the way of her easterly excursions; obviously, she frequently heads in this direction to collect the tithe from her supplicants across the mountains. So if we station a sufficiency of men and warriors here, this will be the second supply route we've obstructed; and possibly Wratha's main route, at that. As for the as yet unseen, unknown regions in the west, beyond the great pass and the strange cold glaring light of that . . . that what? A fallen star?"

"Is that what it is, do you think?"

She shook her head, sending her red hair flying, and lying said, "I don't know what it is. But as for the west—"

"—That is for you and I to explore!" Vormulac exclaimed, with some animation. "Together, I think."

Devetaki shrugged. "Why not? After all, we are the *best* of companions! And when we've taken the high ground—namely these barrier mountains, from east to west—and if we locate observer units out on the plain of boulders, consisting of our fleetest flyers, and lieutenants in tune with their Lord's receptive minds . . . why, Wratha's every twitch will be relayed to us! Thus we'll have her covered from all points."

"Only two things she can do after that." Vormulac nodded. "Or possibly three, if we include a slow and highly improbable suicide by starvation. She'll attempt to break the siege, fly into Sunside and glut her starveling lads in some lush land of plenty; or . . . she'll consume Wrathstack's provisions in one last massive fuelling, and hurl herself into battle!"

"The latter, if I know Wratha." Devetaki nodded. "That's precisely what I meant when I guessed we wouldn't have long to wait before this war got well and truly under way. She's Wratha the Risen, remember? And she's wrathful as ever, be sure! She won't lie low for long. But if I may ignore your creeping starvation solution—which I'm sure she would not contemplate—there is a third possibility, and real, however improbable."

"Oh?"

"That she'll sit tight in the stack till the last minute, then gut the rest of them to fuel her own, and finally make a break for it!"

"She'll run for it? But where?"

Again Devetaki's shrug. "Turgosheim?"

"What, back across the Great Red Waste? With my army hot on her heels? And the Seer-Lord Maglore waiting for her in the gorge, with all the good stuff we left behind to bring to bear against her?" Vormulac couldn't see it.

"Maglore is an old fraud!" Devetaki snorted. "She'd

crush him in a trice—or convert him to her cause! Nor would we be 'hot on her trail,' not immediately. Eventually, perhaps."

"Explain!"

"Her beasts would be well rested; *they* would make it back to Turgosheim. Ours would be exhausted from all the patrolling, watching, flying, and possibly fighting. For remember, we don't know what else we might yet come up against."

"Such as?"

"Such as those men from—I mean of course those men *in*—the pass." (She had caught herself only just in time, before saying "those men from another world.") "So you see, before we could get after her, we would have to build ourselves up again. And meanwhile Wratha would be converting all of our good stuff in the gorge of Turgosheim."

Vormulac scratched his head and made an unhappy growling sound. "*Huh!* You make it all so complicated!"

"War *is* complicated!" Devetaki insisted. "But the answer is simple: we'll send back a stiff complement of men and warriors to the eastern tip of the range. They can shelter during daylight in the same trog caverns where we rested up after our crossing. *Hah!* And we know who would find that to his liking: Black Boris is our man! Then, should Wratha attempt flight to the east, Boris and his contingent would intercept and bring her crashing down in the Great Red Waste."

Lord Unsleep, for all his habitual melancholy (not only a morbid but a self-generating condition, Devetaki felt sure), had been attentive to everything she said. "Good! And now can I take it our plan of containment is complete? Then I'll reiterate:

"We'll have watchers on the plain of boulders, keeping an eye on Wrathstack. We'll put a party down into the pass, so preventing Wratha from sneaking into Sunside for provisions. We'll leave a strong force of men and beasts here, to deny her access to her—or should I say, to *our*—supplicant tribes, and we'll locate other siege components in the western heights. Finally, we'll station Black Boris and his lot in the eastern trog caverns, so cutting Wratha off if she runs for home."

Even as he spoke the words, the warrior-Lord's gloom had seemed to lift a very little; but as he finished, frowned, and his face fell further yet, she saw that he was morose as ever. "What is it, my Lord?"

"Where's my army?" he answered. "I lost some before we'd even left our homeland, others where we paused to refuel, and a good many more over the Great Red Waste. Laughing Zack is no more, and now I am contemplating sending Wamus to his doom, or at best into a terrific scrap where—if your report on these weird weapons is correct—he's bound to suffer severe losses. Nor is that the end of it. You, my good Devetaki, seem intent upon the removal of the . . . *unfortunate* Lady Zindevar, and any and all others who deviate from your 'norm.' Thus, even before the bloodwar begins in earnest, with the bulk of the fighting still to come, I see my army being whittled down left, right, and center."

Devetaki sighed—but understandingly, not impatiently. "I see now your concern for those in our command. Is that all it is?" She sighed again. "For a moment I thought it was some insurmountable problem which I had not foreseen. But in any war men and beasts are bound to be lost, my Lord, while in this one . . . at least we can ensure that the brunt of the damage is suffered by those we can best afford to lose. Why not look at it this way: the weakest make the supreme sacrifice for the good of the strong—indeed, for the survival of the Wamphyri!"

Vormulac narrowed his eyes. "I was talking mainly of the rapid dissolution, the dispersal, of my army: the fact that at this rate I'll soon be left naked, with only my own and a handful of lesser contingents to hand! I was not complaining about the 'sacrifices' of war! Why, if I didn't know you better, Devetaki, I might think you were twisting my words."

"But I shall continue to twist them!" she said. "Or if not twist, I'll supply the *correct* words. Dissolution? Dispersal? I think you mean 'deployment,' my Lord. The tactical positioning of your forces to their best effect."

"Yes, you're right"—Vormulac was starting to feel irritated that she was "right" so often—"but when they're apart from me, out of sight, I know I shall feel that I'm losing control."

"Not all all!" She shook her head. "It's why you have generals: because you can't fight the entire war on your own." She touched his arm. "But here comes Wamus now. Shall you tell him, or shall I?"

"I shall task him; you shall describe the task and define its difficulties. After all, you've been there and I haven't."

Seeing the warrior-Lord and Devetaki through the fretted curtain of pumice that provided a screening facade to his lava cavern camp, Lord Wamus headed in their direction with his lieutenant bloodsons in tow. Though well acquainted with Vormulac and his self-appointed aide, still Wamus screened them in advance; the pair felt a high-pitched whistle—a batlike trill or chittering—striking them at all points and bouncing off, carrying the details of their identities infallibly back to the weird being that was Wamus. A moment later and the singular examination stopped; Wamus stepped closer, acknowledged Devetaki with a nod of his head, and performed a stiff, formal bow in deference to Vormulac. And: "Lord Unsleep?" he inquired.

"Wamus." The other nodded a gloomy greeting. "I see you are settling in. But not *too* well, I hope, not just yet! Now tell me, have you provisioned your men, flyers, and warriors? Are they well fed, up to strength—fighting fit?"

"All is in order, thank you, and . . . I see you have work for me and mine?"

It was less than telepathy or prognostication; more properly a bat-skill: the anticipation of certain requirements in the moment *before* they become physically apparent. As the bat is equipped to calculate an arrow's flight path, thus avoiding a collision, Wamus was aware that this was something more than a friendly visit. He had known it from the moment he glimpsed the warrior-Lord and the

Lady Devetaki through gaps in the pumice curtain, and Vormulac's mode of greeting had confirmed it. Fortunately, however, Wamus was not in the habit of avoidance; he would not shirk his duties. Therefore, and without waiting for his leader's affirmation:

"Good," he said, giving a curt nod, "for I deplore inactivity. What is required of me?"

While Vormulac told him, Devetaki took the opportunity to scrutinize Wamus and his sons through half-shuttered eyes.

Despite the fact that Wamscarp was one of Turgosheim's major manses—an echoing cathedral of a place in a stalagmitic cavern system located high in the wall of the gorge—still its master was something of an unknown quantity; of a solitary nature, he was rarely seen in public. Now, as she looked him over however covertly, Devetaki found herself much in accord with his self-imposed insularity.

That Wamus was of human origin was obvious; his anthropomorphism was plain to see, though his *meta*morphism tried hard to obscure the fact. In this respect Wamus and Vasagi the Suck had been two of a kind: they had both practiced their metamorphic skills to such an extent that flux was effortless and instantaneous. Vasagi, when the acromegalic extension of certain of his facial bones became grotesque, had extruded them in deference to his own freakish design. Wamus, long enamoured of the unerring aerial instinct of bats and determined to achieve similar skills, had guided his metamorphism in that direction.

Almost all of the Wamphyri could fly; though a few, like Lom Halfstruck, were earthbound of their own choice. Some flew with great skill, others less dexterously; a handful performed clumsily, and only when there was no other option, when flight was an absolute necessity. Metamorphic flux allowed transformation of shape; various designs, aerofoils and leaf-shapes, had proved successful. Should a flyer be crippled during an aerial collision (or, in the light of prevailing hostilities, during an attack by warriors), then depending on the altitude, a vampire Lord or

Lady rider might reasonably expect to launch from the injured beast and make a safe descent. Conversely, lieutenants and common thralls would certainly crash to their deaths. For while they had partial metamorphism, only the Wamphyri had truly mastered it.

As for Wamus's mastery: he was, to all intents and purposes, a bat. Some six feet tall, sleekly furred, sharpheaded and with pointed ears curving inwards to the skull; thin as a rake, but flexible as a whip, and light as a feather to boot; with "hands" that reached to his knees, and arms webbed to his body with folding, furred, membranous pinions, so that opening them the webbing formed air-trap wings; with a quivering, convoluted snout, taloned extremities, and crimson pinprick eyes ... Wamus *was* a bat!

But where the creature itself is as one with nature and therefore acceptable, Lord Wamus's imitation made him hideous even in the eyes of his contemporaries. He was a man, but he was also a great bat no less than *Desmodus*; and being Wamphyri, he was a great deal more than both. As for his bloodsons: there was nothing to choose between them and their father; if anything their faces and forms were even less acceptable.

The Lady's observations had taken no more than a moment or two, and meanwhile Vormulac had outlined the task at hand. It was now Devetaki's turn to speak. Describing the location of the keep, she offered to lead Wamus and his raiders to the canyon's rim directly overhead. Because Vormulac was aware of the deadly weapons of the party in the pass (and also because Devetaki did not wish to appear too determined with regard to Wamus's removal), she was not remiss in explaining the perils of the mission. Finally she concluded:

"Lord Unsleep saw at once that this was a task which you alone were equipped to undertake. From the bed of the pass and faced with superior weapons, it might seem impossible. But the keep stands in the sheer face of the canyon from which it was carved, and you may go where lesser 'flyers' may not. To such as you, access should be no more difficult than entering into your own Wamscarp. By window or balcony ... whichever you may choose."

Wamus looked at her, and she at once guarded her secret mind. He made no attempt to probe her, however, but merely inquired. "Entry may not be gained by use of common flyers? Are there no landing bays?"

"None," she answered. "The keep, while fairly extensive, is an observation post or way station, nothing more. But it's also an important vantage point, securing the pass. Also, you should know that great honour attaches: Lord Unsleep and I are agreed that in the event of your taking it, you shall keep it. Thereafter the pass shall be named 'Wamus Pass,' and the keep in the canyon 'Wamskeep'!"

Wamus drew himself up, filled his lungs, and for a moment his tiny eyes glittered more brightly yet. But then, blinking rapidly, he said: "Vormulac and ... you? The virgin grandam of Masquemanse, called Skullguise? Do you say *you* are agreed? But how is it you have the right, Lady?"

"As the warrior-Lord's chief adviser, I have it," Devetaki answered.

The other nodded, blinked again and thought on what he'd been told. "And ... the keep shall be mine—?"

"—To use to our mutual advantage," she reminded him.

"And ... my name shall be on the keep and on the pass?"

Vormulac put in, "In honour of your victory, yes."

"So be it." Wamus bowed from the waist. "Only allow us a few hours' resting time and we shall be ready. I go to make my plans."

"And I to take nourishment in Sunside," Devetaki told him. "Shall we meet here, then, in a matter of—what, six hours?"

Wamus nodded. "Midway between now and midnight, aye." And bowing again to Vormulac, he and his bloodsons turned and went back through the time-carved pumice curtain into their temporary camp.

Then Vormulac said to Devetaki, "Lady, there are things I must see to: the setting up of ambushes, blockades, and observation posts, and so forth. Call me when you've eaten and rested, and I'll be ready. We'll see how well or badly Wamus fares when faced with these deadly weapons of yours."

But as they parted company, Devetaki was aware of Vormulac's hooded eyes upon her. More to the point, she also felt his feeble, inferior telepathic probe—and turned it easily aside.

In a cavelet off Nana Kiklu's care-cave, where she saw to the requirements of the elderly whom Lardis Lidesci had given into her charge, Nathan slept in his Misha's arms "like a dead man"; which wasn't at all the cliché that it sounded. For as Nathan knew only too well, the dead do "sleep" from time to time, not only to escape the ennui of their condition, but to rest their ever questioning minds. For when inquiring *mind*—a no longer physical but metaphysical factory of questioning and reasoning, of calculation and conception—is all that remains, then, uninterrupted, the mental pursuits of a person's lifetime follow exponential curves almost to infinity. But while most questions have answers and problems solutions, others appear insoluble or form merely the nuclei of even greater problems. And even dead minds can become exhausted.

As for Nathan Kiklu, or "Keogh," as he now rightly considered himself: his mind and body were anything but dead, although they felt it, especially his body. For in the last two "days" Earth time—parallel Earth, the Earth beyond the Starside Gate—Nathan had performed the physical work of at least two men, and the metaphysical work of just one man before him: his father, the Necroscope Harry Keogh. And where work such as that was concerned, Nathan was the only one who could perform it, for he was the new Necroscope.

But for all that he was physically exhausted, or perhaps because of it, his sleeping mind—galvanized by the events of the recent past, and the mixed emotions evoked by his return to his homeworld—went on in a whirlwind spiral of recollection, reflection, even reacclimatization to the old-but-new environment of Sunside/Starside. It might best be thought of as a kind of jet lag, but between universes as opposed to continents. And as the sprinter continues to run in his sleep, or the long-distance cyclist goes on pedalling, so Nathan continued to dream, to remember, and even . . . to communicate, eventually.

Not unnaturally his most lucid memories, and the happiest ones, were uppermost in his mind: he dreamed of the occurrences following immediately upon the battle for Sanctuary Rock, after Gorvi the Guile's lieutenant, Turgis, had undergone interrogation by Lardis Lidesci—and after he'd uttered his last curse and died the true death in a Szgany firepit.

And because it was all so fresh, the dream was as real as life, more nearly a vivid recollection than a dream proper . . .

Wearily, they made their way back to the Rock across a battlefield mainly cleared of the debris of war. A warrior burned in its own fats, kept going by the blazing faggots that Lardis's men tossed into the heat and the stench . . . A Flyer seemed grotesquely perched upon an agony-arched framework of red-glowing, skeletal cinder wings, its long neck gradually slumping in the melt, parting from its body and issuing sooty scraps and sparks that drifted to the sky in a column of smoke . . . A lieutenant's bloodied gauntlet lay where he had left it; his clenched fist, severed from the wrist by a keen machete, was still inside.

Noticing this loathsome relic in passing, Lardis growled: "Have someone deal with that, Andrei, if you please. I want no bits left over to contaminate the clean earth. No, for I swear by my star that the very air these bastards breathed was tainted forever!"

Lardis, Andrei Romani, a handful of the Rock's senior men, and Nathan, Trask, Chung, and the three cavers all walked together, many of them shakily, stepping carefully near warrior-traps left untouched by the fighting, whose camouflage of fresh-cut gorse and green-woven withe showed intact through the thinning mist. But as the last of the Rock's defensive systems fell behind, and a path through the scree-strewn approach lay clear ahead . . .

. . . A sudden eruption! From Sanctuary Rock's main cavern entrance! Nathan should have been expecting it, for it wasn't the first time after all. Word of his return had found its way back to his mother in the Rock, where she cared for the Szgany Lidesci's old ones. And knowing that her son was alive, right here and now . . . nothing in earth, air, fire or water could have kept Nana Kiklu from him! Not only his mother but Misha, too, his young wife who shared Nana's duties with her: both of them came at a run, then stumblingly, finally halting even as the men halted. And Nathan looked at them looking at him.

Misha was desperate to be in his arms; her breast heaved and her eyes were full of him, and full of a mist that threatened to brim over, too. But she held back in deference to his mother, who stepped forward and slapped him!—Then gazed at her stinging hand in wonderment and burst into tears! And no one, not even Nathan, had ever seen Nana do that before!

But he knew why, and so did all the others. So that Nana was the only one who was surprised. Then the piledriver force of her as she flew into his arms, so that he must lean forwards to meet her or be knocked off his feet. And feeling her against him, knowing she was safe—and therefore that *he* was safe—as his eyes transferred to Misha. Misha who was calmer now and waiting her turn, but who nevertheless had that look about her that said, *You are really in for it now, my lad!*

Finally Nana released him, and half-flinchingly, blinking his eyes. Nathan turned to Misha. Then . . . all the men with him bursting into nervous laughter as she cocked her head, narrowed her eyes and wagged a finger, gave a strange, whimpering little cry and fell into his embrace; fell to with a barrage of kisses that threatened to slurp his face off! And finally Nathan knew that he was home.

Before they could go off together, however:

"Nathan," growled Lardis. "We've things to talk about. Me and mine, you and yours. Time later for . . . well, proper greetings. But much to say and do, and little enough time as it is. The ladies will have to understand."

"How long?" Nana and Misha were at once anxious. And Misha protesting: "We, too, have questions, things we want to know!" Then, giving Nathan that look again: "I thought you were gone forever—dead, undead, drained of life: a flame-eyed thrall in Wrathstack!"

But his mother shook her head. "She knew you weren't, and so did I."

"You knew?" he looked from one to the other.

His mother shrugged. Her eyes were dry now, but sarcasm dripped as she said: "Of course! The sun continued to come up in the mornings, didn't it?"

And Misha smiled and added, "And the stars shone bright as ever at night!" Szgany fondness.

Then Nana again: "Very well, go and talk. But Lardis, only for an hour—I hold you to it!" He was possibly the greatest Szgany leader ever, whom even the Wamphyri held in some regard . . . but still it was an order. And without waiting for an answer, the two women went off. Then:

"Come," said Lardis. "I have rooms in the Rock." But as he led them in through the main entrance, the Old Lidesci turned and said to no one in particular, and to everyone, "Except for essential duties, get your heads down. Pass it on: you're to get what sleep you can, for before too long I'll be having you all up again. So start dusting off your carts and travois, you lads. Aye, for we'll all be Travellers again by morning!"

Most of Sanctuary Rock's friable, chalky base was buried in the roots of the foothills rising to the barrier mountains. Water action in some earlier age had carved most of its cavern-systems; what else could be excavated by hand had been, and it was scarcely surprising that Lardis had found evidence of prehistoric habitation. Even now the Rock made an excellent camp and fortress; with its constant temperature, and alveoli cavelets to house Lardis's people, it was quite literally a sanctuary—or had been until now. Above the chalky base, however, the material of the Rock was a hard sandstone turning to granite halfway to the dome. Since geology was an unknown science, the Lidescis could scarcely be expected to know that the whole Rock was an extinct volcano's plug that had weathered out and "toppled" from on high, to where it now stood on its head.

But the Rock's caverns extended upwards only to the sandstone level, and to the rear as far back as the foothills bedrock; so that while on the one hand the Rock had seemed a safe place, on the other it had been a trap. Which was why the Old Lidesci had cut escape routes through the chalk and sandstone to the overgrown rising ground of the foothills on both sides: cramped tunnels that were large enough for men, difficult for anything as bulky as a vampire Lord, and quite impossible for their constructs. If ever the Wamphyri, their thralls or monsters should invade via the main entrance, Lardis would escape through his bolt-holes and use crude but effective gunpowder to bring the entire thing down on whatever was behind him!

Lardis had a large low-ceilinged cave high up and to the rear of the maze of caverns and fissures that formed Sanctuary Rock's interior. Since opening the place up, exploring and occasionally excavating its extensive systems, the Lidescis had made room for all of their tribe. But only the fortunate few, with "apartments" on the rim, close to the external wall or face of the Rock, had natural light and "rooms with a view." This occurred where the Rock was pitted right through to its cysts or caves, forming windows or air shafts to the outside world. In the higher caves these windows made excellent view ports, allowing observation of the countryside all around. As leader of his people, Lardis could have had an airier place; instead he had denied himself and apportioned all of the perimeter rooms to the old folk and families—which was typical of him. But at least his place was large, with room to accommodate all of his senior men whenever Lardis called a meeting.

Here it would be dark, black as the pit, but for candles in niches in the walls. One of these was lit but guttered low; Lardis, leading the way with a flaring torch (also with a warning to keep heads low), touched fire to the other candles and set the place to glowing yellow. Now the group could talk and make proper introductions.

Feeling compressed if not claustrophobic, Nathan sat opposite Lardis at a huge, low, oval table. Everything was low; the ceiling, an uneven blotchy surface scant inches overhead, was festooned with stalactite nodes that would raise unpleasant lumps if they should come into sudden, accidental contact with a man's forehead or face. Ben Trask sat on Nathan's left, David Chung on his right; the three cavers sat next to Chung, with four of Lardis's men opposite.

There were faces Nathan knew of old, others he had rarely seen, or never. But he was certainly glad that Andrei Romani was there; and the wiry hunter Kirk Lisescu, grinning ear to ear and eager to have a word with his young friend as soon as the opportunity presented itself.

For of course to the ones Nathan knew, he was a *new* Nathan! First his absence of three long years, when he'd wandered among the desert-dwelling Thyre, and dwelled in the Seer-Lord Maglore's Runemanse in Turgosheim; now his absence of months, since the time when he'd been stolen away by a Wamphyri flyer and no one had known if he was dead or alive—or somewhere in between. And on both occasions there had been changes in him, some fairly dramatic and others less so, but startling anyway to the few who had been close to him in the old days.

For one, he was no longer a bumbling, blushing boy but a man, and one as rare as silver or mirrors or kneblasch in an aerie at that! And for another he was no longer blond as new straw but wore grey streaks in his temples that loaned him years he'd not yet lived and an air of esoteric knowledge even stranger than the unspent years. *And* he was no longer pale but a tan different again from the weathered-in look of the Szgany: the result of his time spent in the more frequent daylight of Earth, especially the light of the Greek Islands. Finally:

"Necroscope!" Lardis Lidesci declared, decisively.

And Kirk Lisescu added, with a wink and a nod in Nathan's direction, "Aye, and your father's son right down to that faraway look in your eyes!"

Kirk sat on Lardis's left, and was rewarded with an elbow in his ribs. "But that's knowledge that stays right here!" Lardis cautioned him, sternly. "It's for us to know—for us *in* the know—and no one else!" He glared all around the table. "Nana Kiklu *lives* with us; she's a good woman whom I'd protect with my life, even as she protected my own Lissa upon a time! No rumours, no wagging tongues, no sniggering old biddies who begrudge Nana her looks and would *definitely* begrudge that she once loved the Necroscope, Harry Keogh!"

Lardis could be outspoken, which was how he preferred it. It was out in the open now and no more pretending. "Anyway, her Hzak was dead—and died a brave man, of the vampire *shit* in a Lord's bloody gauntlet, which poisoned him—and the Lidescis were reduced. *By my own orders* widows were taking new husbands, and widowers new wives . . . so why shouldn't Nana? It wasn't her fault she fell for Harry Hell-lander! So then, let no man criticize Nathan or his mother, and certainly not his father! Without Harry Keogh we were all dead men long and long ago. Well, like father like son: it could be that without Nathan we'd be dead tonight—or stumbling over the boulder plains to Wrathstack—or turned to living slime in some Lord or Lady's vats!"

Again he glared all about. "Is it understood? All regarding Nathan stays here. Nothing of it goes outside. If a man of you has trouble with that, leave now—but when you go, leave anything you heard behind you! If not, you'll have me to deal with later . . ." No one moved, nor even shuffled.

"Good!" said Lardis.

And Andrei Romani, on Lardis's right, said: "Good, aye! And so what anyway? He's not the only bastard here—I'm one myself, and both of us good 'uns!"

The rest of them laughed (including, Nathan couldn't help but notice, Trask and Chung!) But the three cavers sat silent, looking mystified. They might glean something from all of this; at least it gave them the opportunity to hear the Szgany tongue used more extensively, and perhaps pick up a few words. But in any case they were Nathan's men and so should stay with him in his group, where he could translate or instruct as required.

As for the subject of Lardis's stern warning and Andrei's good-hearted joking, Nathan wasn't embarrassed. He might have been, long ago, but no longer. Both the living, and the dead of another world, its Great Majority, had explained to him how there was nothing to be ashamed of in his father. On the other hand, there was a certain something about his ancestry—more properly, his family—that disturbed him; something that remained undisclosed as yet. Desiring it to stay that way, he now took the initiative and said:

"Lardis, before we begin: a little information, if you'll oblige me—to bring me up-to-date?"

The way he said it made Lardis look at him in the flickering candlelight. For surely information was what they were here about, unless there was some secret meaning? And there was, for it was written on Nathan's face plain to see by the Old Lidesci where he sat directly opposite. Wherefore Lardis must give Nathan his head, to see where the lad would gallop. And so: "Aye?" he said. "Go on. What is it you would know?"

"Tonight was a fierce battle," Nathan said. "The Wamphyri came here, to Sanctuary Rock . . . which is something new?"

Lardis nodded. "Indeed, for it seems they've found us out at last. I anticipated it years ago, and we'll move out later tonight."

"I couldn't help noticing that there were a great many of them. The Wamphyri *themselves* weren't much in evidence—not on the ground, at least—but their men and beasts . . ." He let it hang in the air, unspoken.

It was the emphasis he put on *themselves* that told Lardis what this was about. And now the Old Lidesci must find a way to tell him what he wanted to know—without telling the others.

"We've heard rumours out of the east," said Lardis slowly, grinding out the words. "There were always suppliant tribes in the east—cowardly dogs! Well, Wratha and those other bloodsuckers have started them up again! What's more, it seems the Wamphyri are united again; they've been building their forces without letup. Also, we've been hearing that there's a brand-new Lord among them. We don't know too much about *that* one as yet, but what we do know isn't good. Rumour has it that he's a necromancer! He's supposed to have been seen by some of Karl Zestos's people, rummaging in the old mounds and tumuli in the woods. It's only to be expected, I suppose . . . of a necromancer!" (There: he'd done it!)

And Nathan nodded to show he understood. Understood that Lardis knew his brother Nestor was a vampire, and not "merely" a vampire but also a Lord. And now . . . a necromancer? It made sense, in a way: his father's talent was coming out in Nestor just as it had in Nathan. But where in Nathan it had been for the good . . .

The Old Lidesci had kept it to himself so as not to hurt Nana Kiklu, and so as not to damage Nathan's credibility. His reasons were obvious:

While it was not forgotten among the Lidescis how Harry Keogh (called the Necroscope, or Harry Hell-lander, and occasionally Harry Dwellersire) had joined with his son The Dweller to destroy the Old Wamphyri and reduce their aeries to rubble, it was also remembered how in the end Harry had *become* Wamphyri! If it should now be learned that Nestor was this "brand-new Lord" in Wrath-stack, and not only a Lord but a necromancer, too . . .

. . . Perhaps that quaint old adage, "like father, like son," might take on a new and frightening meaning! And how would that affect Nathan? Necroscope now, aye . . . but what about tomorrow? Would it make any difference that he had been born *before* Harry Keogh became Wamphyri? Would anyone remember that, or even consider it, when they discovered that his brother was a monster?

Even Lardis himself had lost sleep worrying about it;

and if he didn't love Nathan like a son, and if he hadn't lost his own son ... but he did and he had, and that was that.

Nathan was still looking at Lardis, but the tense look had finally gone out of the Old Lidesci's face. The secret was theirs to share between them; theirs alone, for the moment at least.

Lardis relaxed, nodded, and said: "Very well, I think I'm ready for a proper introduction to these friends of yours, Nathan, and then we'll hear your story. If memory serves, the one you told us last time was pretty damn good, but I've a feeling this one is going to top it! Only let's get on without delay, for your mother's given us an hour, no more."

He rubbed his chin in mock concern, grinned and said, "A bit of a girl, your mother in her time. I won't be the one to cross her, be sure!"

The introductions, somewhat stilted and complicated by language differences which required interpretation in places, followed ...

PART FIVE:

NATHAN:
A CHAMPION
FOR THE LIVING,
A DREAMER
FOR THE DEAD

I

Old Contacts Renewed

Glancing left and right at Trask and Chung, Nathan spoke to the Old Lidesci: "As they were my father's friends before me, these men are my friends. Hell-landers, if you like, but despite what Zek Föener told you, it isn't really hell. I've met Zek, incidentally, and she remembers you with great fondness!"

"*Ahhh!*" Landis's long drawn-out gasp. "But . . . you actually met Zekintha? Is she well? And Jazz—ah, how that one could *fight*! They should have come together and stayed here! In fact, I think they did get together. Why, I was almost jealous of him upon a time . . . er, it was before Lissa, of course! Jazz and Zek: their blood was good and hot, very nearly Szgany. And their children would have given us new life right across Sunside."

Nathan nodded wryly; Nana and Misha would be lucky to see him in just one hour. Lardis made a wonderful audience (like a small child, all agog), but *just* like a child he would be full of questions. Best to ignore them and get on with it, except—well, the Old Lidesci must be told about Zek and Jazz.

And so: "They *did* get together," he said. "Zek . . . remains; and she's well, yes. She took me to Jazz's grave, in a place so beautiful you'd scarcely believe. I was pleased to . . . *go* there with her." (He had almost said something else: that he had been pleased to *meet* Jazz and speak with the hero of so many of Lardis's tales of the old days, but Lardis and the others wouldn't have understood. To mundane minds a man may only "meet" someone in the flesh, not at that someone's graveside.)

Changing the subject, Nathan clapped a hand to Ben Trask's shoulder. "This man is as brave as they come in any world, and without him I couldn't have returned; why, he even came with me to help you destroy the Wamphyri!" Which was true as far as it went. "He is called Ben—and Lardis, Zekintha misses him very much in the hell-lands! Theirs is a new thing, too soon broken. Ben has talent: he sees the truth of things. Only lie to him, he'll know your betrayal. Show him a false trail, he'll choose the right one."

Lardis studied Trask anew; but what was to study? If Zek found him good, then he was good!

"And this small, yellowish man is David," Nathan continued, and grasped Chung's arm. "You've much in common with him, Lardis: he sees afar. He is a seer! As the talent was in your ancestors and remains in your blood, so it is in David."

Looking from Trask to Chung and back again, Lardis nodded. "All good things, these strange skills of yours, and we can use them. Aye, for the Wamphyri are talented, too. Well, welcome to Sanctuary Rock, Ben and David. A pity you won't get to know it any better, but we'll soon be out of here. Now that Wratha and her lot know we're here, it's no longer safe."

Trask nodded; and carefully, haltingly—mainly in the Szgany tongue—said, "Thank you for accepting us. Obviously, Nathan has your complete confidence. That's not hard to understand: his father, Harry Keogh, had mine those long years ago. I knew him when he was . . . just a man; *and* afterwards, before he came back to Starside. Nothing changed him—not the real Harry—not even at the end."

"I know," Lardis answered, "for I was *there* at the end!" And then, in a surprised tone: "But . . . you speak our tongue! Not very well, but you speak it. I noticed it before: when we joke, you laugh! Now how is that?"

Trask shrugged; he looked somewhat mystified himself.

"I have a way with tongues. In my world there are many languages. I know a little—not much, a word here and there—of most of them. But yours is a strange world and . . . I have to admit that I've surprised myself!"

For once it was Nathan who knew the "truth" of it. "It's your talent," he said. "I've noticed that all espers have this knack with tongues, especially mentalists. Myself, Zekintha—others too, I suspect. Matching words to thoughts makes it that much easier. In you, Ben, it's the fact that you're a human lie detector: you know the truth of things, even the truth of words. I can't explain it any better than that. Ian Goodly has it, too, and . . . David?" He looked at Chung.

"I'm getting most of this, yes." Chung nodded. "I've never questioned my skill. Chinese parents, English upbringing, some German and a little French in school—the rest just seemed to come naturally."

"No," Trask shook his head, "metaphysically! Nathan has to be right: it's our ESP."

They settled down and Nathan indicated the silent, as yet astonished, even shaken, cavers. They were seated to his right, between Chung and Kirk Lisescu. But here Nathan found himself embarrassed; he had met these men at the Romanian Refuge—since when things had moved so fast he hadn't had time to get to know them. Even their names escaped him now.

Their spokesman, aware of Nathan's difficulty, said: "I'm John Carling. My friends are Jim Bentley and Orson Sangster. I think we all understand a little of what's being said but nothing of what's going on. As for this—this what? This parallel world?—it's just a nightmare! What we've seen so far is unbelievable! But for the fact that we're all cavers, used to being underground . . . well, I'm pretty sure we'd all be out of here on the double! Except we wouldn't know where the hell we were running, or what we'd be likely to run into! At least these people here are friendly and . . . well, people!"

Carling was a compact, capable-looking man; small, wiry, dark-haired and crew-cut. His hands were large and strong, and he used them for emphasis when he spoke. He had a small mouth, straight nose, slightly hollow cheeks. If his hair were longer and his skin a shade darker, he could pass for Szgany.

Jim Bentley was also slender and agile, but stood two or three inches taller than Carling. He had a lopsided mouth, a nervous grin, red hair, and brown eyes. A deep, crescent-moon scar on his forehead was the legacy of some minor caving accident.

Orson Sangster was the odd man out. Heavyset for a caver, he was long-armed and lumbering, and shared many features with the Old Lidesci, who might best be described as "simian." Also like Lardis, his looks were deceptive; a good disguise for his sharp mind and ready wit.

Ben Trask found himself feeling sorry for the three, and said: "When we get the chance, I'll fill you in more properly on what you've got yourselves into. But if I tell you that what happens here could well determine the future of our own world, then you might appreciate that this is bigger than all of us. But in any case—like it or not—you're in it for the duration. Listen in and make your best effort to learn the language. We could be here for some time to come."

While Trask was speaking, Nathan had been looking at Lardis's senior men. He was well acquainted with Kirk Lisescu and Andrei Romani, of course, but the rest were new to him. Also, it seemed that several of the old crew were absent.

So before beginning his story—directing his gaze at Andrei, who sat silently now, apparently lost in thought—Nathan began to inquire, "What of your . . . ?"—and immediately paused. It was his telepathy, which he'd learned from the Thyre to use sparingly, so avoiding intrusion into the minds of others. Andrei's thoughts had been so strong, however, that they'd almost spilled over, making Nathan's inquiry unnecessary. Almost without trying, he'd read his answer in the other's mind: that the Romani brothers, Ion and Franci, were dead, killed in a recent attack on Settlement.

Seeing Nathan's confusion—guessing what he'd been about to ask—Andrei nodded, said, "Gone, aye, like so many before them. They were two of a team on decoy duty in old Settlement. They'd been setting small fires and burning beast flesh, sending cooking smells up to lure the Wamphyri down. And it worked. There were a lot of the bastards that night, but what with Dimi Petrescu's exploding powder, and our rockets and all, the Settlement team had their measure. One of our rockets hit a warrior in the gas-bladders and set them on fire; crashing down, the beast was half-stunned on impact. Ion and Franci went to fling boiling tar on him. But . . . there was more life in the devil than they'd thought."

Andrei's eyes had shone misty in the candlelight. Now, as he gave himself a shake, he said: "Well, that's how it goes." And Nathan felt him blank it from his mind so that it wouldn't creep back again . . . not until the next time. It was sobering, saddening, and it brought the situation home to everyone, with the exception perhaps of the cavers.

Out of respect, Nathan waited a moment before starting to tell his story, but once under way he progressed with some speed and wasted as little time as possible. Picking up the tale from where Lardis must have left it at the time, he told how he had been taken by a flyer whose lieutenant rider, for some unknown reason, had thrown him into the glaring Hell-lands Gate. On the other side, in a place called Perchorsk, he'd been taken prisoner but had managed to escape. In enemy territory, hell-lander Travellers (this part was greeted with utter amazement by Lardis and his men. What, Travellers in the hell-lands? And Nathan knew that he'd have to go into greater detail some other time) had befriended and hidden him until Trask and his organization could pick him up and convey him to a place of safety.

Then, with the assistance of his newfound esper friends, Nathan had discovered his Necroscope connections. Learning his father's art of "going places," he had become the ultimate Traveller! Now, by use of a second Gate, he had managed to return home, bringing back hell-lander weapons with him, hopefully to defeat the Wamphyri. As for

Trask, Chung, and the others: they were here mainly by accident, but also because they desired to destroy the Wamphyri. Not unnaturally, the hell-landers in general thought of the Gates as a monstrous threat to their world and desired to close them forever, and as soon as possible.

Therefore Trask and the others must go back to their own world without delay and while they still could, but not before they had trained Lardis's men in the use of their amazing weapons. Later, upon their return to the hell-lands and if it was at all feasible, they would continue to send guns and ammunition through until the Gates were closed.

Nathan also mentioned that the leader of his hell-lander enemies from Perchorsk had also come through, with a good many men, and that they had weapons, too. The Szgany should be aware of this, that not all foreigners were good sorts. As for Turkur Tzonov: Nathan scarcely cared what happened to him at all, but it would not be a good thing if his weapons fell into Wamphyri hands.

"Or into the hands of the Lady Wratha's collaborators, her supplicants beyond the great pass," Lardis rumbled when Nathan had done. And he spat into the dust of the floor.

Nathan frowned. "I had forgotten about them. Perhaps I'll have to see what can be done about Tzonov after all. I have my own reasons for hating him, but I had hoped it would be out of my hands. Apparently not . . ."

"What about these Gypsies, these hell-lander Travellers?" Plainly Lardis was fascinated by the idea. Nathan pondered a moment, looked for the best way to tell it, and finally said:

"They are true Travellers. Aye, Szgany—or their ancestors were, at least. And in the hell-lands, too, they're called Szgany, or Zigeuner . . . they have various names. The Starside Gate has been there a long, long time, Lardis."

"They're from here, d'you mean? From Sunside/Starside?"

Nathan nodded. "Originally, yes. Indeed the chief of the tribe I spent time with—I lived in his caravan a day and a night—was a direct descendant. He was the last of his line, of the true Szgany blood, and carried the history of his forefathers with him. Likewise, it will go with him to his grave. And I know that you will say it's as well."

Lardis frowned. "Really? How do you mean?"

Nathan shrugged. "He was a Ferengi!"

Lardis's eyes bugged. "Ferengi? A *Ferenc*, d'you say?" He turned his face aside and spat again. "The Ferencs were cursed in prehistory, since time immemorial! There were always Ferencs among the Old Wamphyri. Fess Ferenc was one such, and I saw him once during a raid: a giant, bulge-headed and block-jawed, his bones all wrong, and talons for hands. But . . . the Szgany Ferengi?"

Nathan nodded. "But all myths and legends now—to them! Ancestral memory: of a time when their Lord was big in his castle, and they went out across the world to do his bidding. They remember the places where their ancestors came from: the Gates where they emerge into the hell-lands!"

Lardis said: "We have our legends, too. We know that as long as the Wamphyri have been, they've had three dire punishments for transgressors against their own 'laws.' Or in other words, they've had three especially unpleasant ways of getting rid of their greatest enemies! They were banished to the north, to die of hunger and cold in the Ice-lands. Or, they were buried undead in deep pits out on the barren boulder plains, till they stiffened to stones in the earth. Or, they were hurled into the Starside Gate, and sent to hell forever—for no one ever came back from there! Aye, and sometimes their thralls would go with them. Is that what you're telling me: that the hell-lands Travellers were supplicant Szgany?"

Nathan nodded. "Some of them must have been: unvampirized, in order that they could keep watch during the hell-land days, which are shorter and more frequent than ours, to ensure their Lords slept in safety."

Lardis looked at him for long moments. "Just legends, you say. But are you sure that's *all* they are, Nathan, these Lords, in this strange world you've visited—*just* legends?"

Trask cut in, "We believe so. Harry Keogh tracked the last of them down, and killed him. That one was a Ferenczy, too. But Harry must have got too close, which was his undoing."

"Indeed!" Landis nodded. "It doesn't do to get too close to the Wamphyri!" He looked at Nathan. "And so, when this old chief who sheltered you goes down into the ground, it will be the end of his line?"

"Of the *direct* line, yes," Nathan answered.

And Trask smiled and said: "But not of the Ferenczys."

"Eh?" Lardis frowned. "Come again?"

"It's a common name in my world," Trask told him, and he looked at Andrei Romani. "Especially in Romania!"

‹ Andrei drew breath in a great gasp. "Where? *What* did you say?"

Nathan stepped in at once. "It's true enough, Andrei. In the hell-lands there's a Gate—indeed, the original Gate— that opens into a country called Romania. And the Travellers, Gypsies, Szgany, Zigeuner, call them what you will, they are known collectively . . . as Romany!"

Andrei was agog. He glanced this way and that, said to Lardis, "Should I be insulted? Did ancestors of mine go into the hell-lands as vampire thralls?"

But again Nathan was quick off the mark. "Not necessarily. Romani is a common name, after all—you'll forgive my saying so, I'm sure. But all along the mountain flank dwell Romanis, in no way related to you . . . or remotely at best."

Andrei said, *"Phew!"* and sat back.

Trask checked his watch and warned, "Your hour is up."

Lardis stood up. "Enough for now. We're all of us on our knees. It has been a hard enough day for us Szgany, so it must have been—what, 'hell'?—for you lot!" He grinned through crooked ivory teeth, but in a moment was serious again. "I'll have someone show you your places. Get your heads down by all means, but try not to make yourselves too comfortable. Before midnight—*long* before—we shall be on our way out of here; where to . . .

is my business. Sunup will find us in a new camp, which will be soon enough for weapon-training and what all.

"But you six, or seven if the woman was here ..." Lardis held out his long arms as if to encompass Carling and colleagues, then did the same towards Trask, Nathan, Chung. "Listen; I'm not much of a one for saying thanks: there's never been a lot to say thanks for! Still it's plain to me that your being here saved us all tonight. I know that as soon as my lads get the chance, they'll want to celebrate and have a do; aye, and rightly so, for it's been a long time at that! Then you'll be made welcome, be sure!"

And as his men lit torches and prepared to leave the cave, Lardis called out: "Oh, yes, and another thing. I give you fair warning: there's a bunch of fine, brown-limbed lasses here, and many of them without men. So watch your step, you hell-landers! For believe me, *they* will be wanting to make you welcome, too!"

His chuckles followed them out into the mazy ways of the Rock. . . .

Nathan made a small rasping sound in the back of his throat, then clearly spoke a name, however strange: "Thikkoul!" For a moment disturbed, he struggled a little and turned over in his sleep. Misha, wide awake, made room for him, then went back to cradling him when he'd settled down again.

Her arm went across his body; she pressed her breasts to his back; her hand found his manhood where it lay limp now. It was always a wonder to her how an item so small and soft could grow so large and hard, and *so* swiftly! But making love to her this time had been too much for him; physically exhausted even before the act, afterwards he had fallen straight into a deep sleep. It wasn't his usual way, she was sure—not that she'd ever had him long enough to *know* his usual way!—but she had understood. Emptying himself into her had created this void in him: no movement, no thought, nothing but the salving surf of relief rolling over sharp reefs of body and mind. Except Nathan's was a special mind and a stranger to inactivity. And so, in a very little while he had started to dream.

Now he was doing it again, and because she loved him Misha wondered what he was dreaming about this time. As if in answer: "Thikkoul!" he said again. It was a mumble fading into silence—and into a peculiar stillness! Indeed, he lay so very still that she knew he must be listening.

But to what . . . ?

Nathaaan!

It came as from a million miles away, a voice remembered as if from a million years ago; so it seemed to the Necroscope. Yet how may a man recall to mind a voice he never before heard in life, whose owner was dead before he was even born? A normal man—or normal *mind*—may not, except perhaps in flashes of ancestral memory, if a man believed in such things. But normal minds are incapable of communication with the dead.

Nathaaan! The voice came again, like an echo out of space and time, but far more insistent than any dream; and the Necroscope had learned to know the difference. Which was why for the third time, in his sleep, he spoke the name of his real yet incorporeal contact: "Thikkoul!" Except this time he repeated it to himself, under his breath in a language known as deadspeak, which was now as natural to him as breathing.

Had there been living minds in tune with Nathan's at that moment (in fact there were several that were *trying* to contact him), they would doubtless be mystified by a sudden blackout—the fact that where Nathan's subconscious mind had been, there was now a void. For only the dead could hear deadspeak. It was like radio without a receiver, or rather, the receiver was in Nathan's head. It was like semaphor to a blind man, or a distant shout to a man stone deaf; and among the living, there was only one man who could receive, see, hear it. Or perhaps two, if Nestor were included; except his talent took on a different form, where incoming transmissions were not voluntary. No, not at all.

Nathaaan! And then, more clearly, homing in on the Necroscope at last: *Nathan, is it really you? But then, who else can it be?*

And who else could this be but Thikkoul, a Thyre astrologer whose talent was to the precog Ian Goodly what Goodly's was to some fairground faker! Thikkoul: who had read Nathan's future in the stars, and read it true, however obliquely. Nathan remembered what Thikkoul had told him: how first he would be reunited—albeit briefly—with his mother and Misha, before disappearing from the world (from *this* world), "as in the blink of some monstrous glaring eye!" And indeed he had gone out of this world: tossed half-conscious into the glaring eye of the Hell-lands Gate by Nestor's vampire lieutenant.

"But you didn't foretell my return?"

Because I looked no farther! And after all, why should I? For when you are gone you are gone! In my experience the total absence of a man indicates his demise. In all truth, Nathan, I had expected to talk to you again, but from our respective resting places. In any case, are you sorry that I was wrong?

"No, of course not. And I'm not blaming you: your reading was accurate. It's simply as you said: reading the future is a devious thing. That a point will be arrived at is inevitable, but how we arrive there is up to time and the tides!"

The tides?

"An expression from another world." Except Thikkoul had seen it in his mind even before he could begin to explain. For the Thyre were amazing mentalists all, and their Great Majority had been practiced in deadspeak long before the advent of Harry Keogh into their world.

Another world! And didn't you always go in search of one? So why did you return?

"Because this is my world, and because everything I love is here."

Also because everything you hate is here, I fancy.

"The Wamphyri? Oh, yes! And we may have the means to destroy them at last . . ." But here Nathan paused, for even in the seclusion of deadspeak that was something he didn't want to go into. Anyway, he wasn't sure of the details himself—except that the less anyone knew of them, dead or alive, the better. Which was why he now changed the subject:

"Thikkoul . . . how did you know I was back?"

What, you? The one man who stands between life and death? Like a bridge between alien nations, a messenger between different spheres of existence, an envoy of the otherwise unknown? When you went from us, a solitary candle blinked out; when you returned, it burst back into flame! I would have tried to contact you earlier, but at first we did not dare believe.

"We?"

Myself, and all of your friends among the Thyre ancients with whom you have spoken in the past, whose word you passed on to their descendants among the living. But in the Cavern of the Ancients, in Place-Under-the-Yellow-Cliffs, Rogei, Shaeken, and others were suddenly excited! Via deadspeak they spoke to their colleagues in other places. To Tolmia, and to Ethloi the Elder in Open-to-the-Sky, who passed the message on: that in fact you had returned! So it finally reached me, Thikkoul the Stargazer in the Hall of Endless Hours, in River's Rush. And of course I had to speak to you, and offer my services.

"Your services?"

Oh yes! For now that you have *a future—why, I can read it for you! But I admit, it's for myself as much as for you: to see the stars again, through the eyes of the Necroscope!*

Nathan thought about it. "It could be invaluable," he said eventually. And then, rather more cautiously: "But on the other hand, since whatever you see can't be changed . . . ? I mean, since what will be, will be . . . ?"

Of course, said Thikkoul, if disappointedly, and Nathan sensed his slow deadspeak nod. *Of course. And I really can't blame you that you do not wish to know. For after all the future of any man, even the Necroscope, can only be so long . . .*

"But if I should change my mind—?"

—*Yes, yes, that's understood,* said Thikkoul. And after a moment: *I've interrupted your sleep long enough. Only remember that I'm here if ever you should need me.*

"I will," Nathan answered, and felt Thikkoul's incorporeal probe dwindling to nothing in his metaphysical mind. In another moment the deadspeak void had disappeared, too, and the Necroscope's dreaming mind was open again . . .

. . . Open to those several others who had been trying to reach him ever since his return to his homeworld some hours ago, who had known that their best chance would come when he slept. Various obstructions—for one, the mass of the barrier mountains; for another, the fact that Nathan's mind was either fully occupied or totally empty, a deadspeak void; and for a third, the fact that he slept in the Rock, though close to its outer perimeter—had so far kept them from him. But while they waited they had talked among themselves, as was their wont.

In previous times it had scarcely been necessary for them to communicate in this current fashion: living together and as joint leaders of the same pack (in itself a situation unthinkable among previous packs), and brothers out of the same litter, daily contact had more than sufficed. Recently, however, bitter circumstances had forced them apart, which was the reason they contacted Nathan now. That and to welcome him home.

He had been listening to their telepathic conversation for several minutes before true cognizance dawned: that it wasn't a dream but a reality. Had he been awake, Nathan would have made the connection at once; his own telepathy had long developed to that degree where he recognized the thoughts of others for what they were, no longer as the vague static or mental interference he had known as a child. His telepathy and his deadspeak (different talents yet plainly analogous) had always been present in him but undeveloped through lack of practice, or lack of sympathetic minds on whom to practice. The dead wouldn't speak to him, and apart from "his" wolves he had known no telepathic contact—or perhaps some but only with Nestor, which was not an uncommon phenomenon between Szgany kith and kin.

In his travels, however, the "nomadic" Thyre had opened up both of these esoteric channels to him, and in Ben Trask's parallel world he had finally used his talent to befriend the teeming dead in a way superior to all his expectations in Sunside. For as far as Nathan was aware—and with the exception of the Thyre, of course—the Great Majority of his own world had not changed in their attitude: desiring no truck with him at all, they continued to shun him. Wherefore these communications he intercepted now, since they were not Thyre sendings and could not be Szgany deadspeak, were telepathic.

But to speak mind-to-mind with such as these! It resolved a question of old concern whose answer, while it had been made apparent in Trask's world, was one that might only be verified here. And this communication *was* that verification.

It was something that Nathan had always questioned, while in his heart knowing that it was true: his weird "relationship" with certain members of the grey brotherhood, the wild children of the night, the wolves who inhabited Sunside/Starside's barrier mountains. But a relationship in the true and fullest sense of the word, as was now apparent. For Nathan's *older* brother—not Nestor "Kiklu" or whatever he called himself now, no, but a blood brother nevertheless, a true son of Harry Keogh and a woman of his Earth—had been The Dweller himself! And The Dweller had been a werewolf!

Even as Nathan slept on, the last pieces of an old puzzle began slotting themselves into place in his metaphysical mind. The reason his wolves had always called him "uncle." Surely it was as they themselves had often declared it to be: because he *was* their uncle! The reason that he'd always been aware of them as other than "just wolves," and had exercised some power over them (and they over him): because they were of one origin with him, one blood. The reason they had always seemed to watch over him as best they could: because "their father would have wished it," even as they'd tried to tell him, upon a time!

And sleeping still, he remembered something else they had tried to tell him, which thrilled him to his very core! For he knew now that he was not the only Necroscope: what Harry Keogh had passed down to him, and in a yet more morbid manifestation to Nestor, had also been passed to Nathan's nephew wolves.

It had happened on the night of Wratha's very first attack on Settlement, when she and her renegades had flown from Karenstack (as the last aerie had been known then) over the barrier mountains and down into Sunside for the first time; and Nathan recalled what his wolves had revealed to him in the aftermath of that raid, during a similar exhausted sleep:

Things have come to pass (they had told him). *Strange and monstrous creatures are come to dwell in Starside's last great aerie, out of which they raid on Sunside. The woods and mountains are no longer safe, neither for wolves nor men. These are problems for which we have no answers, but . . . there is one at least who might know.*

And Nathan had said, "But there is no answer to the Wamphyri."

You may be right. You may be wrong. But our mother speaks to our father, who is your brother. If anyone would know, he is that one. And so we go to speak to the one who suckled us.

"Your mother, a she-wolf?"

Aye, where her bones lie bleached in a secret place . . .

It had been before Nathan discovered his talent, before he had even known what a Necroscope was. There was no way he could have understood their . . . what, riddles? But now . . . oh, now he understood well enough: that they, too, in their wolf way, were Necroscopes! Necroscopes, all three of them—and just as Nathan talked to his dead, so they talked to theirs!

"Dock," so called because his tail had been shortened by an angry vixen when he was a cub. And "Blaze," after the diagonal white stripe across his forehead, as if the fur there were marked with frost. And "Grinner," whose upper lip was given to curling, so that his teeth were always bared even to friends. Nathan's wolves: "his" wolves—his nephews!

Even now they heard his thoughts, and answered them.

Uncle, Blaze growled, coughed, barked in his mind. *And so you've come back at last. You and your numbers! There could be but one source.*

"My numbers?" Nathan frowned.

Did you not know? But they issue from you like light from a beacon; not so much during the day, but most certainly when you sleep!

That gave Nathan something to think about, something to ponder when he woke up and all of this reverted to a dream or, if he was lucky, to memory. For if the numbers vortex made him apparent to his wolves, then how transparent was he to others? Half-forgotten things, which had disturbed and worried him at the time of their occurrence, now stirred to renewed life:

In the world beyond the Starside Gate, Siggi Dam—not a locator but a telepath—had discovered him easily enough. And the last time he was here in Sunside his vampire brother Nestor had known his whereabouts precisely. But . . . the numbers vortex? Was that it? The metaphysical math he'd been born with: his betrayer? From now on he must suppress it, especially now that he was back with Lardis and the Szgany Lidesci. The last thing he desired to be was a beacon for the Wamphyri!

The shake of a deadspeak head. It was Blaze again. *In all Sunside/Starside there are only five who give off numbers like that, and only five who can read them. If another mind were to touch yours—as mine touches it now—then he might experience your numbers vortex. But to us it has always been a clear signal, revealing your whereabouts. Alas, not only to us, but also . . . to your brother Nestor!*

"Five of us," Nathan answered. "Myself the three of you, and Nestor. All of the one blood!"

The nod of a wolf head—the flash of its white stripe—

registering as clearly as if Blaze were here right now. And Nathan could see him as he'd known him since his childhood: his eyes brown as dark wild honey in the twilight, but feral yellow at night. Lean and muscular; surefooted as a mountain goat, but fleeter far. And intelligent? Oh, way beyond the average intelligence of the pack! Except for individual markings and habits (Dock's tail or lack of one, and Grinner's less-than-affectionate grin), all three of them were much of a muchness. Of course they were, for they were of the same litter, the one blood. As was Nathan of that blood. It made sense.

Yet something—indeed several things—made very little sense or none at all. "Nestor has a numbers vortex, you say? My brother gives off numbers?"

His numbers aura is a weak thing and slowly fading, but we know him by it all the same. Aye, for our senses are keen, and we use them to their full—both our senses and his aura—to avoid him! Now Blaze's wolf voice was a low growl, and bitter.

"Because he's Wamphyri?"

That and more. Nestor and those others in the last aerie, for a while now they've been our problem, too.

"Wait!" said Nathan. "I must be straight on this. If Nestor has numbers, why don't I know it? Why can't I read them? Why have I never sensed them? I mean, Nestor *hated* numbers!" It was so, and now Nathan remembered something Nestor had used to say: that a number was the count of fish he had caught, and division was the share-out after a day's hunting, and multiplication was something rabbits had mastered without once using their fingers and toes!

He doesn't know he has them—or if he does know, then he doesn't care to know. He blames you, Nathan, for the numbers in his head! He always has! For when you are near it sets Nestor's vortex going, and he doesn't much care for the whirling in his brain.

"How can you know this?"

Because it's much the same for us. We have numbers, too, but no use for them! What was in our father is in us;

it's why we are different, clever. But to be what we are doesn't require us to know everything that he knew! And Nestor is the same. Can you not try to understand? Ah, but you were far easier to talk to, upon a time! Nathan sensed great frustration in the other, a certain urgency. But he must have this out.

"I was easier to talk to because I didn't understand; I simply accepted! Now I am beginning to understand. But I tell you this: just as I've never sensed Nestor's numbers, neither have I sensed yours, Dock's, nor Grinner's!"

A despairing wolf shrug. *I have tried to answer for Nestor. Perhaps I am right, perhaps I am wrong. I say how I see . . .*

"And your numbers? Why haven't I sensed them?"

They are subdued, dormant. Our mother told us, "Hide them! They are unnatural! Your father had numbers, too, and where is your father now? Gone in a bang and a great flash of light!" As cubs we put our numbers aside. What were they anyway but a distraction?

"Could you recall them? Show them to me?"

My numbers? (A wolf groan.) *But what a waste of time! Now tell me, Uncle: have you returned to fight the Wamphyri, or to play with numbers?*

"It's important."

Very well, but I must be brief. Watch!

Nathan "watched"—and he saw! Conjured out of nowhere—

—It *was* a numbers vortex, that same mad cone of numbers; yet not the same. For while Nathan's vortex was made up of *real* numbers—from the simple ̶I̶I̶I̶I̶ "gate" marks of the Szgany system, to all the cyphers, symbols, and algebraic jumble of alien, parallel worlds—his wolf-nephew Blaze's vortex was composed in its entirety of *wolf* numbers: paw marks, scratches, moon and star symbols, clusters of five or six rocks, pine trees grouped in threes and fours. The grey brotherhood "counted" only those things that had meaning or use to them! But no meaning at all to Nathan.

Yet the ebb and flow and whirl of the thing was not

without direction . . . indeed it appeared to be all *about* direction. Nathan's own vortex had always seemed to hint of vast distances spanned in a moment, and of all time being NOW. Also, there had been this sense of worlds far beyond. All a puzzle then, but of awesome relevance now: his numbers had proved to be the source material of the Möbius Continuum itself! Could there be a similar case here? For that familiar feeling of worlds beyond was very real—*and* of their direction! Nathan found it of great interest; he would have liked to study it longer . . .

. . . Except Blaze shut it down before he could even begin. *This gets us nowhere.* Again his frustration showing through, so that Nathan dropped the subject and asked instead:

"Where are you now, and why did you seek me out?"

To say hello . . . also to warn you, and to seek your help. Though how you may help is beyond me. You are too full of your own problems, your own questions. Let me answer yet another of them: I am high in the mountains.

"Hello to you, too, then, Blaze high in the mountains—who upon a time was far less irritable!—and Grinner, Dock, if you're listening. But you know that if I can help you with something I will. First, what did you want to warn me about?"

About the Wamphyri, of course!

"Of course, but I already know about the Wamphyri."

Oh? Well, you know about Wratha and hers, at least.

Ice melted on Nathan's spine, and trickled there. "Are you telling me there are more?"

Come from the east, aye . . .

"When?"

A day at most.

"How many?"

More than we can count! But we are wolves, not good with numbers.

The ice trickled faster. "You've seen them?"

Your nephew Dock has seen them. Dock is the leader of the pack that holds the high ground beyond the great pass. Dock has seen them at a place called Stone-Like-a-River, where they camp in great numbers. Grinner, too, has seen something of them. His pack holds the ground from this side of the pass to the heights over Twin Fords. My pack runs in the west, from Grinner's boundary to a place over Tireni Scarp. Beyond that . . . lies the territory of a dangerous old bitch-wolf! She's a common wolf—yet uncommon! Fiercer than a dog, much! Leader of a fine pack, aye! But we hold each other in mutual respect, and confine ourselves to our own places. This way there are no disputes, skirmishes. The grey brotherhood is a brotherhood.

"Or a sisterhood?" Nathan smiled.

She is a rarity. (The other's wry shrug.)

Nathan's levity had been brief. "But you yourself have not seen these eastern Wamphyri?"

I talk to Dock and Grinner; isn't it enough that they have seen them?

Nathan nodded. "Of course. And I may tell you this, the invasion of these creatures isn't unexpected. It's the reason I brought strange weapons out of a strange land, with which to fight them! If you'll work with me and the Szgany—the grey brothers would act as observers, and the Szgany as fighters—that would be invaluable!"

I guarantee our assistance. (A great flood of relief.)

"You've had problems?"

Have I not stated as much? Wratha and the others eat wolf hearts, kidneys, and cubs basted in their mothers' milk! Would you not call that problematic? It's why my brothers and I have split the Great Pack three ways. We were a horde on the mountain slopes: too easy to trap! They chased us over cliffs; they brought down avalanches upon us; they used cubs for lures, and knew that their mothers would follow to their doom. They are a plague!

"They always were, in the old times, too."

I wasn't here then.

"Nor was I, but the Szgany have legends. Men live a long time, if they're lucky, and they keep records." Nathan frowned. "But . . . Nestor has hunted you, you say?"

Nestor himself? I cannot truly say. But the others—all of them! Or if not them, then their thralls. What odds? Nestor is one of them. And as for him . . . there are worse things than the hunting of the grey brothers. Members of my pack have seen him where he digs among the relics of his own kind, to—

"—I know!" Nathan cut in. "I know . . . what Nestor does. I know what he is, a necromancer. I heard it from the Old Lidesci. Nestor . . . can't *help* himself. As for his hunting: he has even hunted me! He caught me, too, for a little while."

Which is why you've been away?

"Yes, locked away, a prisoner in a strange place. Finally I escaped unharmed. But . . ." Nathan could only shrug and repeat, "Nestor isn't responsible. He can't help himself."

Of course not: he's Wamphyri!

That last was like an arrow in Nathan's heart, and Blaze had felt it go home. *I am sorry, Uncle . . .*

Me, too. (A new voice: Grinner's.)

And me. (And this was Dock, but faintly and from much farther away, in the heights beyond the great pass into Starside.)

Then for a while Nathan was silent, mulling over all he'd been told by Blaze. But eventually he asked, "What advice did your mother give you, that time when you went to see her where her bones lie bleached?"

She was the one who said we should split the pack, Blaze answered. *Which was wise of her. And we've been that way ever since. Well, and it worked for a while. Thinned out, we could hide that much more easily when the vampires came a-hunting. But now, with the influx of these newcomers from the east . . .* they *will be the horde!*

"Until they, too, are thinned out." Nathan nodded. "And already we've started."

Grinner came back with some eagerness, and Nathan could almost see his bared fangs gleaming white, salivating in the starlight. *I for one* know *that you have started! I am in the mountains between Twin Fords and the pass. I saw the Wamphyri come like a cloud out of the last aerie, heading west for Settlement or Sanctuary Rock. Ah, yes, but they were a much more ragged cloud when they returned!*

Then Blaze, infected with his brother's excitement: *And I saw the fires of the battle! Thunder and fire-lights in the sky, and noises like splitting rocks!*

Nathan smiled a thin cold smile. "Oh, yes. They got the worst of it this time."

And every time, from now on?

"Let's hope so. Contact me when you have news or difficulties. And remember what I said: as of now we work together. Keep watch on the movements of the Wamphyri. You are the eyes of the hawk, and the Szgany are its talons!"

And what of you, Nathan, in the scheme of things? What will you be: the war-hawk's beak?

"I hope to be, aye."

We will keep watch. (The nod of a wolf head and the flash of its blaze.) *Enough for now. Except ... I should warn you. Be careful how you use your deadspeak. For Nestor has it, too. With him ... it's different: the same and yet the opposite. Like the light of the moon and the light of the sun: one is cold and the other is warm. But Nestor listens to the thoughts of the dead, and eavesdrops on their conversations—and on yours, when you use deadspeak! He could be listening even now. Indeed, I'm sure he is.*

Nathan was at once alert, his mind probing the deadspeak aether. And in the north, Starside ... was that a presence, an intelligence, listening? If so it kept a very low, and a very suspicious, profile. Nathan gave a grim nod. "I'll try to remember that," he said. "But for now, farewell."

Then, from Dock far away, the wag of an unseen tail stump and a far, faint, whispered, *Keep safe, Uncle!*

And: *Aye*, from Grinner, who liked to keep things short. With which they were gone.

But Nathan was not alone, and he knew it. . . .

II

New Contacts Tried, and an Old *Contract* Denied

Misha too was fast asleep by now, clinging to Nathan, automatically adjusting to his body shape as he lived in dreams that were much more than mere dreams, which caused him to moan and mumble a little as he turned in his sleep.

Brief glimpses of the mountain heights, of a fleet moon tumbling on high, and the throats of the grey brothers a-throb with weird, unearthly ululations, their song of adoration. For like all natural creatures of the night in any world, they worshipped their silver mistress moon . . .

The howls faded away and were gone, and Nathan had been the only one to hear them.

Or perhaps not the *only* one, for his conversation with Blaze, Dock, and Grinner had been telepathic after all, not deadspeak, which is private. Sleeping, Nathan had had little or no control over eavesdroppers. The teeming dead knew that he had returned, of course, and although they had no great faith in him—or perhaps because of it?—and trusted his necromancer brother even less, they had listened to his conversation with the wolves in morbid fascination: much as a bird watches a snake. But one among them at least was vociferous.

Nathan knew his voice of old; why, he even remembered a name—Jasef Karis!—but not where he remembered it from: some old dream out of the past. Jasef Karis, yes. But a mere name did not give him rank or authority in such matters. Perhaps one day Nathan would go to him personally—*if* the rest of the Szgany dead would let him! For of all Sunside's Great Majority, Jasef had always seemed to be on his side, invariably to the consternation of his colleagues.

And so—quietly, not daring to speak or even think too clearly—it was the Necroscope's turn to eavesdrop. And once again, if Misha had been awake, she would have sensed her husband "listening" to something. In fact, to the furtive whispers of the dead.

Back again! (An audible shiver—or shudder?—in the incorporeal voice.) *Doesn't Sunside/Starside have enough of monsters?*

Bah! (Jasef Karis.) *You make me want to be sick, the lot of you! Why, for all that he's a youth, and human, the Thyre revere him! You have heard them: their Elders gone from them as we are gone from ours, the way they speak of him! Nathan's a hero to the dead of the Thyre! And to their living. Does it take unmen of the furnace deserts to recognize the saviour in our midst? For believe me, this one* will be *the saving of the Szgany—if you'll let him! How can you lie there and ignore him, when your very children among the living are at risk? He is your one hope: the continuity of the Szgany, and the guardian of your graves, those of you that have them!*

Nathan understood the last few words well enough. Since time immemorial the Szgany had burned most of their dead, certainly those killed by the Wamphyri; it was the only safe way. But if a man or woman died in an accident—or of sickness or old age, or if they were revered among their people and it was deemed safe—then they might be given a decent burial. Some tribes even had their own places of interment: mounds, tumuli, or cavern systems. Unmarked graves out in the forests must be numerous, and Nathan wondered if Jasef Karis had his own place somewhere out there. It seemed likely, for where a majority of these dead voices were literally thin as air (proof that their owners had been burned to nothing, or that they were long gone from the world of the living), some were louder and even substantial: the more *recently* dead, more focussed, more "together" with their mortal remains. And Jasef, despite the fact that his was the voice of an old man, was of the latter.

As for the more *freshly* dead, such as those killed in the fighting at Sanctuary Rock: as yet they'd be confused and unacquainted with their new, dark, incorporeal environment, and so unable to speak out. Nathan hoped to have friends among them eventually, when the truth of their situation had sunk in, but for now he could only suffer the alienation of the Great Majority—and suffer in silence, covertly, if he wished to listen to their conversations.

. . . So much for the Thyre, one dead voice was saying now, with an irritating air of assumed authority as false as his ingratiating tone. *We knew the desert folk all our lives, yet did* not *know of their mentalism! They kept that from us, and doubtless other secrets, too. For what good reason? So that we would continue to believe that they were ignorant desert trogs? Well, and what is it they've been hiding out there in the furnace deserts all this time, eh? And in how many other ways do they make fools of us? Answer me this, why should we put our faith in the opinions of such deceivers as the Thyre? And if this Nathan is a hero to them, then be sure it's to their benefit, not ours!*

And now it was Jasef's turn again. *Benefits? You talk of benefits? Man,* we're dead! *We derive no benefits! The only ones who can win out of Nathan championing them are the living: your sons and their sons! Who gives a damn that the Thyre are secretive? And who cares what they've got in their deserts? They're a race apart, like the shambling trogs in their Starside caverns. And did you envy them their existence, too? Well, I say enough of this; if Nathan Kiklu comes to me looking for answers, I for one shall supply them! What? Why his mother cared for me all my days—the last of my days, anyway. More care than I ever knew before. What was in Nana Kiklu is in her son: the lad's a good 'un! That is my opinion. . . .*

Now the apparent spokesman for the dead, his voice

trembling in fury and perhaps something of fear, too: *'Ware, Jasef Karis! Or earn yourself the detestation of the Great Majority throughout the length and breadth of Sunside! Do not defy us in this!*

Us? But I hear only one voice—yours! And what of the rest of the dead? Or is it that you're all truly dead, in your minds as well as your bodies? And what will you do, shun me if I speak to him? Damn me, but that will hurt! I cradled Nathan Kiklu as a child—would you have me turn from him now?

But . . . (another voice, tremulous) *. . . he talks to wolves, Jasef! And they use deadspeak, too, for we can hear them! What manner of a man may converse with a wolf? And what manner of a wolf, for that matter?*

A man with the same blood! Jasef snapped. *His father was the Necroscope. And their father was the Necroscope's son, the Dweller! What could be more natural than that? Don't your nephews and nieces talk to each other? Wouldn't they talk to you, if they could?*

The self-appointed spokesman was on him in a flash. *Werewolves! He talks to werewolves! The Dweller, their father, was a vampire. Everyone, the living and the dead alike, knows it. Why, those wolves are The Dweller's bloodsons! What, and will you tell us they're not vampires, too? And what about tomorrow? Wamphyri, aye!*

But now Jasef was silent, for the spokesman had found the weak spot in his argument. Or one of them, at least. And a second one was just around the corner.

What's more, and far more to the point, the spokesman continued, sensing that the argument was won. *Nathan's brother is most certainly Wamphyri—and a necromancer to boot! So, what are we left with? We've listened to your arguments, Jasef, all the points in favour; so be so good as to hear ours, the points against:*

One, Nathan has lived among the living Thyre and has doubtless learned their sneaky ways. Two, he has even lived with the Wamphyri and come through it . . . unscathed? Three, he came out of the east on a vampire flyer . . . and like the fools they are, our living descendants ac-

cepted him back among them! Four, his brother is a vampire Lord and his nephews are werewolves. Five, his Wamphyri masters have followed him out of the east, and now ravage on Sunside among our children! And is that last a coincidence? I think not! This Nathan is the harbinger of doom!

Silence from Jasef, but a thoughtful one.

And now the tremulous one again: *We can't take the risk. We daren't chance talking to him. He will know us: our whereabouts, graves, caskets, and urns. His brother is a necromancer! We'll have to leave it at that, for now. Later, perhaps, if it is seen that—*

And so it's decided, the spokesman cut in, with something of satisfaction. *Jasef, you will not talk to this Nathan Kiklu, on penalty of—*

—On penalty of nothing! Jasef spat. *For now at last—I know you!*

You ... know me? But the spokesman for the Great Majority didn't sound nearly so sure of himself now. Yet still he blustered: *What can you mean? In what way do you know me?*

And a sharp edge in Jasef Karis's voice as he answered, *I know you! Aye, for I recognize your voice, even as I knew it in life all those years ago—Arlek Nunescu!**

But I ... I ...

A coward and a traitor in life, and the same in death, or so it seems. Where've you been hiding, Arlek? You, Arlek Nunescu, who would have sold his leader to Shaithis of the Wamphyri!

A lie! the other's deadspeak shout of denial. *The old fool lies!*

Old fool, possibly. So a good many folk believed, anyway. But a liar? Never! And you're the one who would have sold Lardis Lidesci himself to Shaithis. I cannot be mistaken, for I was there! Cowardly, wrongheaded, power-mad Arlek Nunescu. I remember now: you wanted Lardis out of the way so you could lead the tribe and be a

The Source, by Brian Lumley, Tor Books 1989.

Wamphyri supplicant! What's more, I saw how the Lidesci dealt with your treachery. But at least he put you out of your misery before tossing you onto the cleansing fire!

It's . . . not true! Arlek choked, sobbed.

But it is! And as you were a coward in life, so you're a coward in death. And would you still be a Wamphyri supplicant, Arlek? Do you still give in so easily? Or is it that you'd pay Lardis back, even after all this time? Would you see him destroyed, and all the Szgany with him, because you were destroyed—for your treachery?

And as Arlek continued to sob, so the tremulous one—but not so tremulous now—wanted to know: *How, pay him back?*

By keeping from us the only man who can save our children! Jasef thundered, despite that he has less than a sigh. *By denying us access to the Necroscope Nathan!*

Nathan could hold himself back no longer. "Jasef, I thank you," he spoke up, and felt his shock waves ripple through the ranks of the dead. "I don't know you but I feel that I should. Just as soon as I get a chance, I'll come and introduce myself properly. Whatever it is you would tell me can keep till then, by which time the dead may have learned to trust me."

Some of us trust you now, son! a hitherto unheard voice spoke up, but uncertain of itself, unused to its circumstances. *Those of us who were . . . who were killed in the fighting. It's just that it's taken awhile to sink in, that's all—our situation, I mean. But we know that if you'd been on hand a little earlier, a few more of us might still be alive. These others—these . . . what, old-timers?—they've forgotten what they had in life and have come to accept what they have in death. That's why they're scared: in case they lose that, too! But us recent ones, we feel we've nothing left to lose. Well, except contact with what's been left behind. We certainly don't want to lose that. And that . . . why, that's you, Nathan!*

And from some little distance away, but strong in the deadspeak aether as they'd always been in life: *Aye, and there are others, Nathan, men who amounted to some-*

thing, who'll put their faith in you. If you're good enough for wily old Lardis Lidesci then you're good enough for us! For without you, why, who would there be to keep us up-to-date on the doings of Andrei, eh? We don't know about these others, but give us a chance to stay in touch with the living, we'll take it whatever the cost!

It was the dead Romani brothers, Ion and Franci, speaking to Nathan from their cave tomb near Settlement. *We'd have spoken up earlier, except what we heard made us sick! But since you've now seen fit to talk to this rabble and make your presence known—and answer their so-called charges—well, it seems only right that we should get a word in, too. We're the Romanis, or we were, and we're with you!*

By now the dead were in tumult, split into two camps by the various pressures within them. Even the ghosts of Starside trogs joined in, who in certain ways were more akin to men than the desert-dwelling Thyre. A phlegmy grunt, and:

A thousand sunups gone (came the dull deadspeak thoughts of one such Neanderthal), *this Nathan's father and his brother The Dweller, called us up out of our cavern niches to fight for them. Our joints were made supple again, and our skin caused to bend without cracking. But still there was a pain in it unlike the pain of living, and a horror worse than the blackest nightmare! I for one don't wish to know this Nathan; for to know his father was to love him . . . and to love the Necroscope was to do his bidding. Now I'm done with walking, breathing, and all such. Now I'm satisfied to cling to the earth and stiffen to a stone, and dream my fading dreams.*

But another trog voice had it: *That tells only the least of it. A great many of us answered the Necroscope's call— and willingly! What? But we'd been slaves to the Wamphyri from teat to tomb, and they had treated us cruelly! They sent us against the Dweller in his garden, who could have punished us severely. But he said, "Stay with me, and earn my protection." Then, when the Wamphyri came and we were dead, when Harry Dwellersire and his changeling son said, "Come—up out of the earth and fight them that killed you"—you could not·have held us back! Not only for the love of the Necroscope and his son, but for our pride, our souls. Then there was pain, aye. But myself, I say the pain was as nothing. I would do it again, today, now. The Szgany call us unmen, but when the Necroscope called us up out of the earth to fight the Wamphyri . . . then we were men!*

You trogs are men, sure enough! (Ion and Franci Romani, so united that their voice was one.) *Certainly you fought like men that time. We had a common enemy—the Wamphyri—and leaders in common, too: Harry Keogh and his changeling son. Now there's Nathan, another son of the Necroscope, whose enemy is the same as before.*

"Well," said Nathan, still dreaming, "that's true as far as it goes, but this time it's not just the Wamphyri. Men have come out of a strange land into Sunside/Starside, some of whom are monsters no less than the vampire Lords! No, not in their shape or form, but in their minds! I've been to that world of theirs, and returned with some of their weapons, though hardly sufficient to give me the upper hand. And so my task is doubly difficult: to clear *our* world of the Wamphyri once and for all, and to right certain wrongs done in another world, and so make both places safer for our children. Now: if there's that in my motives which you find questionable, by all means continue to deny me access to the knowledge gone down into the earth with you. But if you find justice in my actions, then be my friends. Except I promise you this: that whatever my father or The Dweller did in the past, and whatever my brother does now, I shall *never* call you up out of the earth! If ever you come to me, it will be . . ." (He almost said, "of your own free will," but then thought better of it) ". . . because you want·to."

Again a tumult of incorporeal voices—most of them thin as air and far less substantial—crowded into the void that Nathan's deadspeak had left behind; but rising above the rest, and filled with a new authority, the tremulous one, some chief or elder of forgotten times, made himself heard:

Nathan, you have touched us. It is one of the reasons we would have nothing to do with you: because we knew we would be touched. For you never knew the Necroscope Harry Keogh, despite that he sired you. But we knew him, and I can tell you this: in the end, he wasn't all warmth and light. But you . . . are warm! And you . . . are light! A blanket on a cold night, a candle in the darkness. Now leave us be, for we've much to consider.

Nathan, like his father before him, would never be one to defy the dead. Obediently, he withdrew, and the void behind him filled with fading deadspeak whispers . . .

Time passed and Nathan fell into a deep, dreamless sleep. This wasn't unusual; he rarely dreamed in the true sense of the word but rather used the time (albeit subconsciously, and frequently without remembering the details) to explore the problems of his waking hours, and to "listen" to the whispers of the dead. But not on this occasion, for this was a sleep of exhaustion.

His numbers vortex shield was down, a mere wisp or curl of ciphers as opposed to the accustomed whirlwind of esoteric formulae (which, paradoxically, left him wide open to some, yet mainly invisible to one at least: his vampire brother Nestor). Nathan's mind was empty of deliberate thoughts and therefore receptive as a sponge; he slept in the arms of his love "like a dead man," drawing strength from what food he'd had at his mother's table, and from the loving warmth of Misha's body and being.

But along with the warmth was a cold, too, and while the former was an entirely natural thing, the latter was . . . something other. A metaphysical cold, a chill not only of the mind but of the soul. Or of soullessness? Telepathy of a sort, yes, and yet different; not deadspeak, which is the art of the Necroscope, but . . . something in between? A horror certainly, but as much horrified as horrifying. A creeping cold oozing in Nathan's subconscious "awareness" as pus in a running sore, as if to cleanse itself by contact with the pure. A malignancy which yet recognized its own nature and knew Nathan's as its opposite, but remembered however vaguely, remotely, inaccurately, a time or phase or circumstance other than the nightmare of now—a *place* in the unknown past—when things had been different.

And remembering, it *knew* his mind! So that however empty, the *feel* of his mind galvanized activity in the all-but-erased, echoing caverns of its own. Until yearning to fill the emptiness, finally it—she—*must* know . . .

Nathaaan?

A whisper at first, a question, uncertainty.

And again Nathan's attitude of listening, of subconscious concentration, rapt attention.

Nathaaan!

He felt her probe, knew her identity, recognized the mutation that had occurred, the nightmare metamorphosis; knew too that he should not answer her, should indeed shun her, deny her the right to invade his thoughts. But at the same time he knew the complications of her condition; above and beyond which, he of all people was aware of the curse of ostracism, the desperate loneliness of the outsider. Of course, because for a large part of his life Nathan had been just such an outsider.

"Siggi? Siggi Dam?"

Nathaaan! Her sigh, like the exhalation of some poisonous cloud—with which he knew that he could not be mistaken: Siggi was a vampire.

Ah, no! She snatched at him, clung to him at once with a fierce energy. *Not merely a vampire, Nathaaan . . . Wamphyyyri!* The cold was there—the terrible burning cold of her condition—which was in fact an alien heat; for out in the spaces between the stars even a "dead" sun is hot, and in the aching cold of undeath the heat of the blood is a roaring furnace!

"Siggi," he said. "Siggi . . . I'm sorry."

Why?

Innocence, in a vampire! No, not innocence, but the lack of knowledge. For her mind was as empty as his had been just a few moments ago. Except his had been the emptiness of exhaustion, while hers was that of deprivation. She had been deprived of her past.*

Fiercely eager, she grasped upon that at once. *Nathan—do you know?*

Like deadspeak, telepathy often conveys more than is said. And yes, Nathan knew. But how to explain it? "There are different kinds of vampire, Siggi," he finally told her. "And I don't know which is the worst. The one that got you—the *first* one that got you, in a place called Perchorsk—was a machine. But without the men who built and used it, the machine itself would be nothing."

I—don't—understaaand! (The wail of a lost child.)

"Your . . . your mind was sucked dry." (He could only tell it the way it was.) "And you were thrown out of your own world into this one. You survived, except you survived in the worst possible way: you are Wamphyri!"

Perhaps something of it had come back to her. Partial recognition at least—of the crawling horror of her existence—washed over him; and Nathan felt Siggi's shudders, of loathing and of ecstasy both, racking him, filling him with their freezing fire. Until: *A machine, aye,* she finally said. *A vampire—but the men who used it were worse!*

Then—

Another thrill of horror, as she added, *They still are!*

Nathan knew what she meant. "They're here, yes."

They have come for meeeee!

"No." He shook his head. "I should think the last person or thing Turkur Tzonov desires to see is you, Siggi. You have no reason to fear him now. He is only . . . only a man."

And now she was the one to see his meaning. *And I . . . am Wamphyri?*

"Yes."

Canker will protect me, when he is done with serenading the moon. But until then I'm alone. I am alone,

---

The Last Aerie, by Brian Lumley, Tor Books 1991.

Nathaaan, for this place is not my place. Except . . . with you out there, I am not alone.

"Wrong" (again he shook his head). "You should fear me, Siggi, as I must learn to fear you."

But we were . . . friends?

"You don't remember any of it?"

No . . . yes . . . no . . . perhaps. Did you love me?

In his sleep, Nathan smiled a sad smile. "No . . . yes . . . no . . . perhaps!" He remembered something Zek Föener had once told him, about his mother and Harry Keogh. And like an echo out of the past: "Forces beyond our control threw us together. But yes, we were friends, however briefly."

Then we still are. For in this place I have no friends. Only food. And there's no pleasure in food that screams!

With which the ice was back on Nathan's spine—cold ice this time—as he was reminded who or what he was talking to; and he knew who or what he should *not* be talking to.

"Friends, then," he answered, despite that it was a lie. "For as long as it lasts."

And finally:

Now I rememmmmberrr! she said, with some animation, some excitement. *You . . . escaped? And I helped you.*

"Yes." He could only agree.

Now, I would escape.

"From Canker?" (If so, then Nathan could well understand it! The dog-Lord was his sworn enemy, and he would kill him if he could.)

Run from Canker? Ah, no, for he loves me! Not from Canker, no, but from this place, this world which is not my world, back to my memories. Anyway, you can't kill him. No man may kill the dog-Lord! No, for he's the strong one, Nathaaan. He adores me, but I fear his strength, I fear . . . his ways. And I must flee him, out of here, back to my memories. Confused, she contradicted herself.

Nathan was sad for her, mad at himself, hateful of Turkur Tzonov. But he must try to make her understand.

"Siggi, all of that is beyond you now; there's no returning; you are what you are. Men will not accept you."

You accepted me, upon a time.

"You were a beautiful woman. I was a man."

You were innocent. And afterwards ... your thoughts were warm. You did not think of me as a sucking thing. But now ... I am *a sucking thing!*

With which he knew that she was mad, that the mazy corridors of Siggi's mind weren't merely empty but bereft. Fear was the cause, and fear the spur that prompted her to seek an out now. But of what was she afraid? He sensed nothing of fear of Canker. And as for her present circumstances, they were all she had of memory. She saw the question in his mind and answered:

He—he—has come for meeeee!

"Turkur?" And he saw from the way she cringed that he was right. "But you've nothing to fear from him, not now, not when Canker is your protector."

Canker! Nathan's words had been like an invocation, spawning an image and more than an image in her mind. *The moon music fades ... The dog-Lord returns ... He must not find me speaking to another! ... You shall be my secret ... And we shall be ... ?*

"Friends, yes—if there's a way." (He knew there wasn't, but hid it from her for pity's sake.)

Take care, Nathaaan.

"You, too, Siggi."

And she was gone.

How very odd, how very peculiar, how very talented *you are, Nathan!* said a deep, dark, gurling deadspeak voice from the depths of his sleeping mind, bubbling and festering there like a sucking swamp. *Don't you find it odd, my son? That while I am able to eavesdrop on your conversations with things dead as I am dead, your conversations with the living are quite beyond my range? Oh, I hear what* you *have to say to them, for despite that they are alive the thoughts that accompany your* words *are deadspeak; you're the Necroscope, after all! But I cannot hear their answers! No, for they exist in a different world now—or rather, I do. Peculiar, aye ...*

And painful, too: that I who was once so very much a part of your world—alive! Alive! Or undead at worst—should now find myself excluded entirely from that oh-so-agreeable estate. But death comes to all of us, I suppose. Given time even a man such as I must stiffen to a stone, and undeath turn to the true death. Except—as you and I well know—death is not always the end. Or it doesn't have to be, eh, Nathan? And when there are wrongs to be put to rights, what then? Are we so different, my son? You who would avenge the deaths of so many Szgany, and I who would avenge my own? You who would rid your world of all of the Wamphyri forever (why, it seems almost greedy of you!), and I who desire to destroy just two of them?

Only call me up, I shall be your most powerful ally! And when it's over I'll go down again, just a mound of bones in a refuse pit in Madmanse, in Turgosheim. Just think of the benefits: to fight fire with fear, and destroy with a glance! For you have my word, Nathan: when Eygor walks again, called up by the Necroscope, yours shall be the power, and none shall stand against my killing eye, which I shall gift to you!

From the first word Nathan had known who it was, the only one it could be, with his ghastly, gurgling, suggestive, insinuating, inveigling, and very nearly hypnotic voice. Powerfully talented in death, even as he'd been in life, Eygor Killglance of the Wamphyri, an ex-vampire Lord, reached out with his deadspeak across all the miles from Turgosheim, to offer again his terms as once before he'd offered them in Maglore's promontory aerie, Runemanse.

Because Nathan was deeply asleep his mind was receptive, if not to Eygor's unthinkable suggestions, certainly to his insidious probe, his evil presence. And triggered by the other's voice, pictures were conjured to the mirror of Nathan's memory—from another time, a different dream—of a nightmare Thing in its Madmanse pit:

It leaned or slumped against the wall like some strange stalagmite formation—much like the creatures in the cave at the Radujevac Gate, without their sheaths of glazed dripstone—but its shape was much too irregular and its texture darker than the salty, nitre-streaked, natural stone wall. It was ... that monstrous amalgam, *Eygor Killglance! And even as the picture registered on the screen of Nathan's mind—as his feverish gaze once more took in the Thing's gigantic size, freakish proportions, and the grotesque, almost inquiring angle of its head, fused like a melted candle to the wall—so the eyes in that head began to crack open! And as before, Nathan could well understand and believe their power to kill!*

At that Nathan would have snatched himself awake, but the hypnotic strength of Eygor's deadspeak, his awesome mentalism, was such as to paralyse and hold him rooted; like a man on the edge of sleep who knows he should move but cannot, not even to save his life! And yet again, as the clotted gurgle of Eygor's mind spanned all the miles between, so the monster pleaded his position, pressed his case, and proposed his potentially lethal contract:

Yes, Nathan. My killing eye: it can be yours! Do you remember, in Turgosheim, how we ... discussed it? Ah, you think you don't need me now, Nathan, but you will. Just think: the power of your mind, the mind of the Necroscope, coupled to the seething, searing energy of my eyes! Even the Wamphyri would shrink to a stench, would be blasted to shreds, in the cleansing beams of your gaze!

"Cleansing?" Nathan found his voice at last, if not the strength of will to wake himself up. "*Your* gaze, cleansing? As acid cleans, maybe—except it would sear *my* mind, too!"

No, no, no! Not my *gaze,* yours! *And you would be using it only for ... well, for good, yes! Can't you see the wonderful irony in it? Isn't it what you want: to destroy the Wamphyri?*

"Oh, yes, but not if I must make a monster of myself! Just look what your 'talent' has done to you. Just see what's become of your eyes."

And flinching, Nathan looked again at that mind-picture of Eygor Killglance as he'd seen him before—let his gaze crawl slowly over all eighteen or more feet of that monstrous, mummified anomaly of fused bone, black, corrugated flesh, knobs of gristly cartilage, and massive plates of blue-gleaming chitin like the armour of insects, but insects grown to tanks in the armouries of the not-so-alien world beyond the Starside Gate. Anthropomorphic, certainly, which was all that could be said of Eygor's relationship to humanity. For while men may have a similar shape, they do *not* have additional mouths in . . . various places.

But quite apart from the diseased overall *design* of this monster, the most terrible thing was the knowledge that it was Eygor's *own* design! This was how, towards the end, the loathsome Thing in the pit had shaped himself! Those horny fossiled feet and shrivelled leathery thighs; those withered arms that terminated in talons; the arched back, and those jutting shoulders, and the misshapen screaming skull thrown back and fused to the wall by nitre, jaws frozen in some everlasting rictus. Oh, he'd not wanted this desiccation, this gradual deterioration, this death, never that, but the rest of it was the very *essence* of Eygor!

And finally those eyes, now fully open, exactly as the Necroscope remembered them from a previous dream. And remembering, he heard again Eygor's words just as then, indeed, as Eygor repeated them now:

Only see how I cry, Nathan, because my sons blinded me, because my eyes are blind and white. Ah, but upon a time the right one was filled with blood! See! And at once, the right eye of the gargoyle dripped scarlet. *While the left was full of pus!* And now the left one turned yellow and swollen, like a boil about to burst. And Nathan knew that if it did and the poison splashed him, then he'd be infected, heir to the monster's powers!

And: *Only call me up so that I may take revenge on my bastard bloodsons,* Eygor begged him, *and the power can be yours as easily as that! Do it, Nathan! Do it now!*

Eygor was there in Nathan's head, frantically seeking

out the metaphysical mechanism—the Necroscope's esoteric art—the power to cancel death and return him to
undeath!

CALL . . . ME . . . UP!

Nathan could do it: he could call the dead—this monster
himself—up out of the earth, out of death. And for the
very first time he actually *knew* he could do it! Twice in
the past he had done it, but without knowing. Or perhaps
on those occasions they had come of their own accord, out
of their love for him. But this *One* did not love anyone or
thing, and so must be brought up—by Nathan's art.

He . . . must . . . be . . . brought . . . up!

The massive weight of Eygor's metalism . . .

His hypnotism . . .

His terrible eyes . . .

Nathan tossed in his fever; his mind burned; in the
depths of his *mortal* soul, a darkness seethed. But:

No!!! No, Nathan!

It was as if with that cool but urgent thought, a scented
breeze, a mental fragrance, a waft of fresh air blew across
his burning brain, bearing away the stench of the thing in
its Madmanse pit, in Turgosheim. And:

No, came the thought again, but sighing its relief now as
the danger receded, as Nathan unfroze, drove Eygor out
and the monster's raging voice echoed into a distant denial, a sobbing curse, a fading, chittering *hissss!*

Then he was gone, and the timely intruder spoke again,
however severely:

Nathan! Ah, and didn't I warn *you upon a time: beware
what you would call up to a semblance of life, lest some
things may prove harder to put down?*

"Rogei! Thank God for you!" For it was Rogei of the
Thyre, of course, that dead old . . . *man*, in the Cavern of
the Ancients. The first of the dead to recognize Nathan
and speak to him openly, even to the extent of saving his
life. Twice in fact: then and now. Nathan's thoughts were
deadspeak, and in answer:

The shake of an incorporeal head, Rogei's denial. *No,
the* first *time it was your life, this time your soul—possibly.*

*But did I hear you offer thanks to a god? Didn't your god
die at the time of the white sun? So you told me, at least.*

Nathan was still shuddering from his encounter with
Eygor; he didn't want to go into that now: that the god he
had called upon was an alien god, and the phrase a
frequent—and frequently empty—benediction from an
alien world. The Thyre were far less familiar with their
god; but still, maybe Rogei would understand if he said:

"Perhaps I meant Him Who Listens, if that is permissi-
ble?"

Certainly, for He listens to everyone. And everywhere!
So maybe the wise old Rogei had heard the Necroscope's
thoughts about an alien world after all . . .

As Nathan's nerves settled down, he changed the subject. "Why did you seek me out?—Not that I don't appreciate it."

*Because I was concerned. For long and long, ever since
the time you left us, I searched for you with my deadspeak.
I knew that you were, that you lived. But it has grown to
be a habit. Now that you are back—despite that it's
unseemly—still I search! Except . . . perhaps it's no longer
unseemly, for we all would know how you fare. But all of
that is a feeble excuse; I had no right; I invaded your privacy. Forgive me.*

"Forgive you? Rogei, continue to seek me out. And
promise me that you will, please do!"

As you will, Nathaaan . . .

. . . "Nathan?"

"Yes?"

"Nathan!"

He started massively as he felt a hand on his shoulder,
tugging insistently. *"Wha—!"*

He sat up—sprang upright from the waist in a tumble of
furs! And it was Misha. And he was drenched in sweat.
And she was wet, too. Wet, worried, and huge-eyed where
she stood beside their bed. "You were nightmaring," she
told him breathlessly. "But I was so tired . . . I took a long
time to wake up. By then you'd calmed down. I got up,
heard sounds in the Rock, came to wake you . . ."

Nathan heard sounds, too. A stirring in the guts of Sanctuary Rock, movement, and an echoing voice that cried: "Gather up your things, whatever you will take with you. We're to move out within the hour. Lardis's orders. So gather up your stuff, for we're on the move."

And from the far corners of the labyrinth, other voices faintly echoing, but crying the same sad message. "Gather up your things . . . your things . . . things."

"We're moving out . . . moving out . . . out."

The Szgany Lidesci would be Travellers again.

III

The Return of Vasagi! The Death of Nana Kiklu

In Wrathstack, strange forces were in motion.

The dog-Lord Canker Canison had blocked passageways leading up from Mangemanse into Nestor Lichloathe's Suckscar. And in Suckscar, Nestor's favourite flyer had apparently gone mad, reduced to rubble the cartilage walls of its pen, destroyed a launching bay's safety barrier and launched of its own accord; all of this before the warrior-Lord Vormulac Unsleep's observation posts were in place, so that the escaped flyer had gone undetected, unmolested as it fled southwest by south for Sunside.

Also in Suckscar: Nestor's morbid mood was grown out of all proportion, as if to encompass his entire manse. And despite the fact that Wrathstack must soon come under siege, there was an unaccustomed air of inactivity about

Suckscar—a nameless sense of futility, a breathless, creeping expectancy—with Nestor himself a gaunt grey ghost, listlessly issuing orders that carried little of their former authority; neither weight of will, nor terror of Lord Lichloathe's necromancy. For much like the master himself, his lieutenants and thralls moved as if stricken with the same weird malaise . . .

On the other hand, down below in the shadowy levels of Guilesump, Gorvi the Guile was anything but listless; indeed, his basement manse was witness to a frenzy of industry hitherto unknown! Complaining warriors were hauled prematurely from their vats, cauldrons of urine and wastes were set above the many corbel-chutes over the entrances (with faggots below all ready to be fired), spiked grilles were fitted to windows and bays, and ground-based warriors stationed in the scree-canyon gantlets, where Gorvi ordered them to hide and wait in ambush.

Likewise in Wran and Spiro's Madmanse: except here, too, a noticeable difference. For the Killglance brothers no longer worked in unison; Wran's forces defended the north- and southeastern half of Madmanse, and Spiro's the western half. And if it were not for the fact that at last Vormulac had come out of the east, then possibly they'd be at each other's throats even now. It had much to do with Spiro's killing eye: the fact that he had it while Wran did not. For Wran had always enjoyed playing "big brother," and Spiro wasn't about to let him "Lord" it any longer. They were equals or they were nothing. Except they couldn't be equals, for Wran considered himself superior. And Spiro felt slighted, for he was the one who had inherited his father's killing eye.

From Spiro's point of view: Wran should now consider himself a junior partner, for the boot was on the other foot. And from Wran's . . .

. . . He remembered old Eygor, the way his cruelty had grown apace with his power. And already Spiro was full of a new confidence, so that while Wran was apprehensive about the fighting to come, his brother seemed to welcome, even to invite it. Naturally, for it would give him the chance to exercise his heart-bursting glance, his killing eye. Ah, but when the fighting was done, however it went, what then? Would history repeat itself, Wran wondered? Not if he could help it, for he'd felt the lash of his father's glance once too often. The first time he felt his brother's would be the last—for Spiro. But it might not even come to that, or it might come sooner than that. And from now on, Spiro must never turn his back on Wran the Rage.

So much for Madmanse. While in Wrathspire:

Only the Lady Wratha remained unchanged. Only Wratha the Risen, risen highest of them all, was her own person. And that was just as well for she had a war to plan, and a war that she dared not lose. Indeed losing was an outcome she wouldn't even consider, for then she knew what must *next* be considered. And she remembered how Nestor's love-thrall Glina had puffed into fire and smoulder in the seethe of the sun. She had been a comparative newcomer, but Wratha? Even her bones would calcine in the sun's blast, and all her liquids steam away in a trice!

Then Wratha shuddered; aye, even Wratha. For she knew how Vormulac would deal with her, even as he had dealt with others before her. Lord Unsleep's sigil said it all: a hanging man or what remained of one—a tarry skeleton wrapped in chains—with rotting black flesh sliding from its bones!

But she must not dwell on that . . . there was a war to plan . . . the others would be waiting for her call, to learn Wratha's strategy, or lack of one! She felt momentary anger—with herself—that she'd allowed her thoughts to stray when there was so much to do. But these were strange times as well as dangerous ones, and it took fortitude simply to stand up straight and bear the weight of things. Or did she mean the weight of years? Suddenly, the Lady knew how long she had lived . . . *and at once felt the angry squirming of her leech!*

A long time since *that* had happened; it served to remind her, and only just in time, that she was Wamphyri!

Cunning—tenacity—longevity—*Wamphyyyri!*

What? How long she had lived? She was not old but

young, a mere girl! And while there was blood she would always be young!

Her leech settled down again and began pumping its vampire essence into her veins. Its host was strong; it had nothing to fear; the long red years stretched out before both of them.

And yet, even as the Lady began to make her plans, still she found herself listening to the stack. It sounded, or felt, all wrong. Her telepathic probe went out from her . . . feeling . . . feeling.

Gorvi was a coward; he sweated to block himself in, without realizing that he also blocked his escape routes! Wran and Spiro's thoughts were hateful—of each other as much as their enemies! All previous slander to the contrary, however, the brothers were not mad, except as berserks. But as for the dog-Lord in Mangemanse, Canker and his infernal moon music—that same, simple Szgany tune played over and over, louder and ever *louder* on his instrument of bones—oh, he *was* mad, and growing madder by the minute! That clout he had taken seemed to have been the last straw to break a shad's (or dog's) back. Or his brain.

And finally there was Nestor.

But from neighbouring Suckscar's no longer handsome, indeed scarcely visible young Lord Lichloathe, behind his mummy or cerecloth wrappings, only an echoing mental silence like a sullen veil over his thoughts, a cloud of gloom that had nothing to do with the coming war. Perhaps it was his necromancy (a suspect art at best), which gave him that doomful air. But certainly the change in him was like night into day. And for a single moment Wratha felt some strange emotion or poignancy deep inside which she could not fathom. Regret, perhaps—?

—That he was not the man she'd thought him?

But of course he wasn't; he was only a boy! And as for his Misha on Sunside: how quickly things could change. Wratha couldn't give a damn for this Misha now. Nor for the Lidescis as a whole. Time to rekindle *that* fire later, if there should be a later, when this rabble out of Turgosheim had been dealt with.

Except it would never be dealt with; not if she failed to hold her war council.

Enough!

She sent her familiar bats winging, to call the others up into Wrathspire . . .

Travellers again.

It had been awhile, almost seventeen years in fact, since Lardis Lidesci last sent his people out into the forest trails from Settlement. Then . . . it had been a precautionary measure; the Wamphyri, under Shaitan the Unborn, had returned out of the Icelands and there had been danger. But they never had raided on Settlement. Not at that time, anyway.

And while the Szgany Lidesci had scattered into the woods, Lardis and a small party of his senior men had gone to hold a war conference with Harry Keogh, his son The Dweller, and the Lady Karen in a place called the garden. But they had arrived at the garden too late: Karen and the Necroscope were already at war, and the Dweller and his pack . . . were only wolves.

But at least Lardis, Andrei Romani, and a small handful of others had been there to see the end of it: the brilliant flash of white light in the vicinity of the Starside Gate; the mighty thunderclap that shook the mountains to their roots; the weird lightnings, and the roiling, writhing mushroom cloud that spilled its hot, red and yellow guts as it rose nodding to the sky. And then the warm winds blowing through the passes out of Starside, bringing a creeping sickness and in some cases death.

A small price to pay, in the end; and it had signalled the end, certainly—of the Wamphyri! For they had been there, the last of the vampire Lords, dead centre in the fireball when it blazed into life! Shaitan the Unborn, and Shaithis his descendant, survivors out of the Icelands but survivors no more. They and all of theirs had gone up in the sound and the fury, until nothing was left of them. Alas—or perhaps not—Harry and Karen, and The Dweller too, had gone with them. And for fourteen joyous years the Wamphyri were no more—

—Until Wratha and her renegades had come raiding out of the east . . .

All of which was a story Lardis had repeated yet again, in the night, to Nathan and his hell-lander companions and to anyone else who would listen, as the Szgany Lidesci trekked by the light of the stars along an old forest trail, heading south and a little east from forsaken Sanctuary Rock. And:

"You were four then," Lardis told Nathan after a long silence. "You and Nestor. My Jason was somewhat younger, and Misha Zanesti, too. You probably don't remember. You should ask your mother. I had split the tribe into small parties, sent them out into the woods. Nana had an able-bodied man with her, her sons—that is, you and Nestor—and old Jasef Karis the seer. But it was the end of Jasef, that trip. He was old, and he'd grown too soft in Settlement, in Nana's care."

Jasef Karis! And Nathan's "dream" came flooding back.

"Lardis!" he said, in such a startled tone that the Old Lidesci at once drew to a halt as Nathan grasped his arm. "If I tell you a name . . . ?"

"Eh, a name? What name?"

"Arlek Nunescu!"

"Hah! And where did you hear *that* name, I wonder? Arlek Nunescu was a traitor! He would have sold me—us, all of us—to Lord Shaithis of the Wamphyri! But myself and Jazz Simmons, we caught him out. Well, in those days there was only one sort of justice: rough! Arlek paid the price in full. So what of him?"

"Nothing." Nathan shook his head; but it confirmed that his dream had been real, all the same. "And this Jasef Karis: he was in my mother's care, you say?"

"Aye, Jasef the old thought-thief. A seer and a mental-ist, he was. Perhaps there was something of the Wamphyri in him, but much watered down. He died on the morning of the hellfires at the Starside Gate. So why all these inquiries, eh?"

"Too much to explain now," Nathan told him. And too many of Lardis's men about, who mightn't care to be reminded of Nathan's *other* talent: that he talked to dead people—even in his sleep! Not so bad that he could, well, *go* places in a single instant of time; no, for that was all to the good; any fool could see the usefulness of that! But this other thing, he did . . . was something else.

Lardis looked at him in the forest gloom through wise old eyes well used to penetrating the Sunside night (and possibly, Nathan thought, something of the intricacies of a man's mind, too). But after a moment the Old Lidesci nodded, albeit with a frown, and said: "Very well. Later, perhaps . . ."

"Where is my mother now?" Nathan asked. "I think I might like to speak to her."

"Towards the rear of the column, with Misha and a bunch of the old 'uns." Lardis jerked a thumb over his shoulder. "I gave 'em a handful of good strong lads, to haul their travois and such."

And Nathan said, "I'll catch up later, then," and stepped to one side, letting the column pass him by. Then, as the long line of Travellers moved past him, he stood with his back to a tree and tried to order his thoughts. Easier said than done, for there was a lot on his mind.

Weapons, for one thing.

Nathan seemed to have lost one of the special crossbows somewhere or other; with all the action he'd been engaged in, that hardly surprised him. It might turn up later. As for the other five: Lardis and Andrei had one each, Nathan had claimed another, two more at least had been deposited somewhere along the trail from Radujevac to Sanctuary Rock, most probably in the cache of two bundles stashed in the boulder clump on the Starside plain; or perhaps in the bundle that he had hidden in the gorse atop the Rock. No, cancel that last; he couldn't remember any crossbows among that lot. And since they hadn't been in the bundles from the Cavern of the Ancients, they could only be out there on Starside's boulder plains. Well, and they could stay there, with whatever other weapons had been in those temporarily abandoned bundles, until morning. Even with his powers, Nathan wouldn't consider a Möbius jump into the immediate vicinity of a wounded warrior! If the bundles had been out in the open . . . maybe it would be worth a quick visit and snatch. But not if it meant scrambling among the rocks for them.

Then there was the rocket launcher that had gone over the edge of the Rock with him. That must be written off: shattered into bits, without a doubt, when it struck bottom. Which left one other launcher, also in the boulder plains cache. And atop the Rock: fragmentation grenades, a lightweight flamethrower, a machine pistol and ammo. They, too, would have to wait, at least till the moon was up; Nathan scarcely fancied stumbling about up there in the starlight.

He had seen what personal arms his party of hell-landers carried: John Carling had a self-loading rifle; the other cavers had machine pistols; likewise Trask, Chung, and Anna Marie. And most of them were now equipped with fragmentation grenades stuffed in their pockets. Lardis had also re-equipped himself with grenades, but no one else had been allowed to touch them. The rest of the Old Lidesci's senior men could wait until morning, when Nathan or one of the E-Branch people might find the time to do a little rudimentary weapon training. But not much, not while more than half of Nathan's arsenal was scattered in difficult or dangerous places.

In the shadow of his tree, Nathan gave his head a sharp nod. That was as much planning as he could do for now: either wait for full moonlight, or sunup, and then at his best opportunity recover the arms; and in so doing make the Szgany Lidesci strong as never before. But for how long? The ammunition wasn't going to last forever. By the time it came down to the real thing, hopefully the two warring Wamphyri factions would have already taken the best part of the job out of his hands.

That was about as much as he could hope for.

But at the same time Nathan did have something of a plan, albeit a dangerous one, which might speed his task up somewhat. Some three and a half years ago he'd accompanied Lardis on what had then been an annual pilgrimage to the last aerie, when he'd not only visited Karenstack (now Wrathstack), but also seen the tumbled, fire-blackened remains of all the other aeries of the Old Wamphyri. And seeing those fallen giants, it had been easy to see what had brought them down: explosions in the gas-beast pens and methane chambers.

And of course, Lardis had verified it often enough: that the Necroscope Harry Keogh had somehow sent the rays of the sun blasting in through windows, bays, and every crack and crevice, into the heart of each stack in turn, until they'd exploded in their lower levels like so many bombs.

Well, Nathan held no great sway over the sun, but he knew there were more ways than one to cause explosions. Dimi Petrescu's explosive powder—gunpowder in fact but of a poor quality—mightn't have the power of the real stuff, but it would certainly cause a flash and a bang. As would a couple of fragmentation grenades, for that matter!

Deprive Wratha of her base: at best she'd be killed, and at worst forced into a fight with Vormulac and the others out of Turgosheim. Nathan must give it some thought . . .

And thinking, as his ideas gradually took shape and form, he watched the seemingly endless Lidesci line go by. They were in small parties or packets: a few caravans, a great many travois; family groups, couples, singles; low-talking women, long-striding men, and hushed children. All wary, sharp-eyed in the mercifully cloudless night, trekking under the cover of trees that leaned protectively over the ancient track, but yet able to see in fine-filtered starlight.

And beasts: muzzled shads, and yellow-eyed wolves—not grey brothers as such, but brothers to the Travellers, certainly. All well spaced out, humans, beasts, watchdogs; so that in the event of an attack, each group might break for cover independent of the others. About a half-mile of them, mostly silent, guarding even their thoughts in the treacherous night. Wheels, travois poles, pots and pans all muffled; minds muffled, too, generally. Fearful in a way, yet paradoxically strong. Strong under Lardis Lidesci, a survivor in *his* way no less than the Wamphyri. Or even more so.

Which was the subject of a conversation even now about to take place forward of the line, where Anna Marie English had joined Ben Trask in the gap left by Nathan . . .

"Survivors," Anna Marie said, under her breath, striding out with Trask and David Chung some few paces apart from Lardis's party. Only a moment or two earlier Trask had been talking in lowered tones to the Old Lidesci, asking him various questions:

Why were the Lidescis trekking in the night? Wasn't it dangerous?

Yes, but better than waiting for Wratha to gather together her forces and launch an all-out attack. For she now knew the location of Sanctuary Rock.

Where were they going; were there other places of sanctuary in the woods to the south?

There was a leper colony at the edge of the woods where the forest met the savanna fringe that extended south some miles to the furnace desert proper. South was away from the Wamphyri and towards the sun; also, the vampire Lords feared leprosy, a disease their metamorphism found impossible to handle. The colony wasn't guaranteed to keep them away, not by any means; Wratha probably wasn't even aware of the existence of the place! But it had been a lucky place in the past, and hopefully its luck would still be holding.

What would they do there?

They would make camp close to the colony, dig in, build makeshift defences. At sunup, still some thirty or more hours away, Lardis would give a briefing; then there would be weapon training, and an apportioning of the Necroscope's amazing arms and ammunition. But since the lad was himself a weapon, Lardis must wait and see what he had in mind. Indeed, for to know him was to be certain that something was brewing in there!

But at the same time Lardis's optimism following the battle at the Rock seemed to have dissipated somewhat; despite the advantages of the Necroscope's weapons from another world, and his recently acquired powers, still the future looked grim.

For Lardis knew the worst of it now: Nathan had told him that indeed Vormulac and a mighty army out of Turgosheim were here and the bloodwar already commenced. Now it would be as it had been in the old days: as warring vampire factions depleted each other, so they would refurbish themselves upon the Travellers. Wanton, indiscriminate destruction of human life! Or if not its destruction, its hideous *alteration* to suit the requirements of the Wamphyri . . .

Then a mood had come over Lardis and he'd paced apart for a while, and his silent men had let him be. Trask, too, moving apart to where Anna Marie English had fallen in beside him and just a moment ago muttered her one-word comment: "Survivors."

Trask glanced sideways at the ecopath and was at once arrested by something odd, something new, that he couldn't quite put his finger on. Starlight seemed to suit her; in the night she looked almost . . . attractive? And it was that, simply that—the spring in her step, her newly awakened—what, *joie de vivre?*—that Trask found strange. For it seemed that indeed Sunside/Starside suited her! Nor were his thoughts deliberately unkind; rather, they were "truthful." For it was the nature of her talent that she *not* be attractive but reflect the aura of her surroundings. She was an ecopath, *the* ecopath, after all. Her nature—or *un*-nature?—was the nature of her environment. On Earth she had felt each new ecological disaster as a hammer-blow to her psyche, even to her physical being. And yet here . . .

"Who, survivors?" Trask asked her. "The Lidescis?"

"Oh, *they* are," her silhouette nodded, "for they're human. *We* are survivors, yes, our race as a whole. But I was talking about the Wamphyri. In fact I was thinking out loud."

"One word," Trask answered, " 'survivors'—but enough to give me the impression that you admire them?"

"That's *your* talent." She smiled. "You saw the truth in what I said. For of course I admire them! I admire their form, their vitality, their tenacity, at least."

Trask glanced at Lardis some little way away. "It's a good job he can't understand everything we're saying!"

She shrugged. "If Lardis understood it fully, I think you would find he'd agree. Their form—as a life force, albeit a force for evil—*has been* very successful, indeed admirable."

"Come again?"

". . . But the *real* survivor" (she was determined to finish, and took his arm, gripping it for emphasis), "is this world!"

"You said 'has been.' " Trask was fascinated. He knew that her talent could not be put aside lightly. "The Wamphyri *'have been'* successful? Now what are you getting at? And what do you mean, this world is a survivor?"

"Because it's young, it's strong," she said. "Unlike the Earth, our Earth, Sunside/Starside hasn't yet been poisoned to its core. It can fight back for—oh, a long time yet."

"The planet can fight back?"

"Exactly. It can recover. I feel it *will* recover!"

Trask frowned. "From what?"

She looked at him as if in surprise. "From the 'white sun'—or the grey hole—that gave the moon its wobble, changed the planet's orbit disastrously, created the barrier mountains, furnace deserts and frozen Icelands. Recover from the Great Red Waste suppurating away like some gigantic sore far to the east, which I can *feel* it even from here! And recover—"

"—From the Wamphyri?" He saw that he was right.

She nodded and said, "Even from them. It's just a feeling I have, Ben."

"Just a feeling?"

"It's my talent. I feel that . . . that even without our intervention, they're on the decline." Her voice was a sigh.

"The spring in your step?" He inclined his head questioningly. "Because you feel the years dropping away, you
think it somehow signals the decline of the Wamphyri?
Like, maybe they overstepped Nature's welcome? Survivors no more?"

She shrugged . . . and was her bone-dry, brittle self
again. "Well, maybe it's not as dramatic as all that! And
of course I could be wrong; perhaps I'm simply feeling the
raw youth of the place. I suppose we'll just have to wait
and see what . . ."

But: *"What?"* he gasped, as the night back along the
trail was split by a flash of light and a sharp *crack!*—
definitely an explosive bolt—and the sound of panicked
screaming came clear on the still night air. *"What the
hell . . . ?"*

Trask had an electric torch; using it to light the trail, he
went stumbling back the way they'd walked. Nathan was
back there somewhere. It could only have been him, using
his crossbow.

But on what?

He . . . and she, had witnessed the abortive battle at the
Rock, and afterwards *he* had used superior mentalism to
penetrate Lardis Lidesci's triumphant—and triumphantly
open—mind, and so know his thoughts: that his people
must now become Travellers again. Then, they had
waited . . .

Eventually, they had seen the Szgany Lidesci leave their
warren, the direction in which they headed, and by a cir-
cuitous route had gone ahead to lie in ambush. And it had
pleased *him* to know that *he* could achieve what Wratha
and the rest of her pack of dogs had failed to achieve: to
strike at the Lidescis and feed on their good strong blood!
Oh, *he* had known whose blood *he* would prefer—whose
blood *he* must finally slake *his* vengeful burning thirst
upon, if only to satisfy a craving come into being some

two and a half long years ago—but for that must wait on a more opportune time, and for now be satisfied—

—Satisfied to take by stealth that which Wratha and the others, including Wran the Rage Killglance (ah, Wran the Rage! Wran, Wran, *Wran!* The name burned like some mordant poison in a mind now utterly deranged) . . . which they had failed to take by force.

For *he* was that monstrous being called Vasagi (once the Suck), and his consort was the Lady Carmen Who-Should-Not-Be, but who was. And theirs was an errand of vengeance not against the Szgany Lidesci but against Wrathstack, certain of whose inhabitants were *shit* in their eyes, their mouths, and their putrid hearts, made yet more putrid by their loathing of them.

It was Wran who was Vasagi's fixation, his Great Hatred: Wran who had done his best, or his worst, to kill Vasagi; while paradoxically it was the necromancer Lord Nestor Lichloathe who was the Lady Carmen's. Paradoxically because it was Nestor who had saved Vasagi's life that time in the Sunside foothills! But that was then and this was now, and the dire privations of the years flown between had drawn these outcasts together in their common cause: revenge!

For while Lord Vasagi and the Lady Carmen had suffered, those others in Wrathstack had lived life to the full without a thought for such as the once-Suck, ruined in his body, raped of his leech, and pegged to a hillside as the sun came up. And who had given a damn for Carmen, whom Nestor's grave errors of lust and gluttony had in the first instance elevated, only so that he might later reduce her to a stain? Except she was *not* reduced but *was* Carmen-Who-Should-Not-Be. And Vasagi was . . . Vasagi!

So they'd waited on the woodland trail, these two oh-so-long forgotten and oh-so-recently returned, Vasagi and Carmen; waited for the good strong blood that is the life. And their sinister purpose was as much a matter of warped pride—to do what Wratha and the others had failed to do—as for the rich red blood itself. But it would be *good*, that blood, most certainly, and sustain them while they saw what was what and which way the wind blew, and made their secret plans.

Vasagi had waited on one side of the trail, where the old track bottlenecked between close-grown stands of iron-woods. On the other side, in the utter dark of the trees, Carmen was as a statue carved of night. And they had drawn down the shutters of their minds and reduced their movements, even their heartbeats, almost to nil. Their eyes were shuttered, too, shielding their telltale scarlet glow; yet still they "saw" through the closed, furry lids. They "breathed" with the pores of their bodies, but made no vampire mist lest their scent be in it. They were not required to think or to probe each other's thoughts, for their plan was simple; there was no need for repetition.

Thus they were near-invisible, as one with the darkness of the woods. It said a lot for Vasagi's metamorphic skill, in which he was past master and which he'd taught to Carmen. They imitated the very night! They *were* the forest and the writhing, silvery ground mist. They *were* the rich brown earth and damp swirling air. They were *not* there . . .

The head of the column had passed them by, then the silent, shuffling column itself. Armed men had been present with every group, or interspersed between groups. Guard wolves had come close, sniffing in the trees, but sniffing nothing; for there was no Szgany blood on Vasagi and Carmen—*not yet*—who had survived on the blood of trogs for long and long.

And finally the tail end of the column came into view: a party of old ones, mainly, in the care of two women, "protected" by three brawny but inexperienced youths . . . and quite a gap between them and the party of mature armed men that had passed a short while earlier. This final and most vulnerable group had fallen a little behind.

Many of the old ones rode a creaking open cart hauled by a team of shads; while assisted by the women, the less fragile of the party walked or hobbled. The youths grunted and sweated a good deal, straining to drag heaped travois.

Their crossbows dangled from their belts. To Vasagi and
Carmen-Who-Should-Not-Be, all of this looked very
tempting, very good ...

... Too tempting, too good!

And in unison, without any command being given, they
came to life ... and it was as if the forest woke from a
dream to a waking nightmare! They, Vasagi and Carmen,
were the nightmare! The darkness under the trees on both
sides of the trail pooled, flowed into mobile, swift-moving
stains, formed a pair of red-eyed fiends whose sinuous
movements were fleet as wispy clouds against the stars,
rushing inwards upon the old ones, Nana and Misha, and
the three young men!

The latter were the first, because they had weapons and
were young, strong. Even as they sensed their danger,
cried warnings, let go of travois poles and reached spastically for their crossbows, so the vampire Lord and Lady
fell upon them. And it was slaughter pure and simple.

Despite the fact that Vasagi and Carmen wore no battle
gauntlets (or rather, because they lacked them), they had
formed their hands into talons with nails like sharpened
chisels. Slicing her first target above his belt, Carmen cut
the youth inches deep through his soft leather jacket and
coarse shirt. Crying out, trying to hold his guts in, he fell
gasping, writhing to the ground. And Carmen kicked his
weapon out of reach. Vasagi had meanwhile torn out the
throat of a second youth, so that his soon-to-be corpse
sprayed red even as it vibrated in its death spasm and
crumpled to the dark earth of the trail.

The third young man was backing stumblingly away.
Slack-jawed, babbling, he tried to load his weapon with
fingers that shook like leaves in a gale. But Vasagi sent:
Ah, no! directly into his mind, flowed forward, took the
crossbow from him and tossed it aside. Quick as thought
Carmen joined him, took the youth's face into her hideous
"hands" and breathed her essence into his gaping mouth.
As he collapsed, paralysed with terror, she caught him up
and bore him away into the woods. And Vasagi sent after
her: *Drink deep!*

And you, my Lord, she answered, flowing as darkness back into the dark woods with her prey. And indeed he intended to, but from which of these human vessels? From whom?

All of this had taken but a moment. Many of the old ones—looking the other way, mumbling together, or lolling sleepily on their cart—weren't even aware that anything was happening. But Nana and Misha had seen!

For long, wasted moments they'd clung together, paralysed by the sheer shock of the attack, but as Vasagi's scarlet eyes scanned and settled upon them, so they were panicked into activity. Then, screaming their loudest— screaming not only their horror but an unmistakable warning—they instinctively ran in different directions; for they knew that the monster could not target both of them at once. Nana ran to one side, skirted Vasagi, leapt nimbly forward along the trail. Misha threw herself under the cart and clung to the boards.

Vasagi was undecided. He could turn the cart over, certainly . . . it would be worth the effort, aye, for the girl was a beauty. But so was the older woman, and both of them full of rich red blood!

He made up his mind and pursued Nana, leaning forward and *flowing* in that sinuous, gliding, unnerving lope of the master vampire. And breathing a mist, and calling up a ground mist out of the shuddering earth, he rapidly closed the gap between. But at last, in answer to Nana and Misha's piercing screams, there sounded pounding footsteps; the party of armed men was returning along the trail!

Issuing from Vasagi's pores and from the earth alike, his vampire mist was as good as any he ever made. Even as he caught at the fleeing woman's hair, jerking her to a halt and dragging her to her knees, so his mist enveloped her, clinging like damp cold sweat. But coming the other way, and almost colliding with Vasagi where he snatched up the fainting woman into his arms . . .

. . . An armed youth, all wild and ragged-looking in his anxiety! Blue-eyed and yellow-haired, shiny-damp with mist and the sweat of horror, he gasped his shock and disbelief as he saw:

"Mother!" the youth cried, snarling his hatred and swinging his weapon in Vasagi's direction . . . *but yet hesitating to pull the trigger!* If his crossbow had been of an orthodox kind, he would have fired it, certainly. But Vasagi wasn't aware of his good fortune.

Dropping the woman and lashing out all in one smooth movement, Vasagi caught Nathan a glancing blow, but sufficient to send him flying. And stooping over the fallen youth he glared into half-glazed, startling blue eyes . . . which at once snapped back into furious focus! Then—

—Vasagi reared back as the youth's weapon-hand and arm swung determinedly up from the earth to point his wet-gleaming crossbow at him a second time. Only this time he fired it. The bolt missed Vasagi by a hairbreadth and went *whirring* off into the night. Ah, but this one would never shoot at a Lord of the Wamphyri again, be sure!

Vasagi stooped to grasp the other's throat, fully intending to rip out the pup's windpipe, chords and flesh and Adam's apple, all in a welter of spurting red . . . only to release him in the next moment, shocked rigid by a flash of light and shattering explosion from behind and somewhere overhead!

However momentarily, the flash had lit the forest track with a dazzle of white fire, leaving one of the lower branches of an ironwood splintered as if struck by lightning where Nathan's explosive bolt had shattered it some twenty feet above the ground. And finally, bending under its own weight, with a tortured squeal of torn timber, the weakened branch came crashing down!

The earth shook as the branch smashed down, blocking the trail. And beyond the dust and debris of its falling, figures came running with flaring torches and sweeping beams of light like mirrored sunlight . . . but in the dark of night?

It was all too much for Vasagi!

Snatching up the unconscious woman he left the trail

and fled, or flowed, into the dark maze of the woods, and followed Carmen's scent through the night. But when he was well clear of the Lidescis—and when he came upon Carmen waiting in a clearing, where already she'd commenced to slake her awful thirst—at last it was time to take the edge off his own hunger of more than two long years. For goat meat and trog flesh will suffice when there's nothing else, but there's no real substitute for the sweet red juice of humanity.

And Carmen (even Carmen, a fearful lady of the Wamphyri!) turned her scarlet-smeared face away, shuddering as the *Thing* that was Vasagi fed himself on the mercifully unfeeling figure, the melting shape, and finally the shrivelled corpse, that was once Nana Kiklu.

The rending!—the grunting and slobbering!—the pink-tinged steam that rose up from it . . . !

Misha, witnessing the departure of Carmen and Vasagi, had come out from under the cart and gone to Nathan where he writhed on the misted trail, clutching at his throat and choking. The two youths who had pulled the travois were quite dead; their colleague was missing, as good as dead. Finally Nathan could speak and croaked:

"My mother?" He looked wildly all about through the clearing mist. "Nana?"

Misha had no answer for him, not even a shake of the head. She knew that he wouldn't accept it even if she told him. Looking at her—seeing the drained look on his face—he got to his feet and automatically, uselessly, dusted himself down . . . but in a little while stopped and reeled like a drunkard. And: "Nana?" he said again, hopelessly.

Suddenly there was no strength in him, and he went to his knees, crumpling to one side. Misha fell with him, cradling his head with her breasts. "Oh, Nathan, my Nathan . . ."

"N-N-Nana?" It was a sob, almost the wail of a lost child. But in the next moment it was a choked, outraged roar of sheerest rage, madness:

"*Motherrr! Nanaaaaa! Naaa-naaaaaaa!*"

The party of armed men had arrived. They saw the bloodied bodies, guessed the rest. And in a little while Ben Trask and David Chung came running, their torch beams flashing and Lardis Lidesci not far behind, cursing vividly.

Nathan took Misha's face tenderly in his hands. Unashamed tears washed his own gaunt visage as he begged her, "Which way? Did you see?" His voice was the merest whisper.

She pointed into the woods—then grasped his arm as his face twisted into a snarl and he seemed to lean that way, as if tugged by invisible forces. "Nathan, no!"

He got up again, shakily. "But I have to. I must." And in his metaphysical mind:

Nathaaaan! His sweet mother, calling to him. His poor brave Nana, unafraid even now. And the awful truth like a hammer-blow to his reeling mind, that she spoke to him *in* his mind! And the fact that it wasn't telepathy.

"Ma?" The word fell from his lips like an echo from long, long ago, when another Necroscope had mourned his mother, in a dim and distant world.

And now her words were warm, and Nana's smile was warm in the deadspeak aether: *Nathan, son. Try not to feel so torn. For there was no pain, none at all. And even now we've not been put apart. No, for now I'm another voice to talk to in your pillow. I always knew you were your father's son, Nathan. And what the Necroscope Harry Keogh did, you can do again. Aye, for all of us, the living and the dead alike . . .*

"Look!" Trask pointed.

High overhead, and rising, a pair of manta shapes pulsed through the sky. Wamphyri flyers, scudding like clouds against the stars. They were there, and they were gone, lost over the horizon of treetops.

Nathan snarled, stumbled a pace in the direction the flyers had taken. He would conjure a Möbius door, leap into the sky, go after them! But:

No, Nathan, not in haste or hatred. That way you're fal-

lible. Your father was fiery, too, sometimes. But not when he made war. Then he was cold.

"War," Nathan panted, gritting his teeth. "Aye!" And his empty blue eyes mirrored the ice-cold starlight.

And mustering all the strength of his blasted, bereaved, agonized mind, he hurled a question, a taunt, and a challenge after the unknown Wamphyri thief who had stolen that which was precious beyond words:

You! Bastard thing! Mother-killer! Who are you? Who is it I must seek out to kill?

Eh? came back a mental grunt, perhaps surprised. *A Szgany mentalist—and powerful! Is it you, freak? Blue-eyes, yellow-hair? I see that it is. And she was your mother, was she? Well, and now we're kin, Blue-eyes—for her blood runs in my veins, too! Oh, ha-ha! And so you'd seek me out to kill me, would you? But that's been tried before!* There came a grim chuckle, gradually fading, and finally a hoarse, chilling whisper: *Very well, if you're that tired of life, then seek me out. I look forward to our meeting. But don't forget to ask for me by name . . .*

. . . By the name of Vasagiiiii!

Vasagi! A name to ring, raucous as a cracked bell, in the Necroscope's mind forever. Or if not forever, for as long as it took to still it. Then, to himself, a promise: *Vasagi, you are doomed! I swear it . . .*

Except it was not to himself, for the Necroscope's every thought was deadspeak. And:

All in good time, Nana told him, softly. *But first me.*

"You, Ma?" The anger fled out of him in a moment, for the moment.

Oh, indeed. For while I'm dead, son, we really have to be sure I'll stay that way. Find me, and give me to Lardis. He'll know what to do.

Nathan moaned, staggered, and finally resigned himself to it. He stepped aside from the others, conjured a door, and followed Nana's voice to where her body lay crumpled on the forest floor. And when he saw her, if he hadn't known that it was her, then he never would have known . . .

He took her back to Lardis, handed her into the Old Lidesci's arms ... and passed out cold under the glittering stars.

Ben Trask and Misha caught him, and lowered him onto one of the travois. And: "Thank God for that!" Trask said.

Misha looked at him, until he explained, "Where Nathan is now, there's no more pain. Not for a little while, anyway."

Lardis gave a grunt and said, "And no war either—for a little while, at least. Eh, Ben Trask?"

The other shook his head grimly. "Not yet," he answered, "but it's as well to let him rest. For the war will come soon enough, you can be sure of that."

Looking at the poor shrivelled thing in his arms, then at the man on the travois—his drained face, for the *moment* drained, whose looks were now more than ever Harry Keogh's—Lardis gave a nod of his gnarled old head. Oh, yes, he was as sure of that as he'd ever been of anything ...

PART SIX:

BATTLE STATIONS!

I

Wratha's War Council—
The Attack on the Keep—
New Arrivals

Lolling on the jolting bed of a travois, with a skin tossed over him against the chill of the Sunside night, and his young wife Misha walking alongside, the Necroscope slept a sleep of total exhaustion; this time a far more emotional than physical fatigue. Finally burned out if not actually bereft, there was no room for dreams in the closed-down vaults of his mazed mind now—or rather, no energy for them. Neither dreams, thoughts, nor even esoteric, whispered conversations ... nothing to disturb him. For this was a healing sleep, for a wound as deep as the soul.

The Great Majority knew, of course, and were silent; they had felt Nathan's grief; their whispers no longer echoed in the deadspeak aether. And for the first time in what seemed a very long time, the Necroscope was finally at peace—

—But the rest of Sunside/Starside was not.

Out on the boulder plains, Vormulac's observation posts were being set up in ages-fretted ossuary piles or the rubble of crumpled aeries, wherever man and beast could find shelter from the grim grey light of the coming day. It made little or no difference that the sun never shone on the boulder plains; the mere *proximity* of that furnace orb was enough of a threat in itself. When the barrier mountains turned golden in their peaks, that would be the signal for the warrior-Lord's creatures to cower down and sleep however uncomfortably, irritably, in whatever shade they could find. It was the way of the vampire.

And far down the spine of the barrier range, beyond the dogleg pass, Black Boris pulsed east with his company of lieutenants, thralls, and warriors, to make camp in the caverns of the trogs. Black Boris, at least, was not too displeased with his lot.

While in the great pass itself:

Lord Unsleep and Devetaki Skullguise landed and hid away their flyers, and crept silent as shadows to find an advantageous position from which to watch Lord Wamus's invasion of the gorge's guardian keep.

And fifteen miles east of the pass, a veritable swarm of vampires settling to what remained of Wratha's stunned supplicant Szgany tribes, sacking, raping, and looting indiscriminately, putting on fat and gathering provender against the coming day and all the bloody nights that were yet to be. For in the final analysis the warrior-Lord had seen little or nothing to be gained out of the conservation of these snivelling supplicants; since Vormulac must in any event provision his army, it were best done at Wratha's expense. Moreover, it pleased Lord Unsleep to know that in using up these people he destroyed in short order what must have cost Wratha no small amount of time and effort to implement! Therefore, all in all, such slaughter seemed the logical decision. Or the logic of the Wamphyri, at least. And in any event . . . gratifying?

As for Wratha herself:

Even now, in Wrathspire, that Lady was making decisions of her own . . .

With the exception of Canker Canison, Wrathstack's Lords had all come up to Wratha's war council: Gorvi grudgingly (he felt far safer in Guilesump, where he'd taken additional, personal, and secret precautions against the stack's invasion); the Killglance brothers awkwardly, distanced from each other by reason of Spiro's "superior talent"; and

Lord Nestor Lichloathe gloomily, as was his wont. Indeed such was the necromancer's morbid fascination with death, he now more than ever shrouded himself in cerecloth robes, till even his eyes were scarcely visible in all the wadding! Patently his art had warped him irretrievably. This was Wratha's conclusion, at least.

And despite the fact that Wrathstack had drawn first blood in the war with Turgosheim—namely, the rout, rack, and ruin of Lord Shornskull and his party—it was obvious to Wratha that this was a desultory, even dispirited gathering. Lacking Canker Canison's outrageous antics especially, there was nothing to give it cohesion, not even mutual irritation.

With a cursory wave of a slim hand she bade them welcome and be seated, and inquired of no one in particular: "The dog-Lord?"

"Flown out," said Nestor, low-voiced. "I saw them from a window in my room of repose—Canker and his moon mistress—heading south and a little west, perhaps for the great pass."

Wratha nodded, and snapped: "Well then, it seems we must pray that Canker's lieutenants are free of their master's burgeoning affliction! My Lords, in case it's escaped your notice, we have an aerie to secure and defend against the hosts of Vormulac!"

"No use to bare your fangs at us, Lady!" Gorvi lashed out, noticeably less unctuous than usual. "For *we* are here. Canker's the one who's absent!"

All of them, with the exception of Nestor, glared at one another. But in that quiet way of his, the necromancer merely said, "Time is wasting." And with a shrug: "If Canker returns he returns, and if he doesn't he doesn't. What difference does it make? His men are fierce fighters all."

Again Wratha's nod, and her sigh as she let out something of her pent air. "Very well, then let's to it. And as for Canker: I had nothing for him anyway. Now you see why I allotted him Mangemanse in the first place: it's the least important of all the manses; and central, it's the easiest to defend!"

"Good!" Spiro slapped the table, his scowl like the blaze of hot coals. "Then we can get on? What do you have for me and mine?"

Wratha raised an eyebrow. "Eager, are you?"

"I have achieved my father's killing eye," Spiro answered, "and I can feel its power growing even now! Time it was tested to the full." He looked several inches taller and wore a dirty eye-patch over a bruised, purple-blotched right eye and cheek. Swollen and discoloured, his left eye was a red-veined blob of sulphurous hate.

Wratha stared at him awhile and said, "Your father's eye, Spiro? And so it would appear. Well, and now you must use it to best effect! Wherever your manse's defences are weakest, there make yourself available. And in the event of an attack, unleash your scathing eye upon the raiders! Glare them from their saddles—burst their hearts and obliterate them with a glance—before they can so much as think of landing!"

"Alas," Wran spoke up, smiling sarcastically and plucking at his wen, "I am gifted with no such skills but merely rage a little. Will you also tell me my duties, Madame?"

She nodded curtly. "Your duty is the inspiration of your forces. Show them that your furious madness is not without purpose but directed at enemies who may *not* stand before the rage of Wran!"

Her words prompted him to puff himself up a little. But in a moment he scowled and asked, "Is that all? Have you called us here to instruct us in the obvious, in what is second nature to us? If so, it seems a great waste of time to me!"

Wratha's turn to scowl. "My, but you Lords are edgy! Now tell me, have I led you astray so far? Are your manses full of good Sunside stuff to withstand Vormulac's siege, or what? And listen . . ." She put up a slender hand to a conchlike ear. "Is that the wind or the ghost of Laughing Zach Shornskull I hear? Now whose great works were these, I wonder—yours or mine?"

Wran's scowl became a snarl. "And do you also take credit for that fiasco at Sanctuary Rock? And I would remind you: Zach Shornskull was just *one* of Vormulac's generals . . . but what if he'd sent ten? Lady, I tell you we are lucky!"

Before Wratha could spit an answer, Nestor sighed through his wrappings and said: "My Lords, Lady: Do we really have time for these word games, this carping?"

Wratha glared at him, then snapped at Wran: "Of *course* I have other work for you! But since your arrival here, pale and shivering, my first thought was to boost your flagging morale . . ."

Wran's jaw dropped. He pushed back his chair and made as if to spring to his feet.

"Oh, not just you!" Wratha threw her arms wide. "But *all* of you! Utterly out of sorts, worn down in spirit when by all rights you should be geared for war. Gorvi the so-called Guile in a cold sweat, his former cunning noticeable by its absence, displaced by panic. Spiro Killglance almost *too* eager for war, which makes him irresponsible and easy prey to possibly fatal errors. And Nestor Lichloathe as cold and quiet as one of his beloved corpses! What a sorry bunch! But you three . . ." (Wran, Spiro, Gorvi.) "Is this that same band of renegades I led out of Turgosheim that time? Oh, it is, be sure—but grown fat and idle. What's needed is more of the spirit you showed then. What? For then Vormulac had every advantage, where now he has only the weight of numbers. *We* are the ones sitting pretty in a fortress impregnable! So wake up! Rise up from this morbid mood in which you wallow!"

"So, then!" Wran huffed and puffed. "Now everything comes clear! *We* are to blame for this fix we're in! *We* are the ones at fault, us Lords! Fat, idling cowards, the lot of us! Dull, dispirited dimwits! And Wratha the Risen the only one capable of reasoned thought. Are *these* the insults we must suffer? Is *that* what you're saying, Lady?"

She looked at him and lifted a knowing eyebrow, and her look said it all: *Ah! But just listen to you raving. As if it serves some purpose.* And in a while, out loud and yet quietly, "Remember, those are *your* words, Wran Kill-glance, not mine . . ." And a little louder: "Well then, what's it to be? Do you hear me out—or don't you?"

Wran glared at her for long, silent moments, but finally lowered his voice to growl, "Go *on*, then! We're listening."

Wratha got up abruptly from her bone-throne, strode to a window and beckoned the Lords to follow. And when they had joined her, she pointed out and down at the starlit piles of the tumbled stacks of the Old Wamphyri, strewn over the Starside plain in all directions. Then:

"Aye," she said, turning her gaze on Wran. "And indeed I *do* have work for you—all to be attended to *before* this war continues! Else it could be too late . . ."

"Eh?" He frowned.

"Those fallen aeries all have one thing in common," she went on, "one weakness which brought them down."

"Oh?"

"Don't you see it?"

"That they are fallen, certainly!"

She shook her head. "That they were *caused* to fall! I've known it since the day we arrived here, and I should certainly think that you would know it, too: you and Spiro of all people, since you're living on hell's very doorstep! Also, I know that this stack is no different; it has the same fault; it too can be toppled, brought down onto the boulder plains."

Nestor stood apart from the others, at another window. But his strange, quiet voice was magnetic and claimed their attention as he said, "Wratha is right. I've spoken to the liches of men who told me how it was that time. But . . . let her finish, and then I'll have my say."

"The gas-beast pens," said Wratha, which was explanation in itself. But without waiting for comment she pressed on. "All of the pens on one level, side by side with the methane storage chambers; pens and chambers alike huddled *together*, like chicks in a nest—in *one* nest, Madmanse! And in this instance, well named at that! For upon a time these other gutted aeries of the Old Wamphyri were of a similar flawed design. Ah, but only look at them now! *Huh!* It scarcely takes a genius to fathom how they were brought down . . ."

All the heat had passed out of Wran in a moment. Looking to Wratha for advice, he said, "But what would you have me do? We need the methane for the kitchens, heating, lighting."

She nodded. "By all means let's use this fire to warm our hands—but I for one refuse to *sit* on it a moment longer! Not when it threatens to burn my tail! Two beasts in three must go, leaving plenty of well-aired space between the remaining pens! Now tell me, do I have it right? Are the chambers and pens all on the perimeter?"

"Aye." Wran nodded worriedly. "Of course: to simplify the venting of excess gas."

"Then 'simply' vent it!" she told him. "As much as may be spared! And keeping only a handful of pens occupied, drain the rest of the chambers and stave them in, so that gas can't accidentally gather there. Finally, until this war is over, keep only sufficient beasts for minimal lighting, heating, cooking. We see well enough and there are other ways to keep warm, and burning meat for greedy thralls was always a luxury at best."

"I should simply release my beasts and let them drift out on the air?"

"Their function is to manufacture gas," Wratha answered. "That's all they do, and when they stop they die. You have no choice but to release them . . . or would you rather have Vormulac send in a suicide squad to fire them in their pens? I can see it now: each beast setting the next ablaze—and the methane chambers popping one by one— till all goes up in a titan blast! And finally, this last great aerie of the Wamphyri left teetering on a central stem, or slumping to a stump like these other toppled ruins!"

And now Nestor's voice, gloomy and quiet as ever: "Your picture isn't a pretty one, Lady, but it is accurate beyond a doubt. Moreover, Lord Unsleep isn't the only one whom we need to worry about. No, for I know how it was that time, and that even now events are swinging full circle. History repeats . . ."

"Explain," she said, sharply.

He went back to the table and sat down (wearily, Wratha thought). She and the others followed him, waiting for him to continue. And eventually: "I talk to liches, as you know," he said. "And from them and other sources I've learned something of the recent history of this place. A thousand and more sunups ago there was a war . . . but not between the Old Wamphyri. No, because for once they were united against a common enemy. A very terrible enemy, aye: a Sunside wizard! And it was him who toppled the aeries one by one, and laid them low on the boulder plains."

"What?" Gorvi's eyes had narrowed to slits. "D'you mean a common man, a Sunsider, Szgany? A *man* did all that? How?"

"A man, or men, aye." Nestor nodded. "But common, never! Haven't I said they were wizards? As to how they did it: they caused the sun to shine on Starside, and guided its rays into the great stacks, to the methane chambers and gas-beast pens." Then, seeing Wratha's puzzlement, he paused.

"A thousand sunups gone?" She queried him. "But . . . what has that to do with here and now? And what do you mean: events are swinging full circle?"

"That wizard had sons," said Nestor, "one of which inherited his powers, much as Spiro got his father's killing eye."

"And?" Wratha prompted him.

"The wizard's son still lives!" Nestor turned his head abruptly, and stared at Wratha through the slits in his wrappings. "You even *saw* him, Lady, atop Sanctuary Rock! Why, you knocked him from the rim, which should have put an end to him! But no, he lives there still, on Sunside. For a while he was . . . elsewhere—wherever wizards go, don't ask me—but now he's back, and dangerous!"

For long moments she gaped at him, then slowly shook

her head. "It seems to me your liches have lied, or told you myths and legends. Men can't control the sun, Nestor. That there's a spark of truth in it . . . who knows? Maybe they massed an army in the mountains—men with mirrors, or weapons such as those the Lidescis use—and blasted the stacks with reflected sunlight. But even then, it seems far-fetched to me."

Nestor shrugged. "Well, I've warned you. And I have something else, for Wran. In their war against this Sunside wizard that time, the Old Wamphyri used gas-beasts as weapons, exploding them in the faces of their enemies. Since Vormulac Unsleep has set up watchers on the plain, and Wran has beasts to lose, I thought it was worth mentioning."

Wran grinned, and for once nodded appreciatively.

"And one last thing," said Nestor, but very quietly now.

"Oh?" Wratha waited.

"This wizard's son . . . he comes and goes!" Nestor groaned, flapping his bandaged hands uselessly.

"He does what?" (This from Spiro.)

"He . . . he *moves!*" Nestor cried. "He moves instantly, from place to place. Even miles—a great many miles—in as little time as it takes to tell! He flits like a thought—but in body as well as mind . . ."

And in a little while: "Ah!" said Gorvi, breaking the sudden silence with his sigh. And drily: "Well, there you have it. Didn't I always say that Canker's condition was contagious?"

Nestor took no offence apparently. He stood up, staggered, headed for the exit. He would descend along a well-known route into Suckscar. But at the archway exit, as if remembering his manners, he turned and looked back. "I take it you have nothing for me, Madame?" His voice was hoarse, pained.

For a moment her heart went out to him . . . *handsome young Lord Nestor, as had been*! She wondered what ailed him, then put it aside at once. Whatever, it was none of her concern; she had problems of her own; they all did.

"Nothing," she said. "Except you make your best preparations for war."

"I am prepared," he answered, and left.

"Which leaves me," said Gorvi.

Wratha got her thoughts together, turned her gaze on the Guile, and in a moment said, "Just you, Gorvi, aye. Well, you must guard your wells, and ensure that the water is plentiful. For there's nothing quite like boiling water for poaching the flesh from a would-be invader's bones! We must all be thankful my siphoneers are in fine fettle. And of course you must secure the bottoms; only let a man of Vormulac's in down there—we'd have kneblasch in the water for sure! Also, I foresee a veritable rain of bodies into your territory, men and beasts alike! Make sure your earthbound warriors know the difference between friend and foe. Should fighting men or creatures of Wrathstack fall, give them succor if you can and return them to the battle with all speed. And our enemies . . . but I need not tell you how to use them."

She looked from face to face. "As for myself: my roof is well guarded, with warriors, pitfalls, traps. My landing bays are gantlets for any brave fool who would try them. My lieutenants and thralls will not fail me but fight to the death—for should they fail to fight, they'll die more terribly yet!

"There. Now we must wait awhile, and see what's what."

With which the war council was over—

—But the wars were only just beginning . . .

In the keep in the great pass, Bruno Krasin's night guard had settled into their duties and were watchful. Trained soldiers, they watched the ground for men and scanned the air for flying beasts. But the keep was literally a fortress, and in a world as primitive as this the weapons of Earth were devastating; so that despite the loss of Tzonov and Yefros, of whom the common soldiers had known very little and understood even less, Krasin's men felt strong, capable, and sure of themselves.

Krasin himself felt sure of them. Indeed, it said a lot for his faith in them that having witnessed the Lady Devetaki Skullguise's abduction of his leader, still he could sleep in this place! But Krasin was as hard as they come; he knew that his staying awake could not help matters; far better to be up at the crack of dawn, full of energy, and clear-headed from a good night's sleep.

So he slept in the glow of a hearth fire, and trusted the watchful men he'd left awake. If this were Russia, Krasin knew he would feel secure in the knowledge that nothing could slip by them.

But this was not Russia . . .

A corporal and a private soldier kept watch from their vantage point on the jutting balcony of a slate-roofed turret halfway up the face of the keep. Located centrally between the yawning cavern entrance and the topmost watchtower, the turret projected from the riddled face of the gorge like the beak of a bird of prey. Beneath the sloping slate canopy of the roof, the men were the bird's eyes. Their own eyes gleamed blue in starlight flowing down to them, from the winding ribbon of glittering ice-chip stars overhead. The men had been there for five hours now and were tired; one more hour to go before handover of duties, when they could go to their beds and sleep.

One hundred and fifty feet below, the courtyard sprawled blue-tinged and black-shadowed under its massive walls; a cigarette's telltale glow lit the darkness where shadows gathered; faint footsteps and a hoarse-whispered challenge echoed up from a prowler-guard making his rounds. And a moment later a second glowworm cigarette joined the first, the two seeming to flirt where the shadows pooled close to the keep gates.

The night was quiet. From far away, the occasional hoot of an owl; now and then a red-eyed moth half as big as a man's hand, whirring in the darkness and staying close to the canyon wall to avoid the attention of bats; a sentient-seeming ground mist floating over the bed of the pass, its hesitant tendrils writhing, evaporating, apparently repulsed by the gates of the keep. Then the owl falling silent; the last moth whirring away in a fan of powdered wings; the silence closing in more yet . . .

To break it, the corporal in the turret shuffled and commented, "Private Bykov appears to be late with his signal." He leaned out across the balcony, craning his neck to stare up at the topmost tower, aimed his torch at it and pressed its stud. The beam reached out, picked out a gaunt stone facade and inkblot windows. But although the corporal waited, there was no answering flash.

"Asleep," his 2/IC answered. "But do you blame him, Corporal Zorin? Why, secure in that high tower, who can possibly threaten him?"

The other answered with an irritable grunt, switched off his torch. "I shall charge him anyway. He wasn't put up there for his security nor even ours, but for the safety of the whole keep. From such a vantage point, Bykov can see everything: the pass in both directions, the approaches to the keep, the courtyard and the movements of the prowler-guard . . . everything. Or he *would* see it if he wasn't asleep!"

As if to punctuate Zorin's words, a pebble and some mortar or fine grit fell from on high, clattered against a ledge, went plummeting into the deeps. But while the corporal gave a start, his subordinate merely chuckled and said, "So, he's not sleeping after all but merely distracted."

"Eh?" The corporal frowned. "Distracted?"

"Vasily Bykov carves stone with that army knife of his," the other explained. "It's his hobby. I would guess that he's just this minute brushed a handful of chips from that window-ledge up there."

Zorin's frown deepened. "He should at least have seen my torch beam, and answered it."

A half-seen shrug from the darkness of the turret. "Perhaps his batteries are faulty. I've had to change mine twice!" There came a *click* and the turret was lit from within. Zorin glanced back from the balcony to where his subordinate aimed his beam into his own face, making it look devilish. But overhead, where the beam played on ancient wooden beams and badly gapped heavy slate tiles . . . just darkness, no stars.

Clouds? Zorin wondered. But a moment ago . . . he was sure he'd seen stars through the gaps in those tiles. And over the pass, the sky seemed clear.

The sloping roof projected almost to the full extent of the balcony. Zorin leaned backwards, stood on booted tiptoes, aimed his torch beam upwards along the slope of the roof . . . and saw something stir!

It was as if the roof was furry, inches deep in moss or lichen, mobile as Zorin moved his beam across it—until he realized that it *was* mobile! Then he gave a gasp and reached for his machine pistol, but far too late.

Inverted on the roof—head down, spread-eagled, inching forward like some sentient slug on a rock—Lord Wamus of the Wamphyri formed a deadly living blanket. But feeling the light of the corporal's torch on him, he lifted his head, opened his scarlet eyes, and *hissed* right into Zorin's face! No more than fifteen inches separated them, eye from eye.

Zorin's 2/IC had heard his corporal's gasp and seen his hand snatch at the machine gun's strap across his shoulder. Now he saw something else—something unbelievable— that caused him to snarl his terror and grab with jelly fingers for his own gun: a pair of huge, flat, webbed hands with long, bony fingers and nails like fishhooks! Hands that reached out over the scalloped rim of the roof, grasped Zorin's head and lifted him bodily from the turret! His wildly kicking legs slid from view; his choked-off cry came burbling from above . . . followed at once by his hurtling body, tossed into the gorge! And Corporal Zorin's scream went on and on, "Oh-ah-*aaaaah!*" all the way down, until he hit the bottom.

Panting his terror, alone now in the turret, the private soldier used his gun to prod at a loose tile immediately overhead; it shifted and went sliding into space. And mercifully, the stars were visible again in the gap it left—or perhaps not so mercifully, for the darkness was closing in even now.

The light from the starlit gorge was being shut out as if someone slowly drew a curtain; the soldier held his breath and lowered his gaze towards the balcony ... where Lord Wamus had come into view headfirst, arms reaching, slithering like some rubbery jellyfish, flowing over the rim of the roof into the turret! Upside down, he gripped the scalloped rim with his great bat's hands and *unfurled* himself to the floor. And for a single moment a vampire Lord crouched there with his hunched, black-veined, bat-canopied back to the terrified soldier, who finally pointed his gun and made to squeeze the trigger.

But a ragged, leathery arm and hand reached down through the hole left by the slate to snatch the weapon from his palsied hands. And up there, another face like Wamus's was glaring down. Meanwhile, the vampire Lord himself had turned inwards.

The soldier gazed into the nightmare's furnace eyes, felt the steamy copper-tasting *breath* from its convoluted, flattened bat-snout and yawning red-ribbed cavern jaws, and tried to will his nerveless legs to turn him around and run ... back into the core of the keep, down through its endless stone stairwells to the courtyard, out into the company of other men ... or better still into another world, his own, where he knew he would wake up at last, for things like this only happened in bad dreams. Except, and *exactly* like a bad dream, his legs wouldn't move but felt nailed to the hewn rock floor.

Wamus, however, suffered no such constraints. *He* moved—so swiftly and efficiently that the soldier never even saw the movement or knew what it signified ...

Down in the courtyard, booted feet were running; hoarse voices shouted; torch beams swept the bed of the pass north and south, and reached up to scour the canyon face, the looming facade of the keep, the sky itself. Automatic weapons made their definitive and very threatening ch-*ching*! sounds as they were readied for action.

But against what? Where was the target? Where the enemy?

All movement ceased; breathing stilled; silence reigned. A man lay dead, crushed to the courtyard's bedrock, his blood and brains spattered outwards like a sticky halo around his head, or a painted peacock's-tail design without its beauty, without its life. And in the higher watchtowers no slightest sign of movement or recognition of tragedy, and in the courtyard no one so much as noticing the lichenlike patterning on the sheer walls, or the sentient creep of certain surfaces.

Then:

Hurried movement in the interior of the keep; the clattering of more booted feet; Bruno Krasin and a handful of men appearing from the dark yawn of the entrance cavern like ants from the jaws of a picked skull, pausing briefly to look about, then hurrying down the exterior steps. And a host of wide-eyed faces peering from the lower balconies and windows.

"What?" Krasin shouted as he pushed the prowler-guard out of his way and looked down on the corpse of Corporal Zorin. And again: *"What?"*

"He fell," someone mumbled.

"Or he was thrown!" someone else choked out. "He screamed, but it was—I don't know—the *way* he screamed! He was terrified, I guess, but not just of falling . . ."

"Shut up!" Staff Sergeant Krasin rounded threateningly on the speaker, though he suspected he was right. And a moment later, turning his gaunt face up to the night, the platoon commander let loose with his bull voice:

"Now hear me: we're on intruder alert for the rest of the night, right through till dawn. If you want to live, do *exactly* as I tell you. If something moves and doesn't answer your challenge, shoot it! No second warnings. Any doubt whatsoever, you shoot the bastard dead!"

He aimed a powerful torch up the face of the keep. "You up there, in the upper towers and turrets: what the hell happened? You, Raiken!" (Zorin's 2/IC). "How did the corporal fall?" But there was no answer, and somehow Krasin hadn't expected one.

The third vantage point from the top was simply a natural cave fronted by a rough stone wall. Access was via a precarious exterior staircase carved from the rock. Inside, at the back of the cave, there was also a steep, dark stairwell that in some other time must have connected up various parts of the keep; it was choked now and impassable. But pale in the glare of several torch beams, a pair of anxious faces could be seen peering down at Krasin from behind the wall: a flamethrower team, positioned there so as to offer maximum protection from aerial attack.

"Well?" Krasin yelled, adding his beam to the crisscross pattern of moving light. "Did you see anything?" Except even as he shouted, Krasin himself saw something!

Krasin's eyes were as keen as his memory. A true soldier, only show him a battle zone and his mind would instantly, instinctively lock on, every detail recorded. Earlier, he had committed the face of the keep to memory without even knowing he'd done it. But a moment ago, as his beam swept the naked rock to light on those faces behind the balcony, it had picked out however briefly a detail previously unseen. Ergo, a *new* detail: a large, raised, ragged patch of something that looked like moss or lichen, close to the observation cave with the balcony. And when he swept the beam back the other way to double-check—

—Then he gasped and narrowed his eyes, hunched down and grabbed a rifle from one of his men. And: "All torch beams on the area around that cave!" he snapped. For he'd seen that the patch was closer still—and closing!

Bruno Krasin was a marksman. On a count of three he got off three shots, all of them finding their target. The first bullet hit Wamus in the airfoil webbing between his left arm and side; passing through the soft membrane of the webbing, it splayed to a hot, rag-edged disc of metal against the rock. On the rebound it did more damage, tearing out a fist-sized chunk of furry but mainly unfeeling flesh. The second bullet slammed into Wamus's thigh, splintering and lodging its fragments deep in alveolar bone. The third missed his spine by inches, punctured his right lung and passed right through him. It too richochetted, and Wamus felt its burn against his right breast.

What result Krasin had expected would be difficult to say; he couldn't be sure what he was firing at, might even be making a fool of himself. It didn't matter; he wasn't about to take a chance on losing any more of his men. The bottom line was that their lives were his life. In any case, the result he got was astonishing.

Wamus let out an ear-piercing screech that took over from the echoes of Krasin's fusillade. His nightmare *shape* detached itself from the sheer rock face, kicked outwards, formed arched wings and glided for the balcony. His lashing tail acted like a rudder and seemed almost to propel him to his target; a taloned "hand" closed over the head of one of the keep's defenders; the man was dragged shrieking out across the balcony and dropped.

Wamus sped out of the sweeping beams of light and was lost to sight; the dropped soldier crashed down sickeningly and his screaming ceased; Krasin was shouting: "Light up the keep, the entire face of the fucking place! We need to see what else is there! Anything that isn't right, shoot the fucking thing!"

And fifty yards away on the other side of the gorge where it bottlenecked, Devetaki and Vormulac looked on, watching the action from behind fallen rocks at the top of a scree jumble. In the darkness with their Wamphyri eyes, they saw what Krasin and his men could not hope to see: the injured, enraged Wamus turning in a tight circle—then speeding back to avenge himself! And not only Lord Wamus but one of his bloodsons, launching from a dark crevice, stooping like some weird bird of prey to the cave where his father had suffered hurt and indignity!

But he *was* seen. Converging torch beams picked him out as his wings arched and he hovered over the cave's wall; automatic gunfire sounded; the surviving defender of the cave finally got his act together and lashed out with a gouting, searing, thirty-foot blade of white and yellow fire, which caught the bat-thing squarely and hurled it screaming out over the pass in a ball of scorched, frantically lashing limbs and blazing membrane.

The volatile liquid stuck, burned, ate like acid into fur,

skin, and metamorphic flesh. The great bat uttered shriek after alien shriek as it flopped down the face of the cliff, leaving a trail of fluid fire wherever it made contact and driving back the shadows to the corners of the courtyard as it crashed down. But Krasin and his men weren't about to leave it at that; forming a semicircle, they pumped round after round into the roasting, shrilling vampire, and only stopped when it stopped jerking and twitching. By which time Wamus was back.

But bleeding copiously, made erratic by his pain and fury, Lord Wamus's return was ill conceived in the face of odds and weapons such as these. He appeared from the south, out of the darkness of the pass, and at once targeted a man on top of the courtyard wall where he watched the spectacle of Wamus's burning bloodson. The soldier sensed Wamus's presence a moment too late; horror fell out of the sky and folded him in, and before he could cry out, Wamus's elongated jaws closed on the back of his neck and severed his spine. But even as the vampire Lord dropped his victim and relaunched, he was seen!

Alert, a soldier in the courtyard cried a warning, elevated his automatic weapon, fired from the hip and loosed a stream of hot lead. Shuddering from a score of hits, Wamus was astonished to suddenly find himself weak, drained of energy! Defiant, intent upon scathing among his tormentors, he swooped towards them and was literally hurled back by the weight of lead they poured into him . . . which at once dragged him down! And with his membranous webbing collapsing to rags, he fell in a tangle.

A flamethrower team was now on hand; they stepped forward, one carrying a tank and the other operating the hose, and Wamus became an inferno! But he was a Lord, and the thing inside wasn't going to capitulate that easily.

Out of the fire and smoke, tapering skyward, a pale, pulsing tentacle of leprous flesh quivered and shuddered where it formed; another shot out sideways, knocked a man from his feet and dragged him screaming towards the blazing mass. But he was lucky; even as his combat-suit trousers smoked and licked into blue flames, the tentacle released him and his colleagues were able to haul him out of danger. By then an entire nest of blue-grey appendages was lashing frantically in the roiling heat as the flamethrower team continued to hose searing death on the melting thing that had been Wamus of the Wamphyri.

Finally the hideous commotion stopped; the gouting chemical fire died to a flicker; black, stinking smoke, sparks and sooty scraps gushed up into the night, and the shadows began to creep again in the courtyard under the keep.

But from *within* the keep:

Muffled automatic fire ... then screams ... and a flash of hot white light behind a window space, preceding the coughing detonation of a grenade that shattered part of the keep's facade outwards in a shower of stone and rotten mortar!

"Let's have some light!" Krasin roared, and his men again turned their electric torch beams on the face of the keep.

Up there, framed for a split-second in the eye-socket hole of a window, the awesome silhouette of Wamus's second bloodson! The thing launched, plummeted like a stone, then released something that flailed and went "Ah-aah-*aaah*!" as it fell: a third soldier sent plunging to his doom.

Krasin's men crouched low, hurled lead into the sky, tried to anticipate the flight path of the bat-thing where it swooped only inches overhead, then gained altitude as it headed for the wall of the keep close to the gates. They saw its red, swivelling eyes and heard its chittering laughter—its vaguely human yet utterly *in*human laughter—as it sped for the darkness of the pass and safety ...

... And didn't quite make it!

Two figures—two entirely human figures—had entered through the keep gates. Down on one knee, one of them aimed a rocket-launcher and at point-blank range squeezed the trigger. A lance of yellow light and a ball of white fire ... the chittering laughter was drowned out in a deafening blast of sound greater than any gone before. Chunks of smoking meat and blazing membrane sprayed outwards, and all around a warm red rain spattered black on the ancient stone.

After that:

. . . It took awhile for Bruno Krasin and his men to realize that it was over, but it would take the rest of the night for their nerves to stop jumping.

As for their nightmares: they'd retain those for however long they had left . . .

On the other side of the pass, unseen, a Lord and a Lady made flitting shadows among the darker shadows where they returned to their flyers. The great grey, vacantly nodding beasts were waiting under an overhang, where a compacted scree slope made an ideal launch site. But before going to her flyer, Devetaki searched for a moment among a scattering of loose stones near a jutting, weathered outcrop.

What is it? Vormulac inquired. *What are you looking for?*

In the moment before my captive was taken, he dropped his weapon here, she informed him. Then, stooping to pick something up: *Ah! Good fortune at last: it's still here!* And quickly joining Vormulac—observing him through hooded eyes as he checked his flyer's trappings—she gingerly hooked the machine pistol to her flyer's saddle. If only she were practiced in the use of the thing . . . but that was a thought she dared not even think! Glancing again at Vormulac, she saw that she need not concern herself; the warrior-Lord was lost in thoughts of his own.

As they mounted up and launched, he gloomily sent: *Again I am depleted. Three good men gone the way of all flesh, or most flesh, at least.* His telepathic voice sounded very grim, a low mental rumble.

Darkly, Devetaki returned: *Did you say "good"? And "men"? But they weren't that good, my Lord, as we've seen. And as for men* . . . He sensed her mental shrug. *Freaks, at best. But useful freaks: they tested those weap-*

ons for you, and you've seen with your own eyes the utter devastation they wreak.

Huh! he grunted. *And am I supposed to be reassured? Devastating? Is that how you describe that flame-hurler? Awesome is the only word for it! And if it were used on us?*

To which she slyly replied, *Ah, but if it were used by us—against Wrathstack?*

Narrow-eyed, he glanced at her sideways where they lifted up out of the pass. *Another of your schemes, Devetaki? Perhaps I rely too heavily upon your advice.*

Oh, it's no great burden (she was self-serving in translating his meaning). *And anyway, what are friends for? As for the keep and its defenders: they can wait until morning.*

Morning? Sunup, d'you mean? But how may we work at sunup?

I have a prisoner, an informant, remember? At the crack of dawn those fighting men will head for Sunside. But a mile down the pass our forces will be waiting. It will be light, but as yet there'll be no sunlight! Those men will feel safe; on the contrary, they'll be ours! And their weapons, too . . .

Good! (Vormulac's sour grunt.) *At last I gain something! That makes a change! I grow weary of the many ways in which my army gets thinned out.*

To which she answered, *No, my Lord, it gets* weeded *out—which was surely your intention?*

And after a while: *Your intention, perhaps,* he said, but very quietly, very ominously, and in his secret mind.

Except, of course, his mind was no secret to Devetaki, not with her superior mentalism. But this time she knew better than to let him know she'd heard him . . .

Back in the courtyard of the keep, Bruno Krasin had sent men to assess losses within the keep itself. Now he stood flanked by heavily armed corporals where he eyed the newcomers who had arrived in time to dispose of the third vampire. Their bearing suggested that they were military types, but their too-casual, too-civilian-styled uniforms placed them squarely in a paramilitary category.

"I'm Bruno Krasin," the Russian introduced himself in English, bluntly. "Platoon Commander Krasin to these men. I wasn't aware that your British E-Branch had a paramilitary section."

"It doesn't," the senior man replied. "We're CMI—or we were."

"Were?" But despite Krasin's attempt to maintain a cool, unshakable attitude, still his eyebrows had gone up at the mention of CMI. It was also news to him that this more mundane British intelligence agency had any knowledge of, interest in, or connection with Sunside/Starside.

"Were, yes." The other nodded. "Now we're outcasts. Much like yourself, I imagine. What, mercenaries? You can only be from Perchorsk: Turkur Tzonov's men? Perhaps you'd better take us to him."

But Krasin slowly shook his head. "Take you to Tzonov? I don't think you would want to go even if it were possible . . ." Briefly he explained his meaning.

"I see," said the other, quietly thoughtful when Krasin was through. "A pity. There was a time when Tzonov and I would have had a great deal in common. On the other hand . . . I take it that you're in command now?"

"*Huh!*" Krasin grinned wryly, humourlessly, and offered a fifty-fifty shrug. "For as long as I last, yes. But since getting here . . . we've seen some weird stuff."

"So what's your next move?"

"Sunside, just as soon as it's light."

"Can you use two more guns?"

Before Krasin could answer, a senior corporal appeared in the mouth of the cavern entrance to the keep and called down to him: "Sergeant! In the upper levels, we found three more dead men, sir . . ."

Six fatalities all told. The night wasn't halfway through and Krasin was down to seven men! Signalling a brief acknowledgement, he turned to the newcomers and rasped, "Two more guns? I could use fifty!" And the funny thing was he really would be glad to have these two along. In this alien world of vampires, not only was their firepower a bonus but it was good to see a pair of genuinely human faces!

"Let's go inside," he said, shivering. "I have a fire and we can talk. I need to know more about you. Anything you know about this place will probably be useful. We'll have to pool everything we know."

They skirted the remains of the burning vampire where its stench continued to go up to the sky, and made for the steps to the cavern entrance. Then, pausing with his foot on the bottom step, Krasin asked, "What's your name, anyway?"

"Paxton," said the other, "Geoffrey Paxton. A big gun in Combined Military Intelligence—until recently, when I found out about this place. Mainly about the gold. Now they can keep CMI. All I want is to be rich!"

In fact Paxton wanted a whole lot more than that; indeed, he wanted everything he'd lost and more yet—and believed he knew how to get it, and *intended* to get it on his own terms—but as an explanation for being here, what he'd said to Krasin must suffice for now. The Russian should understand greed well enough; he would accept Paxton's motives without hesitation.

Which was just as well, for he certainly wouldn't understand or accept the other . . .

II

At the Leper Colony—The Fall of Sanctuary Rock— Tzonov: Escape!

When Devetaki and Vormulac got back to the main camp on the lava falls, it was only a few hours before midnight. The warrior-Lord's observation posts had been established out on the boulder plains; his fighting contingents had returned replete from the massed Sunside raids; the army's provisioning was now complete. There was sufficient of good fresh flesh in storage to see men and beasts through the night and coming day, and meat afoot to last another night at least.

Along with Vormulac's other generals, Zindevar Cronesap made report. The Lady's familiar bats had returned out of the west with news of a large Szgany encampment; they'd seen fires and a great deal of human activity; Zindevar's interpretation was that there had been a battle, or if not war as such, then violent bloodletting of one sort or another. Due to obvious limitations in communication, she was able to supply only an approximate description and location for the site: a massive outcropping boulder or knoll situated in the Sunside foothills some eighty miles west of the great pass, something less than two hours' flying time away.

Since the night was still young, and Vormulac edgy about things in generals, he decided to investigate. For after all, Lord Unsleep would *not* sleep, not even come sunup, and he and Devetaki Skullguise had already determined on a joint venture to explore the regions west of the pass. This seemed as good a time as any; it might serve to dispel Vormulac's gloom and take his mind off things awhile. Also, it would let his generals see that he was an adventurous and innovative commander in the fullest sense of the word.

First, however, he must inform Wamus's contingent of the loss of their leaders, and invest them with a new one: one of Devetaki's several senior lieutenants. The Lady had an abundance of them; she herself had "chosen" the fledgling Lord; he already slept the sleep of change.

The fact that from now on Wamus's contingent would have strong connections—even affiliations?—with Devetaki had not failed to impress itself upon Vormulac. It simply did not concern him; he was commander in chief; the virgin grandam had merely taken on another secondary role, that of weaning along a new Lord, thus ensuring that Wamus's men and creatures continued as one body and remained intact as a fighting force.

So that while Vormulac gathered information from the other Lords, and attended to the minutiae of command, Devetaki found herself free for an hour to inspect the progress and well-being of her own lieutenants and thralls, and to visit her alien captives under guard in a crumbling secondary cone.

Alexei Yefros was still asleep; he shuddered and moaned in red, ravaging dreams; he would wake up eventually, entirely in thrall to his mistress Devetaki. Turkur Tzonov prowled to and fro, a fur thrown across his shoulders, his dark mind seething with plans of escape and the retention of his humanity. Ah, he *was* devious, this one . . . well, considering that as yet he was entirely human. Watching him from a distance (or rather, listening to his thoughts), Devetaki smiled. Then, putting on her smiling mask, and taking Tzonov's machine pistol with her, she went to him.

There was that which she would discuss with him. Since

he was so intent upon his freedom and his continuation as an entirely *human* being, maybe they could come to some arrangement? The virgin grandam would deny, renege upon any such agreement, of course, but not until she had what she wanted. Or until she had disposed of what she did not want.

And from now on Devetaki would keep the alien close beside her, leashed and muzzled, like some strange and vicious pet. At least until the most opportune moment, when with a flourish—

—But yet again she must guard her thoughts. For such as they were they could easily get her pegged out on a peak as the sun rose over Sunside, and steamed away in its cleansing glare.

Or on the other hand, they could win her a whole world or perhaps even two . . .

Less than two hours later—secure in the knowledge that Wratha and her renegades were confined by siege to the last aerie of the Old Wamphyri—Devetaki, Vormulac, and a dozen each of their lieutenants and men, escorted by a pair of small, powerful warriors throbbing on the flanks, followed the spiky spine of the barrier mountains west, keen eyes scanning for landmark Sanctuary Rock.

While seven miles south and a mile east, where the forest gave way to savanna, Lardis Lidesci and his Travellers had come finally to the leper colony under the last great stand of ironwoods. Or rather, they'd come to the place where the colony had used to stand, but where even the ironwoods stood no longer.

Lardis couldn't believe it; it wouldn't sink in; his eyes refused to accept it. The smell of death, the devastation, the sheer wanton destruction of it all! But the evidence was unmistakable: trampled underbrush all around, crushed shrubbery and vegetable gardens where warriors had raged, their hideous lingering stench; and the simple, most obvious and damning fact of all: that the terrified inhabitants of this place had tried to flee the holocaust, only to be herded or thrown back into the inferno. For their grotesque, blackened bodies, many still burning, were all lying close to the perimeter. It was the work of the Wamphyri, certainly—but how, why, *what* had induced them to come here, risking infection from the one human disease they feared?

There was just one survivor, dying of his burns; but while he lived Lardis must talk to him. And despite Uruk Piatra's delirium of pain, he *desired* to answer the Old Lidesci's questions and tell of the part he had played in the downfall of at least one of the Starside Lords. But first his own hoarse, coughing question:

"Lardis, tell me—am I the last?" He had been blinded, not by his disease but by the flames. But Lardis had made introduction, and Uruk had identified himself. That last had been necessary; there was no other way a man could know; the leper's burns were terrific, and he clung to life only by the strength of his will. So that Lardis found himself thinking:

Uruk Piatra, aye. Uruk Long-life, they called you, which you always claimed was a misnomer. And yet here you are, last after all of you poor unfortunate lepers—in this colony, at least. And out loud he confirmed it, "You are the last, Uruk, aye. However things go with the Wamphyri, I'll not be beating the bounds out this way again."

"It was your father built this place," Uruk reminded him. "The Lidescis are blessed . . . their stars are the warmest of all the stars in the cold, cold sky. And yet . . . not *all* the Lidescis are blessed . . ."

Perhaps he rambled: "Not all of the Lidescis were blessed"? What could Uruk mean? The Lidescis as a family, or as a tribe? He could only mean the *Szgany* Lidesci, or a member of the tribe, for with Jason gone the only true Lidesci was Lardis himself; and Lissa his wife, of course, through marriage. Fascinated, Lardis leaned forward a little the better to hear the other's broken whisper. "Say on, Uruk, if you can. What is it you would tell me?"

"Are we . . . alone?"

They were out on the prairie a short distance from the still-smouldering quarter-acre of the colony, where even the ironwoods had been reduced to blackened totems. Uruk had been found with his rags burned into his flesh, sprawled in the muddied pool of the colony's spring. Wrapped in a blanket, he had been carried out here, where Lardis had come to talk to him.

Lardis nodded, though Uruk couldn't see it. "We're alone. My men are . . . mazed. They sit about the smoking ruins and feel the horror of it. You people were helpless, crippled, dying. You *were* dead, or as good as: corpses that yet walked, or stumbled. Even without the Wamphyri, there was no hope for such as you. So why did they do this? What could they hope to gain from this? They could not . . . use you. What *reason* could they have had? Or are the Wamphyri utterly without reason?"

"Not . . . not *they*." The merest twitch of Uruk Piatra's blistered, blackened head, because he hadn't the strength to shake it. "Not *they*, Lardis Lidesci . . . but *he*! And aye, we knew his motive well enough: it was revenge!"

Then he told his story.

Some nineteen, twenty sunups ago . . . a lone flyer crashing in the forest in the twilight before the night! Its rider was a vampire Lord, with tiny pellets of silver shot lodged in his ravaged face. Likewise his mount, its face half blown away and hanging in shreds. The work of a Lidesci weapon, no doubt, for who else but Lardis's people could boast these weapons out of an alien world? Hurled from his saddle, the young Lord had suffered in his fall through the trees. Any ordinary man would have been killed, but this one was Wamphyri! And Uruk Long-life had seen a way to pay the Szgany Lidesci back for all the years they'd supported the colony. And not only the Lidescis but the Szgany as a whole; all of them would benefit from a simple yet extraordinary act . . . of mercy!

But there's mercy and there's mercy . . .

And so the lepers had cared for this one who had crashed down into the forest. They had cleansed his wounds, balmed him, teased the silver shot from the raw flesh of his face, bandaged his sore, bleeding places. They had treated him as one of their own, and with their nubs of hands and grey scale fingers had succoured him through the long night. Except he was not one of theirs but Wamphyri, and they were lepers, and their "kindness" was in no way a kiss of life but a bane, a blemish, a blight.

When they coughed, they did not avert their faces; their breath went into his wounds. The balms and ointments they used were theirs, mixed with their hands. They ladled the water he drank and prepared the soup he ate, and generally did whatever they could for him ... glad in the knowledge that their mercy would kill him, and knowing that it would kill him in their way; *that they had made a plague-bearer to carry their curse back into Starside with him, to the last great aerie of the Wamphyri!*

He had been feverish; crying out in the night, he'd named himself as Lord Nestor of the Wamphyri, once Nestor of the Lidescis. And at Uruk Piatra's urging, the young Lord had spoken of deeds and named names. There was this Nathan among the Lidescis—Nestor's Great Enemy— and this Misha who had betrayed him. But Wratha the Risen would make them all pay; yes, and so would Nestor now that Nathan was no more, now that he had been sent to hell! *If* he had been sent to hell!

Then, tossing and turning in his fever, Nestor had ranted and raved at someone called Zahar, making vile threats and constantly demanding reassurance that his orders had been carried out and this Nathan hurled into hell ...

So the night had passed, and in the false dawn the young Lord's fever had broken; he'd woken up and gone blundering off into the grey misty forest. If he died on Sunside ... so what, he died. But if he made it back across the barrier mountains into Starside—

—Who could say? A plague of leprosy could not take all of the Wamphyri; it never had before. But certainly they would be slowed down and the Lidescis and Travelling folk in general would earn something of a respite from them.

The one thing that Uruk and his people hadn't taken into account was the possibility of Nestor's return. For in all the long years of the colony's existence, no vampire had ever come here of his own free will. Until now . . .

Almost from the first few words, Lardis had known what was coming. What, twenty sunups ago? The day of Nathan's marriage to Misha? The night of Nestor's attack on his brother, when Lardis himself had crippled that flyer with a load of silver shot, and even got off a shot at Nestor? Both of them good shots, apparently! Well, and now he knew the whole story—also knew why it had been for his ears only: because Uruk Long-life had not wanted it known that an ex-Lidesci was the author of this deed tonight. Not that it was the fault of any human agency, and certainly no man of the Szgany Lidesci was to blame; but in any case, Lardis understood.

He nodded his head, and whispered gruffly, "My thanks to you, Uruk Piatra. But now . . . I'm at a loss. For there's nothing I can do for you in return."

Again that twitch of Uruk's scorched head, and once more his tortured whisper: "There is . . . something."

And Lardis knew what it was. "But it seems too cruel," he said, "to end it like that. For one whose life has known hardship enough already."

"Would you make that one's death . . . harder still? I desire it, Lardis Lidesci. And by . . . by your hand?"

"Very well," Lardis could only agree. "Afterwards, well, the others must burn—those who are not burned already. You know why, Uruk. But I shall see to it that you are buried in a secret place out on the savanna."

"Ahhh!" Uruk answered, in a dying sigh, the last living, breathing sigh he would ever utter. And with that the matter passed out of Lardis's hands. For which he was glad . . .

For long minutes Lardis sat there before covering Uruk's face. Until suddenly he became aware of Misha standing over him. She hadn't been there for long, he was sure; she'd heard nothing of his conversation with Uruk. Her primary concern lay elsewhere, unconscious under a fur on a Szgany travois.

"How is he?" Lardis asked, standing up and groaning as he felt his joints crack.

"In a fever," she told him. "I'm worried about him."

A fever, Lardis thought. *His brother, too, last time he was here. One a fever of the body, the other of the soul. And when he's awake, must I tell him that Nestor did this? I suppose I must. So that where the one has lost his last vestige of humanity, the other may put aside any last remaining thoughts of love, pity, and do what must be done. Brothers, aye: blood brothers from the same womb. But different from the start, and never more so than now.*

While out loud he said, "Take me to him."

Ben Trask and most of his "hell-lander" companions were there with Nathan, but no one more concerned about the youth than Trask. "It can only be grief." He stood up as Lardis approached. "He loved his mother dearly. Grief, passion, fatigue . . . you name it. These last few days, Nathan has been through a hell of a lot—and in more worlds than one! Now, he needs care, and attention."

"Then care for him," Lardis answered, looking down on the Necroscope where he moaned, sweated, shivered. "We'll *all* have to take care of him. For after all, Nathan's your one hope of ever getting out of here, and he's our one chance of ever living here! And one way or the other, I'm sure it's close now. I can feel it thickening like the air before a storm. Everything has a turning point, and every war reaches a climax. It's coming. I know it . . ." He turned away.

"What will you do now?" Trask called after him.

Lardis looked back. "We have to make camp, build shelters of sorts, prepare defensive positions." He shrugged. "We know how. This isn't the first time."

"And us?"

"Care for yourselves, and for Nathan, as best you can. As the camp takes shape, spread yourselves—and your weapons, of course—around the perimeter. Then sleep as peacefully as you may. I shall set a watch. We won't be caught napping again. Not this night, anyway."

"The Wamphyri have been here once tonight." Trask

appeared doubtful; he wasn't privy to Lardis's knowledge about this most recent atrocity.

Lardis nodded. "Aye, but you must let me be the authority on the Wamphyri. Take it from me, they're not likely to return tonight. On the other hand, we won't be taking any chances."

As he went off to rouse his men up and get them working, a drizzling rain started to fall, hissing among the smouldering fires.

It had started to rain over the barrier mountains, too, where the warrior Lord Vormulac Unsleep and Devetaki Skullguise gentled their manta flyers down out of a lowering sky, and called down their lieutenants, men, and warriors to the rim of a scarp high over Sanctuary Rock.

Then, sniffing the damp air and scanning the dreary night with vampire eyes and senses: "This has to be the place," Vormulac grunted. "Even up here I can smell the smoke of fires, the reek of furious fighting, the sweet scent of Szgany blood. Zindevar's familiar creatures were right: down there was a battleground, and recently!"

He and Devetaki sat in their saddles not far apart, their voices echoing hollowly in the still, damp darkness. But hers was low and thoughtful as she answered: "Your senses are acute as ever, my Lord. But there is blood and blood. Myself, I smell more than Szgany blood. Oh, men died down there tonight, it's true—but so did vampires!"

Vormulac gazed redly across at her where she sat wreathed in mist and drizzle. "What do you think?"

She glanced at him. "Wratha's last throw at provisioning, before we close our jaws on her?"

"And she had to fight to take her share?" He was puzzled. "How so, when so far we've encountered only supplicants?"

"The men in the pass were not supplicants."

"*Ahhh!* You think there are more of these weaponed humans down there! Now that you mention it, Lady, you could be right, for indeed I smell more than blood in the air. A sulphur reek, as when Lord Wamus fell at the keep in the pass!"

"The very same," she nodded. And turning, she looked back into the grey, penetrating, calculating eyes of Turkur Tzonov where he sat at the rear of her long saddle. "But I've someone here who knows the truth of it, who has told me how extremely unlikely it would be to meet up with such weapons here."

"What do you suggest then?" For Vormulac had indeed come to rely upon her far too heavily.

"Why, that we go down and see what's to be seen! For if there's been fighting, patently there was resistance. Perhaps Wratha has softened them up for us, in which case we may profit from her losses."

"Good! And do you care to lead the way?"

Devetaki laughed, and launched, and behind her Turkur Tzonov held tight to her waist, and heard her whisper in his mind: *Ah, my pretty! But those are good strong hands! And is the rest of your body so strong? Perhaps we'll look into that later. Ah! Do you tremble? Well, then, have no fear but be of stout heart ... for remember, we have an understanding, you and I.* In tune with Tzonov's telepathic mind, her words were for him alone.

On arched air-trap wings they floated, stalling and gliding by stages, descending through the mist and the night until the Rock came more clearly into view. Losing altitude rapidly at first, they then glided in a lazy spiral, finally came down and landed in the lower foothills on Sanctuary Rock's approach routes. And as the Lord and Lady, their men, and Turkur Tzonov dismounted from their flyers, so the rumble and sputter of warrior propulsors died away, and the pair of fighting beasts put down on top of the Rock itself.

Signs that others had been here before them were all too obvious; despite Lardis Lidesci's best efforts at cleaning up, the lesser debris caused by Nathan's alien weapons was visible everywhere: soggy scraps of iron- and gold-studded leather, a broken sandal and shattered gauntlet, blood-spattered patches of gorse and heather. And as the rain stopped and the writhing mists rose up, the silence was almost a living thing that Vormulac and Devetaki probed with all of their vampire senses.

Until: "No one here," said Vormulac, shortly. "Not now."

But Devetaki shook her head, and whispered, "They are artful, these people. They have retained what Turgosheim's Szgany surrendered long ago: their pride, their individuality, their skill in concealing themselves—bodies and thoughts alike—their freedom! Oh, they're here, be sure of it! Hiding in that great rock there—I *sense* them! Some of them, at least. And now I begin to see it as it must have been."

He glanced at her. "Your female intuition?"

"If you will." She tossed her head. "Should I go on?"

"Huh!" But he nodded his great head anyway, and followed her where she made for Sanctuary Rock on foot.

Herded along by lieutenants and thralls, Turkur Tzonov went with them and stuck as close as he dared to Devetaki. His machine pistol swung from a strap across his shoulder . . . but its magazine was hooked to Devetaki's belt.

"Wratha and her gang of renegades must have known that these people were here," Devetaki began to outline her theory. "Ah, but Wratha also knew that they were fierce fighters! Well, no matter; as long as Wratha had supplicant tribes in the east beyond the pass, she need not attack the people of this great rock and risk expensive losses. But eventually, when she discovered that *we* were come out of the east—"

"—Then she *must* provision her aerie?" Vormulac finished it for her. "And she did some of that provisioning here! Yes, I see it . . ." And then, more gloomily: "Which means that we're too late. Any good stuff has been stolen into Starside, to the last aerie."

"But not all of it!" Devetaki sniffed the air. "I tell you I sense them in there, deep in the rock!"

And now that they were closer to that massive boulder: "So do I," Vormulac had to agree. "But . . . how many?

And more important, what are we going up against sight unseen?"

"We?" Devetaki looked at him sideways and shook her head. "What, do we keep wolves and do our own howling? *We* go against nothing, my Lord. Our men and monsters go up against whatever awaits them, which by my reckoning isn't much. Wratha has worn them out, which is why they hide in the rock. See, their traps are all sprung or burned up, their defences are unmanned. They wait like chickens in a coop—to have their necks wrung!"

They passed through the outer semicircle of warrior traps (many of which were still smoking, and some issuing the hideous stench of burnt flesh), skirted the inner pits, finally arrived at the drystone wall where Lardis's makeshift rocket-launching tubes stood empty and idle, fronting the mighty cavern entrance or "mouth" of the Rock. And indeed, it was not unlike a pockmarked face, that huge skull of a boulder. As the clouds began to break up, its round window eye sockets gleamed blue in the ice-shard starlight, and its mouth wore a frozen yawn or grimace.

Like a skull, and dead as a skull; no lights were visible anywhere; the Rock might well be deserted. Except—

"—There!" said Devetaki. "Did you not feel it: a tremor of terror? They watch us from those window holes. And they're defenceless as newborn babes, else by now they'd have fired a bolt or two."

At which Vormulac immediately felt vulnerable, and joined Devetaki where she knelt in the lee of the wall. "So, then," he said. "And to flush them out—?"

"—We send our lieutenants and men in, aye." She nodded. "But first, and to ensure that we're not sending them into an ambush . . ." She turned her burning gaze on the high rim of the Rock and sent: *Come, my brave one. For your mistress Devetaki has work for you!*

Then from on high, the answering roar of her warrior, and the sounds of its propulsors sputtering into life; a dark shape launching from the Rock's rim, and a second blasphemous outline close behind as Lord Taintspore followed suit and ordered down his own creature.

Landing room between the defensive positions and the Rock itself was limited; both beasts came down clumsily; they hissed and spat at each other, jostling awhile until Vormulac and Devetaki intervened. Then, turned hind-on to the cavern, they were ordered to prepare their most noxious gasses for release under pressure within the Rock. Poisonous fumes at once began to fill the labyrinth of tunnels and caves, venting in steamy jets from several lower windows, cracks, and crevices.

And from within . . . terrified thoughts! The desire to run, flee, escape! A great leaping, a mad rout of thoughts, this way and that . . . panic! Devetaki's superior mentalism picked up all of these emotions and knew them at once—for lies! Ah, and *indeed* these people were artful, yes! But this time they went too far.

What? Did they really think to play their games with the virgin grandam herself, the very mistress of deception? And she knew that there was nothing in the rock but death. *She* knew it, but on the other hand . . . Vormulac did not.

"I hear them now!" he chortled, his voice a clotted gurgle of anticipation. And to his men: "Spread out. Take them as they emerge!"

"Ah, no!" Devetaki saw her chance. "They're too proud for that, my Lord. These people would rather die than surrender to a stench. If we want them, we must drive them out. Here, let me send in half of my brave lads."

Vormulac glared at her. What? Would she upstage him to the last? "Mine go first!" he cried. "Yours . . . may follow on." And to his dozen lieutenants and thralls: "In, and sort it out!"

Driving the warriors before them, Lord Unsleep's dozen sprang to obey. Devetaki's six followed them in, but the rest stayed close to their Lady. And from within the Rock: was that a sigh, the thrill of pleasurable anticipation, the sure knowledge that a trap was about to be sprung? Devetaki knew that it was, but Vormulac had heard nothing.

The warriors were inside, deep into the larger tunnels,

which would take their bulk. The lieutenants and thralls were exploring lesser caves and burrows, all well within the labyrinth. There was no resistance ... because there was no one to flush out! Oh, there had been: men, minds, human *lures*, within the Rock, whose function Devetaki had read to perfection; she'd used no less a ploy herself! But they were there no longer. Now they plunged along Lardis's bolt-holes to secret exits where the steep slope of the foothills met the Rock's worn-smooth stone; and now they struck flints to send sparks flying into multiple trails of Dimi Petrescu's powder, trails that led sputteringly back into the heart of the Rock.

White-blazing, hissing, smoking fire ran like small bright rivers through claustrophobic confines. And all of these eager, almost sentient tongues of hungry flame licking their way back to an instantaneous feast of sudden, explosive, crushing death; all of them eating distance and darkness as they raced to their targets.

The base of the Rock was itself a massive mine! There were sacks of Dimi's powder in cracks in the ceilings, barrels of it in caves around the perimeter; drifts of it in walled-off corners and niches in the narrow tunnels!

And: *Now!* Devetaki "heard" the exclamation in her mind.

And again: *Now!* Two separate but equally triumphant cries going up; and despite the fact that she couldn't foresee the outcome and wouldn't be able to understand it, certainly not the mechanics of the thing, still she found herself borne along on the waves of excitement generated by these mental declarations of victory. So much so that she reiterated them:

Now!—and waited to see what would be.

But she'd been careless, and Vormulac had heard her.

"Eh?" Scowling suspiciously, the warrior-Lord turned gold-flecked scarlet eyes on her. "Now, did you say? Now what?" But it wasn't Devetaki who answered him ... it was as if Sanctuary Rock itself answered; first with a series of lesser explosions, then several colossal ones!

The earth shook; a hot wind blew from the cavern

mouth, showering pebbles and grit everywhere; lesser gusts hissed in pressured jets from windows and cracks. The windows lit up as white and orange flames spilled out from them. The grimace on the face of the skull became a rictus of agony, or a snarl of vengeance, as the porous chalky rock of the lower levels was fractured and blew outwards in crumbling chunks.

"What?" Vormulac stood up, his bottom jaw falling open.

Devetaki asked no questions but crept away, calling her six remaining men after her.

Turkur Tzonov went with them, cringing down into himself as Sanctuary Rock continued to erupt, spouting smoke and fire as its innards were torn out. Gutted in its soft chalk underbelly, it was finished, and the last and biggest explosion of all saw the end of it.

At the outer row of pits Devetaki stopped to look back. Vormulac came stumbling, clutching his head, bleeding from a cut where a flying rock had struck him. He looked dazed, disbelieving. And behind him the Rock went down, a million tons of it settling into its own foundations, tilting this way and that, easing into the earth, like a great egg tapped gently on a flat stone and left balancing there. The Rock went down, and overhead a signal rocket went up, high into the now cloudless night sky, where it terminated in a great orange starburst.

What the last might signify, the virgin grandam couldn't say—unless it was the death of the Rock. One thing was certain: it wasn't the end of death this night.

"Devetaki! *Devetaki!*" The warrior-Lord staggered closer. "My men, my monsters . . . *and you knew!*" And he would make her pay, right now, if that were possible. But it wasn't.

"My Lord, you have become a burden," she told him with a sigh. "But I've no time for speeches or recriminations. Men come and men go, and we're keeping destiny waiting. But don't be disappointed, for even now I serve you well. After all the long sleepless years that you've known, finally the greatest, longest sleep of all is upon you. And so, farewell!"

Putting on her smiling mask, she glanced at Tzonov meaningfully and tossed him his weapon's magazine.

Vormulac reached for her with hands that could tear her throat out. Bulge-eyed, he stumbled towards her. Blood rained down his forehead and dripped from his hawk's nose; his moustaches hung heavy with blood, and his grinding gash of a mouth was full of it. He was almost upon her, and Devetaki standing there with one slender arm held out to keep him back—as if it possibly could.

At the last moment she stepped back, and Tzonov stepped forward. He aimed his weapon and drew back the cocking lever—ch-*ching*! Vormulac moved to brush him contemptuously aside, and Tzonov let fly with a dozen hammers of hot lead that thundered death and destruction where they ripped through the vampire Lord's armour into his chest, hurling him back and down!

With his heart in pieces inside him, Vormulac Unsleep lay on his back, looked up at the stars and wondered what had happened. He was still wondering as Devetaki's lieutenants fell on him with their murderous gauntlets, and reduced his head to so much pulp. But he was perhaps the greatest of the Lords of the Wamphyri, and they knew it. Despite that Vormulac was dead, *he* was not nearly dead!

Before the *Thing* inside him could recover and activate itself in a final frenzy, they dragged him to a firepit and toppled him in. In the bottom of the pit, embers were glowing still; close to hand, a small pile of Lardis's tarred torches, left unused after the fighting with Wratha, would soon bring the embers back to life.

Vormulac went up in fire, smoke, and something less of a commotion than Devetaki had expected. Nevertheless, just to be absolutely certain, she waited until it was finished. Then she looked for Tzonov ...

... And at first failed to see him! As her lieutenants had busied themselves with Vormulac at the pit, so the alien had taken his chance and slipped away. Then a thrall pointed him out, scrambling up a slope towards a bluff or outcrop of solid rock, where dark fissures showed in the cliff face. Devetaki saw his scheme at once: tucked away in a crack or shallow cave, he could take out her men one by one as often as she sent them in after him! His devastating firepower would destroy them as easily as he'd dealt with Vormulac.

One of her more adventurous thralls was after him even now, scrambling with a vampire's strength and agility up the slope. But at the top Tzonov turned, aimed, and put two shots close together into his pursuer's heart. The thrall cried out, threw up his arms, and came tumbling head over heels down the steep slope.

In a rage, Devetaki looked all about—and saw what was required: a second pile of tarred faggots close to one of the pits. She gave orders, chose an easy route up the slope, and sticking to the shadows went after Tzonov. And her fury was such that she even forgot to change her mask . . .

At the place at the southern edge of the forest, where once a leper colony had huddled under the ironwoods, a gaunt-faced Lardis Lidesci had supervised the layout of his overnight camp before walking out under the stars to where Uruk Long-life lay wrapped in a blanket. It had been Lardis's intention to honour his promise and bury Uruk with his own hands.

But having found a spot at the top of a low, grassy hummock, and before commencing to dig, Lardis had felt some strange premonition and looked north . . . and a moment ago he'd seen the brilliant bomb-burst of the signal rocket over Sanctuary Rock! The flare-up had been dimmed by distance and a little moisture lingering in the air, but the Old Lidesci knew that he couldn't be mistaken. In corroboration, a lookout on a low rocky outcrop close by hallooed down to him: "Lardis, the Rock!"

Other lookouts up in the ironwoods around the camp must have seen it, too; Lardis heard their shouts, and set off back at the run. Uruk Piatra would have to wait for his decent burial, but Lardis was sure he wouldn't mind that now.

He made for an awning under a tree on the camp's perimeter where he knew that Misha looked after Nathan, with Trask and others of the Necroscope's party in attendance. High time the lad was back on his feet. It wasn't that Lardis considered he was being coddled, but simply that his talents were needed. Lardis had friends back at Sanctuary Rock, and he wasn't about to lose more good men to the vampires of Starside. Especially not these men.

Even as Lardis arrived at the makeshift shelter, Nathan was stirring. He had heard the disturbance in the camp, sensed that something was afoot. At first disorientated, his strange blue eyes finally focussed on Misha, and the first word on his lips was a name:

"Nana?" But a moment later he knew that it hadn't been a dream.

"Lad." Lardis couldn't wait a moment longer. "Nathan," he panted hoarsely. "There's trouble at the Rock!"

"What?" Nathan was on his feet now, unsteady but rapidly gaining ground. "Trouble?" he was wan and shaken, but the heat of his fever had finally burned itself out.

"Andrei and Kirk are back there," Lardis explained. "They volunteered. And now there's been a signal rocket. When we left the Rock, it was all primed up as a trap for Wratha and her lot should they return. Well, and it seems they have. But those two brave lads are still back there, and you are the only one who can bring them out."

Now Nathan's mind focussed; he stood straighter, and his resolve tightened to twin fists of iron in his guts and in his heart. For a moment there was a brief surge of pain, a wash of misery, grief; and then a greater surge—of hatred! For the Wamphyri.

Lardis saw his expression, his attitude visibly changing, but couldn't know what it meant. Time was of the essence. The Old Lidesci grasped Nathan's arms and snarled through clenched yellow teeth: "Lad, do you know where you are? Have you understood what I said?"

Nathan shook him off, glared at him. "*Yes*, I understand!" And now his turn to grab the Old Lidesci's arms. "Andrei and Kirk: where will they be?"

"The escape tunnels at the sides of the Rock, halfway up the slope, where the trees begin . . ."

Nathan nodded, pushed him away, stepped free of the group and looked up at the stars. They were his orientation. Now he knew where he was, and he'd known the Rock's coordinates since childhood.

Misha flew to him, said, "Nathan!"

He kissed her and pushed her away, but gently, and said, "Yes, I'll be careful."

Trask said, "Can I help? Listen, why not take me with . . ."

But Nathan had already moved, stepping forward into nothing, into nowhere—

—And into everywhere! Into the Möbius Continuum, the source of The All, which existed before anything else existed, except perhaps The One whose mind it was! He stepped into that space between spaces, which is the junction of everywhere and when. Stepped in, chose his coordinates . . . and stepped out—

—Into the foothills over Sanctuary Rock.

Down there: smoke going up from several of the pits west of the Rock, one fire at least still burning, and a heavy reek of sulphur rising on man- or monster-made thermals. But as for the Rock itself . . . it had settled! Boulders, loosened by the massive convulsion of earth as the Rock's lower levels concertinaed on themselves, were still tumbling from the slopes all around, and even up here in the foothills Nathan could sense minute tremors of the earth.

But he could sense more than that. Extending a telepathic probe, he found vampires—Wamphyri! *And* human thoughts, which was what he had hoped to find: thoughts to home in on. The difference was like night and day. Human thoughts were often light as thistledown, floating. But the thoughts of vampires seethed! They were heavy, clotted, thick as tar. Both sorts were here.

Kirk Lisescu's mind felt stunned, and Andrei's was full of curses. But their confusion following the devastation they'd wrought on the Rock had left them open, not only to the Necroscope's probe but also to the Wamphyri. Whichever Lord or Lady was down there now, they would be able to find Andrei and Kirk as easily as Nathan had found them. It galvanized him to activity.

Focussing on Andrei, he entered the Möbius Continuum and went to him—

—And emerged to the east of Sanctuary Rock in a tangle of bushes and gorse that threatened at any moment to go sliding right into a yawning, grinding, groaning black fissure left by the Rock's settling!

Andrei was cursing low but vividly, clinging to the roots of gorse and shrubs, his legs flailing uselessly in loose soil and unstable earth. Nathan had emerged a little above him in a patch of gorse, which alone arrested what must otherwise be a fall . . . and that was exactly how he would play it.

"Andrei!" he called down to the older man. "Look here!"

The other gasped, looked, said: "Eh? Nathan?"

"Let go," Nathan told him. "Don't fight it—go with me." And without further explanation, he himself let go and plunged down on Andrei!

"*What?* Let go?" The other couldn't believe it. "Have you gone mad?" In these circumstances, it was easy to forget just whom he was speaking to.

But Nathan crashed into him and tore him loose anyway—and at once conjured a door beneath them and fell into it . . .

. . . And out again east of the Rock close to Kirk Lisescu.

This time the ground was firmer; they emerged in a stand of trees; Andrei made an unintelligible sound, sat down in a clump of brambles and stuck his hands deep into the soil.

And there was Kirk, a dark blot in the starlight, panting and wide-eyed, already halfway out of the trees and scrambling madly up the sliding face of the slope . . . until he recognized Nathan's voice, calling: "Kirk, don't be afraid. It's me, Nathan!"

Then he came sliding back down into the trees where Andrei and Nathan grabbed at him. "What in the name of . . . ?" Kirk whispered, slack-jawed. "How in . . . ?" But by now both he and Andrei knew what in the name of, and how.

And without pause Nathan conjured a door and took them up into the foothills again, for orientation and a breather.

Except no sooner were they there—

—Gunfire, from below! The frenzied chatter of an automatic weapon! But who? Whoever, he was an entirely human being, certainly. Nathan could try probing him, except the time taken might prove to be the difference between life and death. And:

"Wait for me," he told the others—as if there were anything else they could do—and took the Möbius route to the old Traveller trails east of the Rock . . .

. . . Where just fifty yards from the firepits, he looked up at the lower escarpments as again the darkness was slashed by bright, staccato flashes of light and the savage *rrrrip!* of automatic fire. Up there, the night seethed with the bloodlusting thoughts of vampires, and even now a red-flaring torch was bobbing among them, igniting other torches. But why? What use did vampires have for torches? Darkness was better than daylight to them!

Nathan Möbius-jumped to the foot of the cliffs some hundred yards from the activity. And now he knew the place; as a child he'd played with his brother Nestor, and with Misha and Jason Lidesci, in those selfsame caves and crevices where now someone had taken refuge.

The night was alight with the torches of vampires. They were igniting them, and throwing them into a certain narrow-necked cave. Nathan knew it well. He pictured it in his mind as he'd known it all those years ago. He was sure he had the coordinates. He jumped . . .

. . . And emerged in the interior of the cave, where even now someone moved in the smoky darkness, stamping out a torch. Whoever it was, he sensed Nathan in the moment he emerged and their eyes met in the flare of another blazing faggot where it landed at their feet.

Their eyes met, their minds locked, and they both knew!

Made aware, alert as never before—galvanized by terror—Tzonov moved like greased lightning. Grabbing Nathan's arm, he rammed the hot muzzle of his weapon up into the soft flesh under his jaw. And: "You!" he breathed.

For answer, and however bitterly, Nathan said the first thing that came into his head. "I . . . I came to recue *you*! To take *you* out of here." Because their eyes were still locked, the Russian knew exactly what he meant—also that he could do it. Of course he could; Tzonov had *seen* him do it, in Perchorsk. And if that wasn't proof enough . . . well, he was here, wasn't he?

More torches were lobbed, came hissing, looping the loop, bouncing and showering sparks. Figures moved furtively in the mouth of the cave, just beyond the bottleneck. Tzonov coughed as acrid smoke snatched at his lungs, and said: "Very well, do it. Get us out of here!"

And hugged close to the Russian, with the hard hot muzzle of Tzonov's machine pistol pressing up into his throat, Nathan had no choice.

He did it . . .

III

Tzonov: Taken Again—Misha: Made to Understand

To Turkur Tzonov, the Möbius Continuum was much as it was to anyone else—astonishing, frightening, an experience beyond experience, bearing no comparison to anything gone before. He was blind, weightless, lost in a darkness utter. And yet, for all his human ignorance, there were things he felt, things he knew instinctively: that the Continuum was infinite, and that in a way beyond comprehension it was sentient (therefore infinitely sentient?), and that he, Turkur Tzonov, had no right to be here. Only one human being had that right, the Necroscope himself, and he had earned it. Anyone else was either a guest . . . or a trespasser.

The Continuum would expel him if it could, or otherwise dispose of him, lose him in places, spaces, undreamed of; he knew it as surely as he knew his own name, knew also that his one hope of survival was Nathan Keogh. Like others before him he clung to the Necroscope, and kept his machine pistol jammed up under his chin. Feeling the hard, warm metal there, Nathan knew that any slight increase of pressure on the trigger would spread his brains across eternity! He could do only as Tzonov had ordered him to do: take him out of there.

But to where? To Lardis Lidesci, Trask, and the others, and risk Tzonov killing one or all of them? To some place in the Sunside forest, and leave Andrei and Kirk defenceless in the foothills? Wherever he took Tzonov, the Russian had the upper hand; he wasn't going to let go of Nathan just yet. An idea played in the Necroscope's mind: to conjure a door and step out, and collapse it before Tzonov could fully emerge.

And in the "mundane" world of Sunside, what would remain of Turkur Tzonov after that? A weapon and a pair of arms, and perhaps a lower leg, sliced off above the knee? And if in the moment of the death-dealing act, there should occur one last nerveless twitch of the Russian's trigger finger?

All of this flashing through Nathan's metaphysical mind, even his secret mind, as he forgot a simple yet all-important fact: that in the immeasurable echo chamber of the Möbius Continuum, even secret thoughts have weight! And the Russian was no mean mentalist in his own right.

Just try it! Tzonov's own thoughts gonged viciously. *But you'd better be sure that if I'm going to die, you're coming with me, Necroscope!*

Andrei and Kirk were waiting; theirs was by no means a secure location; Nathan went to them knowing he would have to move on, and that Tzonov would know it, too. Oh, the Russian might want to kill him, but he wouldn't be able to do it just yet.

They emerged on the crest of a false plateau, beneath the first real cliffs that went beetling up and finally reared into the barrier mountains. And Andrei and Kirk were still there, of course, knee-deep in a writhing ground mist, anxious for Nathan until the moment of his return—then yet more anxious as they saw his fix.

"What the hell . . . ?" Andrei started forward.

But Nathan, squirming in the Russian's iron grip, waved him back. "No," he said. "Do nothing, make no move. This man will kill me if you push him too far. He's a hell-lander, but he isn't a friend. Let's see what he wants."

An esper, Tzonov understood almost everything of what had been said, knew that for the moment he was in no great danger. And now that he felt reasonably safe, a plan took shape in his mind. He knew that his men—if any of them survived—would still be trapped in the keep in the pass. Come daylight they'd strike out south, and eventually emerge from the pass into Sunside. That would be the ideal place to link up with them again. The Necroscope could take him there, a simple one-to-one proposition. And once they were there: good-bye, Necroscope! But if Tzonov allowed these Travellers to be taken along, too— they might fancy their chances during transit, or immediately after.

And in any case Tzonov couldn't let them live. They knew him now as Nathan's enemy. If circumstances were such that he was caused to stay in this world longer than he intended to—and if he should bump into these men again—they would want to know what had become of the Necroscope. They were the only witnesses that Tzonov had ever been with Nathan, and knew the circumstances of their being together. They'd name him as the Necroscope's murderer. Which by then he most surely would be.

Nathan was in the Russian's mind. He saw the whole thing and knew what was coming. All thoughts with regard to his own safety fled at once; he knew that Tzonov couldn't kill him yet, not and get back down into Sunside to wait for his men.

"Run!" he yelled at his friends. "Now, both of you!"

The ground mist was swirling more yet, and for the first time—even as he shouted—Nathan became aware of the *texture* of that mist: how it clung and felt against his skin. And from deep inside a warning voice was telling him, *The Russian isn't the only danger here!*

Tzonov shifted his grip to Nathan's throat, his windpipe. Iron fingers dug in as the Russian swung his weapon's ugly muzzle after the ducking, weaving figures of the Travellers where they fled through the thickening mist. But sensing the Necroscope's sudden tension, and feeling the spasm of fear—which wasn't fear of Tzonov—that stiffened his body and limbs, he glanced into Nathan's sapphire-blue eyes at point-blank range; which was the same as looking through a window into his mind. But if Nathan's eyes were windows, they were also mirrors!

Nathan was thinking . . . absolutely nothing! However momentarily, his mind had gone blank, a wasteland of shock. But his mirror eyes told the whole story:

Riding that vampire mist and settling towards their target on arched air-trap wings *behind* Tzonov, a pair of Wamphyri flyers had zeroed in on him and Nathan! Their long necks were outstretched and their saucer eyes unblinking. And their riders . . .

Him! A powerful vampire voice, female, echoed in the minds of both men. *That one—the hairless one!* And Tzonov knew that telepathic voice as he would know a lover's kiss, or an enemy's hatred—for he *had* known her, and in both senses.

And this time it was no artful ploy of Devetaki Skullguise but the real thing—Siggi Dam! Except the real thing was now just as deadly in its own right; or, considering the incredible being who was Siggi's escort, it was a good deal worse!

He had no choice. Releasing Nathan, he whirled about-face and brought up his gun; the machine pistol jerked in his hands, spitting fire and fury at the closest flyer and rider. His best shots burned deep grooves along the flyer's neck; others expended themselves uselessly in the yawning pouch, or chipped soft cartilage from the leading edge of a wing.

The beast's rider—who in Tzonov's eyes looked like an intelligent, upright wolf!—hauled on his reins and presented his mount's corrugated underbelly. Tzonov threw himself flat as the creature's pouch, thrusters, and belly passed harmlessly but too close overhead, then got up on one knee and took aim at the second flyer and rider.

It was Siggi, but such a Siggi as Tzonov could never have expected to see! Wamphyri, and beautiful—horrifically beautiful—beyond words! Yet even now . . . was that fear he saw in her flaming scarlet eyes? Fear, yes, and loathing! Somehow she remembered him still. Well, fear and loathing were emotions he could deal with. Her weakness gave him strength.

As she turned her mount aside, Tzonov gritted his perfect teeth, narrowed his eyes, and took careful aim . . . and was hit from behind as the Necroscope flew at him in a headlong dive!

Why? . . . Nathan would never be able to say. But whatever she was now, Siggi Đam had suffered enough at the hands of this man. And anyway, she considered Nathan her friend. And what the hell—*she* had saved *him*, upon a time, hadn't she?

Tzonov cursed and went flying but retained his gun. And in the next moment he was back on his feet. Furious, he'd take any target he could get now. And the Necroscope himself was·closest and most readily available. Grinning viciously, Tzonov grunted, "Good-bye, Gypsy!"

Even as Nathan conjured a door he knew he was too late, so that what came next was almost an anticlimax:

A bolas of three eight-inch, razor-sharp hooks came whirling out of the mist and wrapped itself around Tzonov's upper body. The Russian's weapon was jerked aside, its shots deflected. He screamed as the hooks skewered him through combat suit, flesh, and muscle, and screamed again, louder, more desperately yet, as a thin line attached to the bolas tightened and he was drawn up into the air.

And from above, Canker Canison's grunt of monstrous satisfaction in Nathan's mind: *Got you, my friend! Got you at last! What? And did you think to find my silver moon mistress, steal her away and make her your own? If so, then now you* have *found her. Ah, but you've found Canker, too!*

Tzonov dropped his gun, howled his agony and clawed uselessly at the web of ropes that whirled him like a top as they unwound themselves. He would try to unhook himself if he could, which was about as possible as lifting himself by his own bootstraps. Suspended like an animal carcass on meathooks, he was drawn up into the mist and vanished—but his fading screams came back . . . oh, for a long time.

Nathan's door had collapsed. He reached out a telepathic probe, searched for vampires, and found nothing but

Canker Canison's rapidly evaporating mental aura and fading chuckle. That and the Lady Siggi's relief, and ... the first faint glimmer of morbid excitement, unthinkable anticipation, in her changeling mind? But of course, for she was Wamphyri!

Then, hallooing into the mist, the darkness and the echoing night, Nathan called for Andrei and Kirk. In a while they found courage to answer him; he collected them, and took them via the Möbius route back to Lardis's camp.

There on the rim of the savanna, there were a good many people whom Nathan must speak to. First Misha, to tell her—even show her—what must be made known to her. For if he expected her understanding as well as her loyalty, she must be *given* to understand: that her husband was more than even she had suspected him to be. And when that was done he must speak to Lardis, Trask, anyone else with wisdom enough to guide him in the ways he intended to use himself. And finally, last but not least he must speak to ... oh, a Great Majority of others, who were no longer so lively.

But first Misha.

Having delivered Andrei and Kirk safe into the arms of Lardis, and cutting all of the Old Lidesci's and Ben Trask's questions short—promising them that he would tell them all that had transpired at Sanctuary Rock just as soon as he possibly could—Nathan walked with Misha out onto the prairie a little way.

The night was more than halfway through; it had been a long, long night for both of them; Nathan's tiredness was now entirely physical, and therefore something that he could fight. Misha on the other hand was sleepy beyond fighting. She would gladly surrender herself into the Necroscope's arms, and fall asleep with him in the long grasses if he so desired it.

But that wasn't Nathan's plan. Though he loved her desperately, he intended to make her more tired yet—to make her head whirl, to weary her emotionally as well as physically, with feelings she'd never before experienced—and so be sure that she would sleep. Because he had work to do, and his young wife couldn't be allowed to intrude while he did it.

Also, knowing what he was, what he could do, Misha might rest peacefully in the knowledge that her man was "truly invulnerable." Oh, he wasn't, but in a little while she would think he was. And so, hugging her close in the chill of the night—in the light of a rising moon, under ice-blue stars as cold as their colour but warmer far here than in Starside—he turned to face north and looked back at the barrier mountains, a scalloped rim on the horizon, and at the Northstar over Wrathstack, the star of ill omen glittering there, and said:

"Misha, I've told you what I do, but I haven't shown you. You of all people should know. You have the right. I'm not the boy, the youth, the man I was. We've scarcely had time to know each other, not the new people we've become. And I know how you have worried about me for far too long. It's time you stopped."

She smiled at him, that elfin look from their childhood, beguiling, mischievous, loving. *A little girl in the sparkling river shallows, innocent in her nakedness, teasing him to come to her in the water. And later, years later: her hair dark as night, velvet, which in the light of the sun shone black as a raven's wing. Her eyes, so huge and deeply brown under black, expressive, arching eyebrows, that they too looked black. Her mouth: small, straight and sweet under a tip-tilted nose which, for all that it flared occasionally in true Gypsy fashion, had nothing hawkish or severe about it. Her ears, a little pointed, pale against the velvet of her hair where it fell in ringlets to her shoulders. Misha the girl, who was now Misha the woman and his wife.*

The vision from the past faded, and he saw her face as it was now: mature, lovely, longing. For peace. For children. For a chance—hope against hope—to live out her life, to live out *their* lives in freedom, side by side in a free world. All of it was there in Misha's look, so that he didn't have to read her mind. Not that he ever had or ever would, for in this respect he was wise beyond his talent and could gauge only too well the pitfalls of probing the thoughts of loved ones.

"Now tell me," she said. "How am I to stop worrying about you? Will you ever be with me long enough that I can stop worrying?"

He hugged her tighter still and said stumblingly: "Misha, listen. I'm trying to tell you . . . you have to understand that . . . that we go against the Wamphyri."

She offered a small frown, shrugged, and said, "But haven't we always?"

"Yes," he was patient, "we always have. But this time it has to be different. This time all the vows we ever made—all of the Szgany since the beginning of what we call our 'history'—*must* be realized! This time we fight them all the way, until they're finished forever.. We have to, because I want what every man of the Travellers ever wanted: to be able to love his woman every night without hiding in a hole in the ground. To watch my children grow up and know they'll be mine always, not just future fodder for a vampire Lord and his beasts, or materials for his vats of metamorphism."

She nodded. "I've heard Lardis say much the same thing—often . . .". Too often, perhaps. And yes, he could see that Misha needed convincing.

"Misha," he said, "in that world beyond the Starside Gate which we called the hell-lands, Ben Trask promised me a weapon to fight the Wamphyri even as Harry Keogh and his son the Dweller fought and destroyed them before we were born. And he kept his word—Trask gave me that weapon! Now I must discover the best way to use it."

"I have seen your weapons," she said. "Very impressive—and very limited." She was wise beyond her years, but she had read only half of his meaning.

"My love," he said, holding her by the shoulders, looking deep into her eyes, sending her a telepathic message that even a child or the least talented person in the world must surely hear, *the weapon I'm talking about . . . is me!*

"What . . . !" Her gasp, as her hand flew to her mouth. "Nathan, I heard you speak—when you weren't speaking!"

But I was. Misha, I have things to show you. You have to know who I am, what I am.

"I . . . I'm talking to myself!" she said. "In my head! But I'm not thinking my own thoughts!"

He shook his head, smiled and said. *No, you're hearing me! And I can hear your thoughts, too, if I so desire. But I don't and I won't. It's part of the weapon which I am, which I'll use against the Wamphyri. Do you want to see more?*

At first she couldn't answer, but then she nodded. "Oh . . . yes!"

"Then close your eyes, and keep them closed. You know that I . . . go places? You've seen me. But in between those places is a secret place. A place inside and outside time and space. You won't be frightened?" He conjured a Möbius door.

"Not if I'm with you."

"You'll feel that you're floating, like this . . ." He drew her through the door with him.

"Nathan, I . . . AHHHHH!!!" Her voice gonged in the primal night of the Möbius Continuum—but she kept her eyes tightly closed.

Hush! he told her. *In this place, words are like hammers, and they hurt. But thoughts are like words, which we can hear. Anyone could be a mentalist here, except no one else can come here. Now, imagine the deepest, darkest cave you ever saw. No light at all, no sound, nothing. And you are a moth floating in the dark. Do you have it?*

Yes, I think so.

Open your eyes.

Ahhhhh!

It's all right! Don't cling so. Hold my hand. I have you. There!

She was filled with wonder, and her "voice" was the very smallest thing as she said, *This is a very strange place, Nathan.* An understatement, but what else was she to say?

Everything began here, he told her. *This is what was left when time and space flew outwards. In a way, it's the centre.* It seemed the simplest explanation.

The shake of her head. *I don't understand.*

Don't try to, just believe.

He opened a past-time door and held her on the threshold, where their shimmering life-threads of blue light uncoiled out of their bodies and went falling into the past, back into what had been, into the misty blue Origin of Human Life ... and of life that was less, or more, than human. For there were a good many crimson threads among the blue: vampires, of course.

Misha saw him limned in the light of their lives and the misty blue pulse of the past, and asked:

What is it? What are we seeing? Where . . . is it?

Our past, yours and mine, he told her. *These blue threads, they are us. They were us! I can follow my life-line, I think, even to its source in my mother's womb. But what is the use? I can't materialize in the past. Only the Dweller could do that. This was to show you—to try and explain—what this place is. Now, are you ready to look into the future?*

She was eager now. *Oh, yes!*

He closed the past-time door and opened a door on the future. It was different, and it should have been glorious—the expansion of mankind into an ever-brightening future—but it was saddening. For the scarlet lines were there as before, but closer than before, encroaching on the blue. And even as Nathan and Misha looked on, many of the blue threads were blinking out of being, snuffed like candles, wrapped around and extinguished by the Wamphyri!

Misha read in Nathan's thoughts what it meant, and sadly asked him, *Can you go there, too? It seems to me a good place to avoid! But if it's the future, how may we avoid it?*

I think I can probably go there, yes, he told her. *Except*

*it would be dangerous, for the future's a devious thing. But
in any case I can't materialize there. So what would be the
point? What will be will be.* Or, as his father had used to
say: What will be, has been . . .

But will it be . . . like that?

*That's how it must be—how it is—until we can put a
stop to it. I haven't looked too far. Perhaps I haven't
dared. But there is someone who might advise me. Maybe
I'll have to speak to him after all . . . later.*

And now the hardest part of all. *Misha, now I'm going
to take you somewhere else, out into the furnace desert.
We have friends there.*

The Thyre?

Fine people, he told her. *Not at all like you might have
imagined them to be.*

He closed the future-time door, chose coordinates, went
out across the savanna and the furnace desert—*without*
crossing them—to a certain canyon white in the light of a
hurtling moon. And as Misha staggered where he gently
set her down, he spoke telepathically to that faithful one
who he knew would be waiting. And she told him yes, certainly he could bring his lady there . . .

. . . Into the Cavern of the Ancients!

This time Misha *did* stagger, quite helplessly, and would
have fallen if Nathan hadn't supported her. And: "What?"
She looked all about. "Where . . . ?"

"A sacred place," he told her, "where the Thyre remember their dead. For their dead are here."

The place was lit by candles, a great many, in the niches
of the revered dead all around the walls. And in the center of the dusty floor—Atwei, Nathan's Thyre "sister,"
seated at a small table, with the remains of a meal spread
before her. She came to her feet at once, and almost ran to
him . . . then remembered she was Thyre and came in less
haste, which was seemly.

"Nathan, brother. And . . . ?" She knew who, of course,
for he had already "spoken" to her. But it might seem *un-*
seemly to have spoken of another behind her back, as it
were. Especially this other, Nathan's wife. Also, Atwei

knew that the Szgany were not as particular as the Thyre about protecting their names—that indeed casual introductions were quite in order—or she would not have asked in the first place.

"Misha," Misha said, however faintly, her pretty jaw hanging slack as finally she found her feet and gazed about in open astonishment at the Cavern of the Ancients:

The domed ceiling of yellow sandstone with its cat's-eye gash of white quartz crystal, which let in the moonlight like a ghostly swath across the floor; the crystal stalactites descending from the ceiling, and dripstone humps of crystal like frozen men all seated in a circle. And in niches carved out of the walls, *actual* frozen men, but frozen in the rigidity of death: the mummied ancients of the Thyre.

None of which was new to Nathan, who was eager to get on. "Atwei, excuse my impatience," he said, "but will you speak to the elders for me? I have a very great favour to ask of them." And in her mind he showed her what that favour was.

"Of course I will speak to them," she said. "For am I not one of them?"

"You?" He was taken aback. "But you're a girl!" He spoke in haste, but intended no disrespect and she knew it.

She smiled, and explained: "My status is a token of *their* respect! For you are my brother, Necroscope."

It was no small compliment, and he accepted it as gracefully as he knew how. "The Thyre . . . honour me. But Atwei, I need to speak to my wife. Will you go now, and see the elders personally?"

"Of course." She began to turn away, then turned back. "I too, have a favour to ask."

"Then ask it."

"Another time, some time when there *is* time, I would like you to meet my mate, my husband, Alaia—Al-ay-ee-ay. It would be our pleasure to have you share food with us, all four of us together."

Nathan smiled and was glad for her, and for a moment forgot the weight of two worlds pressing down on him.

But then: "I didn't even know!" he said. And as his smile faded, "Time yes; only see how much of it has flown, sister, and how things have changed. And there are a great many things still to be changed. But yes, when there *is* time, then it would be our pleasure and an honour to eat with you and yours."

She was pleased and lowered her head, then turned and ran from the Cavern of the Ancients. In a while they heard her feet pattering briefly in a tunnel that Nathan knew descended to the first Thyre colony he'd ever visited, called Place-Under-the-Yellow-Cliffs.

Then Misha looked at him and blinked. "Brother?"

Nathan nodded and told her. "I'm honoured to be her Szgany brother, yes. Atwei is my Thyre sister. When the Thyre found me dying, she was the one who nursed me back to health."

Again she staggered a little, and said, "My head is reeling!"

"Now see," he steadied her. "I've shown you these things so that you won't worry about me when we're apart, as we must be apart if I'm to work against the Wamphyri. Now that you've seen some of the things I can do, and the power of those weapons out of the hell-lands . . ."

". . . But you're *still* only one man," she cut him off, and at once fell silent. For she knew his purpose now; also that she would never stop worrying about him, not as long as there was danger in the vampire world.

And he knew that he must show her the rest. It was why he'd brought her here, to the one place—the one man— who could do it for him; or rather, who *would* do it for him, willingly and without question. Except, like his father before him, that wasn't Nathan's way. The teeming dead were his friends; he would never take from them, or expect of them beyond that they give him their friendship. And if what he wanted meant pain or even the smallest hurt, then he simply wouldn't want it.

Rogei knew his thoughts, of course, for they were deadspeak. *No pain for me, my son,* he said, *for I am be-*

yond that now. Oh, there is one *who could hurt me, it's true; you know him well enough! But as for you . . . it would be my pleasure. Yes, I believe these old bones can be made to move again, if only one last time.*

Nathan had walked Misha towards a special niche with its dusty ledge and crumbling tenant: Rogei, the first of all the dead to openly converse with him. Rogei the Ancient, in this his last resting place. And placing a hand gently on Rogei's fragile chest, Nathan told Misha, "But I don't have to be just one man, Misha. I have Lardis and the Szgany Lidesci. I have Ben Trask and his people. And I have . . . *other* friends, up in the mountains; you'll be meeting them, too, in a little while. If I so desire it, I can even have an army. But that last . . . that last depends on them."

"Them?" She hugged close to him. For suddenly she'd sensed something different in his voice: a strangeness? A very uncharacteristic coldness, certainly.

"Misha," he continued, "there's something that only Lardis and a few of the others know about me. They know . . . yet don't know; because they *can't* know, not with any real understanding! They accept it, and then they forget it. And because I'm just a man, they accept *me* without thinking about this other . . . business. That's because they don't want to think about it. But you are my wife. You should know, because you must live with me."

She looked into his eyes, this way and that, as if to see if anything were hiding in them. "Is it so very terrible, this thing about you? If so, it's strange I never noticed it before. Is it like your mentalism, something new?"

He shook his head. "No, I've always had it. Ever since we were children. I can't remember a time without it. But you see, I could hear them talking to each other even then, and now they talk to me, too."

"Them? They? Your secret army?" He was so quiet, and his eyes so strange. "Nathan, I think I'm a little frightened."

That broke his mood, brought him out of it. Fear was the last thing he wanted, not in Misha. If he showed her now, she might think him a monster. He would proceed more slowly, take her to the barrier mountains, introduce her to his wolves and let her see the rest of the strangeness first—and save the strangest till last.

"Put it aside," he said, almost sighing his relief as he turned abruptly away from Rogei.

"But you said—"

"No, let it be. It can wait."

"Nathan!" She put her hands on her hips.

And: *She's right, you know,* said Rogei, that extinct old man of the Thyre. *Right to be annoyed—even as I am annoyed! The last time you were on the run it was from Life itself, and this time it's from Truth! What is she, a weakling, this woman of yours? And are you a weakling, too? I think not. Show her, my son—or let me show her.*

"Who are they, who talk to you?" Misha would not be moved, not now.

Nathan held out his arms helplessly. "Them," he said, his eyes moving about the cavern, its niches and ledges. "These ..."

"These," she looked. "These ... *dead* creatures?"

"The Thyre," he said. "Not creatures but men. Oh, different from the Szgany, I know, but still men. And Starside trogs, too. And our own people; I mean, the dead of our people, yes."

"You ... talk to them?"

"Don't ask me to prove it."

But: *Let her ask you!* said Rogei. *For you can prove it!*

"Nathan, I—"

"Come on," the Necroscope said, conjuring a door. "Let's go and talk to some wolves of the wild—my nephews! Perhaps if I can make you believe in that ..."

"Wolves? Your nephews? Nathan, I—"

He had moved her back to the centre of the cavern; now he would take her into the Möbius Continuum again. But as he made to do so—

—*Nathan!* Said Rogei. *Farewell!* But it was the way that he said it, his deadspeak voice hoarse with some nameless emotion,

Nathan looked back, and Misha's eyes followed suit, glancing towards the source of some half-sensed movement: the flickering light of the candles, perhaps? But no, it wasn't that.

Rogei the Ancient lay in his niche as before. Except . . . his skull head had turned to look at them through empty socket eyes, and one slender skeleton hand was raised in a gesture of farewell!

It was the first time that Nathan had seen it for himself. But now he knew beyond any further doubt that it was true. And Misha . . . she also understood.

As she collapsed with a sigh into his arms, Nathan told Rogei: *I don't know if I should thank you or what.*

Nor do I! I did what I thought was right. His bony hand fell loosely to his side; his head lolled on the crumbling column of his neck; he was just a dead thing.

"She'll be all right," Nathan said. "The mountain air will revive her. And anyway, you're right: she had to know."

Was it . . . unseemly?

Nathan shook his head. "I can't believe you ever acted in an unseemly way in your whole life, father," he said. "And certainly not in death." With which he carried Misha through the waiting door . . .

. . . And out again into the heights over old Settlement. But as she stirred in his arms, he sent: *Blaze, where are you?*

Closer than you think, Uncle! Between Settlement and Twin Fords that was. In the heights with your nephew Grinner, where we rest. A few miles, which to you is as nothing.

And you know where I am?

Indeed! I know . . . directions, yes! Myself and my brothers, we all know the directions.

Nathan understood: his nephews had the dog or wolf sense of direction, but enhanced by the blood of the Necroscope, come down to them through the Dweller from Harry Keogh. He'd sensed it in them before, in their wolf equivalent of the numbers vortex. Where he had mastered metaphysical numbers—the math of space and time—their expertise lay in orientation. Blaze had known instinctively where he was. But his way was a two-way talent; Blaze's own coordinates stood out so clearly in Nathan's mind that he could pinpoint the wolf's location within inches.

Wait, he said, and went there.

Misha came to as he arrived and carried her into the moon- and starlit saddle between peaks where Blaze and Grinner had met up to rest awhile. For they and their divided pack had been about their allotted duties: keeping watch on the comings and going of the Wamphyri. Dock, too, beyond the great pass; he had performed the same duties, but closer to the temporary camp of the vampires out of Turgosheim—too close. Dock's story was a sad one, which Nathan had still to learn.

Nathan spread his jacket and sat the bemused Misha down on a flat-topped boulder. It finally got through to her where she was—and in whose company—and she made to spring up again! But Nathan sat beside her, put his arm around her and held her in position.

"You have nothing to fear from them," he said. "These have always been 'my' wolves."

"Your wolves?" She glanced at him out of the corner of her eye; and again, but fearfully, at the animals surrounding them. "I . . . I always thought that was a false memory, or a dream out of childhood. I remember a strange rare time; there was snow on the barrier mountains; the wolves came down and you and Nestor . . . you played with them! We were just children at play. No one else saw. When we went home and I told my father, he laughed! I didn't talk about it again. And afterwards . . . I thought it was a dream, that it hadn't really happened. Also, I seem to remember that you talked to them."

"These are the same wolves," he told her. "In this world they're long-lived—not so in the hell-lands. But here, they have no natural enemies. Not in these heights which are their places."

But: *We have enemies now,* Blaze told him, padding closer, and sitting facing him. *And these mountain places are no longer ours alone. Uncle, Dock is no more!*

Nathan's jaw fell open. "What? Dock? How ... ?"

Grinner had come, too; he sat with his head cocked on one side, grinning at Misha, in his fashion, who crept closer into Nathan's arms. And shivering, she said, "You *do* talk to them!"

"Shhh!" he hushed her. "This is important." And to Blaze: "What about Dock? He has the high ground beyond the pass, am I right?"

He had it, aye. A nod of that unmistakably wise wolf head, with its blaze of frosted fur. *He watched the Wamphyri, their movements, him and three of his best. They watched close up ... too close, Uncle.*

Nathan felt sick; such losses were too great to bear; his mother—Nana, whom he loved so dearly—and now this faithful one, Dock with his bristly stump of a tail. Gone forever ...

... But not too far, Uncle! Dock's deadspeak voice, in Nathan's mind! For a moment it stunned even the Necroscope.

But why? Blaze inquired. *How else could we have known? He is our brother. He is our brother, Uncle, just as your mother is your mother. And he is right: they are not gone too far away.*

Of course, for as Nathan should know only too well, death isn't like that.

Misha had stopped trembling. She looked at them all, the grey brothers, all ringed about the rock where she and Nathan sat. And he *was* talking to them; to these two leaders, anyway! And Grinner with his head cocked, and that sly slavery look on his face ... that almost human look. Until suddenly she remembered a myth or legend from her childhood. Perhaps more than a legend, for Lardis Lidesci had mentioned it time and time over again. But then again, Lardis was full of stories.

About the Dweller in his garden over Starside. A man—a hell-lander—who had become a wolf! Indeed, a

werewolf! More than that, he'd been Wamphyri! A creature with Nathan's powers: a mentalist, a teleport, a wolf
. . . a vampire! And these wolves of the wild . . . ?

"The Dweller's children!" she gasped aloud.

Nathan looked at her where she clung to his arm, and
saw what flashed across her mind. And *they* saw it reflected in his own mind, too. Like a question there, but
such a question that he scarcely dared to ask. Blaze answered it anyway:

*We are not Wamphyri. Something of them is in us, per-
haps, as it is in most of the Szgany of Sunside. But the
essence—that which makes them what they are—is not in
us. The Dweller, our father, was Wamphyri, but he was different. He kept that of the wolf, and that of the man, but
nothing of the vampire, not after his change. Or if he was
Wamphyri, nothing of it got into us. We had it from our
mother that he would not bring vampires into the world,
but only wolves . . .*

And Grinner said, *Your mate fears me, and all I have is
an itch behind my ear, and all I want is that she scratch
it!*

Almost absentmindedly, Nathan reached out to scratch
the place behind Grinner's ear, and Misha watched in
amazement. "A wild wolf!" she said.

Nathan nodded. "But with a mind clever as a man's—
and stranger than you could ever guess!" Then, to Blaze,
as Misha gingerly fondled Grinner's head: "I can't tell you
how sorry I am about Dock. I mean, I know he's still here,
but—he isn't here."

We know. Blaze acknowledged his grief. And in a moment: *Would you know about the Wamphyri?*

That wasn't why Nathan had come here, but knowledge
was always useful. "What of them?"

*They have places out on the plain of boulders, from
which they spy on the last aerie. But as yet their main
force is the east, for they have not crossed the pass; not in
any great numbers, and them that did cross have gone
back. We think they will wait out tomorrow in caves, and
at sundown spread out all along the ridge of the moun-*

tains. Then all of the grey brothers will be in trouble, with nowhere safe for us unless we flee far into the west, or down into Sunside's forests. And the Travelling folk will have problems of their own.

"If you come into Lidesci territory, men won't hunt you, I can promise you that!"

We know it, Uncle . . .

Suddenly the pack was restless; the grey brothers and sisters stirred as one; Blaze and Grinner stood up, however reluctantly. And: *Time we were on our way,* said Grinner. *Now we must hunt to live.*

And Nathan nodded grimly. "So must I," he said . . . but in his mind, for them alone: *But mainly I hunt to kill!*

They understood. *Good hunting, then.* Blaze bared his fangs, and turned away.

They melted into the shadows, were gone into the crags and gulleys in a moment. A few heads turned; triangular eyes flared in the darkness and blinked out. It was as if they'd never been there at all.

But from far away (or so it seemed): *One last thing, Uncle.* It was Dock, his deadspeak. *The Wamphyri of the last aerie kept supplicant Szgany in Sunside's forests east of the pass. I suppose you knew that?*

Yes, Nathan sent. *Traitors to their own kind. What of them?*

The army out of the east descended on them, destroyed them in great numbers! They are no more. Those who survived are fled deep into the woods.

Then they got their just deserts. Nathan could find little of pity for them.

Indeed they did! Dock barked. *But what happened to me and mine was unjust! I make no complaint for myself, but my bitch goes without a mate. You said you would hunt?*

Yes.

Then hunt some for me (Dock's low, threatening growl), *in the place of the lava river east of the great pass. For that is where the Wamphyri butchered us, and ate the smoking hearts of me and my bravest!*

And: *I'll hunt them there,* Nathan promised him, with

his eyes closed and his teeth clenched. *Be sure that I will . . .*

IV

A Plan of Campaign—Final Arrivals—Dead Allies

Back at the temporary camp, Misha was so weary that she could barely find strength to curl up under the stretched skin of an upturned travois and go to sleep. Nathan marked well her exact location, then sought out Ben Trask and Lardis Lidesci.

They were seated around a campfire with David Chung, Anna Marie English, Andrei Romani, and the caver John Carling. At first Nathan wondered about the advisability of the fire, but since the gutted heart of the old leper colony was still smouldering less than a hundred yards away, and sending up columns of dense black smoke into the night air, Lardis saw no harm in allowing one or two rather more friendly fires. Also, the Old Lidesci felt a lot more secure with the hell-landers around; their extraordinary weapons had given him heart.

Nathan sat down with them, and at once opened with: "It's time we struck back. I think I have something of a plan, but I need to know what you think of it."

This was what Ben Trask had been waiting for. Trask had known from the moment of Nana Kiklu's death that it was coming, and soon. Now, seeing the grim set of Nathan's jaw in the firelight—a look that reminded him more than ever of the Necroscope, Harry Keogh—he knew that it was here. And so: "Let's hear what's on your mind," he said.

"We're well through midnight, fast heading for morning," Nathan answered. "The Wamphyri know that, too; indeed they're more surely aware of it than we are. They can feel the steady motion of the sun, its gradual climb, even beyond the horizon and through the heart of the planet. So there isn't likely to be much activity for the rest of the night. And I have it on good authority that the army out of Turgosheim is making camp for the coming day in dead volcanoes and caverns east of the pass."

"Oh?" Lardis grunted. "On whose authority, exactly?"

But Nathan looked at him in that certain way, and Lardis shrugged and immediately fell silent. This wasn't just any man who was talking. "I also have it," Nathan continued, "that the last aerie is in siege; Wratha the Risen is confined to Wrathstack; Vormulac Unsleep has watchers positioned on the boulder plains to report on her movements. If she or any of hers takes leave of the stack, they'll be set upon and destroyed at once. There'll be no more excursions out of Wrathstack, not without someone suffering the consequences." The Necroscope didn't yet know that Vormulac was dead, but in any case what he had said was still correct in its essentials.

"*Huh!*" Lardis grunted. "This warrior-Lord out of the east has cut off her supplies; she can't get at us without fighting him! But if he is the greater of the two evils, how does that benefit us?"

Nathan's turn to shrug. "At least while they're standing each other off, they won't have quite so much time to hunt for us. And come daylight, *both* parties will be in siege— pinned down by the sun! But we won't be, and we'll have to use every scrap of daylight to our best advantage. The sun is the single tried and true weapon which has never let us down. As for Vormulac: I fancy the warrior-Lord has made a big mistake."

"How so?" Lardis frowned. The Old Lidesci would give anything to know where the Necroscope had been and how he'd come by his knowledge, but it was sufficient that he had. And quite obviously Nathan wanted to get on; there were still things he would attend to this night.

"The Turgosheim army is—huge!" Nathan had to rely on what he'd learned from his wolves. "In order to fuel it through the night and coming day, Vormulac has decimated Wratha's supplicant tribes east of the pass."

"Just how . . . *huge* is the army?" Lardis was cautious.

"Hundreds strong," Nathan told him. "All of our hell-land weapons together won't nearly be enough."

Lardis's face fell further yet. "And Vormulac's error?"

"His gluttony!" Nathan answered with a shudder. "The rest of the tribes east of the pass will be scattered and in hiding by now. No more easy pickings for Vormulac—but he still has to feed his army!"

Ben Trask cut in: "So what's your plan?"

"First, to get those weapons all together," Nathan told him. "For which I'll need both you and David. You know exactly where you put those guns in that clump of boulders close to the Gate. Once we're finished talking, I'll go back and check that it's safe. And then . . ."

"We're with you," David Chung spoke up. "We can be in and out in a few moments."

Nathan nodded. "If the way is clear, yes. Then, I'll need Andrei and possibly Kirk. They know Sanctuary Rock better than anyone else. The Rock is still stable—I hope! I left a fair cache of weapons up there, on the dome of the Rock. Hopefully they suffered no damage when the Rock sank down on itself."

"That must have been a sight to see!" Lardis breathed. "I should have been there. Andrei has talked about it, but to have *seen* it . . . !"

And Trask said, "Andrei has also mentioned this, er, hell-lander you tangled with? From his description it could only be Turkur Tzonov."

And now Nathan's face was grimmer yet. "It could only *have been* him, yes," he answered.

Andrei's turn to speak up: "It was Canker! Kirk and me, we saw some of it. The dog-Lord's got him, aye."

But the Necroscope shook his head. "No, it was Canker

who took him, but it's a *Lady* who has him now. The Lady Siggi Dam!" He looked at Trask. "Knowing what Tzonov has done, and for all that I know he's evil, I couldn't have wished worse on him . . ."

But Lardis grunted, "An enemy is an enemy!" As always (or as he always appeared to be) the Old Lidesci was iron. "What's done is done . . . now we get on with what's still to *be* done."

And Nathan agreed with him. "The rest of tonight, when I have the weapons, we go to work on the Wamphyri. And again it will be me, Ben, David . . . and perhaps you, John Carling?" He nodded to indicate the caver. "That is, if you'd like to be in on it? I can only use men who are familiar with these weapons."

Now Chung frowned. "*We* . . . are going to attack the Wamphyri, right?"

"Hit and run," Nathan told him. "Guerilla warfare. I saw film of it at E-Branch HQ in London." He explained his intentions, and Trask excitedly said:

"That would work!"

"It would certainly confuse the hell out of them," Chung agreed.

"That's my intention, yes," Nathan said. "To confuse them—and also to *kill* the black-hearted bastards!" He showed his teeth. "As many as possible!" And then, more calmly, "For you see I . . . I gave my word to someone that I would kill a few of them for him at least. But the idea will be to use our weapons as sparingly yet effectively as possible."

"Very well." Trask nodded. "It's a plan of sorts, anyway. And it will certainly show these monsters that they're not invulnerable, or even safe from attack. In fact it will probably come as a hell of a shock to them! But suppose we get through the rest of the night intact—what then?"

"Tomorrow morning we . . . we practice a game," Nathan answered. "The Szgany Lidesci, all of us. A very special game."

"Oh?" Lardis grunted. "We'll have time for playing

games, will we? What, like children d'you mean? Hide and seek?"

"Exactly like that!" Nathan nodded. "Hide and seek, yes. So that when next the Wamphyri come hunting, they'll find nothing. Absolutely nothing!"

"Explain," Lardis demanded.

"I can't," Nathan answered. "Not without breaking a trust. And anyway, I don't know if my plan will be accepted . . . by certain others. But it may be, and so if the time should come, we must be ready; which is why in the morning we'll play this game of mine. Like children, yes. Like all the children, and for the children. And for the future of all of the Szgany, if they are to have a future . . ."

It was all beyond Lardis, but he didn't press it. Nathan was their one hope now, especially since Sanctuary Rock was no more, and so they must play it his way—including his mysterious "game."

Nathan looked at Trask and Chung. "How long to get ready?"

The two glanced at each other, and Trask said, "I suppose we're as ready as we'll ever be right now. Give us a moment to check our weapons, and—"

"No weapons." Nathan shook his head. "Not going out, anyway. But coming back . . . with any luck, you'll have a lot more than you can handle!"

Trask nodded, licked his lips and said, "Then we're ready when you are."

Nathan stood up, stepped away from the fire and glanced at the sky, the stars in their eternal wheel. And: "Give me a few moments," he said. Which was as long as it took him . . .

. . . To make a Möbius jump out onto the plain of boulders, close but not too close to the Gate, yet close enough that he felt its repulsion—a weird *deflection* even within the Möbius Continuum—which caused his exit door to warp and waver as he stepped through it onto Starside. And a moment more to clamber up onto a natural causeway of boulders and scan the land all about for the Wamphyri or their creatures.

Shielding his eyes against the near-distant glare of the Gate, he looked north and believed he saw . . . was that a manta shape, pulsing against the weave of the northern auroras? Perhaps, but if so it was at least a mile away, or even more. So much for eyesight. But there were other senses, too.

Nathan put out a telepathic probe and felt . . . something? 'No, nothing—not of the Wamphyri anyway—not nearby. He was edgy, that was all. But certainly the psychic aether was alive with their echoes, their afterimages, the slime-trails of their having been here, the taint of their existence. Faint thoughts reached him from far across the boulder plains . . . others from the mountains east of the pass, and . . . *again* that sensation of—of what? Held breath? Or was it simply him—Nathan himself—holding *his* breath?

He checked his location. He wasn't too far from the clump of boulders where Trask and Chung had taken refuge and stashed their weapons. Then, there had been an injured warrior to contend with. But no sign of that creature now.

He climbed back down from the rocks, ran halfway towards the clump, brought a halt and conjured a door. This time it was more stable, but still it trembled a little. Nathan decided to try a little experiment and turned the door in the direction of the Gate; its trembling increased and he could feel the Gate's resistance, the way it pushed at his door. It was like the nervous, fluttering activity of a small magnet with its like pole too close to the like pole of a large magnet; the big one would turn it around if it could, then suck it in! But if it couldn't turn it around it would simply repulse it, shoot it away like a bullet from a gun, into unknown places. In E-Branch HQ, Nathan had read the Keogh files. He knew that his father had done just that: conjured a door too close to the Perchorsk Gate, and been hurled into space! And he wondered:

If a door was big enough, strong enough, and the mind that made it was powerful enough—which would give way first, the metaphysical Möbius Continuum and the mind that controlled it, or the hyperspatial, transdimensional Gate?

Almost automatically, instinctively, he began to study the maths of the problem—until he realized what he was doing and knew that he didn't have the time for it, and that anyway there was no requirement. Then he collapsed his door and moved a few paces farther away from the Gate, where he paused to scan the sky again. The flyer was still there, but if anything the distance had increased. There was no danger that he could see, and so . . .

. . . He returned to the camp on Sunside, held his new door steady as he guided Trask and Chung inside, and so transferred them to Starside. There, when they'd recovered from their momentary disorientation, he led the way to the clump of boulders where all three men saw what had happened to Gorvi the Guile's warrior. Its awful debris was strewn across the uneven ground; bloodied, blue-grey chitin scales as big as dinner plates were scattered everywhere . . . gnawed cartilage . . . grooved, white-gleaming bone . . . and the churned, dark-stained earth. A great many creatures had disposed of the one, in a mighty and monstrous provisioning.

They walked among the remains of the thing, with the starlit silence of Starside pressing down on them—

—Until Trask whispered: "God, what a nightmarish place! Let's collect the guns and get *out* of here!"

"We must consider ourselves lucky," Nathan told him. "The guns might easily have been discovered. But even beast-minders would have kept well out of it while a frenzy such as *that* was in progress!"

Then, as the three approached the entrance gap into the clump—*something suddenly appeared there! Two of them!*

"Ben?"

Trask started and cried out; Chung, too; even the Necroscope felt his blood run cold—and in the next moment warm—as finally he recognized the voice, figure, and telepathic aura of Zek Föener, and understood what he'd sensed when last he was here, what or who it was that had held its psychic breath.

Zek Föener, and Ian Goodly.

She literally flew into Ben's arms; and the spindly, cadaverous precog wasn't far behind, first clutching Trask's hand, then grasping Chung to him in an entirely uncharacteristic hug. "Thank God!" Goodly piped. "Thank *God* it's you!"

Nathan was the only one to keep a level head. "The guns," he reminded them. "Get the weapons!" And while Trask and Chung entered the clump and reemerged, he gave Zek a hug and clasped hands with Goodly. Then—

—All four linked arms, holding tight to the Necroscope as he conjured a door, guided them through its invisible portal, and took them back to the Sunside camp . . .

Between them, Zek and Goodly told their story, how Gustav Turchin had let them use the Perchorsk Gate to come through into Starside. It had been Zek's intention to contact Nathan telepathically as soon as they emerged onto the plain of boulders, but the sight of a flyer in the alien sky of the vampire world had changed her mind; she hadn't dared use her mentalism until she could be sure that the Necroscope alone would hear her.

And as the flyer had passed overhead, heading out across the boulder plains, Zek and the precog had taken refuge in the nest of leaning boulders—where they had stumbled across Ben Trask's cache of weapons. At that they had known that if Nathan lived he must return here sooner or later, but they'd scarcely expected it to be so soon.

Also, and where weapons were concerned, there was now a new cache that Nathan would have to recover at some time in the future. For Zek and Goodly had come through the "white tunnel" from Perchorsk aboard a battery-powered cart or buggy, one of three that Perchorsk's scientists used to trundle heavy instruments from place to place around the core; still aboard were two Russian-built machine pistols and a small wooden box of one hundred and twenty golf ball-size grenades. Buggy and weapons had come courtesy of Gustav Turchin.

The location of the cache: *inside* the Starside Gate! Zek and Goodly had dismounted well within the tunnel, and had left the cart in neutral at the other end of a length of nylon rope whose last six inches protruded from the hemisphere of white light. They had done this because Goodly's talent had foreseen some small problem on the boulder plains: the lone flyer that both Nathan and the newcomers had seen in the aurora-shot distance. And so as soon as Nathan wanted to do it, he could take someone back there to the Gate, haul the cart through, and recover the weapons.

But something was obviously puzzling him, and now he gave it voice. "We've always known that the Gates were one-way systems," he said, "but now we know something else about them."

"Oh?" Trask waited for him to continue.

Nathan nodded. "Obviously they *can* be used more than once, but only in the same direction! Zek has been through the Perchorsk Gate twice."

"Absolutely right!" Zek put in excitedly. "For a while we thought that Ian might have to come through on his own, or maybe with other espers from E-Branch. But Ian's a precog, and he had seen *both* of us coming through from Perchorsk! As soon as we got out there from London, I knew he was correct; close up, I could actually *feel* the pull of that white monster; no repulsion whatsoever. It seems it was something that Harry himself didn't know: that while you can't *return* through the same Gate, you *can* use that Gate more than once. It's like the circulatory system of the heart, with one-way valves to stop blood flowing downhill between beats. The blood circulates time and time over but can't back up on itself. So if I wanted to, I could use the lower Starside Gate to go to Romania, and the Perchorsk Gate to come through into Starside, over and over again!"

"But," said Trask, looking thoughtful, "doesn't that mean that if you had used *both* Gates to get here, you'd probably be stuck here forever? Zek Föener, are you trying to tell me that you were willing to consider that risk?"

She hugged his arm. "Not really, Ben. Remember, the Romanian Gate is temporarily out of action; we couldn't have used it anyway. So I suppose what I'm telling you is that I trust Ian's talent, and that he hadn't foreseen that kind of disaster ..."

"Then what kind of disaster has he foreseen?" Trask glanced at Goodly.

The precog shrugged, looked uncomfortable. "I've only covered what had to be covered," he piped. "I've never trusted the future and don't intend to start now. Don't ask me to look, Ben—and especially not in *this* place! But when I'm needed, then you'll know you can rely on me."

Trask continued to look thoughtful. "So ... that time when Harry Keogh used the Gate at Perchorsk to escape from us—or rather, when he removed his potential plague from our world—in fact he could have used the Romanian Gate a second time?"

"Yes," Zek told him.

Trask nodded, and said, "Then I think perhaps he did know about it. But he was Wamphyri, and he was just cussed enough to want to do it his way, despite—or because of—all the odds against him. To go out in a blaze of glory on a big, motorcycle, shouting 'to hell with you' at the whole damn world!"

And: *"Huh!"* Lardis Lidesci grunted, appreciatively. "That sounds exactly like Harry Hell-lander to me!"

"I'll tell you what *really* sounds like him," Trask continued. "If Harry did know about the Gates, if he suspected deep down inside, with that intuitive grasp of his, then what he did—to use both Gates, and so get himself stuck here—would be the perfect way to ensure that he could never bring the plague of vampirism back into our Earth. That would be *exactly* Harry's kind of sacrifice ..."

After a moment Goodly said, "Was that how the Dweller did it, do you think? Came and went between here and our world on a regular basis?"

"No." Nathan shook his head. "The Dweller found Sunside/Starside—came here, lived here—before the Perchorsk Gate came into being. The Dweller was very special, that's all. In the Möbius Continuum, he . . . he knew the *directions* of places, even of parallel universes."

He looked at Zek and Goodly, and almost accusingly asked: "Why did you come? It could cause—I don't know—complications?"

Goodly explained why, and there were several reasons. For one, he had "seen" that they would come. Two, they'd desired to use their knowledge and talents in the fight against the Wamphyri. Also, they'd come to bring their weapons—and a warning: that Turchin would close Perchorsk permanently in just two and a half to three Sunside days' time. And finally a second warning, different but no less important—certainly no less ominous—that Geoffrey Paxton had followed Nathan and the others through into Sunside/Starside, where he planned to regain his "stolen" telepathy.

"Except it's the *way* we think he'll try to get it back," Goodly gloomed. "For you see, we didn't tell Turchin our worst fear: that perhaps Paxton desires to *be* Wamphyri!" He shrugged helplessly. "But that's what we're obliged to believe. We had an empath go over Paxton's place, get a picture of his psychological profile. And quite simply, Paxton is Keogh crazy! In a way he hates the very thought of Harry, and anything or anyone to do with him, for what Harry did to him; but in another way he loves the idea of the Necroscope's power. Harry Keogh was a telepath, a teleport, finally a vampire. Paxton will try to do it in reverse: become a vampire, regain his telepathy, use Nathan to discover the Möbius Continuum. It's his obsession . . ."

"Power-mad!" Trask nodded. "He always was, right from the start. And that's *before* he's Wamphyri! Just think of it: if he actually got those things he craves, and then took them back to our world, Earth would have a scarlet emperor! And God help us, but if that's what he wants, he can certainly find it here!"

"He's a madman," Nathan summed it up. "You just don't get to be a Lord of the Wamphyri as easily as that. But it's a very simple thing to get drained, eaten, enthralled, or changed utterly into . . . something else. Anyway, let's forget him for now. There's still a lot to be done and time is wasting."

Then he quickly went on to detail most of what had transpired during the course of just one night, since his return to the vampire world. He finished with Turkur Tzonov, how the Russian esper had been taken by Canker Canison and Siggi Dam, and concluded: "I think we can safely say that Tzonov is no longer a problem. For all that he's an evil, resourceful man, there's no coming back from where he is now. I was privy to something of what Siggi was thinking when Canker snatched him. Frankly, I wish I hadn't been . . ." And after a moment's silence:

"As for Paxton, we'll face that problem when/if it comes up. But nothing else has changed, except we now have two extra 'weapons' to add to our list. I mean Zek and Ian, of course."

"And now?" Lardis Lidesci was finally over the fact that Zek Föener was here again, back in the vampire world. Later he would introduce her to Lissa, and if it wasn't too painful they might even talk about Jazz, the Dweller, Harry Hell-lander, the old times . . . but all of that must wait until sunup. For there was still work to be done tonight.

"Now?" The Necroscope Nathan Keogh was looking at Lardis in that new, grim way of his. Looking at him and agreeing with him: "Now we carry on with what we were doing."

After that: a trip to the dome of Sanctuary Rock with Kirk and Andrei, to collect the remainder of the hell-land weapons, and finally it was time to wage war.

Long ago in the half-mythical, crimson history of Sunside/Starside, the Lords of the Wamphyri had christened their interaerie feuds "bloodwars"; now Nathan intended to give that word new meaning. Except he would not be taking and using blood but spilling it, wasting it. The blood of vampires: Wamphyri blood!

First, however, there were those he must speak to, and to him it was like going to church to offer up a prayer. Except of course he had no church but only a private shrine with a secret door. The legend carved upon that door was "deadspeak," and the Necroscope held the one and only key. But knowing how the Great Majority value their privacy, he took the Möbius route out into the desert and chose a lonely place under the stars, where any intercourse with the dead would not be disturbed by the tumult of the living.

And where before, indeed for all of his young life, Nathan had been shunned by the teeming dead, at last he found them to be his wholehearted allies. For recently one had come among them who would have it no other way. And Nana Kiklu had always been—and in death as in life would *continue* to be—a force to be reckoned with. When Nana's voice had been added to those of her son's friends among the dead, and when she had argued on his behalf, then any last trace of opposition had finally crumbled away.

Now the dead could talk to him, and he could ask them for their blessing on the bloodwars to come. He wanted nothing more for now, but that they think it over and seek in their memories—even their racial memories—for anything that might be of assistance in the crusade against the Wamphyri. For the Necroscope knew that all of Sunside/Starside's knowledge lay buried in the ground or blowing in the wind, dust to dust or ashes to ashes, and that the soil and the sky knew all that had been.

And of course there were those who would speak to him at once—urgently, now!—whom he could only thank and promise that he would indeed speak to them as soon as possible, but for the moment must use his resources, especially his time, to best advantage. For the nighttime had always belonged to the Wamphyri, and now he intended to take it back from them!

How many times—on how many nights of terror—had that warning cry rung out in the camps of Sunside's Szgany: "Wamphyri! *Wamphyri!*" A cry of warning, aye, but also the battle cry of the vampires themselves; except to call it a "battle cry" was to glorify it, where in fact there'd been no glory in it at all. A cry of slaughter, more like. Battles? Oh, there had been a few, but in the main—at least until the Old Lidesci's time—the only course of survival had been flight. And so, one way or the other, tonight would be a night to remember. For the Szgany and the Wamphyri both. A night when the Travellers did *not* flee but came, killed, melted away, and came again!

The Great Majority were taken with Nathan's vision. And in their way they cheered him on. He got their blessing and their deadspeak promise both: that if the time came when he required their assistance, then he need only ask. . . .

It was everything that he'd wanted, and with that Nathan would have taken his leave of them; but still there were those among them who insisted that he listen to them if only briefly. Jasef Karis was one; there was that which he must speak of—a secret out of the past, and perhaps important. But Jasef understood Nathan's eagerness to be off on his mission to claim back a little of the enormous debt owed by the Wamphyri. And so his scrap of secret knowledge must keep for now, even as he'd kept it for all of seventeen long years.

Then there was the Thyre ancient, Thikkoul the Stargazer. If only Nathan would take him out again under the stars—if only he could *see* the stars again through the eyes of the Necroscope—Thikkoul felt sure that the future could be made to reveal itself and Nathan would know the way to go. Except both of them (and the precog Ian Goodly, too) knew that the future isn't like that. Immutable as the past, it may not be changed or even tampered with, but will be as it will be. And the *way* it will be is best left unknown. For as had been proved time and time again, tomorrow is a devious place . . .

After Thikkoul, the leper Uruk Piatra had spoken to Nathan; but this time the Necroscope had been especially attentive. Uruk's burned, crumbling shell of a body still lay unburied on the sandy mound where the Old Lidesci had left it; but because Uruk had a plan, the teeming dead ignored the miles between in order to introduce him to Nathan. And the leper's plan was simple. Once, not so long ago, he'd tried to use the disease that plagued the people of his colony as a weapon against the Wamphyri. Now he would do it again: a matter of personal sacrifice, but one whose cause was just. And because Uruk would brook no argument, in the end Nathan could only bow to his wishes. It would be as the leper wished it.

And finally there was a new deadspeak voice; but previously unheard, it was a voice so dour, melancholy, and doom-fraught that it hushed all the others to silence in a moment. Its timbre, texture, and evil resonance were such that the Necroscope could not mistake their source, neither Nathan nor the Great Majority with him. Which was why they had fallen silent. For this was the voice of a vampire—indeed, Wamphyri!

Nathan would not talk to him, not in this place where he had spoken to the decently dead and gone, but yet felt that he *should* speak to him, if only to know what was on the monster's mind. To that end he excused himself and followed the voice to its source, the place where its owner had died . . .

. . . In a firepit at Sanctuary Rock!

Necroscope . . . (Vormulac's voice was even more mournful than it had been in life: like the moaning of the wind into which his smoke had passed.) *I learned of you through the dead, who did not deign to speak to me.* Hah! *I eavesdropped on them anyway, and discovered their deadspeak whispers to be full of the Necroscope, Nathan Keogh: a man who talks to the dead. Even to Vormulac Taintspore, called Unsleep—who once was undead but now is truly dead, and sleeps only too well! Of secret skills and talents, I thought I'd seen them all. But this . . . is something new. A man who brings comfort to crumbling bones in rotting shrouds and lifeless dust in old clay bottles—even to an ancient, evil thing like me!*

"I'm not here to comfort you, Vormulac," Nathan told him. "Indeed I would not be here at all, except you said you wanted revenge on your own kind, the Wamphyri, and especially on that one called Devetaki Skullguise, a Lady. Well, and so do I want revenge on the Wamphyri—for all the Szgany they ever killed or changed, and forever! In fact I desire to destroy them all! So any advice or knowledge you impart that gives me an advantage . . . it will be more than welcome. Even though you yourself are not."

Nathan . . . said the other thoughtfully. *And you speak without fear, as if you were used to conversing with one such as I. Not merely a dead man, but a vampire Lord. Hmmm—Nathan! Now say, have I not heard that name before? Can you use your deadspeak, perhaps, to show yourself to me?*

The Necroscope saw no harm in it, and so showed himself to Vormulac, "I am that one, yes," he said, "who was the seer-Lord Maglore's so-called familiar in Runemanse."

Ah! Vormulac responded. *I remember: you stole a flyer and fled back into Sunside . . . or west, as it now appears. And you are the Necroscope, eh?* (A grim chuckle.) *But it would break old Maglore's black heart to know what he let slip through his fingers! Even if I had not remembered you, still I would know you from the ring in your ear: Maglore's sigil. Why, I myself wore just such a twisted loop, which the Seer-Lord gave to me in friendship.*

At which Nathan gave a start, for he remembered something that David Chung had said to him. And: "I ask a favour of you," he said, in the next moment.

What, you ask a boon of me?

"You desired to speak to me, didn't you?"

Indeed I did: ask away!

"I showed myself to you—now show yourself to me." Vormulac did as requested, and Nathan saw the very duplicate of his earring in the lobe of the dead vampire's conchlike ear!

That makes twice you've started, Necroscope, Lord Unsleep pointed out, curiously. *Now say, what is it that concerns you?*

"Only that he's made fools of both of us," Nathan answered grimly.

He? Maglore?

"The same. That's not merely the Seer-Lord's sigil but his shewstone—which we have worn like fools only inches from the cores of our brains! What we have seen, so has Maglore. What we have thought, he was privy to."

But to what end? In order to watch over us, and know what is become?

"That's one way to put it, yes," Nathan answered. "But far more to the point: to spy on us, and know our every move. He is Wamphyri after all, and so no better or worse than any of you."

For long moments Vormulac's deadspeak presence—his Wamphyri aura—was gloomier than ever. Then: *Hah! And I left him to his own devices in Turgosheim. An error, as it would seem. I see it all now: by now the gorge entire belongs to Maglore! And his sigil no good luck piece but a traitor to sit in my ear and listen to my thoughts! Upon my return—if I returned—that wily old rune-mage would know my every move and counter it with maximum efficiency! Bah! Is there nothing of honour?*

At which Nathan gave a snort of his own. "What, are you playing word games with me, Vormulac? A Lord of the Wamphyri asking a question like that? Honour, indeed! And yet I promise you this: Maglore wields a two-edged sword."

Eh? How so?

"Because he's not the only mentalist in Starside, that's how so. Would you see the shape of Turgosheim now?"

Because deadspeak often conveys more than is said, Vormulac knew his meaning. *Indeed I would!*

"So be it . . ."

And Nathan concentrated on the warped shape of the loop of gold in his ear, and hurled a telepathic probe east . . . far to the east . . . across all of Starside and the Great Red Waste . . . to Turgosheim at the end of the world. And:

"Maglore in his apartments in promontory Runemanse," Nathan whispered. "Secure in his triumph and open in his thoughts, for who remains to spy on them now? No one, for Lord Taintspore and his generals are off on a mighty crusade against Wratha the Risen in the west. The Seer-Lord gazes out from his window. And you're right, Vormulac: Turgosheim is his entirely! Maglore the Mage is master now! *He* commands! His forces are taking all of the great aeries, spires, and manses. His sigil flutters everywhere, from the walls of the lowliest hovel in the bed of the gorge, even to the frowning heights of melancholy—"

No!

"—Vormspire itself, yes! As for Masquemanse: Devetaki's place is now a vast scar on the face of the gorge. Maglore has settled a few old scores with her, be sure!"

Little I care for that, Vormulac grunted. *Indeed I welcome the news; it is something to thank the Seer-Lord for, at least! But Vormspire! Ah, Vormspire . . . !* And angrily: *Do you seek deliberately to torment me, Necroscope?*

"Yes," Nathan said again, without hesitation.

How do I know you're not lying? Obviously Maglore instructed you well. Why, I believe you could play word games with the best of us! How is it that you read him so well, and over such a distance, while he reads nothing of you?

"I was his one great failure," the Necroscope answered. "My mentalism was better than his. It was ever the same, even in Runemanse. He would attempt to read my mind, only to have me read his! He read my dreams instead, but found little of use in them. I hid my telepathy from him, and my deadspeak hid itself. If Maglore had once suspected my talents, he would never have let me go."

He "let" you go?

Nathan nodded. "As I now realize. To be his shewstone in the west—even as you have been his shewstone!"

If only I could live again, Vormulac moaned then. *Ah, to know what I know now, and live again! Devetaki Skullguise, the so-called virgin grandam . . . I would line up my lads to have her one by one. I'd melt her leaden masks and pour the liquid down her lying throat! Virgin?*

I would know where to drive the longest stake of all—and let her writhe upright on an ironwood prick, and steam to a stain as the sun rose over Sunside! And as for Maglore: I would drench him in oil, weight him with stones, and hurl him from Turgosheim's rim—and set a torch to him, to light his shrieking descent! But alas . . .

The fury went out of his voice in a moment, which sobbed now, and moaned as before:

. . . My life is done, and all hope of revenge dead with me.

"Not necessarily," Nathan told him. "You asked me to come here for a reason, but I cannot linger for time is wasting. So now advise me however you will, or say nothing ever again. But *which*ever you do, do it quickly."

You'll help me to redress what was done to me . . . help me take my revenge—even from beyond the grave?

"No, Lord Taintspore—*my* revenge, not yours. But if you can find pleasure in that . . . ?"

I suppose it must suffice. Very well, listen:

Devetaki is treacherous. I've given it some thought. It must be her plan to murder all of my generals one by one, and so command my army out of Turgosheim.

"That sounds like a good plan to me."

Are you always so cold? Is there no humour in you?

"This from you? Your very deadspeak is ice! Maglore told me about you: even Vormspire was a living tomb, a mausoleum to a lost love. And if you lived as long again, do you suppose it would change you? In Turgosheim you were a great shroud covering the gorge with your misery. So don't call me cold. Anyway, what you've told me so far is useless to me."

Not if you tell it over again, to those generals whom the Lady would destroy! (There was sinister cunning, typical of all the Wamphyri, in Vormulac's voice now.) *For then they'd turn on her at once!*

"Tell it to them? How? It's dangerous enough to play word games with the *dead* of the Wamphyri—such as yourself—but utterly impossible with the living or the undead! I was fortunate that time, with Maglore. What do you suggest: that I seek audience with these leaderless Lords, to inform them of Devetaki's treachery?" His deadspeak voice dripped sarcasm.

Audience? Vormulac grunted. *No, scarcely that! Oh, they'd see you, all right—and eat your heart before you uttered a word! But you are a* mentalist, *Necroscope! And there's something of that in all of them. . . .*

It was an idea at least: to use his telepathy to create dissension and cause insurgency in the ranks of the Wamphyri. To get them fighting each other, even as they now fought with the last aerie—which, since war and territorialism were in any case second nature to them, shouldn't be too hard. Nathan gave it a moment's thought, then nodded grimly. "Perhaps I'll be able to work something out after all. So what else do you suggest?"

Vormulac's deadspeak shrug: *Let me think.* And after a moment: *Do you know that Devetaki used weird weapons to kill me? Are you aware of their source?*

"Are you?" Nathan countered.

A force of strange and powerful Szgany—or perhaps not Szgany, but men anyway—in the keep in the great pass. Devetaki has already used one such man and weapon . . . against me*! To destroy* me*! And I fancy that she'll try to take and use the others, too.*

"I know about these strange men," Nathan answered. "Also about their weapons. But I have weapons of my own. Now that the strangers are without leaders, I may be able to sway them to my side. Come dawn they'll head for Sunside, where I shall be waiting to meet them."

Oh? But you're careless with your plans, Necroscope! Does it not trouble you that I know them?

Nathan's cold smile. "And who will you tell them to? You have no friends or allies now, Vormulac. You have nothing and no one—except me. And when our business is done, you won't even have that. For I have better things to do than waste my time with such as you."

Then be about your work, for I am done with you. Let me simply wish you luck, and get yourself gone!

But Nathan shook his head. He'd give no jot of satisfaction to a vampire, nor accept any offer of alleged friendship. "It's not that you wish me luck," he said, "but that you wish evil on all of them who have survived you! You see me as the Great Destroyer that you wish you still were. Worse, you hope that when my work is done, I shall be destroyed, too."

He was right, but Vormulac was finished and would say no more. Nevertheless, before Nathan returned to Lardis's camp he thought to hear one last sigh from the deadspeak aether. It was Lord Unsleep, his final "sentiment":

That perhaps now he really *would* sleep, but he hoped that he wouldn't dream . . .

PART SEVEN:

SETTLING SCORES—
FURTHER
SKIRMISHES—
DREAMS AND DOOMS

I

Nathan's Guerillas—
Seeds of Suspicion

When Lardis Lidesci saw the Necroscope walk out onto the savanna where Uruk Piatra lay wrapped in his blanket, he followed after him and caught up as the youth took up the lifeless body into his arms. And after Nathan had explained:

"But ... is this what Uruk wants?" Even the hardened Lardis was shocked by the Necroscope's explanation.

"It will be no bad thing," Nathan answered, "to know that in life he was helpless, but in death a deadly weapon. It's the way of the dead, Lardis. What they did in life they continue to do after death, albeit to no effect. Except through me there *is* an effect. And Uruk wanted to see the Wamphyri Lords destroyed! For you and the Lidescis, Lardis, who all these years have provided for Uruk and his people in their sickness and seclusion, and for every Traveller everywhere. It *is* what he wants, yes."

"You're certain?"

Nathan sighed. "I have spoken to him, and him to me. Uruk wants to do this for the reasons I've given, and I want to be his instrument in this sacrifice ... for my own reasons."

"Because a Kiklu did this thing?" Lardis knew how Nathan was torn; and yet again he was reminded that this was no ordinary man, but the son of the Necroscope, Harry Keogh. Which was why he stood back, and said, "Then speak to Uruk again, for me, and tell him I never knew the better man, leper or no." In any other world this might seem a very dubious compliment, but not here.

Nathan did as Lardis asked, however silently, then carried Uruk with him through a Möbius door . . .

. . . And out again onto the boulder plains halfway to the last aerie: dark and dreadful Wrathstack glooming there, some miles away, in blue-litten starlight, silhouetted against its eerie backdrop of a writhing auroral curtain. And:

Are we there? Uruk inquired.

"No, but I know the way," Nathan told him. "For I've been here before, with Lardis on his treks. He used to come here in the old times, the good times."

There'll be good times again.

"I pray you are right. But let me look and listen. There may be vampires here: watchers from the army out of the east."

The Necroscope put out probes from his metaphysical mind and at once sensed Siggi Dam and others, in Wrathstack . . . and more vampires on the plain of boulders, hiding there, but none in the immediate vicinity. He made a second Möbius jump, this time to a cluster of ruins, the stump of a toppled aerie, only a mile from the broad base of Wrathstack.

Again his probe went out, and discovered . . . one of Gorvi the Guile's ground warriors, and a lieutenant, and a handful of thralls, deep down in the ruin's basement! An ambush for Devetaki's army (for surely by now the Lady was in command), should any of its elements venture this way. He couldn't linger, not here.

Nathan knew the layout of a stack. The design of all the aeries would be much the same, here as in Turgosheim. But even a simpleton would know that the only possible place for a well is in the earth, in the very bowels of the stack—Gorvi the Guile's domain. Except . . . where exactly? No good to materialize in darkness, or a place of deadly danger.

He mentioned the problem to Uruk, and of course his deadspeak went out across all of Starside—and was heard.

Nathaaan . . .

And the Necroscope gasped, for he would know that sighing deadspeak voice immediately, anywhere, despite the fact that three and a half years had passed since the last time he saw its owner, on the night of Wratha's initial attack on Settlement. Jason Lidesci, Lardis's son, with whom Nathan had grown up!

"Jason," he said. "Where are you?"

Close, but we've been closer. I would have spoken before, but to what good end? Now is different, for at least I can give you some advice. My body rests in a crevice in the earth, where Gorvi put me one night after I . . . after I had spoken with your brother, Nestor, who is now beyond redemption! I'm down in the earth, Nathan—where I belong, as all vampire things belong—slowly stiffening to a stone among stones, aye. But don't feel sorry for me, for I am glad that I'm here now. Better here than in Guilesump! The place is not far from the Starside Gate, but do not seek me out. I'm one with the dark and the cold and the earth.

"Jason, I . . ." But there was nothing, no words, to express the way the Necroscope felt. Since deadspeak conveys more than is said, however, it was in any case unnecessary.

Hush, said the other, *and listen:*

Upon a time I was Gorvi's man, but for a thrall I was rebellious. To punish me, he put me to work tending the wells. No man knows the guts of Guilesump better than I do. Now look upon my mind, and see the secrets of the sump!

Nathan looked, saw, and felt horror creep again upon his spine, even as it had crept in promontory Runemanse. Except the Seer-Lord Maglore's Runemanse had known something of light, at least, while the nether pits of Guilesump were entirely lightless. It made no difference; Nathan saw with a vampire's eyes—the dead eyes but living memory of Jason Lidesci . . .

. . . Saw the siphon-tubes, hollow bones like pipes, descending from the low ceiling to the dark water, letting down the jellylike veins they contained—*human* veins, the Necroscope knew, of some monstrously metamorphosed siphoneer high overhead in Wrathspire's attic—into the water to soak it up. He saw the mindless swimmers: flat and fan-shaped, like lichen spores grown huge, their countless cilia flickering to propel them through the water, cleansing it of microbes, scum, dust, fallen spider- and fly-specks, and foulness in general.

And he saw the ledges where once Jason had worked, removing cobwebs, sweeping dust, and scraping slimy cavern growths from walls and ceilings. But the last aerie was under siege and there were no thralls here now; Gorvi had other work for them.

"Perfect!" he said, and took the coordinates direct from Jason's mind. And because he could feel the stirring of thralls and monsters in the roots of the fallen aerie whose ruins gave him shelter, he lingered no longer but conjured a Möbius door into Wrathstack—

—Into the subterranean cave of Gorvi the Guile's wells. And without pause, despite the fact that he was blind here, he knew precisely where to spill Uruk Piatra's corpse into the dark water! After that, a moment to say his farewell, conjure another door, and return to Sunside . . . where Trask and Chung waited for him.

Nathan had been right: Devetaki Skullguise now commanded Vormulac Taintspore's army out of Turgosheim. In gloomy trog caverns at the eastern tip of the barrier mountains, Black Boris was the only Lord who was not aware that Lord Unsleep slept at last, neither him nor a handful of watchers out on the boulder plains; but the rest of them knew. That Vormulac had lived and died a true warrior, in a massive battle with a savage Szgany tribe west of the great pass. He'd killed fifty before he himself was overwhelmed, staked and beheaded (according to Devetaki's story), and even then the liveliness within him was not finished; there'd never been such an *eruption* of evil as when Vormulac went up in flames!

But as finally the Szgany savages were driven off, Vormulac's last message had passed from his mind into Devetaki's: his plea that she take command of his army and tame these terrible heathen regions. Thus he had given this great task, and the taking of the last aerie, into her hands.

And after all, it was only right. For by now hers was the greatest of all the contingents, consisting of her own forces, and Lord Wamus's, which she'd commandeered, and now Vormulac's otherwise leaderless force, which had been a small army in its own right. So the vampire Lords (*and* the Ladies, for there was still Zindevar Cronesap, Ursula Torspawn, and one or two others to contend with) had finally succumbed to the virgin grandam's leadership.

Zindevar was with her now, and Devetaki had just this moment finished explaining to that Lady her plan: a female conspiracy, to remove all power from the Lords and rule as a matriarchy! The Ladies would have it their way for once . . . and for always! Ursula Torspawn might perhaps rule in Turgosheim (which was after all a piddling place); Zindevar could choose between eastern Sunside/ Starside, from the trog caverns in the east to the great pass, or the as yet mainly unexplored territory west of the pass; Devetaki would be happy to take the other half.

"You have no preference?" Things had swung around so rapidly that Zindevar was still suspicious.

"The land is vast." Devetaki shrugged. "But who knows, in a hundred years' time we might argue over it. It will take that long at least to explore and tame it!"

Zindevar saw the logic of that and laughed—and was serious in a moment. "Devetaki, you have a deal. But some of these men may prove hard nuts to crack. However, and since it appears you've already cracked the hardest . . ." And gazing at the virgin grandam, Zindevar's eyes were hooded.

Devetaki ignored the remark, apparently—but putting on her frowning mask she looked out across Starside. "I can smell morning," she said. "Oh, sunup is way off as yet, but it's coming. And there's work for you tomorrow."

"Eh, for me?"

"For you and yours, aye." Devetaki looked at her. "There are men in the pass with strange weapons. They are a superior breed of Szgany, who were exploring Starside when we came from the east. Knowing that we would pick them off in the open, they took refuge in an ancient keep in the pass. Vormulac gave Wamus the task of clearing them out, but the bat-Lord failed and paid the price. Him and his bloodsons with him."

Now Zindevar's suspicions ran rampant. "Oh? And is it that I should pay the price, too?"

"Not a bit of it. I took one of these men prisoner, and so know their plans. Come sunup they'll head south for Sunside and safety. Ah, but the pass is as a dogleg! This side is darkness and that side is light. You'll ambush them there, take them for your own, grow mighty with their weapons."

Zindevar was astonished. "You do this for me? Why not take the men, their weapons, the pass for yourself?"

"This is the sign of our pact," said Devetaki. "I make it willingly, so that you can see I'm genuine. Now listen: there are only a handful of these men, but their weapons are mighty. However, a crafty ambush should do the job, and there are none so crafty as Zindevar of Cronespire. What's more, when you take them you take the pass itself: from that time forward it shall be 'Zindevar's Pass,' and the keep shall be 'Croneskeep'!"

"You . . . would make me strong!" Zindevar's gasp said much for her mixed emotions.

"But exactly!" said Devetaki. "How can we hope to hold a world if we're weak? Where's the profit in a weak alliance?"

While in her secret mind:

Whichever way it goes, you and yours will be reduced in the fighting. I shall see to that. Nor is your contingent the strongest by any means—what? A handful of hairy women lieutenants and a bunch of cringing eunuchs? I'll

*be waiting as you come out of the pass, when you are at
your weakest.*

Zindevar heard none of this; she saw only that Devetaki
had removed her frowning mask, replacing it with the one
that smiled . . .

Having eaten and rested awhile, Nathan, Trask, and Chung
were ready and armed. Dressed in typical Szgany garb—
dark browns, greens, but mainly greys, to blend with the
volcanic colours of the mountains, their shadowy crags
and slopes—and with their cheeks, foreheads, hands
daubed in the stain of plants and soot of fires, they appeared as desperate a trio as Lardis ever saw.

Looking at the Necroscope's guerillas from some short
distance away, the Old Lidesci folded his hands over his
chest and thought: *Aye, best look out all you Lords and
Ladies, for here comes hell!*

All of Lardis's people knew about the Necroscope's
weird powers now, and most of them were there to see the
heroes off. They formed a silent ring about a central fire,
but stood well back, allowing plenty of room, so that when
Nathan formed his Möbius door it would not suck them in.
This was a fable spread by Lardis to allow the Necroscope
his privacy. Too many people were aware of him, wanted
to talk to him, touch him. The saviour of the Szgany, possibly; he was definitely becoming a legend among Lardis's
people, no less than he was among the Thyre.

Nathan stood with head down, eyes closed, in conversation with Grinner. East of the pass, Dock's survivors kept
watch on the Wamphyri. Grinner had joined them; in the
last seven hours he had crossed the pass, climbed into
the heights, taken temporary command: a massive effort.
The army out of the east had settled in now; sunup was
less than twenty hours away; apart from a handful of ma-
rauders from various contingents, who had gone down into
the east of Sunside to forage for flesh in the forests, the
main body of vampire invaders was here.

Through Grinner, Nathan had passed on his requirements to Dock's vengeful grey brothers; noting his needs,

they'd chosen various vantage points; Grinner passed the coordinates, which entered Nathan's metaphysical mind clear as a picture, so that he knew he could home in on them with the directional instinct of . . . why, of a wolf, of course! And:

"Ready!" he said at last.

As he formed his door, Trask and Chung moved closer, formed a triangle with him. Then the darkness, weightlessness, and even temperature of the Continuum, and a moment later the cold and starlit heights over Starside!

Simultaneously, Trask and Chung drew breath in twin gasps, aimed their weapon. But the Necroscope at once cautioned them: "No!" Trask, however, had already blocked Chung's aim with his own body; he'd read the "truth" of the situation, that this was an ally.

For there on a bluff high over Starside, it was only the "evil" visage of Grinner who greeted them. And silently, whiningly, with his head cocked on one side and fangs showing, the "wild" wolf passed on more details of the vampire encampments to his blood-uncle, Nathan Keogh.

The party farthest to the east . . . camped under a slope of sliding shale . . . only a handful of pines, and an outcropping boulder or two, protect them from a mighty avalanche! If you and your strange new weapons were able to bring down Sanctuary Rock, you'll have no trouble causing havoc there! Also, the Lord who killed Dock . . . that one is located behind a fall in the frozen lava river, where he will keep his men and creatures from the dawn's sunlight. But we have discovered a blowhole into which you can pour your liquid fire from above. Marvelously intelligent, Grinner had read the nature of Nathan's weapons right out of his mind!

Nodding grimly, the Necroscope noted the coordinates of an ancient fumarole over a lava cliff; and in the caves below (according to Grinner's information), a large body of men and monsters. Smiling however coldly, Nathan glanced at the compact flamethrower slung over David Chung's shoulder . . .

"Anything else?" (He was aware of startled glances

passing between Trask and Chung, as he spoke to his "nephew.")

Not for now. In and out, Uncle! Do not overstretch yourself. These are vampires and react with speed! That was Dock's mistake, and we have lost enough of kin ... Good advice—especially from a wily wolf!

Nathan explained the task to his colleagues, then said: "First the avalanche. Grenades, I think. We simply roll them down the slope. I'll drop you off first, Ben, then David, and take my own position at the end of the line. Spaced out fifty yards apart, that will make a line one hundred yards long. And everything beneath us will be swept down onto Starside's foothills. Let Devetaki Skullguise pick the bones out of that!"

The Necroscope's phrasing was perhaps unfortunate, Trask thought; it seemed to him not at all unlikely that indeed the Lady *would* pick the bones out of that! Nor would she let the meat go to waste ...

"Afterwards," Nathan continued, "I'll pick you up and we move to location number two." He explained what was required.

And without further ado, they made the jump—

—And emerged at Grinner's precise coordinates. Above them, the gaunt grey crags, escarpments, peaks; solid ground, all of it. But below them, exactly as Grinner had foretold: a steep surface of sliding shale, built up over many years, and only held back from sweeping down onto Starside by a narrow band of pines, a compacted scree barrier, and jagged outcrops that were the volcanic stuff of the mountains themselves.

And beneath that—in a thicker band of trees and under the protective cover of shallow ledges—the movements of men and beasts ... the mewling of complaining warriors ... a flyer launching even now ... the starlit glint of armour!

Nathan dropped off Trask, then Chung, made another jump and looked back—and signalled!

As their pins were pulled, the grenades made a triple ch-*ching*, almost but not quite an innocent sound in the still of the Starside night. And drawn by gravity, the deadly eggs were lobbed, and went bouncing downhill as the Necroscope collected Chung, and paused at Trask's location to watch the outcome—which was devastating!

The first two grenades went off almost together right in the mass of compacted scree, and a split second later the third exploded just beyond the precarious barrier. Not only the concussion of the triple blasts but also their reverberating detonations rang out and echoed back to shake the mountainside, and the entire surface of the slope immediately beneath the three men at once began to move!

They scrambled hurriedly backwards, away from the sliding ground to the solid rock above, where they sat with jaws hanging open, very nearly appalled by what they had done.

The mountain commence rumbling! Fifty yards west and a hundred and fifty east, the mountainside was on the move! The scree barrier caved in before a wave of cascading rocks, dirt, and shale, and the line of scraggy trees was uprooted without pause or mercy! The piled debris of the heights, undisturbed for decades by anything louder than the mournful howling of a wolf or the pull of an eccentric moon, now found itself stampeded by an uproar manufactured in another world!

Avalanche! And it was all (or even better, or worse) that the Necroscope had hoped it would be. It wiped the side of the mountain clean, right down to solid bedrock. The stand of pines stood no more but was swept away; the vampire encampment ceased to be, was caught up, rolled under, hurled down, and buried. Men and beasts uttered startled cries, but only a few found time to scream, mewl, or rumble. A second flyer, riderless, lofted itself out of danger, but more from astonishment or instinct than fear, for there had scarcely been time for fear to register.

In a way it had been merciful. "More than they deserved," Nathan told no one in particular. Then, because he had learned something about himself, he stiffened his resolve for the next attack. This one would not be so merciful.

* * *

They emerged from the Möbius Continuum at Grinner's precise coordinates and went straight into action. David Chung loped to the grotesque molten-candle rim of a fumarole some eighteen inches in diameter, unslung his flamethrower, primed the pilot light and laid the deadly cylinder aside, then pulled pins and dropped two grenades one after the other right down the throat of the blowhole. And taking up the flamethrower—even as the first muffled detonation sounded—he sent liquid fire roaring straight down into the unseen caverns beneath.

Nathan and Trask had stepped cautiously to the edge of the "falls," a weathered cliff of lava, and waited there with their weapons at the ready. They felt the volcanic rock under their feet shudder twice, and in another moment smoke and fumes came pouring from the dripped candle-fat curtain of the falls fifteen feet below. Screams sounded . . . a hideous bellowing . . . and the pitiful mewling of flyers. But somewhere in there, deep in the suddenly chaotic darkness, Dock's murderers who had *eaten* him might survive still, and Nathan felt no pity.

An eruption of smoke and sulphur stench from breaks in the curtain, and a spew of monstrous life emerged! Human (inhuman?) torches blazed as vampire thralls beat at themselves to put out the flames, and spilled breakneck down the course of the solidified lava river. A small warrior came coughing into view; puffed up, confused, furious and perhaps even a little frightened, it fired its propulsors to get aloft. But its aerial gas-bladders were on fire; exploding one by one, they blew the creature to and fro in midair, until suddenly it lost its balance, capsized, and went crashing down among the howling men. To add to the confusion, Nathan and Trask tossed grenades into the melee.

Then, as Chung continued to pour fire down the blowhole, a trio of bulky, scorched, shouting lieutenants came scrambling into view. There could be no mistaking such as these for common thralls. They were huge men; they wore leather armour studded with gold; war-gauntlets swung from their belts, and their eyes were feral yellow, cored with red. While they were not yet Wamphyri, the time would come when they might be—if they survived. But Nathan didn't intend that they should.

At the Necroscope's signal, Ben Trask opened up with his machine pistol. His fire scythed among the disoriented vampires. Two were cut down . . . and were back on their feet almost as quickly; with such as these, simple bullets wouldn't get it done. But Nathan's vendetta, especially with *these* vampires, was a personal thing, and his weapon was something special.

As the three lieutenants limped to the side of the lava falls and came scrambling, one lurching, up a moonscape jumble of rocks towards their attackers, Nathan took careful aim and fired his first bolt. It took his target through breastplate, sheathing muscle, and ribs, and knocked him backwards onto the man immediately behind him. A split second later, the detonation of the explosive bolt killed both of them, while the third was drenched in their blood and draped in red and black shreds of gristle. Before he could recover, Trask lobbed a grenade.

By the time the flash had burned itself out on their retinas, and the detonation had stopped echoing off the mountains, Nathan's guerillas saw only a grotesque *disassembly*: a crumpled torso, and a tangle of meat barely identifiable as the innards of a man, steaming on the rocks.

But some fifty yards away at the eastern end of the lava falls, other men and monsters were now streaming like hornets from a broken hive out of caverns unaffected by David Chung's firestorm. Even as Trask opened up again with his gun, a small warrior fired its propulsors and throbbed aloft, and a lieutenant leaped to grab his flyer's trappings as the beast skittered skywards. It seemed a good time for the guerillas to make an exit. Except—

Who? What? How—? A vampire Lord appeared from the wreck and reek of the cavern immediately below their vantage point, and probed the night with senses more than the usual five. He must have been in a partitioned, private area that hadn't suffered Chung's cleansing fire. And this was the one—the man himself—that Nathan wanted.

He knew him at once. Eighteen months ago in Rune-manse, in Turgosheim, Nathan had been present at a meeting of Maglore and Lord Grigor Hakson of Gauntmanse. Grigor's luck in the draw for the get out of Sunside had been bad for a long time; his tokens brought him no girls. The Seer-Lord had ample females, and Grigor wanted to trade young males. Maglore needed men for work he was carrying out in Runemanse—the excavation of living and work areas—and Grigor wanted the girls . . . for his own purposes. They didn't call him "Grigor the Lech" for nothing.

This was the selfsame Lord, Grigor the Lech: tall, thin, slate-grey, shifty- and slant-eyed, his black topknot shiny with grease, human fat as Nathan well knew. A loathsome Lord of the Wamphyri. But more than that: this was the creature or the master of creatures who had killed Dock for food!

He was naked; he carried a young woman, obviously Szgany; she was naked, too—and recently dead. Her suffering rang in the Necroscope's metaphysical mind! The deadspeak aether shuddered with it! She wasn't hurting now but the torture she had known would burn in her memory for a long time, perhaps forever.

Hush now! Nathan told her. *Let it go. For all of that's behind you now. And you're not alone, wait and see. Only let them in, and you'll have friends galore. I for one would consider it an honour.* Afraid for now, the girl couldn't answer. But she had heard and would remember.

The sheer power of Nathan's emotional sending was such, however, that she wasn't the only one who heard. Grigor could not know what the psychic disturbance signified, but his vampire probe tracked its source instantly. His grey-gleaming head jerked up; his scarlet eyes swivelled like some weird chameleon's to light on Nathan and the others at the rim of the lava falls. Then, he glanced at the girl in his arms—a lifeless rag thing, a mere distraction—and tossed her down. She went slipping and sliding down the stone river, gathering speed until she hurtled over a lesser rim and plunged from view. With a little luck, no creature would find and devour her.

And: "Eh?" Grigor grunted. "What, men?" As if they could not possibly be the source of this disaster.

Nathan had reloaded his crossbow. Now, without knowing why—or without consciously thinking it, in a moment of red rage—he cried, "Aye, men! Szgany! *Szgaaany!*"

And feeling his passion, Ben Trask and David Chung joined him. "Szgany! *Szgany!*"

Lieutenants and thralls had meanwhile climbed up onto the far lip of the falls and came running, crouching; small warriors were in flight, circling; a flyer and rider came swooping, setting the night thrumming with vibrating air-trap wings.

Nathan got off a shot at Grigor, but his hands were shaking with rage and the bolt flew wide by inches. Striking rock, it was deflected into the air and there detonated with a blinding flash and loud report. It was enough for Grigor the Lech; he took cover at once.

Trask opened up on the oncoming vampires, scything their legs from under them, and Chung torched the air above, driving the flyer off course. But they'd done all they could here and knew it. As Grigor stuck his head out from behind an outcrop, Nathan would make one last effort to get him. "A grenade!" he cried huskily. "Give me a grenade."

"I'm out," said Trask and Chung as one man. "We've used them all." And Trask added, "Nathan, those warriors are descending!"

The Necroscope groaned his frustration—and grew calm in a moment. Then, aiming his telepathic thoughts direct into Grigor's mind, he sent: *We go now; but we'll be back. Tonight, maybe. Tomorrow and tomorrow, certainly. Always!*

And despite that his mentalism surprised Grigor, still he sent back: *Bastard Szgany dogs! You are dead men! You and whoever you serve!*

Oh? Nathan returned. *No, you are wrong. Vormulac was*

*the one to die. And if Devetaki has her way, the rest of you
Lords will be next!*

Warrior stench was falling all around; a monstrous
shadow came sputtering across the lava falls; Nathan conjured a door, guided Trask and Chung inside . . .

. . . And out again at Sunside camp. His exit area was in
a roped-off clump of trees; a cry went up, and Lardis
Lidesci came running. "How did it go?" Then he stepped
back a pace, for he'd smelled warrior!

"It went well," Nathan answered, steadying his colleagues where they swayed and staggered. The Möbius
route was dizzying, even to esper minds. And before
Lardis could question further:

"Where are Zek, Ian Goodly, Andrei Romani?"

Several of Lardis's men had followed him; he sent one
of them to find Andrei and the two latest arrivals in
Sunside. And while the Necroscope waited, he told Trask
and Chung, "Get what rest you can. Don't worry about
me—I'll be resting, too, as soon as I have a chance. But
not until I've caused a deal more havoc!"

"What do you want with Zek?" Trask was worried for
her.

"She and Goodly left weapons at the Starside Gate,
mainly grenades," Nathan answered. "We're running low
and should try to recover them while we can. Just the one
jump, Ben, and then Zek is out of it; I won't use her again
if I can avoid it. But she and I are both telepaths. We can
stay in contact with each other while simultaneously
watching the boulder plains. Remember, I can't get too
close to the Gate personally, not and use the Möbius Continuum. But in any event, I won't take Zek along if Ian
says it's going to be in any way dangerous. Okay?"

Trask nodded. "Look after her, that's all."

Misha came and Nathan walked aside with her a little
way. "Tomorrow morning, you're all mine," she said.
"Hero or not—Necroscope or whatever—you'll lie with
me out on the savanna, in the clean sunlight and sweet
long grass, and like it!"

"I'll love it!" he told her huskily, hugging her close. "But the night isn't over yet, and—"

"—You still have work, I know. How is it going?"

"On the Starside slopes of the barrier mountains, we spilled a deal of Wamphyri blood!"

"And more to spill?"

"A lot of it."

"Where next?"

"After I've recovered a new cache of weapons . . . the last aerie."

"Wrathstack?" Her jaw fell open. "Nathan, that's—"

"—Dangerous? *Living* here is dangerous! But I've seen a free world, Misha—or almost free—and I want the same for us. While Wrathstack and the barrier mountains, Turgosheim and Starside remain safe habitat for vampires, that free world simply can't be. We've been their sustenance for far too long and now it's our turn. So while I may I'll strike at them—again and again!"

She kissed his mouth to a standstill, breathlessly said: "Whatever you say—but tomorrow you're mine."

"But not in the long grass."

"Where, then?"

"In a place you won't believe."

"*That* place?" She meant the Möbius Continuum, and looked wary, uncertain.

But he smiled and told her, "No, but we'll use it to get there—unless you like the idea of a long, long walk across the furnace desert!" At which point the timely arrival of Zek, Goodly, and Andrei Romani saved him from further questions.

The recovery of the weapons at the Gate went without incident. Out on the boulder plains to the northeast, there were signs of some activity: strange shapes in the sky, and what sounded like the echo of a distant explosion, but nothing in the immediate vicinity. Nathan stood off from the Gate with Zek and let the other men drag the buggy out onto the crater rim and collect the weapons. When they were through they toppled the buggy down onto the faintly phosphorescent plain, wheeled it into a small clump of rocks and did their best to disguise it. Then they rejoined Zek and Nathan, and he took all three back to camp.

The Russian-made hand grenades proved simple things to use; they were armed by twisting small projecting fins until the internal mechanism began to tick like a clock; then, for best effect, a count of three before hurling. Nathan let Lardis test just one; it caused a flash, made a loud noise, felled a small tree. The Old Lidesci was satisfied. He and his senior men, the cavers and Nathan's party received four each of these deadly eggs, which used up half of them. The rest of them were to be treated like gold—or on Sunside, like silver!

The remaining ammunition—explosive bolts, and bullets of various caliber—was shared out between the men with hell-land weapons. David Chung had proved himself more than proficient with a flamethrower and retained it; the other "torch" went to one of Carling's cavers. Nathan ordered the remaining rocket launcher wrapped up in an oiled skin, along with its warheads. If the time should come, he would use it himself. And so, finally, the weapons had been apportioned.

Then Trask took Nathan aside and said, "Why so keen to get these arms distributed?"

Nathan looked at him. "Was it that obvious?"

"To me it was. If anything happens to you, you want to be sure these weapons will be put to the best possible use."

Nathan nodded. "I'm going into Wrathstack again," he said. "Oh, I'll be in and out as quickly as possible—but accidents sometimes happen."

"You are going in," Trask repeated him, with the emphasis on *you*. "On your own? Why that nightmarish place again?"

Nathan's shrug was perhaps fatalistic but in no way careless. "I'm going in alone because I can't risk taking anyone with me," he said. "I have to be able to get out fast. As for why I'm doing it: well, we've given the army out of the east something to worry about, so now I want to even up the score a bit."

"But didn't you do that with Uruk Piatra? Lardis told us all about it."

"Yes, but Wratha and the others in the last aerie don't know about Uruk, not yet. I want to do something that's a lot more immediate, dramatic. Something they'll remember, to play on their nerves and throw them off balance." While he spoke, he pocketed extra grenades.

"You'll be careful, of course."

Nathan nodded. "The worst thing about it is I'll have to use Zek again. I know I promised not to, but I need a lookout. She'll be on the boulder plains, in a safe place, just watching, or rather 'listening,' out for me."

"And if something goes wrong? She could be trapped there? Is that why you wanted me to get some sleep?"

"You know it isn't. I hadn't thought it out, that's all."

And of course Trask knew it was the truth. "Then I'm glad I didn't sleep," he said. "Because I'm coming with you."

Nathan couldn't deny him. They went and found Zek . . .

Out on the boulder plain, the Necroscope found a suitable place to leave the two—the vacant ruins of a toppled stack on the very fringe of the miles-wide cluster of ancient Wamphyri tumuli—and went on alone. Keeping well clear of Gorvi's ambush party, he emerged several hundred yards away from Wrathstack's scree- and rubble-bedded base, and moved quickly into the shadow of a massive boulder. The numbers vortex swirled in his metaphysical mind, shielding it and ready at a moment's notice to conjure an escape route. But with less than seventeen hours to sunup, he should be comparatively safe.

In Wrathstack, and wherever Gorvi's ground-based creatures lurked now, the vampires would sense dawn's approach. From personal experience in Turgosheim, Nathan knew that the Lords and Ladies, and common vampires alike, normally took to their beds in the hours before sunup. Maglore himself had been a rare exception. But in the last aerie, the barrier mountains, Turgosheim, and wherever vampires were to be found, they'd be sleepy now. Indeed the Necroscope knew they were; their thoughts were vague, disjointed, and fragmentary where he probed them with a light telepathic touch. But . . . perhaps not all of them? There were rather more active minds, well guarded, on the other side of the stack.

In any case satisfied, he contacted Zek. *All's well?*

Yes.

And it was time. . . .

II

Assault on Wrathstack—The Dog-Lord's Dire Predictions

Nathan used deadspeak to contact Jason Lidesci. *Jason, how is the stack arranged? Not Guilesump but the rest of the levels. Where are the gas-beasts situated?*

Jason came back at once: *In Madmanse. The Killglance brothers have control of gas production. They have the levels over Gorvi's. You'll recognize the gas-beast pens from their round windows: not windows at all but vents! They surround Madmanse in an almost complete circle, like a ring that dips from south to north and follows the slant of the rock strata. This effect is most pronounced in Suckscar—named first after Vasagi the Suck, then for the sloping "scars": where soft rock has weathered out. The rock of the gas-beast level in Madmanse has to be soft, too, for the vents are far too regular to be natural; they were tunnelled in ages past by the Wamphyri!*

Nathan could see the ring of circular openings that banded Wrathstack like a bracelet. The pens were on the perimeter, and so there must be access to them from within . . . *and*, as he now saw, from without! For looking closer in the blue-tinged starlight, he could make out ledges and bone and cartilage scaffolding on the stack's exterior—for maintenance, of course! It was all he needed to know.

Except: *Vasagi the Suck?* he sent, his deadspeak hoarse as a snarl. *He dwells up there, near the top of the stack, where its sides are worn into scars?*

Ah, no—no longer! Suckscar was Vasagi's place, but now it belongs to . . . another.

Vasagi was usurped? There was something here that Nathan couldn't understand.

Usurped, no—he was killed, *by Wran the Rage! And Suckscar went to your brother, the necromancer Nestor Lichloathe!*

But . . . that can't be, Nathan said. *Why, this very night, Vasagi has murdered my mother, Nana Kiklu, in Sunside!*

I can only report what I've heard from the dead of Wrathstack, Jason answered. *For I was already dead when Vasagi and Wran duelled on Sunside. Two flew out, but only Wran returned.*

Nathan would like to explore the riddle further but must let it go for now. In any case, the dead of Wrathstack would be vampires; in death as in life they would be liars; perhaps they had lied to Jason, too.

Jason had heard his thoughts, of course. Quietly he said, *I know that you don't include me in that.*

No, of course I don't, Nathan told him.

The other's deadspeak sigh.

My thanks, Jason, Nathan sent—

—And jumped, to within two hundred yards of the base of Wrathstack. Now the last aerie of the Wamphyri towered over him like some monstrous menhir, a dizzy pile rising up and up, taller than the mightiest building of Trask's Earth and broader at its base than three city blocks.

But Nathan had precious little time to feel awed or even afraid.

. A moment for orientation . . . and he jumped, up onto a high ledge in the face of Madmanse, close to the wide rim or sill of one of the vents, which was all of seven feet in diameter. From within, nothing. No sound, not even the noxious smell of a gas-beast. The chamber was empty.

Disappointed (and aware that he was exposed on the naked face of Wrathstack), the Necroscope crouched down and hurried along the ledge, which was precarious in places where it narrowed or sloped towards the sighing gulf of air. Forty paces took him to a second gas vent, likewise innocent of sounds or smells. Here the ledge tapered out, and he must clamber down onto a flexible walkway of cartilage. Vertigo did not concern him; he knew that even if he fell, it would be through a door into the Möbius Continuum. But still he proceeded cautiously to the third circular shaft . . . where the night air shimmered with expelled methane, and the reek of a gas-beast was all too evident! From within, soft sighing sounds.

Nathan fingered the grenades in his pockets and was tempted, but knew now that his original plan wouldn't work. He had wanted to emulate his father, Harry Keogh, and cause a devastating simultaneous or chain-reactive explosion that would bring down the stack in its entirety. But Wrathstack wasn't right for it. Even if all the gas-beast chambers had been occupied, still the sheer girth of the stack would have protected it. The outer caverns would be blown away, most certainly, but ninety percent of the stem would be left intact. For it had been more than any merely *explosive* force that the original Necroscope had used; it had been the almost nuclear power of the furnace sun itself, which had instantly eaten into the rock of the many fallen aeries like some vengeful, cleansing acid! And so . . . it seemed a lesser plan was now in order. Any action was better than none.

Beyond the occupied gas-beast chamber, the cartilage catwalk spanned the mouth of a landing bay camouflaged with hanging nets of woven rope. Nathan felt sure that even this close to sunup there were bound to be watchers just inside. He made a Möbius jump across the gap, which set the catwalk swaying a little on the other side as it took his sudden weight. Balancing himself, without further pause he went on to the next vent. This chamber was also occupied, which decided Nathan upon his course of action:

Grenades into each of the two "loaded" chambers, and two more into the landing bay itself. Anyone within the bay would see him in the moment that he tossed his grenades . . . and then they *wouldn't* see him. If there were survivors, let them worry about that! If there were none, so much the better; still the rest of Wrathstack's monstrous inhabitants would be inconvenienced, and more than a little concerned over what had happened here. The unfortunate but mainly insensitive gas-beasts would surely be destroyed and their chambers reduced to rubble. With a bit of luck, the landing bay itself would suffer damage and even destruction.

Nathan knew the coordinates of the first occupied chamber and the landing bay, and he had been here long enough. But first:

A quick probe in Zek's direction . . . *Is all well?*

Yes. And almost immediately, with a thrill of horror: *No! Look!*

He read it in her mind, knew where to look—then saw it for himself:

Coming out from behind Wrathstack—at his own level but some three-quarters of a kilometer away—a fantastic sight! A gas-beast, swollen with its own gasses, puffed up and grotesque. A living balloon in tow behind a pair of lieutenants mounted on straining flyers, their necks outstretched with effort! While in the Necroscope's mind Zek shouted: *And behind you!* He looked the other way, to where a second beast was now hauled into view from behind the eastern flank of the stack.

For an anxious moment Nathan thought that the appearance of these creatures must have to do with his presence here, but in the next moment he knew it wasn't so. It was just a coincidence. And as his nerves settled down again he shrank back into a crevice in the aerie's wall and re-membered those mysterious explosions he'd heard out on the boulder plains. Now he knew, or strongly suspected, what they had been.

He had likened the floating gas-beasts to weird bal-loons; in fact they were bombs! And his mind went back to the stories Lardis had used to tell: of the battle at the Dweller's garden when the Wamphyri had used just such tactics against Harry and the Dweller. Now, peering from his hiding place, Nathan could see the payloads at the end of long taut lines where they hung from the flyers' sad-dles: bundles of hooks weighted with large stones. Flint stones, the Necroscope was sure. And pictured on the screen of his mind, the rest of it was clear:

The beast would be towed to its target, then cut free to drift lower. As it descended, the flyer would sweep over-head, raking the living bomb with razor-sharp hooks! *The clatter and clash of metal and flints against metamorphic flesh; a tearing of bloated leather and simultaneous strik-ing of sparks; the sudden hiss of pressured gasses! Then, the deafening, searing blast and outrageous rush of heat and stench!*

The picture faded in Nathan's mind, but not before it had reminded him of why he was here. The flyers, riders, and their grotesque cargoes were heading south; one a lit-tle to the west of south, the other a little to the east. Their target destination: Vormulac's (now Devetaki's) observa-tion posts, of course. It explained why so many methane chambers were empty. And soon two more would be empty, if they existed at all!

He took a grenade, twisted the fins, listened to the om-inous ticking start and without pause hurled the deadly egg right into the vent. Then, without waiting, a Möbius jump . . . back to the first occupied vent. And the second gre-nade was on its way into the stack. Another jump . . . to a spot central on the cartilage catwalk in front of the cam-ouflaged landing bay; two more grenades armed, and lobbed one after the other through the mesh of the hanging nets just inside the mouth of the bay.

There was movement in there, and Nathan opened his mind to let in the startled thoughts of those who guarded the way. *Astonishment! Shock! Outrage! Bloodlust!—Fear?* Yes, because for all these thralls knew, Nathan might be only the first of a huge invading task force, which had somehow managed to creep up on them unseen. But of course he couldn't stay here.

He backflipped from the catwalk into empty air, flattened his body, conjured a door and hurtled through it ... found his coordinates and stepped back into normal space, where Zek and Trask were waiting. And: "Watch!" he breathed. Which was about as much as he had time for.

Four bright flashes lit the south-facing wall of the last aerie a third of the way up. From the explosions on the flanks came stabbing gouts of fire, secondary flashes, hurtling chunks of rock and clouds of smoke and rubble. Centrally, twin bursts of light and fire shook down an avalanche of loose debris from above and both sides of the landing bay; fragile walkways went plummeting; fractured slabs of rock teetered outwards, falling in a deceptive, distance-wrought slow-motion into space.

Then came the *cracks!* of the detonations, sharp as knives in the silence, echoing out over Starside to the barrier mountains and back again. And the rubble blasted out or shaken free of the stack was still falling, bringing down a tangle of flying buttresses from lower levels, more walkways, various ramps and man-made staging areas, all going down in a mighty roiling of dust and a rumble like thunder onto the scree slopes at the foot of the stack.

It went on for a long time ...

When it was over the landing bay was a gaping hole twice what it had been; the ruptured vents on both sides were black, and issued twin columns of smoke; one-sixth part of the south-facing wall had been wiped clean of all artificiality. Natural rock remained, showing a uniform grey among a variety of dull ochres, greens, blacks, and yellows. It served to show how the outer sheath of that great fang had been changed and festooned by its vampire tenants over the long centuries of their habitation. Likewise its interior: carved, hollowed, and whittled out like an old branch full of earwigs. A rotten old branch, yes. And Nathan found himself thinking yet again: *if old Dimi Petrescu's powder—common gunpowder, in copious amounts—could sink Sanctuary Rock, and if I knew ex-*actly *where to locate it in Wrathstack for maximum effect* . . .

But his thoughts were suddenly interrupted as Trask said, "Maybe we can capitalize on the situation." He was armed with a self-loading rifle and sniper-scope, which he aimed into the sky at some twenty degrees. Without look-ing, Nathan knew what Trask's target would be. Reaching up, he pulled the barrel of the gun out of alignment.

"No," he said, glancing at the triangle of flyers and gas-beast maybe a mile away and drawing closer by the mo-ment. "Let them go. It suits our purpose to let them reach their destination. They're on their way to bomb Devetaki's observers, probably a suicide mission. I'm not against these monsters killing each other, and anyway it saves am-munition!"

Trask nodded, however reluctantly, and said, "As you will. So what's next?"

"I'm . . . tired," said Nathan, and Trask saw it in his face. It was going to take a long time for the Necroscope's system to catch up on all the energy he'd expended; one or two days, even Sunside days, wouldn't do it. "I want to get some sleep," Nathan went on. "Normal undisturbed sleep, with my wife in my arms and nothing to think about or worry over. I need—oh, I don't know—eight hours at least. After that, sunup will be so close that we can guar-antee the vampires will be at their lowest ebb. That's when we'll hit them again."

And with that they returned to the camp of the Lidescis.

Apart from the night watch, the camp at the edge of the savanna slept. But in the last aerie—despite the perhaps imagined stain of light already washing the southern hori-zon, lying like a luminous mist between the peaks—Wratha and the vampire Lords were still awake. Time enough for sleeping when the peaks themselves turned from wolf-grey to gold, but for now there was much to occupy them . . . or to occupy their evil minds at least.

Wratha was on the roof of Wrathspire. Attended by a small, personal warrior—a bodyguard that kept itself mainly to the shadows—she paced to and fro, wandering aimlessly in and out of the battlements, towers, and turrets, pausing now and then to gaze south and wonder what the army out of Turgosheim was up to now, and what its next move would be. But quite apart from the constant nagging worry of the bloodwar—the fact that Wrathstack was under siege, and not only that but actually coming under a form of attack, if the inexplicable explosions in Madmanse were anything to go by—there were other, more personal matters to concern her. For her vampire instinct told her that all was not well with Wratha herself. Except . . . she knew that it was more than mere instinct.

Beside a semicircular stone structure on the south-facing rim of the sloping plateau, where an ironwood gantry and hoist stood to one side, its dangling chains clanking in a breeze off the Icelands, she paused at a door to peer inside. In there, a grim reminder of the history of this place:

A massive cage of deadly silver, all tarnished and dark-stained. Its bars were an inch thick, welded, reinforced with iron; the effort of some Szgany metalworker long gone into air or earth . . . or the belly of a beast, or the vats of its Wamphyri master. How many enemies or victims, Wratha wondered, had some ages-forgotten Lord locked in that cage, hoisted on high, and swung out over the rim of the stack to await the dawn? It had been Vormulac Taintspore's wont in the past to do much the same thing. And in the future?

But she must not dwell on such things and so put it aside . . . for now. What had been had been, and no man—or woman—knew the future. The present had surprises enough! And terrors, too. Terror, in the black heart of a vampire. It seemed strange to Wratha, wrong somehow, that she should feel afraid. But not of men, not of the army out of Turgosheim, not of anything outside her own body. Afraid of something within it . . .

Wratha bathed frequently. And recently, ever increasingly. It wasn't that she was unclean (how could she be when she was so scrupulous?), but that she *felt* unclean. And all because of a blemish or two . . . or three. Persistent blemishes that her vampire leech couldn't shift, that her metamorphic flesh couldn't deal with. Let her will the . . . the *marks* away, and they would be back in a matter of hours. Let her scrub the silvery scales from her forearms and calves until her flesh was red under the clean pink of a young girl, and they would return just as soon as Wratha's leech repaired her skin. Yes, she could scrub till her flesh was numb . . . except it was growing hard to tell when it *wasn't* numb, in those certain areas. Under her left breast; the fingers of her right hand; her right thigh where it curved into a once-smooth buttock . . .

And all of this dating from a time, the start of it all, just four sunups ago. But her forearms . . . the Lady Wratha had *prided* herself on her young girl's arms! And now she wore pale cream gloves to her elbows: thin leather trogskin, peeled from living arms, softened and bleached in urine, and scented with oil of roses. It was infuriating, and it was worrying. So that on occasion Wratha had wondered if . . . but that was impossible. She'd had no contact with . . . there had been no sign of infection in . . . in all Wrathstack.

Nestor.

She put the thought aside like so many others. A niggling doubt, that was all. If only he wouldn't wrap himself up so. It was his art, she knew. Nestor talked to the dead, and imitated their cerements . . .

But the original thought would not stay put aside:

He, too, hid his flesh.

But she had seen his body . . . his beautiful body. She had even loved it, frequently. She had rubbed his liquids into her skin, sipped them from his jerking shaft. But "love" had died as all things (except vampire things) must;

finally she'd stopped seeing him, shortly after his brief "sojourn" in Sunside . . .

No, he *had stopped seeing her! But* why *had he stopped seeing her, when his lust had been such a fire in him?*

He had sensed her dwindling desire for him, that was it.

Except it had not dwindled, until recently.

The bloodwar had intervened.

That, too, was a recent thing.

It was the *nature* of vampires, to love and leave!

And was it also the dog-Lord's "nature" to build a wall of stone between himself and his once-great "friend"? Never a word of explanation out of Canker, who now went about his business with such a hangdog expression. And in Suckscar, all of Nestor's thralls creeping like ghouls; the general air of infirmity about the place; the sense of descending doom . . .

"My Lady!" Wratha gave a massive start, and spun cursing on her heel. It was a thrall come up out of Wrathspire to find her. His eyes were full of some strange terror, but not of his mistress.

And he brought a message from Gorvi the Guile.

Following which, Wratha's eyes were filled with the same dark dread . . .

The Lords and Lady flew down into Guilesump. All were there except Nestor who (according to his man Zahar) had retired to bed early leaving instructions that he was not to be disturbed. The Lady Siggi was likewise missing, but her absence was excusable. Siggi had not as yet ascended in the fullest sense of the word; as the dog-Lord's mistress, her role was in any case secondary; her conversation was limited and not entirely . . . well, sensible. Also, she was grown very beautiful—no, *extremely* beautiful—so that Wratha didn't want her there anyway.

Wratha, the dog-Lord, Wran the Rage, and Spiro Killglance were met by one of Gorvi's lieutenants just inside a landing bay in Guilesump's central level a hundred and fifty feet over the sloping scree jumbles. Debris from the Madmanse explosions was still being cleared from the entrance; flanking platforms and stanchions were no longer in evidence; other external fixtures sagged and looked ready to tumble into space at any moment.

As yellow-eyed thralls manoeuvred their flyers aside and tethered them, Gorvi's man took the four callers to his master in an open-roofed annexe to one side of the landing bay, where the Guile stood well back and watched others of his men burning corpses. The stinking black smoke went up, roiling under a domed ceiling, until it was sucked out around a tangle of wreckage into the night.

"Huh!" said the gaunt-visaged Gorvi as he turned and saw his visitors. "This is where I boil up lead, water, piss, and fats, with which to repel invaders." He waved a skeletal hand at a row of fire-blackened cauldrons lining a wall, then indicated the roof. "Once there was a crack in the ceiling, a natural chimney . . . now a gash, and dangerous! Why, all that scrap scaffolding up there could fall in at any time!" The poisonous glance he cast at the Killglance brothers said it all: that in his opinion, they should bear the blame for what had happened to the methane chambers. It was the Guile's way of distracting from his own possible negligence.

"Not only an oily bastard but a cheeky one!" Wran snapped. And Spiro glared through eyes that were now thoroughly dissimilar. Canker seemed subdued, however, and Wratha even more so when she said: "Those burning bodies. Your message said there was a dead leper in the wells: *one* dead leper. But I see three corpses."

Gorvi shrugged. "Just the one leper, aye . . . but it took a pair of clean thralls to carry him up here. Or should I say *once*-clean? What? Should I let them infect the entire stack?"

"Idiot!" Wran shouted. "What difference does it make how many thralls you burn now? The stack's water is infected, and that means the whole damned aerie! Wrathstack *in its entirety* is infected!"

To hell with Wrathstack! Wratha thought numbly, but kept the thought well guarded. *Wratha herself is infected!*

Nestor, too. Indeed, Nestor was the first. Yet . . . how can it be? And out loud, frowningly:

"Gorvi, how frequently do you inspect the wells?"

"A prowler-guard looks in on the wells every two to three hours," he answered, breathlessly. "Normally I'd have a man or men down there all the time, to keep the place immaculate. But . . . these are not normal times! And I must man the gantlets."

Slowly but surely, Wratha was growing angry. Now that the shock—the *fact* of her condition was known to her beyond any further doubt—she could begin to react to it.

This Gorvi . . . ah, what a great liar! Every two to three hours? But Lord Lichloathe had been suffering for—oh, a good threemonth since first he began to wrap himself in rags! Three *months*! The stack must be steeped in plague! Wratha's reaction, typical of her leech, was beginning to make itself plain in her face, form, and voice as she hissed: "How is it then that I seem to recall, and not so very long ago, advising you to watch your wells most diligently? Did I not say that given half a chance, our enemies would poison the wells with kneblasch? Well, and it appears I was wrong—for they have poisoned it *with the body of a dead leper!*" Her voice had risen to a shrill of impotent fury. Or perhaps not impotent, for Gorvi was here within arm's reach.

The Guile would answer but couldn't seem to find the right words. They were all against him: Spiro with his deadly killing eye, the rabid Canker, Wran with his rage mounting in him even now, and Wratha whose own furies made strong men whimper!

"Gorvi the Guileless!" that Lady stormed, grown very tall and thin (the young girl quite disappeared now), with her skin wrinkled and crimson eyes bulging hideously. "And are you also gutless? I seem to remember the necromancer Nestor Lichloathe calling you that upon a time. Are you so weak you can't admit the truth even when it is known to everyone around you? Gorvi, you . . . have . . . *neglected* . . . your . . . wells! In these most difficult of times, you may well have poisoned us all!"

"Including myself?" he panted, backed up against the wall as they turned on him in a body. "Is it likely? Think what you are saying, Wratha! Think, all of you! Would I knowingly—or even negligently—allow the wells to be poisoned—and then bring it to your attention? And did Wran and Spiro bomb their own gas-beasts, too? But isn't it obvious: we are *all* the victims of some weird warfare!"

And this time the truth was obvious. Wran saw it at once, and however reluctantly said: "He's right. The pens and chambers might possibly have been an accident—only *just* possibly—but the landing bay? There was no gas in the landing bay!"

But Wratha snarled, "A moment ago, Gorvi would have given you the blame in order to lessen his own neglect!"

And Canker shook his head and growled, "We are at war—indeed besieged—yet here you stand bickering among yourselves! *Hah*, and you dare to call me mad! Well, make up your minds and decide what if anything is to be done, and then let *me* know! Meanwhile, I'm through wasting my time here. My instrument of bones is finished, perfected at last, and I want to try it out before sunup." He shook his head again worriedly, slapped ineffectively at his ear, whined his frustration (his pain?) and headed for the exit.

Spiro Killglance followed him, snarling, "Extra vigilance! Who or whatever's to blame for these affairs, we must catch him out and punish him! Give him to me, to blast with my eye!"

"Vigilance with regard to this ... this *pestilence*, too!" Wratha was quick to call after them. "Look for the signs, and if you so much as suspect leprosy ..." But deep inside she shuddered.

Wran pointed his finger straight at Gorvi's nose and said, "Gorvi, this isn't finished. You have been saved by circumstances alone: the fact that Madmanse has likewise suffered a weird and inexplicable attack. But how can there be any excuse for a leprous body in the wells? So be advised: that when this bloodwar is over, however it goes, *my* war and *yours* begins. You and I shall see it out together—on Sunside!"

Wran left, and Gorvi stood alone with a furious Wratha. To her he said, "Lady, I am not at fault!"

And in all honesty, despite her rage, she couldn't see how he could be. Calming herself a little, and shrinking back to a girl, she said, "Is it possible that this body has been there a long time? Might it have got stuck under a ledge, out of sight, only recently floating into view?"

"Wratha." He flapped his hands. "I have swimmers! They are fit and well even now! That corpse was put there, deliberately and recently, even within the last three hours."

And: *Nestor!* she thought again. But how could he fit into this? And anyway, she wasn't even sure that he was . . . a leper. But she knew who would be sure. Except how could she inquire of the dog-Lord without explaining her suspicions? If Canker Canison had wanted to say something, he'd have said it by now. But no, he'd left this place in short order, eager to be out of it. He was loyal as a pup, that one—to Nestor.

So . . . why not ask Nestor himself, direct? And if he said yes, then *kill* the bastard!

Gorvi broke into her thoughts. "Wran intends to kill me!"

"He rages," she answered, "as is his wont. We all rage, as if someone had planned it. So maybe you're right, Gorvi, and an alien force is at work. Anyway, let's leave it at that for now. It's all we can do. But from now on, no more errors!"

"I swear I'm not to blame!" he called after her, as she in turn left.

A little later, Canker played moon music. Nestor (who was not in his bed and had not intended to be) heard him, took a flyer and went down to the north-facing wall of Mangemanse where it was pitted into great bays and windows, like the bones of some ancient skull or toothless jaw. Since it was not his intention to land, he caused his mount to form air-trap wings; and hovering on a wind rising in the north, he gazed on Canker across a gulf of air where the dog-Lord worked his baffles to make the bones of monsters sound and fill the aerie with his "music."

As always it was a cacophony; there might be something of a tune in it, though far more a dirge than the original Szgany love song. And Nestor thought: *I gave him this tune. Why is it the Wamphyri murder everything?* There was nothing of humour in his inwards-directed question.

In a little while Canker saw him, and sent: *Well, and do I make progress?* His thoughts had been morose; they brightened a very little at the sight of Nestor.

For as long as the necromancer could remember, the dog-Lord had been his one friend, the only creature he could truly trust. Indeed, Canker had been far more friend to him than he to Canker. For on occasion, Nestor had considered a time when Canker would play the part of a mere lieutenant—to himself. But that was all in the past now. There would be no such time; no future at all, not for Nestor Lichloathe. Anyway, he would not hurt the dog-Lord now, not by word or deed.

Your music is excellent, he answered. *With a talent such as yours, no wonder you've called maidens down from the moon! Except . . .*

Aye?

I didn't come to listen to your music. If so, I could do it from a window in Suckscar.

Canker nodded, continued to work his baffles, create his awesome noise. *I know why you came: because you could not come down into Guilesump. If they'd seen you there . . . it might all connect.*

As you have connected it?

Guilesump, no. But the rest? It wasn't hard. I pity you, my friend. And I have wept: that we can no more run on Sunside together, like foxes among the chickens! Well—(he shrugged, and for a moment his music was sourer still)—*it was all coming to an end, anyway.*

Oh?

Again Canker's nod. *I scry the future in dreams, Nestor, as well you know. And for us . . . there is no future.*

For us? You and I?

The Wamphyri! Canker barked. *It's finished, all of it.*

How soon?

Soon.

Myself?

Nothing specific. Don't ask, for you can't change it. Anyway, I'm not always right.

You'll tell me nothing more?

About the future, no. His music soared and the aerie shuddered; the very air seemed to vibrate; dust came trembling from the high ledges.

Then tell me about this bane, which burns like a cold fire in me, devouring me as a fire devours the forest! Why have they called it the "hundred-year death," when its spread is so swift and wicked?

Canker kept on playing, but between the notes Nestor could hear his sobbing. *In some it's a slow thing,* the dog-Lord said, *but in others—lightning fast! It's as if it were waiting to be triggered, like a bolt in a Szgany crossbow. And in you, the bolt is shot.*

There's nothing I can do?

How may I advise you? Finally Canker stopped playing. His great wolf's eyes were wild, wet, red; his muzzle quivered with some strange emotion. *What words can I say? When my father knew the end was close, he shagged his bitches one by one, saddled a flyer and made for the sun. Myself: I shall head for the moon, to do battle with its puny priests for the love of its maidens! But you . . . you're you, Nestor, and I may not advise you! Maybe you'll be killed anyway, in the bloodwar.*

But out on the gulf of air, Nestor shook his head. *If I'm to die, it'll be my way.*

Oh?

All of this stems from one act, one deed, one betrayal.

That old itch on Sunside?

The same.

Your Great Enemy?

My brother, aye. He comes and goes. He was . . . even here!

What? Canker came to the rim of the bay and leaned out.

In Madmanse, Nestor told him. *The gas-beasts and methane chambers. That was him.*

And in Guilesump? (The dog-Lord had considered the possibility that that might have been an effect of Nestor; but if the necromancer said it wasn't, then it wasn't.)

Of course he was in Guilesump! I burned the leper colony on Sunside; what happened in Guilesump was his reply! I cannot be mistaken . . . I have felt his numbers . . . he . . . he comes and goes! Everything that has happened to me—all that is wrong in my life—I can trace it back to him. And Canker, he knows everything! About me! More, far more, than I do! I have to kill him, my blood brother, and question him with my necromancy, so that I too may know . . . everything!

And again Canker thought: *They call me mad!* But loving Nestor Lichloathe (and . . . missing him, already?), he did his best to keep the thought to himself. *So what will you do?*

Find him, and kill him, as I've said.

In Sunside?

Nestor nodded. *He has a day to live—or I have.*

Your own brother? Your blood brother?

He was my brother. Now, I'm Wamphyri. And he is my Great Enemy.

For a moment, a great wave of sadness washed out from the dog-Lord on the rim of the landing bay. Then a second wash . . . of pain! His ear! His aching head! The thing that ate into his brain! It, too, came and went . . .

And as Canker slapped at the side of his head, Nestor said: *We're a mess, you and I!*

Aye, Canker agreed. *But you are right: it's as well to end things as they have been, to die as we have lived. All my life I have worshipped my silver mistress moon. Now I'll go to her, and join the great ranks of wild wolves and dogs and foxes gone before me. You have loathed for long and long, which is a disease in itself! Well, at least that's something you can cure! I wish you good hunting.*

Nestor said no more, for there was nothing more to say. He reined back, sought a rising thermal, and went up and up, into Suckscar. And in a little while, from below, the sounds of the dog-Lord's moon music sounded again. . . .

Wratha had eavesdropped on all they'd said.

Initially their thoughts had been "loud" to compensate for Canker's music, but they'd both appreciated the danger in that. After a while, however, they hadn't much cared. A sad conversation, between genuine friends. Apart from Devetaki (and that a long time ago), Wratha had never had a friend. In a way she was jealous of the situation, while in another she was afraid of it. It might even seem to defy logic—except her Wamphyri "logic" had already defined it: as the loyalty that a dog gives to his man. But Canker was only part dog and all Wamphyri, wherefore his own safety had been paramount; finally he had wavered and built his wall.

Now that she knew the whole truth, Wratha was surprised to discover so little of anger in herself; not towards Nestor, anyway. And wrily she queried the logic of that, too. What was it, then: the boundless "love" that exists between a *bitch* and her man? Scarcely! But even lacking the human ability to understand it, at least she could appreciate the facts in the case: that as soon as Nestor was sure of his condition, he'd stopped seeing her. And he had been careful to keep himself apart from all of the others, too. Unlike some Wratha could name (if they had been in his shoes), the necromancer had not deliberately tried to spread his curse abroad.

As for this Great Enemy of his—well, and perhaps even in this he was right! "Weird warfare," Gorvi had called it. A "special talent," according to Nestor: of a man who could move instantly from one place to another, even miles apart, without covering the distance between! How else might one explain the damage to a Madmanse landing bay, or a leprous cadaver in Gorvi's wells? (Or a man

thrust from the rim of a mighty boulder to his death,
whom Nestor claimed was still alive?)

So maybe Wratha wouldn't kill Lord Lichloathe after
all. If this Great Enemy of his was real, perhaps Nestor
should be allowed to deal with him in his own fashion—
and at the same time perform a great service for
Wrathstack. Anyway, there was enough dissension in the
aerie as it was; and what would Wratha's excuse be if she
did kill Nestor? And what if his *condition* should be seen
before she could dispose of his corpse? It was general
knowledge that they'd been lovers.

She remembered a legend of old Turgosheim, the story
of Lord Kalk Ingrison. Kalk had been shunned as a leper
for more than one hundred and forty years, and for that
same period of time had used his amazing metamorphism
to hold the disease at bay! For Kalk, the blood really *was*
the life: he had required it by the gallon, to fuel his metamorphism! But following the introduction of an early form
of the tithe system, his plasma intake had been so reduced
that it was the end of him. In the space of a single night
he'd withered to a husk and crumbled into pieces—and his
very leech had been discovered riddled with leprosy!

Ah, but he *had* survived for a hundred and forty years!
And if Kalk Ingrison could do it, so could Wratha. Except
first she must survive a bloodwar. Well, only time would
tell about that. As for Nestor: if *he* survived his rendez-
vous with this nameless enemy, his so-called "blood
brother" . . .

. . . But that, too, must be left to fate and time.

As for now: Wratha could hear the sighing of the sun
even through a thousand miles of planet's rock, and she
was certain that the southern sky was lightening by the
minute. If she was to be strong enough to repel the invaders out of the east, she must have rest; likewise her leech,
in order to find strength to defend her from the thing in
her blood.

She took to her bed, where she tossed and turned for
long and long, aware of all the evil of forgotten millennia.
It was in the very rock: a cement of horror that held the

last aerie erect against gravity, time, and all the immemorial hatred of Sunside's Szgany. But for how much longer? The dog-Lord's predictions seemed ominous. An end to all this? Well, forewarned is forearmed.

But how may one forearm oneself against the Very End?

Or was the knowledge simply there to be used as a last resort (a last chance for glory, perhaps?) by someone wise enough to accept its inevitability?

Once again, only time would tell . . .

Uppermost in Turkur Tzonov's mazed mind was a memory so monstrous it could only be a nightmare; a bad dream that might yet be in progress. He remembered . . .

. . . A place of dusty gloom and creeping, jewel-eyed evil. Held down by men with the strength of giants, and watched over by a woman with eyes red as a desert sunset, he'd suffered the bites—a great many bites—of *creatures* he could no longer bear to think about! And all of this in addition to the agony, indeed the delirium of pain, from his torn body.

Since when, this dreary, bleary malaise—this sinister state of being, of body and mind—from which try as he might he could not raise himself up. He floated, light as a feather yet heavy as lead, in a material void whose only substance was the disjointed, fuzzy imagery of his own mind. Or rather, such *had been* its substance, until recently someone else's mind had impinged.

In itself this wasn't strange. Tzonov was a telepath; he had experienced the thoughts of others; they were usually accompanied by fear—*great* fear—of himself! Yet now, *he* was the one who was afraid.

He had thought it was the darkness, for the unknown dark is a fearsome place. But the owner of the curiously naive yet intrusive mind had lit a candle—following which she'd been a stranger no longer! For then, looking into eyes that bored into his own like crimson drills (this even though he seemed to meet their gaze through a misted window), Tzonov's telepathy, if very little else, had sprung alive! At which the oddly deficient yet malevolent and vindictive mind behind the crimson eyes had at once made itself known—

—As that of Siggi Dam!

And everything had come flooding back, to fill the dull unfeeling void with unbearable truth: the truth of his situation. But only the incomplete truth, as he understood it:

That he'd been poisoned by the paralysing bite of great spiders, and was now in a weird half-comatose condition, cocooned and stored by those same creatures against an uncertain future, a time of need when he would become . . . their food?

And at that precise moment, as suddenly Tzonov knew that this was not a nightmare but a reality, the here and now: *Ah, no!* Siggi told him, smiling like a shark to display her white needle teeth and scarlet gums. *Not their food, Turkur—but nourishment for their young!*

Their . . . their young? The thought floated out from his frozen brain encased in ice.

And in return she sent him an even colder picture, which showed him exactly how it was, and how it would be . . .

Then, as his mental screaming commenced, and went on and on, climbing ever higher along the scales of madness, the Lady Siggi snuffed the candle and floated away into darkness, leaving him with this one last thought:

You are their incubator, *Turkur! Though you cannot feel them, they are in you even now. So save your screams for later when you really* will *feel them, and all too keenly!*

Following which he was alone with the dark and the numbness and the madness, and Siggi's laughter slowly fading. But not really alone, for an alien multitude was right there with him. . . .

III

Devetaki Quells the Lords— Nathan: Further Visitations

In the camps of Devetaki's generals on the north-facing slopes of the barrier mountains, there was trouble . . . certainly there *would be* trouble if Zindevar Cronesap, Ursula Torspawn, and the virgin grandam herself were not there to face it down. For the mood among the lesser Lords was one of insurgency, and Devetaki scarcely required her superior mentalism to sense it. Which was why she now addressed a meeting of all her generals, within the natural amphitheatre formed of an extinct volcanic cone close to her own headquarters.

The principal troublemaker was Lord Grigor Hakson, called the Lech, who, in answer to Devetaki's ostensibly innocent air of surprised inquiry in the face of this undeserved hostility, was first to voice his concern. But there was little or nothing of lechery in Grigor now—only a righteous fury.

"We had an *army*!" his voice rang out from the central area of the cone, where he stood ringed about by restless, scowling contemporaries. "We flew out of Turgosheim under the banners of a mighty *army*! Where is it now? And where are our successes, by way of trade for these considerable losses? If Vormulac Unsleep were here, he would answer for these several failures. But Vormulac is not here, nor is he anywhere! No, he is simply another casualty of his own poor planning and utterly ineffectual command. You, Devetaki, were his right-hand man, or woman—indeed, his adviser. And *you*, madame, chose to take upon your shoulders the glory and responsibility of leadership. Well, so be it; now perhaps you'd care to explain our *in*gloriously diminishing rank and file, and the apparent *lack* of leadership!"

Up on the rim of the cone, Devetaki and the other Ladies formed a matriarchal trio whose elevation in rank seemed emphasised by the terrain; they stood high above lesser personages. Devetaki had been wearing her frowning mask, a bad enough sign in itself. But now, before answering the Lech's rabble-rousing queries, she removed her mask and scanned the assembly with a coldly horrific visage. This unmasking of her flensed face was a sure sign of her vast displeasure, so that she was not required to raise her voice as she answered:

"So, Grigor. We have a bloodwar, and the first time you're blooded you squeal! Well, I suppose it was only to be expected. When a man gives up so much of his time and energy to wenching, he cannot have a great deal left to devote to fighting. Indeed, I have it on good authority that at the time of the attack you were astride some Traveller whore stolen out of Sunside. Is it not so?"

Grigor looked astonished. He opened and closed his mouth, then drew himself up to his full height. "We were told to make camp for the coming day," (his voice was strident now). "Naturally, I took this to mean that the activities of the night were finished! Now tell me: since when is it unlawful to use a woman out of Sunside? And anyway, what has that to do with our army's failure to make inroads on Wratha the Risen in her aerie or the weird, dangerous inhabitants of the lands south of these mountains?"

Devetaki sighed before repeating him: "So, *you* took it to mean . . ." And here she paused. "But did you not also take it to mean that you should post a watch? Also, just how many of these weird and dangerous Szgany attackers set upon you in your camp? A hundred, fifty . . . a dozen?

Just what sort of a mighty horde was it that caused such devastation in the camp of Grigor the Lech?"

Grigor fumed. "They had the advantage of surprise and superior weaponry! And they had taken up an inaccessible strategic position, from which to launch their attack."

"Inaccessible?" She contrived to look puzzled. "But what of your flyers, warriors, lieutenants, thralls? Are you saying that you could not bring a single one of your men or creatures to bear against these vile, murderous attackers? Or is it that you were simply unprepared? Or perhaps your men and beasts were all . . . well, should we say otherwise *engaged*, as you yourself, Grigor?" And for a second time: "Inaccessible? What, like Wratha in her soaring aerie, do you mean? But out in the open, on the lava slopes? Again I ask, just how many of these dangerous, incredibly vicious Travellers were there? Er, three is the number which I have heard bruited—but of course I know that this must be a joke! What, three common men out of Sunside, Szgany, against the might of Grigor Hakson?"

Grigor sputtered, but giving him no time to recover, Devetaki went on, "As for their 'inaccessible position': I take it you mean that this overwhelming force of three wild and heavily weaponed supermen had discovered the weakness of *your* defensive positions—that is, assuming that you had planned to man such positions; also assuming that you'd checked to see if such positions existed in the first place, and if so that they couldn't possibly become available to an enemy—and that somehow, despite all of your most sensible precautions, the barbarians were nevertheless able to use them to their own advantage!"

Grigor was now genuinely furious. His face had turned a purplish grey, his chest heaved, his eyes were wide and wild, and he had difficulty speaking. "I had camped my men and creatures beneath the frozen lava flow to provide protection from tomorrow's sunlight! But . . . do you speak of defensive positions? Now tell me, Lady: Since when have the Wamphyri required to so much as *consider* defensive positions?"

"Since now!" Devetaki remained calm, but her voice

had hardened. "Since my Lord Vormulac is no more, murdered by the very Szgany who attacked you . . . or if not by them, by others of the same blood! What? Are we incapable of learning a simple lesson? And Grigor, do not pretend that you would question Vormulac in this fashion. Why, the mere suggestion would find you fed balls-first to his favourite warrior—as well you know! Ah, but it's easy to be brave after the fact! And Grigor, try not to splutter so; it only serves to illustrate your dismal inefficiency. For if you can't even defend yourself verbally, quite obviously you would be easy prey to far more physical attacks—*as you have been!*"

"Physical attacks?" he blurted, the words slurring from his mouth in an almost drunken fashion. "Lady, I've had more than enough of a tongue-lashing from you! And if it's a *physical* attack you'd like to see . . ." He came striding, thrusting through the ranks of Lords and senior lieutenants, to a place directly below Devetaki and the other two Ladies. But when it seemed he was about to climb up—

"Hold!" said Devetaki. While in her mind she called out: *Come, my darlings!* And her darlings came.

Devetaki's camp was in the immediate vicinity; when she had heard the first rumbles of trouble, she'd been wise enough to call her generals here, and not go to them. While they were a fine body of Lords, still they were mainly on their own, supported by only a small handful of lieutenants. But the virgin grandam was not on her own.

There came warning grunts and a nervous throb of propulsors, a clatter of chitin scales and a thudding on the shallow outer walls of the fretted cone. Behind Devetaki, Zindevar and Ursula, and to left and right of them, ugly snouts were pushed up into view. A pair of small warriors reared, to look down on the gathering with suspicious, swivelling eyes. Flanking them, a large body of minders, lieutenants, and thralls came scrambling, ringing the cone about. There were men of Vormulac's contingent among them, seconded now to Devetaki; also, there were her own lieutenants, several of Wamus's and Ursula Torspawn's men, even a handful of Zindevar's ferocious women.

And Devetaki knew that if she wanted to she could do away with a majority of these Lords right here, right now, and never be concerned with them again. And she would have . . . except she needed them to fight the bloodwar.

She looked down on them:

Lord Eran Painscar, with the ribs and flesh of his left side laid open, displaying his pulsing organs encased in bags of metamorphic skin. Lord Eran had kept this hideous wound or trophy to remind him of the even greater pain of his enemy—whom he had killed by cutting out his spine entire.

Hesta the Hermaphrodite, whose liquid features alternated between a demure, eye-fluttering pout and a bestial snarl, and whose hands were slim and manicured at the ends of arms like a bear's!

Lord Tangiru the Grunt, who swore that he'd never told a lie in his life. Well, and it was true; one does not say much of anything without a tongue.

Lom Halfstruck, the dwarf, whose arms were long to compensate for his shortness of leg. He had hands like clubs of knotty ironwood, and a great passion for striking detractors in their most delicate parts. Three times when he had considered himself insulted, Lom had reached out and castrated the offenders with his bare hands.

Devetaki looked down on all of these Lords and twenty or so more, but not nearly as many as before. In Turgosheim there had been some thirty-six Lords; now they were down to—what? Twenty-eight? Of course, Maglore was not here, and Black Boris was in the trog caverns in the east. But there had also been a good many real, however contrived, fatalities. Wamus, for example, Laughing Zack Shornskull, Vormulac himself: gone the way of all, or most, flesh. And others lost crossing the Great Red Waste, and several more from internal feuding or other causes. Most recently, Lord Zun of Zunspire (called Zun the Lips, despite the fact that he had none): swept to oblivion with most of his men and creatures in a great avalanche whose dust had not yet settled, which was rumoured to be the work of these same guerilla Travellers. Aye, it all added up—to a very satisfying situation, in Devetaki's eyes. Well, with certain reservations. A shame she had a bloodwar on her hands, that was all. Else now she might achieve her life's ambition all in one fell swoop.

And in those dangerous moments while Devetaki gazed down on the restless Lords, there was a sombre silence broken only by the hot snort of one of her warriors . . .

. . . Until, putting on her scowling mask, finally the virgin grandam ordered her creatures down from the wall. *But stay close to hand,* she sent, *for I may yet need you!* Unlikely now, but as well to let these cowed Lords know what was what. Well, she'd done that, all right. Like chastised children, they were surly but silent; they knew their place in the scheme of things now. It seemed a good time to make her peace with them, starting with Grigor Hakson.

"Very well," she said, staring straight down at him. "We know where we stand, and you believe that I've made a fool of you. But you are wrong, for I am in total agreement with you! Ah, surprise on your face, Grigor! But why? For the only mistake you made was to blame me— and that out of frustration, I know. I was Vormulac's adviser? Indeed I was! But think—how many losses had we suffered if I had *not* been? Even the best adviser may only guide a fool."

And before he could speak: "As for the rest of it, you're right. Mistakes have been made. But didn't you ask it yourself: since when do the Wamphyri require defensive positions? It's in our *attitude*, Grigor, don't you see? For while in Turgosheim we were the masters—Wamphyri, whose word was law—here we are only enemies! And not only to Wratha but to Sunsiders who have learned to fight back! Oh, she had tamed a few of them—*hah!* a precious few—and made them her supplants; which we were unlucky enough to discover from the onset . . ."

"Unlucky?" (A lesser Lord's puzzled query.) "How so?"

Devetaki lifted her crimson gaze from Grigor to sweep it over all the assembled Lords, and answered: "Because from that time forward we knew it would be easy—and we were wrong! For while a *supplicant* is easy meat here as in Turgosheim, the rest of these western Szgany are fierce fighters all. If we had come up against the fighters first, then we'd have been on guard—as we will be from this time forward. But now let me tell you how *else* it will be from this time forward. Tomorrow night . . . we go against Wrathstack!"

And from the Lords: "What, the last aerie?" And, "Wrathstack? That impregnable place?" Until someone called out: "As Laughing Zack Shornskull went against it, d'you mean? Oh? And where's Zack now, eh?"

Devetaki gave a shrug. "The choice is yours; to sit here and starve, or to go against Wrathstack. Now listen: the supplicants are gone, used up, and only the fighters remain. Also, we're no longer a surprise; they're ready for us. Now, at the moment, we're well fed and our fighting beasts are fuelled. We are fit for war. And provided we keep a watch during the coming day—on Wrathstack, to hold it in siege, and on our own flanks, to keep them safe—tomorrow night will be our first and best opportunity to take the last aerie and make it ours. So, how do we go about it?" And before they could answer:

"Let me tell you," Devetaki continued. "But first . . . do not speak to me of Laughing Zack Shornskull. He was a madman! What, one Lord against an entire aerie? He deserved to die! A shame he took so many good men and creatures with him, that's all. But tomorrow night . . . I, Devetaki Skullguise, personally guarantee that tomorrow night will be different. I *guarantee* it! For then you'll not only be fighting for your lives, for revenge, and for glory—but for profit! For territory! For the last aerie itself!"

"What?" said Grigor, frowning. "What are you saying?"

"I'm talking about the last aerie," Devetaki insisted. "A single mighty stack whose capacity is almost as great as Turgosheim in its entirety! And if—no, *when*—we have conquered it, whose shall it be?"

"Eh?" Grigor the Lech was not alone in his amaze; a

good many jaws had fallen open. This was something new, that hadn't yet dawned. Or it had, but mainly on Devetaki herself. A near-perfect example of how Turgosheim's immemorial constraints had stunted natural Wamphyri instincts: that the question of spoils, of ownership, of territory had not previously arisen.

"My proposal," said Devetaki, while still their horizons expanded. "That you Lords band yourselves, your men and beasts together into five or six invincible groups, divide the stack between you, choose your target levels—and have at it! And whosoever survives to take this or that level or levels—"

"—Keeps them!" Grigor gasped.

"Indeed!" said Devetaki. "Just and well-deserved rewards for a fight well fought and a bloodwar well won! Just think of it: for when it's over there'll be vampire flesh enough to fill your bellies and your vats, and furnish your new manses richer far than anything you had in Turgosheim!"

A growled, grunted, but mainly appreciative murmur went up from almost every quarter. Except:

"And your part, Lady?" one voice rang out. "Where shall you be in this great and bloody melee? And what shall be your reward?"

"I have already chosen my target," Devetaki replied. "The topmost levels and spire itself—for that's where I'll find Wratha! That is . . . unless *you* would care to face that Lady?"

But there was no answer.

"At first," Devetaki continued, "I'll stand off, observe, command. Free of the fighting, my eyes shall see what you have missed, and my mentalism will reach out and guide all of you in your endeavours. In this respect I shall watch over my children like the very virgin grandam that you've named me! But then, as the fighting moves within the stack and so beyond my range and control, I shall join my troops in the loftiest of all levels, and so be in the thick of it. My reward—

"—Shall be Skullmanse! At the 'head' of the stack, where else?"

There arose an immediate babble of protest, which Devetaki cut short at once with, "See here: the great battle is not yet begun, and yet you're arguing already! Now listen, and mark my words. When all of this is over, we shall do as Wratha tried to do: First recruit Szgany supplicants, then tame Sunside. A task that will take years! Our blood-children will fly back to Turgosheim, to care for our manses in our absence, and ensure they do not fall into foreign hands. Our holdings will be vast, and all the resources of this brand-new Sunside ours! And in those early years, why, there'll be no time for feuding among ourselves ... what, with all the works we'll undertake? The hunting and taming? The tithe-routes to set up and manage; and all the lesser stumps of stacks around going wanting for masters, each one of them greater than many a so-called manse in Turgosheim? Territory galore, and all for the taking!"

Devetaki had the Lords now, and knew it. She had painted them a glorious (however false) picture, and it lured them like stink-gnats to foul-smelling snapper plants. But she knew that even now they'd be able to see at least one major loophole, and so continued:

"Men will die, of course. Oh, yes, some of you Lords *will* die! But isn't that always the way of it? Only the strongest survive. Ah, but think of the profits to those survivors: masters not only of their own manses in Turgosheim, but every one of them shall also be the victorious Lord of a level or two of that mighty stack out there on the boulder plains!" She threw a dramatic arm and hand to the north, which a host of scarlet eyes greedily followed—until she continued:

"So, how will you name your fine aeries, eh? Eranscar!—Trollsump!—Gruntmanse!" And finally, gazing on Grigor again and deliberately donning her smiling mask, "Lechlodge?"

But he was already hooked and wouldn't rise to any more baiting, except to say: "Very well, Devetaki, and so much for the last aerie. Wamphyri against Wamphyri . . . we know how to fight *that* war! But what of these strange Sunsiders and their even weirder weapons? I *saw* the three who caused me such grief and they were like no other Szgany I've *ever* seen! Now how do we fight such as them, when they come and go like shadows?"

She narrowed her eyes. "*Here*, they come and go like shadows," she said. "Here in these barrier mountains, where they know all the trails and hidy-holes. But do you think they are likely to come adventuring across the boulder plains, to the last aerie itself? Also, I've taken one of them prisoner, and he has . . . told me things." She shrugged. "They have a leader, these irritating Sunsiders. But my captive, now my true thrall and disciple, knows where to find him—always! He has a talent, you see, this new thrall of mine: he sniffs men out. And when Wrathstack is fallen, then he'll sniff out the leader of these guerillas . . ."

"You have it all worked out," said Grigor, however grudgingly.

"Indeed," said Devetaki. "But isn't that what a leader is for?" And to the rest of them:

"Post guards. Let's make sure we suffer no more incursions—no more losses—this night. Likewise tomorrow; for we must always remember, daytime is their time! That's it, then. A long day lies ahead. Get your rest while you may, my Lords, but save the best of your provisions till next the sun sets. For then, with well-fuelled men and beasts, we ride on Wrathstack!"

As the Lords departed back to their camps—some of them eager and excited, and others muttering—Zindevar told Devetaki: "Do you know, you almost had me convinced, too?"

And Ursula Torspawn—slight as a Szgany girl, and even dressed like one, but Wamphyri all the way—said, "Some *will* survive, of course."

"But greatly weakened," Devetaki answered. "And by then, if all works out, we'll have control of some of these weapons that Grigor mentioned, which I have seen in use.

For before we attack Wrathstack, Zindevar here will have secured the pass—*and* what it contains! Remember, I have a man, the same captive I spoke of, who understands those weapons."

Still her Lady colleagues looked uncertain, until the virgin grandam sighed and said, "Try to see the whole picture:

"The great pass secured, ours. A number of superior Szgany thralls recruited, their weapons in our hands. Wrathstack taken and only a handful of Lords surviving . . . for a while. The bulk of our army out of Turgosheim—say half of it?—intact, its men and beasts at our command. The fighting just over, and the bloodwar won. But do we stop there?

"No, we sweep on—sweep *over*—the last of the Lords! And finally, the apportioning. Zindevar: we've spoken before, you and I, concerning territories. Now I have a new proposal for you, which I think you'll like."

Zindevar narrowed her eyes and grunted, "Oh? Do you think so? Then say on."

"The great pass shall be yours to take and keep, as previously agreed," Devetaki nodded. "But in addition . . . what say you have *all* these barrier mountains east to west, to explore, carve out, inhabit? Why, it should keep you busy for a century!"

Zindevar made no reply, for she was struck dumb. Ursula on the other hand was not so taken with things. "It seems I have happened late upon these *discussions*, these plans of yours . . ."

"Ah, no, Ursula!" said Devetaki. "Do not be mistaken or feel in any way slighted; you were taken into account from the start. Zindevar is here to corroborate it when I tell you that we had already apportioned Turgosheim to you, *in its entirety*! Every stack, stump, and manse, the whole gorge! Myself, I shall have the last aerie and all the stumps of fallen stacks around. For we are equals, even sisters of sorts after all. And so the grand triumvirate lives on, but as a matriarchy now! Hah! And why not? The Lords have lorded it long enough."

Their talks were at an end; the sky over the barrier mountains was definitely brightening; Zindevar and Ursula returned to their individual camps. Watching them go, Devetaki thought: *Fools! Greedy fools!* But she kept the thought to herself. Then, gazing west, she sought out a distance-misted glimmer where the foothills met the barren boulder plains: a pale luminosity that lay like a glowworm in the night—the Starside Gate.

For despite the alleged "greediness" of her sisters, Devetaki's ambitions were greater far than theirs. Why be satisfied with a mere stack, a mountain range, a piddling gorge, when she could have a world entire? And why be satisfied with *one* world when she could have two? Her smiling mask glinted lead-grey and shimmery blue in the gradually dimming light of the stars, but the eyes behind the mask were red as ever.

Even as red as lust.

And as red as blood, of course . . .

It was five hours before the dawn when Nathan woke up. Misha had crept out of his arms some two hours earlier, but she had let him sleep on. Indeed, when the others would have woken him up, she insisted that he sleep on!

"He's taking it as the dry earth takes rain," she'd told them. "Because it's required. I don't want my husband to crack like the earth. Also, if he wants to find fault that he wasn't awakened, he can find it with me. So don't worry."

And when Lardis Lidesci had stomped forward and told her: "You're coming between him and a bloodwar!"

"Good!" she'd snapped back. "Now go away!"

And he had done just that, muttering: "*Huh!* So she takes over where his mother left off! Hard women are the poor lad's lot, it would seem!"

But in fact Misha's instinct had been right in more ways than one. For even now, as Nathan slept, things were shaping; the dreams of the Necroscope were never as those of ordinary men . . .

* * *

At first, sensing as Misha sensed how much Nathan needed his sleep—a sleep of recuperation, of physical and mental revitalization; of recovery, from his efforts and his losses both; of adjustment, to reassert the balance of his being—the living and the teeming dead alike had granted him the peace he so desired. But Nathan had asked a favour of the desert-dwelling Thyre, which they had considered and now would answer; the grey brothers of the wild were watchful on his behalf, and they had news for him; and there was a restless handful among the dead, too, who were no longer willing to be kept waiting. They *must* speak to him, and now.

Nathaaan! It was the voice of Thikkoul the long-dead Thyre stargazer, who read the future in the eternal stars. He'd read Nathan's future for him, too, upon a time (and accurately, however obliquely), so that the Necroscope was wary of him; or if not of Thikkoul, of his talent and of the future itself, which had proved as immutable as the past. With or without the stars and those who might try to read them, the future was a devious thing; it had its own way of being as it would be.

And: *Nathan,* said Thikkoul. *Your mind was a void, so that I knew you slept well and deep. But now, as you grow stronger, your numbers vortex swirls as before; I know that you receive me, and we must speak! Since your waking hours are filled with works, I come as before—*

—In my dreams, Nathan answered him. *Yes, I hear you. And you know why I've come?*

To show me the future, yes—even though we can't change it.

Thikkoul seemed breathless now. *Nathan, recently . . . there have been portents! I, too, dream, but I don't understand what I see. You can be my eyes and show me the stars again, wherein the secrets may be fathomed.*

You think it's that important?

Oh, indeed!

Then I'll come to you. And if I may, I shall bring someone with me.

Oh? A friend, I take it?

(Nathan's deadspeak nod.) *And one with a wonderful talent. For like you, Thikkoul, he sees into the future— something of it, at least. But he can't read the stars. And in any case, our stars are alien to him. But the two of you together . . . it may be that we'll get a truer picture.*

Then I look forward to meeting your friend. But when?

Soon, Nathan promised . . .

Thikkoul's deadspeak carrier faded, but there was another to replace it. *Nathan* (the eager, even urgent voice of Jasef Karis, an old champion of the Necroscope among Sunside's Great Majority). *If you would visit this Thyre stargazer, surely you must come and see me? For the past is at least as important as the future. Or, if we may not meet . . . well, on my own ground, as it were, then let me tell you what I know here and now. It makes no difference to me—but it might make a great deal of difference to you and the Lidescis. Indeed, to all the Szgany!*

You, too, Jasef, Nathan told him. *As soon as I can, I'll attend you. But—*(and here his voice became very grim, very cold)*—first I have work to do in the barrier mountains.*

Very well (Jasef's sigh of frustration). *But don't leave it too long, Necroscope . . .*

The deadspeak aether cleared, and the dried-leaves whispers of the teeming dead faded, to make room for the telepathic sendings of the living: the wag of a familiar tail, and a low growl in Nathan's metaphysical mind. It was Grinner, who also knew deadspeak and had listened to the Necroscope's conversation with Jasef:

Uncle, a word of warning: you succeeded too well in these barrier mountains. Best to put back your plans awhile. You may not come here now, not if you would live another day!

Where are you? Nathan was eager to talk to this one.

We spy on the Wamphyri, as you ordered, Grinner told him. *In the mountains, east of the great pass as before. But these are worried creatures, Uncle; they take no chances; over each of their camps they have set a watch, and warriors are hidden in the crags and crevices. Even with your talents you may not come among them unobserved. Also, they have One-Who-Scans! We have sensed him, his probe. He knows you, knows where you are.*

A locator? It could only be Alexei Yefros! And Nathan wondered how many others of Tzonov's party had been taken. Maybe he should speak to Zek and Trask. Knowing that he was asleep, he willed himself to remember all that was being communicated to him when finally he woke up. *What else do you have for me?*

Nothing. Apart from the watchers, the vampires prepare for sunup. They are hidden away. They will sleep in the shadows of the mountains.

My thanks, Grinner, Nathan told him. *But it's hard to take your advice. I have scores to settle . . .*

We know. But they won't be settled if you become a victim! Be as a wolf, Uncle: creep up on your prey and strike him when he least expects it—not when he's prepared.

Nathan nodded. *You're right, of course—*

Then you won't put yourself in jeopardy?

No, not yet at least. Anyway, there are a great many other things that I must see to. Tomorrow, perhaps, in the daylight, when the Lords lie sleeping.

Good! Grinner barked, his telepathic probe fading . . .

. . . But only to be replaced by another—the Necroscope's Thyre "sister," Atwei. *Nathan, can you speak to me?*

To you? Any time.

Good news! she told him. *The elders of the Thyre are in agreement; if Sunside is threatened, then even the furnace deserts come under threat, and the Thyre themselves! Wherefore you need no longer hold yourself to old pledges. If you would bring your people to us—if you need to use Thyre colonies as safe, temporary harbours—so be it. We place our faith in you, Nathan. You have our blessing.*

Tomorrow, Nathan answered, unable to hold back his sigh of relief. *I practice my people tomorrow.*

All of them? Her voice echoed her amazement. *You can bring . . . all of them?*

I can only try.

Tomorrow? But where? Will I see you?

Where are you?

In the Cavern of the Ancients.

Then you won't see me. But you can pass on my message.

Some small sadness, before she answered, *Of course.*

At sunup I'll take my people to Crater Lake. It's a trial, that's all. I'll take them—then return them to their forests in a moment. A reception isn't necessary, and it shall be as if we were never there. I only mention it as a courtesy.

And do you know how to find Crater Lake?

Oh, yes! A very beautiful place, which I remember well. I only have to close my eyes and I can see it like yesterday. And I know the coordinates.

He sensed her nod. *I will pass on your message. Farewell, Nathan.*

Farewell Atwei, my sister ...

At this point Nathan rolled over in his sleep and his arm fell across the empty space where Misha had lain. However vaguely, her absence registered in his sleeping mind, causing him to question it and increasing his awareness. His thoughts went out, searching ... but they didn't find Misha!

Instead they found someone else, who by now was practiced in the invasion of the Necroscope's secret mind. Nathan recognized him at once and despite the fact that he was still asleep conjured the vortex to cloak his thoughts in numbers, which was where he gained the upper hand. In Turgosheim, this had always been the way of it: that his telepathy was superior—to Maglore's! It was why he continued to wear his golden earring, because where certain areas of his mind were forbidden to Maglore, nothing of Maglore's was forbidden to him.

And now Nathan gazed on the Seer-Lord's innermost secrets, and saw how utterly the gorge of Turgosheim had fallen into his grasp ... except for one part, one place. Madmanse, that sinister, gloomy, ghost-ridden mausoleum of a dwelling, like a hollow pedestal supporting Maglore's

own promontory Runemanse! And Nathan read in the
Seer-Lord's mind how his failure to annexe and inhabit
Madmanse irritated him. It was not that the place was uninhabitable, rather that it was *already* inhabited—by the
undead spirit of Eygor Killglance! And for all that Maglore was the self-styled "mage," he could neither exorcise
the thing nor bear to be near it. Quite obviously Eygor
must have been a monster among monsters, that not even
others of the Wamphyri could abide to dwell where he had
dwelled! But that was nothing new; Nathan *knew* what
Eygor had been.

But now ... perhaps Maglore sensed that he was discovered or about to be. In any case his probe withdrew,
was drawn back across all the miles, to Runemanse on the
craggy rim of Turgosheim ...

... And in its turn was replaced—by the monster of
monsters himself!

You are unkind. Eygor's deadspeak crawled like a slug
in Nathan's dreams. *Such thoughts do you no credit,
Necroscope. Do I come in silence, furtive as a thief in the
night, creeping in the corridors of your secret mind like
the Seer-Lord? No, for I am open in my approach, well
mannered, and never a sign of menace. Why, I would not
be here even now ... except I sensed Maglore's probe go
out and desired to know what he was about. And so he
spies on you, eh? Ah, and he knows your powers, Nathan,
and would destroy you if he could! You should fear him,
Necroscope, for he's sly, that one.*

But in you I have nothing to fear, eh, Eygor? Nathan
made no attempt to hide his sarcasm, his disgust. *You are
innocent as a child, right?*

He sensed the other's deadspeak shrug. *We've had this
conversation before.* (Eygor was surly now; he pretended
that he'd been slighted.) *Very well, you don't want to speak
to someone whose only desire is to help you. Someone who
brings words of wisdom—and a warning!*

A warning? However convoluted Eygor's Wamphyri
conversation—his word games—might prove to be, any

information had to be better than none. Nathan's thoughts were deadspeak, and:

Indeed! Eygor agreed. *Yet plainly you would prefer that I leave you to your own devices. Very well, I get me—*

Wait! The Necroscope stopped him, even as he pretended to withdraw. *Except I would remind you, Eygor, that the last time we spoke you tried to lure me into calling you up. That sort of thing won't work a second time, be sure.*

Then you're a fool, for I would be your ultimate weapon!

I would *be a fool, certainly, if I believed you!*

Enough! I don't know why I put myself to the effort. Now, do you want to hear what I have to tell you, or not?

If there are no strings, then I'll listen.

There are many new arrivals among the dead of Turgosheim, killed defending their manses against the incursions of Maglore of Runemanse! They, at least, are not above speaking to me. And their message is simple: Maglore would make himself master here—of all Turgosheim!

Nathan's turn to shrug. *He's that already. It was always his plan. Now tell me something I don't know.*

(A pause, then Eygor's hideous chuckle, as black as sin in the deadspeak aether.) *Ah, but you're not as clever as you make out, Necroscope! Or maybe you are. So tell me: What will be Maglore's next move?*

I haven't given it much thought. Time for that when I've time for Maglore himself.

(Feigned astonishment.) *But . . . aren't you the so-called saviour of your people? Can't you see that once Maglore has filled the gorge with fighting beasts, then he must feed them! Or is it that your duties don't extend so far as Turgosheim? Only your western Szgany are worthy of your protection, eh?*

Now Nathan saw the other's meaning: that in order to keep Turgosheim for himself, Maglore must begin to raid *in force* on Turgosheim's Sunside. No more tithe system, which had been bad enough in itself, but a monstrous bloodbath!

He is not so stupid! he gasped. *What? But he could decimate the eastern Szgany!*

Oh? Hah-ha! No, Maglore is not stupid at all! And yet he will *decimate them, at least until he can be certain that Vormulac's army is crushed or otherwise incapacitated and will not return. Only then will he endeavour to maintain a balance, and let the Sunsiders live and multiply in order that he may live. But before then? Even tomorrow night? The blood is the life!*

Nathan could scarcely control his anger. *Why do you tell me these things, Eygor? To torment me? I can't contain what's happening here, let alone in Turgosheim! You know there's no way I can stop him.*

Eygor's deadspeak nod, and his phlegmy grunt of scarcely concealed anticipation: *Exactly! You can't stop him. But I can—if you'll only call me up!*

That again. Nathan's "voice" hardened. *All a subterfuge, to get you up out of your pit.*

To work on your behalf!

Liar! No vampire ever worked for another.

To take revenge on a certain scrawny old bastard in Runemanse, then, Eygor howled, *who all these years has threatened to annexe Madmanse and make it his own!*

But Nathan shook his head. *Think again, Eygor,* he said. *Oh, I don't doubt that you would kill Maglore, and anyone else you could lay your hands on, but when last we spoke your only desire was to murder your bloodsons Wran and Spiro! You are as changeable as the wind, except you blow to suit the situation! Nothing strange in that—you're Wamphyri.*

For long moments there was silence, until finally Eygor's gurgling, even suppurating deadspeak voice sounded again, saying: *Necroscope, you are an infuriating man. I have offered you the greatest weapon ever in your fight against my own kind. And all I ask is to be up and about in the land of the living again—however briefly—to right the many wrongs that were done me in life. Now tell me: What is it you fear? Do you fear for the Szgany? But there is nothing of humanity left in Turgosheim! Only Maglore, whom I would destroy.*

And your bloodsons?

If they should return, yes.

Nathan nodded. *If and when they return—and if I survive what is yet to be—then it might be time to talk again. Meanwhile . . . I've given you enough of my time. Also, the dead have only recently seen fit to talk to me; I can't jeopardize their faith in me by having to do with such as you.*

Leave it at that, then, said Eygor, sighing. *But I've seen inside your head, Necroscope, and know it can be done. There is . . . such a power of mind in you! Only accept my gift—my talent would be yours in a moment, to use for the good of all the Szgany.*

And you would be up again, in the land of the living.

Only until you willed me down.

How can I be sure of that?

What? (Again the sinister clotted quality of Eygor's deadspeak voice.) *But yours is the power, Necroscope—power over the dead—and what am I but a crumbling old dead thing, eh?*

A vampire thing, said Nathan.

Aye, and one who feels the rising sun even now. And so I get me back into Madmanse, in Turgosheim.

Nathan felt Eygor's presence shrinking, the foul fog of his thoughts rolling back, the final echo of his voice like a shudder in the deadspeak aether, coming from a long way away: *Until we speak again, Nathaaan . . .*

Stirring under the canopy of his makeshift shelter, under the trees, Nathan opened an eye, then both of them. His dreams were already fading, so that he wondered which if any had been real, and which had been . . . dreams. Rolling over, he scanned through the forest, across the prairie, to the furnace desert. And then he knew that the last of them at least had been real. For Eygor was right: the sun was rising. However slowly, a pale stain was spreading on the far horizon, and the familiar star-clusters in the sky were just a little dimmer.

The camp was coming awake. A member of the watch went by, yawning, grinning at Nathan where he lay. It was Andrei Romani. "How goes it, Necroscope?"

"Call me Nathan," he answered, with a smile. "Nothing has changed. Let it be just like before."

Andrei shrugged. "The other has a ring to it. It's like a title."

"Aye," said a gruff voice from the side. "But there's only one title that counts around here—and I'm it!" It was Lardis, seated on a tree stump unnoticed. Lardis who for all his pretended pride was armed to the teeth, alert, the very embodiment of a guardian angel, sitting where he'd sat out the hours since Misha left Nathan's bed, watching over the sleeping form of . . . well, of the Necroscope, aye.

Nathan sat up, yawned in answer to Andrei's yawn, asked: "Is the camp awake? I mean, all of it?"

"Most," said Lardis. "Except you and your people from the hell-lands, mainly. They said you should sleep—then used it as an excuse to get their own heads down!"

Nathan yawned again. "They do right, for they're going to be busy enough from now on. No more trouble in the night?"

"None."

Nathan stood up. "Then let's have them all awake, Lardis. For it's time they learned this new game. For the moment we'll call it 'Going Places.' But if or when the Wamphyri Lords ever come looking for us, then we'll call it 'Hide and Seek.' "

"Games!" Lardis grunted—and wondered why the Necroscope looked at him and grinned that way. But before he could ask:

"Where's Ian Goodly?" Nathan was serious again. "While you are mustering the camp, I've somewhere to go, something to do." He glanced at the sky.

"With the tall gaunt one, who scries on future times?"

"Him and one other," Nathan nodded. "And I can only do it while the stars are still clear over Sunside."

"And this other?"

"You don't know him," Nathan said. "He's Thyre—and he's dead."

Lardis opened his mouth but said nothing. Ian Goodly was already coming, making his way through the trees. But then he would be, of course . . .

IV

Out of the Future, out of the Past—Going Places— Trouble in the Pass

Nathan took Goodly to meet Thikkoul of the Thyre; literally a "meeting of minds," if nothing else, and even then the precog must take Nathan's word for it.

As for Thikkoul himself: he was little more than a bundle of venerable rags in a niche lit by a single constantly flickering candle, in a subterranean mausoleum tended by respectful Thyre descendants, the inhabitants of River's Rush. Though the Thyre colony was two thousand miles east of Lidesci territory and twenty miles into the desert beyond the savanna, the distance was of no concern, the journey instantaneous.

Nathan did not go directly to the Hall of Endless Hours; such an abrupt intrusion would have been unseemly, and anyway, he knew that the Thyre of River's Rush would probably make a great fuss of him. It wasn't that he was above their devotion—or above returning it—but simply a matter of time. The days when he could linger in the Thyre colonies for "endless hours" were long since over.

But there was a place in the desert where he'd once lain out under the night sky and spoken to Thikkoul via deadspeak, so that the astrologer had seen through his eyes and read his future in the stars. That was where he took Goodly, and where the mind of Thikkoul was waiting for him.

I knew you would come, Necroscope. Thikkoul was eager to make his presence known.

Thikkoul, said Nathan, *I have my friend with me, of whom we've spoken. He is here—*

—To corroborate and perhaps explain the things that I might see? I remember, yes. But how is he to know what I see, without deadspeak?

Smiling, Nathan answered: *Not only shall I be your eyes, Thikkoul, but also your voice!* He lay down on the slope of a dune and indicated that Goodly should seat himself alongside. And out loud he said:

"Now what of your premonitions? What have you felt that so disturbs you?"

All my life I loved the stars, Thikkoul answered, allowing time for Nathan to repeat his words in a whisper, for the precog's benefit. *The moon, the sun, the stars—all of the phenomena of the heavens—were as a plan to me; the plan of what has been, and what is to be. As a boy I thought I merely remembered the past, but when certain of the things I saw came to pass, then I knew that in fact I read the future!*

In the night, underground in one of the colonies, even in a closed, darkened room, I could feel the moon and stars above me . . . I sensed how the moon was lured in her orbit by the bulk of our planet; also by a stranger force whose focus lies beyond the barrier mountains, in Starside. And as the moon was lured, so was my mind, but by all of the heavenly bodies! So that even when I could not see them, still I could feel their great wheel and whirl! And ever aware of their presence—even though they were frequently invisible to me—still I could read something *of their awesome portents.*

As it was in life, so in death. For as you know well enow, Necroscope, the passions of our lives go on, even into the ultimate darkness. And now that I am dead, still I can feel something *of the things that will be, in the wheel of the stars . . .*

As Thikkoul paused, so Nathan "translated," and then inquired again: "What is it that you feel?"

The strangest thing! the other answered, his deadspeak so faint and shivery that Nathan's flesh prickled. *For instead of the stars in their eternal revolutions, I feel this* very earth itself *moving, leaning towards the sun! The weight of the moon is felt as always, and likewise that of the alien force beyond the barrier mountains, but now a third, irresistible force is present, which even a world entire must answer!*

Nathan was baffled, and Goodly awed—by the thought of what he was listening to, the words of a dead man; but mainly by a thrill of cognizance that ran through his body and brain as Thikkoul's words registered to conjure a previously unrecognized stream of coconscious thought: the fact that he, too, had felt or *precognized* just such a movement of the earth!

The Necroscope saw something in Goodly's face and was at once concerned. "What is it?"

"Just that I . . . know what he means," the other answered. "For I've felt it, too—except I didn't know it until now!"

"What, that the earth is turning?"

"No." Goodly shook his head. "That it *will* turn! But . . . what can it mean?"

Still speaking out loud, Nathan returned to his deadspeak. "Thikkoul, do you have any idea what it means?"

Perhaps if I could see it in the stars . . . ?

"Very well, but I warn you that they're fading now."

That's when I liked them best, in the twilight before the dawn.

Nathan looked on the stars, and his metaphysical mind was one with Thikkoul's . . .

. . . For a moment, until his head reeled and he drew apart in something of shock. And:

There, said Thikkoul. *You felt it, too. The turning of the world! But . . . did you also see it?*

"See what?" Nathan felt a strange dizziness quite unlike any sensation he'd ever known before.

The stars moving in the night sky, from south to north as the earth turned! Thikkoul's deadspeak was full of wonder.

Nathan shook his head. "No, I saw nothing. But was it . . . the future?"

Something of the future, the other groaned. *But this time I don't know what. As to your future, the future of the Szgany in general—I saw nothing! This other thing is too great; it intrudes, obscures, overwhelms, so that the rest is as nothing by comparison.*

And Goodly was equally at a loss . . .

The whole thing had taken minutes; Lardis would scarcely have had time to muster the entire camp; there was time for another visit. This time Nathan had no coordinates, and so must inquire: *Jasef, where are you?*

The answer was a place in the forest, the woods west of Settlement, where a glade formed the southernmost point of an equilateral triangle, with the abandoned Lidesci town to the northeast and Sanctuary Rock in the northwest. This was the spot where Jasef Karis had died of a heart attack when Nathan and Nestor were only four years old, and it was also the spot where Nana Kiklu had buried him.

Not only that, Jasef's spirit husked as Nathan and Ian Goodly emerged from the Möbius Continuum into the glade, *but it's also the place where I witnessed a wonder, a thing known only to me all these long years. But you're a man now—aye, and your father's son to boot—and it's high time you knew. You would have known before, but they daren't let me speak to you; the Great Majority, I mean. Well, you can't really blame them for that. For*

Harry Hell-lander was a necromancer in the end, and it appears that Nestor takes after him. They had to be sure that you weren't the same, that's all.

Nathan and Goodly sat down in the faintest flush of dawn light on the fallen branch of a dead, ivy-clad tree. The Necroscope was alert, intense, and Goodly mystified. But the precog knew enough to stay silent and let Nathan get on with whatever he was doing. And using deadspeak now, Nathan inquired of old Jasef Karis:

What was it, Jasef, that it's been on your mind so long?

It was a strange morning, that one, Jasef answered. *I had been sick for some time, even years. But what is sickness when you're on the run from the Wamphyri? Anyway, we all sicken and die sometime. So, it was a strange morning; aye, but before the morning I'd had an even stranger dream during the night. Except it was so real, I was sure it wasn't just a dream!*

Tell me about it, said Nathan.

Jasef's deadspeak nod. *In my own time, my own way. Now let me think . . .* And in a moment:

I remember coming awake, thinking, "This could be the last time I'll ever wake up!" For something was very wrong; my arms pained me as if in some great cramp, and my chest hurt as if it were crushed by boulders. Why, it was all I could do to open my eyes!

Above me was the oiled skin that Nana had draped over low branches to keep the rain off. But I'd rolled aside and lay uncovered, drenched and shivering. I was hot on the inside, cold out, yet sweating from the pain in my chest. I thought it was probably the end of me, as I've said, but I didn't have to be a seer to know that!

Except—I knew I must tell someone about my dream! And I knew it must be Nana, of course. My dream of—

—Of a corpse, smouldering, its fire-blackened arms flung wide and steaming head thrown back, lifeless, tumbling end over end into a darkness shot through with brilliant ribbons of blue and green and red light—indeed descending or retreating into this tunnel of twining streamers! A tortured thing, but no longer suffering, unknowable

*as the weird things of dream so often are. And yet ...
there was something vaguely familiar about it, about him!
Then, as my dream drifted me closer, finally I knew who
and what he was!*

And Nathan said: *My father, Harry Keogh!*

How do you know? (Amazement.) *Did I make it so obvious?*

The shake of Nathan's head. *No, but I've seen it before.
Is there more?*

Jasef didn't question what Nathan had said, but went on:
*Harry Hell-lander's spinning descent into—into what,
eternity?—speeded up and left me behind. But in the moment after his corpse had sped away and disappeared—*

"—An explosion of golden light!" the Necroscope
gasped, this time out loud, which caused Goodly to start.
"And a rush of golden splinters like living darts, hurtling
in a hundred different directions and blinking out, escaping
into ... into *other* places!"

But if you know this much, perhaps you know it all!

"No," Nathan answered, "but I've a feeling that this is
the part I *must* know, so please tell it."

Well, I was still dreaming, Jasef continued, *but now in
a moment the scene had changed, to Nana Kiklu's four-
year-old twins in a blanket under a tree. To you, Nathan,
you and your brother Nestor! And suddenly, appearing out
of nowhere, one of the golden darts, which hovered first
over one sleeping child, then the other. The pair of them
stirred in their sleep—at which the dart stopped hovering!
There were two little sleeping heads in that blanket, one
dark and the other blond, and the dart seemed to have
made up its mind. It lanced down ... it entered a small
head! But there was no scream, no scar, no blood, nothing
but a smile on the face of that sleeping innocent!*

"The blond head," Nathan nodded. "My head, yes, it
must have been. I was asleep, and in any case too small to
know or remember. But that was only the first time it happened. Since then there's been another time, in the hell-
lands, beyond the Starside Gate. Now it starts to make
sense; those darts have been my protection!"

Oh? said Jasef, quietly. *Are you sure? But if that were the case I needn't feel concerned, for it would explain everything. It would even explain—you! What worries me is that it's* not *the case!*

It stopped Nathan dead in his tracks. "What?"

That golden dart entered into Nestor, *Nathan! That fragment of your father went to him!*

Nathan felt dizzy, disorientated; a different sensation again from the one he had known in River's Rush, when he'd felt the turning of the world. "But . . . how is it then that things have worked out this way?" he asked. "For I know now that my father was . . . *good!* Anything of Harry Keogh that went to Nestor, it could only be good!"

Which might explain something of the fears of the Great Majority, said Jasef. *For what you got from your father naturally—as a child inherits bones, colour, shape—was good, yes. Undeniably so. But what Nestor got . . .*

"All that was bad in the Necroscope? Is that what you're saying? All that was brewing in him . . . at the end?"

Possibly.

"No, I can't believe that." Nathan shook his head. "Those ˙golden shards . . . I've seen them. They weren't evil; they *were* Harry! One of them entered into me, too, and gave me the solution to the greatest problem of my life!"

Then perhaps the darts were simply forces or Powers. And the way they would develop was in you and Nestor yourselves. If that is correct . . . well, we have seen how it developed in him! It's just that I wanted you to know. In the final battle—and you know what that must be—it's as well that you're aware of what you are up against. For the one thing you do have, whether you get it from your father or not, is your compassion, *Necroscope! It's your greatest strength, but it could be your greatest weakness, too.*

Jasef was finished, and having nothing more to say he fell silent. But Nathan continued to ponder it. Was it possible that Nestor had got all the evil in Harry, the dark instincts of the uncontrollable *Thing* within? And might it not explain his lifelong predilection, an apparently morbid yearning or inclination towards the Wamphyri? If so, it would seem that Nestor had been doomed from the beginning.

But still Nathan couldn't believe it . . .

Back at the camp, Lardis wasn't quite ready for Nathan's game. Nathan used the extra time to explain what he'd learned to Ben Trask. Trask, if anyone, would know the truth of it. But after he'd heard it Trask could only shake his head. "If you tell me the truth of something, I'll know it at once," he said. "Also if you tell me a lie. But you're only guessing, and so I'm at a loss the same as you." They left it at that.

The game was a simple thing. On flat ground a little way out on the savanna, Nathan formed the Lidesci tribe up into a fairly tight-packed circle two to three figures deep. The ring was maybe fifteen paces across. Family groups stayed together, likewise couples and friends as best possible. A long rope was passed around the circle, so that everyone could take hold of it, and then Nathan explained:

"If ever we're threatened by the Wamphyri, as soon as we have the first warning, we hurry here and take up this rope. So remember your positions. Now, this rope is your lifeline. Don't let go of it!" As he stepped to the centre of the circle where all could see him, mothers took up their children and husbands held on to the rope and wives both.

"You may have heard something of what I can do," Nathan said. "Some of you, maybe a lot of you, have even seen it. And a few have gone with me into . . . another place. But it's a very dark place and doesn't feel the same as here. It feels like you are falling, but you're not. So in this other place, it's best to keep your eyes closed. Also, it's best not to talk, and not even to think. Close your eyes and keep silent now."

They did so, and he said, "Now this time is just a trial. When I join the circle and pull on the rope, I want to see how fast you can *walk*—don't run—towards me." He did so, and just like trusting children the Lidescis followed his instructions to the letter. As they passed him, he tapped their arms saying, "Good! That's fine. Just keep going. That's very good." Until they stood clustered together in a group with their eyes still closed, holding on to the rope.

"Open your eyes," said Nathan. "Now I'm going to position men and women among you who have been in my secret place before you. As you see, they're not afraid. Neither must you be." The party from Earth took their places in the new circle, likewise Lardis, Andrei, Kirk, and Misha. And Nathan said: "This time is no practice but the real thing. And believe me, you're going to a wonderful place! Just hold on to the rope and remember what I told you, that you may feel like you're floating or falling—but you're not, and it's only for a few moments."

Nathan conjured a door and guided them through it; it took no more than forty-five seconds maximum. The savanna was empty, and Nathan followed his charges into the Möbius Continuum . . .

. . . and led them out again into—

"—A wonderful place!" Misha gasped. One of the first out, she had opened her eyes at once. Of the rest of the Lidescis: a good many had sat down abruptly as the return of gravity unbalanced them. Others staggered a little, blinking their eyes in the unexpected light; all clung to the rope. Some of them—a small handful and mainly curious children—had in fact opened their eyes within the Möbius Continuum; Nathan had heard their gasps of awe, even terror. These were the ones who clung more tightly yet to the rope, and plumped down that much more abruptly as gravity returned! Several little ones cried their shock, their alarm—shortly turning to cries of wonder, in turn rising to a swelling babble, as the Lidescis gazed all about.

They stood on the fertile rim of Crater Lake, rising like a false plateau from the surface of the furnace desert. All of a mile across, with a raised inner caldera, the place was most probably an old meteoric crater. To the west, a river entered through caverns in the base of the crater wall, formed a great blue lake within the basin, emptied through a gap in the reeflike central node, and so down into the earth again. It was the Great Dark River which, during his travels among the Thyre (it seemed several ages ago), Nathan had followed even beyond this place, under the sprawling Great Red Waste, and so into Turgosheim's Sunside.

Now he calmed his charges. "A Thyre place," he said. "And the Thyre are remarkable people. Soon they'll be up and about, out of their deep caverns, working in the oases. Now I'll tell you what's so wonderful about it. It's because—"

"Let me guess!" Misha stopped him. "It's because . . . on the edge of the forest we were in darkness, the twilight before the dawn, while here . . . now we stand in sunlight!" Sunup, yes, and the dazzling southern horizon as fiery as a perfect spiral nebula viewed edge-on, whose golden central blister threatened to supernova at any moment and burn an entire galaxy. But it was a false impression, for as ever this would be a long, tortuously slow rising. And the slower the better, for the longer the day.

Nathan smiled and nodded. "Exactly right. For we're a good many miles south of where we were. Even at night—even if the Wamphyri knew where we were—they probably wouldn't follow us here. South is towards the sun, and therefore dangerous. But as close as this to sunup . . . they'd *never* chance it!"

Looking all around, he saw the children going down to the water's rim, and said, "A wonderful place, yes—but don't let the little ones stray too far for we can't stay. The Thyre have done us a favour: we have the use of this place in time of danger. So let's not abuse their hospitality. This time was simply a visit, an opportunity to try out our escape route in case the time should come when we have to use it in earnest."

He needn't have worried about the children, for Anna Marie was with them. Indeed it seemed she couldn't be separated from them, especially the orphans. Lardis called them all together again anyway, and formed them up; they played the Necroscope's wonderful "game" again; Nathan returned them to the temporary camp at the edge of the forest.

"Wolf!" Zek Föener cried out, her hands flying to her temples, an amazed expression on her face.

Nathan had been momentarily distracted, surrounded by Lardis and his senior men, who seemed intent on pounding his back to a pulp: their way of congratulating him on his new and apparently foolproof safeguard against the Wamphyri. But within a few seconds of emerging from the Möbius Continuum, Zek was on duty, scanning the area telepathically to ensure that nothing had changed during their short absence.

Now Nathan stepped quickly to her side, touched her, and was at once in contact with her telepathic probe. It was Grinner—trying to contact Nathan, not Zek!

Uncle . . . Necroscope . . . I'm trapped!

Zek reeled, and cried again: "Wolf! For a moment I . . . I thought it was *my* Wolf, except he's dead in another world."

"No," Nathan told her. "Not your wolf, mine! Grinner, yes, in trouble with the Wamphyri, on Starside!"

He read the coordinates right out of Grinner's mind, but before he could act on them picked up a *second* probe trying to make contact with him! It was Jasef Karis's deadspeak. *Nathan! There are newcomers among the teeming dead! Men, some of them! In the great pass—a battle!*

The great pass . . . Turkur Tzonov's men, it could only be. Nathan had intended to meet them in a few hours' time, at the Sunside end of the pass. Now, on the gloomy, winding floor of the canyon, they must be under attack from Devetaki's forces, her final throw before sunup.

A wolf of the wild on the one hand, and human beings on the other—yet Nathan didn't hesitate; or only for a moment, to speak to Lardis:

"Get some men ready . . . eight of them . . . with hell-land weapons . . . wait here!" Then he loaded his own crossbow with a now precious exploding bolt, conjured a door, and was gone—

—To a place in the barrier mountains, on Starside.

It took just a moment for the picture to sink in, but it was a near-fatal moment:

A lieutenant and a senior thrall, one red-eyed and the other feral, both gauntleted, closing in on Grinner where he stood stiff-legged on the rim of a sheer cliff that fell away for hundreds of feet! The intention of the vampires was clear: this wolf of the wild was prey. Whether he fell to his doom or they hacked him to death made no difference: wolf heart was a delicacy, and meat is meat whatever its source.

Nathan had emerged from the Continuum just a few paces to one side of the tableau. The lieutenant immediately sensed him, crouched low, swung towards him, and lifted his gauntlet defensively. Simultaneously, the thrall edged closer to the snarling wolf at the edge of the cliff. But Grinner was wounded, panting his pain, his side torn and bloody. His energy was about used up. He had strength for a final leap, perhaps into eternity.

A rock jutted on the rim, almost teetering there. Nathan was separated from Grinner by this volcanic node, also by the lieutenant—who now took two swift paces towards him!

Nathan swung his crossbow to and fro. Shoot at the thrall, and he himself would be at the mercy of the lieutenant. Fire at the lieutenant, and it might be too late for Grinner. He sent a mental picture of his intentions, and an urgent question: *Have you the strength?*

Yes, Grinner answered—and acted!

He leaped for the rock, bounding to its uneven apex. The thrall swung his gauntleted fist while Grinner was in midair, but Nathan had already triggered his bolt. Passing close to the lieutenant, it struck the thrall in his shoulder and threw him off-balance. The crossbow thrummed empty in Nathan's hand, and the lieutenant laughed in his face, showing the great gape of his jaws. He reached out to grab the Necroscope by the throat, drawing his gauntlet back to strike a killing blow. But:

Now! Nathan sent.

The bolt in the thrall's shoulder exploded, cut short his agonized mewling, sent a spray of scarlet up into the startled air. Grinner made his second leap, struck both Nathan and the lieutenant square-on, so that all three fell in a tangle over the rim. The intended blow never fell on Nathan. The lieutenant's scarlet eyes bulged and he tried to grab the cliff face with his gauntleted hand. Briefly he clung, then slipped. But Nathan and the wolf had already fallen away from him, through a Möbius door.

Before the door collapsed behind them, they heard the lieutenant's shriek dwindle to a flutter of air . . .

. . . And angrily, Nathan asked: *How?*

I failed to take my own advice, Grinner answered. *I told you to hold back, and myself went forward! Three grey brothers were with me, but when the vampires appeared I played the lure and separated myself from the rest. I was trying to spy out a few of their hiding places for you, for the morning. Those two followed after me; I was just a wolf and they would try to take me. The lieutenant was lucky enough to strike me with his weaponed hand. Finally, exhausted, I called for help and you heard me.*

No, someone else heard you, Nathan answered. *And you were lucky, too, for she's known wolves before, that one.*

But Grinner didn't answer—or only with an awed silence, as he experienced the Möbius Continuum. And held fast in Nathan's arms, the great wolf whined, growled, finally panted:

Uncle . . . directions!

What?

I sense them . . . here! Everywhere I've ever known . . . all the time I have lived, and times as yet unlived! This place is all places, all times! Directions, yes! This place is—everywhere! My father's world, and yours, and others! They are here, too; and forces that fight with the moon; and powers that were born in the stars! DIRECTIONS!

Nathan would know more, but had no time for it, not now.

He returned to the camp, emerged from the Continuum,

and at once put Grinner down. And to Zek and Misha as they stepped anxiously forward: "See to him. He's not that badly hurt."

Lardis and his men were ready; among them, Trask, Chung, Carling, Andrei, and Kirk. "Trouble in the pass," Nathan told them breathlessly, as he reloaded his crossbow. "Men against monsters. But be careful: We might yet find problems with both sides! Remember, these were Tzonov's men."

He took them to the pass, where as yet dawn's light crept slowly from the south. At the southern end of the pass where it opened into Sunside, no sign of trouble. Nathan made a second jump, deeper into darkness, and as his party emerged—

—A powerful reek of gunpowder, drifting white smoke, and a stumbling, sobbing figure moving towards them through a pale, writhing ground mist. A survivor, human. But in the broad ribbon of sky overhead where the walls of the pass went up, there were things that were not human!

Two manta shapes, Wamphyri flyers, pulsed against the thin and weary stars. One of them had no rider; it listed, and the webbing of its wings seemed patterned with spangles where starlight gleamed fleetingly through tattered membrane. The other creature was a little lower and carried two riders, one of whom was female. Seated forward of the long saddle—wearing armour and a half-mask of lead—she was obviously a Lady of the Wamphyri. Behind her, the slighter male figure held on as best he could.

The half-mask told Nathan the Lady's identity; quick as thought he fell to one knee, aimed his weapon at the swooping manta shape as it slipped north into the shadows of the pass. But too late, for she'd gone. And disgusted with himself that he'd let the chance slip, "Devetaki!" Nathan grunted.

He cast a telepathic probe, caught only her anger as she shielded her mind. But her passenger wasn't as adept as Devetaki; Nathan could hear him as clear as day, telling her, "That was *him* down there on the bed of the pass! The one that Tzonov and I told you about! Now you've seen for yourself how he can simply appear like that! You can forget those weapons, Devetaki, for with the Necroscope and his fighters down there . . ."

But: "Be quiet, fool!" she cut him off. "Can't you heed your own warnings? He *listens*—with his mind!"

Then the silence was shattered as several of Nathan's colleagues opened up with their automatic weapons, sending a stream of bullets uselessly after Devetaki, and another into the sky where the half-crippled flyer gained altitude. Higher still, two more flyers appeared in the ribbon of sky, wheeled on the wind and sped north. Lieutenants of Devetaki, probably.

"Hold your fire!" Ben Trask shouted over the din. "It's a waste of ammunition!" The firing ceased, and its echoes came bouncing back from the canyon walls like a gradually receding drum roll . . .

Trask went to talk to the sole survivor, and Nathan took Andrei and Kirk forward with him into what had been the battle zone; a short jump of a hundred and fifty yards down the pass, to a misty depression just a quarter-mile south of the dogleg bend. And there they found the ugly debris of war.

There, too, they stood still in the thin, swirling mist, while the Necroscope "listened" in his fashion. Nothing lived here that he could tell, not any longer. At least, there were no thoughts to detect with his telepathy—but the deadspeak aether was alive with fear and bewilderment! That was always the way of it, and it would be no use trying to talk to these recently dead. They would be confused for some time to come.

Burning flyers and a small aerial warrior lay crumpled where they'd fallen or been blasted to a standstill and hosed with liquid fire; their smoke drifted up, making the air vile. Several small craters still issued wisps of smoke where grenades had exploded. The rocks were spattered red. The faces of the men, where they *had* faces, were filled with frozen terror.

The bodies *were* . . . terrible! And some of them might

even be dangerous. Not the men, no—not the *human* corpses—but some of the fallen lieutenants had been vampires for . . . oh, a long time. It surprised Nathan to find more females than males. Then, looking at them, it dawned on him who or what these evil-looking women had been: Zindevar's creatures, aye. The Necroscope remembered her reputation from his Turgosheim days. And proving it was simple: the one or two men were eunuchs!

Meanwhile, the remainder of his party with the exception of Trask and Lardis had arrived. "There's work for you here," Nathan told them. "All of these bodies must be burned. But be careful, and don't touch the vampires or their creatures." He let Andrei Romani and Kirk Lisescu show them how to pile pine branches fallen from the heights against the corpses, and as they saw to it went back to Trask and Lardis.

The single human survivor of the fight, a slim, nervous-looking CMI operative, was talking. "So that's what it was all about: greed, a chance for promotion . . . but mainly stupidity, looking back on it. Well, I wasn't the only one. Paxton fooled just about everyone in his command, even the people above him. I was close to him, I admit it—as close as anyone—but I didn't realize how badly gone he was, how obsessed, until the cavern of the Gate at the Refuge . . ."

"How did Paxton and his team get there so quickly?" Trask wanted to know.

The operative looked at him, shrugged. "He knew that an enemy—he called him an 'alien'—had defected to E-Branch from somewhere in the Urals, and that he would be heading for the Refuge at Radujevac. Borders don't count for a lot these days, as you know, and CMI had safe houses in Bucharest, Belgrade, other places. Paxton had been out there for some time, just waiting for it to happen. But no one in his command, his 'select group,' as he called us, knew just what he was up to or how far he would go. He did initially have orders to stop this alien returning to . . . wherever." Again his shrug. "This place I suppose. But after we had taken the Refuge the orders were suddenly rescinded."

Trask nodded. "But that didn't stop him."

"No. Where the way was blocked he blasted his way through. He found spare air-tanks, inflatables, everything we needed, in the Refuge. He took his entire team up the river to the shining Gate thing. And that was when ... when I found out that he was raving! But too late by then. He was so, I don't know ... *plausible*; he looked sane! He told the men they were going through into another world, and that they'd come back rich. Except they had probably seen through him by then; they weren't much interested in rich. They had wives, children, homes, lives to live.

"When they got awkward he ... he simply shot them! All of them, except me. But I knew I'd be next if I gave him any kind of argument. I didn't know why he'd spared me until I saw Starside. *Then* I knew. It isn't the kind of place you'd want to be alone in ..."

Lardis called Nathan to one side, and whispered, "This one *isn't* a survivor."

"Oh?"

"See how he rubs his neck? He has punctures there, beginning to fester. He's been bitten by some lieutenant during the fighting. He'll be just another plague-bearer, *if* we allow it. But of course we can't."

Nathan nodded but said, "Let Trask finish questioning him. And when you do it be merciful. Don't let him know it's coming. He isn't to blame."

"None of us are," said Lardis, showing him the hilt of a razor-sharp machete in his belt. "Don't worry, he won't feel a thing."

"Does Trask know?"

"I don't think so, or he wouldn't sit so close."

"That's odd. Trask usually knows the truth of things."

"The truth is that this one is not *yet* a vampire," Lardis answered. "But he will be when next he wakes up. If he were to wake up. Except he won't."

"He has no idea what that bite means, then? No, of course he doesn't, else Trask would know."

Lardis nodded. "He's an innocent, poor bastard! But he's strong, too, else that bite would have put him down. It's the worst possible combination: a strong physique and a vampire's bite. He would be a menace!"

"Then let me know when you're ready, and I'll call Trask away."

Again Lardis's nod.

Meanwhile Trask had asked, "Where's Paxton now?"

"Dead," said the CMI man. "I don't know what his game was, but after the fighting started he took off after the leader of those nightmarish women. Him and Bruno Krasin, Tzonov's 2/IC. They chased her into a cave back there. There were a couple of explosions—grenades, I suppose—and the cave came down on them. Nothing could live through that."

"You've been lucky," Trask nodded, and for the first time noticed how the man kept rubbing at his neck, the ugly craters there. So . . . maybe he hadn't been so lucky after all. Slowly, then, Trask stood up and moved apart, and Lardis gave Nathan a certain look.

"Ben," Nathan called out. "Can I speak to you a moment?"

Trask went to him and they turned away. But before Nathan could speak, Trask said, "That man. I think—"

"—I *know* what you think" Nathan cut him short, grabbed his arm.

From behind came the *chopping* sound of a meat cleaver and a short, gurgling cry.

Then silence.

As Geoffrey Paxton surfaced through the dark, choking flotsam of unconsciousness, he studied the various pieces floating by: scraps of memory, bits of the past, all leading to his present situation. He was aware of an urgency in himself, without knowing what it signified. In the misty and mainly unexplored zone that lies between the alpha and omega states of consciousness, that area between vacancy and tenancy of mind, he yet felt impelled to advance his rate of ascent, like a scuba diver short on air. And in fact he was short on air—and even shorter on time as an entirely *human* being.

And so he lay in the rubble of fallen rocks, dirt, dust, in the back of the cave, and "dreamed" his past, or fragments of it:

His childhood, when he was ever aware of his developing telepathy, and increasingly aware of the hypocrisy all around him; his failure to understand that the world doesn't turn on what is *thought* but what is said and done. His gradual opposition to mankind, a turning inwards, an acceleration of self-appreciation, egotism. Knowing that he was talented, and his search for a royal road to power. His time with E-Branch, and his eventual rejection by the Branch, coming hot on the heels of the war with the Necroscope, Harry Keogh.

Paxton's part in that war: his telepathy against the awesome powers of Keogh's metaphysical mind, and the fact that he hadn't stood a chance! And afterwards, the knowledge that he'd stood face to face with just such a Power as he sought, an even greater Power than any he'd ever imagined. And from then on his lust for the Power. But how to achieve it? The Necroscope had stolen—or switched off—his telepathy.

The Necroscope: a man, a monster, a vampire ... yet weak (in Geoffrey Paxton's eyes) in that he'd allowed his enemies to banish him from his own world, or one he could have made his own. If Paxton had been in his position, he would not have been banished. By now the world would be his.

It *would be* his!

And so the plan forming, and finally the chance he'd been waiting for: to restore his telepathy, reverse his misfortunes. The coming of the son of the Necroscope!

Between times, Paxton had worked, elevated himself in the world of men; but that was as nothing now, while his dream, his grand plan, was everything. Keogh had been (or could have been) all-powerful, but didn't know how to control his talents. They controlled him; so it seemed to Paxton. But this time it would be different. If *he* were a vampire he would know how to control it, how to get back his telepathy, stolen by a vampire . . . how to extract the necessary knowledge, from Nathan Keogh, to make *himself* a Necroscope!

. . . His coming here, to Sunside/Starside . . . and his subsequent search for an instrument of change, to bring about his own metamorphosis into that most powerful of creatures—Wamphyri! The attack in the pass . . . he could have been killed and all schemes at an end! . . . But no, there'd been a warning: flyers glimpsed in the sky immediately before the attack. And that had struck him as strange: that they would give themselves away like that. Or had they underestimated the alien weapons? Or . . . had they simply been betrayed? Whichever, forewarned is forearmed; when the vampires had sprung from ambush, Krasin's men had excelled in accounting for themselves. Oh, they had died, but they *had* accounted for themselves.

Then, in the battle, the moment Paxton had waited for. A female, hideous, obviously Wamphyri, had her manta mount blown from under her. He had seen her crawl into a cave—but so had Bruno Krasin! And Paxton had known that Krasin would kill her. Well, so would he, but there's killing and killing. Not *all* of her must die. Something of her—of her *inner species*—must live. In Paxton!

But in the cave, before he could act, that idiot Krasin tossing a grenade! Paxton had barely managed to dive behind a shielding hump of rock. And as he'd stood up in the smoke and stink of the explosion, Krasin had pulled the pin on a *second* grenade! Paxton had seen his one great opportunity disappearing before his eyes! At which his outrage—and his weapon—had spoken for him. Tossed back against the wall of the cave, his uniform tunic gouged crimson in a dozen places, Krasin had flung his arms wide . . . the grenade went bounding toward the narrow entrance . . . *an uproar!* . . . and darkness.

Out of which Paxton, the great survivor, now clawed himself inch by monotonously slow inch toward the present, the here and now, the one proof positive of continuing sentience and life: consciousness.

Consciousness! He woke up!

And coughed in the sulphur and cordite stench, the claustrophobic confines of the collapsed cave. He felt the weight of rocks and dirt pinning him down, the multiple hurts of cuts and bruises, the whirling of his scattered senses ... but more than anything else the darkness. And so he knew that he was still in the cave, while his pain told him that he was still alive.

He moved, and the rubble moved with him. The dust rose up, making him cough some more. He used hands crusted with blood to pick rocks off his chest and body. Laying them aside, he lifted his head, felt nauseous and lay it down. And in a little while lifted it again.

Airlessness! Was that why he couldn't breathe properly? Or was it just the weight of the mountain pressing on him? And the darkness. Paxton put aside more rocks, sat up, freed his limbs and felt them in turn. Nothing broken; just cuts and bruises, and a bump like a hen's egg on the back of his head.

He remembered a pencil torch in his pocket. *God* (in whom he didn't really believe) *please let it be undamaged!* And in a moment a smoky beam of light lancing through wreathing cordite stink and trickles of dust from overhead. The interior of the cave was intact; only the entrance had been brought down.

Close to the wall of the cave, Bruno Krasin's uniformed legs and lower trunk stuck out from beneath ten tons of large rocks; his legs and a dark, wet stain. Well, the Russian had been dead anyway. But what of the woman—or the "Lady"?—whom they'd chased in here?

Paxton searched for his weapon ... gone. Lost under all this debris. Stooping, stumbling, watching his aching head, he moved further into the cave, his torch beam flickering before him, picking out the way. And there—

—There she was! Except she had no head. That was missing; her right arm and flabby right breast, too. And the cave wall close to where she lay was spattered red. Dead.

Paxton knew as much as most men about the Wamphyri, but not everything by any means. And just like most men, he knew and remembered the myths better than the facts. He had wanted her alive, to bargain for her life. He had wanted her to give him what he needed to be: Wamphyri! Little chance of that now.

He sat down on a rock to rest awhile and think. The beam of his torch roved over Zindevar, the tattered stump of her fat neck—*and he saw it move!* He swung the beam back again, held it still with a hand that refused to *be* still but shook as in a palsy. Zindevar's neck was pulsing, throbbing, expanding—as something struggled to find its way out!

And suddenly Paxton wasn't so sure about what he wanted, or even why he'd wanted it in the first place. And there in the cramped confines of the cave, Zindevar's vampire leech emerged; that blind, cobra-hooded thing, trailing mucus from the bloody red tunnel of her neck. She was dead but life went on. The vampire is tenacious.

The thing sensed him (his warmth, blood, humanity, availability, something), and came crawling, undulating. And Paxton was sure now what he did *not* want! Oh, and however briefly, he was as sane as the sanest of men, as he drew a long knife from its sheath in his belt. He jammed his torch in a crack, pointing at the horror, took his knife, and pinned the leech to the dirt floor. Which only served to accelerate the process.

The leech whipped to and fro as he jerked back away from it; it issued its egg, which came skittering out of the torch beam into darkness. That pearly, flickering, over-sized planktonic thing—no bigger than his fingernail, but quite deadly—somewhere in the dark, with Paxton.

Sobbing, he scrambled for the torch and knocked it flying. Its beam went out. And something cold crept on his hand, flowed up his right arm inside his shirt, went from his armpit across his nipple to his neck. It moved like lightning! He slapped at it, at himself, futilely. It was on—it was *in*—his ear!

PAIN!

Agony to make him dance, scream, slapping madly at the side of his head again and again, bounding this way and that. Someone was pouring acid into his ear, his brain, melting his head away! He stumbled this way and that, howling his torment . . . until once again his head made contact with something.

Something mercifully hard.

Darkness.

Again . . .

V

Dreams of the Dead— Ethloi's Symbols—Terror in Turgosheim!

It was the dawning of a new day, and conceived perhaps out of urgency and frustration in the face of a period of impending inactivity, a new idea had likewise dawned.

Nathan's original plan had been to wreak maximum havoc in the vampire camps during the long daylight hours. But according to Grinner—who, while recuperating, continued to relay periodic reports from Blaze and others of the grey brothers in the mountains, thus keeping Nathan updated on Wamphyri activity—this was now out of the question.

Starside of the high passes and peaks, in the permanent

shadow of the barrier range, the Lords of Turgosheim had trebled their pickets and, although it was day, were alert as never before. Devetaki had seen for herself something of the fantastic talents of her Szgany foe—a man Alexei Yefros had called "the Necroscope"—and had taken appropriate measures. Further forays against the camps at this time would be sheerest folly, if not actually suicidal.

Thus Nathan found himself stalemated by his own success, and only two days left before Gustav Turchin would close Trask and his colleagues' escape route to Perchorsk. These were Sunside days, of course, which relieved some of the urgency if not the frustration. And if it came down to it, in the face of some insurmountable difficulty, Nathan could always transport Trask, Zek, and the others to within an ace of the Starside Gate, wish them luck and see them on their way. That would mean the end of their obligations to him, yes, and vice versa. But . . . the Necroscope's emotions were very mixed on the subject; friends like these would be hard to come by in any world; he didn't look forward to it. Following which, and if matters were not resolved by the time they left, the rest would be in his hands entirely. But for now there was a new day and Nathan must dream up some new ideas.

He asked Grinner to relay amended orders to all of his grey brothers, withdrew them to safe positions from which to keep a wary eye on the Wamphyri without putting themselves at further risk, then considered other options and objectives—such as Wrathstack.

But here too he was disadvantaged. Twice he had struck at the last aerie, whose inhabitants were not fools. To go against the stack again would be to take an enormous risk; only emerge from the Continuum in the wrong place at the wrong time—disaster! And in any case, Nathan actually desired that Wratha and the others should not be utterly disadvantaged when it came to the all-out war that must ensue at nightfall. The more evenly matched the opposing sides, the more damage they'd be able to inflict on one another.

Which meant that since he dare not attack, his single alternative course of action—action of a sort, at least—was to take defensive measures. And he had the full span of a Sunside day in which to perfect and complete them.

Dressed in the best Szgany clothing he could beg or borrow, and accompanied by Misha, all scrubbed and attired in her finest, he set out to visit the Thyre, to explain and explore the feasibility of his plan, which was far simpler in outline than it would be in execution. But if it were at all possible, then before the onset of night in some one hundred hours' time, Nathan intended to move not just one tribe (albeit the biggest) into the comparative safety of the Thyre colonies, but as many surviving Traveller pockets as he could locate. Except he knew that he should first have the blessing of the Thyre themselves.

Before leaving the temporary camp, he explained his mission to Lardis and the others. Then, leaving Zek and Chung with work to do—work that only they were equipped to carry out: the locating of other Traveller groups in the forests to east and west—he conjured the first of several Möbius doors.

Starting at Place-Under-the-Yellow-Cliffs, the closest of all the Thyre colonies, Misha and Nathan commenced visiting a long itinerary of suitable refuges. Contacted by Nathan in advance, Atwei was there to meet them in the deep sandstone gorge where the Necroscope had first conversed with the philosopher Rogei. Then the gorge had been a dry, inhospitable place. Now . . . it was very different.

On Nathan's last visit, when he had brought members of his party here after their arrival through the Starside Gate, he had not stepped outside the mausoleum except through a Möbius door. This time Atwei had begged him to come to the gorge itself, because she wanted him to see it.

Her reason was simple: against its rear wall, the gorge was now a small but flourishing oasis full of shrubs, flowers, bees, hives, and honey; all thanks to Nathan and to the artisan Shaeken and the gardener Tharkel. Upon a time, the Necroscope had relayed the words and works of these two Thyre Ancients to their living descendants, with the result that Shaeken's Water Ram was now operational, pumping life-giving water up from the Great Dark River; and Tharkel's gardening and beekeeping theories and skills had not been lost beyond the barrier of his last long sleep.

"But the Water Ram keeps breaking down," Atwei told her visitors. "And so the people of Place-Under-the-Yellow-Cliffs are working on Shaeken's 'Hydraulic Hoist.'" She shrugged her thin brown shoulders. "Alas that the things that men make . . . break! And that when they do, there's nothing for it but that we use muscle and put machines aside. It is very hard to keep the oasis going." At which Nathan remembered something.

It had seemed a big, important thing when first he saw it in Trask's world, but now seemed dwarfed to insignificance by the events of the long night. Anyway, it would be something by way of repayment for the very great favours he must ask of the Thyre. Standing some way apart from the oasis, seeing movement in the greenery, he turned to Atwei and asked her: "Are any of the elders in the oasis? The *other* elders, I mean?"

"Petais, grandson of Rogei, is there," she answered. "Petais who was so hard on you when first you came among us. Will you speak to him? He would be honoured!"

"He became my friend in the end." Nathan smiled. "Bring him here into the sunlight, if you will, for I have something to show him. I'll be back." And to Misha: "It will only take a moment." Before they could query him he conjured a door and disappeared into thin air—

—And was back again by the time Petais (thin as all the Thyre, and bald before his time) had been introduced to Misha. Nathan had brought with him a small box, whose location he had marked among the ammunition boxes in the temporary camp. Now, if the box's contents had come through undamaged . . .

They had: a tiny brass model steam engine with a shining steel flywheel and a chain drivebelt, and a square magnifying glass in a frame. It took only a moment to fill the boiler with water from Petais's waterskin, then Nathan placed the engine on a block of sandstone and positioned the glass against a pebble where its lens trapped the sun and focussed it on the boiler.

The sun was very hot; in a little while the safety valve began to whistle; Nathan barely touched the flywheel and the engine chugged into life. The piston hammered to and fro and the spokes of the flywheel became a blur!

And to Petais: "A little water, and sunlight of which you have ample, equals energy! This is only a small thing, a model. But with a big one, coupled to Shaeken's hoist"— he glanced at Atwei and smiled—"no more aching muscles!"

"We have not the skills!" Petais protested. "Thyre understanding of metalworking would not run to this!"

"But the Szgany *do* have such skills," Nathan answered. "And you can avail yourselves of them. With Thyre mirrors to focus the sunlight, and engines like this in caverns in the ground, the desert could be made to bloom!"

Petais's jaw had fallen open. For once he had no words, and so said nothing . . .

The visit went well, with all of the remaining elders of Place-Under-the-Yellow-Cliffs agreeing to a man that the new oasis in the gorge would make an ideal harbour area for threatened Travellers. It was by now generally accepted that the threat to the Szgany was also a threat to Sunside in its entirety, including the people of the furnace deserts.

Nathan thanked them humbly, and asked permission to visit the Cavern of the Ancients. He would speak to Shaeken and Tharkel, and let them know how their visions had come to fruition; also to show them the steam engine. He would keep his visit as brief as possible. Permission was granted, of course.

But in the Cavern of the Ancients:

Nathan, strange times! said Shaeken and Tharkel together, almost talking over the top of each other. *For we have dreamed weird dreams!* Which wasn't in itself peculiar; Nathan knew that the dead grow weary much like the living, and that they sleep, too, and dream much as they did in life.

"You, too?" Still he was mystified, yet perhaps shouldn't be too surprised; these *were* strange times, and when better for portents to have power? "What are these things you've dreamed?" His reasons for being here, to tell them about the oasis and the steam engine, were temporarily forgotten.

I have dreamed . . . of water! said Shaeken.

And so have I, said the other, breathlessly. *Water to turn the desert green!*

Now Nathan remembered why he was here. "But you must know that these weren't just dreams," he said. "Water was your lifelong fascination, both of you. You, Shaeken, in that you were a visionary, and saw the importance of the Great Dark River under the desert: its bounty if it could be brought to the surface. And you, Tharkel, because you were a gardener who explored the nature of growing things. In a way you worked towards the same end, and your obsessions stayed with you in death as in life. What you have dreamed is what you *felt*—an oasis that flourishes even now in the gorge beyond the cliffs which house this mausoleum!" And now he told them his news. But:

That is all exciting, said Tharkel, *except it does little to explain our dreams. Yes, our obsession was with water, and* perhaps *the water flowing in the oasis, pumped up by Shaeken's ram, has shaken his old bones and stimulated his mind. But my dream was of a* world *of water, with the desert itself pushed back for mile upon mile! Why, I even dreamed of a fountain!*

"But isn't that the same obsession?" said Nathan, with a deadspeak shrug. "Water, springing from the dry earth?"

Oh? said Tharkel. *From the dry, dead earth, do you mean? Aye, for the fountain I dreamed was on Starside, where it was lit by a soft white light!*

And Shaeken said: *Also, I dreamed of thunderclouds in the sky over the desert and great rains, which seemed to*

*me to corroborate Tharkel's dreams, yet neither one of us
can reason it out. We do not know what these things mean!*

Nathan shook his head, frowned, and said, "I don't understand either. Are you trying to tell me you've seen into
some kind of future? If I heard it from Thikkoul—"

Thikkoul! they both cried at once. *But we have spoken
to Thikkoul!* And Shaeken explained: *You must remember,
Necroscope, that the Thyre are telepaths in life, and this,
too, continues after death. All of the Ancients of the Thyre
are now more frequently in contact than ever before. And
practice, as they say, makes perfect. What is more, all of
the Thyre dead seem filled with visions and portents! Oh,
yes, we have spoken to Thikkoul, and recently. And you are
right: it appears our talents complement each other!*

"How so?"

We spoke of water, Shaeken answered, *and Thikkoul
spoke of a great turning of the world.*

Tharkel took it up: *It was almost as though . . . it was
as if we animated each other! As if we were linked up,
dead mind to dead mind, each vision building upon the
one gone before!*

As if our total (Shaeken went on) *was greater than the
sum of our parts.*

Nathan was surprised to hear such an expression. "Do
you know," he said, "but that sounds like Ethloi the Mathematician speaking? I talked to him in Open-to-the-Sky, in
the Cavern of Long Dreams. That was . . . oh, a long time
ago."

Ethloi who knows numbers? Shaeken repeated him. *Of
course, for I was the one who sent you to him. You should
speak to him again, for those were Ethloi's words that I
spoke!*

"Oh? Is he in on this, too? And are his dreams filled
with visions and portents?"

Indeed! And we know that he desires to talk to you.

"He hasn't said as much."

*He's a humble man; Ethloi's numbers are humble, and
yours are legendary! Also, there were a great many who*

would speak to you first, Nathan. He did not wish to waste your time with his "puny symbols."

"He said that?"

Yes.

"Symbols? Not numbers?"

Symbols. Water symbols. "The waters that flow between the worlds." That's what he said.

"Then I shall be with him shortly, for Open-to-the-Sky is next on my list."

When will you go there?

"Now, if you'll excuse me?"

Of course, Tharkel and Shaeken told him in unison. *And may the One Who Listens go with you . . .*

Nathan and Misha returned to the Lidesci camp. It was to have been a brief visit, to check on Zek and Chung's progress before continuing with their round of Thyre colonies; except there had actually *been* a deal of progress, and Nathan must look into it. Namely, Zek had picked up human thoughts in the forests to the east, near the ruined, deserted town of Twin Fords. David Chung had felt something, too, and after Lardis had sketched a rough map of the area, Chung was able to pinpoint the source.

"It can only be Karl Zestos," Lardis grunted, "or his survivors, if Karl's dead. The last I heard, Karl led a small band of Twin Fords folk. Sometimes they lie low in cliff caverns; at others they hide out in the woods; by day they travel and scavenge, of course."

"Their thoughts were very well guarded," Zek said.

"Rightly so," Nathan told her. "If it had been night, you would have had your work cut out to find them at all!"

And Lardis asked, "Will you go to them?"

"At once, if only to take Karl a little cheer. I like him. He asked me to join him, upon a time. But now . . . he might be a bit suspicious. I mean, it's a strange thing that I'll be showing him."

"Take me with you," said Lardis, nodding. "If Karl should find something 'suspicious' about me, I'll box his ears! I can remember when his father, Bela, was boss . . ."

Taking Chung, Lardis, and Andrei with him, Nathan made a jump seven miles east, from where Chung was able to narrow the location of the camp down a little. Nathan's second jump took them to within one hundred yards of their target. Then Lardis and Andrei went off on their own through the bushes, and finally hallooed for Nathan and Chung to join them.

Karl Zestos was just as Nathan remembered him: long-haired, jut-jawed, black-eyed and thin as a pole, but strong. Which was just as well; in the years flown between, even the strongest of men had fallen. "I would know you anywhere," Karl said, locking forearms with the Necroscope. "With your blond hair—a little grey now, I note—and your blue eyes, there can't be a great many like you."

"There's *none* like this one," Lardis told him. "He's Harry Hell-lander's son—and he has his father's talents!" The legend of the original Necroscope was known far and wide, throughout all of Sunside.

After that: the easiest way to explain their presence here was for Nathan to give a practical demonstration. He issued the usual cautions—told Karl to close his eyes, ignore any dizziness, keep still—and after the other had followed his instructions, took his arm and walked him two paces forward . . .

. . . And two thousand miles east and sixty south!

It was Crater Lake, but Nathan couldn't stay. He returned to Lardis and the others, and waited until Karl had taken several deep breaths and adjusted to events. Finally the truth of it sank in, and the necessary arrangements were completed. It had been Karl's intention that towards night his people should make for caves in the cliffs behind Twin Fords; now they would wait here for Nathan. There were perhaps a dozen Szgany Zestos in the small camp, mainly women and a handful of children. The rest, the able-bodied men, were out hunting.

"How many people?" Nathan wanted to know.

Karl's mouth turned down. "We were a town upon a time," he said. And, when the truth of that registered in their memories, "Now there are thirty-two of us all told. The dozen or so that you see here, and the rest out earning their keep."

"I can move you all in a single trip," Nathan said. "And I will, tonight! Not as far as Crater Lake; maybe Crack-in-the-Rocks. I'll keep Crater Lake as a refuge of last resort. As for tonight ... I calculate that for the first half of the night at least, the Wamphyri will be occupied with their bloodwar. After that they'll need to replenish, to restock what they've lost or destroyed, refill their temporary camps with thralls and flesh. If Wratha and the others in Wrathstack survive, they will be in the same position: they'll require to refuel. Except they won't discover anything of nourishment in Sunside, not tonight."

Karl passed on information of other survivors to the east, and then Nathan transported Lardis and the others back to camp. The Necroscope's last words to Karl before leaving were these: "Be ready when I come. There may not be much time ..."

With Misha, Nathan visited Open-to-the-Sky. They received the customary Thyre welcome, and in a little while Misha became the first and probably the last Szgany woman to enter the Cavern of Long Dreams. Indeed, of all the Szgany, the Necroscope himself was the only one who had been there before her. While Misha sat quietly and experienced the mystical atmosphere of the mausoleum, Nathan conversed with Ethloi, who told him:

You could have spoken to me from afar, Necroscope.

That wasn't my father's way, Nathan answered, *and except that it can't be helped, it won't be mine. Here ... I am close to you. That's how friends should talk. But time is short, and I have heard that you have something to tell me. I shall value your advice even as I valued your teaching that time.*

My teaching? My numbers? Hah! The other brushed the compliment aside. *But I have seen yours, Nathan! In fact I was the student, never the teacher, except I had not the wit to understand the lessons!*

Ridiculous! Nathan answered. *And anyway, my numbers were born in me, while yours came from learning. But I've been told your dreams are diverse, and that currently . . . these are not numbers that you've dreamed.*

Symbols, aye! Ethloi whispered. *Like, and yet unlike, the symbols you once showed to me in your vortex. If there is meaning in them, you might know it. If not . . . perhaps I am wasting your time. But as you know, we ancients share our thoughts, and our knowledge puts on growth like drip-stone on a skeletal stalactite.*

Nathan was fascinated. *Show me these symbols.*

And this is what Ethloi showed him:

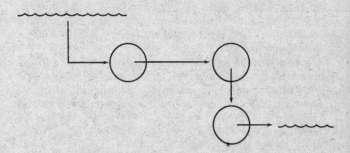

But before Nathan could comment, Ethloi continued, *Which in my dreams always seems to go hand in hand with this:*

Now Nathan said, *I know that one, at least! It is myself, or the symbol by which I know myself. But the other . . .*

I can't say. He shook his head. *The wavy lines look like water . . .*

Ethloi's deadspeak nod. *And I have dreamed of rivers that flow between the worlds!*

There are no such rivers.

I know.

For the moment at least it was all beyond the Necroscope, frustrating beyond reason. If Ethloi's symbols were numbers, it might be puzzled out. But there were no numbers here, just circles, arrows, water. *You could have picked up this water theme from Tharkel and Shaeken.*

Yes, but I don't think so.

And that design (it was impressed on Nathan's mind as if branded there); *could it be . . . a machine? It somehow reminds me of the steam engine; it has a feeling of pistons, pressure, movement, power.*

Ethloi showed him the symbols again, with the Möbius strip laid over or intertwining with them. The Möbius strip . . . like the symbol for eternity . . . like the Möbius Continuum itself: a joining in the fabric of everywhere and -when, where all other places and times come together. A junction of worlds or indeed, of universes. But . . . rivers that flow between worlds?

It was on the edge of the Necroscope's mind like a familiar word that teeters unspoken on the tongue. For a moment his metaphysical mind appeared to grasp it, then let go. And as it slipped away, dissolving to nothing, he sensed all of the same old frustrations mounting, until he felt he must shout, strike out, physically shake them off. The feeling passed, and:

I'll think on what you've shown me, he said, slowly.

Presently, it was time to go . . .

So the day passed.

Together with Misha, Nathan visited as many of the Thyre colonies as were suitable as temporary Szgany refuges, and not one turned him down. It was time that men got to know the ways and customs of their desert brothers and learned to appreciate them, and vice versa. And the best friends are those who make themselves available in time of need. From this time forward, there would always be a much closer liaison between Szgany and Thyre. An era was over; the time when the Thyre of the desert were considered unmen was past.

And the Necroscope was as good as his word. In the night Misha had told him that tomorrow she would lie out in the sun with him, in the long prairie grass, but he had told her there was a better place. And there was: the place where he and she had crept into each other's arms just five months ago, on the day they were married.

One-third of the way through the morning (more than seventeen hours into the long Sunside day) Nathan called a break and carried Misha there via the Continuum, to the spot east of Sanctuary Rock where their nuptial trek had taken them. And as before, in a sea of bracken, he threw a skin over the bole of a fallen tree and made it fast to projecting branches to keep the sun off. And they took their fill of love, drank wine, and ate bread and cheese, just like before. But before they slept she took his head on her breasts, and cradling him said, "Didn't I say you'd remember our first 'little house' for the rest of your days? Didn't I tell you that I would see to it?"

It seemed a long time ago, but Nathan remembered it well. "You did and you did," he answered, dreamily. "And I did, and I always will."

Then they slept . . .

. . . And the Necroscope came awake with something—some*one*—oozing in his mind! He knew him at once, and felt him withdraw like a snake slithering between stones. But by now he knew that he'd had enough of this one.

Without waking Misha, he stole a short distance apart from her through the bracken, put up his hand to the twisted loop of gold in his ear, and sent a thought winging for Turgosheim:

Maglore, I know you. Who else could it be of all the Wamphyri, on the prowl when the sun is up? You kept strange habits, for the beast-thing that you are!

For a moment there was no answer, but then the other put aside all pretense and said: *And so we have made fools of each other. You of me in Turgosheim, when you hid from me your true nature, your powers, and me of you ever since that night when you thought that you "fled" from me. But I will admit, Nathan, that I was the bigger fool, for there was that in you which I should have seen and explored when I had the chance.*

Oh? Nathan answered. *And have you seen enough now? You'll agree that I've given you plenty of time, surely? For you see, you didn't make that much of a fool of me, Maglore. I've known about you for some time, and you have only seen what I wanted to show you.*

The other was silent, and Nathan continued: *Anyway, it's over now. From now on you'll get as little from me as you do from Vormulac, which is to say, nothing! Except where Vormulac is dead, I am very much alive!*

And now Maglore hit back, sneering: *Ah, ungrateful creature, I know well enough that you're alive—and just how much alive you are!* His mental chuckle was black as pitch. *Ask yourself this: Who was it sent his love-thrall to you, in order to instruct you? You virgin! You innocent! You have that to thank me for, at least. But now something you'll never thank me for. Think on this, Nathan: I was with you the night you were wed, and again just an hour or so ago! Oh, I have not enjoyed your woman, your . . . Misha?* (Nathan could picture the mocking flutter of the other's furry eyelashes.) *I have not known her with my own member, no—but I have enjoyed* you *enjoying her!*

Since the game was up, the Seer-Lord would let his spiteful nature hold full sway; whatever he had put over on the Necroscope, he would now use it to belittle him. It was the way of the Wamphyri: if they could not torture their victims physically, they would do it mentally. This time, however, his mockery went too far; Nathan was no longer a shivering thrall in promontory Runemanse but his own free man—and a Power!

Listen to me, he said. *So, you have enjoyed spying on me from afar. You've enjoyed* my *pleasures and hope that*

*by telling me about it they'll be reduced. But you're like a
spoiled child, Maglore! Because you cannot have all your
own way, you seek to subtract from the lives of others.
Hah! And you're the one who counted yourself superior to
the other Lords! Aye, and I remember your silly model of
Turgosheim, its spires and manses: how you would hurl
your so-called spells and imprecations against the houses
of your betters when you thought that they had slighted
you. But in fact they never had slighted you; indeed, they
rarely so much as* noticed *you! What, doddering old
Maglore, who sent young men to service his wenches because he was way past doing it for himself! Well, at least
those young men were* men *by comparison! Scum of the
earth—indeed, vampires, aye—but* men *next to you,
Maglore! Men next to you!*

The part about Maglore's impotency was a lie, of
course, but that too was the way of the vampire, and perfectly acceptable in their taunting and word games; and the
Necroscope had always been good at matching taunts.

Maglore was furious. His telepathic aura seethed with
his hatred. *If I could . . . if I could but reach out across all
of the miles between,* he choked the thought out.

'Ware how you threaten, Maglore! Nathan too was enraged, but somehow managed to control it. His telepathic
voice was a hiss, as if spoken through clenched teeth. *For
you're impotent in more ways than one. No, you can't
reach out, and there's no tool of yours can harm me here.
But as for me . . .*

Eh? the other gasped, sensing a threat.

And quietly now: *I go where I will,* Nathan told him.
And indeed I do *reach out—at will! I speak to the dead . . .
who* listen *to me! But I'm sure you know all this by
now. Except . . . do you know it all? How* little *do you
know Maglore?*

And again: *Eh? But what's to know?*

*Oh, you long suspected that I conferred with some other
in Turgosheim, but has it not dawned on you* with whom
*I conferred? No, you may not "reach out" and strike at
me, but I come and go as I will; I talk to the dead, who*

*advise me; through me, they seek revenge on the living!
Yet how may the dead harm the living? Or is there something more? Do you remember, Maglore, how you told me
that Runemanse was haunted?*

Runemanse? the other gasped. *Haunted?*

Or if not Runemanse itself, Nathan went on, *then
gloomy, shadowed Madmanse in the levels below? No, you
may not strike at me, nor even reach out to touch me from
this time forward. Look!* (He slipped Maglore's sigil from
his ear and pushed it down into a heap of humming beast
droppings.) *There! And will you read me now? Well, good
luck to you! May the stink-gnats entertain you—you have
comparable minds, after all. And so I'm free of you,
Maglore. But . . . are you free?*

Free? (The other gibbered.) *Why I* rule *now in Turgosheim! All is mine! What do I care for Madmanse?*

Care? Ah, no. (Nathan was enjoying it now.) *But fear?
Ah, yes!*

*There is nothing to fear in Madmanse! Just an old and
crumbling dead thing. Eygor may not harm me!*

Really? Nathan's voice was a sly whisper. *Can you be
sure? Well, we shall see . . .*

Maglore pulled himself together and snarled: *When next
we meet, Nathan Seersthrall, you are a dead man. Or a
man changed forever into something hideous!*

But: *I doubt that we shall ever meet,* Nathan told him.
*I doubt that I shall ever speak to you again, not in this
world. Nor am I your thrall—but you may one day be
mine. For after all, I converse with the dead!*

Nathan, I . . .

*. . . Farewell, Maglore. I leave your sigil, your shew-
stone, where it and where you belong—in the shit of a
beast! Spy on that, if you will.*

He withdrew his probe, and the telepathic aether fell silent on the instant.

The Sunside day was a long one, worth more than four of
parallel Earth's days, but the time was not wasted. There
was good, genuinely restful sleep to be had; there were

visits and arrangements to be made; there was a handful of teeming dead whom the Necroscope must speak to. Not least his mother, Nana, who considered herself the most fortunate of all the teeming dead in that she still had her son, and through Nathan, Sunside and the Szgany.

Via his wolves in the heights, Nathan kept a watchful, wary eye on the Wamphyri. Through deadspeak contacts such as Jason Lidesci, he updated himself on the necrology of men and monsters alike. And through the talents of Zek Föener and David Chung, he was able to locate, advise, and make arrangements for the safety of a good many more Travellers. Survivors of Tireni Scarp and Mirlu Township were discovered in the west, and told to prepare for evacuation; others to the east fell in with Nathan's plans.

The Necroscope was relieved to discover large numbers of Travellers in the woods, even though the majority of them trusted only to themselves and kept hidden away. But that was probably as well; after all, it would be impossible to move all of them to safety. Still it was heartening to note that while Wratha and the others had been resident in Starside for three and a half years—a period of prolonged Wamphyri depredations—still the tribes flourished.

And on that theme—the theme of burgeoning against all odds—something else had become very noticeable; not only to Nathan but to everyone who had previous knowledge of it. "What do you make of it?" Ben Trask asked Nathan at Lardis's camp.

The Necroscope smiled and shrugged. "Well, it's plain to see what Andrei Romani makes of it, at least! But, then Andrei doesn't know her as we do."

The subject of Trask's inquiry was Anna Marie English, the previously wilting ecopath. In tune with the Earth (this earth, too, apparently) to such an extent that her own physical well-being was governed by her unique "talent," an incredible metamorphosis now seemed to be at work in her. She was growing . . . younger! Previously drab, arthritic, stumbling, and bleary-eyed—in short, grown old before her time—now the years seemed to be falling off her.

"During the night," Trask said, "no one noticed her. She was with us, that was all. And now, because they'll see her as she *is* now, in the morning light, this is how they'll think of her from now on; they won't realize that there's been a change in her. But back on Earth a week ago . . . well, you saw how she was. She never would have made last night's trek. A few miles would have been enough to cripple her. But take a look at her now . . ."

Nathan looked. According to Trask during other conversations, when the ecopath had been twenty-four she'd looked fifty. When Nathan had first met her just a few months ago, she'd been forty but *still* looked fifty! It had seemed to say a great deal for her homeworld that after years of ecological depredations Mother Earth was struggling to be back on her feet; a fact that seemed mirrored in Anna Marie's "vitality," the abeyance of her physical decline. It had meant that men were learning to abide by rules of ecological conservation and sensible husbandry of a planet's resources, albeit the parallel planet beyond the Gate. So what was going on here?

Anna Marie was forty-one but looked thirty-five! She had put aside her thick-lensed spectacles and hearing aid; her eyes and hair shone; her liver spots were little more than freckles. She who had limped now held herself upright, her head high, and the defect in her hip was barely noticeable. Her movements were flowing, her limbs seemed supple, and her hair—bounced! When she smiled, her teeth gleamed! Anna Marie wasn't beautiful, but she was undeniably attractive.

Certainly Andrei Romani was attracted; he stood watching while she taught a small group of orphaned children a game out of the hell-lands: ring-a-ring-o'roses. Children had been Anna Marie's life ever since the Romanian Refuge: which reminded the Necroscope of someone else who had loved children . . . in Turgosheim's Sunside. So she had told him, anyway.

Orlea, Maglore's love-thrall in Runemanse. For a time

she had been Nathan's lover—albeit wrapped and gifted to him by Maglore. A gift he daren't refuse at first, until in a while he hadn't wanted to! It had lasted . . . for a time, until the Seer-Lord had put a stop to it. Just part of the evil old bastard's game, his plan to corrupt Nathan, subvert him to his cause . . .

"Well?" said Trask.

"Umm? Oh, what do I make of it?" Nathan came back to the present. "Well, this is a young world; an unspoiled world, at least. Ignore the Wamphyri, and the 'Nature' of this world is healthy. However briefly, Anna Marie is now part of Sunside/Starside, and so reflects its quality."

Trask nodded. "I thought that might be your solution. But it feels wrong to me. It could be wishful thinking, of course, but I would like to think she reflects what's still to come."

"Only time will tell." Nathan's shrug was perhaps a little careless, which was hardly intentional. But as Trask was suddenly aware, the Necroscope's mind was on other things . . .

The worst of it was, Nathan couldn't tell anyone where he planned to go or what he would do there. But subconsciously Orlea's plight—her situation in Runemanse as Maglore's "companion"—had bothered the Necroscope for a long time. The Seer-Lord had not changed her (not during Nathan's time with him, at least), for he had valued her humanity; with Orlea, as with Nathan, he had been assured of his own "superiority."

But Orlea's story had warmed Nathan in soulless Runemanse; he still remembered the way she had asked after Sunside's children, and suspected that she'd mourned the warmth and light of times forever past. Well, and if what he planned worked out—

—But even if it failed to work out, why should she suffer the . . . the *hospitality* of that loathsome Lord of the Wamphyri a moment longer? She'd told Nathan she loved Maglore that time, but he had suspected it was a love born out of madness—or of the fact that the Seer-Lord was her only protection in a place void of the light and love of humanity. Well, now there was a choice, something other than Maglore's dubious "protection," if Orlea would only avail herself of it. Wherefore:

In the afternoon, after eating and sleeping, Nathan made sure he was up before Misha in the camp at the edge of the forest. This was deliberate; he couldn't tell her his mission for obvious reasons. She wouldn't understand his motives, or might think she understood them too well! He didn't want to deceive her, but neither could he hurt her. If he could get Orlea out of Runemanse, he would place her in a small Thyre colony until later he could move her back into Turgosheim's Sunside. All of this kept secret, of course. But . . . it was all hit and miss, all ifs and buts. For example: if aught should happen to him, Orlea would be stuck with the Thyre; but even then, would that be any worse than a life of ever-increasing morbidity and madness in promontory Runemanse? No, of course not.

Nor could Nathan mention his mission to Trask or Lardis; so much as hint at it, they would try to dissuade him. Rightly so, for if anything *were* to happen to him . . . what price then Lardis's dreams, his hopes? And what of Trask's chance of returning home? Nathan supposed he was being selfish; but how, if he worked for the well-being of another? Also, he *remembered* Orlea so well; she had been like a breath of fresh air in the otherwise vile atmosphere of Runemanse. It was even possible she'd saved his sanity, so that the very thought of her still trapped there was abhorrent to him.

And so, saying nothing to anyone, he walked out a little way onto the prairie, conjured a door, and moved—

—To the rim of Turgosheim, within the fortifications of the roof of the rearing turret that was Runemanse. It was past noon but the sun was still "high" in the southern sky; its rays burned on the upper ramparts, which cast shade within the walls. The hour was such that in most of the conquered manses a majority of men and monsters alike would be sleeping. Yet still Nathan guarded his secret mind, shrouding it in numbers as he moved swiftly to the low parapet wall, leaned across it and looked down on gloomy, smoking, vapour-wreathed Turgosheim.

He knew that he had the coordinates and could find his way directly into Orlea's locked room. It was simply a matter of familiarity; and certainly (he felt the blood rising to his face at the thought) he had been familiar enough with that room in his time. But what of Maglore? Even the Seer-Lord must sleep at times, and midday was as good a time as any. Also, when Maglore had . . . when he had wanted Orlea, he had used to *call* for her. Her room had been hers alone, where she'd known complete privacy. A singularly rare thing, in Runemanse!

Nathan dared not probe telepathically—but neither could he stand here, wavering on the rim like a boy desperate to swim who fancies the water is too cold. He made up his mind—made to conjure a door, too—and in that selfsame moment saw them: Maglore and Orlea, together on the low-walled platform of a balcony one tier down from his own position, gazing out over Turgosheim. He saw them, and they . . . *sensed* him! His surprise had served to focus his thoughts upon them; as their presence had registered in Nathan's mind, so had his in theirs. Galvanized, their heads cranked back; their widening eyes swivelled up to glare the shock of recognition into his own.

You! Maglore's mental croak rumbled in Nathan's head. And:

Nathaaan! Orlea hissed, her eyes like lanterns in the balcony's shade, flaring to match the Seer-Lord's own!

Gasping his horror, Nathan thought: *I should have known it! She was here too long. She was Maglore's for far too long!* And the Lady Orlea looking at him with uniformly scarlet eyes, her ruby lips slowly forming into a smile that displayed eyeteeth like small curved knives.

And the Seer-Lord pointing a taloned hand, snarling: "See, now! Didn't I tell you he comes and goes like a ghost?" Except the Necroscope knew that Maglore's spoken words were merely a subterfuge, a ruse, a cover for his *un*spoken query and command: *Where are you, dull*

*and stupid beasts, so-called guardians of the roof? My en-
emy is upon me even now! Come . . . see to him . . . destroy him!!!*

This had always been Nathan's main advantage over
Maglore: his ability to read the mage's thoughts while
guarding his own. But even if he had not "heard" Maglore's command, he most certainly would have heard the
grunts of startled enquiry and scrabbling of horny feet on
the vast flat roof. So that turning from the rim he saw his
second error: that he'd failed to credit the oh-so-clever
Maglore with even a modicum of intelligence. Or if not
that, then that he had started to put too much faith in his
own powers, until he believed they'd made him invincible.
What? But *naturally* Maglore would post guards here!
Even in his great triumph he would know better than to
leave unguarded a possible route of entry into Runemanse.

Doubtless these creatures of Maglore's had been stationed in the squat turrets that knobbed the wall at the rear
of the promontory where it bottlenecked into a mighty
bridge of rock. The wall with its turret battlements, and
the precipitous gulf itself, kept Runemanse safe from attack from the great plateau that sprawled for seven miles
to the south before sloping down into the wooded foothills
of Turgosheim's Sunside. The guardians had been keeping
watch outside the wall and to the south, on the lookout for
any creeping incursion; but Nathan had arrived here instantly, north of the wall and *within* its demarcation.
Wherefore the guardians, in tune with their Lord's mind,
had been unaware of the Necroscope's presence until the
moment Maglore himself sensed it.

They were not warriors so much as personal guards,
produce of Maglore's vats, but of recent construction and
utterly nightmarish aspect! And vampires of course. The
Necroscope had never seen anything quite like them before, so that for a moment they unmanned him. They were
spidery things, many-armed and -legged—but their limbs
were those of men, with grapples and pincers in place of
hands and feet! Ravenously hungry, they came scuttling at

great speed and in red-eyed rage from the shadowy doorways of their turret observation posts.

Nathan gathered his wits, conjured a door, glanced down at Maglore one last time and called out, "Enjoy your triumph while you may, Maglore of Runemanse—for it won't last long."

But as the roof's grotesque guardians came scurrying like great grey spiders, he stepped back from the rim and in through his Möbius door, and without pause collapsed it behind him. And as he returned to the temporary camp of the Lidescis in his own Sunside those thousands of miles to the west, he could scarcely help but view his threat (which at best was braggadocio) with dismay. Aye, for with all Turgosheim and its conquered denizens at Maglore's command, the Seer-Lord's triumph might easily last a very long time indeed!

Soured by what he had seen, saddened by Orlea's conversion to vampirism, the Necroscope must leave it at that.

For now, at least . . .

PART EIGHT:

BLOODWARS!

I

Timescan—Two Fly Out—Storm Clouds on Starside

Nathan had no choice but to forget about Orlea, just as he'd been obliged to forget about Siggi Dam. His interest had lain in setting them free, but they were beyond that now. They had become irretrievably part of the vampire world; they *were* vampires, and he was sworn to destroy them.

For the first two-thirds of a long but less than interminable afternoon, he was quiet to the point of being withdrawn. But as the sun dawdled east on its low, slow trajectory, almost imperceptibly losing height, he gradually came out of it. And if his moods were noticed and people wondered about them, nothing was said. For after all, the Necroscope had many problems.

But moods or none, he worked because he had to. Chosen men were trained in the use of alien arms (a good many weapons had been salvaged from the battle in the pass), and transported via the Möbius Continuum into the several camps of Traveller groups who could not bring themselves to trust or accept Nathan's invitation. As support teams these trained men would add firepower to Szgany determination, helping the loner parties to withstand whatever the coming night might have in store.

Through Grinner (now much improved, and eager to be rid of his dressings), Nathan was kept updated on affairs in the barrier mountains, on the boulder plains, and Starside in general. Despite the fact that it was sunup, there had been some movement: Devetaki had replaced the observation posts destroyed by Wran the Rage's bombardiers, and she'd also dispatched men and creatures into selected areas west of the great pass. Flying low over the plain of boulders, and safe in the constant shade of the mountains, they had established a number of camps in trog caverns behind the Starside foothills. It was all part of the continuing containment of Wratha in the last aerie, of course, but the Necroscope was more concerned about the Gate; he worried about the proximity of the vampire camps to that all-important portal.

Finally he took Trask aside to tell him, "Ben, I don't see how you can help anymore. It might be a good idea to get you out of here while we still can. I can have Grinner send a wolf or two to check on movement near the Gate. Then, if the way is clear, I can get you, Zek, and the others as close as possible, and from then on you're on your own."

Trask nodded. "And you, Nathan? Won't you be on your own, too? But we have two whole days, Sunside days, before we have to get back, before Turchin brings the weight of the mountains down on that place in Perchorsk. And the longer the better, if Zek and Ian are to use the Romanian route."

"Two days less travelling time," Nathan answered. "Through the Gate, I mean . . . provided, of course, that the route to the Gate isn't blocked."

"What, *your* way blocked?" Trask cocked his head. "Are you joking?"

"I can only get so close," Nathan reminded him. "But Devetaki's creatures don't suffer the same restrictions." Now more than ever, the Necroscope was aware of the constant danger he was in; he knew that the Lords and Ladies were aware of him!

Trask shook his head. "We've talked about it and we're all of the same mind. While you can use us, we want to stay. And by 'we' I do mean all of us. I'm including John Carling, Jim Bentley, and Orson Sangster. They're good men, and they can handle guns. They—"

"—No." Nathan shook his head, cut Trask short. "Least of all those three. They didn't come of their ... well, I hate to sound like a vampire, but they aren't here 'of their own free will.' They got caught up in things, that's all. And now, well, *they* at least are leaving—and no argument."

Trask set his jaw stubbornly. "Don't think you'll shake me and Zek that easily, or Chung and Goodly—or even Anna Marie, for that matter! We're espers, and you need us. We were a team on Earth—our earth—when you helped us out with that problem in the Nightmare Zone, so we'll continue to be a team here. We're staying until we *have* to go!"

"Even until it's too late?"

"If it comes to it, yes. But I don't think it will. You're Harry Keogh's son, Nathan ..."

"Is that a recommendation? You put faith in that, do you? The Wamphyri killed him in the end." And again Nathan thought of just how close he, too, had come, and how recently. Simple carelessness. But on Sunside/Starside, that was all it took.

Zek was looking for them; she saw them where they stood at the camp perimeter, under mighty ironwoods, and came hurrying. She looked lovely as ever—but they saw that she held a hand to her temple, where the corners of her eyes were creased in a frown. David Chung was right behind her.

"Nathan," she said, closing with the pair. "You are being watched!"

David Chung joined them, and said, "She's right. I picked up a locating probe, one that I'd know anywhere. The last time I came up against him was west of the Urals, when we snatched Nathan from the Russians. It's Alexei Yefros!"

Nathan nodded. "In thrall to Devetaki, yes. It hardly surprises me. We saw them together in the pass."

Chung nodded. "But his talent is that much better now. He can switch it on and off like a light! I've fancied there was a locator at work for some time, but he's been dodging me."

"He's a vampire," Nathan pointed out the obvious. "Even as a lowly thrall, his talent has been enhanced."

Again Chung's nod. "And you're the one he's on to. His probe is a carrier—"

"—For Devetaki!" Zek finished it. And again her hand went to her temple. "She's . . . *powerful!*"

"Stop it!" Nathan told her at once, reaching for her hand, dragging it from her face. "Don't interfere with that one! Devetaki's the leader of the Turgosheim army. And that speaks for itself. She'll know it immediately if you break into her probe—and then she'll try to hurt you!" He had seen enough women hurt, and worse than hurt. Murdered, and worse than murdered. He looked around. "Where's Ian Goodly?"

They found Goodly; Nathan came straight to the point, and the precog agreed with him. "The cavers are out of it." He was matter-of-fact about it. "I don't see them here from now on."

"Is that all?" Nathan asked. And Goodly frowned.

"It's all vague," he said. "It doesn't firm up until it's closer—closer in time, I mean. But I'm going with you to the Gate. Oh, and Grinner, too."

"You see that?"

"Yes, and I'm ready." Which meant they were going now! Zek went off to tell Carling and the other cavers to get ready, and Nathan called for Grinner. The great wolf came, tongue lolling.

Why me? He wanted to know.

It's foreseen. Nathan could only shrug.

Good! For I wanted to see that place again.

The Starside Gate?

Yes, but also the other place. The Between Place!

The Möbius Continuum? Why?

To smell the directions!

Wolf mind-pictures were weird, full of scents and sensations, spacial and even temporal currents. But there was little or nothing of numbers in it, and whatever else it was the Necroscope had neither a nose for it nor the mental compass required to understand it. The thought did cross his mind, however, that the senses of a homing pigeon must be somewhat similar to those of a wolf—minus the hunting instinct, of course.

Waiting for the cavers to get ready, Nathan made a quick jump to a spot just one hundred yards west of the glaring hemisphere Gate; he felt its strange repulsive forces acting on his door, which was beginning to warp even as he exited. But he was there for the merest moment—sufficient to scan the plains in all directions, and send tentative telepathic probes inwards to the barrier mountains and the great pass, and eastwards to the petrified lava camps of the Wamphyri—before conjuring a second fragile door and getting out again.

He had detected the Wamphyri everywhere, but none of them close enough to cause any real concern. He knew, however, that things could change in very short order, so couldn't delay the departure of the cavers a moment longer. Zek had fashioned a rope collar and lead for Grinner—who hated it! But it was the easiest way.

Nathan took the wolf's lead in one hand and guided Grinner and the triple-linked men, Carling, Bentley, and Sangster, with Goodly bringing up the rear, through his entirely invisible door ...

... To Starside.

The men were used to it now, if not Nathan's nephew wolf. Coming out of the Möbius door almost at the run, John Carling and company went loping with their packs bouncing, to the low crater wall, helped each other up, paused for a moment in the sighing white illumination of the Gate to look back. Its glare was such that the Necroscope and Goodly saw the three as dark silhouettes that waved, turned away ... and were gone. They had their instructions: to tell Turchin and E-Branch that others would soon be coming through, both in Perchorsk and in Romania.

"On their way home," Nathan sighed, and glanced at Goodly. But the precog was staggering, which wasn't an aftereffect of their brief Möbius trip! "What is it?" Nathan was at once solicitous.

Goodly straightened up, steadied himself, shook his head. "It will keep," he said. "Until we get back."

Grinner had noticed nothing. He was still fascinated by the Gate, the fact that the three men had vanished within it. He stared at it with his ears pricked up, his head cocked curiously to one side. *Gone,* he said. *To the world of my father's father. Except . . . there are other ways than this!*

Nathan *was* interested in that, but:

We can't stay here any longer, he told the wolf. *The One-Who-Scans will find me if we do, and the Wamphyri will know my business. That's something I can do without.*

Nathaaaaan! There were other voices invading his mind now; the voices of Thyre Ancients, speaking out from their tombs in the burning deserts. He knew the first of them at once: Tharkel the gardener, but excited as never before. *Nathan, I was dreaming again, and . . . you were there!*

Yes, he answered, *I am here.*

No, no! Tharkel shook his head. *I mean, you were there—at the place of the fountain!*

A fountain of light? The Starside Gate? Was that what this was all about? But before Nathan could ask or comment:

Necroscope! (And this was Ethloi, equally excited.) *Forget about Tharkel's fountain for the moment—unless it's significant of a spring—for you are standing at the very source!*

The source of what? (Nathan couldn't stay here any longer, and his frustrations were mounting.)

Where you're standing now—right now, at this very moment—is the shore of a lake! And at your feet, I see a sea of stars! And in their centre, a brilliant sunburst!

"A sunburst?" Nathan repeated him out loud. "A lake? A sea of stars?"

And: "Yes," said Goodly, reeling again.

The answers could be sought later; right now Nathan had to get his charges out of here. Conjuring a door, he led

man and wolf through it and made to return to Sunside.
But on the way:

There, Uncle! Grinner's telepathic voice was a hushed
whimper.

What now? Nathan asked.

Don't you feel them? The directions?

Directions to where?

*To ... other places. But one place especially. Your fa-
ther's world, Nathan—the world of Harry Dwellersire!*

It might make sense at that. For after all, Grinner was a
child of the Dweller; he and Blaze, and poor Dock, too.
And the Dweller had travelled between worlds without using the Gates at Perchorsk and Radujevac. Indeed, there'd
been no Gate at Perchorsk at that time, and the one underground in Romania was still undiscovered.

So, had Grinner inherited something of his werewolf father's metaphysical talents, or was it simply his wolf's or
dog's sense of ... well, direction? Or a combination of
both? Nathan knew that he had to look into it, but he
would drop Ian Goodly off first. He did so, then at once
returned with Grinner into the Möbius Continuum.

But it was a fruitless exercise. Grinner had something of
his father in him, certainly, but he didn't have his metaphysical math, and wolf numbers just weren't sufficient. *I
can feel the way,* he growled in Nathan's mind, *but I don't
know ... how to go there! There is no way to walk, to run.
No way to smell the trail. No spoor to follow. I am lost ...
here.*

Nathan tried scanning Grinner's mind more deeply, his
sensations rather than his thoughts, but it didn't work out.
There was a peculiar feeling of sorrow or anxiety for the
loss of the mountains, the moon and stars, the trees of the
timberline, the rearing crags and moon-silvered passes:
namely, all of the familiar points of reference by virtue of
which a wolf of the wild *is* a wolf—and also an awareness
that was totally *un*wolflike—but never a hint of the real
direction of parallel Earth.

You can't show me the way?

But I can! Grinner protested. *It's ... there!* (It was as if he pointed, but there was nothing there, just the emptiness of the Continuum.) *Except . . . there's no way to get to it!* Now his anxiety and discomfort were such that he was beginning to pant and whine. Nathan knew the other's frustration and sensed there was no answer for it, not yet at least. Regretfully, but unwilling to prolong Grinner's distress, he conveyed him back to the camp. Where Goodly was waiting.

Giving Grinner into the hands of Misha, to care for him, Nathan asked the precog, "What was it all about? I mean, what was it you felt, back there on Starside?"

"What did *you* feel?" Goodly countered.

"Are you so afraid of the future that you can't answer a simple question?" Nathan's frustrations were starting to spill over.

"Yes," Goodly answered, "sometimes I am. It's not knowing what might come about that worries me, it's understanding it."

Nathan had heard all this before. "But you did see something of the future?"

"I saw, and felt . . . something strange."

"The world turning? The wild rush of water, like a river between the worlds? Gardens in the desert?"

"All of those things, yes. Yet nothing definite. The only sure thing is this: you won't be moving any more of us back to the Gate. Not until the end, anyway."

"How do you know that?"

"Because I saw it, and it's the *only* thing I know for certain. At the end, we're all in it together." Goodly's eyes had a faraway look; they were hazy as a river with the morning sun on it, unblinking, as if gazing on the unknown and unknowable.

"When?" The Necroscope could feel the short hairs rising at the back of his neck.

"Soon," said Goodly.

"Was it dark or light, day or night?"

"It was night," Goodly answered with a sigh. "And yet it was . . . it was morning, too!" His eyes cleared and he shook his head. "Nathan," he said, when he could properly focus again. "I know this is difficult for you, but you'll just have to believe me when I tell you that ... that you really shouldn't fool with the future."

Now it was Nathan's turn to be stubborn. "I'm not going to call you a coward," he said, "but there are some things we have to know. And I've been putting it off just like you and for the same reason."

"Putting it off?"

"What we *can't* put off," the Necroscope answered, "not anymore. For it's creeping up on us even now. But me, I believe in forewarned, forearmed. You can help me— you're about the only one who can help me—or you can step aside. It's up to you."

"You'll ... go there?" The cadaverous, gaunt-faced precog backed off a pace.

"And I'd like you to go with me." Nathan nodded. "I don't know what I'll see, or even if I'll understand it. But you and the future, well, there's something between you. So maybe—"

"—I ... don't know," said Goodly. "And anyway, what good will it do? You can't materialize there, can't 'experience' it. You can only travel through it!"

"As far as it goes, yes." Again Nathan's nod; but a curt one this time, and decisive. The meaning was obvious.

"And if it doesn't go ... far?"

"Then I'll know it's all for nothing anyway! But it won't matter, for I'll have nothing to lose."

Goodly relaxed, shrugged, said, "Then I'll go with you." And he sighed, adding, "You don't know how much of a temptation it's been, or how hard I've had to fight not to ask you!"

Nathan was astonished. "What? But aren't you the one who always—?"

"—Yes!" Goodly cut him short. "Even so, we have a saying: 'Better the devil you know.' And if I had been able to go there, instead of having to wait for it to come to me ..."

They both felt something of trepidation then, as the Necroscope made ready to conjure a door. Which was when Ben Trask came over. "What's happening?" he asked conversationally, his face wide open . . . until he saw their looks and knew that something really was happening.

"We're going to have a look at something," Nathan answered before Goodly could speak. But glancing from man to man, Trask knew the truth of it anyway.

"Is it wise?" he said.

"No." They both shook their heads. And Nathan added, "But we have to know." And the fact of it was, Trask wanted to know, too . . .

In the Continuum, Goodly had second thoughts, knew a moment's panic when he felt motion and knew that Nathan was heading for a future-time door. It was strange; in ordinary space-time he could sense the future; but here, so close to it, he couldn't! Because this place *was* the future . . . the present, too . . . and the past. A junction of all times and places.

And he wanted to know, *How do we get back?*

We have blue life-threads, in effect lifelines. They are *us! When we've seen what we want to see—if there's anything to see—we follow them back.*

You . . . you can do that?

Yes, I feel that I can. Else I wouldn't go.

And . . . I can do it?

Just keep a good hold on me, Nathan told him, where they stood framed in the blue light from the threshold of the door. *And look . . . there it is, all of it, going on forever. All we have to do is find out how long* we *go on!*

Despite the fact that the light from the door was blue, it was warm. Not physically warm; just . . . warm. And Goodly knew why. It was the light of human life! For even as he stood or floated there in the metaphysical void, a blue thread of light—like a living neon filament, a weird ectoplasmic extension of himself—issued endlessly out of him, and another out of Nathan, seeming to unwind indefinitely into the future.

Beyond that time-door *was* the future: a chaos of hundreds of thousands of blue threads, all heading for the ever-expanding, hazy-blue, and endless horizons of tomorrow. And even (or especially, or only) in the Möbius Continuum, human eyes could not gaze on that scene without human ears hearing a *sound* that was not there but born of the awesome immensity of the vision: an angelic chorus, an orchestrated, interminable A*hhhhhhhh!*

But not everything was angelic beyond the door. There were scarlet threads, too, among the neon blue (and green, and even golden threads!). For this was Sunside/Starside's future, and it seemed the vampires had a future, too.

Wamphyri! Goodly said, clinging fast to Nathan as the Necroscope launched himself into the future. *Those red threads are vampires!*

Yes, Nathan answered. *The greens are trogs, and the golden ones . . . must be Thyre! Of course, for our futures are mingling even now.*

They sped down the time-stream; blue threads grew dim and blinked out (or worse, turned red) as men died or where changed. And yet there was hope, too, as other threads burst from nothing into brilliant blue life as people were born. Red threads approached, veered off, came again; none of it made any sense, except it told of struggles to come. Scarlet threads clustered close, a horde of them! They fell back, blinking out of existence by the handful. But then:

Nathan jerked to a halt, and Goodly almost fell out of his grasp, *almost* fell into the future! There, somewhere in not too distant time-to-come, they pinwheeled like twin spiders on neon-blue threads, or fallen mountaineers on their ropes. Except it could be seen that all of the strength was in Goodly's rope, in the precog's life-thread; for where it blazed on into an undetermined but ever-expanding future, Nathan's had come to an end! Behind them their threads—*both* of them—went winding back to "the present"; before them . . . only Goodly's thread went on, seeming to beckon him. But now, to him, its twining looked sinister where it merged into the distant haze.

The feeling of hanging from ropes was so real that Goodly cried out "DON'T LET GO!" His words gonged awesomely, mentally, in the metaphysical void. But Nathan said:

It's not a question of letting go. I ... I can't ... "let go," for the thread is me. And this is where it ends.

For a moment Goodly was silent while they spun there, turning endlessly at Nathan's end. Then:

Let's get out of here, he said, quietly. .

Back at the temporary campsite Nathan was more withdrawn than ever. Misha could get nothing out of him, neither his wife nor any of the others. But as the shadows grew longer and the sun sank even lower, until the gap between its rim and the horizon was only a little greater than its diameter, again he snapped out of it. Meanwhile he conversed, however briefly, with Thikkoul the Thyre stargazer, and was reminded yet again: *We're only given to see what will be, not how it will come about, or what comes after.*

Hope springs eternal; something of it, anyway. Even if the Necroscope could not save himself, he had his friends to think of, his loved ones, the Szgany as a race. Also, his nephew wolf Grinner had come to him and reported: *The Wamphyri are stirring in the barrier mountains. Even before the last gold has slipped from the peaks, the bloodwar will be on in earnest!*

It was time now to move the Travellers to safety. It must be now, for Nathan could not say how much time there would be later—or even if there would be a later. The task took longer than he'd thought, but when he was done all of the Szgany who would go were in the safekeeping of the Thyre. In the barrier mountains, only the peaks were gold now, and the gold was swiftly fading. Nathan would like to move his "alien" friends, too, if they would go. But as he had suspected, with one exception the espers were all of a single stubborn mind: they would stay with the Necroscope and see it out.

Anna Marie English was the exception; at Andrei Romani's request, she'd gone with him to a Thyre sanctuary. "There are so many children with no one," he'd told her.

"You are gentle and can tend their needs." His words were valid enough, even though they'd conveyed something else entirely: the fact that he wouldn't be the one to complain if she tended to his needs, too! And she had known it, that for the first time in her life someone wanted her.

And Misha ... had complained bitterly, tearfully, but not until the others had gone. The Necroscope had moved her last, after explaining that if there was danger, her presence would only place him in greater jeopardy. After that, Nathan, Trask, Zek, Chung, and Goodly—and Grinner, of course—had been alone in the camp, in the twilight before the night. Then for a while, weary from all his works and alone with his thoughts, Nathan had sat apart from the others.

But shortly:

Zek came to him and said, "You probably know it already, Nathan, but I'll remind you anyway: Harry Keogh inspired just such loyalty in his time, and your brother the Dweller. Their friends couldn't be persuaded to leave them, either. And they *won* their battles! Perhaps it bodes well, right?" But Zek had missed the point, for they had *lost* their last battle. And of course, she hadn't seen what the future had shown to him.

He said nothing but looked at the sky, in which the first stars were beginning to glitter over Starside. And the biggest of them was the ice-shard Northstar, star of ill omen, like an evil eye watching over Wrathstack. Just seeing it there—its cold blue radiance—was like an invocation. Grinner coughed once low in his throat, lay back his head and howled a moment, then waited for an answering howl to come echoing through the woods, and others from further afield. They carried his message, even to the barrier mountains: that the night would soon be here, and all of its dangers.

And back from the mountains came another message, but this time carried on the telepathic aether: *The Wamphyri Lords under Devetaki prepare to launch against the last aerie!*

Nathan had heard it, too, so that Grinner's confirmation was scarcely necessary when he said: *Uncle, it begins . . .*

An hour earlier, Wran and Nestor had departed Wrathstack on a southwesterly course. Behind them they towed gas-beasts, ostensibly to bomb the most westerly of Devetaki's observer posts on the boulder plains. And indeed they would bomb it, but that was only part of their overall and individual schemes. Each of them suspected the other's true motives, and finally as their target became visible up ahead:

You're fleeing, right? said Wran.

Nestor shook his mental head. *I'm taking my last chance to settle an old, old score—on Sunside. Of all people, you Wran, should understand my position. In your time, you've settled scores of your own. It is . . . oh, a question of honour, I suppose. I was betrayed, and if I'm now to die I want to know that he dies first!* He glanced across the gulf of air. *But on the other hand I think that you are truly fleeing, which isn't like you. What, coward-ice? From Wran the Rage? I might expect such from Gorvi, but you?*

The other's shrug. *As you're surely aware, I'm no cow-ard, Nestor Lichloathe—but neither am I a fool! Nor, de-spite rumour, am I entirely insane . . . but my brother is! Along with his power, his madness waxes. Whatever is to befall the last aerie, sooner or later Spiro will turn on me. Aye, and that murderous eye of his can blind, maim, kill!*

So what will you do?

I won't be the first Lord of the Wamphyri to strike out on my own. The land west of here is unknown, unexplored, by vampires at least. I'll lie low 'til things cool down, then see how the land lies. Maybe Spiro will get himself killed. I hope so, for it will save me the trouble!

Talking of trouble, Nestor answered, *there's just such up ahead!*

I've seen it, said Wran. *Are you ready?*

For answer, Nestor swung a bolas of flints and iron.

The "trouble" was a small warrior, propulsors blasting,

even now spurting aloft from a craterlike depression in the boulder plains only two miles short of the Starside foothills. Down there, the handful of members of a thrall observer group gesticulated, stabbed pointing fingers at the oncoming flyers and gas-beasts, then took cover or scrambled for flyers.

The warrior was up; without pause it blasted for Wran in the lead. Towing a gas-beast, it was hard for Wran to manoeuvre; still he managed to turn his straining mount on its side as the warrior sped by, its spines tearing holes in the membrane webbing of a manta wing. But neither was Wran idle. Even tilting dangerously in his saddle, he swung a bolas of hooks that got caught up in the warrior's bladders, ripping two of them wide open on its left flank.

Bravo! Nestor grunted, hurling his own bolas, seeing it fly true and turning his face away. The stricken warrior throbbed where it redistributed gasses to maintain its balance. But as escaping gas mingled with air to form methane, so Nestor's bolas hit home and struck sparks . . .

. . . There came the great *whuuump!* of ignition as the warrior burst into flame from stem to stern. Roaring its pain, its fury, the Thing angled anal propulsors, keeled over, came head-long in an inverted suicide dive to batter its tormentors from the sky. Before it could reach them more bladders exploded; it tilted towards the ground; its roaring became a whine of frustrated lunacy as, with all propulsors blasting, it smashed down in flames from three hundred feet and burst apart in steaming chunks and a crimson spray!

After that it was easy. Two mounted flyers were off and running, and another, panicked, had launched without a rider. Both escaping riders were thralls, not even lieutenants. They wouldn't have stood a chance against true Lords, and knew it.

Good luck to them, Nestor commented, cutting loose his gas-beast, which joined Wran's in settling towards the earth. Down below, a lone flyer hauled half-heartedly on its tether. In a nearby clump of boulders in the center of the depression, skins had been stretched over a framework of ancient bones to form the post's accommodation. Presumably there were at least two more thralls cowering inside.

But their luck's out! Wran grunted, paying out a line weighted with a net of hooks and flints, and raking the gas-beasts until they screamed and split open from internal pressure. Twin blasts followed, and the Lords were glad of their elevation as smoke-rings hurtled up on superheated thermals. Down below ... the scoops of a freshly gouged double crater issued smoke; a handful of smouldering scraps drifted on the turbulent air; a shattered, blazing flyer crumpled down into its funeral pyre. There were no signs of survivors.

Nestor and Wran split up. *West for me,* said Wran. *But I won't forget you. Who could have foreseen all this, that time I brought you out of Sunside?*

It was my intention to kill you, Nestor answered, coldly, *for the way you "initiated" me.*

Oh, I know that. Wran tossed his head. *Well, who can say? There's always tomorrow and tomorrow.*

But: *Not for me,* said Nestor.

Then I'll not wish you luck.

Of course not. Why lie now?

Wran laughed and sped away. *You did well, Nestor, for a barearsed whelp out of Sunside!*

Nestor made no answer, but set his course for the heights over Settlement.

Wran's mount had suffered damage in the brush with the aerial warrior. They weren't serious injuries but bad enough that he would like to examine them, perhaps apply spittle to the torn areas of membrane wing, and rest the flyer for an hour or two before continuing his flight west.

Preoccupied—knowing that the bloodwar was (or would be) behind him, and all the forces of the opposed Wamphyri factions concentrated at Wrathstack—he saw nothing of danger in landing in the barrier mountains ten miles west of Settlement. But it was a mistake.

It was also a fortuitous event—if not for Wran. For in

a cavern in the crags close by, *someone* had made his temporary home; an awesome someone, a someone who hated Wran with an all-consuming passion. In fact there were two of them, male and female (so far as sexual distinction matters in the Wamphyri), but *his* was the driving force. And the undying force that drove *him* was revenge!

It was a coincidence, then, a trick of fate, Wran's landing here; yet something that had been bound to happen sooner or later, one way or the other. For if he had not strayed into the territory of his enemy, be sure that his enemy would have come for him. And in a while, as Wran sat with his back to an outcropping rock and let his thoughts drift, perhaps dwelling on future problems, a far more immediate problem crept up on him.

Vasagi scarcely dared believe his luck; if a state of grace exists for vampires, then that was what he felt. It was every dream he'd dreamed for two and a half long years, every morbid desire he'd conceived since his fateful duel with Wran on Sunside. And now it was his to savour to the full. And with all the powers of his mentalism restored, blocking the lustful outflow of his thoughts to less than the flutter of a moth, he moved in the shadows and *was* a shadow, until he stood close to Wran, but still unseen, unsuspected in the dark.

Then, unshielding his mind:

Ah, see, he said. *You've learned nothing. A skillful creature may still creep up on you unseen, even to within striking distance—except this time there's no foolish Szgany youth to give warning through his clumsiness!*

Perhaps Wran had been asleep, or drifting with his private thoughts, dozing; whichever, it took only a moment for the oily, oozing message to sink in. When it did ...

... He snatched for his belt, his gauntlet—which wasn't there! It was hanging from the saddle of his snoring flyer! He went to spring to his feet, but a great taloned hand came down on his shoulder, holding him effortlessly in place. And eyes—but *such* eyes—gazed down on him, red and rapacious from under a cowl black and blacker than night!

Again he would stand up, but a second shadow had appeared out of nowhere and stood at his right. His salivating, elongating bottom jaw fell open; he croaked, "What? Who . . . ?"

But he already knew who. Knew too that it was impossible, yet real. Knew that this one was dead—the true death—yet stood here cowled and smiling, with his mind at least, for his face was invisible. And his smile was so monstrous it put even the worst nightmares to flight!

And *"Vasagi!"* Wran answered his own question, in the moment before the female brought a large stone crashing down with all her might onto the crown of his head.

Devetaki launched her forces in two great waves, with only ten minutes between them. But as for the contingents she'd sent out along the spine of the mountains, they remained at their posts. For theirs was a different role, to be determined later at the direction of the locator Alexei Yefros.

Bone horns blared; drummers beat on the sounding membrane of wattles along the sides of their flyers' outstretched necks, causing their mounts to stutter and honk, pacemakers for their own pulsing manta wings; pennants streamed out from the spined backs of aerial warriors bringing up the rear, and the throb of their propulsors was like thunder in the settling dusk. Way out in front, three miles or more in advance of the leading wave, a lone flyer and thrall rider sped to the fore. The rider carried a slender lance; at its tip, a pennant displayed clasped hands: the sign of truce or conference.

The last aerie was no longer disguised as an uninhabited shell; Wrathstack displayed the sigils of its tenants, and its levels were alive with lights, its chimneys roaring with fire, smoke, and stench. Aerial warriors waited to launch from all of the major bays; flyers and riders were likewise positioned in lesser launching bays and heavily defended ledges; the glint of battle gauntlets and sheen of polished leather armour was visible in every nook and cranny of the gaunt, rearing face of the stack.

Devetaki's parley-thrall came on. His mount arched manta wings, rose up on winds off the Icelands; a mote against Wrathstack and the writhing of northern auroras. It flew on a level with the sun-bleached turrets of Wrathspire, gradually descending in a zigzag to and fro across the face of the last aerie.

Wratha herself came out on a jutting balcony and called: *You—why are you so eager to die?*

You have me wrong, Lady (the thrall was nervous but well rehearsed). *Devetaki has sent me to talk. My pennant flies the truce ... well, for what it's worth and however brief a time. But I may not sit here all day; an army waits on your word.*

If Devetaki would talk, Wratha answered, *then let her present herself. Let her come of her own free will to my roof. She knows me, and that my word is good.*

But the thrall shook his head. *It is not the custom for a conqueror to talk to the conquered! Devetaki waits to see what will be her get for letting you and yours live.*

Bah! said Wratha, but without malice. *Your virgin grandam would have me surrender, then cut off my head and melt my body! She seeks to spare herself the bothersome ritual turmoil of the fray—and all of the losses which must surely result. Indeed, she seeks to spare herself, not me, for my forces and position are superior! Wherefore, if Devetaki Skullguise has the heart for it, let her come on. For I am secure in Wrathspire.*

The thrall's careful shrug, and his not-so-careful answer: *But you are only one of several rebels, Lady, and I must speak with the rest.* Side-slipping, his flyer descended until it was level with Suckscar. Wratha had seen Nestor fly out with Wran and knew he would not be back (knew, too, that if Wran did not return within minutes, he must likewise be counted out of it); but she wondered if Lord Lichloathe had left his manse as best possible defended.

He had, for now Devetaki's messenger called loudly across the gulf of air to Nestor's right-hand man Zahar where he stood framed in a broad window. "You there, Lieutenant! I would speak with your Lord and master on behalf of the commander of an army from the east. Her name is Devetaki Skullguise, which I'm sure you'll recognize."

"A Lady?" Zahar called back. "But you must bring her on at once! My Lord Lichloathe, a mighty necromancer, loves only one thing better than a corpse—and that's a good fuck! Moreover, Lady commanders have always been one of his preferences."

"Alas, then he's out of luck," the thrall answered back, more at ease than when conversing with a true Lord (or Lady). "Devetaki isn't called the virgin grandam for nothing. Depending on Lord Lichloathe's *other* preferences, however, she might well consider finding him a well-greased lance to sit upon—upright, of course!"

"Begone," Zahar told him haughtily. "I watch the skies for enemies, not stink-gnats."

"Surrender your manse and live!" offered the thrall.

"On your way, wretch!" growled Zahar.

Less than a mile and a half away now, dark storm clouds were gathering in the south, except Wratha knew they were not clouds but simply a crowded sky. And from where she stood on a flexing cartilage gantry to one side of her main landing bay, the curving double fronts looked like a scythe blurred from the speed of its approach!

Meanwhile, the parley-thrall had side-slipped down to Madmanse, and now called on Spiro in the yawning funnel of a bay: "My Lord, the Lady Devetaki calls on you to surrender. Give up your manse and retain your miserable life!" Successful so far, he was now full of himself. Or as full as he ever would be . . .

Does your Lady have contact? Spiro sent, directly into the thrall's vampire mind. *Is she touching you even now?*

Indeed, Lord, the other answered. *Why, she directs me.*

Then tell her this, Spiro snarled: *that Spiro Killglance is heir to his father's eye. And if she doubts me, here's the proof!*

He crouched down in the mouth of the bay, glared hatred and pus, and murder and shit, and sheer disruptive *corruption* from his terrible eyes. And the thrall and his flyer scarcely knew what hit them!

The flyer crumpled, disintegrated, flew apart in tatters, and the parley-thrall burst open as if sliced by a sharp knife from crotch to mouth, so that his guts bloomed on the air even as his riven corpse commenced to fall.

And up in Wrathspire, Wratha sighed and thought:

Well, that's that. Now for the night's real business . . .

II

The Whelming of the Stack—Vasagi's Story— Desertion, and Just Deserts

Devetaki stood off and directed the fighting. Her flyer was a huge construct fashioned of several men, stretched and warped, metamorphosed and reshaped, *redesigned* in the soup of a Masquemanse vat in Turgosheim. It was the same beast that had borne her safely over the Great Red Waste seated in a natural saddle formed of cartilage flanges (once scapulae) where an elongated, many-knuckled neck met shoulders that curved into mighty manta wings. Insectlike, the body was formed of a trio of stretched torsos, joined end to end, with three massive hearts to circulate the thin blood. Specially designed to glide, the wings had an enormous span, with the once-normal skeleton of arms, legs, and grotesquely extended fingers and toes showing through the sheathing, grey-gleaming membrane. The creature was all heart, muscle, alveolate bone, and flexible cartilage, but mainly wing.

Behind Devetaki, Alexi Yefros clung like a leech to the long horny saddle, which he gripped with knees and heels while aiming his vampire-enhanced locator probe at Wrathstack to seek out its principal centres of activity and its largest, fiercest bodies of fighting men and monsters. Thus by a process of elimination, the Russian's scrying was an invaluable part of Devetaki's intelligence; while she used her mentalism to direct the battle and read the thoughts of the aerie's defenders, Yefros channeled his skills to discover the stack's weak spots.

And there were weak spots, certainly. Devetaki had been quick to detect a lack of morale in the defenders of Suckscar, nor had she found any truly powerful mind there; the penultimate level obviously lacked a Lord, just as she had suspected when her parley-thrall had spoken with a mere lieutenant. And so this alleged necromancer Lord Lichloathe either was a figment of wild imagination, or was himself a lich, dead and departed.

Similarly, the men of the basement levels seemed singularly lacking in guts, and the sump was extremely ill defended. The various gantlets cut through scree and rubble were not so much traps for invaders as for defenders! Devetaki had Tangiru the Grunt land his mightiest warriors on the piled ramps at the sides of the gantlets, where their sheer mass was sufficient to collapse the walls inward, smothering who or whatever waited in ambush and effectively blocking any possible future escape route.

She couldn't know it but Gorvi the Guile had already made his escape along a subterranean watercourse that he'd discovered during his very first night of occupation three and a half years ago. No doubt the tunnel had been excavated in the olden times a bolt-hole for some previous tenant; this wasn't the first bloodwar on Starside, not by a long shot.

Gorvi had resurfaced something more than a mile and a half northeast of Wrathstack, amid the rubble and in the shadows of a toppled aerie where he kept a well-fuelled flyer tethered and waiting. Now, keeping low, the Guile was already speeding east out of trouble, intending to return to the Gulf of Turgosheim to see how things stood there.

As for the rest of the rebels:

Wran's thoughts were noticeable by their absence, as was the Rage himself, but his loathsome brother more than covered for Wran's desertion. Spiro Killglance's evil eye was devastating, and Madmanse was left pretty much alone while the rest of the manses attracted a maximum of attention. As previously reported by the parley-thrall, Wratha was in residence in the topmost levels; she wasn't remiss in sending out a continuous stream of vitriolic taunts, mainly directed at Devetaki. Also, in the third manse down, that matchless hound, that inimitable lunatic Canker Canison! At first he'd been plainly visible in his main landing bay, fighting off invading forces alongside the best of his "pups," but at the rising of a tumbling moon he'd made an exit from the fray. Immediately thereafter, and no doubt inspired by the frenzy of a sudden thunderous uproar of crazy *sounds* from the rear of the stack, Canker's defenders had redoubled their efforts! Their ferocity was such that Devetaki felt obliged to forecast heavy losses in that arena.

So then, lieutenants galore—thralls, warriors, and an apparently endless stream of flyers and riders issuing out of the many bays like hornets from a nest—but a dearth of true vampire masters, the Wamphyri themselves. Well, they were fled and that was all there was to it. All to the good, it made the virgin grandam's task that much easier. Obviously the deserted lesser denizens of the various manses were already much demoralized; with no one to whip them on it wouldn't be long before they began reckoning the value of their undead skins.

Meanwhile the bloodwar was in full swing; the defences of certain levels and manses would soon be swept away, crumbling to nothing, while others were as yet best avoided. (After all, why expend good blood and effort externally when with any luck internal routes would soon be opening up?) Take Guilesump, and work up into Mad-manse. Take Suckscar, and work down into Mangemanse. And finally, take Wrathspire itself—up from Suckscar and down from the plateau roof—until last but certainly not least, the very prize herself: Wratha!

So Devetaki rode the thermals high above the fighting and considered her options, and pointed out the way for her troops. But as for her own ever-expanding contingent (which had formed the bulk of the second wave), they'd been kept back; they now circled and protected her in the sky where she performed lazy, drifting spirals around the great fang of Wrathstack, with all the action clearly visible below.

The minutiae of the battle, however, were neither visible nor known, for there was just too much going on. For in-stance: down on the sprawling boulder plains where they extended from the foot of the stack, Gorvi's ground-based warriors had long since given up trying to distinguish friend from foe. Now, if it fell out of the sky, it was an en-emy. Their thrall minders were either fled into Guilesump or dead from all the snapping and snarling; the plain was littered with all the gory debris of the undead, now truly dead. It was as if a mad painter had taken up a giant brush and daubed the grey and barren boulder plains scarlet! And across this landscape of death the warriors rumbled, glutted yet still killing and feasting, bloated but never sat-isfied and ever lusting; and no one to say them nay, and the dumb beasts themselves too frenzied to know when to stop.

Still the sky rained mauled and mangled horror. Bleating flyers with broken wings crashed down; their thrall and lieutenant riders were tossed or leaped from their saddles, only to be maimed and devoured by lunging, blood-crazed beasts. Aerial warriors with blazing gas-bladders went sputtering and shrieking across the sky like semisentient shooting stars; now and then they would career to earth in mewling red and black tangles, adding to the turmoil.

But the gantlets had been breached; Tangiru the Grunt and Lord Eran Painscar led a surface attack on Guilesump, and despite a molten machicolation from the corbels, fought through to the interior! Up into the stack they struck, and down into the bowels of the place, to the sump itself and the aerie's wells. Devetaki Skullguise had warned them to leave the wells alone, but the Lords were on the sack now and what they couldn't take they'd destroy.

They sliced through a hanging garden of siphons (in fact the extruded veins of Wratha's siphoneers, which drew up water to Wrathspire and from there supplied the entire stack), poisoned the wells with piss, kneblasch, and silver dust, and generally made a shambles of the place ... but expensively. Eran Painscar was gutted by a warrior (fatally this time), and all Tangiru's bones were broken in a booby trap; it was a pitfall, and the *things* in the pit made small work of him. Their passing was scarcely mourned; their lieutenants fought more viciously yet in the knowledge that two at least would ascend to Lords, but first must face a bloody ascent through the basement levels of Guilesump.

Higher, Suckscar was taken! Zahar, Grig, and two lesser lieutenants gave way under the simultaneous assault of half a dozen great warriors that perched in bays and windows to fire their propulsors into the manse. Burned or poisoned, Nestor's demoralized thralls succumbed in droves to Hesta the Herm, Lom Halfstruck, and Grigor the Lech where they secured the landing bays, landed a squadron of flyers and fighting men, and commenced slaughtering the sick and mazed defenders out of hand.

Alas for Grigor, on his way to "inspect" his get in women, he met up with a child of Vasagi's vats and stepped on a carpet that was not. Instantly enveloped by the Thing and drenched in digestive acids, he was badly eaten into by the time he managed to hack himself free—only to be snapped up by the monster's twin! Finally, this latter creature was dispatched by others of Suckscar's invaders; when they opened it up, Grigor was discovered a jumble of clattering bones. So much for the Lech. Later, when Devetaki heard the news of his demise, she would don her smiling mask, however briefly. . . .

The roof of the last great aerie of the Wamphyri was now a bloody battlefield; even Wrathspire's sloping plateau, issuing smoke and jets of flame from burning creatures, awash in blood, guts, and urine as Wratha's men and beasts and Ursula Torspawn's invading forces saw it out hand to hand.

The stack had its limitations and was less than impregnable after all. Exits from Wrathspire onto the roof were few; Wratha had difficulty resupplying her fighters there, and when finally it came to retreating many of them died in the crush on the few steep stairwells. The roof was taken, and in part secured, but Ursula's troops had been reduced to a handful—which Devetaki thoughtfully replaced with her own people.

Only then landing, on the roof herself, in a corner free of fighting, she dined on the hearts of three freshly slaughtered captive defenders, fed and rested her great flyer, transferred to a second mount and was soon airborne again. But during her short visit to the roof, Devetaki had not failed to notice the silver cage and its hoisting gear, which she'd found most appropriate. . . .

While down below, in the sixth hour of the night, Guilesump was finally taken; at which a lesser struggle at once broke out between rival lieutenants, over who should now ascent in place of Lords Eran and Tangiru!

But in the next manse up, Spiro Killglance had already had enough. He was mad, aye, but not *that* mad; his power was waning with each withering blast from his killing eye; he knew by now that Wran would not be back. His brother was dead or fled, and Spiro suspected the latter. (What's more, he guessed that the bloodwar wasn't the only reason for Wran's flight!) But Spiro was only one Lord and Madmanse was vast; he couldn't be everywhere at once; the more he used his eye, the less destructive the result. He wasted his inheritance here, and would be wise to seek a new and glorious future in fields afar.

For by now (he thought), Wran was well on his way back to Turgosheim, to reestablish himself in advance of any return by other survivors. Well, and Spiro would soon be hot on his tail ... to *punish* him, aye, for cowardice in the face of an enemy, and foul desertion of duty! So thinking, and while the battle raged on, Spiro rested his eyes for an hour, then saddled his best flyer and a spare, and flew out on the night wind.

By now Suckscar had been secured; Lom and Hesta had commandeered new flyers and reentered the fray raging around Wrathstack's exterior; seeing and recognizing Spiro, they zeroed in on him. Devetaki saw them go and knew their danger—and gave no warning. Both of them were freaks and had always irritated her. Half-a-dozen other, lesser Lords joined them where they ringed Spiro in, each whirling a bolas of glittering hooks.

Spiro gathered his nightmare energies to him and located them behind his vengeful eyes. He ducked low in his saddle as whirling death whistled overhead—and at once leaned forward as it sliced the air close behind! But sooner or later they'd get him; he'd be pierced through and through, dragged from his saddle and dropped. *Enough!*

He hunched astride his mount like a monstrous toad, settled his gaze on Lom the Dwarf and fixed him with his eyes as in the sights of a weapon. Lom sat rigid as a rod and couldn't look away! Spiro's eyes were magnetic and drew his gaze; they issued a seething mental bile that sped down Spiro's line of sight like a hawk stooping to its prey!

And Lom ... burst like a bomb! Scarlet froth flew every which way as his guts escaped at once, from every exit and in all directions! It was as if he'd been a bubble of blood in a vacuum, whose skin had dissolved in a single moment, letting the void *suck* him apart.

"Hah!" cried Spiro, and rapidly reduced two lesser Lords, and their mounts, to shreds. Then Hesta the Herm wheeled into view, and it was his or her turn. *Ho, great half-and-halfling!* Spiro called out with his mentalism. *And do you have any last words?*

You ... you bully! Hesta pouted—but was unable to look away. *Do your worst!*

And Spiro did. He flicked his head forward as if to lend his mind-bolt greater velocity, speeding it on its way. For a long moment Hesta's eyes stood out from his/her skull, and he/she screamed: "Sp————!" Just "Sp————!" before dying. But the *way* of it! Hesta's manicured hands and female feet shot from their limbs, while his/her head blew off at the neck! And the grotesque corpse sat still awhile, then toppled from its saddle and cartwheeled down the night, spraying red from all five stumps. Spiro stood tall, shook a great fist, glared threateningly all about; but the others had had enough. He laughed long and loud, then headed east, and no one else got in his way or even considered doing so. Not for many a mile, anyway.

And behind him, its thunder dwindling, the bloodwar for Madmanse, Mangemanse, and Wrathspire raged furious as ever . . .

In a collapsed cave two-thirds of the way through the pass to Sunside, Geoffrey Paxton worked like a madman at a great wall of boulders where they blocked his way to freedom. Hands bleeding, nails broken and clothing torn, he wondered why he wasn't exhausted; also wondered why he wasn't blind in the pitch darkness. In fact he knew why, for there was a weird hunger on him, and an even weirder thirst—which wasn't for ordinary sustenance—but the human part of his mind continued to query such seeming anomalies.

Well, he supposed he would get used to most of them soon enough, if not to the hunger. Of course, if he were to get *too* hungry . . . there was always the headless body of Zindevar where she lay crumpled in the rear of the cave, or the crushed corpse of Bruno Krasin. But Paxton wasn't *that* hungry . . .

. . . Not yet.

And then there were other hungers: for life (or undeath), for power, and definitely for revenge. As for life, he clung to it with the tenacity of the vampire. Revenge? Well, as far as he knew the son of Harry Keogh was still alive, and so revenge was by no means impossible. Power? That would come when he had his telepathy back; he was a step closer in that direction, at least. And this had always been his plan, after all: one step at a time.

Again he attacked the wall of boulders, hurling rubble to the rear of the cave as he burrowed his way towards the night and freedom and destiny.

For somewhere out there, in Sunside/Starside, he knew that he could satisfy all of his hungers in one and the same throw, and after that—

—Then there wouldn't be *any* satisfying him ever again. . . .

To give him credit, Vasagi (no longer the Suck) had been very patient. In *one* way he'd been patient, at least, but in another he had acted hastily; because he had many things to do and Wran the Rage was only one of them. But Vasagi and Carmen had dined royally, and their meal had been of the essence—or flavoured with it—of everything dearest to a vampire's stomach. Namely the blood of another vampire; in fact Wran's blood, and especially that of his leech. And since cutting his parasite out of him would probably have sufficed to render him once more unconscious, Vasagi had not delayed the meal but performed the required butchery while Wran still lay in a heap, with his head all dented from Carmen's blow. Which was also the reason why it had taken him so long to wake up. The damaged head, the loss of so much blood (which had not gone wasted), and of course the removal and *wringing out* of his leech; much like squeezing oranges, except oranges don't writhe and slither and try to escape.

But despite the fact that his leech was gone, its essence remained in his blood as it had always been, and being Wamphyri (or *having* been) he was not yet dead. Indeed, and if there were someone to care for him, he might even survive, though much reduced in spirit and no longer a Lord as such. So that as Wran groaned and awakened, and opened eyes as scarlet as ever if lacking in intensity, Vasagi could sympathize with him in part—though only in a very small part.

For Vasagi knew how Wran felt; indeed, upon a time,

he'd felt much the same and worse, and in similar circumstances.

Can you speak? Vasagi spoke with his mind as always, with elegant weavings of his fingers and hands for emphasis. In the long ago, this mode of speech had become necessary after Vasagi had extruded the diseased teeth and bones of his lower jaw, replacing them with a sleevelike proboscis or siphon tipped with a fine, retractable hollow probe: an excellent weapon or tool for feeding, but useless for common speech. That proboscis was no more; severed by Wran during their Sunside duel, it had been reduced to a red-rimmed hole in the ex-Suck's face. And looking up at his dark silhouette against the wheel of the stars—the glowing fire of his eyes, which was all that Wran could make out—he wondered what sort of face there was now, in the seething darkness under his cowl.

And because Vasagi had asked it, Wran also wondered if he could speak. But his mouth was dry as old bones; his tongue was glued to the roof of his mouth; he was barely strong enough to give his head a trembling shake. And even that was an agony he would not have believed, which threatened for a moment to sink him once more into oblivion. His *back*! His ravaged *spine*, out of which Vasagi had torn his leech, to devour its juices!

Good, said Vasagi. *I don't require you to speak, only to listen; for I've a story to tell. A tale of trial, and now—of tribulation! And who better to tell it to than a principal character who featured at the tale's beginning, and as we now see has stayed to its end? Indeed, to* his *end . . .*

And sitting down almost within reach of Wran, who had not the strength to reach, and gazing out over Starside reflectively, in the manner of the storyteller—while close by Carmen fed gorse flowers, honey, and possibly the crushed, empty sac of Wran's leech to a pair of tethered flyers—Vasagi began:

There was a duel, on Sunside, to the death of course, and only one could survive and return home in triumph to the last great aerie of the Wamphyri. The combatants were Wran the Rage Killglance, a wretched creature of little or no refinement, and the noble Vasagi, called the Suck. The outcome should have been certain, would have been but for a trick of fate: the intervention of a callow Szgany youth, who seriously disturbed the balance of events. So much so that the noble Vasagi was defeated. And not only defeated but . . . disfigured, defaced! That were a shameful thing: to be deprived of one's very face, and by refuse such as Wran.

Well, one would think that the maiming of Vasagi, and his grotesque disfigurement, would be enough. Oh, he must also die, of course . . . but surely in a manner worthy of his status, his place in the scheme of things. Put him down by all means, but let him keep what little was left of his dignity. The Wamphyri are, after all, regal creatures. Some of us, anyway . . .

But Wran, was not—is not—one of them. Nor will he be, until relieved of the monstrous burden of his flesh. Soon, ah soon! However:

So Vasagi was raped of his leech, and the leech milked of its egg, and with a grand sense of the "comical" Wran the Rage bequeathed the noble seed to that same callow youth who, however inadvertently, had saved his miserable life. "Enough!" (you will say). "Now Vasagi can be allowed to die in whatever is left to him of peace. Wran will take his head in one clean stroke, and that will be that . . ."

Oh, really?

But no, Wran pegged him down on a hillside to await the rising sun, to melt there in its poison ray, and fled back to Starside before the dawn. Except—what Fate gives, Fate ofttimes takes away! And that same Szgany youth (him again, aye) tore out Vasagi's pegs from the earth, and set him free. So now you know how it came to pass that Vasagi survived, and I can be sharp about the rest of my tale.

Vasagi crawled into a deep cave and stayed there all the hours of the day. With night he killed a small creature (and, ah! the agony of eating—and through that loathsome hole in his face—after so many years of drinking); but at least he was strengthened. And all through the night he climbed the mountains, only sleeping when exhaustion overcame him, and eating what and when he could. But . . . the Starside night is a long one, and Vasagi was determined. And one thought and only one kept him going—as it has done ever since—that Wran the Rage still lived!

Before the dawn he came through a high pass, discovered a deep crevice in the rocks, crawled inside to sleep. Except his sleep was disturbed! Even as the sun crept higher, a flyer landed and a thrall (some Lord's lieutenant) pegged out a woman much as Vasagi had been pegged out. But when the lieutenant departed, then Vasagi cut her free—and found her to be one of his own, Carmen out of Suckscar! It was as if Wran and the others would eradicate every trace of him and his!

He rescued the woman to be his companion, saw that she would be a Lady, and in the next sundown commenced the long trek west. For the noble Vasagi knew what he was about, and that all was not yet lost. Far from it.

The trek took long and long; the way was hard; only the flesh of trogs sustained them. Vasagi was without his metamorphism, which had been fabled, retaining only his tenacity. But his tenacity was enough.

Finally they came to the vampire swamps far to the west of the barrier mountains, and Vasagi cultivated black and especially ugly mushrooms until they were ripe and released their spores—which he breathed! He already had vampire flesh, of course, which would resist the spores if it could. And it did for long and long. But finally a spore took; it must be strong indeed; Vasagi felt its strength and rejoiced!

He fed it the blood of beasts, and of his consort Carmen (given of her own free will), until finally he felt his metamorphism flow back into him! Ah, but it was a long time in the coming, and hardships all the way. Aye, and more to come, during the long trek home.

Then, in the western foothills of Starside, a rare thing! Vasagi came across a starving flyer. A vampire creature, loose in the wild and left to its own devices. And intelligent, aye! Vasagi fed the beast, returned it to full health; why, he even learned its name! Oh, yes, for it had a name, which it remembered from when it was a man. Karz Biteri, fled from Runemanse in Turgosheim, and from his master, Maglore the Mage. So much the noble Vasagi learned, and no more. But from now on he had a beast to share his and Carmen's burden, albeit a very weird beast, which refused the blood of men and trogs and only ate the flesh of animals, gorse flowers, and wild honey.

Well, their relationship was a strange thing; scarcely that of beast and master at all! For this creature had a mind of his own. But companionship and need drew him to Vasagi, and the ex-Suck's need drew him to the flyer. But their understanding was simple: they were their own "men," and whatever came of their partnership, when it was done it was done.

So, by stages, Vasagi and the Lady Carmen, and Karz the flyer, came back to this central region of Sunside/Starside. And when they were here they found a place to live—just a cave, but it was enough—and Vasagi waited and watched, to see what would be. For olden enemies were on their way from Turgosheim in the east, and the outcome would be interesting. But meanwhile, Vasagi reached out with his restored mentalism to the last great aerie of the Wamphyri, to Suckscar and certain of its creatures. Among them a flyer, but just a flyer, and not like Karz at all. Upon a time, however, this had been an exceptional beast in its own right, and faithful. The very mount that Vasagi had flown to Sunside the night of his duel with Wran! And it was still faithful! When Vasagi called, it broke out of its pen and hurried to be with him. So that now both Vasagi and his Lady had mounts to ride into Sunside and prey upon the Szgany, as of old.

Which brings us to the present . . .

Meanwhile, Vasagi's Lady had done with feeding the flyers and come to where her Lord sat with the broken, ravaged Wran. She carried lengths of thin, cutting, near-unbreakable Szgany twine, spun from Kursgrass, one of which had a noose that she placed over Wran's head, winding the rest of its length about the outcrop until it was firmly anchored. Sick from pain, and made impotent by weakness, Wran could only watch as she wrapped his feet with another length, which she made fast . . . to the saddle of Vasagi's flyer?

And in a little while Vasagi continued:

Upon a time, the Lords—and the Lady, too—of Wrathstack had poked fun at Vasagi, naming him a freak because his face and "voice," his elegant and dexterous mode of communication, were so radically different from theirs. But none of them had laughed louder than Wran. And, as stated, Wran was responsible for reducing Vasagi to a genuine freak, with only a hole for a face! Well, since Vasagi had been named for a freak, and also since he'd never much cared for physical looks one way or the other, deeming it a vanity in creatures who have the power to change their looks so easily, he now determined to become a freak! And none had been more gifted in the metamorphic arts than Vasagi.

He stood up, stood tall, and gazed down on Wran. *My tale is told, and it's a true one, of which I am the living proof. The Wamphyri have long made creatures in their own image, but I, Vasagi, have gone one better, and made myself in the image of one of my creatures. Behold, and know that I am Vasagi of the Wamphyri—now Lord Vasagi the Gape!*

He opened his cloak . . . then opened his body!

Wran's agony was all but forgotten in those astonishing moments of revelation. Not the revealing of Vasagi's identity, for of course that was already known, but the limitlessness of Wamphyri metamorphism, now *taken* to the limits. And when Wran *saw* Vasagi, he knew that he was not merely the very master of metamorphism, but also that he had passed beyond the limits of sanity itself. And because Wran knew there can be no reasoning with madness, he didn't even try but merely lay there, staring with eyes that scarcely believed, and his jaws distended in a rictus of awe.

Vasagi had said that he had made himself in the image

of one of his own creatures. Now Wran knew what he
meant. Upon a time (it seemed an age ago), he'd gone
down into Suckscar with Spiro, the dog-Lord Canker
Canison, and Nestor Lichloathe, and had seen one of
Vasagi's guardians of the stairwells. And Vasagi was . . .
similar.

Under the hood of his cloak, thrown back now, Vasagi
had eyes but nothing else of a face. For beneath the shiny-
black, utterly flat, nostril-slitted flange of a nose, a fat-
muscled neck flowed like a column *directly* into the chest.
But central between the nipples, and from there down to
the crotch, which was merely a junction for the legs and
no longer housed genitalia, great rubbery *vertical* lips
opened like a door, displaying Vasagi's pulsing innards! At
the back, sheathed in muscle, his ribs must be hinged to
the spine—but at the front they formed meshing teeth that
drooled and *snapped* at Wran!

And: *Ahhh!* said the monster. *I could eat your face—eat
all of you—but I won't. What? When there's the sweet fresh
dung of a beast going stale under my flyer's tail? Or, I
might peg you out to await the dawn, except it is too far
off. Also, I was pegged out upon a time—Carmen, too—so
that we know it's not necessarily fatal. But that rope
around your neck . . .*

. . . Is!

Without another word Vasagi closed his cloak, put up
the hood, turned and took Carmen on his arm, and walked
her to the waiting flyers. Wran thought to struggle against
his bonds, and was at once stilled by a thousand small
knives in his back: the severed nerve-endings where
Vasagi had cut out his leech. The pair mounted up . . . and
launched!

Something bounded and spurted red against the rocks,
then lay still. And in a while Vasagi used a knife to cut the
line, and sent Wran's headless body spinning. And:

Done! he said, his voice a sigh in Carmen's mind.

You, but not me, she answered. *No, for a certain "callow Szgany youth" made me a Lady, and then would deny*

and destroy me. Well, and you've had your revenge, my Lord.

Aye, he nodded in her mind, *and ah . . . . it was sweet! But I take your point. So let's seek out this Nestor, shall we?*

And climbing on the night wind, they made for Sunside.

Meanwhile, Gorvi the Guile rejoiced that he was off and running! Nothing behind him but a great many empty miles, and nothing ahead but a last crumbling knuckle in the kinked spine of the barrier mountains, the Great Red Waste, and eventually a mainly vacated Gulf of Turgosheim. Back in the last aerie, Wratha and the others would probably believe he was dead and devoured, and his bones littering the boulder plains. If so, good! But he was fairly sure that none had seen him make his escape, and he was certain no one else knew of his bolt-hole escape route. And anyway, it seemed unlikely they'd send a posse all the way back to Turgosheim just for one man.

Therefore, as the last crags fell away and the mountains flattened to earth—when all that *should* lie ahead was emptiness, the seething red wastelands, and their reek—it came as no small surprise when Gorvi saw in the sky another flyer, and heard the gleeful mental chuckle of its rider:

Ho, Gorvi! Well, and wouldn't we know it! Gorvi the Guile, fugitive! All on his ownsome, and on the run, his head full of thoughts of dear old Turgosheim! What, homesick, are you? Our bloodwar was a bit too much for you, eh? All that nasty fighting and such?

Gorvi did some very quick thinking (but this time kept it to himself). And in another moment: *The bloodwar's over, Boris,* he answered. *And I'm the only survivor of any importance. There may be others come straggling eventually—thralls and a lieutenant or two—but that's all. The two sides were too evenly matched, you see, and wiped each other out.*

"Really?" said Boris, assuming the gawp of an idiot. (He was closer now, and didn't require to use his mentalism). Then the gawp slipped from his face. "Yet a moment ago . . . why, I'd have sworn you were wondering if they'd send anyone after you, to settle the score in Turgosheim."

Gorvi knew the game was up; he whirled a bolas of vicious hooks, and released them towards Boris. His target hunched down in the saddle, caused his mount to swerve, gave way. And with a snarled obscenity, the Guile shot through the breach and headed directly out across the Great Red Waste. Glancing back over his shoulder, he was surprised to see Black Boris smiling a knowing smile . . . until he sensed a mental command shoot skywards:

He's all yours. Bring him down!

Gorvi didn't look but leaned far forward along his mount's straining neck and commanded it, *Fly! Fly as never before!*

But a mile or two out over the Great Red Waste, when at last he heard the rumble of propulsors growing louder, then he had to look. There were two of them, two small, highly manoeuvrable aerial warriors. One fell like a stone directly towards him, the other in a steep spiral, holding back a little to see which way he'd jump. It would make little or no difference anyway; however he jumped they'd be too fast for him. Indeed, and by the time he'd thought it, they were already on him!

The torpedo went straight through his mount's left wing, leaving it singed and fraying. The other flattened its spiral, got beneath Gorvi, raised erectile spines along its back, and sliced his flyer open the full length of its belly. That was more than enough, and down they went. And Gorvi's staggering, stumbling mind wondering how this could possibly be happening to him.

He was still wondering when they splashed down in a smoking, searing acid pool. But even if he'd had the time to form an airfoil and leap free, there'd be nowhere to fly. He stood on his flyer's back as it boiled, bubbled and sank, and tried to figure it out. But with all the guile in the world there'd be no getting out of this. He knew it, and at the end, as his mount slipped under, he reached down to grasp the saddle and went down with it.

In a little while his parasite rebelled (the tenacity of the vampire?), causing Gorvi to relax his grip. Or perhaps it wasn't so much his leech's tenacity as the powerful corrosive action of the acid: the fact that his fingers were dissolving to slime knuckle by knuckle and detaching themselves from his hands. Whichever, very little of him made it back to the surface.

And what little there was didn't last too long . . .

Resupplied from Suckscar, Devetaki's forces attempted an invasion downwards into Mangemanse only to find the way blocked, and, like the rest of the manse, impregnable in the short term. All of Canker's defenders, in whichever quarter, fought as mad dogs; for the time being, the dog-Lord was safe. Not so Wratha. Routes from Suckscar up into the ultimate manse were plentiful, as were landing bays and windows for access, and stairwells and passages within. Under attack from both Suckscar and the roof, Wrathspire was eminently accessible to the invaders. Wratha's forces were confined, compressed within, while she herself was slowly but surely floated up towards the roof on the froth of battle.

Down below, Madmanse fell! The desertion of both of the Lords Killglance had utterly demoralized their thralls; they had continued to fight, however halfheartedly, because there was no alternative. Probably doomed to end their days as warrior meal, it would be as well to die gutted in hand-to-hand combat, as *in* some creature's guts, or soup in a vat of metamorphism!

Thus only Mangemanse and Wrathspire remained, with both Canker Canison and Wratha the Risen in residence, and the rest of the last aerie (with the exception of a handful of inaccessible pockets of resistance) was now Devetaki's. Her forces had suffered losses, of course . . . but she was glad of them! Keeping her generals in the front of the fighting, she had seen the bulk of them go down, never again to rise. The handful of surviving Lords were of little consequence; they'd be like pet dogs following her to heel, fighting for the crumbs she dropped.

Now, in the fifteenth hour of the night (even the virgin grandam was astonished at the scale and speed of her success), she gathered her forces out of the sacked, fallen manses, and concentrated them on Wrathspire. But she left one bolt-hole to the roof clear, and kept back her troops from a certain turret, where she'd been informed of a lone flyer saddled and ready for flight. And as fire and the occasional screaming thrall gouted from Wrathspire's windows, and roiling black smoke poured from every exit, Devetaki landed there, gave Alexi Yefros into the care of thrall bodyguards, stationed herself close to Wratha's flyer but out of sight, and waited. And eventually Wratha came.

She came panting, scurrying through the battling crush, and in her urgency to be away never once paused to wonder why she wasn't recognized or stopped. She *had* been recognized, of course, but Devetaki's orders were plain and simple, and left no room for errors: *Wratha the Risen must not be harmed! She is mine!* And now she truly was.

As Wratha entered the turret she saw her flyer stretched there, leaking life from a throat slit to the spine, all flopping and gurgly, and definitely finished with things. And she also saw Devetaki. Wratha's gauntlet, clogged with flesh, was on her hand, strapped to her arm—but in another moment, so were two of Devetaki's strongest lieutenants, one to each arm and a third man behind her with a sharp ironwood stake in the small of her back. Devetaki stepped forward and quickly took the kneblasch dispenser which she had known would be hidden in Wratha's robe, and so the Lady was disarmed.

And despite the fact that she was thwarted and her plans in ruins, for the first time in Wratha's life there was no wrath left in her. The glow beneath the cartilage scarp on her brow was grown dim, and her flesh had lost much of its customary youthful lustre. Devetaki found it odd that even in defeat a woman such as Wratha should be so subdued (so cowed?) and said as much. Then, as if remembering the Gulf of Turgosheim—the fact that they had been friends there upon a time . . . well, friends of sorts, within limits—Wratha looked at her and quietly said:

"So I look down in the mouth, do I?" She shrugged, and in a while continued, "Well, that's how it is: one day up, and the next day down." And now a grim cold smile. "This is a down day, that's all."

"True," Devetaki answered, "but the last of them, I fear." And putting a leather-clad arm around Wratha's shoulders, as if to hold her up, she walked with her towards the rim of the high plateau roof. Wratha was wan; she slumped down into herself and seemed very fragile. Devetaki was not deceived (if any deception were intended), and her men stayed close to hand.

But the worst of the fighting was over now, and the victors mopped up. Devetaki knew she was secure, and Wratha at her mercy. Of which there was very little. Eventually they came to the open turret that housed Wratha's silver cage. Then, seeing where the virgin grandam had taken her, Wratha started and made to draw away. But Devetaki's men took her, and when their mistress nodded put her in the cage, fastened its door, and made to hoist her aloft. At which Wratha cried out:

"Devetaki! We were friends, you and I. I even . . . admired you, and tried to pattern myself after you. I *still* admire you! You are the winner, after all. Of everything."

"It's true." Devetaki put on her smiling mask. "But what's this? Do you seek to plead with me? *You* were the rebel, Wratha. You are the one who caused all this."

Wratha shook her head. "No, I won't plead. My time is up, and I know it. But I want you to know, Devetaki, that I won't hold anything against you."

Devetaki nodded. "You *are* pleading, then, in your subtle fashion?"

Again Wratha shook her head. "No, it's just that . . . all my life I have hated, one thing or another. And now that it's over . . . I wish there had been more love in it, that's all."

"Love?" Devetaki raised an eyebrow. "True love, you mean, as the Szgany know it? Among vampires? Is there such a thing?"

"We were Szgany, upon a time," Wratha answered, sadly.

"That time is past," Devetaki smiled.

"Kiss me once, through these bars," Wratha begged. "Then they can hang me up to wait for the sun."

"Eh?" Despite the fact that Devetaki was wearing her smiling mask, she frowned. "A kiss?"

"A fond farewell," said Wratha (and began to gather a gob of phlegm at the back of her throat). "If nothing else, it will show that we can die with a flourish, flamboyant as our lives." Her voice was choked—but with the phlegm, not from emotion; or a cold, cold emotion at best.

The virgin grandam cocked her head. "I think I like that, aye! So be it." And stepping to the cage, avoiding the silver bars, she pressed her mouth to Wratha's—who quick as thought straightened up, caught Devetaki through the bars, and spurted phlegm into her convulsing throat! Then, as Devetaki choked and struggled, Wratha massaged her throat until the loathsome stuff was down, finally biting her mouth and tonguing the wound! And as Devetaki jerked free, Wratha threw off her robe to display her nakedness . . . and a great deal more than nakedness!

The signs of her curse were plain; Devetaki saw them and her eyes stood out; she pointed, gabbled something unintelligible, turned aside and hurled the contents of her stomach into a corner of the turret. And finally: "Hang the hag!" she cried in her fury, her fear, as tears dripped from her eyes and bile from her mouth. "Hang the plague-ridden bitch on high, to wait for the rising sun!" And sucking furiously (fearfully?) on her torn lips, she spat the contaminated blood away. Then: *Cleanse me!* she commanded her shuddering vampire, willing it to be so; though whether it would be remained to be seen.

Then, shutting out Wratha's shrieking, cackling laughter where she was hoisted up and swung out under the gantry, Devetaki swept regally away, and stumbled only a very little . . .

* * *

Later, when Devetaki had regained her composure and called her generals to her, she saw Ursula Torspawn was missing. Her first thought was that Ursula must have gone down in the fighting, but one of that Lady's lieutenants assured her it was not the case. "Her flyer suffered some injury," he reported. "That was what she told me, as she limped off south."

"South?" Devetaki was suspicious. There'd been times recently when Ursula had given her some funny little looks. "What lies south, except the barrier mountains? Did she have a fresh mount back there? Why didn't she land on the roof?"

Ursula's lieutenant looked blank, or perhaps surprised by Devetaki's outburst. "The roof was awash with blood and fighting," he answered, "of which my Lady had done her share but in the sky. I have no doubt she'll be back immediately."

"Huh!" Devetaki breathed heavily. "Well, and perhaps she will. We'll have to wait and see." Then she set about to detail her plans concerning in part an indefinite siege on Mangemanse, but mainly the saturation and subjugation of Sunside by vampire forces. For now that Wrathstack had all but fallen, the locator Alexei Yefros had come up with a scheme to bring this guerilla, the so-called Necroscope, Nathan Keogh, out of hiding . . .

Crossing the barrier mountains a little west of the great pass, Ursula Torspawn was glad that she'd deserted. A pity she hadn't thought to do it earlier, that's all, when there was still time to fly back across the Great Red Waste and return to Turgosheim all in the one night. For in Tormanse in Turgosheim, she'd left sufficient of thralls and creatures behind that she could start up again and be a Power, while here she was devoid of power—and at the mercy of Devetaki!

Hah! Small mercy there! But cunning? Aye! And Ursula cursed herself that she'd watched it all happening without seeing anything, until Devetaki herself had let it be known what she was about: the "elevation" of the Ladies . . . a "grand matriarchy"! *Hah!* No such thing—she would be Empress! Where was Zindevar Cronesap now? And what of Ursula Torspawn, now that her contingent was reduced to a handful!? Oh, yes: she'd be next on Devetaki's list, be sure. Except when the power-crazed slut looked around for her, she'd be nowhere to be found.

Ursula's plan was simple: since she couldn't make it back to Turgosheim tonight, she'd use the night to hole up, to feed and rest herself and her flyer, then wait out tomorrow in some dark and bitter crevice of a place further east. And tomorrow night, skirting Black Boris at the eastern extreme of the barrier mountains, she'd get a good start back home. After that, all would be in the hands of fate. But right now . . .

At the back of her saddle was a bundle of clothes. Ursula had always affected the Szgany looks and ways, had kept her girlish shape and Gypsy mannerisms. Let her get out of this battle gear and into her patterned skirt, forest-green blouse, and crudely fashioned shad-leather boots, shake down her black hair, shape her flattened vampire nose a little and quench the fires of her eyes . . . she felt certain she could go among them like a genuine waif of the woods, all unnoticed; well, except by the men. Easy to lure a couple of likely lads into the darkness, refuel herself, and carve a little fresh meat for the return trip.

That was all there was to it. Risky? Well, perhaps—but not as risky as staying with Devetaki. That one would not stop now until she had it all, and what she couldn't have . . . she'd destroy. Ursula could only hope that when she failed to return to the fighting, Devetaki would assume her dead of an accident or misadventure. At which the virgin grandam would most likely rejoice . . .

III

Nana, Nestor, Nathan— Confrontation!

Earlier:

Unobserved (it might even seem ignored), the Necro-scope and his party had followed the ebb and flow of the bloodwar in and around Wrathstack. To any outsider they must seem a singularly disparate team: a light-skinned, blue-eyed man of Sunside, four psychically talented people out of a weird parallel world, and a Starside wolf of the wild. But Nathan, Trask, Zek, Chung, and Goodly—and Grinner, of course—*were* a team and there was this mainly unspoken (their situation was scarcely conducive to chatter) but *sensed* camaraderie between them.

Nathan had stuck close to Ben Trask; Ian Goodly and David Chung had passed the time in low-toned conversa-tion; Zek's apparently inseparable companion had been Grinner. For in the devilish-looking wolf's own "words," as conveyed to Nathan: "This one *knows* the grey brothers. She knows *how to be* with a wolf!" It was a compliment, of course.

Their vantage point or observation post had been a room in the stump of a collapsed stack whose jumble lay a mile and a half northwest of the last aerie. Open on two sides and minus its ceiling or roof, still the remaining walls were massive and the one that faced Wrathstack had a vast window that provided an excellent view of the battle. Nathan would rather have been elsewhere, of course (namely, with Misha), but his reason for being on Starside was simple: to watch the fighting as best he might, and determine the next phase of his campaign against whichever side was the winner.

After nine hours it had been obvious which side that must be. Wrathstack was issuing fire and smoke from most of its levels, and the shattered debris of battle was beginning to strew itself across the boulder plains even as far as the ruins from which the Necroscope's party kept score of the fighting. Several injured, riderless flyers had already crashed down within a hundred yards' radius of their hideaway; finally one such creature had fluttered to earth with a lieutenant still rocking in the saddle. Mazed and stumbling, the man had made it a short distance away from his crumpled mount before himself collapsing facedown in the dust. The fact that he'd made it there at all seemed a sure signal to the huddle of humans that they should now move on.

Via the Möbius Continuum, Nathan had then taken his party up onto a plateau in the barrier mountains midway between Twin Fords and Settlement, where Zek and David Chung employed their talents (and the Necroscope his) to scan along the range and try to find out what was going on. The enemy was camped there for certain; from the lava falls beyond the great pass even to a point some miles west of Settlement, they were scattered in a dozen or more secure locations in small but by no means negligible parties. Grinner's fleet-footed, night-prowling pack of covert observers, and that of his brother Blaze, had already confirmed this fact; also that for the moment the vampires were keeping a low profile and seemed unaccountably immobile, inactive . . . as if they waited for something. But for what?

Perhaps Devetaki kept them in reserve for use in the event that the bloodwar against Wrathstack went wrong or took longer than she expected; maybe they would form a blockade if Wratha should attempt to resupply herself out of Sunside. But Nathan didn't think so. There was something very ominous about them, still and silent in the night, with their seething minds all guarded from telepathic intrusion, and their senses alert for any sign of attack upon themselves.

That last might be a clue in itself: for of course they were aware of the Necroscope now, and knew him for a powerful destructive force in his own right. That they would come after him and clash with him sooner or later was a bygone conclusion—indeed a foreseen conclusion!—as Nathan *had* seen it during his brief trip with Ian Goodly into the future. Except . . . he didn't much care to speculate what that "conclusion" would involve. The word itself conveyed a termination, but of what? His life? So it had appeared when he and Goodly had been left spinning in time, "at the end of his tether": the blue lifethread that literally tethered him to a physical existence.

Finally—unsettled, anxious, and frustrated as ever—Nathan had returned his party to the now deserted camp at the edge of the forest, where they would sleep and take it in turn to keep watch. Nathan himself, teamed up with Trask, had taken the first three-hour watch; while the others slept, the pair had also taken the opportunity to talk.

"We seem a long way from, and a long time since, Earth," Trask had opened. "My Earth, I mean. And in fact we have come—oh, a very long way—an entire universe! But on the other hand, the whole thing has taken little more than a night and a day, your time. So paradoxically, I suppose we might say that time has flown!"

Nathan had nodded, and a phrase remembered from Trask's world, which hadn't made much sense to him then, had suddenly sprung to mind. "Doesn't time fly when you're having fun!" he said, however drily. But now the phrase was entirely appropriate—especially the way he'd used it! In fact, and as he now saw, that was the entire point of the thing. So maybe the *sarcasm* of their two worlds at least wasn't that dissimilar.

Trask's turn to nod, and to grin, but he quickly sobered and followed up with: "You haven't said a lot about your trip with Ian Goodly. Was it really that bad?"

Nathan looked at him with that disconcerting, blue-eyed gaze of his, open as the sky, and thought carefully before he answered. Because in the moment of Trask's question he'd realized that he had *been* thinking carefully about that trip ever since returning from it. "It was—I don't know, a dead end? It seemed to be, anyway. But I can't be sure. And of course I don't *want* to be sure! After all, I've been shown the future before, and by an expert. And he was wrong."

Trask remembered the story from the Necroscope's debrief at E-Branch HQ, London, England, Earth, some five months ago. "Thikkoul, the Thyre stargazer?"

Nathan glanced at the ice-chip stars and said, "The same. Thikkoul saw me disappearing through a great glaring door, 'in the blink of an eye!' And I'll never be able to forget the tone of his deadspeak voice when he said: 'Then . . . *you are gone*!' "

"But you weren't."

"But I was! Gone out of this world, into yours—through the Starside Gate."

"But you weren't 'gone,' " Trask insisted. "You lived on. It was just that you were no longer here."

"That's right," said Nathan. "And that's why I can't be sure—and why I'm glad I'm not sure—about what we saw in future time. If Thikkoul could get it wrong, so can I. Oh, he saw the future, all right. But not the way the future saw it! So maybe Ian Goodly is right, about the future being sentient. Certainly it appears to protect itself; it's jealous of being known; it *does* come to pass—of course it does, and must—but in its own way."

"What will be has been?"

"That, too," Nathan answered, "but we're not allowed to know it. We were fashioned to be of three—and *only* three—dimensions; the fourth does its damnedest to keep it that way. So people like Thikkoul, Goodly, and myself, we're kept guessing. And it's done so expertly—so deviously?—that we're even a little, and sometimes a lot, afraid of it."

"As you are now?"

"As I'm trying not to be. Like your saying: hope springs eternal."

"But does it really?"

"For myself, yes. Let's face it, if I didn't believe I'd come through this, what would be the point? But for you ... I don't know. I'll be glad when you've all had enough and I can take you out of here."

"But you must know we have to see it through? It isn't just your world, Nathan, but ours, too. When, if, we get back to our own place, we'll have to report on things here. And if our report isn't just *exactly* so ... then the bloodwar you've seen so far won't even nearly match the one that's to come."

Nathan stared at him. "You think so? But how so? Surely Gustav Turchin will close the Perchorsk Gate, and you espers will continue to guard the one at Radujevac. Won't that suffice?"

Then Trask told him about the Chernobyl Sarcophagus: how a nuclear curse had been visited on Earth by man's stupidity. "So they built a wall around it and a roof over it," he went on, "thick enough to keep all of that weird heat in. It was quite awhile ago. But just containing it wasn't enough; they still had to know what was going on inside—that nothing else was going to escape! So every now and then they open the wall and go back in. They *have* to be sure, you see?

"And it will be precisely the same with Sunside/Starside. Except while a meltdown can't think for itself, the Wamphyri can and do. And while the nuclear monster in that sarcophagus can't deliberately try to break out ..." He paused, but he had made his point.

"In that event, this whole world will suffer."

"It would be ruined!" Trask corrected him. "As you know, rightly or wrongly we used nuclear weapons to bring one of our own wars to an end. From time to time there's been the threat of such usage ever since. But men have to live on the planet, and finally they're seeing sense. Good news for *my* world, yes ... but this one? The men of my world don't have to live here; to them this is an alien place, and if some of them knew what we already know ... I don't think they'd even wait to see how it works out! And honestly, I can't say I blame them. That's another reason why we're staying: to see it through with you, and to know how to report at the end of it."

"If you get back."

"We're putting our faith in you."

Nathan waved his hands helplessly. "But I can't work miracles!"

Now, despite himself and the mood of their conversation, Trask did grin, and broadly. "Oh, really?" he said. "I think some of us might disagree with you!" Then he stopped smiling and sighed. "But ... if you really can't work a miracle, then we'll simply have to trust to luck—or to the future?"

In the Necroscope's mind, the subject had become depressing and so he changed it. "What do you make of this?" he asked. And taking a sliver of charcoal from their small fire, he drew Ethloi's "engine," as he had come to think of it (the mathematician's enigmatic diagram that so reminded him of pistons and pressure, motion and power), on the pale inner wall of a piece of bark.

"What am I *supposed* to think of it?" Trask asked. "What is it, anyway?"

"That's what I hoped you'd tell me," Nathan gloomily answered. And he attempted to explain the inexplicable, the hidden meaning in the thing which all the Thyre ancients had been trying to get over to him without understanding it themselves. "I had hoped that if anyone would recognize it, you would."

"That I'd know the 'truth' of it?"

"Why not?"

"Because *you* don't know it," Trask answered. "And because they don't know it. Show me an algebraic equation with two solutions, one right and one wrong, and I'll choose the right one. *Tell* me what this is, and I'll know at once if you're lying to me. But when you don't know yourself? Why, I'm not even sure if this diagram is a question or the answer to one!"

Nathan was disappointed but understood Trask's explanation of his inability. And it dawned on him: of course Trask didn't know! This thing was of the future, and the future was devious and deliberately obscure!

Again they changed the subject, and for long hours talked of other things . . .

Their watch passed quickly. On Starside, the bloodwar had been raging for a little over thirteen hours; before sleeping Nathan made a quick Möbius jump to see how things stood. It was much the same as before, except the fighting now seemed to be concentrated around the aerie's summit and the stack's central levels. It would be another two to three hours before Devetaki caught Wratha, locked her in the silver cage and hoisted her on high.

Nathan returned to camp but was unable to sleep. He found himself torn two ways. He hadn't seen enough of Misha—could never see enough of her—yet spent the night separated from her; and no way to tell how many nights were left to them. But Devetaki Skullguise had a locator whose special assignment was the whereabouts of the Necroscope, Nathan Keogh. If he went into the desert, to Misha in the new oasis at Place-Under-the-Yellow-Cliffs, Yefros might locate him there. All of the best-kept secrets of the Thyre would then be in jeopardy: their intelligence and the location of their colonies, their vulnerability . . . and their availability.

Previously the Wamphyri (not unlike the Szgany, much to Nathan's great shame) had considered the Thyre no better than desert trogs: inferior creatures scarcely fit for consumption. Only let them discover the truth of it—it might well mean a disaster! The dull trogs of Starside caverns were left mainly to their own devices *because* they were dull, unfeeling, incapable of resistance. What use to torture creatures who couldn't appreciate the pain? Where was the pleasure in hunting beings who didn't have the sense or opportunity to hide? Why fuel oneself on trog blood, when there was always the sweet flesh of higher human beings? And as for trog women—well, there had never been a great many vampires of Black Boris's persuasions.

But only let them get to *know* the Thyre . . .

It was unthinkable.

But indeed thinking about it—and between times turning over and over in his head the puzzles and enigmas posed by the esoteric dreaming of dead Thyre ancients—finally the Necroscope drifted into a deep sleep, and stayed that way for three solid hours. And because his friends (especially Atwei) among the not too distant Thyre knew that he needed his sleep, they made no "unseemly" intrusions through the medium of their mentalism, and it was a credit to Sunside's Great Majority that they didn't disturb him either, despite the fact that one of their number, and a special one at that, was herself disturbed almost to distraction. . . .

Close to a deserted Szgany trail through the forest not many miles from camp, Nana Kiklu had a visitor at the low mound of earth where Lardis had dug a hole and burned her, then buried her ashes. Her visitor's predicament—and Nana's, that she couldn't hug him, comfort him, hold his head to her breast—brought her to incorporeal tears that she somehow kept from spilling into the deadspeak aether. But she *could* feel him, or his presence certainly, and knew the feeling for a sign of his power and a symptom of his predicament both.

For although he was able to speak to her using his own morbid version of deadspeak, and though she felt his presence, there was no warmth in him and he was not a Necroscope. The next best thing, then? Or the worst possible thing. And:

Mother? he said wonderingly, in his breathless whisper of a deadspeak voice, where he stood at her grave. *Did you . . . did you call out to me?* Wonderingly, aye, for none of the dead had ever done that before! And through all Nana's tears—shed for him—he knew that she had and that he, Lord Nestor Lichloathe of the Wamphyri, had heard her. It was why he was here, for in fact he'd been on his way to find and kill Nathan when her crying had drawn him down out of the sky. What's more, he *had* found his brother (the faint but definite trail of his numbers vortex at least) and had known that Nathan lay sleeping only a handful of miles away. So why he'd answered Nana's cry at all was something of a mystery to him, which Nestor couldn't fathom because the humanity was flown out of him and he was Wamphyri.

Then, when she was able, Nana told Nestor the story of his life, which no necromancer's threats might ever have wrung from her, and slowly but surely the gaps in his damaged memory began to fill themselves in. Except, it would make no real difference to him (or so he thought), for the baby, boy, and young man he'd once been were alien to him now, even different identities. And *he* was the Lord Nestor, of the Wamphyri.

So Nestor stood, then sat, and listened, while out of the cold, cold earth something of warmth struggled to find its way into him, as Nana *tried* to warm him with memories that were no longer his. His mother's purpose, a delaying tactic, was apparent, even transparent, yet there was more to it than that; for Nana had never been one for deceit, and was beyond it now that she knew the truth of the grave. Yet still the necromancer sat there, like a small but very dreadful boy at his mother's knee. And while the greater part of him rejected her, other parts soaked up her words like rust loosened by oil, as the ghosts of memory's faded pictures were retouched with living colour and texture on the screen of his mind.

And perhaps somewhere deep inside, the dry cogs of forgotten intelligence, mental machinery, began to mesh at last, and wheels creakingly to turn . . .

Thus Nathan slept on through the night (though shortly he'd be up and about again), and for the moment knew nothing of Nestor at Nana's graveside.

While in Starside:

Only Mangemanse continued to hold out with any measure of success. Throbbing with Canker's moon music and his "singing," and defended by beasts, lieutenants, and thralls (the dog-Lord's "pups," who in truth could only be likened to mad dogs), Mangemanse seemed impregnable.

But on high, Wratha the Risen—who also had been known to use the word "impregnable" from time to time—cackled like a madwoman behind silver bars and set her cage to rocking, and Wrathspire itself seemed all set to fall to the invaders from the east.

While *in* the east, where the jagged spine of the barrier mountains broke into spurs, sank to earth, and buried itself at last, Spiro Killglance flew towards the last jumble of tumbled rocks that marked the eastern extreme of the range. Dressed in his customary rags—with the tails of a blood-spattered headband streaming out behind him—he thought little or nothing. A wingspan to his left, his spare flyer glided effortlessly on breezes out of the north; and lulled by the interminable throb of powerful manta wings, Spiro's power-crazed mind was for the moment weary . . . and blank.

Likewise Black Boris's mind, blank, except he deliberately contrived to keep it so in order to take Spiro by surprise even as he'd taken Gorvi. For having received warning of Spiro's approach from *Desmodus* bats recruited in the trog caverns as familiar creatures, Boris and a lieutenant were hiding in the last of the crags, crouched there astride flyers that hovered on the turbulent updrafts; while high overhead, obscured by a scud of clouds, a keen-eyed warrior floated on fully inflated bladders, shadowing them and monitoring Spiro's progress. Only one warrior this time, aye, for following the attack on Gorvi, Boris was satisfied that one was enough.

And indeed Spiro *was* surprised, no less than Gorvi before him, when Boris and his man drifted free of the crags directly to the fore, blocking his way and facing him head-on. And: *What have we here!* Black Boris called out gleefully with his mentalism, when the fugitive was still some distance apart from him. *But I do believe it's Spiro Killglance! My how you rebels flee the fighting—like bats from a leaking aerie!*

But Spiro had quickly recovered, and at once returned: *Or female trogs from a cavern, when Black Boris drops his pants?*

Boris's turn to be surprised. This was a Spiro he had not seen before. Obviously the years flown between had given him a little self-confidence; something must have, for sure! *Why, it appears you've been spying on me!* Boris chuckled as Spiro sped closer. *Anyway, it's a real treat to see that you've developed a sense of humor at last— though much too late, I'm sorry to say. But at least you can die laughing.*

"I intend to," Spiro was now close enough to shout. "Well, smiling, at least." And his bloodshot, deep-sunken eyes turned skywards as he heard the warrior's propulsors start into life. Then, as the thing came squirting out of the clouds into view, Spiro saw what a monster it was. Albeit of the smaller variety, it was viciously equipped: a real test, at last, for his fresh-forged weapon.

"And are you *still* smiling?" Black Boris laughed over the throb and sputter of the warrior's discharge.

"Oh, there are smiles and smiles," Spiro answered, gathering his alien energies as the warrior came curving down on him from the star-splashed sky.

Now Boris was close enough to see Spiro's face—more especially, his eyes—and to know where he had seen such before: in the fact of Spiro's father, the abominable Eygor Killglance! But that had been long and long ago, and surely . . .

". . . Surely I have *inherited* them at last!" Spiro snarled, hunching down in his saddle.

The warrior was closing with him, zeroing in. Its many eyes were fixed on him . . . then fixed on *his* eyes! It could not look away! And: *Aye, come and get it!* Spiro thought, the while wondering if he really had the measure of this nightmare thing.

Spiro was in the middle; Boris and his lieutenant to the fore, and the warrior curving down out of the sky to the rear. Issuing mental commands, and reinforcing them by hauling on his reins and turning his mount sideways on, Spiro never once took his eyes off the descending monster. Levelling out of its dive, it sped towards him. Spiro was its target—and it was his as Spiro's eyes underwent a weird and hideous metamorphosis. One eye bulged crimson; the other narrowed to a sulphur-dripping slit. Then—

——He let go his energies all in one massive blast!

Spiro's mind-bolt was not visible, but its effect was!

The warrior opened its cavern jaws, as if to snap him from the sky. But its jaws kept on opening! The flesh stripped back from its "face," its flanks, back, and belly. Erectile spines detached from the creature's true spine and flew like darts in all directions. Gas-bladders exploded outwards from under chitin scales and went flapping away like torn sails. The alveolar bone and cartilage skeleton began to buckle as its musculature was stripped away, and breaking in pieces it flew past a triumphant Spiro in a hail of black excrement and crimson plasma!

Flew past him . . . directly into Boris and his man! Boris avoided the worst of it but his lieutenant was less fortunate. Sliced open by free-flying, scything teeth and whirling spines and knocked out of his saddle, he went twirling down the night. His flyer, ripped in its membrane wings, body, and neck, limped away towards the tumbling crags.

Which left Spiro and his spare flyer, and Black Boris, of course, alone in the sky.

And: *There are smiles, and there are smiles.* Spiro's mental voice was a sinister rumble now in Boris's mind, where the trog-fancier sat blood- and shit-streaked astride his startled mount. Boris would turn aside but couldn't; Spiro's eyes held him like a fly in a spider's web.

Sp-spiro, Boris managed to sent at last, *I . . . I was only carrying out my duties . . . !*

But did you have to enjoy them so?

I . . .

Enough! I'm in a hurry.

He hurled his second bolt, and it was as if Boris and his mount had run full tilt into a mountainside. They crumpled up, and their debris went fluttering to earth in rags and ruin.

And: *East,* Spiro commanded his beasts without pause. *East and Turgosheim. For I've a gorge to populate and rule. And whosoever thought* Eygor *Killglance was a* Power . . . *well, just wait until he sees Spiro!*

Far to the west and on Sunside:

Nana and Nestor sensed Nathan's gradual awakening. Nestor felt the strengthening whirl of his brother's numbers vortex, and Nana . . . simply knew. Yet both of them held back from any sort of action: Nana from warning the Necroscope, because that could only accelerate the inevitable confrontation, and Nestor because he wanted to hear his story out in full.

The twin beliefs that formed Nestor's single obsession and major misconception, that Nathan was a Great Enemy from years long forgotten, and that the woman Misha Zanesti had betrayed Nestor to be with him, were so deeply ingrained in his scarred mind that hearing the truth from Nana was much like listening to a pack of lies—which made it hard to explain why he continued to listen; but he did. Perhaps it was the weird calming effect of her voice, the same in death as in life, which more than anything else stirred memories in him; or perhaps he was simply tired, drained by the disease that even now burned the life out of him. Whichever, Nestor sat still and listened as his mother expanded her story into a genuine delaying tactic, now that she knew her other son was awake.

So both of them kept their thoughts to themselves, excluding the living and the dead alike, silent and secretive as lovers whispering in the Sunside night . . .

Coming more fully awake, Nathan sniffed suspiciously at the air. Typical of his Szgany background, this action served to remind him who and what he was—originally. Oh, he was the son of the Necroscope, Harry Keogh, but he was also Szgany, a man of Sunside. All of his old feelings of alienage in his own land were gone now; Trask and the others were the aliens here. But they were also friends and allies.

Nathan yawned and looked around a small clearing lit by flickering yellow firelight, then threw back the cured

skin that was his blanket, stood up and glanced into a clear
night sky. The position of the stars told him the hour of the
night, and that he'd slept his three hours to the full.
Though it wasn't much, for the first time in a long time he
felt that he'd actually had some rest. Ian Goodly, David
Chung, and Grinner had taken over the watch. The former
sat close to the fire with a wolf of the wild sprawled at his
feet; Chung stretched his legs at the edge of the clearing;
Zek slept on, and Trask had just settled to sleep close by.

Nathan stepped to Goodly and said, "I'm going to see
how things are going at the last aerie. I'll be ... as long
as it takes, a few minutes at most."

The precog looked up and nodded. In the ruddy firelight, half-shadowed, his face looked even more skull-like.
"Then we can talk," he said, in that way of his. And Nathan knew that they would indeed be talking, and that
therefore he was safe to make his jump.

He went out onto Starside, to a different location this
time, scanned the last aerie, and saw that things had
changed. There was no fighting in the uppermost levels,
and most of the fires were out. Smoke-blackened landing
bays, windows, various cracks and crevices transformed
the head of the stack into a pitted skull; the plateau roof
was alive with massed movement but no sign of hostilities.
These men and creatures were obviously the victors, and
Wrathspire the vanquished.

Centrally, however, Mangemanse continued to hold out.
Several airborne warriors held the manse in siege, cruising
to and fro, or standing off and hovering on grotesquely inflated bladders. And in the levels immediately above and
especially below that obstinate manse, there was still a
deal of warlike activity where internal fires burned behind
windows like eyes, and smoke poured from scorched,
slitlike nostrils.

Best evidence that Mangemanse continued defiant came
in the form of Canker Canison's moon music: an uproar of
nerve-shredding proportions, a cacophony that swelled on
the bitter wind from the north and poured out from the rear
of the stack as from a hundred lunatic organists. It reached

out to Nathan more than a mile away, passed over him and rebounded from the astonished barrier mountains themselves! Unbeknown to the Necroscope this was the dog-Lord's prelude to flight, when Canker would launch for the moon to do mortal battle with its priests for all of the silver goddesses which he knew he'd find there. What Nathan *did* know or suspect was that by now Siggi Dam and the rest of Canker's people must be stone deaf or at least as mad as their Lord.

Nathan had seen enough and returned to Sunside. He took with him a picture in his mind of all those men and monsters milling on the roof of the last aerie, and wondered what Devetaki Skullguises's next move would be. Indeed, he *knew* what it must be but refused to dwell upon it. Best to answer it when it came . . .

Back at camp he sat by the fire and spoke to the locator Chung. "When I woke up, I thought I sensed something north of here. You?"

Chung shrugged, but not negligently. "Yes and no. I keep getting a feeling that someone is out there, and once or twice I've seemed to detect mind-smog. But it could be nerves. This is some nervy place! Anyway, it was nothing substantial."

Nathan nodded and turned to Goodly. "What do you see?"

The precog looked at him. "Ahead of us? Something so big it won't register. That's as much as I can say."

"That could mean anything."

"That's the way it is. The future can *be* anything. Especially here."

"Oh?"

"It feels all wrong. It *is* all wrong!"

"What is?" Nathan was interested. It was a rare thing to see Ian Goodly agitated, as he was now.

"This world!" The other threw up his hands. "I mean, this parallel *place*! The sun, moon, and stars. In my own world I did a little amateur astronomy. Not a lot, but enough to know that this place is all wrong. We don't see nearly enough of the sun—yet the days are longer than the nights! And the moon tumbles, which means it has an eccentric orbit or rotation or both. Also, I've watched the stars, which move quickly, then slowly. Or we do."

Nathan nodded. "I've always known these things—every Traveller has—without knowing what they mean. But now ... I think I do. Remember, we had little or no science. Then in your world I took in a lot of learning in a short time, and certain things stuck in my mind. The thing is, I've never had my father's instinct for these things; most of what I know came from my studies on Earth, or from the dead ... or from Harry's dart. In your world, I had the time but I didn't have the maths for it. Now I have the maths but I don't have the time. But as I said, I think I do understand ... certain things."

Go on," said Goodly.

"The Starside Gate—the original Gate, at the bottom of the crater—was a black hole that went wrong. When it fell on this world it created havoc, did a lot of damage. Changing from a black to a grey hole, it had a new kind of gravity, a special gravity that becomes apparent and intrudes when I try to form a Möbius door too close to the centre. Anyway, the Gate's gravity and that of this planet hold each other like balls on a bolas, at the opposite ends of a rope. The true gravity of the planet has been interfered with, which causes its eccentricity. When I was at E-Branch, someone showed me how to make what he called a Mexican jumping bean: a tube of silver foil around a small ball bearing, with the ends sealed off. When you roll it lengthwise it wobbles, goes fast then slow, because its centre of gravity is changing. This isn't a precise—what, analogy?—because the opposed centres of gravity of Sunside/Starside are fixed; which is to say, the rope between the balls on the bolas isn't a rope at all but an unbreakable, unbendable bar of invisible super-metal. That's why the balance is all wrong; there is no flexibility."

Goodly gave a nod, of partial understanding at least. "To cut it short, during daylights hours—"

"—The world is turning more slowly," Nathan finished

it for him, "and the days are longer. That's why the stars seem to move so queerly, and it also accounts for the moon's tumbling. The moon is just like the ball bearing in the Mexican jumping bean, trapped in the silver foil of a complicated gravita . . ."

He cut it short as David Chung suddenly jerked alert and came to his feet. "Oh-*oh*!" he said. And Grinner likewise gave a start as Nathan and Goodly quickly stood up. Chung followed up with: "He's back, Nathan—and fixing a powerful probe on you!"

Nathan sent a telepathic thought winging—and immediately made contact. He knew the other at once, and his location! Gasping, he reached for a machine pistol hanging by its strap from the bough of a fallen tree. But Goodly said: "No! You're going to need *that*," and pointed at the rocket launcher, loaded with only one missile, where it lay on an oiled skin. The precog was trembling like a leaf, his eyes wide and wild.

Zek and Trask had come awake. Trask wearily mumbled, "Eh? What . . . ?" But Nathan had no time for explanations. His brother Nestor was at Nana Kiklu's grave—

—And Nestor was a necromancer!

It was the last throw of Nestor's parasite, a final attempt by his weakened, leprosy-infected leech to regain ascendancy: the denial of Nana Kiklu's truth. When Nana had reached that point in her story where it became clear that Misha Zanesti had been Nathan's woman right from the start, and never Nestor's, everything his evil Wamphyri nature was based upon had seemed set to crumble, and Nestor himself to admit the error of his ways like a child confessing a small crime. Except in him the crime would have been enormous—his life dedicated to a lie!

But the vampire is tenacious: Nestor must be made to cling to his beliefs, for his power was tied to them. And the vampire is jealous, possessive, territorial: if he once gives up something that is his, where will it end? Must he then relinquish everything? *And* the vampire is the ultimate liar, to whom the truth is anathema. For the one *great* truth is that the host is not master of his own destiny but the puppet of his leech, and dances to the tune of an alien intruder. And above all the vampire is Evil, and must oppose Good as surely as black challenges white, day night, the sun the stars.

So that when Nana had told him: *You can't put them apart. Not even by killing them. Especially not by killing them! Love will out, even in death. For as I know as well and better than most, what we did in life we continue to do in death. And they will be lovers to The End!* Even as I love you, *with a mother's love for her son!*—then his leech, its essence, the chemical governor of his blood, his brain, and every enhanced Wamphyri emotion, had fought back.

NO! NO! NO! And at last his cry out loud: "Nooooooo!" And the deliberate opening of his mind, the pouring forth of venom into the mental aether, the unutterable stench of pus and poison in his vampire probe where it sped direct to the source of the cursed numbers vortex . . . Nathan in the camp clearing only a few miles away.

And Nana's incorporeal tears as last spilling over, uncaring now except for her boys, for the love of both of them despite the fact that one was grown to a monster.

This was what Nathan had heard or sensed through two simultaneous media: his brother's rage and his mother's anguish. With the result that he had jumped to a logical but incorrect conclusion: that even now Nestor rooted like a pig in the damp earth and ashes of Nana's shallow plot, torturing her for esoteric knowledge—*exactly* what the necromancer had desired him to think! The hunt was over, for Nathan would come to him.

And Nathan did come . . . with a rocket launcher seated on his shoulder!

Nestor was surprised at the speed of Nathan's reaction. Even though he knew his brother had the power to "come and go," Nathan's almost instantaneous appearance in that small clearing in the cold blue light of the stars astonished him where he came slowly to his feet. And at his feet, Nana's grave all undisturbed, so that Nathan knew he'd been fooled into coming here. But with the launcher on his shoulder and his finger on its trigger, maybe he wasn't such a fool after all.

They faced each other across Nana's mound: blood brothers, but as different—more different—as any brothers before them. Nathan was a little over six feet tall, but his brother could give him ten inches more. The first was blond, fair of skin, with eyes of a sapphire blue; the other was morbid grey, raven-haired, and crimson-eyed. And of course, the Necroscope was entirely human.

He looked upon his brother, the two of them motionless, and Nathan's finger unflinching on the trigger. But for all that he was fuelled by hatred, by a dire loathing and natural dread of the Wamphyri, he knew he couldn't make the first and last move, couldn't pull that trigger. Despite what he'd seen in future time, it was out of the question . . . he *couldn't* do it! Not with his mother's pitiful deadspeak cries ringing out in his metaphysical mind: *Nathan, no! Nathan! You would never forgive yourself!*

But her soulful supplications weren't for him alone. *Nestor, son, everything I told you is the truth. If you must die, then die. But not this way, I beg you. This way you'll be cursed by the dead for all eternity!*

And: "So, little brother," Nestor sighed, his voice muffled, a panting rasp from behind gauze wrappings. And inclining his head, he went on, "My Great Enemy, you—a mere man! Betrayer, thief, plague in my mind and curse on my being—you? Such a flimsy thing as you? Well, your mother pleads for you, and rightly."

Nathan daren't so much as blink, but he could speak. "And for you, Nestor. She pleads for you, too."

Nestor stepped aside from the mound, edged closer, and his eyes seemed to drip fire. "But I don't *need* her pleas."

"Nor I, while I hold this weapon. You saw it used before, on the dome of Sanctuary Rock."

Nestor scarcely seemed to move—yet stood all of a long pace closer! "Why should I fear death, even the true death? I'm doomed anyway, as a *leper*, Nathan. That, too, is your fault."

"No, I'll not be blamed for that," Nathan answered. "The Szgany give blame where it's due, but by the same token they also know how to accept responsibility for their actions. They don't accuse their fellow men out of spite. But then, neither have they leeches to appease!" He could have bitten his tongue but couldn't help it; it was tit for tat; he'd fallen into the mode of Wamphyri argument automatically, giving blow for blow.

"Are you saying I'm less than a man?" Nestor was no more than two paces away now.

"I'm saying you're Wamphyri," Nathan croaked from a bone-dry, gulping throat. "Which means that you can't win, for your greatest battle is already lost!"

And: *Nathaaan!* Nana wailed. *Nestooor!*

The tendrils of a mist began to coil from under Nestor's cloak, lapping his feet. "You *are* my Great Enemy!" he breathed, and the mist was also in his breath. Now he stood only a single pace away, at arm's length, and his eyes were like magnets that held Nathan's in an iron grip. But the Necroscope's finger was still cold on the trigger of his weapon. And:

"It seems we must have it out," husked Nestor. Except—

—Suddenly they were not alone!

IV

The Death of Nestor—
Intuition—Deal with a Devil!

The *whup!* ... whup! ... *whup!* of mighty membrane wings as dark manta shadows blotted out the stars and mentalist voices spoke in the trembling aether:

So, Nestor! (It was the voice of Carmen Who-Should-Not-Be.) *And how is my handsome lusty Lord after all this time? For* upon *a time you made a Lady out of a poor thrall—you* loved *her to death, or undeath! And while she slept you pegged her out where the sun would find her. But the Lord Vasagi found her first. As* we *have now found you!*

She came from the south, skimming the trees, wild and weird in her saddle, her scarlet jaws agape! Her flyer dipped ... its belly pouch yawned open ... Nestor had nowhere to run; and suddenly, his legs had no strength to carry him! Full-waxed, his disease was out of control, running rampant through his system.

"Down!" Nathan yelled; and astonished, Nestor knew that his Necroscope brother shouted at him! He fell beside Nana's mound, and Carmen's flyer came on.

But a powerful mentalist was in Nathan's mind, reading the secrets of his awesome weapon there. And: *Carmen, beware! That one is dangerous; he will surely kill you!* It was Vasagi, whose telepathic voice Nathan would know anywhere. Vasagi, his mother's murderer! There was blood and a mutual death-vow between them, and this Carmen was a creature of his.

Before, when he faced Nestor point-blank, nothing short of a direct, full-frontal attack could have induced the Necroscope to pull the trigger of his rocket launcher. Now, nothing could have stopped him! Heeding Vasagi's warning, Carmen swerved and flew off at a tangent, gaining elevation to clear the trees at the side of the clearing.

Aiming twelve inches ahead of her middle, Nathan squeezed off his missile—which hurtled home along a path of sizzling, blinding fire. There came a flash and a hot blast, and Carmen cleared the trees ... in small pieces and a scarlet spray! And Carmen Who-Should-Not-Be was not. Her mount, its thorny spine gouged by a great bite where the saddle had been, issued a single shrilling bleat and crumpled head-on into the trees. While overhead:

One of you is weak as a sick wolf-cub, Vasagi sent, as he began side-slipping his flyer to earth, *and the other is merely human, Szgany, and now weaponless: scarcely a match for Vasagi. But Vasagi was not the one who threw down the gauntlet!*

His mount settled like a leaf on a still day, or a flat stone through water, slipping from side to side with its manta wings arched into air-trap scoops. But despite the fact that Carmen was dead, still Nathan detected *two* alien minds in the telepathic aether. The other ... belonged to Vasagi's flyer!

"Karz!" Nathan gasped. "Karz Biteri!" And at last his old friend knew him, too: Nathan Seersthrall, called Kiklu, who had flown him to freedom out of Runemanse in Turgosheim. Then:

No! said Karz to Vasagi. *I may not take you down. We have journeyed far enough together, you and I.* Amazingly, a vampire flyer defied its Lord and rider!

Take me down now! Vasagi's voice was a grunt, a threat, as Karz plied his wings and rose up a little.

No! Karz denied him yet again. *I have had more than enough of you, Vasagi. As of now we go our own ways, you and I. It was always our agreement.*

Vasagi was furious. *Beast, I order you—take me down!*

Nathan sensed Karz's mental shrug. *So be it . . .*

And somewhat higher than the treetops, Karz did an utterly unthinkable thing and reneged on a Lord of the Wamphyri! Folding a wing and rolling over sideways, he flexed his body like a steel spring and hurled Vasagi from the saddle.

Vasagi the Gape fell; he fluttered through the higher foliage, smashed through lower branches, thumped down in dark green undergrowth. The fall might well have stunned a man, but never a vampire Lord. A mist issued from the night-dark forest and Vasagi was in it. Nestor, too, continued to manufacture his mist, and the clearing lay deep in milky white. Then:

Go! said Nana to Nathan. *Go now, while you may.*

But as the Necroscope conjured a door, he saw the writhing mist part as his brother Nestor flowed upright from it and hurled himself upon Vasagi—where the Gape had tried to creep up on Nathan! And:

Go! Nestor repeated Nana, even as he grappled with the monstrous Vasagi. *This one is mine. Upon a time I gave him life; a mistake I'll now try to correct, before my own wasted existence and body are finished. So go while you can, little brother, and consider yourself lucky!*

Nathan went, but not too far. Time seemed to blur . . . Ian Goodly was waiting at the camp for Nathan with what he needed, or what the precog knew Nathan *would be* needing . . . he was so sure of himself, he twisted the grenade's fins as he thrust it into Nathan's hand. All of which took perhaps five or six seconds; the next four would be crucial.

One: Nathan took the grenade and trusted to the future—or rather, to the understanding Goodly had with the future.

Two: He conjured a door and sped back to the unequal combat in the clearing.

Three: He vacated the Möbius Continuum into a waist-deep sea of mist that lapped like blue-tinged milk but had an ugly living (or undead) texture to it. Somewhere in there, Nestor and Vasagi struggled even now.

Four: His time was up and he must use the grenade!

Meanwhile:

Ten seconds is life or death in hand-to-hand combat, especially when the combatants are Wamphyri! Nestor was weak, *made* weak by his disease, but Vasagi was at the peak of·his power—made even stronger by his madness. And in his madness he hadn't once paused to consider the reason for his opponent's weakness; he knew only that he was under attack, and he must retaliate. Vasagi had no gauntlet; indeed Nestor wore his gauntlet, taken for his own after Vasagi's duel with Wran: just another infuriating factor, on top of the death of Carmen, which had served to madden the Gape even further. Being raked with his own gauntlet as Nestor tackled him had been the last straw! And knocking Nestor down—and falling on him to enfold his upper half in vertical jaws all of three feet long—had been Vasagi's answer to injury added to insult.

But instead of (or as well as) feeling pain in the necromancer's mind, as the Gape's metamorphic flesh plunged a thousand small siphons into him to draw off his vital fluids, Vasagi had sensed ... what, satisfaction? Even triumph? By which time his leech had known that Nestor was a leper! And even in the act of gutting the other, and tearing out his parasite in pieces, Vasagi had recoiled, let go his death-grip on Nestor, and flowed upright in the lake of their mutual mist.

Five: And just a little late, or at the precise optimum moment, Nathan lobbed his grenade into the convulsing mass of Vasagi's innards and hurled himself backwards, away from that reeling monstrosity!

Astonishment and a point-blank refusal, an *inability* to comprehend, to believe, registered in Nathan's mind—along with Vasagi's *Eh? What?*—before a muffled blast and flash of brilliant white light signalled the Gape's end.

Nathan felt himself ... splashed! Not his flesh but his clothing, and with trembling fingers began to strip himself naked. And:

Aye, Nestor gasped in his mind. *Let nothing . . . let nothing of . . . of that one cling to you!* His telepathic voice was so very weak that Nathan knew he was finished. And trembling still—but from the shock of violent action, and otherwise unafraid—finally the Necroscope went to his blood brother, and found his crushed and broken body in the mist.

Don't touch! Nestor warned him. *As Vasagi is unclean, so am I. Indeed, I am twice-tainted.*

"Wait," Nathan husked, and went to the camp, and returned with a cured skin to carefully wrap his brother, who seemed so small, so shrivelled now. And: "Th-there," he said, his voice breaking and surprising him. "W-w-warmth for you, and protection for m-m-me." And cradling the other's head, he thought, *I haven't stuttered in a long time.*

"Ahhh!" Nestor breathed out loud. "Now I remember—how once I *was* your protection!" His head lolled, but he lived on and the fire in his eyes flickered still.

What to do! What to do! Nathan felt crushed inside, even as Nestor was crushed. But his mother told him: *You know what to do.* And her tears were hot as his own, albeit in his mind.

"She has it right," Nestor whispered. "But quickly, while I . . . while *I* have it right! Such pain should never be, and it will go on and on, and I'll fight it to the end, because there is that of the vampire in me even now, what little Vasagi left me . . ."

"Nestor—!"

"*Do it . . .* do it now." Nestor twitched and jerked beneath his blanket.

And Nathan gathered him up and took him there—ten thousand miles south, to a brilliant blue sky high over the endless furnace deserts! And a golden orb like the hearthfire of some alien God standing high on the southern horizon. Then:

"It's done!" Nathan said, his physical voice lost in the fluttering air, as they fell like stones and he pushed Nestor away from him.

So be it, said the other.

Falling through a door, Nathan emerged below in the shade of a sun-scorched outcrop, and watched Nestor plummet down the blinding sky like a meteorite at noon. He left a trail, white at first, rapidly turning black, which boiled for a moment and was gone. And Nestor gone with it.

The blanket flapped empty wings, like a strange mad bird tumbling to earth.

Then:

A flash of gold! A golden dart spearing down from the sky—from Nestor! And Nathan had seen just such a dart before. It struck home, found its target and came home, like a soft silent arrow to the Necroscope's head. . . .

Intuition! The very essence of intuition! His father's intuition, which in Harry Keogh had made him a Master of Numbers and of the Möbius Continuum! It was everything that had been missing from Nathan's makeup, his personality; that which he *might* have had right from the beginning—*if Nestor had not needed it more than he did!*

It was the instinct to *know* these things and to understand almost everything else that had baffled Nathan to distraction. Nestor had not been the strong but the weak one, and the dart had "known" it . . . instinctively! That was why, on the day of Harry's death, the dart had gone to Nestor. Even Nestor's dark and tortured future had probably been known, but as a descendant or "continuation" of the Necroscope Harry Keogh, he must be given a chance. Except Nestor had not been like Harry or Nathan but had his own nature—or the dark side of his father's? Whichever, he was omega to Nathan's alpha; and once his course had been set, there was no help for it but that the dart must see it through with him.

And Nestor's instinct, his intuitive empathy since childhood, had been for the Wamphyri! Because of that he would have ascended to a Lord anyway, even without the dart; but with it . . . little wonder his awakening had been so swift, his metamorphosis so all-consuming!

Nathan saw it all now: he *understood* those shards,

those fragments of his father. They were guides to see him and his brother on their way through life. But the knowledge had been in Nathan already, and he had not needed; not until that time in the Mediterranean, when at last a door had been opened for him! And all that time *his* dart waiting, buried in the heart of a dead machine at E-Branch HQ, ready to spring to life at the moment of his greatest need.

Just how *much* of the future was known, then—how much had been charted—by those incorporeal inhabitants of Möbius-space, Möbius-time, those pieces of the Necroscope Harry Keogh? Or was it a mystery even to such as them? Had they been allowed a glimpse along Nestor's blue life-thread, to see it turn scarlet? "Instinctively," Nathan knew they had; also that they must have known the end of it: how when the hour was right, Nestor's hitherto wasted dart ... *would come home to him!*

And the hour was right. Sunside/Starside's hour of greatest need! Now!

He stepped naked out of the shadow of the rock and felt the heat of the desert under his feet. And with his head ringing with new thoughts, he conjured a Möbius door and returned to the night. ...

Keeping his mind shielded as best he might, Nathan went to the oasis at Place-Under-the-Yellow-Cliffs and alerted Atwei, who found clothes for him. He didn't dare to stay, not even to speak to Misha, but at once returned to his "hell-lander" colleagues in their camp—

—Where indeed all hell seemed to be breaking loose! Ben Trask acted as coordinator, frantically directing the efforts of Zek and David Chung respectively where they listened in on, or tracked ... who else but their vampire enemies, who finally were on the move! And Grinner was in telepathic contact with Blaze and the grey brotherhood somewhere in the barrier mountains, receiving a mass of information and warnings but unable to pass them on with clear definition to anyone but the Necroscope.

They're coming, Uncle! Grinner barked in Nathan's

mind, as he saw him materialize. *Those in the foothills: they've spread themselves out along the range, beating upwards into the peaks and driving the grey brothers before them! And the others from the last aerie, that vampire army out of the east: the sky is thick with them, on their way to Sunside!*

A mass attack on the Szgany, it could only be. Now that Wrathstack (with the exception of Mangemanse, if Canker Canison continued to hold out) had been taken, Devetaki Skullguise would use the rest of the night to monstrous advantage! She'd be looking for Nathan, of course, but while searching for him her troops would rain terror on Sunside. Indeed, that was probably a major part of her plan, so that the Necroscope would be drawn into the open.

"Alexei Yefros is on to you, Nathan!" Zek and Chung called out almost as one voice. "Not only that," Chung added, "but he has *been* on you all the time you've been away. At a site a few miles north of here—your mother's grave?—and even out in the desert; in fact, wherever you go! Yefros was one hell of a locator before, but now that he's a vampire . . ."

Nathan was aghast. "Are you telling me he knows about the Thyre?"

"Maybe not about them," Chung answered, "but it's an even bet he knows where you've moved all those Szgany groups! Even I would know that: I can feel their massed minds in the night, away in the south, like a soft-glowing cloud of fireflies. And . . . *ahhh!*" Chung gasped, crouching down as a dark and pulsing manta shape passed overhead. And: "Jesus!" the locator continued, "but that's not *all* I feel!"

Trask was down on one knee in a moment, his SMG aimed up towards the stars. The Necroscope stopped him with two words: "No, Ben!" Not even the fleetest of the enemy's flyers could have got here that fast. This could only be Karz Biteri. And to confirm it:

Nathan; Karz sent, from where he hovered on a night wind. *Devetaki's army is on its way. The aether seethes with their lust! You're in great danger, but I can take you out of here.* He did not know how good the Necroscope was at taking care of himself.

My thanks, Karz, Nathan told him. *But this is my fight and I have to stay here.*

Karz sensed his determination, and perhaps something of his power. *Can you win?*

I can try. I have weapons that . . . that I can't even begin to explain!

Good fortune then, said Karz, *and my thanks. For seeing how strong you are, yet again you've given me strength to go on. I, too, have a fight to fight.*

Nathan nodded. *Yet the last time we spoke, you only wanted to die.*

But no longer, not yet. For now I have a mission—in the east! Aye, now that Turgosheim is empty . . . or almost empty.

Maglore?

The same. (Karz sounded grimly determined.) *And since I'm on my own again, I go there now, tonight.*

Too late, Nathan told him. *The night's half done. The sun will find you out before you clear the Great Red Waste.*

Is it so? Then I must wait on another chance.

Nathan thought fast, for he had enough to do here. But on the other hand, how long would it take? The answer was simple: no time at all! *Karz,* he sent. *Land out there if you trust me. That hummock on the rim of the savanna.* And even as Karz came down he went there himself, via the Möbius Continuum.

How . . . !? said Karz, astonished, uncoiling his belly thrusters as he settled to earth. And: *What . . . !?*

Nathan said, "Upon a time, you carried me out of Turgosheim to safety regardless of the risk to yourself. A favour for a favour, Karz. Now I'll take you back." He climbed up into the saddle. "Lift me up." And in a moment they were airborne. "You do trust me, then?"

In Turgosheim, and ever since. But about returning there: didn't you tell me just a moment ago the sun would find me out over the Great Red Waste?

"There's another route. So if you really *do* trust me, do exactly as I tell you, however strange it may seem."

Nathan told him, and Karz obeyed. Gaining altitude, and folding back his manta wings, he sped like an arrow for earth, and passed through the biggest door that Nathan ever conjured! A second door lay only an instant away, but in the moment Karz soared through it—

—*WHAAAT?* It wasn't only the way they'd got here that confused him, but also the sight of the place.

"Turgosheim," said the Necroscope, and realized immediately that it wasn't what Karz had expected. Turgosheim, right enough . . . but deserted? Oh, really?

They floated high above the rim of the gorge, while down below the signs of war were plentiful. Black smoke coiling from burned-out stumps in the gloomy bottoms, and fires still ablaze in many a manse in the towering, honeycombed walls. So that even to a dazed Karz Biteri it was all too clear what had happened here. *Maglore had his opportunity for glory, and like any or all of the Wamphyri . . .*

". . . He couldn't resist it," Nathan finished it. "Yes, I know. What did you expect, Karz? That the place would be derelict, wind-blown, dead except for Maglore?"

Something like that, aye.

Nathan shook his head. "Not so. There are thralls and creatures galore down there. Only the Lords and Ladies are missing. Except, as you rightly suppose, Maglore in Runemanse. So . . . do you still intend to stay here? What will you do now?"

A mental shrug. *I shall hope that my time will come,* Karz answered, *then take my chance for glory—and revenge—even as Maglore has taken his.*

"Then before I go I had better warn you," Nathan told him, "that there may not be a lot of time. Things are going to happen, Karz. Things of great moment."

They can only be an improvement, said the other. *But you, Nathan—these amazing powers of yours?*

"Alas," Nathan shook his head. "I've neither the time nor the means to explain them. But indeed, they are the weapons I mentioned. Farewell, Karz!" He tumbled himself from the saddle.

Karz angled his great head to watch the Necroscope turn over twice in midair before flattening out—and disappearing through an entirely invisible Möbius door! Then Karz Biteri, once a man and perhaps still a man, soared alone in the reeking updrafts out of Turgosheim. . . .

It had taken a minute, maybe two. Nathan scarcely considered the time wasted as he materialized back at the camp. But Trask and the others might disagree. "Nathan, what's going on?!" Zek started as he appeared, then grabbed his arm.

"Something I had to do." he answered. "And here?"

He loosened her fingers, looked her steadily in the eyes. She knew how tense she must appear, slowed down and calmed herself. And: "Remember," she said, "that it's different for you. But we aren't ... we don't ... we're not—"

"—Necroscopes? All right, I'm sorry," Nathan said. "And I know I shouldn't just leave you like that. But I have a feeling that everything will be fine. It's going to be okay."

Ben Trask had heard their conversation, likewise the precog and locator. All of them eased off and gathered to Nathan, and Trask asked him, "Are you going to explain?"

"Let's get around the fire," Nathan answered, and they did. And when they were settled:

"The aerial vampire army is on its way from Wrathstack," Nathan started. "Also, they have several advance parties made up of those camps in the Starside foothills; by now they could be in the high peaks. Devetaki has Alexei Yefros, whose talent has been enhanced by his vampirism. They know where I am—or where *we* are—and they probably know where a good many Szgany are, too, all gathered together for them in Thyre harbour areas like bunches of grapes! But there are a lot more of the Travellers right here in Sunside, hiding in the forests, and they'll be more difficult to find and flush out. Also, what Devetaki doesn't know: several pockets of humanity in the forests are equipped with weapons out of Earth, and men who can use them. That's the current situation. Now, timings:

"If the foothills parties come right for us, they'll be here in a little over an hour. If they hold back and wait for Devetaki's main force, we'll be safe here for at least two and a half hours or more. So there's no need for panic right now. But there are still some thirty-odd hours of night and morning twilight left before sunup, when Nature swings over to our side. And a lot can happen in half a Sunside night.

"Now listen: the vampires *can't* trap us! For we have our own talents, which are equal to theirs. Zek and I are able to 'hear' them; Grinner smells them out; David knows where they are, and Ian can sometimes see what's coming. And if they get too close, I can move us out of here. So in general—as an overview?—that's about the scheme of things.

"But the overall, original plan wasn't to hide from them or evade them but destroy them, utterly! And if we fail to see it through then all this is for nothing—especially now that Devetaki knows there's something south of here, namely my desert-dwelling friends the Thyre! But the south spells danger to a vampire, and we have to hope she'll think twice before committing her forces in that direction. Which leaves us with one conclusion: that she intends to saturate Sunside, flush us out, add our talents to hers, and consolidate her position tomorrow night. That's how I see it, but I could be wrong and only time will tell . . . unless you can tell me otherwise."

"Us?" Trask stared at him.

"You're the ones with the talents!" Nathan answered. "We have two hours maximum to formulize new plans—but sweeping plans—to decimate and even destroy any last trace of Wamphyri contamination. Let's start with you, Ben. Do you find any fault in what I've said? Was it a true or a false scenario?"

Trask shrugged. "The best I can tell you is that you yourself believe in it," he answered. "But as you've already said, time alone will tell ... that is, if Ian Goodly can't tell in advance." He looked at the precog.

Goodly was gaunt as ever. "We have to plan of course," he said, "despite the best-laid plans ... and all that. What I mean is, the future *will* be, but it's always governed by the present. So I simply can't tell you *what* to do—or even not to do anything—but only to do what you must. In other words, Nathan's scenario seems sound to me. And if the future doesn't like it, it will be changed accordingly. There's only one thing I know for sure: that something big is coming. Oh, I've said it before, I know, but it's *so* big it obscures everything else. And it has to do with what Nathan's dead Thyre friends told him."

Nathan nodded and excitedly took over. There was something he'd been wanting to show them, and now seemed the perfect opportunity. "Let's take another look at that, then." He found the piece of bark he'd drawn on for Trask, and showed them Ethloi's no longer mysterious symbols, for this time his newfound intuition prompted him to make changes.

"The arrows suggest movement," he said. "From A to C, or from one to three. But if you *number* the phases like this" (he scrawled with a piece of charcoal), "it's at once apparent that this ... isn't an engine!"

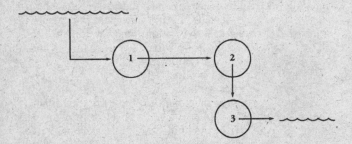

And now the whole thing was simplicity itself. But to be absolutely sure the Necroscope explained it anyway, then went on to describe the system as: "An unending, self-perpetuating cycle, which gives total protection to two worlds but damages and depletes neither. It's just like the Möbius strip that I was shown superimposed over this diagram: a single system transcending and blending disparate dimensions yet interfering with neither one of them. The strip was my father's life; it became my symbol and saved *my* life; now it will be the salvation of a world, even a universe . . ."

As he listened and looked, Trask's jaw had fallen open as he recognized the "truth" of this thing. Finally he jumped to his feet. "But this presupposes that we're going to get back to our own world. We *have* to, in order to initiate it!"

Nathan grinned wolfishly at him, at all of them, and said, "Did you ever have any doubts, any of you?"

One of them had at least. Ian Goodly said, "It's possible, of course, that Gustav Turchin has figured it out for himself. Which would mean our return isn't necessarily a foregone conclusion . . ."

As they pondered that, Nathan said, "Now has to be as good a time as any. I can take a quick look at the Gate, and if it's safe move you out there right now on the first leg of your trip home. Then we can be sure that this," he indicated the diagram, "*will* definitely happen, whether Turchin has already thought of it or not. At least one of our problems—*your* main problem—will have been solved."

Zek reached out and patted his hand. "But yours will still remain. Haven't you given up trying to get rid of us yet, Nathan? Don't you know it's not going to be that easy?"

He sighed out loud and said, "Very well, but from now on you've got to stay close together, all four of you, and at all times. From this moment on I've got to be able to move all of you in one bunch, and at a moment's notice."

"Agreed," said Trask. "And meanwhile?"

"Now," Nathan looked at them in turn, "I could use a

situation report." He patted Grinner's head where the wolf of the wild lay close by.

I've lost my observers, Grinner said. *The grey brothers are scattered in the mountain heights, broken up by the vampires in the foothills. But the reports of several individuals all tell the same story: the flyers out of Wrathstack are coming in great waves, turning the sky black!*

There can't be that many! Nathan was perplexed.

A wolf shrug. *Wolves are sometimes like men, or dogs: they like to exaggerate. They bark at shadows . . .*

Zek had got something of this, and now said, "There isn't a peep out of them. They're not talking, and they're shielding their minds."

"Radio silence!" said Trask.

Nathan looked at him, but Trask shook his head. "An Earth tactic," he said. "Apparently it applies here, too."

And frowning, Chung said, "There *are* a great many of them. But it's a funny thing . . . I mean, if this Devetaki creature is mainly interested in you, Nathan, then why doesn't she concentrate her forces on us? Why are they spreading out, evenly, like a great blanket?"

"Are they?" Nathan was keenly interested, anxious.

"Yes. From the petrified lava falls beyond the great pass, their front extends many miles west of here."

"Like a miles-long wave rolling in on a beach," Zek said, half-closing her eyes and reaching out with her mind.

Nathan's turn to frown as he added, "Or like a net, being draped over us . . ." Suddenly he was worried. "But what if they go right *on* over us, and head out into the desert, to the harbour areas and the Thyre? I've placed a good many hundreds of men, women, and children in Thyre colonies out there, all on a line roughly east to west. Devetaki's wave would hit them more or less simultaneously, and there's no way I can be in four or five different places at the same time!"

It was Trask's turn to calm him down. "Son, take it easy. You painted a picture a few minutes ago, and it was a true one as far as it went. There's nothing more to be done right now. If you make a Möbius jump out into the colonies, to alert your people and the Thyre, Yefros will know of it at once. For you can't make a move without stirring up your numbers vortex, and it gives you away every time. But if or when the first vampire wave passes over us heading out across the desert, then you'll know the worst of it and that will be your signal to take some kind of action to save your people. Until then you can't give the show away."

Nathan nodded. "And after that—if it happens—I'll have no more than half an hour to visit all those Thyre locations and take my people out of there. Except this time I won't make any mistakes but move them right away from here: east, to the very limits of the barrier mountains, and fifty miles out into the desert! Devetaki won't be able to reach them there, not and get back to Wrathstack before the sun rises again."

Trask nodded approvingly.

Goodly, on the other hand, merely grunted and turned his face away. Nathan looked at him until the precog felt his gaze and returned it. And:

"Well?" said Nathan.

"We've arrived at the one conclusion we had to arrive at," Goodly said. "And as you can see, the only action we can take is what we would have taken anyway, without all the discussion! The talk is fine and lets us all know where we stand, but the future is narrowing down on us and will be as it will be. Just don't believe for a moment that we're in charge, because we're not. And don't forget, the Big One keeps getting closer minute by minute."

"But you still don't know what this Big One will be?"

Goodly shook his head. "Good or bad, I can't say. I only know that it's close, and we're all in it together. But I have to remind you, Nathan—even though I *hate* to remind you—of what we saw in future time, you and I. I mean, I'm not worried for myself, but . . ."

"I know what you mean," Nathan stopped him. "I've already been into it with Ben here. Now I don't want to think about it anymore until it comes."

He threw a dead branch onto the fire, leaned back

against the bole of a fallen tree and closed his eyes. "In fact I just want to clear my mind of all this and see what else comes into it. One thing I can guarantee, though: I'm not about to reach the end of my tether just yet awhile . . ."

The Necroscope wasn't trying to sleep, wasn't trying to do anything. He literally cleared his mind, relaxed, and took a mental breather—and slept. After a few moments, when Zek said something to him in a low voice, his only response was when his hand slid from his chest to nestle open-fisted in the grass by his side. A glance into his mind disclosed the "white noise" of human sleep prior to the dream state and a dispersing, collapsed whirl of numbers as mental exhaustion returned him to the basic state of mind.

Mentally, even possessing his metaphysical mind, the Necroscope was little more than a mote now, drifting wherever the eddies of dreams and fancies might take him.

Trask draped a blanket over Nathan's shoulders, looked at the others and shrugged. "I feel weary, too. Tension, and anxiety, I suppose. Let alone all the physical stuff that he's been going through. God only knows what his talent is taking out of him! We can let him be for an hour or so, recharge his batteries, so to speak—but let's all of us stay on the alert. And as soon as we have something, we wake him up."

Grinner seemed to understand. He got up, loped to the rim of the clearing and began circling, sniffing the air, "listening," not only with keen, mobile wolf ears, but with who could tell how many other wolf senses, all tuned for danger. Zek and Chung likewise began pacing back and forth, their wild talents reaching out into the north, to discover whatever they might.

And Ian Goodly sat by the fire not far from Nathan, glancing at the sleeping Necroscope now and then, and perhaps trying to catch the occasional glimpse . . . of other things.

* * *

Eygor Killglance wasted no time; his previously developed rapport with Nathan took him direct to his target's mind, and the monster's panic and confusion told of the state he was in, in his Madmanse pit in Turgosheim.

Necroscope, what terrible thing is this you've wrought? What have you done to me? Eygor's deadspeak voice was as evil as ever, like the methane-belching slurp and gurgle of a quagmire, but his anxiety was very real.

Nathan knew him at once, of course, and although he sensed Eygor's genuine but as yet unexplained alarm returned: *Oh? And is this a new approach, Eygor? Are you claiming to be the victim of some act of mine?*

What—did—you—tell—Maglore!? the other hissed. Which had the effect of jogging Nathan's memory, and bringing alive the screen of his mind until Eygor saw its pictures. *So!* (His voice was black as pitch.) *And now all is explained.*

Then explain it to me. Nathan gave a mental shrug.

You threatened him with me. Do you deny it?

No, it was a word game. He taunted me and I returned fire. He made threats, and I—

—Threatened him with me, aye! Eygor finished it for him. *Except it was more than a word game to him. Maglore knows your powers, Necroscope, and those he doesn't know he suspects. You hinted that he wasn't yet safe from a dead old thing in a pit, that in certain circumstances—under the right conditions—a ghost may be more than a mere ghost. To you this was a word game, a careless jest or taunt, as it would be to many a Lord of the Wamphyri. But to Maglore?*

Nathan knew what he meant: that Maglore of Runemanse was a seer, a supernaturalist even beyond the scope of Wamphyri knowledge and talents; a believer in omens, signs and sigils, dooms and damnations. Of course he was, else Nathan's threat had carried no weight! But how much weight *had* it carried?

His thoughts were deadspeak, and Eygor was in tune with them. *Oh, I can tell you that, all right,* the monster said. *A lot of weight! A world of weight! The weight of all*

*the rubble and boulders that choke the throat of my pit!
For even now he digs his way down to me! He comes to
discover and disassemble me in this stifling, stagnant, ni-
trous place. To break me up, burn what will burn, and
scatter the rest to the four corners of Turgosheim! Because
he fears old Eygor as never before with a fear that you
gave him, Necroscope! It's all your doing, your fault! And
only you can put it right; only you can . . . call me up?*
(The last a whisper, even a prayer?)

Not good enough, said Nathan, while in his secret mind
he turned it over. He had never once deliberately called up
a dead creature—though past events and now his "intuition" told him that indeed he had the power. Yet on two
occasions the dead had returned of their own volition, to
come to his aid in desperate circumstances. And when he
was safe they'd gone down again, "of their own free will."
So apparently the talent worked independent of Nathan
himself: it was that which the Great Majority's love of his
father had transferred to him because like Harry before
him he was the single light in their eternal darkness. Eygor
Killglance on the other hand couldn't come up, because
even if Nathan were threatened there wasn't enough love
in the vampire—indeed *not any*—to motivate and mobilize
him! He must therefore be brought up by the incredible re-
generative power of the Necroscope.

And (it now occurred to Nathan) why not? Why not
fight fire with fire? Hadn't he been the one to stop Trask
shooting at the flyer, rider, and gas-beast bomb out of
Wrathstack, because he liked the idea of vampires destroying each other? Wouldn't this be the same? And didn't
Maglore deserve all of it and more, for what he'd done to
Karz and Orlea and hundreds of others; not to mention
what he *would* do to Nathan if ever he had the chance?

Nathan's mind-shield slipped a little as he became engrossed with the idea; Eygor read him, and urged, *Just
think: what better way to stop the old bastard raiding on
Turgosheim's Sunside? Give him something better—or
worse—to think about, eh? At the moment the Seer-Lord is
glutted, and all his creatures, too, but sooner or later he'll*

need to reinforce Turgosheim blood with fresh stuff out of Sunside. Do you really want to wait that long?

How long? Nathan wanted to know.

When he's finished with me, I should think! Right now I'm the one thing that stands between Maglore and an easy mind and peaceful dreams! Except . . . there is one other he'll be needing to deal with soon enough.

Oh?

I sense it, said Eygor. *My own flesh and blood, returning out of the west. One of my bloodsons—Spiro!*

Out on the boulder plains the teeming dead were listening to their conversation. Now Jason Lidesci said: *It could be that he's telling the truth, Necroscope. Wrathstack has all but fallen, but Spiro is not among the dead. The other brother, Wran, is dead, and raging still! But not Spiro.*

He has fled the fray, Eygor insisted. *He's on his way back to Turgosheim even now!*

If it's true, Jason continued, *then you have real trouble on your hands—for Spiro has inherited his father's evil eye! The victims of that eye lie scattered around the foot of Wrathstack . . .*

Vampire victims, Nathan said. *I feel nothing for them.*

No, but you do feel for the Szgany of Turgosheim's Sunside, Eygor reminded him. *So how's it to be, Necroscope? Will you not call me up to put paid to both Maglore and Spiro? And remember, you don't come out of this empty-handed. We'll strike a bargain: not an eye for an eye, but an eye for a moment of life, or however long it takes me.*

Nathan was tempted. There was nothing of a healthy nature in Turgosheim for Eygor to corrupt; he felt sure that the Thing in its Madmanse pit could handle both Spiro Killglance and Maglore the Mage; if only he could be sure that once Eygor was up, he could be put down again as easily . . .

But you have the power! Eygor was persuasive. *And anyway, what is there for an old dead thing in his pit in the world of the living? Nothing but revenge on Maglore, who dares to covet Madmanse, and my bastard bloodson*

Spiro, who blinded and murdered me! As for Wran . . . he's dead, you say? Good! But I wish that I had got to him first!

Nathan was half-convinced. Eygor's killing eye would make a powerful addition to his arsenal of metaphysical weapons. *If I make a deal with you . . . how will you give me your eye?*

Only let me into your mind, and it shall be done!

Except Nathan knew that upon a time his father had made a similar mistake. Again Eygor read him, and said: *But how may I possibly harm you? I'm dead in Turgo-sheim and you are alive in the west!*

Give me your eye now, Nathan answered, *and if or when Maglore reaches you in your pit, or Spiro makes it back across the Great Red Waste, then I'll call you up.*

What?! (Eygor was outraged.) *What is that for a bar-gain?*

The only one you'll get from me, the Necroscope answered.

For long moments Eygor was sullenly silent; he was over a barrel, and knew it. But eventually: *So be it,* he said, however grudgingly. *Sleep on, Nathan, but leave your mind open to me so that I may invest it with mine.*

Nathan did as instructed, and knew evil dreams awhile . . .

Then:

Done! said Eygor.

Suddenly Nathan's brain seethed; there was an unholy power in him; he felt it there like a cancer in his mind, eating away at the good in him. Eygor had put something into him: the power of his evil eye, of course. And Nathan knew that the monster in his pit had hoped it would make him as evil as Eygor himself.

Given time, perhaps it would!

With a cry of alarm, Nathan sprang awake . . .

V

Shaking the Web—Siege on Settlement

Ben Trask had been about to wake the Necroscope. Leaning over Nathan, touching his arm, Trask felt the brief vibration that shook him—then heard his cry of alarm as he snatched himself sideways away from Trask! Then . . . his eyes opening wide, wider . . . as something monstrous stirred behind them, something awful and awesome *about* them in the shifting firelight! Trask jerked upright and made an inarticulate, questioning sound in the back of his throat. He went to step back a pace—and found himself lifted bodily from his feet and *hurled* back! His heart felt as if someone had jabbed it with a live electrode!

Zek and Ian Goodly had seen something of it; they made to go to Trask, but Nathan was there first. His eyes were normal now. "Ben! Are you all right?"

Trask got up slowly, staggered, looked at the Necroscope curiously, cautiously, and gasped, "Jesus *Christ!* How the . . . ? What in the name of . . . ? Something *hit* me!"

Nathan said nothing but he knew. Knew, too, that from now on people must tread warily about him, try not to take him by surprise—and *never* shock him! Zek read something of it in his mind and said, "Ben, this is all part of it . . ."

"Part of the Big One," Goodly came to her help. "An important part."

Chung had arrived from the perimeter; Grinner loped at his heels. "Something's coming right now," the locator said. "Nothing big, but nasty as all hell!" Whatever had happened was put aside for now, as in. the next moment:

Bats—huge *Desmodus* bats with wingspans a yard across—swerving and dancing overhead. There were four of them, advance reconnaissance, probably recruited in Wrathstack. Trask's machine pistol made its distinctive ch-*ching* sound as he cocked it, but Nathan was wide awake now and stopped him. "Save your ammunition. They're more or less harmless. You can't get them all, and in any case their failure to report back would tell Devetaki just as much."

But as the bats made off Nathan held back a curse of frustration. In all likelihood *he* probably could have got them all—and all it would have cost was a glance! On the other hand, he didn't have the measure of his new "talent" yet; it might be as well to use it sparingly lest it grow on him. Another glance (but at the star-strewn sky) told him he'd been asleep for well over an hour. "What's been happening?"

Chung was first to answer. "Flyers have landed, warriors too, in the Sunside foothills perhaps twenty-odd miles east of here." (Twin Fords, Nathan thought.) "Also due north" (Settlement, and/or Sanctuary Rock), "and other parties in the west." (Tireni Scarp and Mirlu Township, or what burned and shattered ruins were left of those locations.) "And there've been plenty more landings, too, all regularly spaced out along the barrier range."

"Only in the foothills?"

"No." Chung shook his head. "Small packets have been putting down every few miles or so into the woods, forming a sort of grid system. Getting closer all the time."

Nathan nodded. "Like the squares of a large silk net settling gently to earth right across Sunside. Only it's not silk, and it won't be gentle, not for long . . ."

"They're still mainly silent," Zek told him. "With no apparent or specific interest in our group."

Nathan looked at Goodly, who gave a shrug. "Time is—"

"—I know!" Nathan cut him short. "it's narrowing down."

And Grinner took the opportunity to put in, *My grey brothers are scattered throughout the heights. The vampire army has mostly passed over them* . . .

Chung was alert as never before. "North of here, but approaching fast in a direct line . . . something . . . coming at us straight as an arrow!"

There came a distant throb of propulsors and, carried on a soughing breeze out of the northeast, the *crack! crack! crack!* of automatic fire to disturb the night's comparative silence.

"It's beginning," Nathan said. "But this time, at least my people have the means to fight back."

"I don't understand," said Chung. "This oncoming party is just another thread in the net that's being laid down. I don't get the feeling that we're a specific target. *Why* are we being . . . what, ignored?"

"It's like they're waiting for us to show our hand," Trask said. And Nathan agreed:

"They're trying to draw me into it. And meanwhile the net—or web—spins itself ever wider over Sunside."

"Very close now!" Chung's voice showed his alarm. "Are we just going to sit here?"

In the north, spied over a horizon of tall trees, several menacing manta shapes scudded with the last handful of clouds. And: "Time we were on our way," said the Necroscope. But even as he spoke he felt an unaccustomed anger—even rage—deep inside, and his eyes felt hot where cold sweat stood out suddenly upon his brow. Briefly he fought with emotions that were his yet alien to him (the urge to stay and fight, and try out his dreadful eyes?). But before the urge could win he conjured a Möbius door and guided his companions through it . . .

. . . And took them out five miles into the night-dark desert—where, as they exited from the Continuum into sand and brittle scrub, Zek clapped a hand to her forehead and gasped:

"They weren't ignoring us after all! Or they're not *now*, anyway! Their minds are open; messages pass between them; they recognize your signature—the numbers vortex, Nathan—and they know we've moved!"

"But are they still advancing?" He looked at Chung.

"Yes," said the locator in a moment. "Their net is being dragged out into the desert, but it's staggered now. And this is their main spearhead. They're pushing on us!"

"Or on the Thyre harbours," Nathan groaned. "Place-Under-the-Yellow-Cliffs . . . the new oasis . . . Atwei . . . *Misha!*"

"You can move Misha and the Lidescis," Trask told him.

"And pinpoint their hideout!" Chung warned.

"Another five minutes maximum and we'll have to move on anyway," said Zek.

"How big is this spearhead?" Nathan felt his anger growing again, a burning behind his eyes despite that he tried to keep them cool.

"Not big," Chung said after a moment. "This net of theirs is really stretching them. The bloodwar cost them heavily."

The Necroscope made up his mind. "I'll move Misha, Lardis and the Lidescis. Then . . . we'll defend Place-Under-the-Yellow-Cliffs. We have to. I won't have vampires in the Cavern of the Ancients. The Thyre would never forgive me. And to me, their culture is at least as important as any of this . . ."

He conjured another door, and they were on their way. . . .

The Thyre were expecting them; therefore so were Lardis, Misha, and the Szgany Lidesci. The best of the Thyre mentalists, Atwei included, had been keeping surreptitious, sporadic watch on the Necroscope and his friends—and on the Wamphyri, of course.

Lardis and his people were waiting in the new oasis,

ready to play Nathan's game of "hide and seek." And Nathan told them, "This time I'm taking you far enough away that the vampire army can't possibly get to you. Not tonight, anyway."

But as they took up their rope in preparation, Lardis and Kirk Lisescu spoke up almost as one man. "We're not going."

"What?" Nathan looked at them.

"We're fighters and we have weapons," Lardis growled. And Kirk added:

"We're sick of hiding and not knowing what's going on. Out there in the forests there are Szgany who could use our skills. We've been idle too long. Take the rest of our people where you will, but take Lardis and me where the fighting is!"

Nathan looked around and Lardis knew what he was looking for. "Andrei will stay here, help protect the Thyre. Since you and your friends are going to be here awhile, I know he'll be safe enough. Also, he has this woman—this Anna?—who will stay with him."

So, Andrei Romani had been hooked at last, and Anna Marie English had found a new cause: the Thyre. Nathan was glad both ways. Anyway, he had no time to argue; he supposed he must consider himself fortunate that Misha wasn't giving him problems, too!

Except, she was! "I'm staying here with you," she said. And her tone told him she'd brook no denial, that nothing would shift her. He could only shrug his shoulders helplessly.

And so, leaving Trask and his colleagues in the oasis with Lardis and Misha, and telling the Old Lidesci, "I'll be back for you and Kirk . . . be ready," he led the rest of the Travellers into and through the Möbius Continuum—

—To Crater Lake far in the east, and sixty miles out in the supposed desert "wasteland"! Devetaki couldn't possibly get here before dawn; should she be so foolish as to try it, she'd *never* make the return journey home again to the last aerie!

Word of the Necroscope's coming had gone out in advance of him (barely), passed telepathically down the line of Thyre colonies by Atwei and other powerful Thyre mentalists, so that his arrival was anticipated. No time was wasted in handing over his charges into Thyre care, and he returned immediately to Place-Under-the-Yellow-Cliffs.

Armed to the teeth with hell-land weapons, Lardis and Kirk were waiting. "Where do you want to go?" Nathan asked them.

"East of the great pass," said Lardis, without hesitation. "There are people scattered there, afraid, inexperienced. It's likely they're in trouble and could use our help."

Nathan frowned. "Supplicant territory? Vormulac wiped most of them out—and I thought you were glad to see them go!"

"They're Szgany!" Lardis snapped. "This could be our opportunity to win them back from the Wamphyri forever."

"You're sure you'll be all right?"

"No, but there again I've never been sure of that in fifty years! Enough talk. Take us there." So Nathan took them . . .

. . . To a place due south of the lava falls on Starside, but on this side of the barrier mountains, the foothills where they sloped down into the forest in supplicant territory. From perhaps a mile away there came shouts, crashing sounds, a veritable uproar. The Old Lidesci nodded his grim approval. "Supplicants they might have been in their time, but it seems they're fighting well enough now!" And to the Necroscope, "You'll know where to find us come morning."

He clasped forearms with Nathan. "Take care, lad."

"Go to it, Lardis," Nathan told him in the terminology of an alien world. Then, as if realizing his error: "Tear down the mountains, old friend!" He watched the pair slip silently into the woods, then returned to the starlit oasis—

—And arrived with only a minute or two to spare.

Of all the Thyre, Atwei was the one who had chosen to wait with Trask and the others. "They're coming," she told him.

"I know," he nodded. "We make a stand here, in the oasis. Upon a time my father defended a garden such as this, with just such weapons and friends as I have. But especially friends: men and a woman—even the same woman—out of an alien world. It seems . . . seemly?"

Atwei was reluctant to leave. Nathan asked her, "How many routes go down under the earth, to your colony?"

"Several. The one you know lies through the Cavern of the Ancients high in the cliffs there, at the back of the oasis. I won't tell you the others. What you don't know—"

—Can't hurt the Thyre?"

"Or you," she answered. "My people have turned the secret ways into traps! If the vampires attempt to descend . . ."

Nathan understood. The routes were booby-trapped. "And the Cavern of the Ancients?"

"The way stands clear for you and yours."

Nathan shook his head. "It won't come to that. I'll take my friends . . . oh, somewhere else. But the Wamphyri—"

"—We'll be ready for them, if they dare descend."

He took her—and Zek and Misha, too, despite all their protests—up into the Cavern of the Ancients, and returned to the oasis. A moment later, spied as silhouettes against a starry horizon, the vampires came!

"It would seem . . . just two flyers!" Trask husked.

"*And* their thrall riders," Chung noted. "But up there . . ." A dark blot circling in the blue-tinged sky, its booming thunder reaching down to them in the moment of Chung's warning: a warrior, small of its sort but deadly.

"They'll see the oasis." Goodly knew it, of course. Knew what was coming, too. He could hear the uproar, see the fire, smell the blood!

"They have backup!" Chung shouted, as the warrior's main propulsors fired and it began a spiralling descent towards the oasis. "A mile or two back . . . more of them!"

"Ben," Goodly gasped, his Adam's apple wobbling, "we're to take the flyers and riders. You, me, and David. But the warrior is Nathan's!"

Chung was carrying his flamethrower. Nathan asked him, "Do you have fuel for that thing?"

"A little, and then there's this!" A machine pistol. They all had machine pistols, compact and easy to handle. But Nathan had only a conventional Szgany crossbow . . . plus a weapon he'd not yet put to the trial.

"Grenades?" (The flyers were diving on the oasis, and the warrior circled the gorge just above the rim of the cliffs, its many evil eyes swivelling this way and that.) The three nodded in unison; they all had grenades. "Good luck!" said Nathan.

He needed elevation, room to focus his eyes—his anger, hatred—on the warrior. It seemed like madness, but there was nothing else he could try. He transferred himself to the narrow ledge in front of the tunnel to the Cavern of the Ancients, and from there sent a stream of mental abuse directly into the warrior's tiny brain. And:

I'm here, he told the thing. *Right here on the cliff, you ugly son of all that's filthy! You steaming issue of a cesspit!*

The nightmare thing circled to the far side of the canyon, but its eyes swivelled to focus on Nathan. It slipped below the rim of the cliffs, turned inwards, commenced a run on him! This was how he would take the warrior out of the fight. Behind him, the tunnel wouldn't take its bulk; below him, the others were free to engage the flyers and riders.

And they *were* engaging them! Gunfire and the shattering blast of a grenade; a flyer shrilling like a baby, lifting up on shredded, blazing wings, then crumpling back out of sight; a grounded lieutenant or thrall yelling, "Wamphyri, *Wamph—!*" Drowned out and changed by the obscene chatter of a machine pistol to a scream that jarred like syrup on a bad tooth.

The warrior came on, and Nathan took a long shot with his crossbow. If he found his target, it made no difference; it was less than a pinprick to this thing. How he hated the bastard! His lips drew back from his teeth and his brain seemed to burn as he fell into a crouch; his loathing was poison that must be *out* of him! Almost without knowing it, he fired his mind-bolt!

The warrior gurgled—made a weird, somehow questioning sound—but kept coming, except now it had a visible list to the left. From below came the flash of a grenade, which lit up the warrior's prow. Nathan saw its forward-facing eyes—*raw craters streaming blood and brains!*—and its jaws gaping open in a rictus of agony! He could scarcely take it in as the thing tilted more yet, swerved off course, and instead of climbing to clear the rim, dipped towards the floor of the ravine. A moment later, at seventy or eighty miles an hour, it slammed into the sheer cliff and burst into a welter of flying chitin scales and crimson scrambled guts. But Nathan knew it had been dead before it hit, from the moment he'd lashed out with his killing eye.

As Atwei, Zek, and Misha came running along the passage from the Cavern of the Ancients, he went down to the oasis. A riderless flyer limped off over the desert towards the distantly leering Northstar, and David Chung was using up the last of his fuel on Things that crackled and sent up black smoke at they burned.

"But more flyers are on their way," the locator said, his fire dying even as he spoke.

And Ian Goodly gasped: "Nathan, you have work elsewhere!"

"Will you be all right here?" Nathan looked at the three.

"Yes," Trask answered. "Especially if you take us up into that tunnel mouth before you go. It looks easy to defend: flyers can't land there, and it's more or less safe from warriors." Trask was wearing that curious speculative frown of his again. "And while we're talking about warriors, I—"

"—No time for that now." Nathan shook his head. "Later, when I understand it better myself."

He took them up into the mouth of the tunnel, and looking out anxiously over the ravine and oasis, asked Chung, "I don't suppose you can tell me where the next spearhead is?"

Atwei stepped forward. "I can. The elders are passing messages up and down the line. The psychic aether is full of them! But of course the Wamphyri hear them, too, and so our secret is out. Unless the vampires are stopped, their bloodwars must now carry to us."

Nathan took her arm, but gently. "Where will they strike?"

"Strike? I can't say. They seem too few for a task force. But they're advancing on Crack-in-the-Rocks, forty miles east."

"When will they get there—and *how* few?"

"Any time now!" Atwei told him, her eyes huge and unblinking. "No more of them than were here."

There were a handful of Szgany, Karl Zestos's people, at Crack-in-the-Rocks. Nathan knew he could move them out in one packet. He might even leave them there if the Thyre had booby-trapped the several narrow entrances. Crack-in-the-Rocks would not need much defending. He began to conjure a door, paused to crush Misha to him as she flew into his arms.

"Take care," she told him breathlessly. "If anything happens to you, I'll never forgive you!" And then, looking at him more closely: "Did you get smoke in your eyes? Your right eye is bloodshot."

"Probably, yes. Or a little dirt, maybe . . ." He kissed her, and over her shoulder looked at Trask in time to see him begin frowning again. But saving the moment, Goodly said:

"Nathan, I'm coming with you."

Another kiss for Misha—rough, almost hurtful, something to remember—and then they were on their way. . . .

In the Möbius Continuum, Nathan asked, *Why did you come? Is it that close?*

Just that I saw that I would come. Goodly's mental shrug. *Also, if I'm with you, you'll be the first to know if something extraordinary happens. Everything hinges on you, Nathan.*

Or on Devetaki, Nathan answered. *I get the feeling she's setting me up.*

Almost certainly! Now that Wrathstack's gone, you're her biggest threat.

But how can she hope to trap me? She can't fix me in one place long enough to do anything!

Then logically she has to cover all places. If I were her I'd station troops at all of your coordinates.

She doesn't know them all!

But if she makes you move often enough, she'll soon know an awful lot of them. Maybe she doesn't know your choices are—well, almost infinite . . .

They emerged from the Möbius Continuum at the geological fault that the Thyre called Crack-in-the-Rocks. In ages past great plates of bedrock had folded, pushing up through lesser strata and deep desert sand to form granite outcrops. Beneath the earth in this place, far underground, the principal Thyre water-course, called the Great Dark River, flowed east through countless canals over eel-infested shallows of shattered bedrock, under mighty arching ceilings of impervious stone. That was where the Thyre had their colony, in caverns on the banks of the winding river. Nathan could have transferred directly into caves he remembered from his travels with the Thyre, but he'd wanted to see the nature of the attackers and their numbers first.

There were just two of them, flyers and riders, still airborne in the great dark bowl of the sky where they blotted the stars in their criss-crossing. But they'd sensed the swirl of Nathan's numbers vortex as he vacated the Möbius Continuum and so knew he was there. A mentalist himself, he sensed their telepathic transmission flash north, reporting his presence.

So, another of his coordinates was now known to them. Good! Let them thin themselves out even more as they attempted to cover all of them, which was patently impossible. But these were thoughts he kept to himself.

"Observers," he said to Goodly. "I doubt if they'll land. There's nothing here for them."

Earlier Nathan had moved Karl Zestos's people here, plus two of Lardis's men armed with weapons of Earth. Now, without pause, he took the precog down into the earth, where first he checked that indeed the routes from the surface had been camouflaged and booby-trapped, and that the Thyre and the Szgany Zestos were as safe as possible from attack.

Then he relieved one of Lardis's men of his weapon—a self-loading rifle—and transferred out of the place. And to be certain the vampires would know he'd moved on, he deliberately made a brief appearance on the surface before heading for Place-of-the-Beast-Bones.

Place-of-the-Beast-Bones was one of the few mistakes that Nathan had made during an incredibly busy Sunside evening. Now—not necessarily too late—he had realized the error; also that going there at this time might possibly compound it. That was a chance he must take. The error was geographical and lay in the colony's location only thirty-eight miles southeast of the great pass: well within Devetaki's reach. Worse, as a surface settlement it was vulnerable to attack.

Set in a stony desert depression, the colony was housed in flat-ceilinged caverns in the walls of a canyon cut by the resurgent Great Dark River. Where the strata had been sluiced away by water action, fossils of mighty prehistoric creatures were revealed: hence the name of the place. But in the canyon walls, descending tiers of wide ledges would make ideal landing and/or launching sites for flyers and warriors alike. And there were no subsurface escape routes; where the river plunged back into the earth again, its course was an inhospitable, unnavigable borehole.

Possibly Nathan's earlier visit—to deposit a small community of forest-dwelling Travellers here—had been monitored by the Wamphyri; if not, they would certainly know the location of the place now. Which meant that Place-of-the-Beast-Bones was going to need defending—which in turn meant a further series of dizzying Möbious jumps collecting armed men from other locations! But as Goodly pointed out along the way:

Or you could have moved the Thyre and the Szgany out of there; except . . . that would make the place a Wamphyri stronghold if or when they ever get to it. But in actual fact I don't see that any of this does any harm. I mean, surely by now Devetaki has got the message: that she can't possibly cover all of your coordinates? The more places you visit, the thinner she has to spread her net—or web! And all the time the night is moving on towards morning.

And the Big One?

That, too.

And she—I mean Devetaki—will be involved in it?

The very cause of it, yes.

Finally the job was done, and Nathan satisfied that he had put as many armed, trained men into Place-of-the-Beast-Bones as he could spare. But as he and the precog stepped from the Möbius Continuum back into the Cavern of the Ancients, he shook his head worriedly. "The Wamphyri aren't stupid," he said. "Especially Devetaki. She's got Yefros, and together they're plotting something. All that's happened so far is only a small part of a much greater scheme."

In the Thyre mausoleum, Atwei, Trask, Misha, and the others were waiting for him; now they could update him in person.

"Zek and I have managed to pinpoint Devetaki and Yefros!" Chung told him excitedly. "She's directing all of this from a plateau over the great pass midway between Sunside and Starside. Large vampire contingents are en route to most of the Thyre colonies, but the bulk of them have put down on the rim of the forests."

Zek added: "They're maintaining their net formation—"

And Trask finished it: "—Covering as much territory as possible. There's a lot of fighting in the Sunside woods, Nathan: all those Travellers who didn't trust you to move them to safety. Meanwhile we're here, armed and dangerous . . . and useless!" His voice was sour. "I know now how Lardis felt."

Suddenly the Necroscope was desperate; he simply

couldn't be everywhere at the same time; and he could see no end to it. "I have to draw their fire," he said, "and lure them away from both the Travellers in the forests and the Thyre colonies."

"But that's exactly what Devetaki wants!" Zek told him.

"Then let's *give* it to her!" Nathan growled, and his voice hardly seemed like his at all. His blood was up now, and behind his sore eye his mind ached from the pressure of it all . . . or from something else.

"Settlement!" Goodly hissed, staggering as his hand went to his brow. "It . . . it will be Settlement!"

Nathan bared his teeth and said, "Well that's good enough for me! That's where it all started more than three and a half years ago. Now let it finish there, one way or the other!"

Andrei Romani and Anna Marie English had come up from the subterranean colony. Pushing forward, Andrei said, "You're not leaving us out of this one. Indeed, if it's going to be Settlement, then *all* of the Lidescis will want to be in on it! There are caches of Dimi Petrescu's powder there, pitfalls, warrior traps . . . rockets! We can put up a real fight!"

Trask grabbed Goodly's arm. "Settlement? You're sure?"

The precog nodded. "Yes."

And Trask said grimly, "All of us, then, and we'll need all the Earth-weapons you can get together. Nathan, we'll be a focal point of resistance that the Wamphyri *can't* resist!"

There was nothing else to be said. With the exception of Misha (whose only talent was to love Nathan dearly), and Anna Marie English who wanted to stay with the Thyre, Nathan moved them to Settlement. Then he collected the Szgany Lidesci from Crater Lake, the Szgany Zestos from Crack-in-the-Rocks, and weapons from wherever he could find them.

What with all the explaining he must do en route, it took the best part of two hours, until he was sick and disoriented from it . . . even the Necroscope, disoriented!

But by the time he was finished Andrei Romani already had everyone working at a frenzied pace in the shattered old town. When finally the Wamphyri came, Settlement would be ready for them.

Hours passed; reports reached Nathan from the Thyre: the Wamphyri had definitely stopped advancing on them across the night-dark desert. It looked like their colonies were safe, at least for tonight. The vampires had not moved off entirely, however, but rested in the forest fringes where they met the savannas. They were still within striking distance, even now.

As for the bulk of Devetaki's forces: David Chung reported plenty of furtive movement, mainly hidden under what Trask had termed "radio silence." But as time went by, so Zek and Chung began to piece together a picture of what was happening.

Devetaki's "web" was more truly web-shaped now: concentric semicircles of vampire elements, flitting or spurting over the forests, taking up planned positions and hemming Settlement in where the old place nestled in the lee of the foothills. Other "covert" contingents had landed in the heights overlooking the town, but vampire mists were not in evidence; the virgin grandam kept her movements as discreet as possible.

In the town itself: discretion was flown to the wind! The men couldn't be expected to work by starlight alone in what the Old Lidesci had long since transformed into a deadly trap for men and beasts alike! Andrei Romani had lit fires—literally beacon fires—by which the men worked. Bomb-hurling ballistae and giant crossbows were back in working order; fragile-seeming rocket-launching frameworks (complete with their all-too-frequently treacherous missiles) had been hauled into position where stockade walls had been destroyed; men with amazing alien weapons patrolled equally treacherous catwalks atop swaying walls. And Nathan Keogh, called the Necroscope, was at an utter loss to explain why nothing was happening. His nerves were on edge . . . but nothing was happening. Settlement was full of people, lit up brighter than at any time in four years; it was surrounded by vampires . . . and nothing was happening!

Nathan called Trask and the other espers together to ask them: "What in hell is—or isn't—going on? Why is Devetaki waiting? The twilight before the dawn is only seven hours away. Sunup in less than twelve hours' time! What is she doing? The way her web is laid down, she could hit us with one wave after another endlessly, until eventually we'd be overwhelmed. What *is* she doing?"

Zek Föener had the right answer. "Keeping you guessing," she said. "Waiting for you to panic. Watching to see which way you'll jump."

And: "Shaking her web," said Trask. "Trying to tangle you up or startle you into doing something against your better judgement. Maybe trying to force your hand." The words had seemed to leap to his lips unbidden, surprising even him.

Nathan turned to him. "How, forcing me? How can she force me to do anything by *not* moving?"

Trask couldn't answer; but suddenly the precog Ian Goodly was pale in the gouting firelight. "Who said she isn't moving?" he said. And his great wide eyes went outwards to the night.

In the next moment Wamphyri "radio silence" was broken—indeed shattered! Zek, whose mind was wide open, reeled from a sudden telepathic onslaught. But not against her; the vampires were simply "talking" to each other, and their messages could scarcely be clearer:

Ignore the Szgany! They'll keep. But take the Others, the outsiders, the talented ones!

They have weird weapons but their numbers are few.

And the harsh, threatening sendings of some lesser Lord: *You lieutenants, you thralls: success means glory! But failure means death! This last I can promise you, and by my own hand! Wherefore you have everything to gain, nothing to lose. Devetaki wants the Necroscope, and the female mentalist* especially! *Take them alive!*

"She wants me!" Zek gasped, and groped in a pocket

for a lone bullet which she'd placed there right from the beginning. She'd been the property of a Lady once before, but not a Lady like the one who commanded this army.

Nathan had heard the sendings, too. His mouth was dry as a hard-baked riverbed as he looked at Zek, Trask, the others from Earth. Uppermost in his mind was a picture of Ethloi the Ancient's diagram of a device to close the Gates forever, the saving of one world at least. Which meant the saving of Trask and the others' lives was imperative.

"I have to take you—" he began, but they were already crouching down, taking up positions, spreading out.

And David Chung's warning a malediction in the suddenly electric atmosphere, as a mist rolled down from the foothills and swirled in through gaps in the battered stockade, and the air grew heavy, and a growing rumble of thunder that wasn't thunder sounded from the forests and mountains:

"Here they come!"

The Gate on Starside!

The thought was like a brand burning in Nathan's brain: he had to get his friends to the Gate, and now! In one sense the Necroscope felt like a traitor—the thought of leaving the Szgany Zestos and the Lidescis to battle on alone—but in another there was the chance it would have the beneficial side effect of diverting the attack. For right now, Devetaki wasn't much concerned with common Travellers; it was Nathan, Zek, and the other alien talents that she wanted to recruit.

Also, Nathan himself wasn't going. Not very far, anyway, and not for long. He would be back just as soon as he saw the others through the Gate. Except even as he worked it out they were scrambling for previously arranged vantage points. Then, to further distract him:

A warrior crashed down from a suddenly leaden sky on top of a ramshackle structure that only roughly resembled a house. Obviously this creature had instructions to destroy any Szgany refuges. Its furious bellowing turned to roars of agony as the flimsy shell collapsed, pitching it into the pit waiting below, where it impaled itself on sharp six-foot stakes. Gas-bladders burst and released their stench; the doomed creature's propulsors fired sporadically and sputtered into silence; some brave Traveller loped forward, hurled a torch that spun end over end like a ring of fire before falling directly into the pit amid a chaos of tortured vampire flesh and splintered timbers. The ensuing blast hurled the Necroscope from his feet, but he was up again in a moment.

A flyer came pulsing over leaning stockade walls; its lieutenant rider's visage was the leering, bloodlusting mask of a primal beast where he leaned forward in his saddle, swinging a bolas of vicious hooks and seeking victims. Zek was halfway across a rubble-strewn square. The lieutenant saw her and his jaws gaped wider yet in nightmarish anticipation as he swerved his mount in her direction. Skimming lower, the beast arched airtrap wings; its belly-pouch yawned open.

NO! Nathan sent directly into the lieutenant's mind. Feral eyes glanced his way, opened wide, were immediately trapped by *his* eyes! And: *No—you—fucking—DON'T!* the Necroscope told him, crouching down and unleashing his mind-bolt.

Still seeking a place to hide, a hole in the ground, any scrap of cover, Zek saw it happen: saw the lieutenant *cave in* as if crushed by a giant hand ... saw scarlet gush from ears, eyes, mouth ... saw his head compress into his chest, and his upper torso into his lower body, before he was swatted like a fly sideways from his saddle! But the flyer came on.

She twisted the fins on a grenade and forced herself to stand tall, stand still and wait. The flyer's belly-pouch was zeroed on the middle of Zek's body; there were only inches to spare between the lip of the pouch and the lapping white lake of the vampire ground-mist; Zek lobbed her grenade, and threw herself flat. The flyer scooped at empty air, then closed its pouch and rotated its manta wings for elevation.

It passed over Zek, climbing into the reeking air ...

. . . And pressured smoke jetted like the steam from the scalloped gash of the flyer's pouch, in the split second before internal lightning gutted the creature, driving lances of fire and shards of steel up through its spine! Its rubbery neck slumped at once; its mighty manta wings began to fold upwards; collapsing like a pack of cards, it drifted on, rapidly losing height as it disappeared in mist and distance.

By which time Nathan was at Zek's side, looking this way and that to locate the others. And by then, too, the night was alive with the throb of propulsors, dark with the pulsing shadows of flyers, shocked to full, awful awareness by the urgent shouting of men, the stutter and cough of automatic weapons.

Trask had seen the incident with Zek, the flyer and rider. To hell with his position on the stockade wall! With his heart in his mouth, he came running—

—As behind him that section of the great fence buckled and fell inwards, and the ugly shape of a warrior was silhouetted against the misted forest, its pincers and stabbers all mobile as it prepared to launch itself upon Settlement's defenders! Rockets were hastily aimed and fired; Travellers tossed grenades; a burst of automatic fire ripped into exploding gas-bladders before the heat of a rocket's exhaust turned the monster into a raging inferno.

A moment later and Goodly stumbled out of the smoke and stench with David Chung close behind. "I knew it was time and that you wanted us," he shouted at Nathan. "David knew where to find you!"

Nathan took them with him through a Möbius door . . . just forty paces, to where Andrei's men worked at a battery of four makeshift rockets. "When you've finished with those," he told them, "try these." Retaining Zek's machine pistol and the grenades in their pockets, the five dumped the rest of their alien weapons and ammunition on the ground. Where Trask and his colleagues were going, they wouldn't be needing them anymore.

That was the idea, anyway.

Then Nathan took them to Starside.

* * *

Checking his coördinates, the Necroscope got them as close to the Gate as possible: maybe forty-five yards northwest of the low crater wall and its core of white light, like the shining eye of some blinded, paralysed Cyclops gazing upwards into the Starside sky. The weird interference of the Gate, amplified by its proximity to the natural Gate at the bottom of the crater, was stronger far than that of its Perchorsk twin; Nathan's Möbius door writhed like a snake, threatening to warp back out of existence as he hastily guided his charges out onto the barren boulder plains. If he'd tried to get any closer than this, he knew there would have been a problem. What he didn't yet know was that he and his friends had a problem anyway.

Without pause as they cleared the door, Zek, Trask, Chung, and Goodly crouched down and went running towards the blinding hemisphere of cold light. Caught up in the urgency of the moment, Nathan ran with them; he was intent on seeing them safely on their way, Zek and Ian to Romania, Trask and Chung to Perchorsk. Perhaps too intent . . . and perhaps, too, all of the action back in Settlement had glutted their sensibilities, blunted their natural talents.

Clumps of boulders, silhouetted in dazzle from the Gate, appeared as concentric rings of menhirs going out across Starside towards the northern auroras, also to east and west, and south to the foothills and barrier mountains. Facing the Gate, the rocky terrain reflected its brilliance. By contrast, away from the Gate, the shadows of these boulder clumps were etched as sharp as knives and black as pitch—ideal hiding places, as Zek and Goodly could testify. And not only for men.

After a handful of long, loping paces, the group passed between two such clusters . . . and at once sensed the shadows moving there! It was very much a group thing: a sudden shared awareness, a sensation of intense danger. In actuality it was the relaxation of massed vampire minds— the opening of channels of communication—*the springing of the trap!*

VI

The Big One!

Goodly's *"Ahhh!"* was all the warning they got, as in the precog's mind:

Jesus! Of course she knew that Nathan's choices were infinite! Alexei Yefros had told her as much! That's why she had to narrow his choices down and bring him here—to the Gate!

Nathan was thinking just one thought, one word: *Trapped!*

Zek and Chung, too: their talents likewise springing to the fore as the ambushers lifted their "radio silence." Zek's mentalism: the telepathic aether vibrant with the presence of monstrous minds! Chung's lodestone skill: locating the source of the threat—and discovering it all around them!

As they came to a startled, stumbling halt, Trask saw the truth written on all their faces and gasped, "The clever bitch! She made us jump from the fat into the fire."

"Better than that," the Necroscope told him. "She knows it's the one place I can't jump back out of! Not this close to the Gate!" And now Nathan understood the reasoning behind Devetaki's small detachments in the Starside foothills. These were the same men! Their mission: to disperse the grey brothers into the heights, then to deploy here, keep silent, wait.

He looked back the way they had come, between the boulder clumps, and saw figures moving languidly, even tauntingly, into view out of the shadows; a bulky lieutenant, well over six feet in height, and two male thralls, all three of them wearing murderous gauntlets. And from rocky hiding places all around, more vampires appearing, very sure of themselves, unhurriedly moving closer.

The lieutenant was a mentalist; Zek and Nathan's eyes met in grim acknowledgement as they heard his thoughts fly south: *We have them, my Lady!*

And Devetaki's answer: *I know ... well done ... hold them there ... I'm on my way!*

"The Perchorsk Gate," Trask snapped. "You've used it one way, Nathan—but *only* one way. So you can use it again. You can come with David and me, through into Perchorsk!"

Breaking into a run, the five made for the crater wall— and again skidded to a halt. They were cut off. Vampires were emerging from the magmass wormholes all around the Gate, where they had been waiting in ambush. Two concentric rings of vampires, and the five caught between them.

Nathan was frustrated, afraid, angry; his eyes were burning in his face, hurting him with their stored energy. "All of you get behind me," he said. "Don't look at my face!" The unaccustomed, ugly *tone* of his voice—its threatening quality—caused them to obey at once. Behind him the four formed a small circle facing outwards; Trask took Zek's weapon and switched it to short burst; the familiar ch-*ching!* rang loud in the unnaturally quiet night as he cocked it. Zek passed him a spare magazine which he pocketed, sure that he'd be able to use it. The trouble was that it took too many bullets to knock these bastards down, and even then they wouldn't stay down!

In front, towards the Gate, a row of vampires—mainly thralls—were up out of their magmass wormholes; others were still emerging. Behind, among the scattered rocks, the night was alive with sinuous motion and the gleam of feral eyes. The nearest of them was less than forty-five feet away, and their numbers were ... far too many.

But Nathan had the answer to that. "Beware!" he told them, sounding more like one of them now. "My eyes contain the power of life and death." It was no idle boast.

"Oh really?" said the lieutenant, with an oily, glutinous chuckle. "Yet here we stand, untouched. Powers you surely have—we are all witness to that—but you are not the long-dead Eygor Killglance, or his cowardly bloodson Spiro!"

The lieutenant was in command here. Swat him and the rest would be a rabble; they might panic, attack en masse, overwhelm by sheer weight of numbers. But show him something unpleasant, give him an example, teach him a lesson . . .

Nathan crouched down and concentrated his hatred into his eyes. His face became a tortured mask; his lips drew back from his teeth; he glanced at the thralls to left and right of the lieutenant, hurled two bolts in rapid succession, and snarled: *"Die, then!"*

And they did.

The one on the left threw wide his arms and opened his mouth to scream—but only blood emerged as his skull caved in, driving his brains out forcefully through his eyes and ears! And the one on the right coughed a single unintelligible word, then staggered, hands fluttering like trapped birds. His body *vibrated*, his ribs and spine making audible crackling sounds as bones shivered into shards. Finally he crumpled, shuddering to earth like a lightning-struck tree!

And Nathan . . . *liked* it!

"There!" he said, his hideous face split by an even more hideous grin. But in the next moment:

Necroscope! (A well-known voice in his head.) *Bring me up now. Your promise! Do it now, Necroscope—for the fiend Maglore has broken into my pit!*

No! said Nathan, while still his intelligence was his own. *This eye of yours is a power, it's true, but it's also a nightmare—which you knew when you gave it to me. So stay in your pit, Eygor. For after all, it's the best place for you!*

WHAT!?

All of this in the Necroscope's metaphysical mind, while in the physical world:

The vampires were slipping back into their magmass wormholes; the lieutenant was loping for cover; thralls were scattering under the hot gaze of a man who was suddenly a monster. From behind a clump of boulders, briefly a target appeared; a thrall, who whirled a bolas over his head. Nathan was too late to catch him in the act; the man ducked back out of sight; his hurled weapon came whipping through the air towards the group of humans. Goodly cried his pain—*before* the bolas hit him!

The thing had three vicious, six-inch, razor-sharp hooks. Two of them clanged together, catching harmlessly in the precog's clothing; the third whirled around him and hooked itself through his trousers into his inner right thigh. Goodly went down yelping.

The blurred glint of more bolas; a man stepped from cover to release his weapon; Nathan struck at him with his killing eye—but nothing happened.

I take it back! Eygor told him. *I take back my eye! Liar! Cheat! You have robbed me of my vengeance, robbed even a dead thing of his one tomb, however inglorious! For Maglore shall give me* many *tombs, and all of them depleting me! His men are into my pit even now! You've doomed me, who did you no harm!*

Vampires were creeping back out of their wormholes, their rockpile hiding places. Trask's machine pistol came coughing alive in short, staccato bursts; three thralls howled as they were knocked backwards, disappearing below the smooth rims of their chutelike refuges. Perhaps they would slip all the way to the bottom, shoot into the subterranean Gate and end their days as dripstone fossils in a Carpathian foothills cavern.

Then, abruptly, the chatter of the machine pistol came to a halt; Trask swore as he tossed aside the empty magazine and slapped a new one—the last one—into its housing. And the Necroscope knew that he *must* have Eygor's eye.

Give it back!

When you bring me up. But it's now or never Necroscope, for they are on *me! And they will break—me—in—*

pieces! Call me up now or it's the end of you . . . and of meeeee!

Damn you! Nathan ground his teeth. *Damn your black heart to hell! Very well then, hear me now, Eygor Killglance. I command you: come up from the dead. Be* alive, *mobile in the world of the living—and return to me your eye!*

And: *SO BE IT!* said the other, his lunatic laughter ringing out through all the deadspeak aether . . .

And in Madmanse, in Turgosheim:

The Runemage Maglore leaned on the shallow wall of an ancient refuse pit amid the piled rubble of excavation, and called down, "Well, how goes it?" For just a moment ago there'd come a lull in the murmur of excited voices reaching up from the reeking gloom, where his thralls had discovered the incredible fossil, the gigantic *amalgam* that was Eygor Killglance.

"Do you not hear me?" Maglore raised his voice. "I asked, what have you discov . . ." At which point he paused open-mouthed in the middle of a word, as a vast sigh went up or was *sent* up (sent, yes) by a mighty, monstrous mind into *his* mind! In that selfsame moment Maglore knew, even before the previous babble of thrall voices became a ripple of horror, and the ripple an uproar, and the uproar a mad scramble for the dozen ropes that hung down into the pit.

For suddenly there was mist down there in that mausoleum pit where no mist should be, a cold, cold mist that writhed up into the shaft, even to Maglore at the rim. He felt it . . . and felt what was *in* it! Faces appeared—the faces of men coming faster up the ropes than ever they'd gone down—gasping men, panting men, not screaming but saving their breath for climbing, as they fled the nightmare that was—

"—Eygor!" Maglore breathed, snatching himself back from the low wall, aware that his limbs had turned to rubber. And:

Maglooore! came the answer. *What, and do you dare invade me in my own manse, Maglore?*

Sounds from below—a strenuous grunting, a squelching, the crunch of ancient bones under some monstrous weight! The mist grew thick where it swirled from the pit; the ropes went taught, stretched, snapped at the rim! All save one. The last of Maglore's thralls reached up a hand to him, gasping, "Master, he lives! He . . . *uh*!" Then his eyes went wide, his rope also parted . . . he was gone! Eygor's mist swirled where he had been.

And Maglore likewise gone. Gone in a trice from the rim of the pit. Gone up through haunted Madmanse, into Runemanse, where he called—where he shrieked, and gibbered—for his lieutenants, his men and monsters, and ordered them down into Madmanse in a body, to do battle with the dead and alive and undead thing that was Eygor Killglance! But:

Ah, no! Not yet, my friend, Eygor told him. *I'll not be coming for you just yet. Live awhile, Maglore, and see what I learned down here in the bowels of the rock: about the* fusion *of disparate things, and the skills of artistic creation! No, no, don't think it—I would not put you apart from the world, nor even apart from me. Instead I shall make you* a part of me! *Watch me if you will, Maglore—if you dare—while I* put on flesh *in the Gulf of Turgosheim!*

Eygor had already "put on flesh" in his pit: the flesh of Maglore's thralls. But how, in what way? What *manner* of thing was he now? Maglore went to a window, to peer down with seer's eyes through the fogs and reek, into the gloomy gulf.

Turgosheim: all of its creatures in all its manses were Maglore's now, except Eygor. But then, who would want Eygor? And the Seer-Lord shuddered—even Lord Maglore of the Wamphyri, shuddering at the thought of the fate of his thralls in that pit—and shuddered again at the thought of what by now had surely come up *out* of that pit!

Then, down in the bottoms . . . what? A *resurgence*? Maglore "saw" it, he sensed it: an outflowing, certainly. An exudation—spewing out like pus from a boil—from the lower levels of Madmanse, down its ramps and through its gantlets, into the scree and rubble of the bottoms. Good! For several of Maglore's warriors prowled down there, set loose in the bed of the gorge to keep him safe. Because they were his he knew their minds and could follow their progress as they, too, sensed this . . . *eruption*, and rushed to investigate.

He was with three of them—well, in part, given the limited capacity of their minds—as they came upon this strange new force, this swift-flowing *Thing*. With them, aye, as one by one they blinked out, or became one with it! What was it Eygor had talked about? The "putting on" of flesh? And the *fusion* of disparate things? And what had he threatened? *I shall make you a part of me!* What? The absorption of creatures—even men—within himself? All vampires were eaters of life; indeed, the blood *is* the life! But this . . . was something else.

Maglore's throat was dry. Perhaps he was mistaken. He must try again to penetrate the mists and reach his monsters' minds. He did . . . and met a different sort of monster! *Ah, no! Don't be in such a hurry, Maglore!* the Thing told him. *Your turn soon enough . . .*

The creature—this loathsome, flowing mass—was now at the gates of the squat, square gargoyle hump of Trollmanse, Lom Halfstruck's place, or what had been his place, on the bed of the gorge. Now its inhabitants were lieutenants and thralls of Maglore's. Indeed his man Karpath was there in residence—caretaker, "master" of a manse of his own at last—or until the Seer-Lord deemed otherwise. Or until something *else* deemed otherwise.

And Maglore sent directly into Karpath's mind: *Beware! A Thing approaches across the bottoms. It is at your gates even now!*

The answer came at once:

Lord, there are *no gates! They are fallen! And I . . . have* seen *this thing! Trollmanse, too, must fall; it cannot stand!*

Maglore stood aghast. *Karpath, listen to me. Do as I—*

Too late! said the other, his faint, unequal mental voice

a groan. Then silence. A vacuum . . . which swelled at once into an obscene chuckle! Eygor's, of course.

Enough! Maglore no longer felt safe in his own manse! Such a horror as this, loose in Turgosheim! And the Seer-Lord knew whom to blame: that sapless freak Nathan! Except he wasn't sapless but a power—and *such* a power!

Maglore's dreadful premonitions multiplied themselves tenfold, even as Eygor Killglance was at this very moment putting on flesh and multiplying *him*self! Hurrying to his landing bay, Maglore bumped into Orlea.

"My Lord, what is it?" The Lady's eyes were wide. She felt the terror in him, in this place, in all Turgosheim. He thrust her aside; she must take her chances with the rest.

"I've this and that to do," he said. "Don't bother me now. There's . . . oh, I don't know, some small trouble below, in the bottoms." He did indeed have things to do: saddle a flyer, fly deep into the gorge, see how the nightmare progressed, its rate of acceleration. He should visit the higher spires and manses, advise their barricading, their defences. Could they *be* defended? Could *anything* be protected? If not he must flee west and report this invasion-from-within to whoever commanded whatever was left of Vormulac's army. One thing for certain: the Thing-That-Had-Been-Eygor could not follow him there, over the Great Red Waste! And no one in the west knew of his treachery.

Perhaps he should not even delay to inspect the bottoms but go there now, far into Wratha's land of milk and blood and honey in the west. Except he couldn't set out tonight; dawn was too close; he must fly to the western extreme of the range and find a place to hide during the long day, then set off west at sundown. So *great* was Maglore's terror of Eygor Killglance!

He was in such a hurry, so preoccupied with his problems, that he scarcely noted that a mount was waiting in the landing bay, unattended, saddled and ready for flight. Climbing into a saddle that he hadn't seen for years, he gave the silent, nodding beast only a cursory glance, then dug in his heels, urging the creature to flight.

· But airborne, when he would descend, the flyer *ascended*; it gained altitude, cleared the rim and rose up on Turgosheim's queasy thermals! Now what in the name of . . . ? *Down,* he demanded. *Skim the bottoms. I will observe.* Except:

So, Maglore, I have you at last, Karz told him: an almost electric shock to the Seer-Lord's system! *You who having made a man into a monster, never trusted to climb upon his back—and with good reason.* He stalled, tilted, commenced a nosedive into the gorge. *But I have seen what is happening here, and it suits my purpose admirably. For now* I *make a monster out of you!*

Maglore clung on for dear life, or grim death. Drained by fear, he knew he wasn't up to metamorphosis. He didn't have the energy to change his shape to an airfoil and fly. Not a "physical" sort by Wamphyri standards, he'd only rarely used the art, and then in his youth.

"Karz Biteri—once-historian to the Wamphyri!" Maglore choked the words out loud; they were whipped away by dark wind and dank fog. Below, the humped, gargoyle bottoms took on shape through the wreathing mists; also, a mobile half-acre of horror that rumbled over the bed of the gorge full of terrible intent! It was composed of many things, none of them clean, healthy, or alive in the truest sense of the word. Debris of long-dead warriors, flesh of men, the undying mind of the maniac Eygor.

Karz was done with this world. But at least he was avenged. He flew straight for the centre of the mobile *Thing*, feeling only a momentary horror when it pulsed and turned its many eyes upwards to him, and sent the flung spume and froth of its tossing to meet and engulf him. Also to engulf his once-master—empty now of thoughts and words, runes, sigils, and symbols—plunged to his death in a moment and blended with filth and oblivion . . .

While thousands of miles to the west, at the Starside Gate:

The Necroscope and his charges had taken temporary refuge in a shallow depression with a hard earth rim and a low wall of stones. What cover they had protected them from hurled Wamphyri weapons; the vampires must step out into the open to direct and release their bolas. Whenever this happened, either Nathan with his killing eye or Trask with his machine pistol would cut them down. Trask was low on bullets; the only advantage of Nathan's weapon was that its results were permanent.

"Is that what I felt when I woke you up?" Trask asked him.

The Necroscope glanced at him (but carefully) with a face that was now totally alien: shrivelled and hateful, even luminous with evil power. "Yes. It was instinct in me, as it is in Eygor Killglance."

Trask didn't understand that last so said nothing, but Zek read Nathan like a book; she squeezed his arm where he crouched beside her in the hole. She knew what he feared: that the eye's influence would be too strong for him; that having resisted all else life in the vampire world could throw at him, finally he'd succumb to this. "You're stronger than that," she whispered.

"Oh?" He didn't look at her, but his voice was a low purr, a rumble, a growl.

"Yes, for you have your father's strength." Zek knew she was right to believe it. After all, like Harry before him, Nathan had saved her life.

The precog Ian Goodly did nothing (he had no weapon), said nothing, did his best *not* to feel the agony of the great barbed tine in his thigh. It couldn't be removed here; Zek had wrapped it with strips of cloth from her skirt; amazingly she'd stopped the worst of the bleeding. While David Chung comforted him, the precog could only grit his teeth and wait for the Big One. Nodding, feeling faint, his head swaying, he groaned it out loud:

"The Big One . . . coming!"

"*What?*" Chung couldn't believe his ears. "Do you mean this isn't it?"

The tumbling moon had come up. Silver, bloated, it floated well above the horizon; its full face told mockingly of a sunup that was still six or seven hours away. But the moon itself—its strange, eccentric orbit—told more than that, to Nathan if to no one else.

So close to the Gate, trapped here between two camps of vampires, unable or not daring to make use of the Möbius Continuum, and vulnerable to viciously cruel weapons if he should try to make a break for it in either direction—which was out of the question anyway, because of Goodly—the Necroscope had found time to think. Rather, his intuitive math, both physical and metaphysical, had been at work within him.

Before . . . he'd often wondered at the weird physical properties of his vampire world, where some of the "universal laws" he'd discovered in Trask's world didn't seem to work, or where they had been bent out of shape by the advent of an immemorial "white sun" that fell out of the sky and buried itself in the bottom of a crater—the original Gate. And he'd likened the world's wobble to that of an ill-balanced bolas, whose connecting rope had stiffened to a bar of unbreakable metal.

The math of the thing was now clear in his mind; he simply "knew" it, without knowing what to do with it or even if there was anything he *could* do with it. *Knowing* that it takes twelve thousand bricks to build a house doesn't get it built. *Knowing* that $E = mc^2$ isn't enough in itself to create a brief but very destructive star in your garden. On the other hand, how often had he been told that "numbers don't do anything, they simply are"? Time and again, by everyone from the mainly innumerate desert-dwelling Thyre to a highly sophisticated Earth mathematician. And he was the living proof that all of them were wrong!

Which was why now, as once before, he wondered what would happen if he conjured a door so strong it challenged the alien, immutable gravitational force of the Gate or Gates? If he were to make one of his "usual" Möbius doors in the immediate vicinity of the Gate it would tremble, collapse, and get sucked into the Gate or hurled away from it; in all probability he and his friends would go with it, perhaps into a place where life simply couldn't exist.

Two magnets, their like poles facing each other, pushed or held apart by equal forces. But if they were driven *towards* each other, there must come a point when something had to give.

The Necroscope decided to try an experiment. At the moment nothing was happening, had been happening ever since they took cover here. The vampires seemed happy enough simply to harass them, hold them *in situ*, make them keep their heads down. But that was self-explanatory: these creatures hemming Nathan and the others in knew better now than to show themselves too frequently. The fugitives had been in possession of a handful of grenades which they had used, unfortunately, less than effectively. But there were fresh blast marks around several of the wormholes near the Gate, and there must have been *some* damage at least in the surrounding boulder clumps.

Also, there was no urgency on the part of the ambushers now, no need to take any further action. Devetaki Skullguise wanted these fugitives alive, and she would soon be here. Her main forces were pulling out of Sunside, all heading for Wrathstack. David Chung was able to guarantee that last: the siege of Settlement had been lifted, and the fighting stopped. There was no profit wasting good flesh and effort now that the birds were flown, especially since they'd flown into the trap! Sunup was still a long way off, but the vampires knew it was coming and would feel a lot safer Starside of the barrier mountains.

So Nathan had time on his hands, however little. . . .

He let his numbers vortex swarm free, to surround his mind with a maelstrom of once-esoteric equations. Except, of course, they were no longer secret to him. Only call them down onto the computer screen of his brain, he could decipher all of them in as much time as it takes to tell.

But even the vortex warped away from the Gate's influence, disturbed by its proximity: the physical affecting the metaphysical. But if the metaphysical were stronger? Could it affect, even overpower, the physical? Certainly! Hadn't the Necroscope proved it every time he'd travelled in the Continuum? The math of the problem was right there, waiting for him to unravel it. But at a time and in a place like this, why even bother?

It was partly instinct, intuition, but more than that it was what the Thyre had told him, and what Goodly had corroborated. In fact, and if it worked, it was the Big One. The very, *very* Big One! The correction of a disordered world, which had gone wrong when an alien body mutated to a dimensional singularity (or multiplicity?) and fell on Starside!

Again he thought of what Thikkoul and others of the dead Thyre ancients had told him, remembering the way Thikkoul had expressed what to the Ancient was an unthinkable concept:

Instead of the moon, the sun, the stars in their eternal revolutions . . . I feel this very earth itself moving, leaning towards the sun! And: *The turning of the world, Nathan! Stars moving in the night sky, from south to north with the turning of the earth!*

Also what Goodly had said when Nathan had asked him when the Big One was scheduled, night or day? He'd answered that it would happen in the night, *and* in the morning!

Was there a clue there? Of course there was!

Nathan's numbers proved it; he held the equations steady on the screen of his mind and followed them through, saw their solution and knew its truth! Except . . . his mind simply wasn't big enough, wasn't strong enough. He knew the number of bricks it would take to build his house, but he had no mortar! Unless the mortar of his anger, and the strength of Eygor's evil eye, and—

"—And *our* strength?" Zek's hand closed over his where it was clenched, trembling. "Our *combined* strength?" He knew what she meant. He'd heard the idea broached back at E-Branch HQ in her world: in times of extreme danger, the joining of ESP talents into one super-ESP identity, one POWER.

Could his friends provide the extra bit of mortar that he

needed to hold his bricks together? All of their metaphysical energy together, against the Gate?

The moon was fully up now, and borne on a wind from the northeast (it could only be from Wrathstack) came a tumult of sound: thunderous music and an indescribably mournful howling. It was like an omen on the Necroscope's decision—or maybe a warning of Devetaki's imminent arrival! "She's almost through the pass," Chung gasped. "Fifteen minutes at the outside!"

Nathan quickly explained what he would do, but he needed their help. The immovable centre of gravity at the core of the world would be his fulcrum; the invisible, unbendable force it exerted on the Gate would be his lever; effort would come from the combined energy of their minds, concentrated upon the most powerful door he'd ever conjured. And the task—

—Would be to turn a world, correct its eccentricity, make the stars move through the sky, *and turn a night into morning!*

They didn't understand, but neither did they question him as they stood up and linked arms, and glared back at the glaring Gate through narrowed eyes; all of them with the exception of Trask, who must mind their backs while they worked. Watchful, he stayed down between their legs, weighing his precious magazine and wondering how many bullets were left in it, then forgetting to wonder anything as the Necroscope fortified his numbers vortex and conjured his Möbius door!

"Now!" Nathan said, as the thing warped and fluttered and rippled like water in his mind. They held, and glared, chewed their lips, and weighed their minds against the weight of the Gate. And held, and the door held with them! It shaped up; it glowed with the energy of their combined effort; it was *visible*!

For the first time ever, people who were not of the Necroscope Harry Keogh's flesh *saw* a Möbius door: a hole in nothing, going nowhere, and everywhere. But it fluttered like a flag; it must collapse at any moment, or be hurled away, or be shredded and drawn into the Gate. But it didn't and it wasn't, for Nathan held it with *his* mind and *Eygor's* eye—the most powerful combination of wills ever to exist in the vampire world.

And: "Hold it!" Nathan husked. *"Hold it!"*

And: "Yes," Goodly gasped the single word. *"Yes!"*

And: "A black cloud in the heights over the pass," Trask said. Then: "Cloud nothing! It has to be Devetaki!" The ruination of everything, if she should get here first. It galvanized the Necroscope to greater effort. And as Trask's machine pistol barked a single shot, and barked again, Nathan groaned:

"Push! We have to do more than just hold it—so *push!*"

And: "Yes," said Goodly. *Yes!*

Trask thought he felt the ground trembling under his feet where he knelt, but nothing was happening. Nathan's metaphysical door had firmed up and shone and shimmered like a fiery portal, but that was all. The energy the four were burning made the air hum, but nothing had changed. Trask groaned, saw motion in the corner of his eye—the glitter of whirling bolas—snapped off a shot and brought the thrall down before he could release his weapon. But a moment later and Trask saw a different kind of motion, an impossible kind of motion:

The moon, performing a slow *curve* across the sky! Not its weird orbit, but a *curve* from south to north!

"Jesus!" Trask sobbed raggedly, the breath catching in his throat as a wild wind blew out of nowhere, tugging at his hair. "Oh, sweet Jesus!" The very vault of the heavens seemed to be moving; the ice-chip Northstar was *receding* over the last great aerie of the Wamphyri; the rest of the stars were following on behind, uniformly marching south to north across the sky!

"Push!" Nathan's voice was a whisper.

"Yes!" Goodly's, too.

"My God! *My God!*" Zek heard the moaning of the wind, and the moaning of a hundred vampire voices in her head. The world was turning and a far faint flush limned the high peaks of the barrier mountains.

Then, through all the telepathic tumult of fearful vampire moanings, one voice sounding loud and shrill with the realization of what was happening and who was making it happen. Devetaki Skullguise, commanding: *Kill them! Do it now, before they doom us, each and every one!*

And up out of the magmass wormholes came five feral-eyed thralls, and out from behind the boulders stepped the lieutenant and others of the ambush crew. Trask knew he couldn't possibly have more than three or four rounds left, but he'd make every one of them count. He would have to, for Nathan was out of it and most continue confronting the Gate with his irresistible door. And the world continued to turn, the wind to howl, the thunderous music from Wrathstack to blare like the trumpets of hell.

The whirl of a bolas: *crack!* And a thrall, leaking brains from a hole between his eyes, went toppling.

Another bolas: *crack!* Trask took his eye out.

The lieutenant came loping, ducking, weaving. He wore a gauntlet. *Crack!* The man spun around in a complete circle; his eyes went to the scarlet-pumping hole in his shoulder; he kept coming. *Crack!* He was knocked over backwards, flipping from his shoulders where they hit the dirt, came springing to his feet. *Crack!* And this one took him in the heart, which finally swatted him.

The five thralls were closing from the direction of the Gate. Seeing Trask aiming at them, they crouched low, spread out, came zigzagging towards the fugitives. One of them made a sideways leap when he saw Trask lining up his sights; somehow, he got between the Gate and Nathan's door. His body was illuminated in a golden glow for a split second—like a flash of lightning—before he disintegrated like a sheet of paper in a shredder! He was there and he was gone, disrupted, vanished without a trace!

The others came on; Trask squeezed the trigger; the bolt flew forward and—nothing!

Zek touched Trask's head, managed to grin at him even through her tears as she passed something down to him—her bullet. "Fuck it!" she said. He yanked back the bolt, pushed the bullet home with his thumb, looked at her. His heart was in his mouth. The vampires from the wormholes were coming.

One of them started to swing his bolas and Trask didn't think twice. *Crack!* The man went down spraying red.

Half a mile away, towards the pass, the sky had turned black with flyers. Devetaki! But the world was still turning, the wind still howling, the defenders of two universes still standing to the end. Except this *was* the end, surely?

But if so, why had the vampires from the magmass stopped advancing? What was that look on their faces? What could it mean? Trask glanced behind—and saw what it meant. That the dead of Starside weren't about to let this happen, not to the Necroscope Nathan Keogh!

Trask's jaw fell open. The vampires from the rock piles were fighting with dead men . . . with mummified *pieces* of men . . . with the desiccated *debris* of men! It was a rebellion of the dead against that which must never be: the destruction of their one champion in the world of the living.

The teeming dead, not called up but *come* up of their own accord. All of the countless Szgany who over a thousand years had trudged the dreary road to the aeries of the Wamphyri and never made it, suffering the true death out here on these barren boulder plains. All the victims of vampire bloodwars long forgotten by the leaning menhirs of Starside. All the ragged scraps and dust of men long gone, knowing that they *must* come up to a semblance of life at least, else life itself had not been worth it.

Jason Lidesci was their leader; albeit a slender lich, he was a true Lidesci to the end. But there were many others the Necroscope had never known. Glina Berea was among them, who in her time had vowed vengeance on Nestor, and now fought for his brother. Oh, their names were legion, which they sang to Nathan like a battle cry even knowing that he couldn't answer, for he was engaged in a battle of his own.

As for the vampires: the blinding dust of dead men was in their eyes, choking dust in their nostrils, throats, ears. And they knew how unequal was the battle—because dead men can't die twice. But Devetaki and hers did *not* know that, not yet.

All she knew was that the world was turning, the peaks of the barrier mountains gleamed golden in her wake, and the furnace sun was rising like a great blazing meteor to fry her eyes and scorch her undead bones! Ahead of the rest, she came swooping over and through and around the glare of the Gate, driving her mount in what was very nearly a suicide dive right at the group of aliens in the shallow depression.

Nathan saw her coming and his gaze, his mind, his strength was diverted from the glowing Möbius door— which at once collapsed! There was nothing he could do about it; he couldn't concentrate on two problems at the same time, and Devetaki was now the most immediate threat. He went into his killing crouch and glared doom and destruction at the Lady, her flyer, Alexei Yefros, where the Russian locator hung on behind her.

The merest pulse of his former power, there was little of strength in it; fuelling the door had drained him to the dregs. Still, his mind-bolt was not entirely without effect: Devetaki gave a small choking cry, yanked on the reins to haul back her mount's head, climbed up, up into a sky no longer black, where now the stars were the merest flecks of flickering light—

—And yet a sky blacker than the blackest night to Devetaki, for she was blind! Blind, her eyes ruined . . . yet she saw quite clearly. *Saw* that it was the end. *Sensed* cessation. *Felt* finality—as her soaring blinded beast lofted her into sighing, searing sunlight!

"*Ahhh!*" Devetaki herself sighed wonderingly, groped for her scowling mask, didn't quite make it. And at last the pain (but briefly), the rapid devolution: a drift of smoke and slow, silent rain of smouldering ashes. Along with a faster rain, of leaden trappings, leather, iron, and a few charred bones. Alexei Yefros, not long a vampire, fell with the saddle, shrieking until he hit, then lying still. The sun would do the rest.

The sun! For it had risen on Starside, and despite that

Nathan's door was no more, it was *still* rising. And the moon a strange pale orb where it hung in the sky, no longer tumbling. And in the north, Wrathstack a golden finger pointing toward a glorious future, or perhaps at the Northstar, more properly a "north" star now: a blink of silver against faded auroras ...

The dawn had happened first and fastest, of course, Sunside of the barrier mountains. It had come as something of a surprise, to say the least; *not* least to the Lady Ursula Torspawn. Standing a discreet distance from her funeral pyre, Lardis Lidesci wondered very briefly who she'd been, then put her out of his mind forever. She'd been Wamphyri, definitely, else at the end there'd been much less of a commotion.

In fact, nothing had gone right for Ursula. Earlier, she'd taken up with a party of ex-supplicant Szgany, and trembling in every beautiful limb (from fears that weren't entirely feigned and so served to lend her story veracity), she had told how she was the lone survivor of a family group slaughtered by the Wamphyri. That had been several hours ago, shortly after the party itself had survived an attack, which made Ursula's story doubly acceptable. If she had known it at the time, however, she might have tried her luck elsewhere. The skirmish had made these people extra vigilant; they clung together; she'd not had a chance to lure anyone away and ... tend to her needs.

What's more, these were the folk that Lardis Lidesci and Kirk Lisescu were helping, and Lardis's reputation in respect of vampires had been hard-earned. Still, it was a credit to the Old Lidesci's powers of observation that in those weird moments as the stars commenced their march across the sky, and the horizon was suddenly aglow with a dawn all of six hours early, he had noticed something strange about one lone, lovely woman.

Then, as she'd made "casually" away (for she too had seen what was happening, and knew that survival depended upon finding a deep, dark place to hide from a sun gone mad), Lardis had asked the young leader of the group: *"Who is she?"* And his tone of voice had been such that the other had forgotten for a moment the miracle that was taking place, to blurt:

"A stranger, a survivor. What does it matter? She's a girl who'll breed children to replace the many we've lost or given away ... aye, and a *curse* on our cowardly leaders for that!"

"And she came to you as you see her now? Unmarked, clean, and in good clothes?"

"Aye. What of it?"

At which Lardis's eyes had narrowed, and he'd signalled to Kirk Lisescu. "Her bells make no sound!"

"Bells? Decorations that make pretty noises? Man, we were *supplicants*; we wore no silver!"

"But she does—except her bells don't ring. Because they aren't silver—*they're lead!* Kirk!" That last loudly, explosively, so that Ursula would hear him. She did, and knew that it was all up. The sun was rising in the night, and she was in the camp of the enemy. Then: the dark of Ursula's eyes turning red! And a spontaneous *eruption* of dagger teeth, as the gape of her jaws yawned open to house them!

Kirk Lisescu had put three shots into her as she turned to run, but still she'd made it halfway up a hillside before the sun caught up with her. Aye, and a hell of an uproar then! For she had been a vampire for ... oh, for a long time.

When most of the din was over they'd tossed branches over what was left and torched the lot.

It was much the same for Geoffrey Paxton, caught in the sun's golden net halfway back to Starside, in a broad section of the great pass where sunlight never penetrated before. The same, but it could have been worse. For Paxton was a very recent convert, and it might have taken a lot longer.

At first he had felt the furnace heat on his back: the way his hair grew hot, the stretching and splitting of skin already torn from digging his way out of the collapsed cave, the sudden and rapid blistering of his ears and neck. Then, without thinking what he was doing—as if the seething golden stain crawling through the bed of the pass wasn't evidence enough—he'd turned to see what was wrong.

A moment later ... he'd been blind, and all the skin peeling from his eyeballs! Then his screaming and tottering to and fro, the heat of his body turning the space inside his clothes to a furnace, his flesh beginning to broil. But moving blindly in and out of shadowed areas, it might easily have lasted for hours ... if he hadn't got his ankle trapped between boulders and broken it, so that he flopped there in full sunlight. And that way it had been easy on him.

His unbearable agony put an end to him; by the time the sun moved on a little, the shadows found his clothing stuck to the rocks with black tar. Gluey hands, with some bones showing through, protruded from the frayed cuffs of his combat suit ...

In Wrathstack, Wratha had seen the sun come up so swift she'd known she was insane; which of course she was. Her crazed cackling was now at an end, however; her cage swung on high, *almost* empty, its silver-lattice floor dribbling a reeking oily substance into the abyss.

On the south face of the stack, scorch marks and a few puffs of smoke were all that remained of the Mangemanse siege, while the last scrap or two of bubbling, smouldering, *devolving* matter went spiralling down to the blood-soaked scree and rubble slopes. And yet—while still the sun rose up and its light cut deeper yet, searing all down the length of the last aerie—the bone-song from Wrathstack's dark side continued. For the dog-Lord Canker had witnessed a wonder, and knew that he, Canker Canison, was its author! The moon-priests were so afraid of him that the lunar orb itself had turned pale!

Canker's throat was raw but his song was at an end; now he could fly to the moon to claim her for his own! Deaf and bleeding from his ears, Canker went stumbling to find the Lady Siggi and say a fond farewell, and tell her that soon he would return with all her silver sisters. And he knew where to find her. She was bringing on the hatchlings in the cave of spiders.

Normally Turkur. Tzonov's screams would have led Canker to Siggi at play, but he no longer heard them; stumbling and moaning, he heard nothing but his bone-song despite the fact that he was not playing! And Siggi, poor Siggi . . . would she even know him? It seemed unlikely, for she had bathed in his light too long, and was no longer sensitive to mundane things. While Canker . . . he was *too* sensitive by far! And his head hurt, and his ears. And the singing, the singing! It seemed the stack itself was swaying, as if his playing had shaken the foundations or the great fang itself danced to the tune in Canker's head.

And now the sun was fully up, standing higher in the sky than ever before, and its rays lit on all Starside. But Canker in the dark of his manse couldn't know it, or that golden rays were even now eating into the very *heart* of rock that had known the horror of ages, the works and working of vampire Lords, the harrowing and hollowing of unhallowed hands. All the shocks the stack had taken: the centuries of tunnelling and endless whittling of Wamphyri inhabitants, explosive heat of fires and blast of alien bombs. And last but by no means least, the thunder of the dog-Lord's songs.

All it had needed was a push, albeit the push of a giant. The shifting of the earth, causing the stack to rock, and the Great Destroyer sun, burning out every last trace of evil vampire influence until the rock itself was calcined. And now the pull of the moon in a strange new orbit. It was all too much.

Wrathstack went down in rubble, rot, and ruin, crumbling as it toppled, its various levels splitting apart and crashing down onto the shuddering boulder plains, adding its terrible tonnage to all the tumult of olden stacks gone before.

At last, there *was* no last aerie. . . .

* * *

Earlier, in Turgosheim:

Spiro Killglance had left his second mount spread-eagled on the rim of the gorge, utterly exhausted from its flight, while he descended first into promontory Rune-manse, looking for Maglore, then into Madmanse. But the aeries were empty; the gorge itself seemed devoid of life and even undeath; nothing stirred in that haunted old place.

Haunted, aye, by Spiro's demented father, Eygor. Oh, how Spiro had feared that old devil upon a time, but no more. Now, indeed, he felt grateful! What? But he had inherited the cruel old bastard's evil eye, and even the Seer-Lord Maglore was in hiding from him. Laughing, and hearing the echoes reverberate away and back (which changed the tone somehow, until the laughter hardly sounded like his at all), he went to the choked refuse pit where he and Wran had trapped their father after they had blinded him. He went there—*and found the pit dug out!*

And the silence of the place unnatural—breathless?—and nothing exactly the way Spiro remembered it, as suddenly what little light there had been began to dim. But how? There were no curtains at the windows in the perimeter rooms, and no one to draw them if there had been. And the stone floors rubbery under Spiro's feet . . . and the walls and dripstone columns feeling damp, slimy, even *sweaty* to his touch. Like raw meat. *But stone doesn't beat like a great heart, or pulse and shudder when you touch it!*

The light continued to dim. Spiro ran on trembling legs from room to *unremembered* room, breathing stale air that tasted . . . already breathed? Looking for the source of the darkness, to discover who it was that slowly shut out the light, and how. He found a room with windows—

—Which closed themselves one by one as he arrived! And yet no drapes had been drawn for there were none. The holes in the solid rock walls had simply sealed themselves . . . because the walls weren't of rock! And:

WELCOME HOME, BLOODSON, said Eygor, from all around him. *FLESH OF MY FLESH—RETURNED AT LAST TO MY FLESH!*

In answer to which: "No!" said Spiro, drooling spittle on the floor, in the moment before the room that wasn't a room in a manse that was only a manse on the outside closed on him to make him one with it . . .

And shortly:

Six hours of night left—and Eygor quicker, more fluid, elastic, than any creature before him. And *hungry*!

He was dead, undead, alive; he was an animal, an amalgam, an all-consuming organism. He was an animalgamism, and hungry! But Sunside meant blood, and the blood is the life!

A thing whose tendril extensions and frothing extrusions reached down into every crevice, spire, and manse in Turgosheim, Eygor pulsed up through Runemanse on the rim and gushed like a lake of living lava onto the plateau that sloped to Sunside—where he flowed headlong into the searing gaze and golden rays of the sun. And where evil eyes were concerned, to Eygor Killglance especially, *nothing* could be more lethal than the burning yellow eye of that ultimate orb!

What happened then was lightning-fast—a total, instant catabolism, the dispersal of the Eygor-thing into vile gasses that mushroomed up in a cloud as if some mighty explosion had occurred, though that was not the case—a chain reaction of dissolution, going down into Turgosheim wherever Eygor's tendrils reached, transforming them to slime, dust, finally the very elements of their constitution.

And Eygor, and indeed Turgosheim, were no more; just a barren gorge remained, where the shadows were driven back as the sun rose higher still . . .

At the same instant but several thousands of miles away, as the rumble of Wrathstack's fall subsided, the Necroscope and his party stood in an awesome silence at the Gate, where all around the landscape was dotted with smoking ashes. But after a while the precog Ian Goodly said, "Nathan, I . . . I'm sorry, I mean, I—"

"I know." Nathan nodded. "It's soon now, right? 'The end of my tether'?"

Goodly looked away, but Nathan only smiled. And his smile and his eyes were his own, for the awful *Power* within had gone with Eygor's going, dissolved with the monster's dissolution.

They carried the precog a safe distance from the Gate and Nathan conjured a door, and took them back to Settlement. There he called for Grinner, and as the wolf came loping spoke to his friends. "If this fails," he said, "you know where the Gate is. And you still have time. But I won't say good-bye, and don't you say good luck! The first is premature and the last just doesn't count. The future has it all worked out for me, one way or the other."

Smiling again, at Goodly, he conjured another door . . .

EPILOGUE

In the Möbius Continuum, Grinner said:

Why, Uncle? Since we've done this before, is there any point?

I hope so, Nathan told him. *You see, back there on Starside, at the Gate, I discovered something I really should have known before, except this time I had the "intuition" to recognize it: the fact that there are many different types of doors. Thikkoul of the Thyre knew it a long time ago but without knowing that he knew it! He told me: "I see doors ... but liquid, drawn on water, formed of ripples. And behind each one of them, a piece of your future ..." My doors are commonplace compared to others that exist, or that can be caused to exist.*

Other doors exist? Grinner seemed surprised. *Without that you make them?*

That's the whole point, Nathan answered. *Some that exist, and others that are made. Of course, I've known for some time now that there were future- and past-time doors, and doors that I could conjure to get me into and out of the Möbius Continuum. But I'd never thought to make a door here, within the Continuum itself! You see, the Continuum is like a large manse, with many rooms I've never visited. Perhaps I'm not supposed to, for I've only been shown one of those rooms—two, if you include Sunside/Starside.*

I ... don't understand, said Grinner.

But you will. Your father knew those doors, and so do

*you; you sniff them out. Except you don't understand them!
You're a wolf of the wild, who understands trails and
tracks and spoor. You understand . . . directions!*

Ahh! said Grinner. *My father's world—and yours, Uncle.*

Exactly. Nathan nodded. *You showed me the way before,
but there was no trail for you to follow. I had not made
one! Now, if you show me it again, I'll remember it always
as one of my coordinates.*

But it's there. It's right there! Grinner told him, pointing
the way.

Without pause Nathan made his door, and as it opened
felt a warm sweet wind rush out of it to ruffle his hair . . .
one of the many winds of Earth! Then, as he stepped
through the door with Grinner, he thought: "The end of
my tether—in the parallel dimension of Sunside/Starside at
least. But if Ian Goodly and I had gone on awhile, then we
would have come to where it starts again!"

And on the other side of the door:

He knew where he was at once; a place he'd found
magical, which now he had found again, but in a magical
manner: a sunlit hillside overlooking Zek's house at Porto
Zoro on the island of Zante in the Mediterranean. Standing
in the shade of a gnarled old pine, the Necroscope
breathed deeply of resin-laden air and gazed out across the
incredibly blue Ionian. But as for Grinner . . . he sat down
abruptly on his rump and whined. For all of his directions
were gone now, and *he* was the stranger in a strange far
land.

"It's all right," Nathan told him, stroking a flattened,
trembling ear. "We won't be here long."

Just long enough to talk to Gustav Turchin . . .

And six months later, Earth time:

It was nighttime, and again they stood by the Starside
Gate, except now they must find a new name for the land
north of the barrier mountains, and perhaps even a new
name for the barrier mountains! Now they were only a
barrier in the sense that they obstructed eager Travellers,

holding them back from a rapidly developing territory and a land free of vampires.

In the far east and west (at least as far as men had yet to journey) the vampire swamps were drying out, cracking open in their beds, cleansed by the sun. And in all the length and breadth of the vampire world, no vampires existed—at least so far as men knew. But that was not to say that men wouldn't keep watching. Not while Lardis Lidesci lived, anyway!

Nor was the transformation confined to the swamps; water released from the Icelands, drifting in clouds on high, bringing great rains to the scrubland savannas and lesser precipitation even to the deserts, had already turned the land green as far as most of the Thyre colonies. All of which processes of an altered Nature, and others, would go on for a long time yet.

So things were very different, not least at the place where the adventurers were gathered together: the Hell-lands Gate, on Starside. Scarcely a gate to hell now, and no longer a Gate in any sense; or a *one-way* Gate at best, of sorts, and utterly impassable to man or beast . . . or vampire! No longer a Gate, no, but a lake; and all the stars of night mirrored in its shining, whirling surface, whose waters formed small whirlpools that went down through the magmass wormholes to the subterranean Gate, and on into another world. As the Necroscope had pointed out: an unending cycle, protecting the privacy and integrity of two worlds, but depriving neither. A closed circuit, much like the Möbius strip itself. For the waters would return, of course, from the great dam in Perchorsk, whose torrent had been diverted into the now abandoned Projekt by Premier Gustav Turchin!

A fountain of light, reaching up a hundred feet into the Starside night, illuminated by the Gate at its core, and raining its soft white waters on the land and into the lake! Of all the wonders in the vampire world, surely this was the greatest of all?

Nathan thought so, certainly, where he crushed his Misha so tightly she held her breath; and Lardis, Trask,

Zek, Goodly, Chung, Kirk, Grinner, and Blaze. And especially Andrei. But the greatest wonder to Andrei was not the lake itself but the firm-bodied woman who laughed and danced and pirouetted there where wavelets lapped a once-dustbowl shore—

—A woman far younger than her years, whose name was Anna Marie!